THE ORCHARD KEEPER

SUTTREE

BLOOD MERIDIAN

BOOKS BY *Cormac McCarthy*

The Orchard Keeper
Outer Dark
Child of God
Suttree
Blood Meridian
All the Pretty Horses

THE ORCHARD KEEPER

SUTTREE

BLOOD MERIDIAN

CORMAC McCARTHY

QUALITY PAPERBACK BOOK CLUB
NEW YORK

THE ORCHARD KEEPER

The tree was down and cut to lengths, the sections spread and jumbled over the grass. There was a stocky man with three fingers bound up in a dirty bandage with a splint. With him were a Negro and a young man, the three of them gathered about the butt of the tree. The stocky man laid aside the saw and he and the Negro took hold of the piece of fence and strained and grunted until they got the log turned over. The man got to one knee and peered into the cut. We best come in this way, he said. The Negro picked up the crosscut and he and the man began sawing again. They sawed for a time and then the man said, Hold it. Goddamn, that's it again. They stopped and lifted the blade from the cut and peered down into the tree. Uh-huh, said the Negro. It sho is now, ain't it?

The young man came over to see. Here, said the man, look sideways here. See? He looked. All the way up here? he said. Yep, the man said. He took hold of the twisted wrought-iron, the mangled fragment of the fence, and shook it. It didn't shake. It's growed all through the tree, the man said. We cain't cut no more on it. Damned old elum's bad enough on a saw.

The Negro was nodding his head. Yessa, he said. It most sholy has. Growed all up in that tree.

I

For some time now the road had been deserted, white and scorching yet, though the sun was already reddening the western sky. He walked along slowly in the dust, stopping from time to time and bobbling on one foot like some squat ungainly bird while he examined the wad of tape coming through his shoesole. He turned again. Far down the blazing strip of concrete a small shapeless mass had emerged and was struggling toward him. It loomed steadily, weaving and grotesque like something seen through bad glass, gained briefly the form and solidity of a pickup truck, whipped past and receded into the same liquid shape by which it came.

He swung his cocked thumb after it in a vague gesture. Little fans of dust scurried up the road shoulder and settled in his cuffs.

Go on, damn ye, he said to the fleeting mirage. He took out his cigarettes and counted them, put them back. He turned his head to the sun. Won't be no use after dark, he said. Windless silence, not even a rustle from the dusty newsprint and candypapers pressed furtively into the brown wall of weeds at the road edge. Further on he could see the lights of a filling station, some buildings. Maybe a fork where the traffic slowed. He jerked his thumb at a trailer truck as it whined past, sucking up dust and papers in its wake, watched it wrench the trees farther up the road.

You wouldn't pick up Jesus Christ, would you, he asked, rearranging his hair with his fingers.

When he got to the filling station he had a long drink of water and smoked one of the cigarettes. There was a grocery store adjoining and he wandered in, cruising with a slithery sound up and down the aisles of boxes and cans and filling his pockets with small items—candy bars, a pencil, a roll of adhesive tape . . . Emerging from behind some cartons of toilet paper he caught the storekeep eying him.

Say now, he said, you don't have any, uh—his eyes took a quick last inventory—any tire pumps, do ye?

They ain't in the cake rack, the man said.

He looked down at a jumbled mound of bread and cakes, quietly lethal in their flyspecked cellophane.

Over here—the storekeep was pointing. In a crate at the back end of the counter were jacks, pumps, tire tools, an odd posthole digger.

Oh yeah, he said. I got em now. He shuffled over and fumbled among them for a few minutes.

Them ain't the kind I was lookin for, he told the storekeep, making for the door now.

What kind was that? the man asked. I didn't know they was but one kind.

No, no, he said, musing, standing just short of the door, rubbing his lower lip. He was inventing a new tire pump. Well, he said, they got a new kind now you don't have to pump up and down thisaway (pumping) but what's got a kind of *lever* handle you go at like this (pumping, one hand).

That a fact, said the storekeep.

Bet it is, he said. Makes it a whole lot easier on a feller too.

What kind of car you drivin? the storekeep wanted to know.

Me? Why I got me a new Ford. Brand-new thirty-four, V-eight motor. Scare you jest to set in it . . .

Lots of tire trouble though, hmm?

Well . . . no, jest this one time is the only first time I ever had me any tire trouble . . . Well, I better . . . say now, how fer is it to Atlana?

Seventeen mile.

Well, I reckon I better get on. We'll see yins.

Come back, the storekeep said. Shore hope you get your tire blowed up. It would be a sight easier with a pump.

But the screendoor flapped and he was outside. Standing on the store porch he studied the hour. The sun was already down. A cricket sounded and a squadron of bullbats came up out of the smoldering west, high on pointed wings, harrying the dusk.

There was a car pulled in at the filling station. He cussed the storekeep for a while, then walked back down and had another drink of water. From his pocket he produced a candy bar and began munching it.

In a few minutes a man came from the restroom and passed him, going to the car.

Say now, he said. You goin t'wards town?

The man stopped and looked around, spied him

propped against an oil drum. Yeah, he said. You want
a ride on in?

Why now I shore would preciate it, he said, shuffling
toward the man now. My daughter she's in the hospital
there and I got to get in to see her tonight . . .

Hospital? Where's that? the man asked.

Why, the one in Atlana. The big one there . . .

Oh, said the man. Well, I'm jest goin as fer as Austell.

How fer's that?

Nine mile.

Well, you don't care for me to ride that fer with ye,
do ye?

Be proud to hep ye out that fer, said the man.

Coming into Atlanta he saw at the top of a fence of
signs one that said KNOXVILLE 197. The name of the
town for which he was headed. Had he been asked his
name he might have given any but Kenneth Rattner,
which was his name.

East of Knoxville Tennessee the mountains start, small
ridges and spines of the folded Appalachians that contort
the outgoing roads to their liking. The first of these is
Red Mountain; from the crest on a clear day you can
see the cool blue line of the watershed like a distant
promise.

In late summer the mountain bakes under a sky of
pitiless blue. The red dust of the orchard road is like
powder from a brick kiln. You can't hold a scoop of it
in your hand. Hot winds come up the slope from the valley like a rancid breath, redolent of milkweed, hoglots,
rotting vegetation. The red clay banks along the road
are crested with withered honeysuckle, peavines dried
and sheathed in dust. By late July the corn patches stand

parched and sere, stalks askew in defeat. All greens pale
and dry. Clay cracks and splits in endless microcataclysm
and the limestone lies about the eroded land like schools
of sunning dolphin, gray channeled backs humped at the
infernal sky.

In the relative cool of the timber stands, possum grapes
and muscadine flourish with a cynical fecundity, and the
floor of the forest—littered with old mossbacked logs,
peopled with toadstools strange and solemn among the
ferns and creepers and leaning to show their delicate
livercolored gills—has about it a primordial quality,
some steamy carboniferous swamp where ancient saurians
lurk in feigned sleep.

On the mountain the limestone shelves and climbs in
ragged escarpments among the clutching roots of hickories, oaks and tulip poplars which even here brace themselves against the precarious declination allotted them by
the chance drop of a seed.

Under the west wall of the mountain is a community
called Red Branch. It was a very much different place
in 1913 when Marion Sylder was born there, or in 1929
when he left school to work briefly as a carpenter's apprentice for Increase Tipton, patriarch of a clan whose
affluence extended to a dozen jerrybuilt shacks strewn
about the valley in unlikely places, squatting over their
gullied purlieus like great brooding animals rigid with
constipation, and yet endowed with an air transient
and happenstantial as if set there by the recession of
floodwaters. Even the speed with which they were constructed could not outdistance the decay for which they
held such affinity. Gangrenous molds took to the foun-
dations before the roofs were fairly nailed down. Mud
crept up their sides and paint fell away in long white
slashes. Some terrible plague seemed to overtake them
one by one.

They were rented to families of gaunt hollow-eyed and darkskinned people, not Mellungeons and not exactly anything else, who reproduced with such frightening prolificness that their entire lives appeared devoted to the production of the ragged line of scions which shoeless and tattered sat for hours at a time on the porch edges, themselves not unlike the victims of some terrible disaster, and stared out across the blighted land with expressions of neither hope nor wonder nor despair. They came and went, unencumbered as migratory birds, each succeeding family a replica of the one before and only the names on the mailboxes altered, the new ones lettered crudely in above a rack of paint smears that obliterated the former occupants back into the anonymity from which they sprang.

Marion Sylder labored with hammer and saw until late September of that year and then he quit, knowledgeable in purlins and pole plates, and with his savings bought some clothes and a pair of thirty-dollar boots mail-ordered out of Minnesota, and disappeared. He was gone for five years. Whatever trade he followed in his exile he wore no overalls, wielded no hammer.

At that time there was a place in the gap of the mountain called the Green Fly Inn. It was box-shaped with a high front and a tin roof sloping rearward and was built on a scaffolding of poles over a sheer drop, the front door giving directly onto the road. One corner was nailed to a pine tree that rose towering out of the hollow—a hollow which on windy nights acted as a flue, funneling the updrafts from the valley through the mountain gap. On such nights the inn-goers trod floors that waltzed drunkenly beneath them, surged and buckled with huge groans. At times the whole building would career madly to one side as though headlong into collapse. The drinkers would pause, liquid tilting in their glasses, the structure would shudder violently, a broom would fall, a bottle, and the inn would slowly right itself and assume once more its normal reeling equipoise. The drinkers would raise their glasses, talk would begin again. Remarks alluding to the eccentricities of the inn were made only outside the building. To them the inn was animate as any old ship to her crew and it bred an atmosphere such as few could boast, a solidarity due largely to its very precariousness. The swaying, the incessant small cries of tortured wood, created an illusion entirely nautical, so that after a violent wrench you might half expect to see a bearded mate swing through a hatch in the ceiling to report all rigging secure.

Inside there was a genuine bar, purportedly of mahogany, that had been salvaged from a Knoxville saloon in 1919, done service in a laundry, an ice cream parlor, and briefly in a catacombic establishment several miles from Red Branch on the Knoxville road that failed early in its career due to an attempted compromise between graft and cunning. With the exception of two Doric columns of white marble set in either end the bar was of plain construction. There were no stools, and along the front ran a high wooden foot-rail chucked between wagon-wheel hubs. Four or five tables were scattered about the room attended by an assortment of wrecked chairs, milkcases, one treacherous folding campstool. When the inn closed at night the proprietor opened the back door and swept all litter out into the yawning gulf, listening to the crash of glass on glass far below. The refuse collected there cascaded down the mountain to a depth undetermined, creeping, growing, of indescribable variety and richness.

One evening late in March the drinkers blinked in a sweep of lights on the curve, watched a glistening black Ford coupe pull up across the road. It was brand new. A few minutes later Marion Sylder came through the door of the inn resplendent in gray gabardines, the trousers pressed to a knife edge, the shirt creased thrice across the back in military fashion, his waist encircled by a strip of leather the width of a whip-end. Clamped in his jaw was a slender cheroot. On the back of his neck a scarlike gap between sunburn and hairline showed as he crossed to the bar.

There he propped one pebbled goat-hide shoe upon the rail, took from his pocket a handful of silver dollars and stacked them neatly before him. Cabe was sitting on a high stool by the cash register. Sylder eyed the coins briefly, then looked up.

Come on, Cabe, he said. We drinkin or not?

Yessir, Cabe said, clambering down from his stool. Then he thought: Cabe. He studied the man again. Wraithlike the face of the lost boy grew in the features of the man standing at the bar. Say, he said, Sylder? You the Sylder . . . you Marion Sylder, ain't you?

Who'd you think I was? Sylder asked.

Well now, said Cabe, don't that jest beat . . . Where you been? Hey, Bud! Looky here. You remember this young feller. Well now. How about this.

Bud shuffled over and peered up at him, grinned and nodded.

Here, Sylder said, give these highbinders a drink.

Sure thing, Cabe said. Who's that?

Sylder gestured at the dim smoky room. They all drinkin, ain't they?

Well now. Sure thing. He looked about him, uncertain as to how to proceed, then suddenly called out into the tiny room: All right now! All you highbounders got one comin on Marion Sylder. Better get up here and get it.

. . .

When Rattner reached the road he stopped and lit a match by which to examine his shin. In that small bloom of light the gash in his leg looked like tar welling. Blood trickled in three rivulets past the black smear his trouser had made, deltaed, rejoined; a thin line shot precipitously into his sock. He let go the match and jammed his scorched thumb into his mouth.

Aside from the torn leg his elbow was skinned and stinging badly. A low strand of barbed wire had been his undoing. Now he pulled a handful of dried weeds, crumpled and struck a match to them. They crackled in quick flame and he hiked his trouser leg again. Wiping the blood away with his palm he studied the rate of flow. Satisfied, he patted the sticky cloth back against the wound and took from his front pocket a billfold. Holding it to the light he pulled out a thin sheaf of folded notes and counted them. Then he ripped the billfold open, scattering cards and pictures. These he examined carefully along with the insides of the ruined purse, then kicked them away and tucked the money into his pocket. The weeds had burned to a ball of wispy cinders, still glowing like thin hot wires. He kicked them away in a burst of dying sparks. Far up the road a pale glow hung in the night like the first touch of dawn. He had left Atlanta at ten . . . it could not be past midnight. He patted his leg once more, sucked at his thumb, and started off in the direction of the lights.

Jim's Hot Spot, the sign said in limegreen neon. He circled catlike among the few cars, peering in at their black insides and keeping one eye weathered to the door where in a dome of yellow light an endless whirlpool of insects aspired. He came past the last empty car to the door and by this light checked his furrowed leg once again and then made his entrance.

. . .

The little coupe could be seen leaving or entering the Sylder place at strange hours, or in the heat of the day parked glistening and incongruous before the house, sleekly muscled and restless-looking as a tethered race-horse. Saturday evenings he collected parcels of town-ward-walking boys in new overall pants from the road-side as you might gather hounds the morning after a hunt—them leaping awkwardly in, riding solemnly or whispering hoarsely one to another until they gained speed. Sylder could feel their breath on his neck—those in the rear, wedged in like crated chickens—as they peered over his shoulder. A long silence as they watched the needle vanquish the numerals on the dial in a slow arc to hover briefly at 80 on the last and long straight stretch before reaching the city limits. Sometimes one of them would venture a question. He always lied to them. Company itself don't know how fast she'll go, he'd say. They plannin to take one over to the Sahary Desert to find out.

At Gay or Market he would pull to the curb and yell: One stop! and watch them erupt from the car like circus clowns—five, six, as many as eight of them, all bound for the show, farmboys with no more farm than some wizened tomato plants and a brace of ravenous hogs. In the rearview mirror he could see them watching the car scoot away, hovering and bobbing on the sidewalk like a flock of curious birds.

Sundays the Knoxville beer taverns were closed, their glass fronts dimmed and muted in sabbatical quietude, and Sylder turned to the mountain to join what crowds marshaled there beyond the dominion of laws either civil or spiritual.

Jack the Runner's mouth was blue, his tongue blue-black as a chow's. At the table by the door of the Green

Fly Inn he sipped blackberry wine from a liniment bottle.

Where'd you leave em? Sylder was asking.

Ahh, Jack gurgled. Over on mountain.

You're on the mountain now, Sylder said.

Over, Jack emphasized. Hen'son Valley Road.

Henderson Valley Road? Whereabouts?

Top o mountain, like I tol ye . . .

You reckon he's tellin us right? June asked.

Sylder looked from him to the runner again. Jack studied a huge and evil-looking cigar he had found in his shirtpocket and fell to turning it against his tongue with drunken singlemindedness. Yeah, Sylder said. Most likely he is.

Right feisty, Jack was saying, holding now the cigar at arm's length. A loop of spittle woggled mucously from its underside. Right feisty.

Caught in the yellow glare of the headlights they had the temporarily immobilized look of wildlife, deer perhaps, frozen in attitudes of surprise predicating imminent flight. Sylder drove past and up the mountain.

Ain't you goin to stop? June asked.

Comin back, Sylder said. Behind em, like I was goin their way. I never figured they'd be headed wrong. Way they're goin, through Sevierville, it's near thirty mile.

Between them in the crevice of the seat nestled a mason jar of whiskey. Sylder heard the skirling tin sound of the lid being unscrewed and he reached out his hand for June to pass the jar. Moths loomed whitely before the windshield, incandesced, dusted the glass with mica. A ballet of gnats rioted in the path of the headlights. He drank and handed the jar back. Under the black hood the motor hummed its throaty combustions.

Sylder thought about old man Tipton saying it wasn't

sensible as any fool could see that with the pistons going on an angle like that—lop-ass-sided, he'd said—they were bound to wear through on one side. Pistons were supposed to go up and down. Street's are full of em, he said, if it's any comfort to know you wadn't the only one took.

They turned at the quarry and came back down the mountain coasting silently, the tires making a soft slapping sound at the cracks in the asphalt. When the lights picked them up they began to group and sidle to the ditch as cows will. Sylder brought the coupe to a stop slowly alongside of them.

Howdy, said June right into the ear of the girl on the outside. You-all need a ride?

The other one was standing next to her then. They looked at each other and the first one said, Thank ye, I reckon we can make it all right. The boy hung back behind them. Across June's shoulder Sylder could see him looking not at them or at the women either, but at the car.

How fer ye goin? June wanted to know.

The two exchanged glances again. This time the taller one spoke up. We jest goin down the road a piece, she explained.

Tell her let's all go down the road for a piece, Sylder suggested.

What? the short one said. Then the boy piped up and they both turned to glare at him.

How fer is it to Knoxville? That was his question.

Knoxville? June couldn't believe it. You say Knoxville? Why you-all cain't *walk* to Knoxville. It's twenty mile or better—ain't it, Marion?

A groan went up from the travelers. Sylder was already motioning him out the door.

Here, June said, climbing out. You'ns get in here. We goin to Knoxville, proud to hep ye out.

Sylder presented them each with a welcoming smile as they climbed in and studied each in turn his face under the domelight.

He dropped into the Hopper—the steep twin fork road—without braking. The little one between him and Tipton squealed once and then hushed with her hand clapped over her mouth as they swerved across the pike and shot out into blackness, the lights slapping across the upper reaches of trees standing sharply up the side of the hollow. The coupe dropped, squatted for a moment in the gravel of the lower road, sprang again and slithered away obliquely with the exhaust bellowing from the cutout and gravel popping and rattling in the woods like grapeshot.

The one in the back was making small sobbing noises. No one spoke for a few minutes and then the little one said, Where's this go?

Goes to the gettin pla . . .

Town, June broke in. Goes to town. Shorter this way. He thought she seemed to have edged closer to Sylder although she turned and was talking to him. He saw Sylder's hand greenly phosphorescent under the dashlights pulling out the choke.

They reached the first bridge before it began to sputter enough for her to notice. Above here the road began to climb again and Sylder let it buck a time or two before he shifted to second. She didn't move her leg. He was watching her out of the corner of his eye, her sitting forward on the seat and peering out intensely at the unfamiliar night. A moth whipped beneath the windscreen, brushed her cheek. He cranked the glass in a turn. When the car bucked again she flinched and asked what was wrong.

He started to tell her the generator was out of water but thought about the boy in the back seat. No word from him at all. The tall one in the back had leaned forward, breathing in Tipton's collar and fixing the windshield with a look grim and harassed as if contemplating one desperate leap at the black passing night country.

Vapor lockin, he said finally. Overheats on these hills and you have to stop and let her cool off.

She looked at him and then looked away again, not saying anything. A phantom rabbit froze in the headlights, rolled one white eye, was gone. June was talking to her in a low voice, her still looking straight ahead, saying nothing. The one in the rear had sat back. No sound from her. In the mirror Sylder could see half a head dark and bushy in silhouette as a bear's. He recognized the smell then. A tepid odor of urine, musty-sweet, circulated on the air now as they slowed.

They jerked around the last curve below the pine thicket and shuddered to a stop in front of the Olive Branch Negro Baptist Church. Sylder switched off the ignition. I guess that's all she wrote, he said.

He opened the door and started to get out when he felt her hand on his leg. He stopped and turned.

Not him, she said. Not the other one.

No, he said. O.K. Come on.

He switched off the lights and then they were gone, negated in the sudden darkness.

Marion, June whispered hoarsely. Hey, Marion?

From his porch Arthur Ownby had watched them pass and now he heard the slam of the car door up the road where they had stopped. It had begun to rain. A yellow haze in the woods flicked out. He could hear low voices, near-sounding on the warm night air. With one foot he tapped out the time of some old ballad against the corner post of the porch. From under the brim of the roof he studied the movements of stars. A night for meteors tonight. They cannonaded the towering hump of Red Mountain. Rain falling now from a faultless sky. A girl's laugh on the road. He remembered her sitting high on the wagon seat Sunday morning that the mule broke wind in his ear while he unhooked the singletree and he stove two fingers in on a rib and it never even flinched. Late hours for an old man. Arthur Ownby had watched from his porch. He dozed.

When the boy came past on the road he looked up at the house on the sidehill, dark and abandoned-looking. He could not see the old man and the old man was asleep.

It was near daylight when they started back from Knoxville, a pale cold graying to the east.

Where'd you take her? Sylder asked.

June reached for the cigarettes riding in the visor. Goddamn she's ugly, he said. You know what she told me?

What's that, said Sylder, grinning.

That I was the nicest boy ever needled her. *Needled*, for God's sake.

Where at?

Huh?

Where'd you take her. You come down from the church but I never heard you come up. Where'd you go?

Ah. Up in the backhouse.

Backhouse?

Shithouse then.

Sylder was looking at him in amazed incredulity, acceptance and belief momentarily suspended, unable to picture it yet. He had one more question:

Standing up?

Naw, well . . . she sort of sat down and leant back

and I . . . she . . . But that was beyond his powers of description, let alone Sylder's imagination.

You mean to say you—Sylder paused for a moment trying to get the facts in summary—you screwed her in a nigger shithouse sittin on the . . .

Well Goddamnit at least I never took her in no Goddamn church, June broke in.

The coupe wobbled to a halt at the side of the road and Sylder collapsed against the door epileptic with laughter. After a while he stopped and said:

Was she the one that . . .

Yes, Goddamn you, she was the one.

Whooeee! Sylder screamed and rolled out the door where he lay in the wet morning grass shaking soundlessly.

The place was dimly lit and barnlike. A polished dance floor in which at the far end fell the reflection of the jukebox lights and those of the bar. Behind the bar a long mirror in which he was surprised to see himself, silhouetted in the doorframe, poised nimbly atop a stack of glasses. He came down and crossed the floor, limping slightly, and clambered up on the corner stool.

The bartender was sitting in a captain's chair reading a magazine. He folded it carefully and shuffled down to where the man was sitting.

Beer, Rattner said. His tongue swept his lower lip in anticipation. The bartender went to the barrel and drew off a schooner, flicked away the foam with a stick and brought it to him. He reached and tilted one side of the glass up and lowered his face into it; his lips sought the glassrim and fastened on it white and fat as leeches while under the yellowgray skin his throatcords jerked spastically, pumping the beer down. He drank it all, lifting the glass finally to drain it, and slid it back toward the bartender, who had been watching with both fascination and disgust, as one might watch pigs mate.

Say now, that sure was all right. Yessir, jest believe I'll have me anothern.

Ten cents, said the bartender.

He struggled with his pocket and came up with a dime. You betcher, he said.

The bartender took the glass, gingerly, and refilled it.

Rattner had been gone for a year this time. He had moved from Maryville to Red Branch, taken up quarters in an abandoned log house with his wife and son, and left there four days later with twenty-six dollars in his pocket, alone and southbound in an empty L&N reefer. An incident at the Green Fly Inn had been his windfall:

The rear door through which Cabe swept the night's litter had once given onto a porch that ran the width of the building, supported by joists that were extensions of the floor timbers and braced frugally with two-by-fours angled up beneath them. On summer evenings the drinkers gathered here, bringing with them their chairs or cases or perching riskily upon the narrow railing like roosting birds. Weather and termites conspired against this haven and brought it to ruin. This was in 1933 then, a hot summer night, that Ef Hobie came to the Green Fly Inn. A prodigal return (Petros—Brushy Mountain— eighteen months, illegal possession of liquor) that attracted a great number of well-wishers. One by one they retired through the rear door to take up their stations on the porch. Hobie was a favorite and carried on a running monologue of anecdotes. He was telling how his old lady had loaned the family soupbone to Mrs Fenner, who had cooked peas with it and ruined it, when a sharp dry crack issued from somewhere in the floor. It was a calm windless night, laden with heat, and the sound had an ominous quality about it. The talk paused a moment, resumed.

He came through the door and onto the porch, circumspectly, nodding across them all with diffidence, as if someone he knew might be there, beyond the railing itself and suspended mysteriously in the darkness, leaned against the doorframe and lifted the bottle to his mouth, his eyes shifting among them or when they looked closing or seeking again that being in the outer dark with whom only he held communion, smiling a little to himself, the onlooker, the stranger. The talk eddied and waned, but he offered neither comment nor question and after a while they ignored him. He came from the doorway and took a seat on the rail at the near end of the porch.

There was a long creaking sound like a nail being pulled and again the sharp detonation of strained wood giving way. There followed a dead and immobile silence during which the faces searched from one to the other uncertainly. A few began to rise and mill about, still not saying anything. Already they had begun to eye the narrow door, the one point of egress, weighing in their minds not so much numbers as tonnage and freight of men, calculating speed and congestion with the concern of traffic experts.

With the third report a section of flooring listed visibly.

Fellers, Ef started, rising himself, I think this here . . . But that was all, or as much as anyone heard at least. There ensued a single rush as of so many marionettes on one string being drawn in violent acceleration toward the door while above the noise of their retreat the joists popped like riflefire, snapping off in rackety succession, and the floor drooped in long and gathering undulations in their wake.

They hit the opening in one concerted mass and wedged there tight as a peg at the same instant that the far end of the porch came away, swung out from the building in a long swooping and not ungraceful arc.

Now from the knot of men clawing at the door single figures began to be sucked away in attitudes of mute supplication one by one down the dangling incline of the porch, gaining momentum among leaping cans and bottles, and dropping at last with wild cries into the pit below. A few caught at the rails and dangled there with stricken looks eying their fellows rocketing past into the night.

From within the building Cabe and a few others were trying desperately to untangle the mass that writhed in the doorway, resorting finally to taking hold of what limb presented itself and pulling until something gave. Thus the survivors came aboard bereft of one shoe, or both, or pants, or as with Hobie himself naked save for one half of a shirt. Until the frame of the door exploded inward carrying a good section of wall and they entered in a roil of bodies and crashing wood.

The porch had swung out and downward and now tottered for a moment on the strength of a single two-by-six before it too snapped and the whole affair slewed away with a great splintering sound. The figures clutching at the rails began to turn loose their holds, coming away by ones and twos like beetles shaken from a limb, and the entire wreckage descended in a slow tableau of ruin to pitch thunderously into the hollow.

The atmosphere inside seethed with an inchoate violence. Scared men, torn, unclothed and crushed, breathing loudly and sweating the sweat of subsiding panic, mounting outrage and indignity. One by one the fallen

*were entering through the front door red with blood and
clay and looking like the vanquished in some desperate
encounter waged with sabers and without quarter. As
they gathered strength from below two factions became
apparent and they fell upon each other murderously
and fought far into the night.*

*Kenneth Rattner nursed a slashed hand as he squatted
in a blackberry thicket below the inn and listened with
quiet bemusement to the thrashings and curses of the
victims. Someone had brought a light; he could see the
flicker and sweep of it through the bramble wall. He
pulled a kerchief from his pocket and tied it around his
hand, pulling the knot to with his teeth. Then he worked
his way carefully up to the road and started for home.
Small groups of men were running up the mountain to
the scene of disaster bearing lanterns and whispering
hoarsely.*

I got a job, he told her.

Praise God, she said. Whereabouts?

*Greenville South Carolina, showing her the money
now. Trainfare, he said. But he gave her five of the
thirty-one dollars and they went to the store. He bought
the boy an orange drink, lifted him onto the box where
he sat holding it in both hands, watching. Mrs Eller
was telling about it.*

*That Coy Tipton showed up here this mornin looked
like he'd fell in a combine. Said they's three or four
of em what lost their britches—I'd like to know how
they done that my own sef—and when they clumb
down in the holler to get em somebody had beat em
there and stole their pocketbooks. She sat atilt in her
rocker, fanned slowly with a church tract. Thiefs and
drunks runs together I expect, she said. Ain't none of
em but got what they's lookin for.*

Mildred Rattner pinched from loaf to loaf across the

bread rack. When them as wallers in sin thinks they's gettin by with it, she said, that's when He strikes em in His holy wrath. He jest bides His time.

Kenneth Rattner stroked his stiffening leg, flexed his ankle. It was past midnight and people were coming in now. The bartender had abandoned his magazine and was moving nervously up and down the counter and filling glasses for the newcomers.

He drained the last of the beer and set the glass upon the bar. Hey, buddy, he called. Give us anothern over here. Hey, old buddy.

Saturday afternoons Marion Sylder would come in the store fresh-looking in starched khakis or overall breeches and go to the glass case and point out the socks to Mr Eller. Mr Eller would put the box on top of the counter and Sylder would hold up a pair and say: How much are these?

Quarter, Mr Eller would say. No change in price, still a quarter. All a quarter, ain't got no other kind.

Sylder would spin a quarter on the glass, take his socks and sit down on a milkcase in front of the stove. He would do them one at a time, taking off one shoe and sock and waving his bare foot about while he reached for the stove door, opened it, and swung in the old sock, holding it delicately. Then he would put on his fresh sock, lace up his shoe, and proceed to the other foot, the one with the big toe nailless and truncate. He was working in the fertilizer plant now. Noontimes he ate in the café the regular lunches, the thirty-cent specials with the lightbread that clove gluily to the palate, three slices with a thumbprint in the center served on a piece of waxed paper. Beans and fatmeat oozing grease into the greasy gravy that leaked down from the potatoes, a beaded scum of grease on the coffee, everything in fact lubricated as if all who ate there suffered from some atrophy of the deglutitive muscles which precluded swallowing. In late afternoon he returned, parked the coupe and crossed the gullied and wasted clay of the yard where an old tire still hung from the one knobby and leafless oak, and so into the unpainted house.

Within the hour he was out, washed and combed, blasting away the peaceful cricket sounds with the open cutout, tooling carefully down the corroded drive and onto the pike and gone.

To Happy Hollow or McAnally Flats. Mead's Quarry or Pennyroyal. Smoking shacks yellow with coal-oil light and areek with the sweetmold smell of splo whiskey.

Drinking, courting with ribald humor the country slatterns that hung on the city's perimeter like lost waifs; his favorites the ill-shapen: Wretha, white lisle uniform, thighs the dimensions of oiltuns. The too thin. A nameless one, bony rump that cut into his leg. Experimentally he wet a finger and cut a white streak on the grime of her neck.

Some nights he made it to the Green Fly Inn and rocked away with those old boozers to the last man, this affluent son returned upon them bearing no olive branch but hard coin and greenbacks and ushering in an era of prosperity, a Utopia of paid drinks.

He was hard-pressed now on eighteen dollars a week, who had spent that in an evening. He turned twenty-one in August.

The following Friday he lost his job at the fertilizer plant. Aaron Conatser needled him into a fight, and he fought, not out of any particular dislike toward Conatser, or even in any great anger, but only to get the thing over with, settled. Conatser was the only man in the plant his size and had been looking to try him.

He was on one knee with his arms locked around Conatser's neck when he heard Conatser's hoarse breathing stop. There was no sound in the shipping room and when he raised his head he saw that the men standing around them were looking past him at something else and knew before he turned that Mr Petree had joined the circle. Not the dock foreman, or even the supervisor, either of whom would have said Break it up. He turned loose of Conatser and stood. Conatser came up too, stretching his neck like a mute rooster, and put his hands in his back pockets with elegant indifference.

He licked at the trickle of blood from his nose, tasting it salty and metallic, and turned to see what the old man would have to say. But Petree spun on his square leather heel and stalked briskly back down the aisle, the shipping-room floor echoing his hollow footfalls among the tiers of bags.

The three or four men who had gathered to watch the fray dispersed in silence, faded or slunk away in the dark malodorous aisles, less brazen than the rats that nested beneath the pallets. He and Conatser stood glaring at each other for a small minute, breathing laboriously. Then Conatser turned his head and spat, looked once obliquely across his shoulder at him and sauntered away toward the dock.

The dock foreman came down just before quitting time and told him. I tried to put in a word for you, he said, but he wadn't hearing any.

Sylder doubted him but muttered a thanks anyway and started for the office.

Where you goin? he asked.

Get my pay.

Here, he said. Sylder turned. He was holding out the envelope toward him.

Sylder went to Monk's and drank beer till six or seven o'clock, and finally went home. By eight o'clock he had packed some clothes into an old cardboard grip and was sitting grimly behind the wheel of the little coupe with the headlights clearing out the night ahead and a narrow strip of asphalt numbered 129 slipping away beneath him like tape from a spool. He stopped once at a grill outside of Chote, drank two warm beers from coffeecups and bought cigarettes. In the mountains the road was thin and gravel and he slewed down the curves on drifting wheels. Once a bobcat stood highlegged and lanterneyed in the road, bunched, floated away over the roadbank on invisible wires. For miles on miles the high country rolled lightless and uninhabited, the road ferruling through dark forests of owl trees, bat caverns, witch covens.

He smoked continuously, cranking in the windshield to light a fresh cigarette from the old stub and studying in the glare of their union his shadowed muzzle in orange relief on the glass, watching the point of light fade when he exhaled and climb slowly up the dark mirror like a sun risen inexplicably by night as he turned the glass out again to let in the damp rush of air, the retired butt curving past the cowl to be swept away in a swift red arc. At Blairsville he filled up with gas and did not stop again after that. Out across the flats he could see the moon on the river curling under the black fall of the mountain, plating the riffles in chain-work, hordes of luminous snakes racing upriver over the sounding rocks. The air came cool and damp under the windscreen.

He reached Atlanta some time after midnight but did not go into town. He pulled in at a roadhouse just short of the city limits and sat in the car for a few minutes flexing his eyelids. There were three or four other cars parked in front, dimly lustrous in the neon ambience.

He passed through a fanfall of moths under the yellow doorlight and inside. Above the heads of the dancers he could see himself hollow-eyed and sinister in the bar mirror and it occurred to him that he was ungodly tired. He skirted along the high booths lining the walls and got to the bar where he ordered and drank straight four shots of whiskey. He began to feel better. He was sitting with the fifth drink before him when sounds of breaking glass issued from the dance floor and he turned to see two men circling warily with clenched bottles. A huge figure hulked up from the end of the bar and shuffling out through the gathering spectators seized the combatants one in each hand by the belts and turkey-walked them out the door, them stepping high, unprotesting, their bottles dangling idly.

Whooee! see them turkeys trot, a man down the bar called out. The bouncer came back down the floor wearily, not smiling, faded again into the shadows. Sylder tossed off the drink, watched the blur of faces for a few minutes, not even high on the liquor, just feeling waves of fatigue roll from him. He didn't even think he was mad any more. A few minutes later he left, wondering vaguely as he stepped into the air again why he had come here and where he thought he was going. Louisiana or anywhere else, his job had gone off the market December fifth 1933.

He walked out in the quiet darkness, across the gravel, limping just a little on the bad ground. He got to the car and opened the door.

By the phosphorous glow, more like an emanation from the man's face than from the domelight, Sylder froze, his hand batting at the air stirred by the outflung door. The face stared at him with an expression bland and meaningless and Sylder groped for some, not cause or explanation, but mere association with rational experience by which he could comprehend a man sitting in his car as if conjured there simultaneously with the flick of light by the very act of opening the door.

The mouth stretched across the lower face in a slow cheesy rictus, a voice said: You goin t'wards Knoxville?

—A strained octave above normal, the pitch of supplication.

Sylder's hand found the door and he expelled a long breath. What in the Goddamn hell you doin in my car, he croaked. Something loathsome about the seated figure kept him from reaching for it violently, as a man might not reach for bird-droppings on his shoulder.

The mouth, still open, said: I seen your plates, Blount County—that's where I'm from, Maryville. I figured you might be goin thataway. I need a ride bad . . . 'm a sick man. The tone cloying, eyes dropped to Sylder's belt as if addressing his stomach. It was not presentiment that warned Sylder to get shed of his guest but a profound and unshakable knowledge of the presence of evil, of being for a certainty called upon to defend at least his property from the man already installed beneath his steering wheel.

You're sick all right, Sylder said. Scoot your ass out of there.

Thanks, old buddy, the man said, sliding across the seat to the far door without apparent use of any locomotor appendages but like something on runners tilted downhill. There he sat.

Sylder leaned his head wearily against the roof of the car. He knew the man had not misunderstood him.

I knowed you wouldn't turn down nobody from home, the voice said. You from Maryville? I live right near there, comin from Floridy . . .

Sylder lowered himself into the car, the hackles on his neck rising. He looked at the man. I would have to put you out with my hands, he said silently, and he could not touch him. He slipped the key into the switch and started the motor. He felt a terrific need to be clean.

Shore is a nice autymobile, the man was admiring.

Swinging the little coupe through the rutted drive and out onto the paving he thought: He'll be a talker, this bastard. He'll have plenty to say.

In immediate corroboration the man began. This sure will help me out, old buddy. You know it sure is hard to get a ride nights.

Morning, Sylder muttered under the vehement shift to second.

—specially not much traffic and what they is folks won't hardly pick you up even . . .

Ah, Sylder thought, shouldn't have thrown that shift. He could see the knee out of the corner of his eye, cocked back on the seat, the man sitting half sidewise watching him.

—My mother been real bad sick too, she . . .

Sylder's hand moved in stealth from wheel to shift-lever, poised birdlike. The hand on the speedometer climbed with the hum of the motor.

—doctor's bills is higher'n . . .

His left foot dropped the clutch. Now. Under his

cupped palm the gearshift shot down viciously, quivered where a moment before the man's knee had been.

—so I shore do preciate it . . . The man went on, droning, his legs now crossed with an air of homey comfort, slightly rocking.

Sylder hung his elbow over the doorsill and leaned his ear to the rush of wind, the pockety rhythm of the open exhaust and the black road slishing oily under the wheels, trying to lose the voice.

No cars passed. He drove in almost a trance, the unending and inescapable voice sucking him into some kind of oblivion, some faltering of the senses preparatory to . . . what? He sat up a little. The man had not taken his eyes from him, and yet never looked directly at him.

You bastard, Sylder thought. It began to seem to him that he had driven clear to Atlanta for the sole purpose of picking up this man and driving him back to Maryville. His back hurt. I must be crazy, he said to himself, reaching in his pockets for cigarettes. This son of a bitch will have me crazy anyway. He jiggled one from the pack, spun it leisurely between thumb and forefinger to his lips. He had the pack in his other hand then riding the top of the steering wheel. I'll bet I don't make it, he wagered, don't reach it. His right hand having delivered the cigarette to his mouth was creeping slowly for the pack to put it away. It was halfway up the steering wheel when the voice, suddenly clear, hopeful, said:

Say, wonder could I get one of them from ye . . . (leaning forward, already reaching) . . . I run out a while back and ain't . . .

Sylder chuckled and straight-armed the pack at him. Sure, he said. Help yourself. He waited a few seconds, listening to the paper rustle, the man getting the cigarette. He could feel him hesitate, the eyes turn on him. Then the package came back.

Thanks, old buddy, the man said.

Sylder waited. The man didn't say anything more. Waiting too. Sylder produced the matches with painful deliberation. Catching up his knee to the underside of the wheel he steered that way and with studied slowness fumbled a match from the box and struck it. Shielding the flame with his hands he lit the cigarette, then dropped the dying match over his elbow into the slipstream boring past the open windwing and took the wheel once more, exhaling luxuriously and repocketing the matches. He waited.

Say, old buddy, I wonder if I could get a . . . why thanks, thank ye.

The match scratched and popped. Sylder meditated in the windshield the face of the man cast in orange and black above the spurt of flame like the downlidded face of some copper ikon, a mask, not ambiguous or inscrutable but merely discountenanced of meaning, expression. In the flickery second in which Sylder's glance went to the road and back the man's eyes raised to regard him in the glass, so that when Sylder looked back they faced each other over the cup of light like enemy chieftains across a council fire for just that instant before the man's lips pursed, carplike, still holding the cigarette, and sucked away the flame.

They smoked, the heat of the night air moving over them heavy as syrup. In the dark glass where the road poured down their cigarettes rose and fell like distant semaphores above the soft green dawn of the dashlights.

He stopped at Gainesville for gas which he didn't need and went into the men's room taking the keys with him. The man sat in the car. Inside, Sylder lit a cigarette, smoked it in long pulls and flipped the butt into the toilet. He splashed some cold water on his face and went out again, paid the sleepy-eyed attendant and got in the car. The man was sitting as he had left him. An unmistakable trace of fresh tobacco smoke hung on the wet air.

Dawn. Fields smoking where the mist shoaled, trees white as bone. The gray shrubbery hard-looking as metal in the morning wetness. Beads of water raced on the windscreen and he turned on the wipers, watched the arms descend in slow benediction, was mopping at the glass with the back of his hand when the right rear tire went out with a sudden hollow detonation and they flapped to a stop.

Later Sylder realized that the man had passed up one chance with the jack handle, had waited until he took the jack from under the car and handed it himself to the man to put in the trunk. And realized too that the man had only miscalculated by part of a second the length of time it would take him to bend and slam the hubcap back on the rim with the heel of his hand. So although he never saw it, had no warning, he had already made a half turn and started to rise when the jack crashed into his shoulder and slammed him into the side of the car. Something crashed alongside his head into the quarterpanel—he remembered that too, but couldn't know until later that it was the base of the jack. He didn't duck the second time either, but only slid down the door of the coupe when the man swung, sideways —he was watching him now—tearing a ragged hole in the metal. Then he was sitting on the ground, his head leaned back against the door, looking up, not yet outraged but only in wonder, at the figure above him, his arm trailing in the dirt like a shattered wing. But when the man jerked the shaft of the jack from the punctured door he reached up, slowly, he thought, and laid his hand on the jack and still slowly closed his fingers over it. The man looked down at him, and in the gradual suffusion of light gathered and held between the gloss of the car's enamel and the paling road dust he saw terror carved and molded on that face like a physical deformity. They were like that for some few seconds, he sitting, the man standing, holding either end of the jack as if suspended in the act of passing it one to the other. Then Sylder stood, still in that somnambulant slow motion as if time itself were running down, and watched the man turn, seeming to labor not under water but in some more viscous fluid, torturous slow, and the jack itself falling down on an angle over the dying forces of gravity, leaving Sylder's own hand and bouncing slowly in the road while his leaden arm rose in a stiff arc and his fingers cocked like a cat's claws unsheathing and buried themselves in the cheesy neckflesh of the man who fled from him without apparent headway as in a nightmare.

Whether he fell forward or whether the man pulled them over he did not know. They were lying in the road, the man with his face in the dirt and Sylder on top of him, motionless for the moment as resting lovers. Something in Sylder's shoulder traveled obliquely down to his lungs with each breath to cut off the air. He still had one hand locked in the man's neck and now he inched himself forward and whispered into his ear:

Why don't you say something now, bastard? Ain't you got some more talk to spiel for us?

He was jerking at the man's head but the man had both hands over it and seemed lost in speculation upon the pebbles of the road. Sylder let his hand relax and wander through the folds of the neck until they arrived at the throat. The man took that for a few minutes, then suddenly twisted sideways, spat in Sylder's face, and tried to wrench himself free. Sylder rolled with him and had him then flat backward in the road and astride him, still the one arm swinging from his broken shoulder like a piece of rope. He crept forward and placed one leg behind the man's head, elevating it slightly, looking like some hulking nurse administering to the wounded. He pushed the head back into the crook of his leg, straightened his arm, and bore down upon the man's neck with all his weight and strength. The boneless-looking face twitched a few times but other than that showed no change of expression, only the same rubbery look of fear, speechless and uncomprehending, which Sylder felt was not his doing either but the everyday look of the man. And the jaw kept coming down not on any detectable hinges but like a mass of offal, some obscene waste matter uncongealing and collapsing in slow folds over the web of his hand. It occurred to him then that the man was trying to bite him and this struck him as somehow so ludicrous that a snort of laughter wheezed in his nose. Finally the man's hands came up to rest on his arm, the puffy fingers trailing over his own hand and wrist reminding him of baby possums he had seen once, blind and pink.

Sylder held him like that for a long time. Like squeezing a boil, he thought. After a while the man did try to say something but no words came, only a bubbling sound. Sylder was watching him in a sort of mesmerized fascination, noting blink of eye, loll of tongue. Then he eased his grip and the man's eyes widened.

For Christ's sake, he gasped. Jesus Christ, just turn me loose.

Sylder put his face to the man's and in a low voice

said, You better call on somebody closer than that. Then
he saw his shoulder, saw the man looking at it. He dug
his thumb into the man's windpipe and felt it collapse
like a dried tule. The man got his hand up and began
with his eyes closed to beat Sylder about the face and
chest. Sylder closed his eyes too and buried his face
in his shoulder to protect it. The flailings grew violent,
slowed, finally stopped altogether. When Sylder opened
his eyes again the man was staring at him owlishly, the
little tongue tipped just past the open lips. He relaxed his
hand and the fingers contracted, shriveling into a tight
claw, like a killed spider. He tried to open it again but
could not. He looked at the man again and time was
coming back, gaining, so that all the clocks would be
right.

The man had been dead for perhaps a quarter of an
hour. Sylder staggered to the car and sat on the runningboard, stared unblinking into the brass eye of the sun
ponderous and unreal on the red hills until he lost
consciousness.

Morning. Lying with his cheek in the dust of the
road he had a child's view, the jack looming like a fallen
tree and beyond that the man face-upward like a
peaceful giant composed for sleep. The rocks in the
road threw long shadows and the first birds were about.
Sylder had already started dragging the heavy body
off into the johnson grass and poison ivy when he heard
the sound of a motor somewhere on the curves behind
him. He stopped, then turned and started toward the
coupe again trying to run and dragging the carcass
behind him with one hand, stumbling, knowing halfway
there that he would never make it, that he had made a
mistake. So he didn't even open the door but dropped

the body as he reached the car, squatted over it, and gripping the underside of the runningboard for support jacked his feet up into the man's armpits and slid him toes up beneath the car for three-fourths his length just as a truck rounded the far curve and caught him struggling to his feet.

The sun was well up. Across the open country, the wale of pines shedding scarves of mist like swamp gases rising on the steamy air, some crows were hawking their morning calls. Sylder scooted from under the car, stood and was idly toeing out the drag-marks when the truck pulled alongside. He knew they would stop and already he began to think that he had done the best thing, that they would have seen the man inside, would insist on helping when they saw his . . . His arm: he snapped his head and two faces peering from the halted truck blurred and he looked down and saw the great smear of blood on his arm and dried and blackening on his shirtfront, was still looking at it sickly when a voice from the truck said:

Kin we hep ye?

He didn't look up for a second, caught in the pain of his wrecked shoulder raging now as if loosed by the voice from the truck cab, and not lost either to the irony of it. Then he raised his face to the curious sympathetic eyes watching him with a bland serenity that not even the bloody vision of himself could ruffle.

They were on the far side, he looking at them across the incline of the open turtledeck, so that even as he said *We* he thought: They can't see him. Yet he couldn't get his mind that far ahead, and even afterwards could not trace the possibilities on their separate courses. He reconciled the whole thing by this: that there was no way to keep them from getting out of the truck anyway.

So he said: We had a little accident, and thought Yes, they will get out anyway. These bastards will jest have to get out and see good.

The truck doors spread simultaneously like rusty wings and fell to in a rattle of glass uncushioned by any upholstery. They were a man and his son, the elder heavy and red, with creased skin, the younger a tall and thinner duplication. They came shuffling around the rear of the car with an air of infinite and abiding patience. Sylder turned slowly, his eye raking over the scene, trying to imagine what it looked like: the feet protruding solemnly from under the car, the car itself with the hole torn in the quarterpanel and in the door, the dent where the base of the jack hit and the jack lying in the road . . .

You hurt bad? the man asked.

Naw, Sylder grunted. The man was looking past him. What happent?

Car fell, Sylder said. No-account piece of a jack give way on me. He kicked at the handle.

The man eyed the strewn jack. Shore did now, didn't it, he said. Whew. Them things'r dangerous as a cocked gun. Always have maintained it. How about your buddy there? Nodding at the upturned feet.

Yeah, Sylder said to himself. How about him now. Then to the man: He's all right. Knocked the muffler down when she fell. Soon's he gets her wired back we'll be set. The man was moving around him; Sylder cut him off. Say, he said, tell you what you might do.

What's that?

Get your dead ass out of here, Sylder thought. He said: Well, you might carry me down to Topton, see a doctor. Durned arm's bleeding pretty bad.

Shore, said the man, I guess we might better at that. Looks pretty bad. You come on.

They started for the truck, Sylder behind them, herding them. He moved around to the cab, hung back till the older one got in, then stooped to one knee and spoke loudly to the corpse:

Listen, these fellers going to carry me in to Topton to the doc's. You come on when you get done . . . You all done? He rose and turned to the man sitting now in the truck, the motor already started. Listen, he said. He's about done, I'll jest go on in with him. You fellers go on, we'll be all right now . . . and thinking *Will you go now? Will you go?*

Well, the man said, leaning across the boy (wide-eyed, still silent, getting into the truck), you sure you okay now?

Sure, Sylder said, already waving to them. Much obliged.

You're more'n welcome, the man said. His face moved back, the boy nodded. The gears shifted with a grating sound and the motor died, hushed suddenly in the blue stillness of the broken day.

Sylder stood there listening to the tortured cranking of the starter and thinking: Ah, God. I should've knowed. That raggedy-assed son of a bitch ain't goin to . . .

But it did. The motor coughed a few times, then clattered to a low roar. The gears raked again and the truck pulled away sifting up dustspurs from the rear wheels and was gone almost instantly beyond the curve of the road.

They never seen the hole, Sylder said. They must never of even seen it. Then he thought: How in hell would they know how long it'd been there if they had?

He turned and made for the far side of the car, listing badly, staggerfooted, reeled at the rear bumper and collapsed into the trunk whacking his broken shoulder against the spare tire. There he sat for some minutes dazed and his mind threatening unconsciousness again.

Got to get the hell out of here, he said, shaking his head and wobbling to his feet. He steadied himself with one hand against the cool skin of the coupe, worked his way to the other side and squatted there above the brogans. He cursed them for a while, then took hold of one worn heel and bracing a foot against the running-board began to pull the man out. He tried not to look when the head emerged, then gave up and had a good look. The eyes were leaping from their sockets, an expression of ghastly surprise, the tongue still poking out. Sylder pulled him to the back of the car, got his hand in the shirt collar, lifting him bodily, and jerked him into the trunk. Only the legs dangled over the bumper and these he folded in after. Then he collected the jack and threw it in, dropped the lid, went to the switch for the keys and locked the trunk.

Night. The coombs of the mountain fluted with hound voices, a threnody on the cooling air. Flying squirrels looped in feathery silence from tree to tree above the old man sitting on a punk log, his feet restless trampling down the poison ivy, listening to Scout and Buster flowing through the dark of the flats below him, a swift slap slap of water where they ghosted through the creek, pop of twig or leaf-scuttle brought to his ear arcanely —they were a quarter mile down—and the long bag-throated trail-call again.

When Sylder turned the key, the handle, and swung the lid up, he didn't expect the stench that followed, poured out upon him in a seething putrid breath. He didn't even have time to step back. The spume of vomit roiled up from the pit of his stomach and he staggered

The Green Fly Inn burned on December twenty-first of 1936 and a good crowd gathered in spite of the cold and the late hour. Cabe made off with the cashbox and at the last minute authorized the fleeing patrons to carry what stock they could with them, so that with the warmth of the fire and the bottles and jars passing around, the affair took on a holiday aspect. Within minutes the back wall of the building fell completely away, spiraling off with a great rushing sound into the hollow. The rooftree collapsed then and the tin folded inward, the edges curling up away from the walls like foil. By now the entire building was swallowed in flames rocketing up into the night with locomotive sounds and sucking on the screaming updraft half-burned boards with tremendous velocity which fell spinning, tracing red ribbons brilliantly down the night to crash into the canyon or upon the road, dividing the onlookers into two bands, grouped north and south out of harm's way, their faces lacquered orange as jackolanterns in the ring of heat. Until the stilts gave and the facing slid backward from the road with a hiss, yawed in a slow curvet about the anchor of the pine trunk, overrode the crumpling poles, vaulting on them far out over the canyon before the floor buckled and the whole structure, roof, walls, folded neatly about some unguessed axis and dropped vertically into the pit.

There it continued to burn, generating such heat that the hoard of glass beneath it ran molten and fused in a single sheet, shaped in ripples and flutings, encysted with crisp and blackened rubble, murrhined with bottlecaps. It is there yet, the last remnant of that landmark, flowing down the sharp fold of the valley like some imponderable archeological phenomenon.

II

II

Curled in a low peach limb the old man watched the midmorning sun blinding on the squat metal tank that topped the mountain. He had found some peaches, although the orchard went to ruin twenty years before when the fruit had come so thick and no one to pick it that at night the overborne branches cracking sounded in the valley like distant storms raging. The old man remembered it that way, for he was a lover of storms.

The tank was on high legs and had a fence around it with red signs that he had been pondering for some time, not just today. From time to time he sliced a bite from one of his peaches. They were small and hard, but he had good teeth. He propped one foot up in the limb with him and fell to stropping the knife slowly on the smooth-worn toe of his boot. Then he wet a patch

of hair on his arm and tested the blade. Satisfied, he
reached for another peach and began peeling it.

When he had finished this one he wiped the blade of
the knife on his cuff, folded and pocketed it, passed a
handful of loose sleeve across his mouth. Then he got
down from his limb and started up through the wreckage of the orchard, threading his way among the old
gray limbs and stopping to look out over the valley now
and again, at the black corded fields and the roofs winking in the sun. When he came out on the road he turned
down to the right, his brogans making small padding
sounds in the red dust, his huge knobby-kneed trousers
rolling and moiling about him urgently as if invested
with a will and purpose of their own.

This was the orchard road red and quiet in the early
sun, winding from the mountain's spine with apple trees
here along the road and shading it, gnarled and bitten
trees, yet retaining still a kept look and no weeds growing where they grew. Farther up was a side road that
went off among the trees, shade-dappled, grass fine as
hair in the ruts. It went to the spray-pit, a concrete tank
set in the ground that had once been used to mix in-
secticide. These six years past it had served as a crypt
which the old man kept and guarded. Passing it now he
remembered how he had been *coming up from the hollow with a gallon bucket when a boy and a girl, neither
much more than waist-high to him, had rounded the
curve. They stopped when they saw him and it took
him a while, coming toward them with his pail, to see
that they were scared, huge-eyed and winded with
running. They looked ready to bolt so he smiled, said
Howdy to them, that it was a pretty day. And them
there in the road, balanced and poised for flight like
two wild things, the little girl's legs brightly veined
with brier scratches and both their mouths blue with*

berry stain. As he came past she began to whimper
and the boy, holding her hand, jerked at her to be still,
he standing very straight in his overall pants and striped
jersey. They edged to the side of the road and turned,
watching him go by.

He started past, then half turned and said: You'ns find
where the good berries is at?

The boy looked up at him just as though he hadn't
been watching him all the time and said something which
cracked in his voice and which the old man couldn't
make out. The girl gave up and wailed openly. So he
said:

Well now, what's wrong with little sister? You all
right, honey? Did you'ns lose your berry bucket? He
talked to them like that. After a while the boy began to
blubber too a little and was telling him about back in
the pit. For a few minutes he couldn't figure out what
was the pit and then it came to him and he said:

Well, come on and show me. I reckon it ain't all this
bad whatever it is. So they started up the road although
it was pretty plain they didn't want to go, and when they
turned down the road to the spray-pit the boy stopped,
still holding the little girl's hand and not crying any
more but just watching the man. He said he didn't want
to go, but for him, the old man, to go on and see. So
he told them to wait right there that it wasn't nothing.

He saw the berry pails first, one of them turned over
and the blackberries spilled out in the grass. A few feet
beyond was the concrete pit and even before he got to
it he caught a trace of odor, sour . . . a little like bad
milk. He stepped onto the cracked rim of the pit and
looked down into the water, the furred green top of
it quiet and touched with light. Sticks and brush poked
up at one corner. The smell was stronger but other than
that there was nothing. He walked along the edge of the

*pit. Down the slope among the apples some jays were
screaming and flashing in the trees. The morning was
well on and it was getting warm. He walked halfway
round, watching his step along the narrow sandy concrete. Coming back he glanced down at the water again.
The thing seemed to leap at him, the green face leering
and coming up through the lucent rotting water with
eyeless sockets and green fleshless grin, the hair dark
and ebbing like seaweed.*

*He tottered for a moment on the brink of the pit and
then staggered off with a low groan and locked his arms
about a tree trying to fight down the coiling in his
stomach. He didn't go back to look again. He got the
berry pails and went back to the road, but the children
weren't there and he couldn't think how to call them.
After a while he called out, Hey! I got your berry
buckets . . .*

*Some wind turned the apple leaves, shadow of a
buzzard skated on the road and broke up in the fencing
of briers. They were gone. He walked up the road a
way, then back down, but there was no trace of them.*

*Three days later when he came back it was still there,
no one had come. With his pocketknife he cut a small
cedar tree with which to put it from sight.*

It was still there, what of it had weathered the seasons
and years. He went on along the road, an old man
pedaling the scorched dust.

The sun was high now, all the green of the morning
shot with sunlight, plankton awash in a sea of gold. Even
late spring had dried nothing but the dust in the road,
and the foliage that overhung either side had not yet
assumed its summer coat of red talc. In the early quiet all
sounds were clear and equidistant—a dog barking out in
the valley, high thin whistle of a soaring hawk, a lizard
scuttling dead leaves at the roadside. A sumac would

turn and dip in sudden wind with a faint whish, in
the woods a thrush, water-voiced . . .

The old man took a sidepath that led along a spur
of the mountain, cutting a spiderstick as he went to
clear the way where huge nets were strung tree to tree
across the path dew-laden and glinting like strands of
drawn glass, bringing them down with a sticky whisper
while the spiders fled over the wrecked and dangling
floss. He came out on a high bald knoll that looked
over the valley and he stopped here and studied it as a
man might cresting a hill and seeing a strange landscape
for the first time. Pines and cedars in a swath of dark
green piled down the mountain to the left and ceased
again where the road cut through. Beyond that a field
and a log hogpen, the shakes spilling down the broken
roof, looking like some diminutive settler's cabin in
ruins. Through the leaves of the hardwoods he could
see the zinc-colored roof of the church faintly coruscant
and a patch of boarded siding weathered the paper-gray
of a waspnest. And far in the distance the long purple
welts of the Great Smokies.

If I was a younger man, he told himself, I would move
to them mountains. I would find me a clearwater branch
and build me a log house with a fireplace. And my bees
would make black mountain honey. And I wouldn't care
for no man.

He started down the steep incline. —Then I wouldn't
be unneighborly neither, he added.

The path followed along the south face of the mountain and came out on the pike; a dirt road dropped off
into a steep hollow to the left. The old man went this
way, down under the wooded slope where water dripped
and it was cool. Half a mile farther and the road turned
up a hill, emerging from the woods to poke through a
cornfield where a brace of doves flushed out and faired

away to the creek on whistling wings. Beyond the field and set back up from the road was a small board shack with the laths curling out like hair awry, bleached to a metal-gray. It was to this place that the man came, carrying the stick across his shoulders now as one might carry a yoke of waterbuckets, his hands flapping idly.

The hillside in front of the house was littered with all manner of cast-off things: barrel hoops, a broken axehead, fragments of chicken-wire, a chipped crock . . . small antiquated items impacted in the mud. There was a black hog-kettle which he didn't use any more; it was flecked with rust. The porch was shy the first step and he had to climb up, using his stick for support. The front of the house in the shade under the porch roof was green with fungus and the old man sat wearily on the floor and leaned back against it, stretched his legs out flat and opened his collar. It was damp and cool. The house faced to the north with a slope of trees behind it and snow lay in his yard longer than in most places.

In spring the mountain went violent green, billowing low under the sky. It never came slowly. One morning it would just suddenly be there and the air rank with the smell of it. The old man sniffed the rich earth odors, remembering other springs, other years. He wondered vaguely how people remembered smells . . . Not like something you see. He could still remember the odor of muskrat castor and he hadn't smelled it for forty years. He could even remember the first time he had smelled that peculiar sweet odor; coming down Short Creek one morning a lot more years ago than forty, the cottonwoods white and cold-looking and the creek smoking. Early in the spring it was, toward the close of the trapping season, and he had caught an old bull rat with orange fur, the size of a housecat. The air was thick with the scent of musk and had reminded him then of something else, but he could never think what.

He dozed, slept, for a long time. Late in the afternoon clouds began to pile up in the gap of the mountain and a fresh breeze came past the corner of the porch to rock gently the gourds swung from the eaves.

He woke before the rain started. The breeze had cooled and cooled, fanning his face and the beads of sweat on his forehead. He sat up and rubbed his neck. A pair of mockingbirds were pinwheeling through the high limbs of the maples, were still; and then, arriving as if surprised themselves in the greengold heat of the afternoon, the first drops of rain splatted dark on the packed mud below the house. A flat shade undulated across the yard, the road, and climbed the mountain face with an illusion of sudden haste; the rain increased, growing in the distance with the wind and leaching the trees beyond the creek lime-silver. The old man watched the rain advance across the fields, the grass jerking under it, the stones in the road going black and then the mud in the yard. A gust of spray wet his cheek and he could hear the roof-shakes dancing.

When the one gutterpipe wired to the porch roof overflowed, the water fell in a single translucent fan and the landscape bleared and weaved. The rain splashed in until there was a dark border about the porch. He took out his tobacco and rolled a cigarette with trembly hands, neat and perfect. The wind had gone and he sat back with his head against the green plankings and watched the smoke standing in the air under the dampness and very blue. After a while the rain began to slacken and it was darkening, the sky above the mountain black but for a thin reef of failing gray, and then that was gone and it was night, staccato with lightning in the distance. The old man began to feel a chill and was ready to go in when something cracked on the mountain and he looked up in time to see the domed metal tank on the peak illuminated, quivering in a wild aureole of light. There was a sound like fingernails on slate and the old man shivered and blinked his eyes, the image burning white hot in the lenses for another moment, and when he looked again it was gone and he stood in darkness with the sound of the rain slipping through the trees and a thin trickle of water coming off the roof somewhere to spatter in a puddle below. He waggled his hand in front of his face and couldn't even see it.

He stood up and batted his eyes. Far back beyond the mountain a thin wire of lightning glowed briefly. Corner post and porch began to materialize slowly out of the murk and he could see the hound when it loomed up over the edge of the porch, snuffling, ears flapping and collar jingling as he shook the rain from his reeking hide. He came up, toenails clicking on the planks, and snuffed at the old man's trousers.

Where you been, old dog? the old man said. The dog began to rub against his leg and the old man pushed him away with his foot, saying Go on, Scout. Scout moved over against the house and settled. The man rubbed the back of his neck, stretched and went in.

The house was musty, dank and cellar-like. He felt his way to the corner table and lit a coal-oil lamp, the ratty furniture leaping out from the shadows in the yellow light. He went into the kitchen and lit the lamp there, took down a plate of beans and a pan of dry cornbread from the warmer over the stove. He sat at the table and ate them cold, and when he had finished went outside with a handful of biscuits and threw them to the dog. The rain had almost stopped. The hound bolted down the biscuits and looked up after him. The screendoor banged to, the square of light on the porch floor narrowed and went out with the click of the latch. The old man did not appear again. The dog lowered his head on his paws and peered out at the night with wrinkled and sorrowing eyes.

Cats troubled the old man's dreams and he did not sleep well any more. He feared their coming in the night to suck his meager breath. Once he woke and found one looking in the window at him, watching him as he slept. For a while he had kept the shotgun loaded and lying on the floor beside the bed but now he only lay there and listened for them. Very often they would not start until late and he would still be awake, his ears ringing slightly from having listened so long. Then would come a thin quavering yowl from some dark hollow on the mountain. He had used to trot to the window and peer out at the hills, at the silhouette of pines in the low saddle above Forked Creek like a mammoth cathedral gothically spired . . . Now he only lay in his gray covers and listened. He did not sleep much at night and he was sore and bone-worn from napping in chairs, against logs and trees, sprawled on the porch.

When he was a boy in Tuckaleechee there was a colored woman lived in a shack there who had been a slave. She came there because, as she said, there weren't any other niggers and because she felt the movements and significations there. She wore a sack of hellebore at her neck and once he had seen her on the road and hadn't been afraid of her, as he was very young then, so she put three drops of milfoil on the back of his tongue and chanted over him so that he would have vision. She told him that the night mountains were walked by wampus cats with great burning eyes and which left no track even in snow, although you could hear them screaming plain enough of summer evenings.

Ain't no sign with wampus cats, she told him, but if you has the vision you can read where common folks ain't able.

He related this to his mother and she held the cross of Jesus against his forehead and prayed long and fervently.

The old man lay on his back listening to the heart surge under his ribcage, his breath wheening slow and even. In the fall before this past winter he had come awake one night and seen it for the second time, black in the paler square of the window, a white mark on its face like an inverted gull wing. And the window frame went all black and the room was filling up, the white mark looming and growing. He reached down and seized the shotgun by the barrel, spun it around and thumbed the hammer and let it fall. The room erupted . . . he remembered the orange spit of flame from the muzzle and the sharp smell of burnt powder, that his ears were singing and his arm hurt where the butt came back against it. He got up and stumbled to the table, dragging the gun by its warm barrel, found and struck a match and got the lantern lit. Then he went to the window, the light flickering thin shadows up the wall, playing to the low ceiling and whitening the spiderwebs. He held the lamp up. Above the window the boards were blasted and splintered clean and honeycolored. He didn't keep the shotgun by the bed any more but over in the corner behind the table.

The old man lay awake a long time. Once he thought he heard a cry, faintly, beyond the creek and the field, but he wasn't sure. A car passed on the road and he wondered about that but then he dozed and the crickets had already stopped.

Deep hole between her neck-cords, smokeblue. Laddered boneshapes under the paper skin like rows of welts descending into the bosom of her dress. Eyes lowered to her work, blink when she swallows like a toad's. Lids wrinkled like walnut hulls. Her grizzled hair gathered, tight, a helmet of zinc wire. Softly rocking, rocking. A looping drape of skirt slung in a curtain-fold down the side of the chair swept softly at the floor. She sat before the barren fireplace stitching buttonholes in a shirt of woolen millends. From out his scrolled and gilded frame Captain Kenneth Rattner, fleshly of face and rakish in an overseas cap abutting upon his right eyebrow, the double-barred insignia wreathed in light, soldier, father, ghost, eyed them.

With the lamps aligned one on either side she had a ritualistic look, a nun at beads perhaps. Later he watched from the kitchen lean-to because it had a tin roof and a wind had come up now and was blowing the rain across it with long ripping sounds like silk tearing. He turned the pages of his magazine but he had read it so much that he scarcely looked at the pages any more; mostly he watched how the lampflame quivered and the polished work that bound the stove, burnt to peacock colors of bronze and copper, violet-blue, changed patterns, ran to whorls and flamepoints. He waved his hand over the glass and the blue canisters above the stove bowed.

In the kitchen the man on the mantel couldn't watch him any more either. After a while he put down the magazine and turned around in the chair, sat with his elbows propped on the back and watched out the window for lightning. Thin cracks of it far back over Winkle Hollow like heat lightning. There was no thunder, only the rain and wind.

The boy thought he could remember his father. Or perhaps only his mother telling about him . . . He remembered a man, his father or just some other man he was no longer sure. His father didn't come back after they moved from Maryville. He remembered that, the moving.

It was a house of logs, hand-squared and chinked with clay, the heavy rafters in the loft pinned with wooden pegs. There had been a loom in the loft but it had since been burned piece by piece for kindling. It was a huge affair of rough-cut wood that under the dust had retained even then a yellow newness. The rafters still looked that way. In the summer wasps nested over the boards, using the auger-holes where dowels had shrunk in some old dry weather and fallen to the floor to emerge out into the hot loft and drone past his bed to the window where a corner of glass was gone and so out into the sunlight. There had been mud-dobber nests stacked up the wide planks too but his mother had raked them all down one day and aside from the wasps there were only the borers and woodworms, which he never saw but knew by the soft cones of wood-dust that gathered on the floor, the top log beneath the eaves, or trailed down upon the cobwebs, heavy yellow sheets of them opaque with dust and thick as muslin.

The house was tall and severe with few windows. Some supposed it to be the oldest house in the county. It was roofed with shakes and they seemed the only part of it not impervious to weather and time, for they were blackened and split, and now curling in their ruin they seemed victims of a long-ago fire which the house had somehow escaped altogether, for it was sound and the logs were finely checked and seasoned. They sagged and bellied and seemed supported only by the chimneys of clay and river rock at either end, but the house was strong and settled and no wind could bring a creak from it.

They paid no tax on it, for it did not exist in the county courthouse records, nor on the land, for they did not own it. They paid no rent on either house or land, as claimants to either or both properties were nonexistent in deed as the house itself. They paid Oliver Henderson, who brought water to them three times a week on his milk route.

The well hidden in the weeds and johnson grass that burgeoned rankly in the yard had long shed its wall of rocks and they were piled in the dry bottom in layers between which rested in chance interment the bones of rabbits, possums, cats, and other various and luckless quadrupeds.

· He didn't know that, but only guessed because he had found a young rabbit in the well one spring and was afraid to climb down after it. He brought green things

to it every day and dropped them in and then one day
he fluttered a handful of garden lettuce down the hole
and he remembered how some of the leaves fell across it
and it didn't move. He went away and he could see for
a long time the rabbit down in the bottom of the well
among the rocks with the lettuce over it.

She had finished now and put one lamp on the mantel
and was looking at it with the shirt in her hand held up
against her. She stood that way for a while and then she
turned and saw him watching her over his shoulder, each
of them touched with light and the space between them
through the narrow door dark. He couldn't see her eyes
and he made out that he was looking at something else
and finally turned back to the window and the rain.

Boy, she said.

Yesm.

You get to bed.

Yesm, he said again. He did not move.

Your bed ain't got wet, is it?

No mam.

It would be wet, always was when it rained even if it
didn't blow. It was musty and smelled good then and
cool enough for the blanket. This year, this summer, he
had moved to the porch off the kitchen, carrying his bed
down one Sunday evening while she was at church and
in it by the time she got back, breathing deeply when
she stopped at the door on her way in. Then he could
hear her at the dishes in the kitchen humming to herself,
and she never said anything about it except she made
him carry out the two boxes of bottles and cans he had
evicted from the corner. The lean-to porch was screened
in from waist-high up; after he was in bed a while
he could see even the acorns in the yard oaks. Some
nights a tall gaunt hound came and peered in the screendoor at him and he would speak to it, it standing there

high-shouldered and flat-looking, not moving, and then
it would be gone and he could hear its feet padding off
through the yard and the clink of its collar.

He pulled the bed out from the corner, turned back
the spread and felt the pillow. Then he turned it over
and took the blanket from under his arm and put it on
the bed and got in. That was the last night of that summer. He fell asleep to the water and metal sounds of the
rain runneling over the tin and sluicing through the gutterpipe, the rapid slash of it in a gust of wind and the
fine mist spraying his face through the bellying screen.
The oaks stirred restlessly, low admonitions, shhh . . .

In the morning the rain had stopped and there was a
chill in the air and smoke. He smiled at that, for he was
waiting and weathers and seasons were his timepiece
now. There were still warm days but that didn't matter
to him. Jays were in the blackoaks mornings and the
grackles had come back, great flocks of them bending
the trees, their feathers glinting dark metal colors and
their calls harshly musical, like a rusty swing. Or they
would be on the ground, the yard rolling blackly with
them, and he would run out and pop his hands once and
see them explode sunward, a flapping shrieking horde
bearing leaves and debris into the air on the updraft of
their wings.

The first weeks of September went and the weather
held and no frost. The veins were coming up in his arms
and he would press them and then raise his fist and feel
the blood in the soft tubes.

He was pushing time now and he could feel it give.
She canned the remainder of the garden in two days and
was after him to get his bed back up to the loft before
he took cold. It rained and the pond went blood-red and
one afternoon he caught a bass from the willows in water

not a foot deep and cleaned it and held the tiny heart in the palm of his hand, still beating.

His bed was still on the porch. These nights he could not bear to be in the house. He would go out after dinner and come back at bedtime—and then out again directly she was asleep, walking the dark roads, passing by the shacks and houses, the people illumined yellowly behind the windowlights in gestures mute and enigmatic . . .

One night cutting through a field he came upon two figures struggling in the grass, naked, white and frantic in the gloss of the quarter-moon as stranded fish. He went on. They did not see him. When he got to the road he began to run, his shoes slapping loud on the asphalt till they burned and stung, ran till his chest was seared. Below the forks of the road in Stiefel's yard was a great tulip poplar. He crawled up the kept-grass bank and folded in the shadows of the trunk like a malefactor gone to earth, his breath dragging coals through his lungs.

He sat there for a long time, watching the lights go out one by one over the valley. Sound of voices close and urgent on the acoustic night air, doors falling to, laughter . . . An encampment settling for rest, council fires put out . . . In caverns by torchlight a congress of fiends and warlocks rattling old dry bones in wistful hunger.

You goin to hunt him out. When you're old enough. Goin to find the man that took away your daddy. (Remember: fierce and already aging face downthrust into his, sweetsour smell . . .)

How can I? He had begun to cry.

Your daddy'd of knowed how. He was a Godfearin man if he never took much to church meetin . . . The Lord'll show you, boy. He will not forsake them what believe. Pray and the way will be made known to ye. He . . . You *swear* it, boy.

His arm was growing numb with pain . . . could feel her tremble through the clutched hand . . . I swear, he said.

You won't never forgit.

No.

Never long as you live.

Long as I live.

Yes, she said.

Long as I . . .

I won't forgit neither, she said, tightening once more on his arm for a moment, leaning her huge face at him. And, she hissed, he won't forgit neither.

I live . . .

He never forgot. From somewhere in the darkness came the sound of a banjo, tentative chords . . . a message . . . what news? Old loves reconsummated, sickness, a child's crying. Silence now in the houses. Repose. Even to those for whom no end of night could bring rest enough. And silence, the music fled in the seeping amber warmth of innumerable dreams laid to death upon the hearth, ghostly and still . . . The morning is yet to the nether end of the earth, and he is weary. Bowing the grass in like sadness the dew followed him home and sealed his door.

Still the weather held, and the rain. The days were gray and misty and in the night the trees dripped and spattered. The pond had been bottled and he watched them drifting about one morning while still-fishing from the limestone ledge at the upper end. Later a man came in a skiff poling through the fog and he saw him stop what bottles skittered and jerked and lift up the lines to take off the fish. The man saw him and nodded his head and he nodded back. The skiff circled at the upper end and returned down the pond, silent but for the thud of the pole on the stern-boards.

He was pushing hard now and the days were bending under and cold weather came. His cot was still on the porch and daily he checked the undoing of the yard trees, woke to a red world with the sun wedged huge and squat in the mountain gap and the maples incandesced. Couched in his musty blanket he sniffed to test the air. A limp breeze water-wrought and tempered with smoke came lisping through the screen with no news yet.

He waited. In the slow bleeding month of October he watched, looking torpid and heavylidded as a toad, his nerves coiled and tuned like a waiting cat's.

One evening coming from the store he saw her on the road and she smiled at him and said Hidy. He nodded and went on, heard them giggle behind him. He hadn't seen her since late in the summer.

He was crossing Saunders' field and bound for the creek, the homemade crokersack seine riding his shoulder like a tramp's dunnage. He never saw her until she spoke, leaning against a post with her hands capping the top of it and her chin resting on them. She looked as if she might have been standing there for days with an incalculable patience just waiting for him to come by.

Well, he thought, she ain't old enough to own the land to want to run me off of it even if she is big enough. So he said Howdy back to her.

Your name's John Wesley, ain't it?

He started to say, Yesm, but he said, Yep, that's my name.

She moved down from the post and came toward him, unhurried, sauntering. She wore a cotton print dress that buttoned up like a housecoat and where it stretched across her belly or strained to cover her rolling breasts white flesh and pink silk pursed out between the buttons. She pulled a weed and began chewing on it, eying him sidewise, standing in front of him now and favoring one leg so that her hip tilted out. What you doin? she asked.

Jest messin around, he said.

Messin around?

Yeah. That's all.

She nudged a stone with the toe of her slipper. Who you messin around with?

Why, nobody. Jest me.

The tips of her breasts were printed in the cloth like coins. She was watching him watch. You ain't supposed to mess around with yourself, she told him, part of a smile at her mouthcorners and eyes squinting in mischief.

Who says that? he asked.

Me. Preacher says that too.

I got to get on, he said.

You goin to mess with yourself some more?

He started on and she fell in alongside him. Where you goin? she asked.

Pond, he said.

What you goin there for?

Fish.

Fish. Fishin? You ain't got a pole.

Got one over there, he told her. Hid.

You don't carry your pole with you?

Nah.

She giggled.

They were walking along slow, much slower than he walked. After a while when she didn't say anything he asked her where she was going.

Me? she said. I ain't goin nowhere. Jest messin around.

Who you goin to mess around with?

Hmph, she laughed. You'd like to know, wouldn't you?

Nah. I don't care who you mess with.

He walked on, looking up at the trees, the sky.

You carry your fish in that?

What's that?

She was pointing at the croker seine. *That, she said.*

Oh. Naw, that's a seine. I got to seine me some minners first afore I go to the pond.

She didn't leave. Wading up the creek poking the pole of the seine up under the banks he would see her walking along or standing and watching. Where the honeysuckles thinned at one place she came up to the bank and took off her shoes and kicked at the water with her toes as he went by. When he looked back she was in the creek to her knees with her skirt hiked up and tucked under in the waist of her bloomers and her thighs were incredibly white against the surge of brown water where she walked unsteadily into the current, leaning, her breasts swinging. She caught up to him and splashed water at him. She said:

You don't know my name, do you?

All right, he said. What's your name?

What do you care?

I don't care, you jest . . .

What'd you ast me for then?

You . . . I never . . . He stopped. You was the one ast me if . . .

Wanita, she said. If you jest got to know. Wanita Tipton. I live over yander. She motioned vaguely beyond the creek, across the late summer ruins of a cornfield, a stand of walnut trees surrounding a stained house with a green tin roof. He nodded, fell to seining again.

*He didn't have enough floats and the minnows kept
going over the back. Still he had half a dozen in the can
tied to his belt.*

You like to do this? she asked over his shoulder.

*He turned around and looked at her. She was standing
on a rock with her legs together. The back of her dress
had come down and was dark and wet.*

You got a leech, he said.

I got to what?

Leech, he said. You got one on your leg.

*She looked down; it didn't take her long to find it, a
fat brown one just below her knee with a thin ribbon of
blood going pink on the wetness of her shin. She put her
hand to her mouth and just stood there looking at it. It
was a pretty good-sized leech for the creek although the
pond leeches came much bigger. She just kept looking
at it and after a while he said:*

Ain't you goin to take him off?

*That moved her. She looked up at him and her face
went red. Goddamn you, she said. Goddamn you for
a . . . a . . . Goddamn you anyway.*

Hell, I never put him there.

Take it off! Damn you! God . . . will you take it off?

*He sloshed over to where she was. Standing like that
in water halfway to his waist and her up on the rock he
could see up her thighs to where the skirt was tucked
into her bloomers. He got hold of the leech, trying to
look up and not to at the same time, and feeling giddy,
shaky, and pulled it loose and flipped it past her onto the
bank. He said: You ought not to wade barefooted.*

He had felt for a minute that he wasn't even afraid of
her any more and all he could remember now was running. *The huge expanse of flesh and the bloomers and
her holding him by the collar with her feet somehow in
the water on either side of him until he jerked away with*

his shirt ripping loudly and splashed back through the creek to the bank and out and across Saunders' field shedding water and minnows from his bucket with the foolish little seine still in his hand and water squishing in his shoes, running.

She said something to the other one and they giggled again. He went on with his bread, home, his face burning in the chill of the low October sun. When he came in through the porch he saw that his bed was gone. She was in the kitchen. He put the bread on the table and went up to the loft, his tread hollow on the boxed steps, up to the cobwebby gloom under the slanting eaves where the bed had been set and made with fresh linen.

By now in the early mornings the pond was steeped in mist, thick and coldly swirling, out of which sounded the gabble of phantom ducks. At sunrise the whole valley would be glazed white and crystal and the air smoked and tangy from the stoves and later from the open fires where women gathered about the kettles with long wooden paddles, elvish-looking in their shawls and bonnets, a clutch of trolls at their potions. First days of frost, cold smoky days with hogs screaming and now and again the distant hound-calls of geese howling down the south in thin V's flattening on the horizon to a line and then gone. He cut wood, went out early to the rising stacks of new pine kindling rimed and shining in the morning frost like wedges of frozen honey. He worked hard at it and the days went. For that much time he would have buried the yard house-high in stovewood.

If he'd lived, she told him one evening, you wouldn't want for nothin. And him disabled in the war with that platmium plate in his head and all—turned down the govmint disability, he did. Too proud. Wouldn't take no handout from nobody even if it was the govmint. He was a provider all right, may the Lord God Jesus keep him.

Yes, she said, eying him doubtfully, you make half the man he was an you'll be goin some.

The fire ticked on in the little stove, cherrying softly the one side of it till the cracks in the old iron showed like thin spiders sprawled there.

Rocking quietly in her chair she had the appearance of one engaged in some grim and persevering endeavor in which hope was the only useful implement. Not even patience. As if perhaps in some indistinct future the chair itself would rise and bear her away to glory with her sitting fiercely sedate and her feet maybe tucked under the rung, her skirt gathered about her. She was humming something in her high nasal hum, faint evocation of summer bees. The coals chuckled, settled with easy sifting sounds. She rocked. That was how winter came that year.

Through the weary slide of the wiper on the glass, the water sluicing away, Sylder watched the rain dance in the lights, flash from the black road. Behind him the siren sounded again, louder and with a new sense of urgency. I never tried it in the rain, he was thinking. The accelerator pedal was crushed hard under his foot and he watched the needle strain upward to sixty before he let off for the next curve. Got to do it afore I start up the mountain, he told himself, or I'm in a sling. So it would have to be at the forks of the road.

Lightning glared in threatful illusions of proximity and quick shapes appeared in the road, leapt from ditch or tree in configurations antic and bizarre. Ghosts of mist rose sadly from the paving and broke in willowy shreds upon the hood, the windshield. One curve more.

Behind him the rear window blackened, then the slow inexorable reach of lights crept out and fingered their way across the hillside off to his left, remarking scrub pines, ropes of limestone stretched in a yellow path like rows of somnolent sheep. When he reached the top of the hill the lights dropped away and the siren sounded again.

I can take a wide sweep, he told himself hopefully. The road looked like oil. Then there was no more time and he was there, nerve and muscle on their own and him just watching. He went into it at forty by the speedometer, saw the store blink its square eyes, cut the wheel to the left, one hand locking for just a moment the handbrake.

He couldn't see any more then. He brought the wheel back, the brake already released. Except he couldn't pull it sharp enough and the front end was sliding away and not turning. Then it gave and a streaming herd of trees swam past in the lights as if rushing headlong off the very rim of the earth and the store loomed again, glazed onto the green frieze, spinning past starkly white and in incredible elongation. And yet once more, trees and building in one long blur and then he was jarred from the rear by a solid whump of a sound and heard something snap like a dry stick cracking and then a rattling spray of glass. The lights had come to rest straight back down the road and he already had the shiftlever up in second, the tires whining, inching forward, when the cruiser leapt over the hill before him. Then the tires bit and he was gone, raking a fender of the other car on the way out with deliberate skill. Behind him the store squinted with half a post leaning in through one window and a corner of the porch sagging down, abject and humble in the pounding rain.

Sylder popped a match on the dash and lit a cigarette.

Adios, John, he said. He sang quietly to himself: Long gone, ain't he lucky? Long gone, from Kentucky . . . rocking slightly with the car's motion as it strung the curves.

*I*t was in August that he had found the sparrowhawk on the mountain road, crouched in the dust with one small falcon wing fanned and limp, eying him without malice or fear—something hard there, implacable and ungiving. It followed his movements as he approached and then turned its head when he reached out his hand to it, picked it up, feeling it warm and palpitant in the palm of his hand, not watching him, not moving, but only looking out over the valley calmly with its cold-glinting accipitral eyes, its hackles riffling in the wind. He carried it home and put it in a box in the loft and fed it meat and grasshoppers for three days and then it died.

Saturday he went into town with Mr Eller, holding the bag in one hand and sitting up high in the cab of the old truck watching the fields go by and then houses and *more of them and finally stores and filling stations, the river-bridge, and beyond that the shape of the city against the hot morning sky.*

How you gettin back? Mr Eller asked.

I'll get back, he said. I got some things to do.

He was standing on the runningboard, one foot in the street at the corner of Gay and Main. Here, Mr Eller said, leaning across the seat, holding his hand down.

What?

Here.

I got money, he said. It's okay.

Go on, damn it, the man said. He was shaking the quarter at him. Behind them a horn sounded.

Okay, he said. He took the quarter. Thanks, I'll see ye.

He slammed the door and the truck pulled away, Mr Eller lifting his hand once in parting; he waved at the back of his head in the rear glass, crossed the street and went up the walk to the courthouse, up the marble stairs and inside.

There was a woman at a small desk just inside the door fanning herself with a sheaf of forms. He stood for a few minutes looking around the hall and reading the signs over the doors and finally she asked him what it was that he needed.

He held the bag up. Hawk bounty, he said.

Oh, she said. I think you go in yander.

Where's that?

Over there—she pointed to a hallway.

Much obliged, he said.

There was a long counter and behind it were other women at desks. He stood there for a while and then one of them got up and came over to him and said, Yes?

He hefted the ratty little bag to the counter. From the sweat-crinkled neck exuded an odor rich and putrid even above the stale musty smell of the old building. The

*woman eyed the package with suspicion, then alarm, as
the seeping gases reached her nostrils. Delicately with
two fingers she touched the pinked mouthing of the
bag, withdrew. He upended it and slid the malodorous
contents out on the polished wood in a billowing well
of feathers. She stepped back and looked at it. Then she
said, not suspiciously or even inquiringly, but only by
way of establishing her capacity as official:*

Is it a chickenhawk?

Yesm, he said. It's a youngern.

*I see. She turned sharply and disappeared on a click
of heels behind a tier of green filing cabinets. In a few
minutes she was back with a little pad of printed forms,
stopping further down the counter and writing now
with a pen from a gathering of inkstands there. He
waited. When she had finished she tore the form from
the pad and came back and handed it to him. Sign where
the X's are, she told him. Then take it to the cashier's office. Down the hall—she pointed. He signed the two
lines with the pen, handed it back and started away when
she called him back.*

*I wonder if you would mind, she said, wrinkling her
nose and poking a squeamish finger at the little bird,
mind putting it back in the bag for me. He did. Holding
the slip of paper delicately in one hand and waving the
ink to dry he went to collect his bounty.*

*He left through the open door with the wind hollow-
ing through into the hall and skirmishing with the papers
on the bulletin board, warm wind of the summer forenoon fused with a scent of buckeyes, swirling chains of
soot about on the stone steps. He held the dollar in his
hand, folded neatly twice. When he got outside he took
it and folded it again, making a square of it, and thrust
it down between the copper rivets into the watchpocket
of his overall pants. He patted it flat and went down the*

*walk past the grimy trees, the monuments, the poised
and interminably peering statue, and out to the street.*

*A band was playing, wavering on the heat of the city
strains of old hymns martial and distantly strident. Rows
of cars were herded in shimmering somnolence beneath
a vapor of exhaust fumes and at the intersection stood a
policeman at parade rest.*

*He crossed the street and the music came suddenly
louder as if a door had opened somewhere. When he got
to the corner he could see them coming, eight and ten
abreast, a solemn phalanx of worn maroon, the drill-
cloth seedy and polished even at that distance, and their
instruments glinting dully in the sun. In a little knot to
the fore marched the leader, tall-hatted and batoned,
and the four guidons bracing up their masts, the colors
furling listlessly. A pair of tubas in the mass behind
them bobbed and rode like balloons, leaped ludicrously
above the marchers' heads and belched their frog-notes
in off-counterpoint to the gasping rattle of the other
instruments. Behind the marchers came a slowly wending caravan of buses through the windows of which
flocks of pennants waved and fluttered.*

*He watched, gathered up and pressed in the crowd,
the people sweating in their thin summer clothes, a maze
of shapes and colors similar only in the dark patches
under their armpits, straining their necks, toe-standing,
holding up children. The marchers passed them under
the canopy of heat, sweaty and desperate-looking. He
saw the near tuba player redfaced and wild as if perhaps he were obliged to puff at his instrument to keep
it from deflating and drooping down over the heads of
his fellows. They passed in an enormous shudder of
sound and the buses came, laborious in low gear, churning out balls of hazy blue smoke, their windows alive
with streamers, pennants, placards, small faces. Long*

paper banners ran the length of the buses proclaiming for Christ in tall red letters, and for sobriety, offering to vote against the devil when and wherever he ran for office. One by one they passed and again the multicolored flags in small children's hands waving at the spectators who in turn mopped listlessly at their necks and faces with handkerchiefs. A blue and yellow card legended: Don't Make My Daddy a Drunkard fell to the street like a stricken bird, leaving an empty hand clutching at the window. The next bus splintered and ground the flagstem and printed tiretreads over the sign.

Then the music stopped abruptly and there was only the uneasy shifting of the crowd, the slow drone of the buses. The pennants and signs came gradually to rest, to a collective embarrassment as if someone had died and they went on that way until the last bus was by, the little faces looking out solemn as refugees, onto the bridge and so out of the city. The crowds ebbed into the streets and thinned and the traffic began, the cars moving and the streetcars clicking past.

He was still standing on the sidewalk and now he saw the city, steamed and weaving in heat, and rising above the new facings of glass and tile the bare outlandish buildings, towering columns of brick adorned with fantastic motley; arches, lintels, fluted and arabesque, flowered columns and crowstepped gables, baywindows over corbels carved in shapes of feet, heads of nameless animals, Pompeian figures . . . here and there, gargoyled and crocketed, wreathed dates commemorating the perpetration of the structure. Rows of pigeons dozed on the high ledges and the heat rose in visible waves up from the paving. He patted the folded dollar again and started up Gay Street. When he got to the Strand he stopped and studied the pictures advertising the Saturday serial and fingered the quarter. Then he turned left and went up to Market Square. On the corner a man was screaming incoherently and brandishing a tattered Bible. Next him stood an old woman strapped into an accordion, mute and patient as a draft horse. He crossed the street behind the half-circle of spectators. The man stopped screaming and the accordion began and they sang, the two voices hoarse and high-pitched rising in a sad quaver to the calliope-like creaking of the instrument.

He went up the far side of the square under the shadow of the market house past brown country faces peering from among their carts and trucks, perched on crates, old women with faces like dried fruit set deep in their hooded bonnets, shaggy, striated and hooktoothed as coconut carvings, shabby backlanders trafficking in the wares of the earth, higgling their goods from a long row of ancient vehicles backed obliquely against the curb and freighted with fruits and vegetables, eggs and berries, honey in jars and boxes of nuts, bundles of roots and herbs from sassafras to boneset, a bordello of potted plants and flowers. By shoe windows where shoddy footgear rose in dusty tiers and clothing stores in whose vestibules iron racks stood packed with used coats, past bins of socks and stockings, a meat market where hams and ribcages dangled like gibbeted miscreants and in the glass cases square porcelain trays piled with meat white-spotted and trichinella-ridden, chunks of liver the color of clay tottering up from moats of watery blood, a tray of brains, unidentifiable gobbets of flesh scattered here and there.

Among overalled men and blind men and amputees on roller carts or crutches, flour and feed bags piled on the walk and pencil pedlars holding out their tireless arms, past stalls and cribs and holes-in-the-wall vending tobacco in cut or plug, leaf or bag, and snuff, sweet or scotch, in little tins, pipes and lighters and an esotery of small items down to pornographic picture books. Past cafés reeking with burned coffee, an effluvium of frying meat, an indistinguishable medley of smells.

Under the Crystal's marquee of lightbulbs a group of country men stood gazing hard past the box office where a tired-looking woman sat beneath a sign: Adults 25— Children 11—watching the film through a missing panel of curtain. Sounds of hooves and gunfire issued onto the street. He couldn't see past or over them and went on by, up the square, until he stood before a window garnished with shapes of wood and metal among which he recognized only a few common handtools. He held his hand up to one eye to break the glare of light on the glass and he could see them in the dim interior, hanging from their nail on the wall. He checked the dollar and went in. His footfalls were muffled on the dark oiled floors, bearing him into an atmosphere heavy with smells of leather and iron, machine-oil, seed, beneath strange objects hung from hooks in the ceiling, past barrels of nails, to the counter. They were hanging down by their chains and looking fierce and ancient among the trace chains and harness, bucksaws and axehelves. A clerk passed behind the counter and waited on a man idly turning a brass doorknob in his hand. Together they disappeared into the gloom, ducking under a fringe of dangling strap leather, to the rear of the store. A few minutes later a grayhaired man came up the aisle and leaned on the counter looking down at him.

Can I hep ye, son? he said.

How much are they? He motioned vaguely past the man as if there were but one item of merchandise displayed there. The traps . . . your traps there.

The man turned. Traps? Steel traps.

Yessir.

Well, he said, let's see . . . what size?

Them. He pointed. Number ones.

The man studied the dull metal shapes as if aware for the first time of their existence, seemingly puzzled not over their price but as to how they came to be there in the first place. Then he said, Yes. And lifted one down and set it on the counter before the boy at a quarter-angle, straightening the chain, as one might show a watch or a piece of jewelry.

The boy touched the oiled smoothness of it, pan, trigger, jaws, spring. How much? he asked again.

Thirty cents.

Thirty cents, the boy repeated.

Lessen you buy by the dozen. They're three dollars the dozen.

The boy turned that over in his mind. That would make em twenty-five then, wouldn't it?

Well, the man said, twelve and three . . . four for a dollar . . . is right, twenty-five cents is right.

Well, he said, I aim to get a dozen but I cain't get all of em together at the same time. So I wonder if I couldn't get four of em today and then get the rest later on . . . ?

The man looked at him for a minute and then he smiled. Why I reckon you could, he said. Course you'd have to sign a pledge for the whole dozen so as for me to let you have the four at the dozen price.

The boy nodded.

He reached up and unhooked three more traps and put them on the counter, their chains rattling angrily, reached under the cash register and came up with a book of old order forms. He wrote in it for a while and then tore off two copies and handed one to the boy. Sign that, he said. He was holding out the pen.

The boy took it and started to write.
Better read it first, the man cautioned.
He read it, ciphering out the tall thin handwriting:

I, the undersigned, do hereby agree to purchase
8 (eight) Victor no. 1 traps from the Farm & Home
Supply Store prior to Jan. 1, 1941. Price to be @ 25
cents ea.

Signed..............

signed his name to the bottom and handed back the pen.
The man took the signed paper and handed him the
other one, the carbon. Thisn's your copy, he told him.
The boy took it and folded it, then took the dollar from
his watchpocket and smoothed it on the counter. The
man took the dollar and rang it up in the register. Wait
till I get you a poke, he said.
He pulled a sheet of brown paper from a roll and
wrapped the traps in it and tied them with string. The
boy took the package, hefting the weight of it in his
hands. I'll be back to get the othern's afore long, he told
the man.
Then he was gone, out into the blinding sunshine
among the high-shouldered crowds, sped and well-
wished by an old man's smile.

They were still tied up in the brown paper and
wedged in back of the rafter. On the morning of the
fifteenth of November he got up early and crossed
the icy floor of the loft, reached in and pulled them
out and went back and sat in bed, feeling the shape of
them through the dusty paper. Then he undid the
string and dumped them out on the blanket. He set
them one by one and touched them off with his
thumb under the lower jaw and they leaped in his hand
and rang shut viciously. After a while he hung them
on a nail over the bed and went down to breakfast.

He was at the creek all that day wading in the steely water, poking among the dried honeysuckles, noting tracks and droppings, slides and dens. One sleeve was wet past the elbow where he had reached to feel an underwater hole and his toes were numb in the leaky knee-boots. By the time he got home he was chilled and shaking but he had his four sets laid.

When he left the house the next morning, quietly out through the lean-to, letting the door back softly, light was just coming low in the east, breaking along the gray ridges, and a cold rim of moon still hung over the mountain. The oaks were black and stark and the leaves in the yard were frosted and snapped under his feet with thin glassy sounds. He cut straight through the woods to Saunders' field, hoary and pale in the hazy cold of that first light, the dead grass sheathed in ice like slender bones, rock shoals lapped in mist and crows ambling stiff-legged on the far side where willows marked the creek's course. He crossed the fence, the icy wire in the web of his thumb like a cut. The crows skulked off on hooked wings to a clump of gray cedars. He quartered across the field, crossed another fence, near to the creek now, under the mountain, past the slain corn in hushed and battered flanks where doves had fed till late. Already he could hear the riffle and purl of the water and then he was out on the high bank where the slide went down —a slash of packed clay casehardened with frost and pressed with the scrabble-marks of muskrats—and below in the water his trap lying in wait still. He went on up the creek, crossed a shelf of limestone where periwinkles crowded and watercress swayed in the current. In a honeysuckle tunnel reeds and grasses were tramped down and a tangled sheaf of white weed stalks floated over his second trap. The other two were close together just below the pike bridge and there were no sleek muskrats in them either. The creek clattered down through green stone grottoes, over the rocks, curling, eddying under the white roots of cottonwoods where crawfish peered out with stemmed eyes. And the sun running red on the mountain, high killy and stoop of a kestrel hunting, morning spiders at their crewelwork. But no muskrats struggled in his sets.

After five mornings he pulled one trap and carried it to the bridge. There were fresh tracks on a siltbar there and he set his trap in the shallow water where they came and went. Two mornings later the trap was pulled out in the creek and there was a toenail clamped in the underside of the jaws. He reset it and was at the creek an hour before daylight in the morning with a flashlight.

Light pale as milk guided the old man's steps over the field to the creek and then to the mountain, stepping into the black wall of pine-shadows and climbing up the lower slopes out into the hardwoods, bearded hickories trailing grapevines, oaks and crooked waterless cottonwoods, a quarter mile from the creek now, past the white chopped butt of a bee tree lately felled, past the little hooked Indian tree and passing silent and catlike up the mountain in the darkness under latticed leaves scudding against the sky in some small wind. Light saw him through the thick summer ivy and over windfalls and limestone. Past the sink where on a high bluff among trilobites and fishbones, shells of ossified crustaceans from an ancient sea, a great stone tusk jutted.

The old man kept to a steep path off to the right and

came through the last thick brush to the mountain road, breathing heavily. He stopped there to lean on his cane and the first slant light of moon topped the mountain on the far side so that the crest of it was washed in a watery silver and the dust of the road shone like mica. A half mile to his left was the circle at the end of the road and beyond that the fence and the installation. The road to the spray-pit was but a few yards to the right of where he stood in the road now, hearing his breath soar out in the silence. He looked as one peering from vast heights, the sky seeming to lie below him in a measureless spread, flickering like foil by half-light and gleaming lamely into shadow where it folded to the trees.

Years back on summer nights he used to walk with neighbor boys two miles to the store to buy candy and cigars. They would come back over the warm and deserted roads talking and smoking the cigars. One night taking a shortcut they passed a house and saw through one window a woman undressing for bed. The others had gone back for a second look but he would not go and they laughed at him. The old man remembered it now with dim regret, and remembered such nights when the air was warm as a breath and the moon no dead thing. He started down the road to the orchard path and to the pit for this second look.

The moon was higher now as he came past the stand of bullbriers into the orchard, the blackened limbs of the trees falling flatly as paper across the path and the red puddle of moon moving as he moved, sliding sodden and glob-like from limb to limb, fatly surreptitious, watching as he watched. His feet moved ahead of him, disembodied and unfamiliar, floating through the banded shadows, and the limecolored grass swished and folded, breaking to light-shivered undersides like glass splintering softly, catching the pale light and then rushing to darkness. Excepting the counterpoint of crickets there was no other sound.

Where the road curved to bring into view the clearing, the dim outline of the pit, the old man paused. The glade seemed invested with an aura of antiquity, over-hung with a silence both spectral and reverent. He could feel something cold rising up in him and was almost of a mind to turn back. Taking a little tighter grip upon his cane he stood so for a while, then stepped into the clearing and came to the edge of the pit, ushering his own presence forward like a child to the pale gray lip of concrete stretched in the grass like a fallen monument, stepped up on it and looked into the black square of the pit incised geometrically into the earth.

The old man had visited here in the years past but never by night. Each winter he came and cut a cedar to serve for wreath and covering, the waxed and ciliate sprigs holding their green well into the spring before the heat blasted them and even then they held their shape, like reproductions in dull copper. It took a year's weather to fret them into the aromatic humus which steeped in what rainwater the pit held and so rendered in turn a tannic liquor dark as pitchblende by which the old man fancied had long been stained the wormscored bones that lay here. These things he observed, for he was a watcher of the seasons and their work. By the coming Christmas he would have cut the seventh cedar and with this he felt might come an end to his long deadwatch.

So he stood, looking down, and now he thought it less eerie than he had supposed, the half-darkness about him almost sheltering. Seeing that the range of his visibility extended at least partially into the pit he even sat down on the concrete edge and dangled his feet. He tugged a pipe from the folds of his overalls, filled it from a small sack of tobacco and lit it, puffing deeply, watched the smoke pale against the night by the matchflare. Then he held the match out over the pit and peered down, but he could not see even the rustcolored tips of the cedars and the match burned down to his thumb and he dropped it.

There was nothing. The dead had risen and gone; no revenant mourned here the unburied remains. Slanting down the near wall was a half square of light and he could see the blotches of moss and fungus on the pale concrete like land-shapes from some ancient atlas. But that was all. Then in the silence there came from the pit a single momentary water-sound, softly, a small, almost tentative slosh.

He got to his feet and stepped back, then turned and trotted back up the path with his queer shambling gait, neither a run nor a walk, waving his cane about curiously.

Back in the road he slowed his steps; his breath was rasping and his chest tight.

He wandered up the road a way and came to a cleared place where he could see down through the thin trees faced with light the slope of the ground pouring over like a waterfall to break somewhere below, and the small yellow pinholes, lights from shacks and houses, warmth and life, burning steadfast among the fitful lightning bugs. A dog barked. He squatted on one heel in the road, tilted his cane against his shoulder, laved a handful of the warm dust through his fingers. A light breeze was coming up from the valley.

To his right, off beyond the last black swatch of trees in silhouette cresting the nob, he could hear a long cry of tires on the curves; in a little while the sound of a motor racking the night. The car came through the cut of the mountain, howling brokenly in the windgap.

Fine pencils of light appeared far below him, swinging an arc, shadows racing on the lit trees and then lining down the road and the car hurtling into sight, small and black, pushing the lights ahead of it. It rocketed down the grade and in a thin and slowly fading wail of rubber slid to darkness again where the road curved at the foot of the mountain.

The old man's legs began to cramp under him and he rose and stood about trying to work the stiffness out of them. He balanced on one leg and bent himself up and down by the strength of his knee. Then he stooped all the way down and tried to raise himself, an old man, exercising at midnight on a mountain top—too old to get up that way, and that was the good leg too. He hadn't been able to do it with the other leg for years and it creaked like dry harness. It still had birdshot in it, above the knee and higher, almost (he could remember yet the doctor pointing to the last little blue hole) to where a man surely oughtn't to be hit. Years later the leg had begun to weaken. The head too, the old man told himself, and got up, looked out over the valley once more before starting up the road.

Toward Red Branch a dog barked again. Another answered, and another, their calls and yaps spreading across the valley until the last sound was thin and distant as an echo. No dogs howled in the Hopper or down along Forked Creek where the old man lived. He thought of Scout bedded under the house, old and lame with his tattered hide half naked of hair, the bald patches crusted and scaly-skinned as a lizard. Scout with his hand-stitched belly and ribboned ears, split their length in places, whose brows so folded over his eyes that he could see at all only by holding up his head—which gave him an inquisitive air as he walked, as if he followed forever some wonderful odor strung out before him.

Big even for a redbone, a strong dog in his day, but he
was seventeen years old. The old man had traded a
broken shotgun for him when he was a pup.

He walked and ruminated and furrowed the dust
absently with his cane until he came to the circle at the
end of the road and the knoll beyond where the trees
had been plucked from the ground and not even a weed
grew. A barren spot, bright in the moonwash, mercurial and luminescent as a sea, the pits from which the
trees had been wrenched dark on the naked bulb of the
mountain as moon craters. And on the very promontory
of this lunar scene the tank like a great silver ikon, fat
and bald and sinister. When he got to the fence he
stopped and leaned his cane and hooked his fingers
through the mesh of the wire. Within the enclosure
there was no movement. The great dome stood complacent, huge, seeming older than the very dirt, the
rocks, as if it had spawned them of itself and stood
surveying the work, clean and coldly gleaming and
capable of infinite contempt.

He clung there wrapped in the fence for some time,
perhaps the better part of an hour. He did not move
except that from time to time he licked the cold metal
of the diamonded wire with his tongue.

When the old man reached home again the moon was
down. He did not remember coming back down the
mountain. But there was the house looming, taking shape
as he approached, and he felt that he had come a great
distance, a sleepwalker who might have spanned vast
and dangerous terrains unwittingly and unharmed.

As he turned his steps up the path a shadow swirled
past his knees and fled soundlessly into the night.

In one corner of the front room there was an old
wooden footlocker and the old man cleared away papers

and clothes from the top of it and set the lamp on the floor close by. Then he undid the broken hasp and lifted it open. He rummaged through it, stopping now and again to examine some object: a brass watch weighing perhaps a quarter of a pound, a pair of cock-gaffs, a .32 rimfire revolver with owlhead grips and the hand broken so that the cylinder spun smooth as a barrel in water. Reams and sheafs of old catalogs and lists he thumbed through. An eight-gauge shotgun shell. At length he came up with a small square box decorated with flying ducks and this he set on the floor beside the lamp. He dropped the lid of the locker closed and the lamp flickered, on the wall a black ghoul hulking over a bier wavered.

He took the lamp and the box to the kitchen and placed them on the table. From the drawer he took a short curved meat knife and tested the edge on his thumb, pulled the drawer out further and reaching back in it came out with a worn gray piece of soapstone. With this he honed the knife, trying it from time to time on the hair of his arm until he was satisfied, then replaced the stone and opened the box. There were twelve bright red waxed tubes in it and he set them out on the table one by one, their dull brass bases orange in the lampglow. He selected one and with the knife made a thin cut around the base of the paper where the brass met. He examined it carefully, then deepened the cut, turning the shell against the blade. He checked it again, nodded to his nodding shadow and put the shell back in the box. He performed the same operation on the remaining eleven, putting each in turn in the box again. When he had finished he replaced the knife in the drawer and returned to the front room where he took them one by one, the twelve circumcised shotgun shells, and deposited them in the pocket of his coat.

Ef Hobie's father had been dead too long for the people who admired Ef to remember him. They were a whiskey-making family before whiskey-making was illegal, their family history mythical, preliterate and legendary. They had neither increased nor prospered and now Garland was the last surviving son. Ef had died in a car wreck in 1937, less than a year after coming out of Brushy Mountain. Not in the wreck either—he lived three weeks and was even back on his feet, where he wasn't supposed to be at all, and in the store where people looked uneasily at his gaunt frame, who had weighed just short of three hundred pounds. He had been thrown clear of the car and then the car had rolled on top of him and they had removed a good part of his insides in the process of restoring him to health. He was showing them the slick red scar that angled across his withered paunch and sucking long drafts from an orange dope.

They performed a autopsy on me and I lived, he told them. Then he laughed and got down off the drink box, emptied his orange and reached to put it in the rack. The bottle clattered on the floor, he lurched once, wildly, collapsed into the bread rack and went to the floor in a cascade of cupcakes and moonpies.

So there were only two Hobies, Garland and his mother, and hard luck dogged them. Within the month Jack the Runner was arrested and sent up to Brushy for three years himself and county deputies broke into their smokehouse and took off what whiskey was there and took Mrs Hobie, aged seventy-eight, off to jail, sending her back home only when it was discovered she had cancer of the duodenum.

So Garland had to carry the whiskey up the mountain now to a den in the honeysuckles just below the circle and leave it there for Marion Sylder to pick up and haul to Knoxville. There was a gate across the orchard road since the installation had been set up on the mountain and only official carriers were permitted access —olive-painted trucks with gold emblems on the doors, passing in and out of the gate, the men in drab fatigues locking and unlocking the chain sedulously. With like diligence Sylder bolted and unbolted the ring-plate that held the chain on his comings and goings in the old Plymouth. But the two parties using the road kept different hours and they never met.

It was four o'clock in the morning when Sylder heard the old man shoot the first hole in the tank. He almost let go the case of whiskey he was carrying and then when the second shot came, hard upon the first, he set the case down carefully and stood dead still, waiting for cries, commands—an explanation. All was quiet. The birds were stilled in their first tentative and querulous chirpings. Low in the east and beyond the town a gray soulless dawn gnawed the horizon into shape. He was braced for another report, holding his breath, echoing the outrageously loud concussion in his inner ear before it came—two more shots, evenly spaced, something deliberate about them. Sylder made his way stealthily along the edge of the honeysuckle jungle, crossed an open space, arm of the orchard, going in the direction of the shooting.

When he got to the edge of the clearing where the installation stood he could see the man with the muzzle of the gun sticking through the fence-wire. He fired and the barrel came up short, sending waves out along the woven mesh and back. The man jerked under the recoil and the smoke spurted, slowed and billowed in the damp air. There were six neat black holes in the polished skin of the tank, angled up across it in a staggered line. The man broke the gun and picked the shells out. Slyder saw him hold them up for brief inspection before throwing them to one side, and saw them dance in the new light and knew what they were: the brass bases of the shells only, flicking and turning like coins as they fell.

The man was putting two more shells into the breech of the shotgun and Sylder could see them now, and the dull red of the waxed cardboard tubes that had been missing from the extracted cases. The man didn't hesitate; he raised the gun and breeched it in one quick motion. Two more blasts ripped the silence and two holes appeared now in the lower corner. He was making a huge crude X across the face of the tank. Again he examined the bits of brass before reloading.

Sylder watched wide-eyed from his retreat in the bushes. He could hear the solid whop of the full cases lamming into the tank and the tank seemed to reel under the impact like a thing alive. There was something ghostly and horrific about it and he had the impression that this gnomic old man had brought with him an inexhaustible supply of shells and would cease his cannonading only when he became too weary to lift the gun. He backed out of his hiding place and returned to the car. Daylight was coming on fast and he began to worry lest the old man's shooting bring investigation. He was late anyway and didn't know but that the legal, the official, carriers might use the road at this hour even if a crazy old man wasn't shooting holes in their responsibility with a shotgun and rung shells. There were six cases of whiskey still in the honeysuckles and he brought them out two at a time with a hobbling half-run. The firing had ceased. He got the turtledeck loaded and fastened, got in and started the motor. When he pulled out of the weeds and into the road he looked back and there was the old man standing on the hill above him at the turnaround, holding the shotgun in one hand and leaning on a cane. Sylder lowered his head and floorboarded the gas pedal.

When he was safe around the first curve he relaxed and drove slowly to the gate so as to leave as few signs as possible. He refastened the ring-plate and chain, got back in and turned onto the pike and toward Knoxville. Just beyond the creek he passed an olivecolored truck, the driver and the other man in the cab looking serious and official, but somewhat sleepy and not in any particular hurry. Genial, unofficial, and awake, Marion Sylder drove to town.

His light played on the wet mudbanks among roots and stumps, a sheaf of brown honeysuckle hanging down

and trailing in the water like hair. His boots made sucking sounds as he waded against the slight current, walked
softly the silted floor of the creek. He could hear a car
on top of the mountain coming down, the exhaust rattling and the tires sounding on the switchbacks. He
came to the bridge and waded to the spit of loam filled
in against the concrete wall. Throwing his light to the
set he could see the trap with the jaws cocked and the
pan, all brown-looking under the water and wrinkling
in the small ebb and lap of it. He put the flashlight in
his pocket and squatted on the sand among tracks of
feet and tails, wiggling his numb toes, huddling down
in his mackinaw and breathing slowly into his cupped
hands, listening in the darkness to the water curling past
his feet with small muted water-sounds, to his cough
echoing hollow and blankly among the beams overhead.

The tires sounded again, closer, and then the motor
revving between engagements of the clutch and the
explosive sound of the shift to high gear as the car came
out of the last turn at the base of the mountain. He followed with his muscles the downward thrust of the
lever, locked the shift home arm and shoulder. The car
was on the straight stretch approaching the creek and he
could feel the vibrations of it, waiting for it to pass overhead. It did not. He heard the motor building speed and
then there was a sudden explosion, a doglike yelp, followed by a suspension of all sound, a momentary eclipse
of animation even to the water and his own breathing.

The trees at his left leaped, wild with light, went out
again. There came an eruption of limbs cracking, splitting, of wrenched metal screaming like slate, a heavy
and final concussion like a steel drum bursting. Silence
again through which filtered a thin and diminishing rain
of glass. By the pulsing wash of water at his feet he
knew that it was in the creek and he tugged his flash-

light free and poked the beam out along the bridge, the bank of the creek where broken saplings and peeled trunks stood out whitely all about like markers and finally to the sleek black flank of the car, upturned in the creek with the hood tilted into the water and the off-wheel still spinning idly. The side window-glass was laced with myriad cracks, shining in the beam like dewed spiderwebbing, and he could not see inside. The waterline angled across it, from cowl to centerpost, giving it an inverted look of anger.

By then he was already in the creek again, scrambling low under the beamed flooring of the bridge and dipping water into his boots with gentle sluicing sounds where he floundered in over the tops, squatting down too far under the canopy of sumacs broken over the bank, and the water on his backside icy as alcohol. He was thinking: I'll have to pull *up* on the doorhandle. Then he was at the car, stepping and threading the brush it had pulled into the creek with it, reached for the doorhandle, crammed it upward, and jerked back on it with his full weight.

It catapulted outward as if something inside had been galvanized into violent effort. shot open and pitched him backward through a tangle of down saplings and into the creek. In the darkness the water closed over him thickly as running oil, choking off his breath, filling his nose. He floundered to his feet streaming and numb, coughing up creek water. Wiping water from his eyes he looked about and saw the flashlight, still lit, scuttling downstream over the bed of the creek like some incandescent water-creature bent on escape. He waded after it, tearing recklessly about in the freezing water with the boots leaden and rolling about his shins, reached for it, his hand like a bat's shadow poised over the dome of light, and then it was gone, sucked down through the silt and mire inexplicably, and he was left balancing on one foot in the darkness with his arm and shoulder deep in the water. He groped about and finally came up with the flashlight and shook it. The metal cylinder sloshed softly water among the batteries. He stuck it in his pocket and surged noisily back upstream to the car.

He was aware for the first time now of a sickly-sweet odor, faintly putrescent, and by the time he reached the car again it was thick in the air and he knew it was whiskey without having ever smelled it. Then he could see the man taking shape out of the gloom, sprawled on the upturned headliner and half out through the open door, one arm hanging into the water. The sour smell of the whiskey, the mustiness of the old car upholstery, and what he perceived to be blood on the man's face— these burned such an image of death into his brain that he made for the bank, panicky, clawing wildly at the brush, up to the field where light in fragile shellpink reefs broke on an unreal world.

But the man wasn't dead. The boy was already on the bank, catching his breath and teetering with the dry rollings of his breakfastless stomach, when he heard a voice out of the void, hollow and half lost among the chatterings of the creek.

Hey, the call came.

He turned, hanging to a jagged sapling, saw in the shade below him a movement among the wreckage, a pale face against the dark interior of the car, the man propped up on his hands looking at him. Hey you, he said.

He hung there looking at him. A sweep of lights tracked the shadows of the mountain and a car hammered the bridge, echoing the noise of its passage in the creek. Finally he said: What do you want?

The man groaned. There was a moment of silence

and then he said, Goddamn, man; how about giving me a hand.

Okay, he said. He wasn't afraid any more, just cold, sliding down the mud and into the creek again and then squatting in the water facing the man, wondering what he should say. He could see him quite clearly now, there was a dark smear of blood down the side of his face. The man looked at him, a suggestion of a grin breaking painfully on his face. Played hell, didn't I? he said.

You hurt? His own words rattled like bb's through a clatter of teeth. He started to say something else but a further chill rendered him inarticulate, his palsied jaw jerking like an idiot's.

I don't rightly know, the man was saying. Yes. Here . . . he reached out one hand and the boy steadied it on his shoulder while the man drew up one knee and stepped out into the water. Then he pulled the other leg out, his face wrinkling with pain, and so was standing in the creek, his hand still on the boy's shoulder in an attitude of fatherly counsel. When he started for the bank the hand withdrew for a moment, one faltering half-step, and then flew back and clamped there like a predatory bird striking. Whew, the man said. I must of busted the shit out of my leg.

It took them some time to get up the bank, the boy trying to push him up and him pulling himself along by trees, roots, handfuls of dead grass, holding the leg out behind him. Then they sat in the weeds at the edge of the field breathing white plumes into the cold morning air. In the quarter-darkness the fields looked like water, flat and gray. The boy was wet and cold; everything was wet and very cold. The man ran his hand along his leg trying to tell whether it was broken or not. His trousers were clammy against his skin. The boy sat in front

of him hugging his shoulders and shivering, his toes lifeless, squishing in his boots when he wiggled them and
sand and grit rasping in his socks. He said: Your head's
bleeding.

The man ran his hand along the side of his face.

Other side.

He reached across and his hand came away sticky
with blood and he wiped it on his trouser leg and turned
to the boy. You want to do something for me?

Sure, the boy said.

Go down and get them keys then, and let's get the
hell out of here.

The boy disappeared over the cut of the bank; the
man could hear him in the water. Presently he came back
and handed the keys over.

Thanks, he said. Here. He took the boy's hand and
turned it over. What'd you do here?

The boy looked down at his palm. There was a black
and jagged line across it.

You jest do that? the man asked.

The boy looked at it dumbly. No, he said. I don't
think so. I must of done it when I fell in the creek.
Before . . .

The man dropped the keys in his pocket and struggled
to his feet. Well, come on, he said. We better get ourselves patched up. This way, he added, seeing the boy
start for the road. He motioned toward the field and
set off with a hopping gait, muttering under his breath
Whew, Mother.

The boy followed him for a few paces, then quartered
off to the creek again and the man watched him go, his
legs disappearing in the mist, then the rest of him, so
that he seemed to be gliding away toward the line of
willows marking its course like some nightwraith fleeing

the slow reaching dawn until the man wasn't sure that he had really been there at all. Then he came back with a pole and handed it to him.

Thanks, the man said.

They moved on across the field, through vapors of fog and wisps of light, to the east, looking like the last survivors of Armageddon.

Their path led them up the creek, along the edges of the fields that terminated there—a curve of fields and the creek and the cupped slope of the mountain rising up to their right along which shafts of light now appeared laterally among the ghostgray trees. They struggled through the last fence, the boy holding the wire and trying to help him and him cussing, crossed a plank bridge at the fork of the creek, out through a cattle gate and onto the road, Henderson Valley Road.

The boy fastened the gate behind them and the man said, We got to stay off this road. They might of found it by now what with the light and all.

They crossed the road and started up a steep dirt drive on the other side. We can call here, the man said. The boy could see him better now. He needed a shave and the blood crusted on the side of his face was broken in fine cracks like old dark pottery where he winced with the pain of his slow progress, leaning heavily on the pole and breathing hoarsely. He was leanhipped and tall and his poplin jacket hung loosely about his shoulders. The boy thought he must be awfully cold dressed no warmer than that and wet to the knees besides. His own feet he couldn't feel at all now; they were like hooves rattling inside his boots. He hadn't stopped shivering the whole time. The drive climbed and turned and then there was a house.

It was an older man came to the door, a tremendous paunch slung in a gray and ragged undershirt drooped

pendulously over the waist of his trousers like a sacked
hog carcass. Out of a meaty face, jowled and white-
stubbled with beard, two porcine eyes regarded them,
blinking. Hot-toe-mitty, he said, slow and evenly.
Then: Well, come on in if you're able. They entered,
the man hobbling in with his pole and the boy following. The room was warm and suffused with odors of
cooking meat.

Hey, old woman, their host called out, they's two
fellers here jest fell out of a aryplane.

A woman came to the door at the far end and looked
at them. Lord God, she said. She looked as if she might
be going to say something else, then she clamped her
jaw shut and disappeared with an air of briskness.

The room itself was comfortable with the new catalog
store prosperity of china lamps, linoleum floors, a Warm
Morning heater in front of which he installed himself
while the two men stood talking. They paid little attention to him and he just watched them, the injured man
waving his arms, telling the story, the other scratching
alternately belly and head and saying Godamighty softly
to himself from time to time by way of comment. After
a while the woman came to the door again and called
them in for coffee.

As they started for the kitchen the younger man
motioned at him. This here is . . . he nodded to the boy.

John Wesley, he said.

John Wesley. This here is June Tipton—and this is
his Mrs.

Mrs Tipton nodded back at him as they entered the
kitchen and said, How do, John Wesley.

They sat down at the table and June said to the
woman: John Wesley's the one what pulled Marion out
of the creek.

She looked at her husband and then to him and smiled

appreciatively. The one called Marion was fishing through his pockets for cigarettes. That's right, he said. I might near of drownded.

She smiled again. After a while she turned to her husband and said, What all was he doin in the creek?

Jest laying there, June said. He blowed a tire and his car fell in.

She looked at the boy again and smiled and went on sipping her coffee demurely. The boy lowered his face to the steaming mug before him. Small waterdrops tripped down from his thawing hair, beaded and dropped from his earlobes. He was still in his soaked mackinaw and a puddle of water was gathering on the linoleum beneath his chair. Raising his eyes above the rim of the cup he saw the woman looking at him, leaning forward. She reached out and squeezed his coat. It made a funny squishing sound.

Lord God, she said, this youngern's wet clear through. He's a-fixin to take pneumony. She set down her cup and began pulling at the coat, trying to help him off with it. He seemed bent and tottering under the sheer weight of it.

They got him out of his coat and by then the man had finished his coffee and stood and he said he was ready to go if June didn't mind taking them.

So they thanked the woman, declining breakfast two or three times, and filed through the door, him holding the mackinaw in his arms now like a great bundle of wet wash, and got into a pickup truck parked behind the house and pointing down the drive. June kicked the blocks from under the front wheels and got in and they began rolling silently, gaining speed, and then he let in the clutch and the motor came to life angrily and they catapulted down to the road, turned left toward the mountain, the truck coughing and lurching and a bluish haze boiling up in the cab. He sat in the middle between the two men, trying to keep his knees clear of the gear-shift. Through a missing slat in the floorboard he could see the gray road sliding under and a slip of bitter wind angled up one jean-leg.

They drove a mile or so up the mountain and turned into another drive not unlike the one from which they started. June turned the truck around in the yard and stopped and Marion opened the door and climbed painfully down. The boy waited.

Better come on in, Marion said. The boy turned and started to say something and then June said, behind him:

Reckon I better get on back.

Well, he said, I sure am much obliged. John Wesley, you better come on in and get dried out some; your old lady'll skin you for shoe leather.

So he clambered out of the truck and slammed the door, the truck already moving and June waving at them, and he and the man started for the house. It was full light now, the air smoky and cold. A woman was standing in the door with her arms crossed, holding her shoulders. She let them past and came in, closing the door behind her.

Mornin, the man said cheerfully.

Are you hurt? she asked. She was small and blond and very angry-looking.

Breakfast ready? he wanted to know.

She looked like she might be going to cry, her face crumpled a little and her chin quivering. Damn you, she said. Won't nothin do till you've killed yourself, is they? Why you ain't dead afore now is a mystery to me and God too I reckon, as I don't see why He'd have any call to look out after the likes of you any more than . . . she broke off suddenly and looked at the boy, standing there holding the coat in his arms and still dripping water. What about him, she pointed. Your helper. He hurt?

The boy looked down at himself, soggy and mud-splattered, seeds and burrs collected on his waterdark jeans like some rare botanical garden being cultivated there, at his rubber kneeboots with twigs and weeds sticking out of them, feeling the blisters they'd worn and the cords in his ankles pulled from walking in them. One sock was completely off and scrunched down somewhere in the toe of the boot. I ain't no helper, he said. I jest found him.

He shot a glance up at the man. He was grinning. Don't let him fool you, he said. He was drivin. But he ain't hurt I don't reckon. I ain't neither, my leg is jest wore out fightin that dashboard.

Your head's wore out is what's wore out, she said. You get out of them clothes. Here, set down. She guided him to a sofa and began trying to undo the laces of his shoes.

The boy stood about uneasily, wondering what he was supposed to do. She got the man's shoes off and his socks. Now she was unfastening his belt. He just sat there, quiet and unresisting, as if engaged in some deep speculation. She kept saying Damn you, damn you, in a tone of despair and solicitude at once.

She was pulling his trousers off. The boy began to look about him wildly.

What are you doin? the man said in mock indignity. You raise up, damn you!

Here! he said. I'm in no shape for this kind of carry-in-on.

Marion Sylder, I'm not puttin up with your foolishness, you hear me? Now you get out of them britches and get out of them now and quick. God rest your poor mother I don't know why she ain't dead either puttin up with you long as she did . . . lift your feet. You . . . here, wait. I'll get you some shoes too. She disappeared through a door and the man winked hugely at him, sitting there with his trousers in a pile under his feet.

She came back and dumped some clothes into his lap —then she saw the great bruise on the side of his calf, livid in hues of red and purple against the bare white of his naked legs. She knelt and touched it, whimpering softly. She went out again and returned with a basin of water and a cloth and bathed it carefully, the man crying out from time to time in simulated anguish. But she didn't cuss him any more. When she finished she turned to the boy. What about you? she said.

Yesm?

Yesm? She looked from him to the man and back. You goin to die standin there I reckon, Yesm. She narrowed her eyes at him. Start shuckin, she said.

What?

The man on the couch giggled. He was pulling on a clean shirt.

Here, she said, go in yonder. She pointed behind her. I'll get you some clothes in jest a minute.

He started past her with strange sluicing sounds.

Empty them boots first, she told him.

He stopped.

Outside.

He said Yesm again, went to the door and returned, one sock on and one off, leaving odd unmatched tracks on the raw pine flooring.

The door she pointed him through led to a bedroom. There was a fireplace with a coal grate and a faint warmth still issuing from it. He stood in front of it on a small hooked rug for a minute, then softly eased the door to.

Get that blanket, the woman called to him.

He peeled off his wet clothes, piling them on top of the mackinaw which he had laid carefully on the floor, took the rolled blanket from the foot of the bed and wrapped himself in it.

He was standing at the window looking out at the gray morning when she came in with the shirt and pants and handed them to him. Then she scooped his things off the floor and went out. He unfolded himself out of the blanket and got into the dry clothes. There was a pair of army socks too and he put these on and sat on the bed, wondering if it was all right to walk on the floor with them. She didn't bring any shoes though and after a while he ventured out into the front room again. The man was dressed, his head bandaged, and he was sitting with his feet in a pan of water and reading a magazine. He looked up and saw the boy standing there in the drooping shirt and the trousers turned up at the bottoms and gathered at the waist by the expedient of fastening the front buttonhole to a suspender button on the side.

They ain't much of a fit, are they? the man said.

Nosir.

Marion.

What?

Marion. Sylder. That's my name, Marion Sylder.

Oh, he said.

Pleased to meet ye.

Yessir.

Well, the man said, get ye a chair.

He pulled up a cane rocker from beside the stove, sat quietly with his hands on his knees. The man leaned back on the sofa, a huge shapeless affair draped with a flower-print cover. Behind him on the wall in an oval frame hung a picture of him and the woman, the wife, peering out upon the room with tentative and uncertain smiles. There were small rugs scattered about the floor, some pieces of furniture—a sideboard, a table and chairs. On a small cabinet in one corner stood a walnut trophy with a small bronze automobile perched on top of it.

You know what was in the car?

The boy looked back at him. Yessir . . . Marion.

Well, the man said. He returned to his magazine, leafed a page over slowly, looked back at the boy. He grinned. It was good stuff too, he said. Sixty gallons of it.

Then the woman called them to breakfast and he put down the magazine and reached for a towel to dry his feet with. The boy noticed that part of the big toe was missing from the man's left foot. It was nailless, curious-looking, sort of like a nose. The man eased his slippers on and stood up, supporting himself on the couch. Come on, he said, let's eat some. And hopped off to the kitchen. The boy followed.

They sat down to a breakfast of eggs and grits, biscuits and pork tenderloin and huge cups of coffee. The coffee was black and bitter and there was no milk or sugar on the table. The boy sipped it slowly, watched the man. The woman didn't eat with them. She hovered about the edge of the table resupplying eggs and biscuits to their plates, filling their cups. The man didn't say anything until he had finished except that from time to time he would nudge a plate toward the boy and frown and grunt, urging him to eat. He finished off with biscuits and dark honey and got up from the table. In a few minutes he was back with coats and boots and handed a set to the boy. Come on, he said, I got somethin to show you you might like. The boy pulled on the coat and stepped into the cavernous brogans and they went out the kitchen door into the new morning, the air clear and cold as springwater, shreds of mist lifting off the mountain above them and light pouring through the gap like a millrace. The man hobbled ahead of him to a smokehouse where he pulled a bent nail from the wood and swung out the door, hinge, hasp, lock, and all, and went in. Come on, he said. The boy followed him into the musty gloom. Hello, gal, the man said. The air was rife and fetid with dog smells. Sounds of snuffling. Thin mewlings from somewhere in the corner. A small hound poked her face around the man's knee and looked up at him. This here's Lady, the man said. Lady sniffed at his billowing trousers.

He could see now: a broken lantern swung from a beam, a clutter of tools, a grindstone, an anvil fashioned from a section of rail . . . The man was squatting in the corner, the hound skitting nervously behind his back, poking her nose under his arm. She got around him and settled in a pile of crokersacks and he could see the puppies then too over the man's shoulder. They crawled over each other and fell to nursing. Lady blinked her mild hound eyes and gazed at the roof.

The man picked out one and handed it to him. He took it, the fat slick little belly filling his palm, legs dangling, took it and looked at the quiet and already sad eyes, the pushed-in puppy face with the foolish ears.

Four weeks old, the man was saying. That's the best'n, but you can pick whichever one you want.

Do what?

His daddy's a blooded bluetick—half bluetick half walker, the pups. Makes as good a treedog as they is goin. You like that'n?

Yessir, he said.

Well, he's yourn then. You can take him home with ye in about another month, say.

Jefferson Gifford thumbed his galluses onto his shoulders, took a last swallow of coffee from the still full

earthenware cup and crossed with heavy boot-tread the
curling linoleum of the kitchen floor to the rear en-
tranceway where he took down his hat and jacket from
a peg.

A Plymouth? he repeated.

Legwater was buttoning his coat. That's what he said.
I ain't been down there. All I know is he said it was a
Plymouth. He come straight to my place on account of
it was on his milk route and he ast for me to call you.
So I jest come on over. He said it was a Plymouth.

Gifford adjusted his hat and opened the door. Well,
come on, he said. I sure never heard of nobody hauling
whiskey in a Plymouth.

Ain't you goin to call the Sheriff?

Reckon I'll see what all it is I'm callin him about
first, Gifford said.

They parked the car just beyond the creek and
climbed through the wire fence and walked along slow,
studying the swath the car had cut through the brush
and small trees. It had cleared the fence completely,
peeling a limb from a cottonwood that grew by the
bridge, and come to earth some thirty feet from the
road. It was upside down in the creek against the far
bank and facing back the way it came. Gifford couldn't
see anything yet but the undercarriage, but he knew it
wasn't a Ford this time by the two semi-elliptic springs
at the rear axle. They had to go back to the road and
cross the bridge to get to the car. It was smashed up
against some roots on the bank and they could see the
glass leaking from the trunk lid.

Later when they got a truck down and winched the
wreck out the lid fell off and glass poured into the creek
—someone said later for thirty minutes—for a long time
anyway. There were even two or three jars unbroken,
which pleased Gifford—evidence, he said . . .

It was a Plymouth, a 33 coupe; there was a hole in

the right front tire you could put three fingers in. Other than that there was nothing remarkable about it except that it was wrecked in Red Branch with the remains of a load of whiskey in the back end.

Gifford examined the ground carefully, walking back and forth along the bank as if he had lost something there. He had written the license number down on a slip of paper but on looking closer saw that they were last year's plates repainted and threw the paper away in disgust.

Looks to me like he'd of been hurt, Legwater was saying.

They.

They what?

Them, Gifford said. They's two of em.

You mean tracks? Them's most likely Oliver's; he come down to see was they anybody hurt . . .

Cept he never clumb down into the creek to . . . See? Here . . . Gifford paused, staring at the ground. After a long minute he looked up at Legwater. Earl, he said, I reckon you're right.

Figured I was . . .

Yep. The othern wadn't in the car. He jest come along and got whoever was in out.

It wadn't Oliver, Legwater persisted. He never even seen nobody around when he come by. He . . .

Ain't talkin about him, the constable said. Come on, if you're ready.

It had begun to rain a little by then.

Believe it may warm up for a spell, Gifford said. If it don't turn snow.

In the store the old men gathered, occupying for end-less hours the creaking milkcases, speaking slowly and with conviction upon matters of profound inconsequence, eying the dull red bulb of the stove with their watery vision. Shrouded in their dark coats they had a vulturous look about them, their faces wasted and thin, their skin dry and papery as a lizard's. John Shell, looking like nothing so much as an ill-assembled manikin of bones on which clothes were hung in sagging dusty folds, his wrists protruding like weathered sticks from his flapping prelate sleeves, John Shell unhinged his toothless jaw with effort, a slight audible creaking sound, to speak his one pronouncement: It ain't so much that as it is one thing'n another.

An assemblage of nods to this. In the glass cases roaches scuttled, a dry rattling sound as they traversed the candy in broken ranks, scaled the glass with licoriced feet, their segmented bellies yellow and flat. Summer and winter they patrolled the candy case, inspected handkerchiefs, socks, cigars. Occasionally too they invaded the meat case, a medicinal white affair rusted from sweat where the lower edge of the glass was mortised, so that brown stains like tobacco spit or worse seeped down the enamel, but they soon perished here from the cold. Their corpses lay in attitudes of repose all along the little scupper to the front of the case.

Leaning against the case John Wesley could see the car pull in alongside the rusty orange gas pump and the two men get out. When they came through the door the nasal clacking voices paused, the chorus of elders looking up, down, back to the stove. Some fumbled knives from their overalls and fell to whittling idly on their milkcases. John Shell struggled to his feet, opened the stove door with kerchiefed hand, dropped in a small chunk of coal from the hod. A draft of sparks scurried upwards. He spat assertively at them and clanked the loose iron door closed.

The two men crossed to the dope box in close order,

on the raw subflooring their steps heavy and martial.
They selected their drinks and the taller man came over
to the counter and spun down a dime. The other one
closed the lid and hiked himself up on the box where he
sat taking little sips of his drink and smirking strangely
at the old men.

John Shell turned to the man at the counter and said,
Howdy, Gif.

Howdy, said Gifford, nodding in general to the group.
He took a drink of his dope.

Mr Eller came from his chair by the meat block and
rang up the dime. Gifford said Howdy to him too and
he grunted and went back to his chair taking with him a
newspaper from the counter.

Warmin up, Gifford said. Outside the rain had stopped
and a cold wind feathered the red water puddles in front
of the store. He tilted his head and drank again. A fly
rattled electrically against the front window. The fire
cricked and moaned in the stove.

Gifford hoisted his dope to eye-level, examined it, his
mouth pursed about the unswallowed liquid, swirling the
bottle slowly, studying viscosity and bead, suspicious of
foreign matter. In the folds of flesh beneath his chin his
Adam's apple rose and fell.

See where somebody lost a old Plymouth down in the
creek, he said.

A few looked up. That a fact, someone said.

Yessir, said Gifford. Seems a shame.

Legwater, the county humane officer, finished now
with his drink, sat leaning forward, hands palm-down-
ward, sitting on his fingers—an attitude toadlike but for
his thinness and the spindle legs dangling over the side
of the box. He was swinging them out, banging his heels
against the drink case. A longlegged and emaciated
toad, then. He kept leering and smirking but no one paid

him any attention. Most of the old men had been there the day he shot two dogs behind the store with a .22 rifle, one of them seven times, it screaming and dragging itself along the fence in the field below the forks while a cluster of children stood watching until they too began screaming.

He said, Sure does . . . brightly, enjoying himself.

Gifford passed him a sharp glance sideways and he hushed and fell to watching his heels bounce.

I don't reckon anybody knows whose car that is, do they, Gifford went on.

A few of the elders seemed to be dozing. The fly buzzed at the glass.

I got a towtruck comin to take it on in to town. Sure would like to get that car to the rightful owner.

What kind of car did you say it was? It was the boy leaning against the meat case who spoke.

Gif drained the last of his dope with studied indifference, set the bottle carefully on the counter. He looked at the boy, then he looked at the boy's feet.

You always wear them slippers, son?

The boy didn't look down. He started to answer, but he could feel the cords in his throat sticking. He coughed and cleared his throat noisily. His feet felt huge.

Them ain't enough shoes for wet weather, Gifford said. Then he was moving across the floor. Legwater eased himself down from the drink box and fell in behind him. At the door Gif stopped, the door half open, studying something obliquely overhead. Yessir, he said, looks like it's fixin to clear off. Legwater hovered behind him like some dark and ominous bird.

Well, we'll see ye, Gifford said.

By the meat block Mr Eller dozed with his paper. He had not looked up nor did he now. Come back, he said.

And they were gone. The fly rattled again at the

window. The congress of ancients about the stove stirred one by one. The boy stood uneasily by the meat case. Some of the old men were rolling smokes with their brown papery hands. It was very quiet. He went to the door and stood there for a while. Then he left.

Her first high yelp was thin and clear as the air itself, its tenuous and diminishing echoes sounding out the coves and hollows, trebling to a high ring like the last fading note of a chime glass. He could hear the boy breathing in the darkness at his elbow, trying to breathe quietly, listening too hard. She sounded again and he stood and touched the boy's shoulder lightly. Let's go, he said.

The strung-out ringing yelps came like riflefire. The boy was on his feet. Has she treed yet? he asked.

No. She's jest hit it now. Then he added: She's close though, hot. He started down the steep hummock on which they had been resting, through a maze of small pines whose polished needles thick on the ground made the descent a series of precarious slides from trunk to trunk until they got to the gully at the bottom, a black slash in the earth beyond which he could see nothing although he knew there was a field there, pitched sharply down to the creek some hundred yards further on. He dropped into the gully, heard the beaded rush of sliding dirt as the boy followed, came up the other side and started out through the field at a jog-trot, the heavy weeds popping and his corduroys setting up a rhythmic zip-zip as he ran.

The cottonwoods at the creek loomed up stark and pale out of the darkness; he crossed a low wreck of barbed wire, heard again the resonant creak of the rusty staples in the checked and split cedar post as the boy crossed behind him. They were in the woods above the creek then, rattling through the stiff frosted leaves.

Lady's sharp trail-call still broke excitedly off to their right. They moved out under the dark trees, through a stand of young cedars gathered in a clearing, vespertine figures, rotund and druidical in their black solemnity. When the man reached the far side, the woods again, he stopped and the boy caught up with him.

Which way is she going? He was trying not to sound winded.

The man paused for just a moment more. Then he said, Same way he is—motioning loosely with his hand. His back melted into the darkness again. The boy moved after him, keeping his feet high, following the sound of the brittle leaves. Their path angled down toward the creek and he could hear at intervals the rush of water, high now after the rain, like the rumble of a distant freight passing.

Watch a log, the man called back to him. He jumped just in time, half stumbled over the windfall trunk, lost his balance, ricocheted off a sapling, went on, holding his head low, straining to see. Trees appeared, slid past with slow gravity before folding again into the murk

beyond. They were climbing now, a long rise, and when
he came over the crest he caught a glimpse of the figure
ahead of him, framed darkly for an instant against the
glaucous drop of sky. Below him he could make out the
course of the creek. They dipped into a low saddle in
the ridge, rose again, and the man was no longer there.
He stopped and listened. Lady's clear voice was joined
by another, lower and less insistent. She was much closer
now, quartering down, coming closer. He could follow
her progress, listening between the explosions of his
breath. Then she stopped.

There was a moment of silence, then the other dog
yapped once. Sounds of brush crashing. Two wild yelps
just off to his right and then a concussion of water. A
low voice at his side said: He's got her in the creek, come
on. The man started down the side of the hill, the boy
behind him, and out onto a small flat set in the final slope
to the creek and dominated by a thick beech tree. Something was coming down from the ridge above them and
they halted. A long shadow swept past in a skitter of
leaves and on toward the creek bank. There was one
short chopped bark and then a splash. They followed,
sidling down the slope and out along the bank where the
water gathered a thin membranous light by which they
could see, directed by frantic surging sounds and low
intermittent growls, some suggestion of figures struggling there, and the new dog striking out in the water
now to join them. The fight moved down, out in deep
water and under the shadow of the far bank. The snarls
stopped and there was only the desperate rending of
water.

A light blinked through the trees to their right, went
out, appeared again, bobbing, unattached and eerie in the
blackness. They could hear the dry frosted crack of

sticks and brush, muted voices. The light darted out, peered again suddenly down upon them, sweeping an arc along the edge of the creek.

Howdy, a voice said.

Cas?

Yeah . . . that you, Marion?

Bring that light; they're in the creek.

They came down the slope, four dismembered legs hobbling in the swatch of light as they descended.

Thow your light, Sylder said.

They came alongside, dispensing an aura of pipesmoke and doghair. The shorter one was working the beam slowly over the creek. Whereabouts? he said.

Down some. Howdy, Bill.

Howdy, the other said. In the glare emanating from the flashlight their breath was smoke-white, curling, clinging about their heads in a vaporous canopy. The oval of the flashbeam scudded down the glides against the far bank, passed, backed, came to rest on the combatants clinching in the icy water, the coon's eyes glowing red, pin points, his fur wetly bedraggled and his tail swaying in crestfallen buoyancy on the current. The big dog was circling him warily, trudging the water with wearying paws and failing enthusiasm. They could see Lady's ear sticking out from under the coon's front leg, and then her hindquarters bobbed up, surging through the face of the creek with a wild flash of tail and sinking back in a soundless swirl.

Cas swung the beam to shore, scrabbled up a handful of rock and handed the light to the other man. Hold it on him, he said. He scaled a rock at the coon. It cut a slow arc in the beam and pitched from sight with a muffled slurp. The big hound started for shore and Lady's tail had made another desperate appearance when the second rock, a flitting shadow, curving, flashed water under the coon's face.

He turned loose and struck out downstream, stroking with the current. The big dog, on the other bank now, had set up a pitiful moaning sound, pacing, the man with the light calling to him in a hoarse and urgent voice, Hunt im up, boy, hunt im up. He turned to the men. He's skeered of rocks, he explained.

Hush a minute, Sylder said, taking the light from him. She was already some thirty yards below them. When the light hit her she turned her head back and her eyes came pale orange, ears fanned out and floating, treading the water down before her with a tired and grim determination. She had her mouth turned up at the corners in a macabre and ludicrous grin as if to keep out the water.

Ho, gal, Sylder called. Ho, gal. They were moving down the creek too, raking through the brush. She's fixin to drownd herself, someone said.

Ho, gal, Ho . . .

He never even felt the water. He couldn't hear them any more, hadn't heard them call since he left them somewhere back up the creek when he hit the bullbriers full tilt, not feeling them either, aware only of them pulling at his coat and legs like small hands trying to hold him. Then he was over the bank, feet reaching for something and finally skewing on the slick mud, catapulting him in a stifflegged parabola down and out into the water, arms flailing, but not falling yet, not until he had already stopped, teetering thigh-deep, and took a first step out into the current where he collapsed forward like a shot heron.

But he didn't even feel it. When he came up again he

was in water past his waist, the soft creek floor squirming away beneath his feet as if he were walking the bodies of a colony of underwater creatures clustered there. He could see a little better now. There was no light on the bank and he thought: I come down too far. And no voices, only the sounds of the creek chattering and rocking past all around him. Then he went in again, over his head this time, and came up treading water and with something heavy pushing against his chest. He got his arms under it and lifted. Lady's head came up and her eyes rolled at him dumbly. He reached and got hold of her collar, the creek bottom coming up and sliding off under his feet, falling backwards now with the dog rolling over him and beginning to struggle, until his leg hit a rock and he reached for it and steadied himself and rose again and began to flounder shoreward with the dog in tow.

They came with the light and Sylder looked at him huddled in the willows, still holding the dog. He didn't say anything, just disappeared into the woods, returning in a few minutes with a pile of brush and dead limbs.

One of the men was kneeling with him and stroking the dog, examining her. She looks all right, he said, don't she, son?

He couldn't get his mouth open so he just nodded. He was beyond cold now, paralyzed.

The other man said: Son, you goin to take your death. We better get you home fore you freeze settin right there.

He nodded again. He wanted to get up but he couldn't bear the rub of his clothes where he moved.

Sylder had the fire going by then, a great crackling sound as the dry brush took, orange light leaping among the trees. He could see him in silhouette moving about, feeding the blaze. Then he came back. He gathered the quivering hound up in one arm and motioned for the boy to follow. You come over here, he said. And get them clothes off.

He got up then and labored stiffly after them.

Sylder put the hound by the fire and turned to the boy. Lemme have that coat, he said.

The boy peeled off the leaden mackinaw and handed it over to him. He passed it around the trunk of a sapling, gathered the ends up in his hands and twisted what looked to be a gallon of water out of the loose wool. Then he hung it over a bush. When he looked back the boy was still standing there.

Get em off, he said.

He started pulling his clothes off, the man taking from him in turn shirt and trousers, socks and drawers, wringing them out and hanging them over a pole propped on forks before the fire. When he was finished he stood naked, white as a slug in the cup of firelight. Sylder took off his coat and threw it to him.

Put it on, he said. And get your ass over here in front of the fire.

The two men were behind him in the woods; he could hear them crashing about, see the wink of their light. One of them came back toting a huge log and dropped it on the fire. A flurry of sparks ascended, flared, lost in the smoke pulling at the bare limbs overhead, returned tracing their slow fall redly through the dark trees downwind.

He sat in a trampled matting of vines, the long coat just covering his buttocks. Sylder made a final adjustment to the pole and came over. He lit a cigarette and stood regarding him.

Kind of cool, ain't it? he said.

The boy looked up at him. Cool enough, he said.

The clothes had begun to steam, looking like some esoteric game quartered and smoking on the spit.

Then he said, What'd you do with the coon?

Coon?

Yeah. The coon.

Goddamn, the boy said, I never saw the coon.

Oh, Sylder said. But his voice was giving him away. Hell, I figured you'd of got the coon too.

Shoo, the boy said. Over his teeth the firelight rippled and danced.

The two men were warming their hands at the fire, the shorter one grinning goodnaturedly at the boy. The other hound had appeared, hovering suddenly at the rim of light and snuffling at the steaming wool and then slouching past them with nervous indifference, the slack hound grace, to where Lady lay quietly peering across her paws into the fire. He nosed at her and she raised her head to look at him with her sad red eyes. He stood so for a minute, looking past her, then stepped neatly over her and melted silently into the black wickerwork of the brush. The other man moved over to her and reached down to pat her head. One ear was mangled and crusting with blood.

Coon's hard on a walker, he said. Walker's got too much heart. Old redbone like that—he motioned toward the blackness that encircled them—he'll quit if it gets too rough. Little old walker though—he addressed the dog now—she jest got too much heart, ain't she?

When Sylder let him out of the car his clothes were still wet. You better scoot in there fast, he told him. Your maw raise hell with you?

Naw, he said, she'll be asleep.

Well, Sylder said. We'll go again. You got to stay out of the creek though. Here, I got to get on. My old lady'll be standin straight up.

All right, we'll see ye. He let the door fall.

Night, Sylder said. The car pulled away trailing ropy plumes of smoke, the one red taillight bobbing. He turned toward the house, lightless and archaic among the crumbling oaks, crossed the frosted yard. His shadow swept upward to the lean-to roof, dangled from a limb, upward again, laced with branches, stood suddenly upon the roof. He slid downward over the eaves and disappeared in the black square of the gable window.

III

Some time after midnight on the twenty-first of December it began to snow. By morning in the gray spectral light of a brief and obscure winter sun the fields lay dead-white and touched with a phosphorous glow as if producing illumination of themselves, and the snow was still wisping down thickly, veiling the trees beyond the creek and the mountain itself, falling softly, and softly, faintly sounding in the immense white silence.

On that morning the old man rose early and stared long out at the little valley. Nothing moved. The snow fell ceaselessly. When he pushed the screendoor it dragged heavily in the drifts packed on the porch and against the house. He stood there in his shirtsleeves watching the great wafers of snow list and slide, dodging the posts at the corner of the house. It was very cold.

The hiss of the coffeepot boiling over on the stove brought him in again.

All day it darkened so that when night came no one could tell just when it had come about. Yet the snow fell, undiminished. Windless, pillowed in silence, down-sifting . . . No one was about. All the dogs were quiet. In his house the old man lit a lamp and settled back in a stout rocker near the stove. He selected a magazine from a rack alongside, an ancient issue of *Field and Stream*, limp and worn, the pages soft as chamois, spread it on his lap and began to leaf through it who knew it now almost by heart—stories, pictures, advertisements. From time to time he could hear scuffling sounds beneath him, scratchings in the darkness under the floor where Scout turned uneasily in his nest of rotting sacks.

He turned the pages for a while and then got up and went to the kitchen where from a high cupboard above the tapless sink he fetched down a molasses jar near filled with a viscous brickcolored liquid opaque as clay. He screwed off the cap, took a clean jelly jar from the sideboard and poured it full. Then he went back to his chair, settled the drink on its broad arm, adjusted the magazine in his lap and began to rock gently back and forth, the liquid in the glass lapping sluggishly with the motion. Now and again he took a sip, staining the white stubble beneath his lip a deep maroon. The oil-lamp glowed serenely at its image, a soft corolla, inflaming the black window-glass where a curled and withered spider dangled from a dusty thread.

The old man rocked, dwarflike in his ponderous chair. He seemed to be weighing some dark problem posed in the yellowed pages before him.

Toward late morning a rooster called and the old man's window blushed in a soft wash of rose. He slept and color drained from the glass and the east paled ash-gray. The rooster called once again, questioningly, and shortly the old man jerked awake in his chair, knocking the jelly glass to the floor where it rolled about woodenly.

He peered through the hazy light of the room. It was morning, the lamp out and the stove too, and he found himself stiff and shivering with the cold, rubbing his eyes now, then his back. He rose gingerly and opened the door of the stove, poked among the feathery ashes. He went to the window and looked out. The snow had stopped. Scout was standing in snow to his belly, gazing out at the fantastic landscape with his bleary eyes. Across the yard, brilliant against the façade of pines beyond, a cardinal shot like a drop of blood.

There were three of them coming up the trackless road past the house, and two dogs. One of them carried a rabbit, holding it loosely by the hind legs, its head jerking limply as they went. The other two carried guns and the boy knew one of them. He hadn't seen him since school started in September.

They were talking and gesturing and they didn't notice him standing there in the yard so he moved out toward the road, making for the mailbox, plopping his feet into the dazzling and unbroken drifts. The one carrying the rabbit had his feet wrapped—wound and encased in burlap sacks to the knee and held with twine. He saw him coming and then Warn turned and saw him too and waved.

Heyo, John Wesley.

Howdy, he said, sliding down the bank.

He met Warn Pulliam in the summer, headed toward the pond one afternoon when he saw the buzzard circling low over Tipton's field and noticed that there was a string looping down from its leg. He came up through the field to the crest of the hill and there was Warn holding the other end of the string while the buzzard soared with lazy unconcern above his head.

Howdy, Warn said.

Howdy. He was looking up at the buzzard. What you doin?

Ah, jest flyin the buzzard some. He cain't get up lessen they's some wind. So when we get a little wind I gen'ly fly him some.

Where'd you get him, he asked. The back of his neck was already beginning to ache from staring up at the wheeling bird.

Caught him in a steel trap. You want to see him?

Sure.

He pulled the bird out of the sky by main force, heaving on the cord against the huge and ungiving expanse of wing, lowering him circle by circle until he brought him to earth. There the buzzard flopped about on its one good leg and came to rest eying them truculently, beady eyes unblinking in the naked and obscene-looking skull.

Turkey buzzard, Warn explained. They's the ones got red heads.

Where do you keep him?

Been keepin him in the smokehouse, he said.

Don't nobody care for you to keep him?

Naw. The old lady set up a fuss but I told her I was goin to bring him in the house and learn him to set at table and that calmed her down some. Here, don't get too close or he'll puke on ye. He puked on Rock and Rock like to never got over it—stit won't have nothin to do with him. Don't nobody think much of him I reckon but me. I like him cause he's about a mean son of a bitch and twice as ugly. What's your name?

The two dogs were beagles, shortlegged and frantic, leaping in and out of the chest-high fall of snow, or plowing their noses through it and furrowing snow up and past their ears, their tails spinning, then looking up with white brows and whiskers, gnomic and hoary-faced as little old men.

Where you-all goin? he asked them.

T'wards the quarry, Warn said. Come on go with us—I got me a skunk in a hole I got to get out. This here's Johnny Romines—motioning at the tall boy with the shotgun—and that there's Boog.

Howdy, he said. They nodded.

We done got us a rabbit, Boog said, holding up the snow-dusted and stiffening quarry. Johnny shot him in the field yonder.

The dogs circled him, sniffing his cuff. Them's Johnny's dogs, Boog added. Rabbit dogs. Bugles.

Beagles, idjit, Warn said.

Yeah, Boog said. Them's what they are.

Where's Rock? the boy asked.

He's layin up under the house still lickin his foot where he accidental stepped in the snow this mornin. Cain't get him to stir a stump. Sides he won't run rabbits noway. He's a bear dog.

I got me a dog now, he told them. Half bluetick and half walker. Makes as good a tree dog as they is goin. They were moving up the road, the beagles for outriders prancing and frisking.

You run him? Boog asked.

Naw. He's jest a pup. I been keepin him with a feller over on Henderson Valley Road raises dogs. He's the one give him to me.

You don't need no more excuse to run wild at night. That was what she said to him standing there in the kitchen with the pup under his arm. She must be a pis-

tol, Sylder said when he returned with it, embarrassed, explaining why he couldn't keep it. Don't make no difference though. He's still yourn; you jest keep him here is all and come get him any time you've a mind to.

I got me a old musket at home belonged to my greatgrandaddy, Boog said. It's nigh on long as me my own sef.

They left the road and crossed a field dotted with scrub cedars, the beagles coursing now and Johnny Romines calling to them to hunt. He and Warn trampled the brush piled all down a rock draw and scouted the frozen drainage ditches but no rabbits appeared. They crossed a fence and came out onto the railroad, following it south across the white quilted fields, the sun on them now glinting and the last traces of icefog dispersing in myriad blue crystals on the shining air.

At the sinkhole they stopped and skittered down the bank to test the ice; it was black and evil-looking and woven with sticks and weeds. The beagles came to the edge and whined, pawing tentatively. After a while they came out too and rushed wheeling and sliding in a game of tag, their hindquarters spinning from under them as they turned. Boog couldn't skate because of his feet being wrapped so he sat on the bank holding the rabbit and watching them. Later he built a fire, making a platform of hickory bark and piling dead cedar branches on top and they came and sat around it.

This here's where Johnny caught the bullfrog, Warn said. Right over yander off the end of that log. By the ass in a mousetrap.

How'd he do that? John Wesley asked.

He bet me a dope on it. I seen him come by the house with this mousetrap on a piece of bailin wire. Said he was fixin to catch him a bullfrog. We come on over and he set it on the end of that log there and then we went

on to the store. I thought the poor bastard had done lost
his rabbit-assed mind . . .

Johnny Romines grinned. He told everybody in the
store, he said.

Yeah, we all like to of fell out laughin. So the son of
a bitch bets me a dope he's caught one by the time we
come back and sure as hell there he is. Pinched right by
the ass. I like to never got over it. And wouldn't nothin
do but we come straight back to the store frog trap and
all and me buy him the dope right there.

It's a old Indian trick, said Boog.

What's that?

Puttin bark down like that. To lay your fire on.

When he reached the fence he rested again, removed
his gloves and blew into his cupped hands. Along the
face of the mountain and down the valley floor guns
were sounding, echoing in diminishing reiteration. The
trees were all encased in ice, limbless-looking where their
black trunks rose in aureoles of lace, bright seafans shimmering in the wind and tinkling with an endless bell-like
sound, a carillon in miniature, and glittering shards of
ice falling in sporadic hail everywhere through the woods
and marking the snow with incomprehensible runes.
Something flicked rapid and invisibly past and struck
with a soft pock into the bark of a poplar above him.
The thin spat and whine of a rifle followed.

The old man paid no attention. He pulled his gloves
on, gathered the wire in one hand and stepped through,
the posts on the downhill side jiggling where they dangled in their wires like sticks in a spiderweb, the earth
having long been washed from about their moorings.
Some dogs were trailing and after a while he could see
them below him where the last finger of bleak trees

reached into a cut and met the barren fields, the dogs coming out from behind the timber, moving slow and diminutive, their voices small as a child's horn, two of them. They dipped into the cut and swarmed up the other side and out, across the fields, their brown and white shapes losing definition in the confectionary landscape of mudclods and snow until only their motion was discernible, like part of the ground itself rumoring upheaval.

He went slowly, the snow heavier now, drifted and billowing in the honeysuckle and breaking it down into the path so that he had to skirt below it in places, teetering with edged steps along the incline, uncovering in his footsteps wet patches of leaf black as swampwater, not even frozen. When he reached the top of the mountain, the road curving away in a white swath through the trees, he paused to brush the snow from his shoulders and turn out the lumps of ice gathered in his cuffs. He plowed his way down the drifts some hundred yards and re-entered the woods to the other side, carrying in his hand now the huge handleless knife forged from an old millfile, receding among the small trees in his stooped and shambling gait, apparitional, a strange yuletide assassin.

A quarter hour later he emerged back into the road again still carrying the knife and dragging behind him a small cedar tree. At the curve below the orchard he stopped and looked back, then relegated the knife to some place in the folds of his coat and shouldered the tree. A little further on he entered the woods again, trace of a path or road leading off to the right. This time he was gone for only a few minutes. When he came back, unburdened of the tree now, he followed his tracks to where he had first come onto the road and so

disappeared once more into the woods, down the slope
of the mountain the way by which he came.

They threaded their way over the jumbled limestone
of the quarry, Warn in the lead, until they came to the
cave.

It don't look like much, Johnny Romines said.

It opens up inside, Warn said. Here, let me hang him
up here and I'll show ye. He wedged the skunk in the
fork of a sapling and then disappeared down into the
earth, crawling on hands and knees through a small hole
beneath the rocks. They followed one by one, the stiff
winter nettles at the cave door rattling viperously against
the legs of their jeans. Inside they struck matches and
Warn took a candlestub from a crevice and lit it, the
calcined rock taking shape, tonsiled roof and flowing
concavity, like something gone partly to liquid and
frozen back again misshapen and awry, their shadows
curling threatfully up the walls among the dried and
mounded bat-droppings. They studied the inscriptions
etched in the soft and curdcolored stone, hearts and
names, archaic dates, crudely erotic hieroglyphs—the
bulbed phallus and strange centipedal vulva of small
boys' imaginations.

They followed the strip of red clay that traced the
cave floor into another and larger room, hooted at their
lapping echoes, their laughter rebounding in hollow and
mocking derision. Water dripped ceaselessly, small ping
and spatter on stone. The two dogs hung close to them,
stepping nervously.

This'n here's the biggest room, Warn said. Then I
got me a secret room on back with a rock in front of it
so you cain't see it. Then they's a tunnel goes back, but

I ain't never been to the end of it. Ain't no tellin where-all it goes.

Boog came up dragging a load of dead limbs and presently they had a fire going in the center of the big room. This here is the way the cave-men used to do, Boog said.

They used to be cave-men hereabouts, said Warn. Pre-storic animals too. They's a tush over on the other side of the mountain stickin out of some rock what's long as your leg. Ain't no way to get to it lessen you had ropes or somethin.

Johnny Romines took out a packet of tobacco and rolled a cigarette. Boog borrowed it and rolled one too and they sat smoking in long steady pulls. Which'd you rather be, Boog asked John Wesley, white or Indian?

I don't know, the boy said. White I reckon. They always whipped the Indians.

Boog tipped the ash from his cigarette with his little finger. That's so, he said. That's a point I hadn't studied.

I got Indian in me, Johnny Romines said.

Boog's half nigger, said Warn.

I ain't done it, Boog said.

You said niggers was good as whites.

I never. What I said was *some* niggers is good as *some* whites is what I said.

That what you said?

Yeah.

I had a uncle was a White-Cap, Johnny Romines said. You ought to hear him on niggers. He claims they're kin to monkeys.

John Wesley didn't say anything. He'd never met any niggers.

Tell John Wesley here about the time we dynamited the birds, Warn said. This is last Christmas, he explained.

His daddy give him a electric train one time and they got it out for his little brother.

Johnny Romines told it, slowly, smiling from time to time. They had wired the transformer of the train to a dynamite cap stolen from the quarry shack and buried the cap in the snow.

We had us a long piece of lightwire, he said, and we set in the garage with the transformer all hooked up. Warn here claimed it wouldn't work. Well, we'd sprinkled breadcrumbs all round over where the cap was buried out in the yard and directly you couldn't see for the birds. I told Warn to thow the switch.

Goddamn but it come a awful blast, said Warn. I eased the switch on over and then BALOOM! They's a big hoop of snow jumped up in the yard like when you thow a flat rock in the pond and birds goin ever which way mostly straight up. I remember we run out and you could see pieces of em strung all out in the yard and hangin off the trees. And feathers. God, I never seen the like of feathers. They was stit fallin next mornin.

Lord, whispered Boog, I'd of liked to of seen that.

John Wesley had begun to cough. Ain't it gettin kindly smoky in here to you? he asked. Above their heads smoke roiled and lowered and they noticed they could no longer see the walls of the cave.

Believe it is some, Warn said. He stood up and was closed from sight by the smoke. Hell's bells, he said, let's get out of here.

This is the way the cave-men done it, Boog said.

Cave-men be damned, we're fixin to get barbycued.

They crawled and stumbled to the mouth of the cave—a shifting patch of murky light weaving beyond the smoke combers, came red-eyed and weeping from their crypt, their jacket fronts encrusted with slick red mud. When they had dried their eyes and could see again they were in some volcanic and infernal under-region, the whole of the quarry woods wrapped in haze and smoke boiling up out of the rocky ground from every cleft and fissure.

Mr Eller stood at the counter and watched them come in, the clothes steaming on the backs of the men as they stomped off the slush from their shoes and stood about the stove making cigarettes with chilled fingers, the stove popping and whistling with the snow-wetted coal, the women excited with the cold, making their pur-chases with deliberation, some towing small children about in the folds of their skirts, leaving again, young boys with shotguns and rifles buying shells not by the box but by fours and sixes and lending to the bustle a purposeful and even militant air. He rang the money up in the cash register or marked it in his credit books.

Odor of smoke and cold, wet clothing and meat cooking. The snow was falling again and they watched it. Lord, Mr Eller said, reckon it's ever goin to quit.

Boog and Johnny Romines came in with a rabbit and they each got a dope.

Whereabouts you get him, Johnny? Mr Eller asked.

Over on the creek.

Warn Pulliam caught a skunk in a hole, Boog said.

That right? How's he smell?

He don't smell too purty.

The men laughed. He's a fat'n, one said, nodding toward the rabbit. How's them pups run? Purty good?

Purty good little old rabbit dogs, Johnny said. They jumped two more but I never got a clear shot.

Them's beagles, said Boog.

. . .

The old man came out on the pike road at the gap where the Green Fly Inn had stood. There was no trace of the inn now but the black and limbless pine trunk that stood in the hollow. Snow had started again, dropping like a veil over the valley or riding the wind through the gap, stinging his face a little. He walked down until he came to the Twin Fork road and took it into the Hopper and homeward. From a lightwire overhead, dangling head downward and hollowed to the weight of ashened feathers and fluted bones, a small owl hung in an attitude of forlorn exhortation, its wizened talons locked about the single strand of wire. It stared down from dark and empty sockets, penduluming softly in the bitter wind.

At the head of the hollow there was a springhouse and they stopped to drink, the water green and pulsing up from the rocks where a scalloped fringe of ice jutted just above the waterline.

I figured to set here, Warn said, but they's too many people come by and you'd get your traps stole. Come on I'll show you where I got my culvert-set. He dipped up another mouthful of the numbing water, took the rifle and trap and handed the skunk to the younger boy. He don't smell so bad out in the air, he said. The old lady'll pitch a hissy when she gets a whiff of me though.

They came out on the road and crossed to the other side where the creek ran. Warn got down on one knee and peered back through the culvert under the road where the spring run trickled through.

It don't never freeze in here, he said. I done caught me one muskrat here but what I'm lookin for is a mink. See? I got the trap jest back inside where nobody won't notice it.

The boy peered into the dark tunnel, the water loping

slowly down the corrugated metal and flaring where it passed over the trap.

I seen mink sign here back in the fall and some lately, Warn said. They's mink on Stock Creek too. Used to be some on Red Branch but they ain't any more is how come I don't trap it no more. You ready to go?

See, they ain't been no cars in here yet, Warn said. Ain't but jest a few people live over here in the holler and mostly they ain't got cars. You see that house up yander?

He looked where Warn pointed. Set back off the road was a squat saddle-roofed structure with a thin wisp of smoke swirling and circling about the top of the chimney.

That's where Garland Hobie lives, he told him. You mess around there you get your ass shot off.

How come?

On account of he makes whiskey, Warn said. Him and his old lady. Here. I'll show you somethin directly.

Beyond the curve of the road there was an old frame church and Warn pointed it out. See that church? Well, that was a nigger church. They used to be a bunch of niggers lived in the holler and they built this here church and commenced singin and hollerin of a night till old man Hobie, he's dead now, he run em ever one off. He's been dead since afore you and me was born and they ain't none of em come back yet. That's how strong he was on niggers. They say Ef was even meaner'n the old man. He died right at the store back a few year ago. Jest got out of Brushy Mountain. Garland, he's meaner'n hell too. They raided em one time here back and he give em the old lady to take off to jail. His own mama. That's how bad he is. Then they's Uncle Ather lives up here—nodding ahead of them—he's a purty good old feller.

Is he your uncle?

Naw. Him and Grandaddy Pulliam worked together cuttin sleepers for the K S & E. So the old man always called him Uncle. He's purty old. Got a dog pret-near old as you and me both.

That's purty old, the boy said. How old is he, Uncle . . .

Uncle Ather? He must be ninety or better. He's older'n Grandaddy Pulliam and Grandaddy Pulliam's daddy fought in the Civil War. He owned a lot of land in Knox County and when the war was over they took it away from him on account of him bein a Confederate. Grandaddy Pulliam says they wouldn't even let nobody vote ceptin niggers and yankees.

Why was that?

On account of back then this was the North I reckon.

Late in the afternoon the old man was sweeping the snow from his front porch when he saw them coming up the road, two small figures dark against the unbroken fall of snow, laboring through the drifts. One of them was carrying a dead skunk. They came abreast of his mailbox and the taller one raised his hand. Heyo, Uncle Ather, he called.

The old man squinted his milkblue eyes against the glare. Hiram Pulliam's grandson. He grinned and waved them up and they came, toiling on the slope, bowlegged for a better grip in the snow, the Pulliam boy leaning on his rifle and the other one sliding and waving the skunk about in the air.

They sat around the stove with their shoes off, their socks steaming. The old man wrinkled his nose and laughed.

I believe you must of fit that there polecat hand to hand, he said.

Can you smell it? Warn said. I cain't smell it myself.

He had to crawl back in a hole to get him out, John Wesley said.

I crawled past where he was at, Warn said. I thought he was way on back and then I come to see the wire and it went off into a little side-hole, but I was already past it then. I was all hunkered up down in there and couldn't hardly turn around, but directly I got to where I could poke my pine knot in the side-hole there and I seen his eyes. I got my rifle turned around and aimed the best way I could and when I shot, it like to busted out my eardrums.

We could hear him shoot, John Wesley said. It sounded like a little old popgun or somethin from on the outside.

Well, when I shot he cut loose too. I mean it really steamed things up in there. I come scootin out hind-end first and we waited a while and then directly I went back and got holt of the wire and come draggin him out and he's shot between the eyes.

The old man laughed. That puts me in mind of a coon hunt I was on one time, he said. Feller with us shot a coon in a tree and it hung in a limb. So I helt the light and he went up after him. Time he got to the limb where the coon was at it come to life and made at him. He figured purty quick he didn't want no part of it, but stead of comin down he scooted up another limb and there he set. Ever time he made like he was comin down the coon'd go at him, growlin like a bear. Well, directly he got mad and he decided he'd come on down anyway. So here he come. He was goin to kick the coon off of the limb is what he hollered down to us. We had the lannern on him and could see purty good. He made two or three swipes at the coon and about that time the old coon latched on to his foot. I never heard the like of hollerin. He commenced swingin that coon around on the end of his toe and he got so took up with it he kindly eased up his holt on the tree. Well, wadn't but a few minutes one of us hollered to Look out! and here they come pilin down out of the tree. He hit the ground like a sack of feed and jest laid there and the dogs piled on to the coon and they commenced walkin all in his face and fightin till we got em kicked off. We thought he's dead, but directly he begun to breathe a little and his eyes to flitter some and we seen he wadn't hurt, jest the wind pooched out of him and scared purty bad. We all laughed considerable and he set there and cussed us, but he was a purty good old boy and I reckon he never helt it against us. I remember he used to tell it on his own sef for years and years and laugh jest like anybody.

The old man sighed. Used to be good coon huntin hereabouts, he said.

What about painters? Warn asked. Was that a painter was hollerin around here one time?

The old man leaned back in his rocker, a wise grin settling among his sagging skinfolds. Well now, he said. Shore, I remember that right well. Been about ten year ago I'd say. There followed a moment of silence in which he seemed to be contemplating with satyric pleasure some old deed. Then he crossed one knee over the other and leaned forward. Shore, he repeated, I heard it. Many's the time. Had folks stirred up and scared all of one summer. Yessir, stirred up a blue fog of speculatin.

What'd it sound like? the boy asked.

Oh, purty fierce . . .

Well, you reckon it was a painter?

Nope, the old man said.

After a minute Warn said, What was it?

The old man had begun to rock gently, a benign look upon his face, composed in wisdom, old hierophant savoring a favorite truth . . . He stopped and looked down at them. Well, I'll tell ye. It was a hoot-owl.

He studied their fallen faces, the hopeful incredulity. Yep, he said, a hoot-owl. One of them big'ns, screechin and a-hollerin on this mountain of summer evenins like any painter. They's folks said painter, folks said not. But I knowed what it was right along. So I let em do their speculatin and arguin . . . I recollect one evenin I was at the store gettin some things, late summer it was and nigh dark, bout eight o'clock I reckon, when it commenced hollerin. Well, I never said nothin. In a little bit it come again. Boys, I mean it got quiet in that store to where you could hear the ants in the candy jar. Stit I never let on nothin and after a while Bob Kirby—he's there—he hollered at me and he said, Hey! Uncle Ather. You fixin to walk crost that mountain tonight?

Well, I turned to him kind of surprised-like and I said, Why shore. A feller's got to get home sometime, and the best way he can. How come you to ast me that?

He jest looked at me for a minute, then he kind of grinned and he said, Cain't you hear that wampus cat?

Why, I said, shore I hear it. Anybody't wadn't deaf could hear that, I reckon.

Well, he kind of figured he had me then so he says, Ain't you skeered of painters, Uncle Ather?

Why shore, I says. Anybody ceptin a fool'd be skeered of one, a full-growed one leastways.

Then I never said nothin, jest went to the dope box and got me a dope and commenced drinkin it and lookin at my watch ever oncet in a while. I could see he was plenty puzzled and he tried to slip a grin to the rest of the fellers there once or twicet cept they wadn't grinnin and I reckon was more puzzleder'n he was. So he never said nothin neither, but after a while they's a young feller there, he piped up and ast me if that wadn't a full-growed one that was raisin all that hell out there. Well, about that time it come again, hollerin, and I looked at him and I said, They Lord God, son, I don't know what you'd do if a growed one was to squall. Why that ain't nothin there. But then course they ain't painters round like they used to be. Back fifty, sixty years ago they'd sing out back and forth crost these mountains all night of a summer till you got to where you couldn't sleep lessen you did hear em. But it takes a big old tom painter to set up a fuss. That there ain't nothin. I told him that and about that time shore enough that owl let out another screech couldn't of been a hundred yards off and I could see the hackles come up on his neck and on Bob Kirby's too.

I finished my dope and set it down and made like I was fixin to leave then and Kirby, he says, stit grinnin kind of, You mean, Uncle Ather, that you can tell one painter from anothern by its squall?

Well, I said, I don't reckon I can so good any more. He grinned right big at that.

But, I says, since I seen this'n t'other night I guess it jest don't worry me none.

Well, they all jumped up with somethin to ast then, how big it was and all. I was already half out the door, but I figured to give em somethin to think about while *they* walked home, so I turned to em and I says, Why it ain't more'n a kitten. It's right up here in the gap not even dusk-dark t'other night I seen it scoot crost the road. Old Scout was layin there on the concrete. Now he's fell off some of late but used to be he come a good bit higher'n my knee—to where you jest could straddle him, and weighed better'n a hunderd pound. So I looked around and I seen him there and I jest pointed to him and I said, Why he ain't a whole lot bigger'n Scout here, and said em a good night and went on.

Down the small panes of glass behind the old man's chair the sun lowered, casting his head in silhouette and illumining his white hair with a prophetic translucence. A little later he rose and went to the table and lit the lamp.

You boys care for some . . . here, jest a minute. He excused himself and went flapping off to the kitchen from where issued in a moment sounds of cupboards and glassware. When he came back he was carrying two glasses and a cup, a mason jar of some dark red liquid. Here, he said, handing them each a glass. He unscrewed the lid of the jar and poured their glasses. A heavy and evil-looking potion the color of iodine. Muskydine wine, he said. Bet you-all ain't never had none.

It beaded black and sinister in the soft lampglow. He settled himself in his rocker and filled his cup, watching them taste it.

Mighty fine, Warn said.

Yessir, said the boy.

They sipped their wine with the solemnity of communicants, troglodytes gathered in some firelit cave. The lamp guttered in a draft of wind and their shadows, ponderous and bearlike upon the wall, weaved in unison.

Uncle Ather, said the boy, was they really painters back then?

Warn's face, a harlequin mask etched in black and orange by the lamplight, turned to the old man. Tell him about that'n, Uncle Ather, he said. That'n you had.

Uncle Ather had already started. Oh yes, he said, allaying doubt with an upthrust of his chin. Yes, they was, long time back. When I was a young feller, workin on the road crew at that time, I caught one.

Caught one?

Yep. He smiled mysteriously. Shore did. Caught him with my bare hands, and I got the scars to prove it. Here he extended a leathery thumb for inspection. The boy slid from his chair and bent studiously over it.

Right here, the old man said, pointing to a place on the inside just above the web. See?

Yes, he said. The skin was wrinkled like an old purse; in that myriad cross-hatching any line could have been a scar. He sat back down and the old man chuckled throatily.

Yessir, he said. He was a vicious critter. Must of weighed all of five pound.

Warn laughed softly. The boy raised his head. The old man sat complacent and mischievous in his rocker, his eyes dancing.

Well, he said, this is what happent. They was a place called Goose Gap—it's up t'wards Wears Valley. Well, it was when we was blastin in there. Bill Munroe, he's dead now, he went up right after, soon as rock quit fallin, and then he hollered for me to come up and look see. They's stit lots of smoke and dust and I couldn't see too good but I got on up a little ways and directly I seen he's holdin up somethin. Looked like a groundhog or a little old dog. When I got to where he was at I seen what it was. I hadn't never seen one afore and it was all tore up and bloody, but I knowed right off what it was. Bill, he couldn't make nothin out of it. What it was was a painter kit.

We started up through them rocks and directly we come up on anothern. It wadn't tore up as bad and Bill allowed as to how it must not of been blowed as fer and so we was headed right. Anyway it turned out he was right and in a little bit we come up on the den-hole. It was all blowed out in the front and about a yard and a half of bones layin all around, and back in the back under some rocks we found this'n, the third'n, he's alive and mewlin jest about like a housecat.

Old Bill, he backed off some, said that old she-painter might be around. Well, I was younger'n him and likely didn't have as good sense, so in I goes and grabs the little feller up by the scruff of the neck. That's when he hung his tushes in my thumb here. I turnt loose right fast, I'll tell ye. Well, I figured a minute, and then I took off my shirt and scotched him up in that and brought him on home with me.

Here the old man paused and helped himself to a chew of tobacco from a huge paper pouch. I lived five mile this side of Sevierville then, he continued. I—you boys don't chew, do ye? no—I had bought me a place off a man named Delozier—twenty acres, mostly side-hill and not much of a house neither, a old piece of a barn . . . I was married then and that was my first place so I reckon I was kindly what you might say proud of it. I kep some hogs and chickens and later on I had me a cow and a wore-out mule, put me in some corn . . . I never had nothin, ain't got nothin now, but I figured it was a start. I wadn't a whole lot older'n you fellers, nineteen, I think I was. But anyway what I was fixin to tell was about that painter. I brought him on home and give him to Ellen. She took to it right off, kep it in a box and give it milk and sech as that. It got to where it'd folly her around the house like a everday walkin-around cat. It wadn't but about the size of a cat too . . . I recollect he's speckled kindly like a bobcat. Well, they's even a feller come out from the newspaper and wrote it up about us havin him; folks come from pret-near everwhere to see him.

I reckon it was about two weeks we'd had him when one evenin I heard one of the hogs squeal. I got the lannern and went out but I couldn't find nothin wrong and went on back in and never thought no more about it. Well, next mornin they's a hog gone. I hadn't never heard of nobody stealin hogs but I figured maybe they's hog thieves jest like ary other kind, up in Sevier County leastwise as that was purty woolly country at that time. But they wadn't a whole lot I could do about it, not knowin where to even start lookin. Then two nights later anothern of em went. Well, I says, they gettin slicker now. The secont one never even squealt.

Next night I laid up on the roof of the house with the shotgun—a old single-barrel muzzleloader and me with not enough money to buy caps with even—I was usin matchheads and cottonseed hulls—and here's somebody stealin my hogs. So I laid up there all night, no further'n from here to the porch yonder from that hogpen. I never seed nothin nor heard nothin. Come mornin I never even looked at the hogs even. Then when she, Ellen, went out later on and slopped em she come back in and she says, Ather, they's another hog gone.

I was settin in a chair about half asleep and I come from there. I don't recollect how many hogs it was that we had but seven or eight I reckon anyway, and I run out and counted em and come up short one more hog. I'd been mad afore but now I was scared.

Here the old man found the cup of wine in his hand and he regarded it for a moment with mild surprise, raised it and took a drink. He closed his eyes for a moment,

the high wagon and them coming up to the house,

wagon and house both belonging to his uncle, and him owning nothing more than he could carry in his two hands, her things in an old leather trunk tied down behind the seat.

That her? he asked.

Yessir.

He walked around the wagon slowly, studying her as a man might a horse. Then he said, Well, light.

He got down and she was still sitting there.

What's she? goin to put the mule up?

Nosir, he said. Ellen. Here.

He took her hand and she got down.

You go on with Uncle Whitney, he said. I'll get the things.

Helen, he said.

It's Ellen, she said. The wagon moved away behind her.

Ellen.

Daddy said he'd kill him, she said.

Ain't nobody goin to kill nobody, he said. Here, watch the mud.

She said something else. He watched them go in.

What happent then, Uncle Ather, Warn said.

Hmm? Oh, well I'd done lost three of them I think it was then. That was three more'n I was willin to lose and two more'n I thought I would lose without I caught somebody. Aside that it looked like I would lose jest as many as whoever I was losin em to was willin to take, which probably meant all of them. So I was mad-scared. Ellen, she claimed I'd gone to sleep on the roof, but I knowed better.

That was late of a summer. I was stit on the road crew and workin twelve and fourteen hours a day and here I got to come home nights and set up with a bunch of hogs. But we never lost no more for a week or better. Then one night Ellen went to the door to thow out a pan of water and I heard her holler. I run out and she grabbed on to me like she'd seen a hant or somethin, and I ast her what it was but she jest stood there and shook like she's freezin to death. I walked her back in and went out and looked but I never seen nothin, so I got the pan and come on in. Somethin had scared her real bad but she couldn't tell me what all it was. After a while all she'd say was *I don't know,* or *I couldn't tell what it was.*

The old man paused again, arrested but for the rise and fall of his breathing, the slow mechanical rotation of his jaws, gazed upward—the image of the lampflame on the ceiling, the split corona a doubling egg, like the parthenogenesis of primal light.

He kept on for a week, coming back each night to the dark and empty house. Then he stopped going to work. That morning he took out the few things she had left—a housecoat, odds and ends, and put them on the bed. He sat and looked at them for a long time. When he got up it was evening.

He stayed for five more days, wandering about the house or sitting motionless, sleeping in chairs, eating whatever he happened to find until there wasn't any more and then not eating anything. While the chickens grew thin and the stock screamed for water, while the hogs perished to the last shoat. An outrageous stench settled over everything, a vile decay that hung in the air, filled the house.

On the sixth day he went out and knocked a plank from the back of the barn with the poll of his axe, cut from it two boards. On one he carefully incised her name with the point of his knife. Then he chopped a stake-point on the other board and nailed the two together in the form of a cross. He took it and took her clothes and a spade down to a corner of the lot where he scooped a hole, buried the clothes, and with the shank of the spade pounded the cross into the ground. Then he walked straight through the house and out again, across the yard, to the road and toward Sevierville. He had gone half a mile before he noticed the shovel in his hand and pitched it into the weeds.

I know you cain't, he said.

I ain't goin back.

I'll go out tomorrow. Come on, you clean up and eat some.

What?

And get some rest, sleep. I'll go out tomorrow.

Well, you can. I ain't.

I was goin out anyways. R. L. come by yesterday mornin to see if you was comin back. You goin back?

I don't know. No. I ain't goin back.

You aim to sell your place?

It don't . . . I don't care.

Well. I do.

He looked at him for the first time, the older face, dark and hard as a walnut. Why? he asked.

Count of you owe me two hunderd dollars, mainly.

Oh. He thought for a minute, then he said, Yes. Here, I got to clean up.

The old man was swaying slowly in his rocker holding the cup before him in both hands like a ciborium. After a minute Warn said, Did you ever find out what it was?

The old man turned and spat into a coffeecan.

That goddamned bibledrummer, wadn't it?

Don't say nothin else.

Well, nobody never died from it.

Don't say nothin else I told you.

Yessir, he said. It was the old she-painter, come after the little one. You boys care for some more wine?

They still had some. The old man labored up from his rocker and went to the table where he had set the wine, refilled his cup. Yep, he said, that had to of been what she seen.

Did you shoot it? the boy asked.

Nope. Never even seen her. I lost one more hog and then I give it up. I turnt the little one loose and that's the last I ever seen of it and the last hog I lost. You see, he said slowly, darkly, they's painters and they's painters. Some of em is jest that, and then others is right uncommon. That old she-painter, she never left a track one. She wadn't no common kind of painter.

Early next morning the old man worked his way up the mountain, following the prints of the two boys. The snow was drifted deeply in places and it was hard going. He stopped often to catch his breath, leaning on the shotgun, the stock sunk cleanly through the crust to the depth of the triggerguard. By the time he reached the road he was winded and leg-weary. From here he could see out into the valley, through the stark trees standing blackly in an ether of white like diffused milk, glazed and crystalline as shattered ice where the sun probed, the roofs thatched with snow, pale tendrils of smoke standing grayly in the still air.

He could smell smoke, but he didn't think about it until it occurred to him that it had a sharp and pungent quality about it and he realized that it was cedar burning—postwood, not firewood—elusive in the cold air, in his nostrils, faintly antiseptic.

He turned up the road and walked steadily until he

came to the cut-off to the pit. The snow was dry and powdered as marble-dust on his trouser legs. Now he could see the faint pall of smoke through the trees. The tracks turned here and furrowed in two drunken lanes, curving into the woods. He followed them, moving faster, stumbling in and out of the snow ruts, shadowed by some presentiment of ruin, into the clearing.

When he saw the smoke rolling up from out of the pit he stopped for a moment and he could feel the old fierce pull of blood in power and despair, the pulse-drum of the irrevocable act. And it was done, what soul rose in the ashes forever unknown, out of his hands now. He squatted on one knee in the snow, watching. On his face a suggestion of joy, of anguish—something primitive and half hidden. The pale eyes burned cold and remote in their hollows like pockets of smoldering gas.

He rose and retraced his steps back to the road. In the pit the amber coals glowed molten in their bed beneath the charred skeletons of the cedars.

Because the car was pulled over up the road and I couldn't see it from the creek. And he wadn't on the bridge when I come down but after I waded through and come out the other side he was standin on it lookin down at me and I seen him then and he said Come here.

So he took your traps.

All of em ceptin one, the boy said. He'd of had to of waded to find it so I never told him about it. He took the three of em. I didn't have but four.

Lowlife son of a bitch, Sylder said. What'd you tell him?

I never told him nothin. He said he was goin to take me to jail for trappin without license and bettin criminals. I told him I didn't know nothin bout some criminals.

Legwater, what'd he say?

Not much. Jest sort of grinned like a possum. Yeah, he said it'd go a lot easier on me if I was to tell em about it. That it was the same thing—bettin a criminal—as bein one your ownself. Then Gifford said that was right, how I'd likely get three to five years but that if I'd hep em out and tell who it was I might get off with jest a suspendered sentence.

But they didn't take you in?

No. He turned me loose at the forks, the store. He said soon as they got the rest of the evidence they'd pick me up and how it wouldn't do me no good to try to run.

He sat back in the chair, finished now and waiting to know what to do, just beginning to be not so scared.

Sylder leaned toward him. Listen, he said. You know that's all horseshit, don't you? You know what a ass it'd make him look to come draggin a fourteen-year-old boy in? Even for helpin a runner, let alone trappin without license? He's jest tryin to scare you. I know him. He cain't prove no way in the world you helped me and if they caught me it'd have to be with a load, in which case they wouldn't need nobody's testifyin, let alone yours, and even if they did I'd swear I never seen you before in my life and you'd do the same thing so they still couldn't bother you. It's all horseshit, tryin to bluff and scare you into helpin him poke his nose where it don't belong. He bothers you again you tell him nothin, tell him you'll get him for false arrest. Cept I don't think he's goin to bother you no more.

He said he'd catch you anyway.

He couldn't catch cowshit in a warshtub. It ain't even his business; he ain't the A. T. U. Anyway don't you let him bother you. I'll tend his apples for him my ownself. He knowed you didn't have no daddy, nobody to take up for you in the first place is the reason he figured he could jump on you. He's a lowlife son of a bitch and a caird to boot. Here, come take a look at your pup; he's fat as a butterball. Come on, I got em on the back porch on account of it bein so cold.

The pike had been cleared some time in the afternoon so that he didn't even need the chains after he came off the orchard road, dark now, something after six o'clock, the rear end of the car heavy and swaying low over the wheels even with the lovejoys set up as far as they would go. It was very cold and his toes had not yet thawed under the gas heater. He thought how the stump of a toe in his left boot was particularly sensitive, re-membering again *the sweep of the cutter's lights on the stanchions of the bridge, the glazed and blinding eye of the spotlight when it picked him out, standing on the forward deck under a canopy of mangrove with his foot braced on the cleat and holding the anchor rope. When the light caught him he yelled once down into the cabin and began hauling in on the rope. The starter whirred and the motor coughed gutturally at the water, the boat jostling, already moving. He got the anchor in and watched the cutter lights. Even above the high wheening of their own motor he could hear her revving the big double Gray engines as she swung about, then voices, commands, detached and sourceless on the steamy calm of the Gulf. The cutter's spot followed them, swamping them in light as they came out of the back-water. He might have been a ballerina pirouetting there. He could see the twin spume flaring from the prow of the cutter, rising as she took speed, and the running lights bobbing and bobbing again in the black wash of the cutwater. He heard the shots too, quite clearly, but made no association between them and himself. It didn't occur to him that he was being shot at until a real flurry broke out and he could see the muzzleflashes minute and intermittent like cigarettes glowing and hear the pebbly thoop thoop of the bullets in the passing water. Then he jumped and started for the cabin. Instantly there came the sounds of splintering wood and then something tore at his foot and threw him to the deck. He crawled to the companionway and slid down it on his belly.*

Jimmy, he called, a hoarse whisper as if someone might hear them. Ho, Jimmy.

It was dark in the compartment except for the skittering glow of the searchlight passing and repassing the portholes, the portholes in bright silhouette wandering back and forth on the far wall.

Hey, kid. What you say?

Jimenez standing in the passageway. The tiller momentarily abandoned, the craft tilting full throttle across the water, the pulsing slap slap of it under the keel.

I'm shot, he said.

Jimenez holding the flashlight while he removed the shredded shoe, the sock sticky with blood, examined the pulpy mess of his big toe.

Where else, Mario?

I reckon that's it, he said.

Jimmy patting his shoulder commiseratingly. Is hard on the feets that, he said.

They went forward and he wrapped his toe in a strip torn from his shirt and sat there miserably, watching Jimenez's face green and serious in the glow of the panel lights.

He drove slowly, coming through the gap with the moon riding low over the pines that edged the long and barren slash of white beneath the power line, ice-fog coming up from the hollow, scintillant in the lights. Here where the inn stood, *the carnival atmosphere with the few cars strung alongside the road, the heat flickering over them and the men standing about passing the last of the bottles back and forth, talking quietly now, their faces flushed and convivial. Some late arrivals claimed the blaze to have been visible from Vestal. Someone saying You done missed it, Marion.*

Was it a good'n?

Best you ever seen.

Nothin to be done there. A drink of whiskey, sneaking it now, Gifford having arrived. Gifford with a long pole poking steaming holes in the melt of glass. Gloop gloop. Vitreous tar. Damndest thing I ever seen. One brogan toe began to blister and blacken and a moment later he was hopping away snatching at his shoelaces. Goddamn. Whew. Leaning against a tree with his naked foot cradled in his hands like a hurt bird he dared a snicker with fierce eyes.

And two days later the charred shaft of the pine tree still smoldering, pitch bubbling gently from the shell of the bark and small electricblue flames seeping and curling, the spire of smoke standing straight up in the motionless air like a continuation of the tree itself.

On the curve below the gap the rear wheels drifted slightly and he realized that there was a thin sheet of ice on the road. He sat up over the wheel and wiped the glass with a rag. He passed Tipton's, the lights above the road warm and friendly-looking through the trees. Old married men. Sylder chuckled, reached for his cigarettes. *He was the nicest boy . . . the rain peening steadily the tin roof of the church, obelisks of light slanting down from the high windows like buttresses. After the creak of the door nothing but the huge breath-*

ing silence, musty odor, the patient and quiet abandon-
ment, chairs, benches, the pulpit, all orderly and still
in their coats of dust, an air of mild surprise about them
at this late visitation. Their steps ghostly on the warp-
ing boards, rousing an owl from the beams, passing over
them on soundless wings, a shadow, ascending into the
belfry like an ash sucked up a flue and as silently. She
gripped his arm. Together to the mourners' bench. O
Lord, O Lord. Witnessed by one nightbird.

Topping the hill above the creek he came upon a
half-ton truck with a horse on it, the long bland face
peering down at him over the slatted tailgate with eyes
luminous and round as bottlebottoms in the carlights.
The truck was laboring at the hill with beetle-like industry, the gears grinding out a low whine. He watched
the snow swirling over the road behind it, serpentine,
white wisps like smoke on glass, eased up the shiftlever
and passed them, the horse's off eye rolling wildly, past
the cab, the driver dimly lit within, puffing at a cigar,
looking down at him once.

One side for the hooch man, Sylder said. New Year's
whiskey comin. Figure ten headaches to the gallon,
makes . . . a thousand . . . about twelve hunderd real
hat stretchers. How about that, old man?

Old man puffed his cigar, receding rearward, dimmed
his lights to one dull orange globe.

He drove straight down Gay Street, halting obedi-
ently at the stoplights, gazing at the numbed traffic
officers with insolent bemusement.

Howdy, Blue-boy. Keer for a drink?

Out on the west side of town he pulled into a drive
and around behind an aged and ill-kept frame house.
He backed the coupe up to the garage and got out,
stretching a little. Two men came from the house, the
kitchen, where a small window was lit. Another man

came to the door and stood there leaning against the
jamb, his shirttail out, smoking a cigarette and taking
the air. A woman's voice small and shrill somewhere in
the house behind him: Shet the door, idjit. You raised
in a barn? He didn't move.

Howdy, Sylder, the first man said, going past him to
the garage, not even looking at him.

Howdy, Sylder said.

The other one stopped. How's the new car? he asked.

All right.

Ward says it come out of Cosby.

Could be.

Ward says it's plenty fast. Says they blockaded the
feller on the Newport highway is the only way they
ever come to catch him at all.

Let's go, Tiny, the other man called from the garage.

Sylder went to the rear of the coupe and opened the
decklid. They began to unload, carrying the cases back
into the garage, the car creaking and rising bit by bit
until they had finished and it stood with its rear end
high in the air like a cat in heat.

Sylder took a flashlight and wrench from the glove
compartment, stooped by the rear wheels each in turn
and lowered the car. Then he undid the chains, got in
and drove off them, came back and put them in the
trunk. The motor was still running and as he slid behind
the wheel once more Tiny came to lean on the door.

Don't she sound sweet though, he said.

Sylder looked up at him. That what Ward says?

Tiny grinned. Naw, he said. Seems to me that's what
McCrary said. When Ward loant him the money to buy
it.

Tell Ward good cars costs good money. Even at a
government auction. Or even if you done paid for em
oncet.

He set the gears and ran the motor up once and Tiny stood up. Come back, he said.

Sylder was rolling up the glass. We'll see ye, he said, switched on the headlights and pulled away down the drive.

He drove slowly back to the mountain, past the forks and the store, the porch posts dead-white as plaster casts of those untrimmed poles, the huge carved lion's head in fierce cameo upon the door, the brass knocker brightly pendant from its nostrils, and the barred panes buckling in the light planeless as falling water, passing out of the glare in willowing sheets to darkness, stark and stable once again. Past his own house, dark but for the light on the porch, and then across the mountain, still slowly, pulling the grades down under the wheels easily.

The road was glazed with ice on the far side and he amused himself by drifting the coupe from curve to curve like a boat tacking. At the foot of the mountain he left Henderson Valley Road and turned right down Bay's Mountain Road, driving on gravel now, slowing to some ten or fifteen miles an hour and finally switching off the headlights. He drove that way for half a mile, the coupe rolling ghostly over the road, black and silent against the snow. Then he turned the car around in a drive, pointing it back down the road, and got out.

He walked up the road until he came to the next drive and here he turned in, plodding through the snow to the lightless house where it brooded in a copse of trees, solitary above the empty fields, over and around it the naked branches tangled like ironwork.

He walked around the house twice. No dogs barked. At the back again he tested a window, lifted it, the weights slithering in the sashes, stepped through and inside. He found himself in an areaway off the kitchen, two doors in front of him, one leading to a large open room, the other one closed.

Hola, Jeffo, he called, whispered, in mock and inaudible greeting. *Dorme?* On downpointed cat's feet he stepped the three steps to the closed door and folded his hand over the knob. Oh, Jeffo, he whispered. *Es muy malo que no tengas un perro.* Turned the knob and opened the door.

There was one small high window in the room, a square of gray standing out of the blackness, and other than that he could see nothing. He stood at the door for a few minutes, listening to the rumbling breath of the man asleep. After a while he could make out the shape of the bed, directly in front of him.

It was warm in the room, he could feel the sweat in his armpits, but the man was swathed heavily in blankets. Thickness of them under his hand . . . here shape of arm, of shoulder, chest . . . sleeping on his back. Gifford snuffled. One gluey eyelid came unstuck as the covers receded from his chin with maternal solicitude.

He even raised his head a little, wonderingly, sleep leaving him in slow grudging waves, so that he seemed to be coming up to meet it, the shut fist rocketing down out of blackness and into his face with a pulpy sound like a thrown melon bursting.

When he got home it was past midnight and had turned off colder yet. He parked the coupe at the back of the house, scotched the wheel and went in through the kitchen. He took some biscuits and a jar of preserves from the icebox and ate them, walking up and down a little, flexing his knuckles. When he had finished he put the preserves back, took a long drink from a jar of buttermilk, and then went into the bedroom. His right hand was swollen and he picked delicately at the buttons of his coat.

Marion . . .?

Yeah, he said.

Oh . . . what time is it?

Late, I reckon. I got tied up.

Are you okay?

Yeah.

He stepped out of his trousers and crawled in beside her.

She could feel him laughing silently. What? she said.

He kept astin who it was.

What? Who did.

Hmm? Naw, nothin. Just some feller. Go on to sleep.

She turned over and put her hand on his chest. She said, Hush.

He lay on his back, his hand over hers, the other hand stiffening. Suddenly he had a bile-sharp foretaste of disaster. *Why was that old man shooting holes in the government tank on the mountain?*

You sure have got cold feet, she said.

He stared up at the dark ceiling. *I'll be damned if I do,* he whispered to himself.

IV

VI

A warm wind on the mountain and the sky darkening, the clouds looping black underbellies until a huge ulcer folded out of the mass and a crack like the earth's core rending rattled panes from Winkle Hollow to Bay's Mountain. And the wind rising and gone colder until the trees bent as if borne forward on some violent acceleration of the earth's turning and then that too ceased and with a clatter and hiss out of the still air a plague of ice.

The old man looked out through a veil of water fringing his hatbrim, beadwork swinging as he turned his head. The hail had stopped and the wind was coming up again with the rain. He had set forth from his refuge under the claybank and already he was wet through. The road had gone from dust shocked up in dark water-balls to geysers of erupting mud, a sluggish flow beginning in the wheelruts and blistering under the rain. The old man began to run, hobbling in an odd bandylegged progress through the blinding rain, great windblown sheets of it sweeping over the road. The air was filled with branches and foliage of trees and the trees whipped and cracked. By the time he left the road and entered the woods they were coming down, the dead and leafless trunks, grasping with brittle gray fingers and going prone on the earth with the muffled thunder of their fall half lost in the fulminations overhead. The old man kept to his course, over last year's leaves slick with water, hopping and dancing wildly among the maelstrom of riotous greenery like some rain sprite, burned out of the near-darkness in antic configuration against the quick bloom of the lightning. As he passed it thus a barren chestnut silver under the sluice of rain erupted to the heart and spewed out sawdust and scorched mice upon him. A slab fell away with a long hiss like a burning mast tilting seaward. He is down. A clash of shields rings and Valkyrie descend with cat's cries to bear him away. Already a rivulet is packing clay in one ragged cuff and a quiff of white hair depending from his forelock reddens in the seeping mud.

Rainwater seeped among the porous boards of the outhouse until the windrowed leaves in the cat's corner were black and lifeless and the cat left through the leaning door to seek new shelter. Pools of black water stood in the path swirling slowly their wrack of straw and weeds, armadillo beetles coiled round as shot and strangely buoyant. She skirted them on wincing feet, bore squeamishly the wet slide of last year's limp and slime-brown weeds.

Arthur Ownby's hound rooted and burrowed in his wad of ripe sacks, slept again, his tail clasped to his

hairless stomach. He did not see the cat that came to
the door of his cellar and stood on three legs.

Such light as there was to announce the new day
filtered thinly through a mizzle of rain and remarked the
fluff of her taupe fur curled in a cleft treebole on the
south slope of Red Mountain. Hunger drove her out in
the late afternoon, cautious, furtive, dusted with wood-
rot.

Still the rain, eating at the roads, cutting gullies on
the hills till they ran red and livid as open wounds.
The creek came up into the fields, a river of mud
questing among the honeysuckles. Fenceposts like the
soldiers of Pharaoh marched from sight into the flooded
draws.

In Saunders' field a shallow marsh, calm and tractable
beneath the dimpling rain. And yet rain. What low
place did not hold water? At the little end of McCall's
pond water fell thunderously into the sinkhole that
drained it. Along Little River the flats stood weed-deep
in livercolored water flecked with thatches of small
driftwood and foam that coiled and spun near imper-
ceptibly, or rocked with the wind-riffles passing under
them. By day flocks of rails gathered. A pair of bitterns
stalked with gimlet eyes the fertile shallows. At night
the tidelands rang with peepers, with frogs gruffly
choral. Great scaly gars from the river invaded the flats,
fierce and primitive of aspect, long beaks full of teeth,
ancient fishes survived unchanged from mesozoic fens,
their yellowed boneless skeletons graced the cracked
clay-beds later in the season where the water left them
to what querulous harridans, fishcrow or buzzard, might
come to glean their frames, the smelly marvel of small
boys.

Rafts of leaves descended the flowage of Henderson
Valley Road, clear water wrinkling over the black as-

phalt. The mud-choked gullies ran thick with water of
a violent red, roiling heavily, pounding in the gutters
with great belching sounds. The cat trod the high crown
of the road, bedraggled and diminutive, a hunted look
about her.

A low sun fired the pine knots in the smokehouse
wall till they glowed like rubies, veined and pupiled
eyes, peering in at the gloom where the cat gnawed
a dangling side of pork-ribs. The salt drew her mouth
but she kept at it, pausing now and again to listen at
the silence. Mildred Rattner's mule-slippers carried her
with care past the bad spots in the mud, chancing rather
the dampness of the ragged grass that grew along the
path. What with the pat of rain on the tarpaper overhead the cat heard nothing until the keys jangled just
beyond the door and the lock rattled. She leapt to a
high shelf, poised, sprang again, making for the air vent
under the peaked roof. As the door let in she was hanging by one toenail from this opening, hindclaws flailing
desperately for purchase, and then a sliver of the molding wood gave way and she lost her grip.

When Mildred Rattner swung open the door and
stepped into the smokehouse she saw a cat drop with
an anguished squall from somewhere overhead, land
spraddle-legged facing her, and make a wild lunge at
her, teeth gleaming in the dimness and eyes incandesced
with madness. She screamed and fell backwards and the
cat with a long despairing wail flowed over her and was
gone.

In Tipton's field four crows sat in a black locust,
ranged upon the barren limbs with heads low between
their wingblades, surveying the silvergray desolation, the
silent rain in the country. They watched the cat come

across the field at a slow lope, an erratic dancing progress where she veered and leapt, keeping to the spotty
dry ground. Their calls in the afternoon stillness had
a somber loneliness about them, the mournful quality
of freight whistles. They came from the roost and defiled low over her head, dipping and swooping. The cat
spun low on her haunches, batted at them. So did they
harry her out of the field, her pausing at each attack to
make a stand and grapple at the wind of their passage,
hard-pressed to preserve dignity, the birds flaring, wheeling, setting to again in high crude humor. They left her
at the bank of the creek to return, settle with treading
wings among the locust branches. She marked them
down, her yellow eyes narrowed in contempt, turned
downstream and followed the swollen creek to the
bridge. Here she crossed and continued, taking the high
wooded ground on the south bank, pausing here and
there with random inquisitiveness at holes and hollow
logs to smell, shake herself or lick the water from her
chest, until a strong odor of mink musk brought her
to the creek proper again.

The mink was dead, swaying in the shore currents
among the swamped and flaring grass. She crept to it on
cocked legs, leapt to a mud hummock and swatted it
with a long reach downward. She stood up and watched
it. It bobbed lifelessly. The chain was hung on a stob
somewhere out in the water and when she hooked her
claws into the mink to pull it toward her it did not
come. Finally she ventured one foot into the water and
bit into the neck of the animal. The grit impregnated
in its fur set her teeth on edge and she attacked it sav-
agely, then stopped suddenly as if her attention had
wandered or returned to something of importance which
she had forgotten. She left the mink and set a course
across the fields toward the pike road.

The rain had plastered down her fur and she looked very thin and forlorn. She gathered burdock and the curling purple leaves of rabbit weed as she went, a dead stalk of blackberry briar clung to her hind leg. Just short of the road she stopped, shivered her loose skin, ears flat against her head. She squalled once, hugging the ground with her belly, eyes turned upward at the colorless sky, the endless pelting rain.

On the afternoon of the third day the rain slacked and through the high pall of faint gray, blades of light swung like far beacons, cutting slowly the wisped cloud edges, lace-tatter or swirl of sea mist. Dark fell early, and later as he lay quilted and awake in his black loft the rainless silence of the roof seemed to measure time, something lying in wait. He had already decided to go to the creek in the morning. The water might even have fallen some.

So it was the morning of the fourth day before he went to his traps again, passing the pond and skirting the lower end where it flared out into the field with the weeds standing in the water like rice, then down along the limestone ledges, past the hail-shattered floats of water lilies, shoals of new green leaves, on across the field and out to the road.

Before he came to the bridge he left the road, turned down a steep bank and crossed a fence, following a mud path until he came out on the creek bank. It had not fallen any. Troughs of clayey water rocked through the shallow field on the far side, seething in the matted honeysuckle, the tops of milkweeds and willow shoots quivering in the pull of it. The creek itself was a roily misshapen flume more like solid earth in motion than any liquid, cutting past him, each dip and riffle, eddy, glide, uncurling rope coil fixed and changeless and only the slight oily tremor of the water and the rush of noise testifying to motion at all. Unless a limb or stick came down, or here: a fluted belt of water curling upward in a long scoop like a snarled lip broken suddenly by a tree branch lashing out of the perfect opacity of it, rapid and deft as a snake striking, subsiding again and invisible with no ring or ripple to trace it by. He sat down for a few minutes and watched it all. A kingfisher came up the creek, tacking back and forth, saw the boy and flared, veered away over the watery fields trailing in the morning quiet his high staccato call.

He got up and started along the path over the shelf of woods between the creek and the mountain, by hickories feathered in mist, by cottonwoods still coldly skeletal for all the new green of the spring. He began to climb, his approach forewarned by the patter of nut hulls, a dipping branch, scrabble of small feet on bark. He crossed the spine of the ridge and started down, seeing the horseshoe bend of the creek below him distended with blisters of brown water spread out into the fields, down the slope to the creek again—a shortcut he took, who measured only horizontal travel.

He couldn't find it. The creek was none that he had ever seen before, and when he turned his back to it at what looked like a place he knew he was surprised to see a draw, a fence-corner, a stand of locust oddly mis-located. He passed the place and came back. He had been too far down. He hurried along upstream for another fifty yards and then stopped short. The rock where his trap had been was submerged, but a dome of water rose over it and now he saw the wire reaching up to the sapling on the opposite bank. Just above here the creek narrowed—it was the place where he usually crossed on a long and mossy pier of stone, that too lost now beneath the floodwaters. In the narrows the current leaped in a slick chute, plummeted into the pool below, churning a chocolate-dark foam and spreading again, a hissing sheet of flecks and bubbles, small twigs, bark and debris. A naked and swollen young bird turned up its round white belly briefly, rolled and folded into the thick brown liquid like a slowly closing eye. And below the rock something roiled darkly to the surface, sank again, as if struggling with some unseen assailant. He watched. A moment later it flared again and he could make it out better, the hair floating undulant as black grass wracked in the eddies. He looked along the bank until he found a stick, came back and leaned on tiptoes out over the water, poking. He found the ledge of rock, tested along it with his stick and then stepped out, panicky for a moment as his foot sank. Then he was straddle-legged with one foot on the bank and the other in the creek, the water boiling between his legs, ribboning high on his calf. He got the other foot down and turned, carefully, facing upstream, standing with the thin brown wings of water flying over his shins with a slicing sound, standing so in an illusion of fantastic motion. He worked his way crabwise to within a yard of the other bank, to the channel where the rocks terminated, launched out wildly across the remaining stretch of water. He went in nearly to his waist, his feet chopping rapidly at the slick and steep-pitched mud, flailing mightily with his stick before he could get a proper foothold. Then he was across, pulling himself up the bank by what roots or weeds would hold his weight, cold and mud-slavered.

He hobbled down to where the sapling was and slid down the bank to it, catching himself with one foot against the slender trunk, took hold of the wire and undid it, the wire humming electrically in his hand, took a good grip on it and climbed the bank again pulling

it after him. When he got to the top and turned around
he could see his catch floating in the grass and even before he pulled it up to him he could see the white places
on it like hanging leeches. Then he had it in his hand,
feeling the fur gritty with mud, the cusped bone-end
jutting from the foreleg wrecked between the jaws of
the trap, the white bib smeared with clay and the fine
yellow teeth bared in a fierce grin. And turning it slowly
in his hand, studying dumbly the clean ugly slits, white
and livid. Wounds, but like naked eyelids or dead
mouths gaping.

He took it from the trap and put it in his pocket,
wound the wire around the trap and put that in the
other pocket. The sun was well up, but already the
promised light was drowned in a sweep of wet clouds
rolling and building darkly to the southeast. He did
not recross the creek but headed out into the field. Before he reached the woods the first drops of rain had
already spattered his shoulder. When he got to the road
it was black and slick with water and he hunched his
shoulders forward against the mounting downpour, shivering a little. Sheets of spray gusted over the smoking
road and over the swamped land—the houses standing
bleak and gray—a final desolation seemed to come, as
if on the tail of the earth's last winter a well of water
were rising slowly up through the very universe itself.

It had been raining for six days steady when Marion
Sylder finally left the house. He came down the drive
sideways, slewing sheets of mud from under the cavort-
ing wheels, got straightened out on the road and drove
to the forks. A small pond had formed in front of the
store and customers were obliged to tread a plankwalk
to get to the porch. The rain had settled into a patient drizzle and the people of Red Branch sat around

their stoves, looked out from time to time at the gray wet country and shook their heads. Sylder backed his car up to the gas pump and got out, sloshing the mud from his boots in the puddle, waded to the porch and went in. There was a mesh of welding rod over the front windows now and he smiled a little at that.

Mr Eller looked up from his chair by the meat block. Well, he said, ain't seen you for a while. Bring some money with ye?

Sylder ignored that. Gas, he said. Where's the keys?

Mr Eller sighed and rose from his chair, went to the cash register, rang open the drawer, handed the keys across the counter.

Hope you don't keer to wade, he said.

Sylder took the keys and went out to the pump. He unlocked it and began cranking the lever, pumping gas up into the glass bowl at the top of the rusty orange tank. When he had it full he unscrewed the cap from the fender, let in the hose and depressed the lever. The gas in the bowl surged and bubbled, sluiced into the tank of the car. After the bowl emptied it remained beaded on the inside, a greasy look to it. Sylder didn't notice. He re-hung the hose and locked the pump, waded back to the porch and inside to give the keys to Mr Eller. A loosed box of kittens came tottering aimlessly over the floor, rocking on their stub legs and mewling. Their eyes were closed and festered with mucus as if they might have been struck simultaneously with some biblical blight.

Them's the nastiest-lookin cats I ever did see, Sylder said.

That's what Mrs Fenner said, droned the storekeeper. Young Pulliam told her she ought to see the ones back in the back propped up with sticks. He picked the keys up off the counter and rang them back in the cash drawer again.

Put it on the bill, Sylder said.

Seems like they ought to be a handsign for that, Mr Eller said. Like for Howdy or we'll see ye. Save a lot of talk in here.

If I had your money I'd retire for life.

It'd pay about the same.

Sure it would, Sylder said.

Seems to me like, Mr Eller began . . .

Never mind, Sylder said. I got to get on. Poor folks don't have time to stand around jawin all day.

He waved and went out, stopped at the door a minute and looked back. Say, he called.

What's that?

A Christian'd of drownded em.

What's that? Mr Eller asked again.

Leaning in the door and grinning Sylder pointed at the kittens bobbing over the floor like blown lint.

Mr Eller shooed his hand at him and he left.

The storekeeper drummed his nails on the marble ledge of the cash register for a minute. Then he turned and went back to his chair. He had been resting for only a short time when the clock among the canned goods began a laborious unwinding sound as if about to expire violently in a jangle of wheels and leaping springs, stopped, tolled off four doomlike gongs evocative of some oriental call to temple, then hushed altogether.

Mr Eller stirred from his chair, went to the clock and wound it with a key hanging down from a string. It made a loud ratcheting noise. Then he seized it from the shelf and slammed it back. It set up once more a low wooden ticking.

One of the cats had wandered behind the meat block and on his return to the chair he stepped over it carefully. It went by in a drunken reel, caromed off the meat case, continued. Lost, they wandered about the floor, passing and repassing each other, unseeing. One staggered past a coffecan set next the stove, slipped, fell in the puddle of tobacco spittle surrounding it. He struggled to his feet again, back and side brown-slimed and sticky, tottered across to the wall where he stood with blind and suppurant eyes and offered up to the world his thin wails.

Mr Eller dozed and his head rocked in small increments down his shoulder, onto his chest. After a while a little girl in a thin and dirty dress came through the door behind the counter and gathered up all the kittens, now wailing louder and in broken chorus, carried them out again, talking to them in low remonstrances.

Mr Eller dozed, the clock ticked. The flypaper revolved in slow spirals. The wind had come up again and the rainwater blown from the trees pattered across the tin roof of the store, muffled and distant-sounding through the wallboard ceiling.

Sylder closed the gate behind him and started up the orchard road. It was guttered and channeled and sluices of water still seeped along the myriad mud deltas that filled the flats between the inclines. The car slewed giddily on the turns, bogged finally to a frantic stop skittering quarterwise like a nervous horse and the rear wheels unwinding thick ropes of mud that broke and shot precipitately across the low hem of brush and on into the woods where they slapped up against the trees with a sound oddly hollow. Sylder cut the motor and stepped out into the bright mud. It was a quarter mile to the turnaround and he started straightaway, his leather boots sucking.

There were apples on the trees the size of a thumb-nail and green with a lucent and fiery green, deathly green as the bellies of bottleflies. He plucked one down in passing and bit into it . . . venomously bitter, drew his mouth like a persimmon. If green apples made you sick, Sylder reflected, he would have been dead long ago. Most people he knew could eat them. Didn't take poison ivy either. The boy John Wesley, he was bad about poison ivy. Bad blood.

It took him until dark to get done, joggling the cases two at a time back down the road, nine trips in all. When he had stacked the last two cases in the turtle he locked it and opening the door of the car sat down and took off his boots, shapeless with mud, and stood them on the floor just behind the front seat.

He got the car rocked loose and then had to back down for almost half a mile before he could find a place that looked wide and solid enough to turn around in. By the time he got out on the pike a wind had come up and small spits of rain were breaking on the glass. He propped his left sock foot on the handbrake and drove leisurely down the mountain.

The lights of the city hovered in a nimbus and again stood fractured in the black river, isinglass image, tangled broken shapes: the shapeless splash of lights along the bridgewalk following the elliptic and receding rows of pole lamps across to meet them. The rhythmic arc of the wipers on the glass lulled him and he coasted out onto the bridge, into the city shrouded in rain and silence, the cars passing him slowly, their headlamps wan, watery lights in sorrowful progression.

Sylder's motor spat and jerked, caught again for a handful of revolutions, died with a spastic sucking noise. He let in the clutch and coasted for a minute, engaged it again. The motor bucked and the car shuddered violently and came to a stop.

He sat at the wheel of the motionless car for a minute

or two before he tried the starter. It cranked cheerfully, caught and sputtered once or twice without ever running. He flipped the switch off, reached a flashlight from the glove compartment, took a deep breath and surged wildly out into the rain. Waist-deep in the engine compartment with the upturned hood sheltering him like the maw of some benevolent monster he checked the wiring, the throttle linkages. Then he removed the floatbowl from the fuel pump, held the flashlight up to the glass and looked at it. The liquid in it was a pale yellow. He poured it out and replaced the bowl, dropped the hood and got back in the car. He had to crank the engine for some time before the bowl filled again and then the motor caught and he engaged the gears. He drove along cautiously, listening. The streetlamps passed bleary whorls along the window; there was no more traffic. Before he got to the end of the bridge the motor rattled and died again.

The old man awoke to darkness and water running, trickling and coursing beneath the leaves, and the rain very soft and very steady. The hound was lying with its head on crossed forepaws watching him. He reached out one hand and touched it and the dog rose clumsily and sniffed at his hand.

The wind had died and the night woods in their faintly breathing quietude held no sound but the kind rainfall, track of waterbeads on a branch—their measured fall in a leaf-pool. With grass in his mouth the old man sat up and peered about him, heard the rain mendicant-voiced, soft chanting in that dark gramarye that summons the earth to bridehood.

They came three times for the old man. At first it was just the Sheriff and Gifford. They were one foot up the porch steps when he swung the door open and threw down on them and they could see the mule ears of the old shotgun laid back viciously along the locks. They turned and went back down the yard, not saying anything or even looking back, and the old man closed the door behind them.

The second time they pulled up in the curve of the road with three deputies and a county officer. The old man watched them from his window darting and skulking among the bushes, slipping from tree to tree like boys playing Indians. After a while when everyone was set the Sheriff called from his place under the bank of the road.

Come out with your hands up, Ownby. We got you surrounded.

The old man never even turned his head. He was in the kitchen with the shotgun propped over the back of the chair and he was watching one of the deputies hunkered up under a lilac bush in the west corner of the lot. The old man kept watching him and then the Sheriff called out again for him to surrender and somebody shot out a window-glass in the front room so he didn't wait any more but pulled the stock in against his cheek and cut down on the deputy. The man came up out of the bushes like a rabbit and hopped away toward the road with a curious loping gait, holding the side of his leg. He'd expected the man to yell and he didn't, but then the old man remembered that he hadn't yelled either.

The kitchen glass exploded in on him then and he got behind the stove. There was a cannonade of shots from the woods and he sat there on the floor listening to it and to the spat spat of the bullets passing through the house. Little blooms of yellow wood kept popping out on the planks and almost simultaneously would be the sound of the bullet in the boards on the other side of the room. They did not whine as they passed through. The old man sat very still on the floor. One shot struck the stove behind him and leaped off with an angry spang, taking the glass out of the table lamp. It was like being in a room full of invisible and malevolent spirits.

He had the shotgun across his knees, broken, still holding the empty shell in his hand. The firing died in a few minutes and he crawled along the cupboard and got his shells off the table and came back and reloaded the empty chamber. Then he rolled a cigarette. He could hear them calling to one another. Someone wanted to know if anyone was hurt. Then the Sheriff told them to hold up a minute, that the old bastard hadn't shot since the first time, and hollered loud, as if a person couldn't hear him anyway, wanting to know if Ownby was ready to come out now.

The old man lit his cigarette and took a deep pull. Outside all was silence.

Ownby, the Sheriff called, come out if you're able.

There was more silence and finally he heard some voices and after that they fired a few more rounds. The stick propping up the glassless window leaped out on the floor and the window dropped shut. He could hear the bits of lead hopping about in the front room, chopping up the furniture and scuttling off through the walls and rafters like vermin.

They stopped and the Sheriff was talking again. Spread out, he was saying. Keep under cover as much as you can and remember, everybody goes together.

That didn't make much sense to the old man. He pulled twice more on his cigarette and put it out and crawled under the stove. Through a split board he could see them coming, looking squat above the grass from his low position. Two deputies were moving down from the south end with drawn pistols. One of them was dressed in khakis and looked like an A T U agent. The old man marked their position, wiggled back out from under the stove, riposted to the window and shot them both in quick succession, aiming low. Then he ducked back to his stove, broke the shotgun, extracted the shells and reloaded. No sound from outside. The Sheriff did not call again and after a while when he heard the cars starting he got up and went to the front room to see what they'd shot up.

Toward late afternoon it began to rain again but the old man couldn't wait any longer. Black clouds were moving over the mountain, shading the sharp green of it, and in the coombs horsetails of mist clung or lifted under the wind to lace and curl wistfully, break and trail across the lower slopes. A yellowhammer crossed the yard to his high hole in the jagged top of a lightning-wrecked pine, under-wings dipping bright chrome.

The old man carried out the last of his things and piled them on the sledge, buckled them down with the harness straps he had nailed under the sides. He went back in one more time and looked around. Some last thing he could save. He came out at length with a small hooked rug, shook the dust from it and put it over the top of the sledge. He took up the rope and pulled the sledge to the road and called for Scout. The old dog came from under the porch, peering with blue rheumy eyes at his indistinct world of shapes. The old man called again and the dog started for the road, hobbling stiffly, and they set out together, south along the road, until they were faint and pale shapes in the rain.

So when they came for the old man the third time he was not there. They lobbed teargas bombs through the windows and stormed the ruined house from three sides and the house jerked and quivered visibly under their gunfire. A county officer was wounded in the neck. He sat on the muddy ground with the blood running down his shirtfront, crying, and calling out to the others to Get the dirty son of a bitch. When they came back out of the house no one would look at him. Finally the Sheriff and another man came to where he was and helped him up and took him to the car.

No, the Sheriff said. He got away.

Got away? How could he get away. The man asked two or three times but the Sheriff just shook his head and after that the man didn't ask any more. They left in a spray of mud, four cars of them, with sirens going.

. . .

When the old man came out upon the railroad the rain
had moved off the mountain and in the last light under
the brim of the clouds he could see the long sharp ridges
like lean burning hounds racing down the land to the
land's end westward, hard upon the veering sun. He
turned his back to them, going east on the railbed, the
sledge rocking over the moldering ties. It was still raining and dark was coming on fast. From time to time
he stopped to check his load and cinch the harness
straps up. For two hours he followed the tracks, down
out of the darkening fields through cuts where night
fell on the high banks and fell upon the honeysuckle
drawing shadow forms there, grotesques, shapes of
creatures mythical or extinct and silently noting his
passage. The old man bent east along the tracks, leaning
into the rope, into the rich purple dusk.

By full dark he had left the tracks and turned into
the woods to the south, feeling out the path with his
feet, shivering a little now in his wet clothes. They came
past the old quarry, the tiered and graceless monoliths of
rock alienated up out of the earth and blasted into
ponderous symmetry, leaning, their fluted faces pale and
recumbent among the trees, like old temple ruins. They
went silently along over the trace of the quarry road,
the sledge whispering, the gaunt dog padding, past the
quarryhole with its vaporous green waters and into the
woods again, the limestone white against the dark earth,
a populace of monstrous slugs dormant in a carbon
forest. Groups of trees turned slowly like masted
carousels, blending shadows and parting in darkness and
wonder. The rain stopped falling. They passed, leaving
a trail of foxfire shuffled up out of the wet leaves like
stars plowed in a ship's wake.

Morning found them on the south slope of Chilhowee

Mountain, the dog buckled down on top of the sledge now and the old man pulling them tree by tree up the steep and final rise. From his high place on the slope he could see the first strawcolored light sourceless beyond the earth's curve, the horizon warped in a glaucous haze. An hour later and they had gained the crest of the mountain and stood in a field of broom sedge bright as wheat, treeless but for a broken chestnut the color of stone.

The sun was up by then and the old man rested, leaning against the tree. After a while he fell asleep, the sledge's painter still wrapped in his blistered hand. The dog stretched out in the sun too, wrinkling his ragged hide at the flies. Far below them shades of cloud moved up the valley floor like water flowing, darkened the quilted purlieus, moved on, the brushed land gone green and umber once again. The clouds broke against the mountain, coral-edged and bent to the blue curve of the sky. A butterfly struggled, down through shells of light, down to the gold and seagreen tree tips . . .

The old man came awake late in the afternoon and ate some cold cornbread, sharing it with the hound. He did not eat much and the cornbread was enough. Then he started down the mountain, trucking behind him his sorry chattel, picking a course through the small trees and laurel jungles. Some time after midnight he came out on a road and turned south along it, crossed a wooden bridge, a purling clearwater stream, climbed with the road into the mountains again, the sledge drifting easily behind him and the hound plodding.

The light at the house the old man came to that morning he could see a good while before he got to it. He caught glimpses of it once or twice somewhere on the ridge above him as he was coming through a mountain meadow, a huge pool in the darkness swept with the passing shadows of nightbirds, but he had no way of knowing that the road would take him there. He didn't see the light again until he topped the hill where the house stood and where a section of road was banded out of the night in a tunnel of carlights. Some men were talking and he could hear the sound of the motor running.

He kept on, into the light. The voices stopped. The old man looked up at them, two men leaning against the side of the automobile, another seated inside. He didn't stop. They faded behind the glare of the headlights, re-appeared filmily, not moving, watching him. With the lights out of his eyes the old man stopped and nodded to them. Howdy, he said.

You ain't lost, are ye?

Don't reckon, he said.

One of them said something. The car eased down the drive, the two men walking alongside. The man in the car leaned out toward him. This road don't go thew, he said. It jest loops and comes on back.

How fer is it to the Harrykin? the old man wanted to know.

The man turned out the lights. The other two had come up now and said Howdy, each in turn. Scout clambered up onto the sledge and eyed them balefully.

Wants to know how fer is it to the Harrykin, the driver said.

What fer?

The other one stepped forward and eyed the old man with bland curiosity, the sledge heaped with his worth-less paraphernalia and topped by the prone and wasted hound. You cain't hardly get there from here, he said. You ort to of come thew Sunshine, crost the river there . . . it ain't easy to get to from nowhere but that-there'd of been a nigher cut. What you aim to do in there, cut timber?

No, said the old man. Jest fixin to put up some kind of a piece of a house and kindly settle there.

In the Harrykin?

Yessir.

Where-all you from? the man in the car wanted to know.

From t'wards Knoxville.

The man in the car was silent for a minute. Then he said, I'm goin in to Sevierville here in jest a minute. I can carry you that fer if you don't keer to ride in a old beat-up car such as it is.

Much obliged, the old man said, but I reckon I'll jest get on.

Well, the man said. He turned to the other two. I got to get, myself, he said. We'll see yins.

They nodded. You come back. The car eased away, the lights coming on again, rattled out of sight down the road. The old man had the sledge rope in hand and was saying a goodbye to the men.

You best come on in and have some breakfast with us, one of them said.

Much obliged, the old man said, but I reckon I'll jest be gettin on.

Might as well eat some with us, the other said. We jest fixin to.

Well, the old man said. If you-all don't care.

The house the old man entered that morning was no shotgun shack but a mountain cabin of squared logs rent deeply with weather-checks and chinked with clay. It was long and saddle-bowed, divided into two rooms of equal size, and at the far end of one a fireplace of river rock, rocks tumbled smooth as eggs, more ancient than the river itself. From a door to the right a woman's face peered at them furtively as they sat, the taller of the men motioning the old man to a chair cut from a buttertub and padded in hair-worn cowhide. They produced tobacco and papers and passed them to him not ceremoniously but with that deprecatory gesture of humility which country people confer in a look, a lift of the hand. The old man began to feel right homey.

Say you from t'wards Knoxville? the tall man said.

Yessir, he answered, taping down the paper of his cigarette.

I got a sister lives over thataway. Meanest kids I ever seen. Married a boy from Mead's Quarry—you know where that's at?

Shore, the old man said. I come from Red Mountain my ownself. We used to whup Mead's Quarry boys of a Sunday afternoon jest to keep a hand in.

The man grinned. That's what he told me about you-all, he said.

Then the old man grinned.

The other one broke in. Don't reckon you'd keer fer a little drink this early of a mornin?

Not lessen you fellers is fixin to have one.

He disappeared through the door into the lean-to and presently came back with a mason jar. Less see if this here is the one I wanted, he said, tilting it, watching the slow-rising chain of beads. He took off the cap and stretched a draught down his lean corded neck, swallowed deep, cocked his head in a listening attitude, then passed the jar to the old man. That's the one, he said. It's right good drinkin whiskey.

The old man accepted the jar and took a good drink. His legs were beginning to feel a little heavy and he lifted first one and then the other, slightly, testing their weight. He raised the jar again, drank and handed it back to the man. Now that's a right nice little whiskey, he said.

The two men relayed the jar between them and then it was capped and set on the floor. The shorter man was looking out the tiny window. Gettin daylight, he said.

He turned to the old man. You get a right early start, don't ye?

The old man recrossed his legs, taking a look out himself.

Well, he said, kindly early, yes.

You come up from Walland this mornin I reckon?

No, the old man said, Knoxville.

I mean on foot, comin up the mountain . . .

I come straight acrost, the old man said.

They looked at each other. The tall one hesitated a moment, then he said: You say you goin to the Harry-kin?

Aim to, the old man said.

Cain't say as it seems like much of a place to jest go to, he said. I've knowed one or two people at different times what was there and would of give some to of been away from it though. Daddy I remember would leave dogs treed there of a night rather'n go in after em. He said they was places you could walk fer half a mile thout ever settin foot to the ground—jest over laurel hells and down timber, and a rattlesnake to the log . . . I never been there myself.

You aimin to stay there long? the other one asked.

But before the old man could answer that, the woman thrust her face through the door and announced break-fast. Both men rose instantly and started for the kitchen, then paused, remembering the old man still seated with the slow words forming on his lips. They had the uneasy look of boys sneaking to table with dirty hands. The old man stood and walked between them, the shorter one smiling a sort of half-smile and saying: I reckon we jest about forgot how to act, ain't we?

Pshaw, said the old man.

At the foot of the mountain the old man found himself in a broad glade grown thick with rushes, a small stream looping placidly over shallow sands stippled with dace shadows, the six-pointed stars of skating waterspiders drifting like bright frail medusas. He squatted and dipped a palmful of water to his lips, watched the dace drift and shimmer. Scout waded past him, elbow-deep into the stream, lapped at it noisily. Strings of red dirt receded from his balding hocks, marbling in the water like blood. The dace skittered into the channel and a watersnake uncurled from a rock at the far bank and glided down the slight current, no more demonstrative of effort or motion than a flute note.

The old man drank and then leaned back against the sledge. The glade hummed softly. A woodhen called from the timber on the mountain and to that sound of all summer days of seclusion and peace the old man slept.

Yessir, the storekeeper said. Yessir, now I believe I do recollect who tis. You some kin of hisn?

No, the man said. No kin. Jest somethin I got to see him about.

He was dressed in clean gray chinos and had a neat felt hat tipped back on his head. Huffaker stole a look out the window to where his car was parked at the side of the porch, a plain black Ford, a late model.

The man saw him look, watched the glint of suspicion narrow the storekeeper's eyes.

Well, Huffaker said, I couldn't tell you offhand where-all you might find him at. He lives up yander somewheres—a random gesture at the brooding hills that cupped in the valley.

He trade here? the man wanted to know.

Well, I couldn't rightly say he did, nosir. Not regular at all. I ain't seen him in here but once or twicet and that's back several week ago. He's a right funny old feller, don't have no money at all I don't reckon.

What'd he buy then?

Well, he got him some backer and a sack of cornmeal. Little sidemeat last time he's in.

He got credit?

Well, no. I don't give out a whole lot of credit. He brings in sang. Ginseng roots. Had some goldenseal too but it ain't worth a whole lot. I give trade on that.

Roots?

Yessir, Huffaker said. I send em off to St. Louis. Same place as I send hides.

The man looked puzzled but he didn't ask any more about that.

You from around here? the storekeeper asked.

From over t'wards Maryville.

Oh, Huffaker said. I got kin over there myself.

He still got that dog?

Who's that?

The old feller . . . the one . . .

Oh. Yessir, did have one with him. A old redbone looked like he'd been drug half to death or warshed in lye one. Didn't have no hair hardly at all. Right pitiful-lookin, like.

Well, the man said, you say you don't know where-all he lives at?

Nosir, I shore don't.

Well, much obliged.

Yessir. You come back.

He did. He came every day for seven days.

He was there next morning early among the un-churched Sunday idlers, hovering on the edge of the circle they formed about the fireless stove, their conviviality so broken by his presence that they took on the look of refugees grimly awaiting bulletins of some current disaster, the news of flood or fire or plague. From time to time he got a drink from the box and stood sipping it, hand on hip, gazing up at the phantasmagoria of merchandise hung about the ceiling beams. Or peered solemnly out the window, beyond the river and the narrow bridge to where a broad green hollow rose and rose into the mountains.

Monday when Huffaker came down he was not there yet but half an hour later when he went out to unlock the gas pump the car was parked on the gravel ramp approaching the store and the man was perched upon the fender in the same creased and tireless clothes sipping coffee from a paper cup. The sun was coming up behind him and to the west fog was breaking, lifting off the slopes to leave the laurel balds burning with the fierce green light of morning. The man was watching again, the peaks across the river, as if with those slategray eyes he might mark out an old man and a hound somewhere on the face of a mountain not less than four miles distant.

When Huffaker let the door to, the man turned. He lifted a palm in greeting and the man nodded. He went down to the pump and undid the lock.

Looks like another purty day, don't it? he called.

Does at that, the man said. He drained the coffee and pitched the cup away, got down from the fender and took a few steps up and down the gravel, stretching himself. Huffaker returned to the store.

Around eleven o'clock he came in, nodding once again to the proprietor. He bought a box of soda crackers and some cheese, looked for a long time at the cake rack and finally took a moonpie. He laid his lunch on the counter and Huffaker began to total it laboriously on a scratch pad, adding the figures aloud.

And a quart of sweet milk, the man said.

He put that down, then went to the cooler and brought back the milk in a quart mason jar. The man looked at it, turned it around on the counter.

That's Mrs Walker's milk, he reassured the man. It's good as ever you drunk, garntee ye.

The man nodded and pulled a clip of bills from his pocket.

Forty-five cents, Huffaker said.

He paid it and went out on the porch where he sat back against a post and ate his lunch. After he had finished he squatted there a long time smoking cigarettes. Then he brought the jar back inside and set it on the counter. Huffaker took it out again and washed it under the tap at the side of the building. Some customers were coming up toward the store and he waved at them and went in.

Later on in the afternoon the man came in again and drank a Coca-Cola. Before he went back out to his car he asked Huffaker what time it was that the old man usually came in.

The old feller?

The one I was astin you about.

Oh. Well, times he come in it was genly of a mornin. But then he don't come regular enough for me to say when a feller be most likely to expect him.

Light gained on the high peaks and in the dawn quiet first birdcalls fell like water on stone. In the wood mists like old gray spirits paled and scattered, by moss coverlets the dark earth stirred and nightfurled wildflowers unbent their withered fronds all down the path where came the derelict hound shambling along in an aureole of its own incredibility, the old man picking his steps over the schist and quartz chines, his hex-cane bobbing lightly on his shoulder, carrying a limp and greasy paper bag of the curious twisted roots with which he bartered. They crossed a broad rock slide emblazoned with sun and threaded by a trickle of water in a rock channel rusted copper-dark. The old man paused to scale a slate down into the gorge where trees lay tossed and broken. The dog peered down, looked at the old man inquisitively, studied the empty gorge again and then moved on, the old man taking up his cane and following. The sole of his brogan was all but off now and he limped, favoring the odd shoe to save the binder twine with which he had tied it together.

Crossing the slide they entered the deep woods once more, the sun winnowed in tall fans among the spiring trunks, greengold and black vermiculated on the forest floor. With his cane the old man felled regiments of Indian Pipe, poked the green puffballs to see the smoke erupt in a poisonous verdant cloud. The woods were damp with the early morning and now and again he could hear the swish of a limb where a squirrel jumped and the beaded patter of water-drops in the leaves. Twice they flushed mountain pheasants, Scout sidestepping nervously as they roared up out of the laurel.

The path the old man took was a fire trail that had been built by the C C C. From the glade in which he now made his home he had to climb nearly a thousand feet to reach it, but once on the trail the walking was easy and excepting the injured shoe he would have swung along at a good pace. It was six miles to the river where he crossed and came to the highway and the same ubiquitous crossroads store with the drunken porch, the huge and rock-battered Nehi signs, the weather-curled laths, the paintless stonecolored wood—but the old man had taken an early start. Through a gap in the trees he could see the valley far below him where the river ran, a cauldron in the mountain's shadow where

smoke and spume seethed like the old disturbance of the
earth erupting once again, black mist languid in the
cuts and trenches as flowing lava and the palisades of
rock rising in the high-shored rim beyond the valley—and
beyond the valley, circling the distant hoary cupolas
now standing into morning, the sun, reaching to the
slope where the old man rested, speared mist motes
emblematic as snowflakes and broke them down in
spangled and regimental disorder, reached the trees and
banded them in light, struck weftwork in the slow uncurling ferns—the sun in its long lightfall recoined again
in leafwater.

Brogan and cane and cracked pad clatter and slide
on the shelly rocks and stop where a snake lies curled
belly-up to the silent fold and dip of a petal-burst of
butterflies fanning his flat and deadwhite underside.
Scout smells cautiously at the snake, the butterflies in
slow riot over his head, flowery benediction of their
veined and harlequin wings. With his cane the old man
turns the snake, remarking the dusty carpet pattern of
its dull skin, the black clot of blood where the rattles
have been cut away.

They go on—steps soft now in the rank humus earth,
or where carapaced with lichens the texture of old
green velvet, or wet and spongy earth tenoned with
roots, the lecherous ganglia of things growing—coming
down, pursuing the shadowline into the smoking river
valley.

Huffaker would have said it was by chance that he
happened to be looking out the window toward the
river the morning the old man came, but he had been
watching not much less keenly than the patient and
taciturn visitor in the pressed gray chinos. So he had
been looking for him for a week and there he was on

the bridge with the crudely carved staff, carrying a small paper bag in his hand, a moldy crokersack tied at his waist in front like an immense and disreputable sporran, and the wreckage of dog padding at his heels, raising its bitten muzzle into the air from time to time in a sort of hopeless and indomitable affirmation—proceeding on the weathered sun-washed bridge, jaunty and yet sad, like maimed soldiers returning. Huffaker stepped to the door and the man, coming from the car with slow bootcrunch in the gravel, shot him a quick look. Huffaker walked to the broken thermometer on the tin snuff sign at the corner of the store and pretended to check it, gazed at the mounting sun and sniffed at the air, went back in. The old man was on the road, coming toward the store. The man was standing on the porch with one arm hooked loosely about a post, his forefinger in his watchpocket, chewing a straw slowly and watching his approach with the composed disinterest of a professional assassin.

The old man climbed onto the porch and the man said:

Arthur Ownby.

Arthur Ownby's eyes swam slowly across, fixed upon him.

Yessir, he said.

Get in that car over yonder. Let's go.

The old man had stopped. He was looking at the man, and then he was looking past him, eyes milk-blue and serene, studying the dipping passage of a dove, and beyond, across the canted fields of grass to the green mountain, and to the thin blue peaks rising into the distant sky with no crestline of shape or color to stop them, ascending forever.

You hear?

The old man turned. You don't keer if I trade first, do ye? he said.

You're under arrest. You don't need to trade nothin.

The old man turned back toward the store with an empty gesture, holding the sack of ginseng in his hand.

Let's go, the man said again.

So he started down off the porch with a forlorn air and the dog, bland, patient, turning behind him with myopic and near-senseless habituation until, led by the man in the starched and rattling clothes, they reached the car. The man swung the door open and the old man fumbled and climbed his way onto the front seat. As the door was closing it began to occur to him that the dog was still out and apparently not under arrest as he was and he flailed violently at the glass and upholstery swinging toward him and checked it. The man looked at him questioningly.

He didn't know how to begin so he sat there for part of a minute with his jaw going up and down as if he couldn't breathe and the man said, Well, what now?

The old man nodded his head to where in the gravel the ancient hound stood gazing up at the machine before him with a baffled look. What about him? the old man said.

What about him?

Well, you don't keer if he rides, do ye?

You're resistin arrest, Ownby, now get on in there. He slammed the door but the old man's cane was hanging over the runningboard and in mutual defeat the door rocked open again as the cane cracked. The old man pulled it in the car with him and studied the lower part of it, stooping to examine the whiskers of wood standing up from the break. The man slapped the door again and it bounded in snugly upon the old man and all but took his breath.

The man was coming around the car and he hadn't much more time so he pulled at the handles and got the right one and opened the door again and leaned out and called to the dog, standing off a few feet now and rocking back and forth in consternation.

Hya, Scout, the old man whispered. Come on, get in here.

Hey! the man called. What in the hell you think you're up to now?

The dog started, backed away. The man paused midway in his passage from door to door, returned. The old man straightened up and watched him come.

I told you oncet, the man said, coming up fast and reaching for the door. The old man recoiled, waiting for it to buffet shut against him, but instead it wrenched outward and the man's face jutted in and stared at him in a mask of classic anger. You tryin to excape? he wanted to know.

Nosir, the old man said. I was jest gettin my dog in . . .

Jest what! Dog? He turned and seemed to see the hound for the first time. They said you's crazy. Dog's ass, you cain't take no dog . . .

He cain't shift for hisself, the old man said. He's too old.

I ain't no dog catcher and this ain't no kennel, the man said. And I wadn't sent here to haul no broken-down sooner around. Now get in the goddamned car and stay put. He said it very slowly and evenly and the old man really began to worry. But he suffered the door closed to once more and didn't mention it again until the man came around and got in beside him.

It wouldn't hurt nothin for him to ride, he said. I cain't hardly leave him jest a-standin there.

Old-timer, the man said, I advise you jest to set still

and hush up cause you in plenty of trouble already. He cranked the engine and slid the gearshift upward and the old man felt himself rocketed backward violently with a welter of dust boiling and receding before him and the dog standing there in the drive with the gravel dancing about him and then they cut one long rattling curve and were on the road and leaving, and the old man, clutching his cane, holding the dirty little sack between his knees, looked back at the dog still standing there like some atavistic symbol or brute herald of all questions ever pressed upon humanity and beyond understanding, until the dog raised his head to clear the folds above his milky eyes and set out behind them at a staggering trot.

Warn blew little cone-shaped thistles into the fur. No, he said. Ten maybe. See here —he blew again, cotton mink. Takes a first-class mink to bring twenty dollars.

The boy nodded.

Fur's slippin, Warn said. Whew, here. He handed the mink back. Sure raised hell with it, didn't he?

The boy took it and pitched it underhand back up onto the shelf in the woodshed. He clambered down the pile of logs and they went out together. Some wasps were hovering beneath the eaves with their long legs dangling. Small buds already on the locust trees. It would soon be nothing but bones, but he wouldn't come to see, like when he dug up the flying squirrel he had buried in a jar and found only bones with bits of fur rolling around inside the glass like bed-lint.

They took the road to Warn's house, the fields still
too wet to cross, passed the store.

You got any money? Warn asked him.

No, he said. I ain't sold my hides yet. You?

Naw. I sold my hides but I ain't got nothin left. I
blow it in quick as I get it. Got me some new shoes for
school is about all.

What you get for em?

For the hides? I don't know; two dollars on most of
em. That big rat got three I think it was and some of
em the man said was kits and they didn't bring but a
dollar. I had eighteen hides and I think it come to thirty-
one dollars.

I should get six dollars, the boy said. I owe out two.

Who you owe?

Sylder. He loant me the money for traps when Gifford got mine. I'd done signed a paper to buy em
uptown—on account of the man let me have those first
ones I bought at lot price.

You keep messin with Sylder and signing papers uptown and sech shit as that and you goin to get your ass
slung in the jail after all. Lucky Gifford didn't do it.

Gifford's chickenshit.

Oh, Warn said. I didn't know you had him scared
of you.

Warn had his own room in the back of the house.
The boy sat on the bed while he went through the top
drawer of an old-fashioned sewing cabinet. He dredged
up: a hawkbill knife, three arrowheads, a collection of
rifle-balls velvety gray with oxidation, a scalpel, rocks,
some dynamite caps, miscellaneous pieces of fishing
tackle, dried ginseng, a roll of copper wire . . . Rifling
through the mass he at length came up with a thin and
dog-eared pamphlet, its cover decorated with an archaic
and ill-proportioned ink sketch of a trapped lynx. Across

the top in black script was the title TRAPPING THE FUR
BEARERS OF NORTH AMERICA. Warn handled the treasure
reverently. I got this from Uncle Ather, he said. It'll
have something in it.

Under a section entitled *Lynx and Bobcat Sets* they
found a plan of such devious cunning as appealed to their
minds. The bait was to be suspended from a limb and
overhanging a stump. The trap would be set on top
of the stump, so that when the victim stood—the illus-
tration depicted a great hairy lynx sniffing at the bait
on hind legs—his paw would come to rest on the stump
and so into the trap—also illustrated, in broken-line,
straining beneath a handful of leaves.

Warn nodded in solemn approval. That's the one,
he said. The boy studied the set carefully and then
Warn tucked the book away in the sewing cabinet.

You reckon it really was a bobcat?

I don't know what-all else it could of been, Warn said.
Ain't nothin else around here got sharp claws that I
know of.

I sure could of used that ten dollars, the boy said.

The desk sergeant studied Marion Sylder's angular
frame with a hurt look, as if he were being put upon.
Sylder looked back at him with a suggestion of good
humor. The desk sergeant rebent his head to his papers,
his lips working in patient disgust. He pondered for some
minutes, replaced a folder in the filing drawer of the
desk and reached for a pen. Name, he said, gazing at
the inkstand with weary boredom.

Fred Long.

Marion Paris Sylder. Occupation.

Iron and steel . . .

None. Married?

No.

Married. Address.

Red Mountain Tennessee.

Route Nine, Knoxville. Mm . . . Age.

Twenty.

—eight. Previous convictions.

Silence.

Previous convictions.

The sergeant looked up at Sylder as if surprised to see him there. Previous convictions, he said again, slowly.

Again a moment or two of silence. Far to the rear of the building a remote clanking sound. The sergeant waited. Then he nodded wearily to the patrolman sitting in a chair by the door. The man rose and sauntered over to the prisoner, something of the laconical about him. Sylder turned to look at him. When he turned back to the man at the desk the patrolman jabbed his nightstick into his ribs.

Ow! Sylder said.

The patrolman looked aggrieved.

Previous convictions, droned the sergeant, stifling a yawn.

You seem to know all about it, Sylder said. Oof!

The patrolman studied his face with an eager look, holding the stick in readiness again.

Previous con—

None, Sylder said.

None.

The sergeant leaned back with closed eyes, a rapt and serene look. The patrolman returned to his post at the door. From the cells to the rear of the building came bits and pieces of a sad voice singing. The sergeant turned papers over. In the outer corridor men were coming in, stamping their feet and rattling their raincoats, cussing the weather. A furnace pipe clattered.

At length the sergeant regarded Sylder again. I reckon that's all for now, he said. You're booked on illegal possession—untaxed. I got somebody comin down wants to see you, have a little talk kindly.

Who's that? Sylder said.

Fella name of Gifford. Ever hear of him?

Jailer!

Sylder's third visitor was the boy, wide-eyed and serious before the smirking usherance of the jailer.

Here's your uncle, the jailer said. Little buddy come a-callin.

The boy stared at the man seated on the steel bunk. The jailer followed his gaze. Well now, he said, he don't seem too peart, does he? Looks kindly like he's been sortin cats. Step on in and say howdy. Cheer the poor feller up some.

The boy stepped in. Sylder's eyes focused onto him, he managed a small grin, a nod. Howdy there, Hogjowls, he said. The door rattled to behind them, the jailer departing, heelclack, keyjangle, echoing down the corridor.

Howdy, said the boy. What happent to you?

Well, I had a little disagreement with these fellers . . . as to whether a man can haul untaxed whiskey over tax-kept roads or whether by not payin the whiskey tax he forfeits the privilege of drivin over the roads the whiskey don't keep up that ain't taxed or if it was would be illegal anyway. I think what they do is deeport you.

No, the boy said, I mean . . . you wreck?

Oh. No . . . I was wrecked all right, but I didn't wreck. He fingered sorely the particolored swellings on his cheek and forehead. Kindly a bang-up job, ain't it?

Mutual acquaintance helped out with the decoratin . . .
the deacon Gifford. With two buddies to hold me.
Wadn't even much spirited about it till I kicked him in
the nuts. Now they got to worry about gettin me
unswole so as I can appear in court. I got some busted
ribs too that they don't know about yet. I'm sort of
holdin em for a ace. Here, set down. He grimaced and
dropped his feet down off the bed to clear a seat.

The boy hadn't said anything else. He lowered himself onto the bunk, still staring at Sylder. Then he said:

That son of a bitch.

Ah, said Sylder.

How'd they . . . you said you never wrecked, how
did they . . .

Catch me? It wadn't hard. I had my choice though, I
could of jumped off the bridge. They live ever oncet
in a while.

What?

Water in the gas. A little too much rain, I reckon.
Too much for old Eller's leaky-assed tank leastways.
There's one bill the son of a bitch'll play hell collectin.
—It quit in the middle of the Henley Street Bridge.

Oh.

Sylder had leaned back against the concrete wall and
was tapping a cigarette from its package. Ain't that a hell
of a note? he said.

I'll get him.

Hmm?

I'm goin to get the son of a bitch.

What! That old fart? Why I'll be dipped in . . .
Then he said Oh.

That's right, the boy said. The deacon.

The smile had fallen from Sylder's face. Wait a
minute, he said. You don't get nobody.

Him, the boy said.

No, Sylder said. He was looking very hard at the boy but the boy knew he was in the right.

Why? he said.

You jest stay away from Jefferson Gifford, that's all. You hear?

You jest think I'll get in trouble, the boy said. That I . . .

Stubborn little bastard, ain't you? Look.

Sylder paused, he seemed to be trying to think of something, a word perhaps. Look, he said, what's between him and me is between him and me. It don't need nobody else. So I thank ye kindly but no thank ye, you don't owe me nothin and I ain't crippled. I'll tend to my own Giffords. All right?

The boy didn't answer, didn't seem to be listening. Sylder lit the cigarette and watched him. He turned and looked once at Sylder and then he seemed to remember something and he reached into the watchpocket of his jeans and took out two folded dollar bills and handed them to him.

What's that? Sylder said.

The two dollars I owe you. That you loant me for traps.

Naw . . . Sylder started. Then he stopped and looked at the boy still holding out the two dirty bills. Okay, he said. He took the money and crammed it into his shirtpocket. Okay, that makes us square.

The boy was silent for a minute. Then he said:

No.

No what?

No it don't make us square. Because maybe I lost the traps on your account but that's okay and I earned em back and paid for em and that's okay . . . but you got beat up on my account and maybe in jail too that . . .

and that's why it ain't square yet, that part of it not square.

Sylder started to reach for the money, thought better of it and sat up, grinding the cigarette out beneath his heel. Then he looked at the boy. Square be damned, he said. I ast you to stay away from Gifford, that's all. Will you?

The boy didn't say anything.

Swear it? Sylder said.

No.

Sylder watched him, the still childish face set with truculent purpose. Look, he said, you're fixin to get me in worse trouble than I already am, you . . .

I won't get no . . .

No, wait a damn minute.

He did. They sat looking at each other, the man's face misshapen as if bee-stung, him leaning forward gaunt and huge and the boy perched delicately on the edge of the metal pallet as if loath to sit too easily where so many had lain in such hard rest.

Look, Sylder said, taking a long breath, you want to talk about square, all right. Me and Gif are square.

The boy looked at him curiously.

Yes, he said. I busted him and he busted me. That's fair, ain't it?

The boy was still silent, calmly incredulous.

No, Sylder went on, I ain't forgettin about jail. You think because he arrested me that thows it off again I reckon? I don't. It's his job. It's what he gets paid for. To arrest people that break the law. And I didn't jest break the law, I made a livin at it. He leaned forward and looked the boy in the face. More money in three hours than a workin man makes in a week. Why is that? Because it's harder work? No, because a man who makes a livin doin somethin that has to get him in jail sooner or later has to be paid for the jail, has to be paid in advance not jest for his time breakin the law but for the time he has to build when he gets caught at it. So I been paid. Gifford's been paid. Nobody owes nobody. If it wadn't for Gifford, the law, I wouldn't of had the job I had blockadin and if it wadn't for me blockadin, Gifford wouldn't of had his job arrestin blockaders. Now who owes who?

His voice was beginning to rise and he had about him a look almost furious. But you, he went on, you want to be some kind of a goddamned hero. Well, I'll tell ye, they ain't no more heroes.

The boy seemed to shrink, his face flushing.

You understand that? Sylder said.

I never claimed I wanted to be no hero, the boy said sullenly.

Nobody never claimed it, Sylder said. Anyway I never done nothin on your account like you said. I don't do nothin I don't want to. You want to do me a favor jest stay away from Gifford. Stay away from me too. You ought not to of come here. You'll get me charged with delinquency to a minor. Go on now.

He leaned back against the wall and stared at the emptiness before him. After a while the boy got up and went to the door and tried it, and Sylder, not looking up or speaking to the boy, called for the jailer. He heard him come and the clank of keys, the cell door grating open. Then quiet. He looked up. The boy was standing in the doorway, half turned, looking at him with a wan smile, puzzled, like one who aspires to disbelief in the face of immutable fact. Sylder lifted one hand in farewell. Then the door clanged to.

He sat up, half rose from the cot, would call him back to say *That's not true what I said. It was a damned lie ever word. He's a rogue and a outlaw hisself and you're welcome to shoot him, burn him down in his bed, any damn thing, because he's a traitor to boot and maybe a man steals from greed or murders in anger but he sells his own neighbors out for money and it's few lie that deep in the pit, that far beyond the pale.*

Softly and with slow grace her leathered footpads fell, hind tracking fore with a precision profoundly feline, a silken movement where her shoulders rolled, haunches swayed. Belly swaying slightly too, lean but pendulous. Head low and divorced of all but linear motion, as if fixed along an unseen rail. A faint musty odor still clung to her, odor of the outhouse where she had slept all day, restless in the heat and languishing among the dusty leaves in the corner, listening to the dry scratch and slither of roaches, the interstitial boring of wood-beetles. Now she came down the patch obscure with parched weeds shedding thin blooms of sifting dust where she brushed them. At dusk-dark from her degenerate habitation, emerging to make her way down the narrow patch as cats go.

She passed through the honeysuckles by a dark tunnel where the earth still held moisture, down the bank to a culvert by which she crossed beneath the road and came into a field and into a dry gully, the cracked and curling clay like a paving of potsherds, and turned up an artery of the wash, grown here with milkweed and burdock. following a faint aura of vole or shrew, until she came to a small burrow in the grasses. She scratched at the matted whorl, caved it in and trod it down, moved on across the field, crickets scuttling, grasshoppers springing from their weed-stems and whirring away. A shadow passed soundlessly overhead, perhaps a flock of late-returning birds.

Near the center of the field was a single walnut tree bedded in a crop of limestone which had so far fended it against axe and plowshare. Among these rocks she nosed, in their small labyrinths undulant as a ferret. Odor of walnuts and ground squirrels. But she found nothing.

When she left the rocks, was clear of the overreaching branches of the tree, there grew about her a shadow in the darkness like pooled ink spreading, a soft-hissing feathered sound which ceased even as she half turned, saw unbelieving the immense span of wings cupped downward, turned again, already squalling when the owl struck her back like a falling rock.

Mr Eller closed the lionheaded door behind him and rattled the latch to see that it was secure. Then he checked the plaited fob on the notecase in his hip pocket, adjusted his straw hat, and started up the road toward the house. At the mailbox he was arrested by the high thin wail of a cat coming apparently from straight overhead. He looked up but there were no trees there. He shook his head and went on, stepping carefully in the gutted drive. The squall sounded once more, this time more distant and to the ridge of pines behind the house. He continued on, to the porch where a yellow bulb held forth its dull steadfast light, to a place of surcease.

A young social worker recently retained by the Knox County Welfare Bureau, having been notified through his office of the detention of one aged and impecunious gentleman at the county jail pending hearing of his case (charges ranging from Destruction of Government Property to Assault with Intent to Kill) proceeded to make such investigation as would determine whether the gentleman had relatives, and if not, to what department or agency he might properly be assigned as ward. The agent, having been admitted into the cell where the elderly gentleman was confined, addressed him:

Mr Ownby?

Yessir.

I represent the Welfare Bureau for the county.

Welfare?

Yes. We . . . you see, we help people.

The old man turned that over in his mind. He didn't seem to be paying much attention to the thin young man standing just inside the door. He scratched his jaw and then he said, Well, I ain't got nothin. I don't reckon I can hep yins any.

The agent made a fleeting effort at comprehension, passed it over. All we need, he said, is some information.

The old man turned and looked at him. You another policeman? he asked.

No, said the agent. I represent the Welfare Bureau for . . . I have been asked to see you—to see if perhaps we can help you in any way.

Well, the old man said, I kindly doubt it. I'm what you might call Brushy bound.

Yes, said the agent. I mean . . . you see, Mr Ownby, there are certain benefits to which you may be entitled. You seem to have been overlooked by our department for some time and we would like to have a record of your case for our, our, records, you see. And so I have some forms here that I need your help in filling out.

Hmm, the old man said.

Do you mind answering a few questions?

Don't reckon, the old man said. Here, set down.

Thank you, said the agent. He lowered himself gingerly onto the cot and began to unstrap his briefcase. His hand disappeared inside and emerged with a sheaf of printed forms intershuffled with carbon paper. Now, he said comfortably, first of all, your age.

Well, I don't rightly know.

Yes. I beg your pardon?

Don't know for sure, that is. There's a part of it I don't remember too good.

Well, could you tell us when you were born?

The old man eyed him curiously. If I knowed that,

he said patiently, I could figure how old I was. And tell us that.

The agent smiled weakly. Yes. Of course. Well, could you estimate your age then? You are over sixty-five?

Considerable.

Well, about how old would you say?

It ain't about, the old man said, it's either. Either eighty-three or eighty-four.

The agent wrote that down on his form, studied it for a moment with satisfaction. Fine, he said. Now, where is your present residence?

If'n I'm eighty-four I'll live to be a hunerd and five providin I get to eighty-five.

Yes. Your . . .

When was you born?

The agent looked up from his forms. Nineteen-thirteen, he said, but we . . .

What date?

June. The thirteenth. Mr Ownby . . .

The old man tilted his eyes upward in reflection. Hmm, he said. That was a Friday. Kindly a bad start. Was your daddy over twenty-eight when you was born?

No, please, Mr Ownby. These questions, you see . . .

The old man hushed and the agent sat watching him for a minute. Now, he said. Your present address?

Well, the old man said, I did live on Forked Creek —Twin Fork Road, but I moved to the mountains. I got me a little place up there.

Where is that?

That's all right where it's at.

But we have to have an address, Mr Ownby.

Well, put down Twin Fork Road then, the old man said.

You live alone?

Jest me and Scout. Or we did.

Scout?

Dog.

The agent continued to write. You have, I believe, no family or relatives.

Yessir.

The agent looked up. Well, he said, we'll need their names then.

I mean yes I don't have none, the old man said wearily.

The agent continued with his questions, the old man answering yes or no or giving information. Upturned upon his knee his right hand opened and closed with a kneading action, as though he were trying to soften something in his palm. Until at length it stopped and the old man sat upright, fist clenched and quivering and the veins like old blue thread imprinted in the paper skin, sat erect and cut the agent off with a question of his own:

Why don't you say what you come here to say? Why not jest up and ast me?

I beg your pardon? said the agent.

Why I done it. Rung shells and shot your hootnanny all to hell? Where *you* from, heh? You talk like a God-damned yankee. What you do for a livin? Ast questions?

Mr Ownby . . .

Mr Ownby's ass. I could tell you why—and you stit wouldn't know. That's all right. You can set and ast a bunch of idjit questions. But not knowin a thing ain't never made it not so. Well, I'm a old man and I've seen some hard times, so I don't reckon Brushy Moun-tain'll be the worst place I was ever in.

Mr Ownby, I'm sure you're upset and I assure you . . .

Ahh, said the old man.

Mr Ownby, there are only a few more questions. If you'd like I could come back another time. I . . . We at the agency feel . . .

I reckon you could, the old man said. I ain't goin
nowhere. He leaned back against the wall and passed
one hand across his eyes as if to wipe away some image.
Then he sat very still with his hands on his knees, his
shaggy head against the bricks, restored to patience and
a look of tried and inviolate sanctity, the faded blue eyes
looking out down the row of cages, a forest of sweating
iron dowels, forms of men standing or huddled upon
their pallets, and the old man felt the circle of years
closing, the final increment of the curve returning him
again to the inchoate, the prismatic flux of sound and
color wherein he had drifted once before and now beyond the world of men. By the time the agent had
gathered his forms and tucked them once again into his
briefcase the old man had closed his eyes and the agent
called quietly for the jailer and left him.

The jailer walked with him down the corridor. The
agent had regained his composure. Well, he said cheerily,
he's a cantankerous old rascal, isn't he?

The old feller? I reckon. Been pretty quiet here, but
then they shore had a time gettin him here.

How's that? said the agent.

Why, he shot four men. Luther Boyd's stit hoppin
around on crutches.

Did he kill anyone? the agent asked.

No, but it wadn't from not tryin. That old man's
ornery enough.

Yes, the agent said, musing. Definitely an anomic
type.

Mean as a snake, said the jailer. Here, watch the door.

The agent thanked the desk sergeant as he passed
through the outer room. He swung the briefcase to his
left hand and dabbled his handkerchief upon his forehead. Over the worn runner on the flagged hall floor his
steps were soundless and he moved with a slender grace
of carriage, delicate and feline.

In the spring of the year you may see them about the grounds walking or sitting perhaps in the wake and swath of the droning mowers lifting up strewn daisyheads white and torn, softly fallen in the grass. Long monologues rise and fall, they speak of great deeds and men and noble eras gone. The mowers return along the fence in martial formation drowning the babble of voices.

The brick buildings atop the hill are dark with age, formidable yet sad, like old fortress ruins. Families come from the reception room into the pale sun, moving slowly, talking, grieving their silent griefs. The unvisited amble hurriedly about the grounds like questing setters, gesticulant and aimless.

There are others who sit quietly and unattended in the grass watching serene and childlike with serious eyes. Tender voices caress their ears endlessly and they are beyond sorrow. Some wave hopefully to the passing cars of picnickers and bathers. The eldest of all sits a little apart, a grass stem revolving between his yellowed teeth, remembering in the summer.

The mountain road brick-red of dust laced with lizard tracks, coming up through the peach orchard, hot, windless, cloistral in a silence of no birds save one vulture hung in the smokeblue void of the sunless mountainside, rocking on the high updrafts, and the road turning and gated with bullbriers waxed and green, and the green cadaver grin sealed in the murky waters of the peach pit, slimegreen skull with newts coiled in the eyesockets and a wig of moss.

The old man paused at the door, the attendant leading him by one arm through and into the room apparently against his will, peered at the boy through slotted lids as if unused to light of any intensity. He looked older than the boy remembered him. The attendant pulled him into the room, him shuffling in the old brogans with the paper-thin soles, a rasping sound on the concrete floor.

They came over to where the boy sat. Here's your nephew, the attendant said loudly into the old man's ear. You remember him?

The old man flashed a glint of blue eyes from deep beneath the closing lids. I reckon, he said.

The attendant pushed him down into the wicker chair next to the boy and left them, going back through the door, high squeak of crepe diminishing in the corridor. The old man sat in his chair staring across at the unrelieved spanse of whitewashed plaster.

Uncle Ather?

He turned. The boy was holding at him a huge bag of chewing tobacco.

I brought you some tobacca, he said. Beech-Nut, like you like.

The old man took it from him slowly and slid it inside his shirtfront. Thank ye, son, he said. I'm much obliged.

They sat quietly. The mowers passed again beneath the window, droning louder and then fading. Laughter and distant voices, someone crying, quite softly, like a child who is just lonely.

Kindly warmin up a little, ain't it? the old man said.

We had a little rain out to the mountain, the boy said. Sunday week I believe it was.

Yes, the old man said. Well, be little of it this year I reckon. Done had it all at oncet. They's a good warm spell comin on. Won't nothin make, won't nothin keep. A seventh year is what it is.

He gazed at the floor between his shoes, out of the bell-flared tops his shinbones rising hairless, pale and polished as shafts of driftwood and into his trouser legs. Get older, he said, you don't need to count. You can read the signs. You can feel it in your ownself. Knowed a blind man oncet could tell lots of things afore they happent. But it'll be hot and dry. Late frost is one sign if you don't know nothin else. So they won't but very little make because folks thinks that stuff grows by seasons and it don't. It goes by weather. Game too, and folks themselves if they knowed it. I recollect one winter, I was jest a young feller, they wadn't no winter. Not hardly a frost even. It was a sight in the world the things that growed. That was a seventh year seventh and you'll be old as me afore it comes again.

The old man paused, consulted a trouser button. Then he said: I look for this to be a bad one. I look for real calamity afore this year is out.

When the boy asked him the old man explained that

there was a lean year and a year of plenty every seven years. The boy thought about it. Then he said: That makes it over fourteen year then, don't it?

Well, said the old man, depends on how you count I reckon. If'n you count jest the lean and not the plenty, or the other way around, I reckon you could call it ever fourteen year. I reckon some folks might figure thataway. I call it the seventh my ownself.

He gazed at the wall above the line of wicker chairs. The attendant passed through the room with a young man and a woman. She was drying her eyes with a yellow lace handkerchief. They went out. After a while the boy said:

They got Marion Sylder.

The old man turned his head, the fine white silk of his hair lifting slightly with the motion as if a breeze had touched it. Who's that? he said.

Sylder. The . . . the feller used to haul whiskey for Hobie. They caught him with a load and sent him to Brushy.

Thought his name was Jack, the old man said.

No, Sylder. Marion Sylder. He was a friend of mine.

Yes, the old man said. I recollect seein him on the mountain time or two. Had a black car. Kindly a new one I believe it was. Say they sent him to Brushy.

Three years. For runnin whiskey.

That's pitiful, the old man said. Feller nowadays you don't get by with much. Yes, I recollect the boy, don't know as I ever did meet him. Well, I hope he fares better'n me. I cain't get used to all these here people. The old man looked like he might be going to say more but he stopped and he looked at the boy, his wiry and tufted brows bunched whether in pain or anger and eyes blanched with age a china-blue, but fierce, a visage hoary and peregrine.

How long do you have to . . . stay in?

Here? he said, looking about him. Likely a good while, son. They ain't never said what I was charged with nor nothin but I suspicion they think me light in the head is what it is. I reckon you knowed this was a place for crazy people. What they tend to do with me when they come to find out I ain't crazy I couldn't speculate. He patted the front of his shirt where he had put the tobacco. How's young Pulliam? he said.

He's gone up in the country to stay with his grammaw, the boy said. Ain't nobody much left around no more.

No, the old man said. He ever catch him a mink?

No. I caught one though.

Did, eh? What did it bring?

It never brought nothin. They was a bobcat or somethin got aholt of it and tore it up.

That's a shame, said the old man. Did ye lay ye a set for that old cat?

Me and Warn did. But we never caught nothin but a big old possum.

Cats is smart, allowed the old man. Course it could of been a common everday housecat. They'll tear up anything they come up on, a cat will. Housecats is smart too. Smarter'n a dog or a mule. Folks thinks they ain't on account of you cain't learn em nothin, but what it is is that they won't learn nothin. They too smart. Knowed a man oncet had a cat could talk. Him and this cat'd talk back and forth of one another like ary two people. That's one cat I kept shy of. I knowed what it was. Lots of times that happens, a body dies and their soul takes up in a cat for a spell. Specially somebody drownded or like that where they don't get buried proper.

But not for no longer than seven year so he would be

*gone now and I don't have to fool with him no more
except he ought not to of got burnt, that ought not to
of happent and maybe I done wrong in that way to of
let that happen, but it's done now and he's gone, that
had to of been him Eller was supposed to of heard, wonderin what all it could of been squallin thataway, not
that I'd of told anybody—him leavin out cat and all and
bound most probably for hell and I hope they don't
nobody hear no more from him never. So that man put
him there either justified or not is free too afore God
because after that seven year they cain't nobody bother
you, what that lawyer said and I had been scoutin nine
year he said was two year longer than needful but this
time I was too old and they catched me.*

Yes, he said, they's lots of things folks don't know
about sech as that. Cats is a mystery, always has been.
He stopped, passed a hand across his face dreamily.
Then he turned to the boy. Believe you've growed some,
ain't ye? he said.

The boy ran his palms along his knees. I reckon, he
said.

Mm hm, the old man said. What do you figure you'll
make?

I don't know, he said. Not much of nothin.

Well, the old man said, it's always hard for a young
feller to get a start. Does seem like they's any number
of ways to get money nowadays, not like when I was
growin up cash money was right hard to come by.
They's even a bounty on findin dead bodies, man over
to Knoxville does pretty good grapplehookin em when
they jump off of the bridge like they do there all the
time. They tell me he gets out fast enough to beat anybody else to em only not so fast as they might stit be
a-breathin. So they tell it leastways.

But I never done it to benefit myself because I knowed

I'd have to scout the bushes if they found I done it as I allowed they would and if I did have my reasons stit they cain't a man say I done it to benefit myself.

A man gets older, he said, he finds they's lots of things he can do jest as well without and so he don't have to worry about this and that the way a young feller will. I worked near all my life and never had nothin. Seems like a old man'd be allowed his rest but then he comes to find they's things you have to do on account of no-body else wants to attend to em. Like that would make em go away. And maybe they don't look like much but then they lead you around like you might start a rabbit dog to hunt a fence-corner and get drug over half the county against nightfall. Which a old man ain't good at noway. He eased himself slightly in the chair and shifted his weight. Most ever man loves peace, he said, and none better than a old man.

Or even knows they need attendin to. But I never done it to benefit myself. Shot that thing. Like I kept peace for seven year sake of a man I never knowed nor seen his face and like I seen them fellers never had no business there and if I couldn't run em off I could any-way let em know they was one man would let on that he knowed what they was up to. But I knowed if they could build it they could build it back and I done it anyway. Ever man loves peace and a old man best of all.

Do they allow you to chew in here?

I kindly doubt it, the old man said. I ain't a-fixin to ast noway. I'll jest slip me one when I see clear to. They's some in here I wouldn't put past tellin on a feller. Half loonies. The real loonies wouldn't. Some here that ain't crazy, like me, but I doubt they'd want to tell.

I wonder how come them to be here, the boy said.

The old man ran a lank and corded hand through his

hair. I couldn't say, he said. The ways of these people is strange to me. I did mean to ast you, you ain't seen my old dog I don't reckon?

No, the boy said, I've not seen him. You want I could go out to your place and hunt him.

Well, ever you're out thataway might holler for him. I don't know what to tell ye to do with him. I ain't got no money to ast nobody to feed him with and I couldn't shoot him was he too poor to walk, but might could somebody else . . .

I see him I'll take care of him, the boy said. I wouldn't charge you nothin noway.

Well, the old man said, refolding his hands in his lap. They looked up together, an orderly crossing the room with prim steps and bearing in tow an odor of disinfectant, cleaning fluid redolent of sassafras from the corridor where two Negroes mopped backwards toward each other. They could hear the measured slap of the mops on the baseboard above the door's long pneumatic hiss until it closed and they sat again in quiet, the sunlight strong and airy in the room.

That wasn't the one. He said:

What are these? the stethoscope still about his neck and jerking about rubbery when he moved.

Shotgun done it, said the old man, seated half naked and in decorous rectitude upon the examining table with his feet just clearing the floor and looking straight ahead —so that the intern had moved him about roughly without speaking either as you might a cataleptic wasted thin with years until the old man had asked him quietly if he intended to kill him.

What were you doing, robbing a henhouse?

The old man didn't answer. He said again:

I know she's here.

If she is she don't want to see you.

I mean to see her.

Then the barrel of the gun shortening and withdrawing in the cup of his shoulder and his face bent to the stock and him walking into it, the black plume of smoke forming soundlessly about the muzzle and the shot popping into his leg, audible and painless in his flesh and him taking another step with the same leg and pitching forward as if he had stepped in a hole and then he could hear the shot.

You reckon you'll come back to the mountain, the boy said. When you . . . come back?

Oh, said the old man, well. Yes. Yes, most likely I will. I allowed I might go back up yander in the mountains where my new place is at but I don't know as I will. A man gets lonesome off by hisself he ain't used to it. I spect I'll jest come on back if the old house ain't fell down. Yes.

He shuffled his feet on the floor. A shadow fell over them and he looked up to see the boy standing. Are ye leavin? he said.

Yes, the boy said. I got to get on back.

Well. I thank ye for the tobacca.

It's all right.

Well.

I'll come again.

No, the old man said.

Yes. I will.

Well.

He stopped again at the door and lifted his hand. The old man waved him on, and then he was alone again. The mowers came back. A little later the attendant to lead him away.

He stood in front of the courthouse again, again the

heat and the sulphurous haze in fixed and breathless
canopy above the traffic. He took the dollar from his
pocket and pressed out the creases between his palms.
It would leave him two dollars and what was left of
the fifty cents, since he had gotten five and a half for
the hides of which, he had paid the two to Sylder and
now this dollar which he hadn't even known that he
owed. Then he climbed the walk, the dollar in his hand,
past the arch and past the tireless bronze soldier and
under the new shade of the buckeyes. He mounted the
gritty footworn steps upward in a rush, into the hall,
turning left and coming again to the long counter with
the desks behind it. There was only one woman there,
not the one he had traded with before. She was at a type-
writer, the machine clacking loudly in the empty room.
He stood at the counter watching her. After a while
he coughed. She stopped and looked up. Can I help you?
she said.

Yesm.

She still sat, hands poised over the machine. He stared
back at her. She lowered her hands into her lap, swiveled
the chair about to face him. He said no more and she
rose and crossed slowly to the counter, adjusting her
glasses as she went.

Well, she said, what can I do for you?

It's about the bounty, mam. Hawks.

Oh. You have a hawk. She was looking down at him.

No mam, I done give it to ye. He had the dollar out
in his hand now and waving it feebly, wondering could
the price have gone up. I was figuring on trading back
with ye if you-all don't care, he said.

Her brows pinched up a small purse of flesh between
them. Trade back? she said. You mean you want to
get the hawk back?

Yesm, he said. If you-all don't care.

When did you bring it in?

He looked to the ceiling, back again. Let's see, he said. I believe it was around in August but it could of been early in September I reckon.

They Lord God, son, the woman said, it wouldn't still be here. Last August? Why . . .

What all do you do with em? he asked, somehow figuring still that they must be kept, must have some value or use commensurate with a dollar other than the fact of their demise.

Burn em in the furnace I would reckon, she said. They sure cain't keep em around here. They might get a little strong after a while, mightn't they?

Burn em? he said. They burn em?

I believe so, she said.

He looked about him vaguely, back to her, still not leaning on or touching the counter. And thow people in jail and beat up on em.

What? she said, leaning forward.

And old men in the crazy house.

Son, I'm busy, now if there was anything else you wanted . . .

He smoothed the dollar in his hand again, made a few tentative thrusts, pushed it finally across the counter to her. Here, he said. It's okay. I cain't take no dollar. I made a mistake, he wadn't for sale. He turned and started for the door.

You, she called. Here! You come back here, you cain't . . .

But that was all he heard, through the door now, running down the long hall toward the wide-flung outer doors where a breeze riffled the posters and notices on the wall and past them and again into the candent May noon.

The boy had already gone when they came from Knoxville, seven years now after the burial and seven months after the cremation, and sifted the ashes, since whipped to a broth by the rains of that spring and now dried again, caked and crusted, sifted them and there found the chalked sticks and shards of bone gray-white and brittle as ash themselves, and the skull, worm-riddled, vermiculate with the tracery of them and hollowed and fired to the weight and tensile cohesiveness of parched cardboard, the caried teeth rattling in their sockets. And a zipper of brass, fused shapeless, thick-coated with a dull green paste.

That was all. They were there four hours, the two officers deferential before the coroner, dusting the pieces with their handkerchiefs and passing them on to him who placed them in a clean bag of white canvas.

Mr Eller bit with his small teeth a piece from his plug of spiced tobacco, refolded the cellophane and put it again into his breast pocket. And the skull, he said. With all the fillins melted out of the teeth.

Okay. And the skull. Johnny Romines stopped, the cigarette half rolled in his left hand and leaking as he gestured with it. So, he said, what I want to know is did the boy know about it or not, and would he know was it his daddy?

I don't know, Mr Eller said. If he did I never heard it. Asides he's been gone off now since May or June and this is the fourth day of August they jest now gettin up there. I figure maybe the old man was the only one that knowed.

Old man Ownby? Was he the one done it?

No, Mr Eller said. Course they liable to thow it off on him to save huntin somebody else.

But he was the one told it?

Near as I can find out he was.

Johnny Romines passed the paper across his tongue and folded it shut. Well, do you reckon it was him? he said.

His daddy you mean? Room for speculatin there too I reckon. Miz Rattner claims that it was and that the boy has gone off to hunt whoever it was put him there. She says it all come to her in a dream—a vision, she called it.

Wonder if she had a vision about him bein wanted in three states, Gifford said.

Mr Eller turned on the constable. No, he said, I doubt she has. I don't reckon she needs any sech either. She's a good Christian woman don't matter who-all she might of been married to and not knowed no better.

The constable looked at the storekeeper.

Or the boy either, Mr Eller added.

Never you mind about the boy, Gifford said. Me and him is due for a nice little talk anyway.

Well, you'll have to find him first.

Wonder who it was, Johnny Romines said. That put him in there I mean. Reckon it was somebody from around here?

I doubt it was somebody from New York City, the constable said. He turned to Mr Eller. And what about that fancy plate he was supposed to have? In his head from the war.

What about it?

Well, they wadn't none. How's she account for that?

I don't reckon she ever thought to ast about it. She jest never would of doubted or wondered about it in the first place. About whether he had one, if he said he did, or about whether that was him in that dittybag if she'd decided that it was either one. Mr Eller rolled his cheeks and spat soundlessly across the constable's bow and into a coffeecan. Seems like you ought to tell your sidekick about it though, he said.

Who's that?

Legwater.

He ain't my sidekick, Gifford said. And I don't have to tell nobody nothin cept as I see fit.

Mr Eller studied a passing fly, apparently ruminating on some obscure problem in the dynamics of flight. Well, he said agreeably, I reckon you're right. Keep him out of mischief anyhow.

Gifford's eyes narrowed suspiciously. What? What will?

Campin up on the mountain. With his shovel and his winderscreen.

Some coughs went their rounds. A milkcase settled floorward creakily.

Humph, said Gifford, unleaning from the counter

with studied ease. He fingered cigarettes deftly from
one straining pocket. Then: What's he doin up there?

Mr Eller waited while the match rocketed across the
counter. Then he said: Huntin platymum I reckon. Lessen he's siftin them ashes for to make soap.

Legwater was on the mountain three days before anyone could get close enough to him to tell him it wasn't
so, that the man never had any platinum in his head
and that he was wasting his time, it was all a mistake.
The first night he built his fire and was sitting by it
with his shotgun leaning against a tree and was sipping
coffee from a canteen cup when the hound staggered
into the clearing on the far side of the fire and stood
with his blind head swinging back and forth like a
bear's, muzzle up to catch what clue the wind might
bring.

Ha! cried Legwater, leaping up, the coffee flying. Ha!
he said, stepped to the tree and snatched up the shotgun.
But before he could get a proper sight the dog was gone
again, absorbed quietly into the darkness. Legwater
leveled the gun at the night and fired, listened after the
compounding echoes of the shot for a long time and
then stepped to the fire and got the cup and poured
it full from the pot, squatting, the shotgun leaning
against his knee. He listened some more, but could
make nothing out. He set the pot back on the little
circle of stones he had constructed and tried the hot
rim of the cup against his lip. The hound did not reap-
pear. When he had finished the coffee he rolled his
blankets out, reloaded the empty chamber of the gun
and settled for sleep.

Toward early morning he woke, sat up quickly and
looked about him. It was still dark and the fire had

long since died, still dark and quiet with that silence
that seems to be of itself listening, an astral quiet where
planets collide soundlessly, beyond the auricular dimension altogether. He listened. Above the black ranks of
trees the midsummer sky arched cloudless and coldly
starred. He lay back and stared at it and after a while
he slept.

When he woke again the sun was up. He was still
lying on his back and now in the depthless blue void
above him a hawk wheeled. He got to his feet and
began to walk around, feeling stiff and poorly rested.
He scouted in the woods and came back with a load
of dead limbs, snapped them to length under his foot
and soon had a fire going and coffee warming. When it
had perked he sat blowing at a cupful and shifting it
from hand to hand as it got too hot or he found a new
mosquito bite to scratch at. There was an army rucksack hanging from the tree near his blankets and from
the pocket he took some cold biscuits and ate them.
Then he got to work.

The ashes in the pit were better than a foot deep
and the ground all about was strewn with them. He
worked all day, shoveling out piles of ash and then
climbing from the pit to sift them with his windowscreen. Late in the afternoon some boys came into the
clearing and stood for a time watching him. He kept
at it, the clouds of ash billowing up out of the pit.
Before long they began to comment. He looked at them
sharply, not stopping, sifting the ashes, examining
charred bits of cedar wood. Soon they were giggling
among themselves. He ignored them, adopting an official air about his work. It was no good.

Might be gold teeth too, one of them sang out. A
flurry of titters surged and died. Legwater stood up
and glared at them. They were five, standing together

just at the edge of the trees with grinning faces. He climbed back into the pit with his shovel. From time to time he would stretch his head up over the top of the hole to see what they were about, but about the third time one of them gobbled like a turkey and they all howled with laughter so he gave it up and tried not to look their way. He kept at his shoveling. After a while he heard something clatter near the pit. He looked up and the boys had gone. Then an apple dropped into the ashes at his feet with a soft puff. He stopped and craned his neck up. Sure enough, here came another. He marked its course, leaped out of the pit and seizing the shotgun as he went began a fast walk in the direction from which the apple had come. Brush began crashing. A voice called: Run, fellers, run! He'll shoot ye down and scalp ye. Another: You got silver in your teeth you're a dead'n. He stopped. The sounds died away. On the road further down the mountain high laughter, catcalls. He went back to work. By nightfall he was a feathery gray effigy—face, hair and clothing a single color. He spat gobs of streaky gray phlegm. Even the trees near the pit had begun to take on a pale and weathered look.

The hound came back after dark. He could hear it padding in the leaves, stop, shuffle again. He had eaten the last of what food he had brought and could hardly sleep for the cramping in his belly. He held the shotgun and waited for the hound to enter the firelight. It did not. Finally he went to sleep with the shotgun lying across his lap. He was very tired.

When he went to the pit the following morning the first thing he saw was an old goatskull, the brainpan crammed with tinfoil. He pitched it away in disgust and fell to shoveling.

By late in the afternoon his hunger had subsided and he had cleared the pit so that in one end the bare concrete was visible, blackened and encrusted with an indefinable burnt substance that scaled away under the shovel and showed green beneath.

He was shoveling faster, approaching desperation as the residue of unsifted ashes diminished, when Gifford showed up, badly winded from his climb up the mountain. Legwater stopped and watched him come across the little clearing, his shoes weighted with clay, his face inflamed with a red scowl. When he got to the pit Legwater leaned on the shovel and looked up at him. Well, he said, you want shares I reckon? After I done . . .

Idjit, Gifford said. Goddamn, what a idjit. He was standing on the concrete rim now looking down at the humane officer gaunt and fantastically powdered with ash, and looking at the great heaps of ashes and the screen, the bedroll, rucksack, shotgun.

You think so? Legwater said.

I know so. He wadn't no war hero. It ain't for sure it was even him, but if it was he never had no—no thing in his head.

I'll be the jedge of that, Legwater said, bending with his shovel.

Gifford watched him, moving around to the upwind side to keep clear of the dust. In a few minutes the humane officer leaped from the pit and began shoveling the new ashes onto the screen, then shaking it back and forth to sift them through, a fevered look in his eye like some wild spodomantic sage divining in driven haste the fate of whole galaxies against their imminent ruin. The constable lit a cigarette and leaned back against the tree.

Legwater threw out two more piles of ash and sifted them and then when he disappeared into the pit again Gifford could hear him scraping around but not shoveling. He ventured over and peered in. Legwater was on

hands and knees, going over the scraped floor of the
pit carefully, scratching here and there with the tip of
the shovel. Finally he stopped and looked up. The little
bastard was lyin, he said. He got it his ownself, the
lyin little son of a bitch.

Let's go, Earl.

His own daddy, the humane officer was saying.

Gifford started toward the road with long disgusted
strides. When he got to the apple trees he turned and
looked back. Legwater was standing in the pit, just his
head showing, staring vacantly.

Well, said the constable.

He kept staring.

Hey! Gifford called.

Legwater turned his head to give him a dumb look,
the incredulous and empty expression common to victims of tragedy, disaster and loss.

You want a ride or not?

He pulled himself from the pit and began walking
toward the constable, then he was hurrying, loping
along, the shovel still in his hand and bouncing behind
him. Gifford let him get all the way to him before he
sent him back after the shotgun and the camping gear.

They went down the orchard road together, their
steps padding in the red dust, the constable swaggering
slightly as he did and the humane officer, haggard-look-
ing, his black and sleepless eyes all but smoking, grimly
apparitional with the shotgun and the spade dangling
one at either side from his gaunt claws. Gifford carried
the other's rucksack and blanket roll with light effort
and from time to time he sidled his eyes to study Legwater with pity, or with contempt. Neither spoke until
they saw the dog and that was very near to the pike,
on the last turn above the gate. They had overtaken it
and even in the few minutes in which he was allowed

to watch it alive Gifford was struck by its behavior. It was walking in the wheelruts with an exotic delicacy, like a trained dog on a rope, and holding its head so far back, its nose near perpendicular, that Gifford looked up instinctively to see what threat might be materializing out of the sky. The shovel bounced in the road with a dull bong and when he turned it was in time only to see Legwater recoil under the shotgun and to recoil himself as the muzzleblast roared in his ears. He spun and saw the dog lurch forward, still holding up its head, slew sideways and fold up in the dust of the road.

The few small windows were glassless but for a jagged side or corner still wedged in the handmade sashes. The roofshakes lay in windrows on the broad loft floors and this house housed only the winds.

Dervishes of leaves rattled across the yard and in the wind the oaks dipped and creaked, and in the wind even the spavined house hung between the stone chimneys seemed to give a little. The doors stood open and wind scurried in the parlor, riffled the drift leaves on the kitchen floor and stirred the cobwebbed window corners. He did not go to the loft. The lower rooms were dusty and barren and but for some half-familiar rags of clothes altogether strange. He came back into the yard and sat quietly for a while beneath one of the trees. Watched a waterbird skim beneath the shadowline of

the mountain, cupped wings catching the slant light of
the sun, then holding the wide curve in a wingset sweep
low over the trees to the pond, homing to the warm
black waters. He watched it down. What caught his
ear? The high thin whicker of a feather, a shadow passing, nothing. Light was breaking in thin reefs through
the clouds shelved darkly up the west. Old dry leaves
rattled frail and withered as old voices, trailed stiffly
down, rocking like thinworn shells downward through
seawater, or spun, curling ancient parchments on which
no message at all appeared.

Young Rattner finished his cigarette and went back
out to the road. An aged Negro passed high on the seat
of a wagon, dozing to the chop of the half-shod mule-
hooves on the buckled asphalt. About him the tall wheels
veered and dished in the erratic parabolas of spun coins
unspinning as if not attached to the wagon at all but
merely rolling there in that quadratic symmetry by pure
chance. He crossed the road to give them leeway and
they swung by slowly, laboriously, as if under the
weight of some singular and unreasonable gravity. The
ruined and ragged mule, the wagon, the man . . . up the
road they wobbled, rattle and squeak of the fellies climbing loose over the spokes . . . shimmered in waves of
heat rising from the road, dissolved in a pale and broken
image.

He followed along behind, going toward the forks.
Once at the top of the hill he paused and looked back
and he could see the roof of the house deep-green with
moss, or gaping black where patches had caved through.
But it was never his house anyway.

Evening. The dead sheathed in the earth's crust and
turning the slow diurnal of the earth's wheel, at peace
with eclipse, asteroid, the dusty novae, their bones brin-

dled with mold and the celled marrow going to frail
stone, turning, their fingers laced with roots, at one
with Tut and Agamemnon, with the seed and the un-
born.

It was like having your name in the paper, he thought,
reading the inscription:

MILDRED YEARWOOD RATTNER
1906 — 1945
If thou afflict them in any wise,
And they cry at all unto me,
I will surely hear their cry.
                                    Exod.

the stone arrogating to itself in these three short years
already a gray and timeless aspect, glazed with lichens
and nets of small brown runners, the ring of rusted wire
leaning awry against it with its stained and crumpled
rags of foliage. He reached out and patted the stone
softly, a gesture, as if perhaps to conjure up some image,
evoke again some allegiance with a name, a place, hal-
lucinated recollections in which faces merged inextri-
cably, and yet true and fixed; touched it, a carved stone
less real than the smell of woodsmoke or the taste of an
old man's wine. And he no longer cared to tell which
were things done and which dreamt.

His trouser legs were wet and clammy against his
ankles. Sitting on the small square of marble he removed
one shoe, testing the sock for dampness, resting as any
traveler might. From across the tall grass and beyond the
ruins of the spiked iron fence came the click of the
lightbox at the intersection. A car emerged from the
trees at his right and rolled to a stop. There were a man
and a woman. She looked at him across the man's shoulder, then turned to the man. They both looked. The
box clicked. He waved to them and the man turned,

saw the green light and pulled away, the white oval of the woman's face still watching him. So he waved again to her just as the car slid from sight behind a hedgerow, the wheels whisking up a fine spray from the road.

He sat there for a while, rubbing his foot abstractedly, whistling softly to himself. To the west a solid sheet of overcast sped the evening on. Already fireflies were about. He put on his shoe and rose and began moving toward the fence, through the wet grass. The workers had gone, leaving behind their wood-dust and chips, the white face of the stump pooling the last light out of the gathering dusk. The sun broke through the final shelf of clouds and bathed for a moment the dripping trees with blood, tinted the stones a diaphanous wash of color, as if the very air had gone to wine. He passed through the gap in the fence, past the torn iron palings and out to the western road, the rain still mizzling softly and the darkening headlands drawing off the day, heraldic, pennoned in flame, the fleeing minions scattering their shadows in the wake of the sun.

They are gone now. Fled, banished in death or exile, lost, undone. Over the land sun and wind still move to burn and sway the trees, the grasses. No avatar, no scion, no vestige of that people remains. On the lips of the strange race that now dwells there their names are myth, legend, dust.

SUTTREE

The author wishes to express his gratitude to The American Academy of Arts and Letters, The Rockefeller Foundation, and The John Simon Guggenheim Memorial Foundation.

*D*ear *friend now in the dusty clockless hours of the town when the streets lie black and steaming in the wake of the watertrucks and now when the drunk and the homeless have washed up in the lee of walls in alleys or abandoned lots and cats go forth highshouldered and lean in the grim perimeters about, now in these sootblacked brick or cobbled corridors where lightwire shadows make a gothic harp of cellar doors no soul shall walk save you.*

Old stone walls unplumbed by weathers, lodged in their striae fossil bones, limestone scarabs rucked in the floor of this once inland sea. Thin dark trees through yon iron palings where the dead keep their own small metropolis. Curious marble architecture, stele and obelisk and cross and little rainworn stones where names grow dim with years. Earth packed with samples of the casketmaker's trade, the dusty bones and rotted silk, the deathwear stained with carrion. Out there under the blue lamplight the trolleytracks run on to darkness, curved like cockheels in the pinchbeck dusk. The steel leaks back the day's heat, you can feel it through the floors of your shoes. Past these corrugated warehouse walls down little sandy streets where blownout autos sulk on pedestals of cinderblock. Through warrens of sumac and pokeweed and withered honeysuckle giving onto the scored clay banks of the railway. Gray vines coiled leftward in this northern hemisphere, what winds them shapes the dogwhelk's shell. Weeds sprouted from cinder and brick. A steamshovel reared in solitary abandonment against the night sky. Cross here. By frograils and fishplates where engines cough like lions in the dark of the yard. To a darker town, past lamps stoned blind, past smoking oblique shacks and china dogs and painted tires where dirty flowers grow. Down pavings rent with ruin, the slow cataclysm of neglect, the wires that belly pole to pole across the constellations hung with kitestring, with bolos composed of hobbled bottles or the toys of the smaller children. Encampment of the damned. Precincts perhaps where dripping lepers prowl unbelled. Above the heat and the improbable skyline of the city a brass moon has risen and the clouds run before it like watered ink. The buildings stamped against the night are like a rampart to a farther world forsaken, old purposes forgot. Countrymen come for miles with the earth clinging to their shoes and sit all day like mutes in the marketplace. This city constructed on no known paradigm, a mongrel architecture reading back through the works of man in a brief delineation of the aberrant disordered and mad. A carnival of shapes upreared on the river plain that has dried up the sap of the earth for miles about.

Factory walls of old dark brick, tracks of a spur line grown with weeds, a course of foul blue drainage where dark filaments of nameless dross sway in the current. Tin panes among the glass in the rusted window frames. There is a moonshaped rictus in the streetlamp's globe where a stone has gone and from this aperture there drifts down through the constant helix of aspiring insects a faint and steady rain of the same forms burnt and lifeless.

Here at the creek mouth the fields run on to the river, the mud deltaed and baring out of its rich alluvial harbored bones and dread waste, a wrack of cratewood and condoms and fruitrinds. Old tins and jars and ruined household artifacts that rear from the fecal mire of the flats like landmarks in the trackless vales of dementia praecox. A world beyond all fantasy, malevolent and tactile and dissociate, the blown lightbulbs like shorn polyps semitranslucent and skullcolored bobbing blindly down and spectral eyes of oil and now and again the beached and stinking forms of foetal humans bloated like young birds mooneyed and bluish or stale gray. Beyond in the dark the river flows in a sluggard ooze toward southern seas, running down out of the rainflattened corn and petty crops and riverloam gardens of upcountry landkeepers, grating along like bonedust, afreight with the past, dreams dispersed in the water someway, nothing ever lost. Houseboats ride at their hawsers. The neap mud along the shore lies ribbed and slick like the cavernous flitch of some beast hugely foundered and beyond the country rolls away to the south and the mountains. Where hunters and woodcutters once slept in their boots by the dying light of their thousand fires and went on, old teutonic forebears with eyes incandesced by the visionary light of a massive rapacity, wave on wave of the violent and the insane, their brains stoked with spoorless analogues of all that was, lean aryans with their abrogate semitic chapbook reenacting the dramas and parables therein and mindless and pale with a longing that nothing save dark's total restitution could appease.

We are come to a world within the world. In these alien reaches, these maugre sinks and interstitial wastes that the righteous see from carriage and car another life dreams. Illshapen or black or deranged, fugitive of all order, strangers in everyland.

The night is quiet. Like a camp before battle. The city beset by a thing unknown and will it come from forest or sea? The murengers have walled the pale, the gates are shut, but lo the thing's inside and can you

4

guess his shape? Where he's kept or what's the counter of his face? Is he a weaver, bloody shuttle shot through a timewarp, a carder of souls from the world's nap? Or a hunter with hounds or do bone horses draw his deadcart through the streets and does he call his trade to each? Dear friend he is not to be dwelt upon for it is by just suchwise that he's invited in.

The rest indeed is silence. It has begun to rain. Light summer rain, you can see it falling slant in the town lights. The river lies in a grail of quietude. Here from the bridge the world below seems a gift of simplicity. Curious, no more. Down there in grots of fallen light a cat transpires from stone to stone across the cobbles liquid black and sewn in rapid antipodes over the raindark street to vanish cat and countercat in the rifted works beyond. Faint summer lightning far downriver. A curtain is rising on the western world. A fine rain of soot, dead beetles, anonymous small bones. The audience sits webbed in dust. Within the gutted sockets of the interlocutor's skull a spider sleeps and the jointed ruins of the hanged fool dangle from the flies, bone pendulum in motley. Fourfooted shapes go to and fro over the boards. Ruder forms survive.

Peering down into the water where the morning sun fashioned wheels of light, coronets fanwise in which lay trapped each twig, each grain of sediment, long flakes and blades of light in the dusty water sliding away like optic strobes where motes sifted and spun. A hand trails over the gunwale and he lies athwart the skiff, the toe of one sneaker plucking periodic dimples in the river with the boat's slight cradling, drifting down beneath the bridge and slowly past the mud-stained stanchions. Under the high cool arches and dark keeps of the span's undercarriage where pigeons babble and the hollow flap of their wings echoes in stark applause. Glancing up at these cathedraled vaultings with their fossil woodknots and pseudomorphic nailheads in gray concrete, drifting, the bridge's slant shadow leaning the width of the river with that headlong illusion postulate in old cupracers frozen on photoplates, their wheels elliptic with speed. These shadows form over the skiff, accommodate his prone figure and pass on.

With his jaw cradled in the crook of his arm he watched idly surface phenomena, gouts of sewage faintly working, gray clots of nameless waste and yellow condoms roiling slowly out of the murk like some giant form of fluke or tapeworm. The watcher's face rode beside the boat, a sepia visage yawing in the scum, eyes veering and watery grimace. A welt curled sluggishly on the river's surface as if something unseen had stirred in the deeps and small bubbles of gas erupted in oily spectra.

Below the bridge he eased himself erect, took up the oars and began to row toward the south bank. There he brought the skiff about, swinging the stern into a clump of willows, and going aft he raised up a heavy cord that ran into the water from an iron pipe driven into the mud of the bank. This he relayed through an open oarlock mounted on the skiff's transom. Now he set out again, rowing slowly, the cord coming up wet and smooth through the lock and dipping into the river again. When he was some thirty feet from shore the first dropper came up, doubling the line until he reached and cast it off. He went on, the skiff lightly quartered against the river's drift, the hooks riding up one by one into the oarlock with their leached and tattered gobbets of flesh. When he felt the weight of the first fish he shipped the dripping oars and took hold of the line and brought it in by hand. A large carp broke water, a coarse mailed flank dull bronze and glinting. He braced himself with one knee and hefted it into the boat and cut the line and tied on a fresh hook with a chunk of cutbait and dropped it over the side and went on, sculling with one oar, the carp warping heavily against the floorboards.

When he had finished running the line he was on the other side of the river. He rebaited the last drop and let the heavy cord go, watching it sink in the muddy water among a spangled nimbus of sunmotes, a broken corona up through which flared for a moment the last pale chunk of rancid meat. Shifting the oars aboard he sprawled himself over the seats again to take the sun. The skiff swung gently, drifting in the current. He undid his shirt to the waist and put one forearm to his eyes. He could hear the river talking softly beneath him, heavy old river with wrinkled face. Beneath the sliding water cannons and carriages, trunnions seized and rusting in the mud, keelboats rotted to the consistency of mucilage. Fabled sturgeons with their horny pentagonal bodies, the cupreous and dacebright carp and catfish with their pale and sprueless underbellies, a thick muck shot with broken glass, with bones and rusted tins and bits of crockery reticulate with mudblack crazings. Across the river the limestone cliffs reared gray and roughly faceted and strung with grass across their face in thin green faults. Where they overhung the water they made a cool shade and the surface lay calm and dark and reflected like a small white star the form of a plover hovering on the updrafts off the edge of the bluff. Under the seat of the skiff a catfish swam dry and intransigent with his broad face pressed to the bulkhead.

Passing the creek mouth he raised one hand and waved slowly, the old blacks all flowered and bonneted coming about like a windtilted garden with their canes bobbing and their arms lifting dark and random into the air and their gaudy and barbaric costumes billowing with the movement. Beyond them the shape of the city rising wore a wrought, a jaded look, hammered out dark and smoking against a china sky. The grimy river littoral lay warped and shimmering in the heat and there was no sound in all this lonely summer forenoon.

Below the railway trestle he set to running his other line. The water was warm to the touch and had a granular lubricity like graphite. It was full noon when he finished and he stood in the skiff for a moment looking over the catch. He came back upriver rowing slowly, the fish struggling in a thin gray bilge in the floor of the boat, their soft barbels fingering with dull wonder the slimed boards and their backs where they bowed into the sunlight already bleached a bloodless pale. The brass oarlocks creaked in their blocks and the riverwater curled from the bowplanks with a viscid quality and lay behind the skiff in a wake like plowed mire.

He rowed up from under the shadow of the bluffs and past the sand and gravel company and then along by barren and dusty lots where rails ran on cinder beds and boxcars oxidized on blind sidings, past warehouses of galvanized and corrugated tin set in flats gouged from the brickcolored earth where rhomboid and volute shapes of limestone jutted all brindled with mud like great bones washed out. He had already started across the river when he saw the rescue boats against the bank. They were trolling in the channel while a small crowd watched from the shore. Two white boats lightly veiled in the heat and the slow blue smoke of their exhaust, a faint chug of motors carrying the calm of the river. He crossed and rowed up the edge of the channel. The boats had come alongside each other and one of them had cut the engine. The rescue workers wore yachting caps and moved gravely at their task. As the fisherman passed they were taking aboard a dead man. He was very stiff and he looked like a window-dummy save for his face. The face seemed soft and bloated and wore a grappling hook in the side of it and a crazed grin. They raised him so, gambreled up by the bones of his cheek. A pale incruent wound. He seemed to protest woodenly, his head awry. They lifted him onto the deck where he lay in his wet seersucker suit and his lemoncolored socks, leering walleyed up at the workers with the hook in his face like some gross water homunculus taken in trolling that the light of God's day had stricken dead instanter.

The fisherman went past and pulled the skiff into the bank upriver from the crowd. He rolled a stone over the rope and walked down to watch. The rescue boat was coming in and one of the workers was kneeling over the corpse trying to pry the grapnel loose. The crowd was watching him and he was sweating and working at the hook. Finally he set his shoe against the dead man's skull and wrenched the hook with both hands until it came away trailing a stringy piece of blanched flesh.

They brought him ashore on a canvas litter and laid him in the grass where he stared at the sun with his drained eyes and his smile. A snarling clot of flies had already accrued out of the vapid air. The workers covered the dead man with a coarse gray blanket. His feet stuck out.

The fisherman had made to go when someone in the crowd took his elbow. Hey Suttree.

He turned. Hey Joe, he said. Did you see it?

No. They say he jumped last night. They found his shoes on the bridge.

They stood looking at the dead man. The squad workers were coiling their ropes and seeing to their tackle. The crowd had come to press about like mourners and the fisherman and his friend found themselves going past the dead man as if they'd pay respects. He lay there in his yellow socks with the flies crawling on the blanket and one hand stretched out on the grass. He wore his watch on the inside of his wrist as some folks do or used to and as Suttree passed he noticed with a feeling he could not name that the dead man's watch was still running.

That's a bad way to check out, said Joe.

Let's go.

They walked along the cinders by the edge of the railroad. Suttree rubbed the gently pulsing muscle in his speculative jaw.

Which way do you go? said Joe.

Right here. I've got my boat.

Are you still fishin?

Yeah.

What made you take that up?

I dont know, Suttree said. It seemed like a good idea at the time.

You ever get uptown?

Sometimes.

Why dont you come out to the Corner some evenin and we'll drink a beer.

I'll get out there one of these days.

You fishin today?

Yeah. A little.

Joe was watching him. Listen, he said. You could get on up at Miller's. Brother said they needed somebody in men's shoes.

Suttree looked at the ground and smiled and wiped his mouth with the back of his wrist and looked up again. Well, he said. I guess I'll just stick to the river for a while yet.

Well come out some evenin.

I will.

They lifted each a hand in farewell and he watched the boy go on up the tracks and then across the fields toward the road. Then he went down to the skiff and pulled the rope up and tossed it in and pushed off into the river again. The dead man was still lying on the bank under his blanket but the crowd had begun to drift away. He rowed on across the river.

He swung the skiff in beneath the bridge and shipped the oars and sat looking down at the fish. He selected a blue cat and fetched it up by the gillslots, his thumb resting in the soft yellow throat. It flexed once and was still. The oars dripped in the river. He climbed from the skiff and tied up at a stob and labored up the slick grassless bank toward the arches where the bridge went to earth. Here a dark cavern beneath the vaulted concrete with rocks piled about the entrance and a crudely lettered keep out sign slashed in yellow paint across a boulder. A fire burned in a stone cairn on the rank and sunless clay and there was an old man squatting before it. The old man looked up at him and looked back at the fire again.

I brought you a catfish, Suttree said.

He mumbled and waved his hand about. Suttree laid the fish down and the old man squinted at it and then poked among the ashes of the fire. Set down, he said.

He squatted.

The old man watched the thin flames. Slow traffic passed above them in a muted rumble. In the fire potatoes blistered and split their charred jackets with low hissing sounds like small organisms expiring on the coals. The old man speared them from the ashes, one, two, three black stones smoking. He grouped them in a rusty hubcap. Get ye a tater, he said.

Suttree lifted a hand. He did not answer because he knew that the old man would offer three times and he must parcel out his words of refusal. The old man had tilted a steaming can and was peering inside. A handful of beans boiled in riverwater. He raised his ruined eyes and looked out from under the beam of tufted bone that shaded them. I remember you now, he said. From when you was just little. Suttree didnt think so but he nodded. The old man used to go from door to door and he could make the dolls and bears to talk.

Go on and get ye a tater, he said.

Thanks, said Suttree. I've already eaten.

Raw steam rose from the mealy pith of the potato he broke in his hands. Suttree looked out toward the river.

I like a hot dinner, dont you? the old man said.

Suttree nodded. Arched sumac fronds quivered in the noon warmth and pigeons squabbled and crooned in the bridge's ribbed spandrels.

The shadowed earth in which he squatted bore the stale odor of a crypt.

You didnt see that man jump, did you? Suttree said.

He shook his head. An old ragpicker, his thin chops wobbling. I seen em draggin, he said. Did they find him?

Yes.

What did he jump for?

I dont guess he said.

I wouldnt do it. Would you?

I hope not. Did you go over in town this morning?

No, I never went. I been too poorly to go.

What's the matter?

Lord I dont know. They say death comes like a thief in the night, where is he? I'll hug his neck.

Well dont jump off the bridge.

I wouldnt do it for nothin.

They always seem to jump in hot weather.

They's worse weather to come, said the ragpicker. Hard weather. Be foretold.

Did that girl come out to see you?

Aint been nobody to see me.

He was eating the beans from the tin with a brass spoon.

I'll talk to her again, said Suttree.

Well. I wish ye'd get ye one of these here taters.

Suttree rose. I've got to get on, he said.

Dont rush off.

Got to go.

Come back.

All right.

A slight wind had come up and going back across the river he braced his feet against the uprights in the stern and pulled hard. The skiff had shipped enough water through her illjoined planks to float the morning's catch and they wandered over the cupped and paint-chipped floorboards colliding dumbly. Rag ends of caulkingstring flared from the seams and ebbed in the dirty water among bits of bait and paper and the sweeps dipped and rose and a constant sipe of riverwater sang from under the tin of one patched blade. Half awash as she was the skiff wallowed with a mercurial inertia and made heavy going. He turned upriver close to shore and went on. Black families in bright Sunday clothes fishing at the river's brim watched somberly his passage. Dinner pails and baskets adorned the grass and dark infants were displayed on blankets kept at their corners by stones against the wind.

When he reached the houseboat he shipped the oars and the skiff slewed to a stall and settled ponderously against the tirecasings nailed there. He swung himself up with the rope in one hand and made fast. The skiff bobbed and slid heavily and the bilgewater surged. The fish sculled sluggishly. Suttree stretched and rubbed his back and eyed the sun. It was already very hot. He went along the deck and pushed open the door and entered. Inside the shanty the boards seemed buckled with the heat and beads of pitch were dripping from the beams under the tin roof.

He crossed the cabin and stretched himself out on the cot. Closing his eyes. A faint breeze from the window stirring his hair. The shantyboat trembled slightly in the river and one of the steel drums beneath the floor expanded in the heat with a melancholy bong. Eyes resting. This hushed and mazy Sunday. The heart beneath the breastbone pumping. The blood on its appointed rounds. Life in small places, narrow crannies. In the leaves, the toad's pulse. The delicate cellular warfare in a waterdrop. A dextrocardiac, said the smiling doctor. Your heart's in the right place. Weathershrunk and loveless. The skin drawn and split like an overripe fruit.

He turned heavily on the cot and put one eye to a space in the rough board wall. The river flowing past out there. Cloaca Maxima. Death by drowning, the ticking of a dead man's watch. The old tin clock on Grandfather's table hammered like a foundry. Leaning to say goodbye in the little yellow room, reek of lilies and incense. He arched his neck to tell to me some thing. I never heard. He wheezed my name, his grip belied the frailty of him. His caved and wasted face. The dead would take the living with them if they could, I pulled away. Sat in an ivy garden that lizards kept with constant leathery slitherings. Hutched hares ghost pale in the shade of the carriagehouse wall. Flagstones in a rosegarden, the terraced slope of the lawn above the river, odor of boxwood and mossmold and old brick in the shadow of the springhouse. Under the watercress stones in the clear flowage cluttered with periwinkles. A salamander, troutspeckled. Leaning to suck the cold and mossy water. A rimpled child's face watching back, a watery isomer agoggle in the rings.

In my father's last letter he said that the world is run by those willing to take the responsibility for the running of it. If it is life that you feel you are missing I can tell you where to find it. In the law courts, in business, in government. There is nothing occurring in the streets. Nothing but a dumbshow composed of the helpless and the impotent.

From all old seamy throats of elders, musty books, I've salvaged not a word. In a dream I walked with my grandfather by a dark lake and the old man's talk was filled with incertitude. I saw how all things false fall from the dead. We spoke easily and I was humbly honored to walk with him deep in that world where he was a man like all men. From the small end of a corridor in the autumn woods he watched me go away to the world of the waking. If our dead kin are sainted we may rightly pray to them. Mother Church tells us so. She does not say that they'll speak back, in dreams or out. Or in what tongue the stillborn might be spoken. More common visitor. Silent. The infant's ossature, the thin and brindled bones along whose sulcate facets clove old shreds of flesh and cerements of tattered swaddle. Bones that would no more than fill a shoebox, a bulbous skull. On the right temple a mauve halfmoon.

Suttree turned and lay staring at the ceiling, touching a like mark on his own left temple gently with his fingertips. The ordinary of the second son. Mirror image. Gauche carbon. He lies in Woodlawn, whatever be left of the child with whom you shared your mother's belly. He neither spoke nor saw nor does he now. Perhaps his skull held seawater. Born dead and witless both or a terratoma grisly in form. No, for we were like to the last hair. I followed him into the world, me. A breech birth. Hind end fore in common with whales and bats, life forms meant for other mediums than the earth and having no affinity for it. And used to pray for his soul days past. Believing this ghastly circus reconvened elsewhere for alltime. He in the limbo of the Christless righteous, I in a terrestrial hell.

Through the thin and riven wall sounds of fish surging in the sinking skiff. The sign of faith. Twelfth house of the heavens. Ushering in the western church. St Peter patron of fishmongers. St Fiacre that of piles. Suttree placed one arm across his eyes. He said that he might have been a fisher of men in another time but these fish now seemed task enough for him.

It was late evening before he woke. He did not stir, lying there on the rough army blanket watching the licking shapes of light from the river's face lapse and flare over the ceiling. He felt the shanty tilt slightly, steps on the catwalk and a low trundling sound among the

14

barrels. No shade, this. Through the cracks he could see someone coming along the walk. A timorous tapping, once again.

Come in, he said.

Buddy?

He turned his head. His uncle was standing in the doorway. He looked back at the ceiling, blinked, sat up and swung his feet to the floor. Come in, John, he said.

The uncle came through the door, looking about, hesitant. He stopped in the center of the room, arrested in the quadrate bar of dusty light davited between the window and its skewed replica on the far wall, a barren countenance cruelly lit, eyes watery and half closed with their slack pendules of flesh hanging down his cheeks. His hands moved slightly with the wooden smile he managed. Hey boy, he said.

Suttree sat looking at his shoes. He folded his hands together, opened them again and looked up. Sit down, he said.

The uncle looked about, pulled the one chair back and sat carefully in it. Well, he said. How are you Buddy?

Like you see. How are you?

Fine. Fine. How is everything going?

All right. How did you find me?

I saw John Clancy up at the Eagles and he said that you were living in a houseboat or something so I looked along the river here and found you.

He was smiling uncertainly. Suttree looked at him. Did you tell them where I was?

He stopped smiling. No no, he said. No. That's your business.

All right.

How long have you been down here?

Suttree studied with a cold face the tolerant amusement his uncle affected. Since I got out, he said.

Well, we hadnt heard anything. How long has it been?

Who's we?

I hadnt heard. I mean I didnt know for sure if you were even out or not.

I got out in January.

Good, good. What, do you rent this or what?

I bought it.

Well good. He was looking about. Not bad. Stove and all.

How have you been John?

Oh, I cant complain. You know.

Suttree watched him. He looked made up for an older part, hair streaked with chalk, his face a clay mask cracked in a footman's smile.

You're looking well, said Suttree. A tic jerked his mouthcorner.

Well thanks, thanks. Try to keep fit you know. Old liver not the boot. He put the flat of his hand to his abdomen, looked up toward the ceiling, out the window where the shadows had grown long toward night. Had an operation back in the winter. I guess you didnt know.

No.

I'm pulling out of it, of course.

Suttree could smell him in the heat of the little room, the rank odor of his clothes touched with a faint reek of whiskey. Sweet smell of death at the edges. Behind him in the western wall the candled woodknots shone blood red and incandescent like the eyes of watching fiends.

I dont have a drink or I'd offer you one.

The uncle raised a palm. No, no, he said. Not for me, thanks.

He lowered one brow at Suttree. I saw your mother, he said.

Suttree didnt answer. The uncle was pulling at his cigarettes. He held out the pack. Cigarette? he said.

No thanks.

He shook the pack. Go ahead.

I dont smoke.

You used to.

I quit.

The uncle lit up and blew smoke in a thin blue viper's breath toward the window. It coiled and diffused in the yellow light. He smiled. I'd like to have a dollar for every time I quit, he said. Anyway, they're all fine. Thought I'd let you know.

I didnt think you saw them.

I saw your mother uptown.

You said.

Well. I dont get out there much, of course. I went at Christmas. You know. They left word at the Eagles for me to call one time and I dont know. Come to dinner sometime. You know. I didnt want to go out there.

I dont blame you for that.

The uncle shifted a little in his chair. Well, it's not that I dont get along with them really. I just . . .

You just cant stand them nor them you.

A funny little smile crossed the uncle's face. Well, he said. I dont think I'd go so far as to say that. Now of course they've never done me any favors.

Tell me about it, said Suttree dryly.

I guess that's right, the uncle said, nodding his head. He sucked deeply on his cigarette, reflecting. I guess you and me have a little in common there, eh boy?

He thinks so.

You should have known my father. He was a fine man. The uncle was looking down at his hands uncertainly. Yes, he said. A fine man.

I remember him.

He died when you were a baby.

I know.

The uncle took another tack. You ought to come up to the Eagles some night, he said. I could get you in. They have a dance on Saturday night. They have some goodlooking women come up there. You'd be surprised.

I guess I would.

Suttree had leaned back against the raw plank wall. A blue dusk filled the little cabin. He was looking out the window where nighthawks had come forth and swifts shied chittering over the river.

You're a funny fella, Buddy. I cant imagine anyone being more different from your brother.

Which one?

What?

I said which one.

Which what?

Which brother.

The uncle chuckled uneasily. Why, he said, you've just got the one. Carl.

Couldnt they think of a name for the other one?

What other one? What in the hell are you talking about?

The one that was born dead.

Who told you that?

I remembered it.

Who told you?

You did.

I never. When did I?

Years ago. You were drunk.

I never did.

All right. You didnt.

What difference does it make?

I dont know. I just wondered why it was supposed to be a secret. What did he die of?

He was stillborn.

I know that.

I dont know why. He just was. You were both premature. You swear I told you?

It's not important.

You wont say anything will you?

No. I was just wondering about it. What the doctor says for instance. I mean, you have to take them both home, only one you take in a bag or a box. I guess they have people to take care of these things.

Just dont say anything.

Suttree was leaning forward looking down at his cheap and rotting shoes where they lay crossed on the floor. God, John, dont worry about it. I wont.

Okay.

Dont tell them you saw me.

Okay. Fair enough. That's a deal.

Right John. A deal.

I dont see them anyway.

So you said.

The uncle shifted in the chair and pulled at his collar with a long yellow forefinger. He could have helped me, you know. I never asked him for anything. Never did, by God. He could have helped me.

Well, said Suttree, he didnt.

The uncle nodded, watching the floor. You know, he said, you and me are a lot alike.

I dont think so.

In some ways.

No, said Suttree. We're not alike.

Well, I mean . . . the uncle waved his hand.

That's his thesis. But I'm not like you.

Well, you know what I mean.

I do know what you mean. But I'm not like you. I'm not like him. I'm not like Carl. I'm like me. Dont tell me who I'm like.

Well now look, Buddy, there's no need . . .

I think there is a need. I dont want you down here either. I know they dont like you, he doesnt. I dont blame you. It's not your fault. I cant do anything.

The uncle narrowed his eyes at Suttree. No need to get on your high horse with me, he said. At least I was never in the goddamned penitentiary.

Suttree smiled. The workhouse, John. It's a little different. But I am what I am. I dont go around telling people that I've been in a T B sanitarium.

So? I dont claim to be a teetotaler, if that's what you're getting at.

Are you an alcoholic?

No. What are you smiling at? I'm no goddamned alcoholic.

He always called you a rummy. I guess that's not quite as bad.

I dont give a damn what he says. He can . . .

Go ahead.

The uncle looked at him warily. He flipped the tiny stub of his cigarette out the door. Well, he said. He dont know everything.

Look, said Suttree, leaning forward. When a man marries beneath him his children are beneath him. If he thinks that way at all. If you werent a drunk he might see me with different eyes. As it is, my case was always doubtful. I was expected to turn out badly. My grandfather used to say Blood will tell. It was his favorite saying. What are you looking at? Look at me.

I dont know what you're talking about.

Yes you do. I'm saying that my father is contemptuous of me because I'm related to you. Dont you think that's a fair statement?

I dont know why you try and blame me for your troubles. You and your crackpot theories.

Suttree reached across the little space and took his uncle's willowing hands and composed them. I dont blame you, he said. I just want to tell you how some people are.

I know how people are. I should know.

Why should you? You think my father and his kind are a race apart. You can laugh at their pretensions, but you never question their right to the way of life they maintain.

He puts his pants on the same way I do mine.

Bullshit, John. You dont even believe that.

I said it didnt I?

What do you suppose he thinks of his wife?

They get along okay.

They get along okay.

Yeah.

John, she's a housekeeper. He has no real belief even in her goodness. Cant you guess that he sees in her traces of the same sorriness he sees in you? An innocent gesture can call you to mind.

Dont call me sorry, said the uncle.

He probably believes that only his own benevolent guidance kept her out of the whorehouse.

That's my sister you're talking about, boy.

She's my mother, you maudlin sot.

Sudden quiet in the little cabin. The uncle rose shaking, his voice was low. They were right, he said. What they told me. They were right about you. You're a vicious person. A nasty vicious person.

Suttree sat with his forehead in his hands. The uncle moved warily to the door. His shadow fell across Suttree and Suttree raised his head.

Maybe it's like colorblindness, he said. The women are just carriers. You are colorblind, arent you?

At least I'm not crazy.

No, Suttree said. Not crazy.

The uncle's narrowed eyes seemed to soften. God help you, he said. He turned and stepped onto the catwalk and went down the boards. Suttree rose and went to the door. The uncle was crossing the fields in the last of the day's light toward the darkening city.

John, he called.

He looked back. But that old man seemed so glassed away in worlds of his own contrivance that Suttree only raised his hand. The uncle nodded like a man who understood and then went on.

The cabin was almost dark and Suttree walked around on the little deck and kicked up a stool and sat leaning back against the wall of the houseboat with his feet propped on the railing. A breeze was coming off the river bearing a faint odor of oil and fish. Night sounds and laughter drifted from the yellow shacks beyond the railspur and the river spooled past highbacked and hissing in the dark at his feet like the seething of sand in a glass, wind in a desert, the slow voice of ruin. He wedged his knuckles in his eyesockets and rested his head against the boards. They were still warm from the sun, like a faint breath at his nape. Across the river the lights of the lumber company lay foreshort and dismembered in the black water and downriver the strung bridgelamps hung in catenary replica shore to shore and softly guttering under the wind's faint chop. The tower clock in the courthouse tolled the half hour. Lonely bell in the city. A firefly there. And there. He rose and spat into the river and went down the catwalk to the shore and across the field toward the road.

He walked up Front Street breathing in the cool of the evening, the western sky before him still a deep cyanic blue shot through with the shapes of bats crossing blind and spastic like spores on a slide. A rank smell of boiled greens hung in the night and a thread of radio music followed him house by house. He went by yards and cinder gardens rank with the mutes of roosting fowls and by dark grottoes among the shacks where the music flared and died again and past dim window-lights where shadows reeled down cracked and yellowed paper shades. Through reeking clapboard warrens where children cried and craven halfbald watchdogs yapped and slank.

He climbed the hill toward the edge of the city, past the open door of the negro meetinghouse. Softly lit within. A preacher that looked like a storybook blackbird in his suit and goldwire spectacles. Suttree coming up out of this hot and funky netherworld attended by gospel music. Dusky throats tilted and veined like the welted flanks of horses. He has watched them summer nights, a pale pagan sat on the curb without. One rainy night nearby he heard news in his toothfillings, music softly. He was stayed in a peace that drained his mind, for even a false adumbration of the world of the spirit is better than none at all.

Up these steep walkways cannelured for footpurchase, the free passage of roaches. To tap at this latched door leaning. Jimmy Smith's brown rodent teeth just beyond the screen. There is a hole in the rotten fabric which perhaps his breath has made over the years. Down a long hallway lit by a single sulphurcolored lightbulb hung from a cord in the ceiling. Smith's shuffling slippers rasp over the linoleum. He turns at the end of the hall, holding the door there. The slack yellow skin of his shoulders and chest so bloodless and lined that he appears patched up out of odd scraps and remnants of flesh, tacked with lap seams and carefully bound in the insubstantial and foul gray web of his undershirt. In the little kitchen two men are sitting at a table drinking whiskey. A third leans against a stained refrigerator. There is an open door giving onto a porch, a small buckled portico of gray boards that hangs in the dark above the river. The rise and fall of cigarettes tells the occupants. There are sounds of laughter and a bloated whore looks out into the kitchen and goes away again.

What'll you have, Sut.

A beer.

The man leaning against the refrigerator moves slightly to one side. What say Bud, he says.

Hey Junior.

Jimmy Smith has opened a can of beer and holds it toward Suttree. He pays and the owner deals up change out of his loathsome breeks and counts the coins into Suttree's palm and shuffles away.

Who's back in the back?

Bunch of drunks. Brother's back there.

Suttree tipped a swallow of the beer against the back of his throat. It was cold and good. Well, he said. Let me go back there and see him.

He nodded to the two men at the table and went past and down the corridor and entered an enormous old drawing room with high sliding doors long painted fast in their tracks. Five men sat at a card table, none looked up. The room was otherwise barren, a white marble fireplace masked with a sheet of tin, old varnished wainscoting and a high stamped rococo ceiling with parget scrolls and beaded drops of brazing about the gasjet where a lightbulb now burned.

Surrounded as they were in this crazed austerity by the remnants of a former grandeur the poker players seemed themselves like shades of older times or rude imposters on a stage set. They drank and bet and muttered in an air of electric transiency, old men in gaitered sleeves galvanized from some stained sepia, posting time at cards prevenient of their dimly augured doom. Suttree passed on through.

In the front room was a broken sofa propped on bricks, nothing more. One wonky spring reared from the back with a beercan seized in its coils and deeply couched in the mousecolored and napless upholstery sat a row of drunks.

Hey Suttree, they called.

Goddamn, said J-Bone, surging from the bowels of the couch. He threw an arm around Suttree's shoulders. Here's my old buddy, he said. Where's the whiskey? Give him a drink of that old crazy shit.

How you doing, Jim?

I'm doin everybody I can, where you been? Where's the whiskey? Here ye go. Get ye a drink, Bud.

What is it?

Early Times. Best little old drink in the world. Get ye a drink, Sut.

Suttree held it to the light. Small twigs, debris, matter, coiled in the oily liquid. He shook it. Smoke rose from the yellow floor of the bottle. Shit almighty, he said.

Best little old drink in the world, sang out J-Bone. Have a drink, Bud.

He unthreaded the cap, sniffed, shivered, drank.

J-Bone hugged the drinking figure. Watch old Suttree take a drink, he called out.

Suttree's eyes were squeezed shut and he was holding the bottle out to whoever would take it. Goddamn. What is that shit?

Early Times, called J-Bone. Best little old drink they is. Drink that and you wont feel a thing the next mornin.

Or any morning.

Whoo lord, give it here. Hello Early, come to your old daddy.

Here, pour some of it in this cup and let me cut it with Coca-Cola.

Cant do it, Bud.

Why not?

We done tried it. It eats the bottom out.

Watch it Suttree. Dont spill none on your shoes.

Hey Bobbyjohn.

When's old Callahan gettin out? said Bobbyjohn.

I dont know. Sometime this month. When have you seen Bucket?

He's moved to Burlington, the Bucket has. He dont come round no more.

Come set with us, Sut.

J-Bone steered him by the arm. Set down, Bud. Set down.

Suttree eased himself down on the arm of the sofa and sipped his beer. He patted J-Bone on the back. The voices seemed to fade. He waved away the whiskeybottle with a smile. In this tall room, the cracked plaster sootstreaked with the shapes of laths beneath, this barrenness, this fellowship of the doomed. Where life pulsed obscenely fecund. In the drift of voices and the laughter and the reek of stale beer the Sunday loneliness seeped away.

Aint that right Suttree?

What's that?

About there bein caves all in under the city.

That's right.

What all's down there in em?

Blind slime. As above, so it is below. Suttree shrugged. Nothing that I know of, he said. They're just some caves.

They say there's one that runs plumb underneath the river.

That's the one that comes out over in Chilhowee Park. They was supposed to of used it in the Civil War to hide stuff down there.

Wonder what all's down in there now.

Shit if I know. Ast Suttree.

You reckon you can still get down in them Civil War caves, Sut?

I dont know. I always heard there was one ran under the river but I never heard of anybody that was ever in it.

There might be them Civil War relics down there.

Here comes one of them now, said J-Bone. What say, Nigger.

Suttree looked toward the door. A graylooking man in glasses was watching them. I caint say, he said. How you boys? What are ye drinkin?

Early Times, Jim says it is.

Get ye a drink, Nig.

He shuffled toward the bottle, nodding to all, small eyes moving rapidly behind the glasses. He seized the whiskey and drank, his slack gullet jerking. When he lowered it his eyes were closed and his face a twisted mask. Pooh! He blew a volatile mist toward the smiling watchers. Lord God what is that?

Early Times, Nig, cried J-Bone.

Early tombs is more like it.

Lord honey I know they make that old splo in the bathtub but this here is made in the toilet. He was looking at the bottle, shaking it. Bubbles the size of gooseshot veered greasily up through the smoky fuel it held.

It'll make ye drunk, said J-Bone.

Nig shook his head and blew and took another drink and handed over the bottle with his face averted in agony. When he could speak he said: Boys, I've fought some bad whiskey but I'm a dirty nigger if that there aint almost too sorry to drink.

J-Bone waved the bottle toward the door where Junior stood grinning. Brother, dont you want a drink?

Junior shook his head.

Boys, scoot over and let the old Nigger set down.

Here Nig, set here. Scoot over some, Bearhunter.

Lord boys if I aint plumb give out. He took off his glasses and wiped his weepy eyes.

What you been up to, Nig?

I been tryin to raise some money about Bobby. He turned and looked up at Suttree. Dont I know you? he said.

We drank a few beers together.

I thought I remembered ye. Did you not know Bobby?

I saw him a time or two.

Nigger shook his head reflectively. I raised four boys and damned if they aint all in the penitentiary cept Ralph. Of course we all went to Jordonia. And they did have me up here in the workhouse one time but I slipped off. Old Blackburn was guard up there knowed me but he never would say nothin. Was you in Jordonia? Clarence says they aint nothin to it now. Boys, when I was in there it was rougher'n a old cob. Course they didnt send ye there for singin in a choir. I done three year for stealin. Tried to get sent to T S I where they learn ye a trade but you had to be tardy to get in down there and they said I wasnt tardy. I was eighteen when I come out of Jordonia and that was in nineteen and sixteen. I wisht I could understand them boys of mine. They have costed me. I spent eighteen thousand dollars gettin them boys out. Their grandaddy was never in the least trouble that you could think of and he lived to be eighty-seven year old. Now he'd take a drink. Which I do myself. But he was never in no trouble with the law.

Get ye a drink, Sut.

Nigger intercepted the bottle. You know Jim? He's a fine boy. Dont think he aint. I wisht McAnally Flats was full of em just like him. I knowed his daddy. He was smaller than Junior yonder. Just a minute. Whew. Damn if that aint some whiskey. He wouldnt take nothin off nobody, Irish Long wouldnt. I remember he come over on what they used to call Woolen Mill Corners there one time. You know where it's at Jim. Where Workers Cafe is at. Come over there one Sunday mornin huntin a man and they was a bunch of tush hogs all standin around out there under a shed used to be there, you boys wouldnt remember it, drinkin whiskey and was friends of this old boy's, and Irish Long walked up to em and wanted to know where he's at. Well, they wouldnt say, but they wasnt a one of them tush hogs ast what he wanted with him. He would mortally whip your ass if you messed with him, Irish Long would. And they wasnt nobody in McAnally no betterhearted. He give away everthing he owned. He'd of been rich if he wanted. Had them stores. Nobody didnt have no money, people couldnt buy their groceries. You boys dont remember the depression. He'd tell em just go on and get what they needed. Flour and taters. Milk for the babies. He never turned down nobody, Irish Long never. They is people livin in this town today in big houses that would of starved plumb to death cept for him but they aint big enough to own it.

Better get ye a drink there Sut, fore Nigger drinks it all.

Give Bearhunter a drink, Suttree said.

How about givin Bobbyjohn a drink, said Bobbyjohn.

There's a man'll take a drink, said Nigger. Dont think he wont

Which I will myself, said J-Bone.

Which I will my damnself, said Nigger.

Jimmy Smith was moving through the room like an enormous trained mole collecting the empty cans. He shuffled out, his small eyes blinking. Kenneth Hazelwood stood in the doorframe watching them all with a sardonic smile.

Come in here, Worm, called J-Bone. Get ye a drink of this good whiskey.

Hazelwood entered smiling and took the bottle. He tilted it and sniffed and gave it back.

The last time I drank some of that shit I like to died. I stunk from the inside out. I laid in a tub of hot water all day and climbed out and dried and you could still smell it. I had to burn my clothes. I had the dry heaves, the drizzlin shits, the cold shakes and the jakeleg. I can think about it now and feel bad.

Hell Worm, this is good whusk.

I pass.

Worm's put down my whiskey, Bud.

I think you better put it down before it puts you down. You'll find your liver in your sock some morning.

But J-Bone had turned away with a whoop. Early Times, he called. Make your liver quiver.

Hazelwood grinned and turned to Suttree. Cant you take no better care of him than that? he said.

Suttree shook his head.

Me and Katherine's goin out to the Trocadero. Come on go with us.

I better get home, Kenneth.

Come ride out there with us. We'll bring you back.

I remember the last time I went for a ride with you. You got us in three fights, kicked some woman's door in, and got in jail. I ran through some yards and like to hung myself on a clothesline and got a bunch of dogs after me and spotlights zippin around and cops all over the place and I wound up spendin the night in a corrugated conduit with a cat.

Worm grinned. Come on, he said. We'll just have a drink and see what all's goin on out there.

I cant, Kenneth. I'm broke anyway.

I didnt ast ye if you had any money.

Hey Worm, did you see old Crumbliss in the paper this mornin?

What's he done now?

They found him about six oclock this mornin under a tree in a big alfalfa field. He found the only tree in the whole field and run into it. They said when the cops come and opened the door old Crumbliss fell out and just laid there. Directly he looked up and seen them blue suits and he jumped up and hollered, said: Where is that man I hired to drive me home?

Suttree rose grinning.

Dont run off, Sut.

I've got to go.

Where you goin?

I've got to get something to eat. I'll see you all later.

Jimmy Smith fell in with him to see him to the door, down the long corridor, mole and guest, an unlatching of the screendoor and so into the night.

It is overcast with impending rain and the lights of the city wash against the curdled heavens, lie puddled in the wet black streets. The watertruck recedes down Locust with its footmen in their tattered oilskins wielding brooms in the flooded gutters and the air is rich with the odor of damp paving. Through the midnight emptiness the few sounds carry with amphoric hollow and the city in its quietude seems to lie under edict. The buildings lean upon the dim and muted corridors where the watchman's heels click away the minutes. Past black and padlocked shopfronts. A poultrydresser's window where half-naked cockerels nod in a constant blue dawn. Clockchime and belltoll lonely in the brooding sleepfast town. The gutted rusting trucks on Market Street with their splayed tires pooling on the tar. The flowers and fruit are gone and the sewer grates festooned with wilted greens. Under the fanned light of a streetlamp a white china cuphandle curled like a sleeping slug.

In the lobbies of the slattern hotels the porters and bellmen are napping in the chairs and lounges, dark faces jerking in their sleep down the worn wine plush. In the rooms lie drunken homecome soldiers sprawled in painless crucifixion on the rumpled counterpanes and the whores are sleeping now. Small tropic fish start and check in the mossgreen deeps of the eyedoctor's shopwindow. A lynx rampant with a waxen snarl. Gouts of shredded wood sprout from the sutures in his leather belly and his glass eyes bulge in agony. Dim tavern, an alleymouth where ashcans gape and where in a dream I was stopped by a man I took to be my father, dark figure against the shadowed brick. I would go by but he has stayed me with his hand. I have been looking for you, he said. The wind was cold, dreamwinds are so, I had been hurrying. I would draw back from him and his bone grip. The knife he held severed the pallid lamplight like a thin blue fish and our footsteps amplified themselves in the emptiness of the streets to an echo of routed multitudes. Yet it was not my father but my son who accosted me with such rancorless intent.

On Gay Street the traffic lights are stilled. The trolleyrails gleam in their beds and a late car passes with a long slish of tires. In the long arcade of the bus station footfalls come back like laughter. He marches darkly toward his darkly marching shape in the glass of the depot door. His fetch come up from life's other side like an autoscopic hallucination, Suttree and Antisuttree, hand reaching to the hand. The door swung back and he entered the waiting room. The shapes of figures sleeping on the wooden benches lay like laundry. In the men's room an elderly pederast leaning against a wall.

Suttree washed his hands and went out past the pinball machines to the grill. He took a stool and studied the menu. The waitress stood tapping her pencil against the pad of tickets she held.

Suttree looked up. Grilled cheese and coffee.

She wrote. He watched.

She tore off the ticket and placed it facedown on the marble counter and moved away. He watched the shape of her underclothes through the thin white uniform. In the rear of the cafe a young black labored in a clatter of steaming crockery. Suttree rubbed his eyes.

She came with the coffee, setting it down with a click and the coffee tilting up the side of the pink plastic cup and flooding the saucer. He poured it back and sipped. Acridity of burnt socks. She returned with napkin, spoon. Ring of gold orangeblossoms constricting her puffy finger. He took another sip of the coffee. In a few minutes she came with the sandwich. He held the first wedge of it to his nose for a minute, rich odor of toast and butter and melting cheese. He bit off an enormous mouthful, sucked the pickle from the toothpick and closed his eyes, chewing.

When he had finished he took the quarter from his pocket and laid it on the counter and rose. She was watching him from beyond the coffee urn.

You want some more coffee? she said.

No thank you.

Come back, she said.

Suttree shoved the door with his shoulder, one hand in his pocket, the other working the toothpick. A face rose from a near bench and looked at him blearily and subsided.

He walked along Gay Street, pausing by storewindows, fine goods kept in glass. A police cruiser passed slowly. He moved on, from out of his eyecorner watching them watch. Past Woodruff's, Clark and Jones, the theatres. Corners emptied of their newspedlars and trash scuttling in the wind. He went down to the end of the town and walked out on the bridge and placed his hands on the cool iron rail and looked at the river below. The bridgelights trembled in the black eddywater like chained and burning supplicants and along the riverfront a gray mist moved in over the ashen fields of sedge and went ferreting among the dwellings. He folded his arms on the rail. Out there a jumbled shackstrewn waste dimly lit. Kindlingwood cottages, gardens of rue. A patchwork of roofs canted under the pale blue cones of lamplight where moths aspire in giddy coils. Little plots of corn, warped purlieus of tillage in the dead spaces shaped by constriction and want like the lives of the dark and bitter husbandmen who have this sparse harvest for their own out of all the wide earth's keeping.

Small spills of rain had started, cold on his arm. Downstream recurving shore currents chased in deckle light wave on wave like silver spawn. To fall through dark to darkness. Struggle in those opaque and fecal deeps, which way is up. Till the lungs suck brown sewage and funny lights go down the final corridors of the brain, small watchmen to see that all is quiet for the advent of eternal night.

The courthouse clock tolled two. He raised his face. There you can see the illumined dial suspended above the town with not even a shadow to mark the tower. A cheshire clock hung in the void like a strange hieroglyphic moon. Suttree palmed the water from his face. The smoky yellow windowlight in the houseboat of Abednego Jones went dark. Below he could make out the shape of his own place where he must go. High over the downriver land lightning quaked soundlessly and ceased. Far clouds rimlit. A brimstone light. Are there dragons in the wings of the world? The rain was falling harder, falling past him toward the river. Steep rain leaning in the lamplight, across the clock's face. Hard weather, says the old man. So may it be. Wrap me in the weathers of the earth, I will be hard and hard. My face will turn rain like the stones.

He came up from the back lot threading his way among the shapes of castoff and broken and useless debris rotting under the late summer sun. Old tires and bricks and broken jars. A rusty chicken-feeder. He squinched his nose at the rank odor of washwater in the air and he threw a rock he was carrying at the tethered goat. The goat raised its chin from the grass and looked at him with its strange goat's eyes and lowered its head to graze again. He went on around the corner of the house to the front porch where a green and white washingmachine shuddered and churned and over which stood a young woman with a soapy paddle clubbed in her hands as if defying the first insurgent rag to rear from the slateblue and foamless water in which the week's wash moiled.

Hidy, he said.

She moved, her weight bringing up out of the spongy boards beneath her shoes a black seepage. She did not look nor answer.

Old Orville aint been by is he?

She laid the paddle across the washer where it slurred into concatenate images with the motion of the machine and began to slide off slowly. She wiped her forehead with the hem of her apron. No, she said. He aint been here.

He looked toward the open door of the house. What does she want now? he said.

What do you care?

I just ast.

She didnt answer. He propped his foot on the porch and spat, watching out across the dead clay yard at nothing at all.

The paddle dropped to the floor and she stooped and got it and began to dig at the clothes, her breasts pendulous and bobbing with the movement of her shoulders. Blue curded washwater dripped from the end of the porch into a puddle of gray scum. When she looked at him he had not moved. She tossed her hair and tilted one shoulder forward, blotting the sweat from her upper lip. She pouted and blew the hair from her eyes. Why dont you grub some of them weeds out of the tomatoes for me if you aint got nothin else to do, she said.

He sat down facing out across the yard. He put one finger in his ear and jiggled it and she bent to the washer again.

After a while a thin voice came again from the rear of the house. She stopped and looked at him. See what she wants, will ye?

He spat. I didnt take her to raise, he said.

She lifted her bleached and wrinkled hands from the water and wiped them on the front of her dress. All right, Mama, she called. Just a minute.

When she came back out he was hanging by his elbows in the wire fence that ran along the little lane the house faced and he was talking to another boy. They left together. He came back for his supper and went out again and stayed until past dark. Just before midnight she heard him leave the house again.

He listened at her door and then went on to the front room where he sat on the daybed and donned his shoes. Then he was out in the warm August night, lush and tactile, the door set shut with a faint cry of the keeperspring, down the path through the gate and into the lane. When he came out on the pike he could feel the day's warmth from the macadam through his thin shoesoles and he could smell it, musky and faintly antiseptic. He went up the pike at a jog.

He went solitary and starlit through the sleepfast countryside, trotting soundlessly on his softworn shoes, past dead houses and dark land with the odor of ripe and humid fruits breathing in the fields and nightbirds crying in the keep of enormous trees. The road climbed up out of the woods and went on through farmland and he slowed to a walk, his hands slung in his hippockets and his elbows flapping, taking a dirt road down to the right, padding along soft as a dog, sniffing the rank grass and the odor of dust the dew had laid.

He crossed the tracks of the railway and loped into the growth on the far side wiping his nose with his sleeve as he went and casting his eyes about, passing along a high revetment of honeysuckle and then through a patch of cane and coming at last along the edge of a field where his old tracks had packed the clay in a furrow you could follow in the dark and his shape washed shadowless across a backdrop of sumac and sassafras. He could see the house beyond in darkness against the starblown sky and the barn behind it rising outsize and stark. He was going along the troughs in the heavy turned earth, past cornrows, the shellbrown spears on his arms with fine teeth, into the open field where the melons lay.

There were no more than a quarteracre of them, a long black rectangle set along the edge of the corn in which by the meager starlight of late summer he could see the plump forms supine and dormant in spaced rows. He listened. In the distance a dog was yapping and in his keen ears the blind passage of gnats sounded incessantly. He knelt in the rich and steaming earth, his nostrils filled with the winey smell of ruptured melons. To steal upon them where they lay, his hand on their warm ripe shapes, his pocketknife open. He lifted one, a pale jade underbelly turning up. He pulled it between his knees and sank the blade of the knife into its nether end. He shucked off the straps of his overalls. His pale shanks kneeling in a pool of denim.

A whippoorwill had begun to call and with his ear to the ground this way he began to hear the train too. A star arced long and dying down the sky. He raised his head and looked toward the house. Nothing moved. The train had come on and her harpiethroated highball wailed down the lonely summer night. He could hear the wheels shucking along the rails and he could feel the ground shudder and he could hear the tone of the trucks shift at the crossing and the huffing breath of the boiler and the rattle and clank and wheelclick and couplingclacking and then the last long shunting on the downgrade drawing on toward the distance and the low moan bawling across the sleeping land and fading and the caboose clicking away to final silence. He rose and adjusted his clothes and went back along the rows of corn to the woods and to the road and set himself toward home again.

Brogans stood in the tracks he left. Walking up, back, turning. Toeing the bunged melons lying in the sun. A slow spout of black ants pluming forth. A yellowjacket.

He came again that night. In a persimmon tree at the edge of the field a mockingbird whistled him back but he would not hear. Down past the corn he came and into the dark of the melonpatch with stark wooden lubricity, looking once toward the lightless house and then going to his knees in the rich and wineslaked loam.

When the light of the sealedbeam cut over the field he was lying prone upon a watermelon with his overalls about his knees. The beam swept past, stopped, returned to fix upon his alabaster nates looming moonlike out of the dark. He rose vertically, pale, weightless, like some grim tellurian wraith, up over the violated fruit with arms horrible and off across the fields hauling wildly at the folds of old rank denim that hobbled him.

Hold it, a voice called.

He had no ear for such news. The dry bracken that rimmed the field crashed about him. He crossed the stand of cane in a series of diminishing reports and went over the top of the honeysuckle in graceful levitation and lit in the road in the lights of a car rounding the curve. The car braked and slewed in the gravel. A crazed figure dressing on the run blown out of the dark wall of summer green and into the road. In the distance the train called for the crossing.

Two pairs of brogans went along the rows.

You aint goin to believe this.

Knowin you for a born liar I most probably wont.

Somebody has been fuckin my watermelons.

What?

I said somebody has been . . .

No. No. Hell no. Damn you if you aint got a warped mind.

I'm tellin you . . .

I dont want to hear it.

Looky here.

And here.

They went along the outer row of the melonpatch. He stopped to nudge a melon with his toe. Yellowjackets snarled in the seepage. Some were ruined a good time past and lay soft with rot, wrinkled with imminent collapse.

It does look like it, dont it?

I'm tellin ye I seen him. I didnt know what the hell was goin on when he dropped his drawers. Then when I seen what he was up to I still didnt believe it. But yonder they lay.

What do you aim to do?

Hell, I dont know. It's about too late to do anything. He's damn near screwed the whole patch. I dont see why he couldnt of stuck to just one. Or a few.

Well, I guess he takes himself for a lover. Sort of like a sailor in a whorehouse.

I reckon what it was he didnt take to the idea of gettin bit on the head of his pecker by one of them waspers. I suppose he showed good judgment there.

What was he, just a young feller?

I dont know about how young he was but he was as active a feller as I've seen in a good while.

Well. I dont reckon he'll be back.

I dont know. A man fast as he is ought not to be qualmy about goin anywheres he took a notion. To steal or whatever.

What if he does come back?

I'll catch him if he does.

And then what?

Well. I dont know. Be kindly embarrassin now I think about it. I'd get some work out of him is what I'd do.

Ought to, I reckon. I dont know.

You reckon to call the sheriff?

And tell him what?

They were walking slowly along the rows.

It's just the damndest thing I ever heard of. Aint it you? What are you grinnin at? It aint funny. A thing like that. To me it aint.

Once she had moved beyond the shadow of the smokehouse he could not see her anymore. He could hear the dull chop of the hoe among the withered yardflowers as she progressed with bland patience along the little garden she had planted there, her and the hoe in shadow oblique and thin. And the chop and clink of the shadow blade in the stony ground. Or she came up from the springhouse lugging a shrunken bucket that sprayed thin fans of water from between the slats and left a damp and trampled swath out to the flowerbeds and back. He sat on the porch with his feet crossed and fashioned knots in weedstems.

Finally it rained. It rained all one afternoon and at dusk the burnt grass stood in water and it rained on into the night. By the time he left the house it had quit and the sky was clearing but he would not turn back.

He waited and waited at the field's edge watching the house and listening. From the dark of the corn they saw him pass, lean and angular, a slavering nightshade among the moonsprung vines, over the shadowed blue and furrowed summer land. They gripped each other's arm.

It's him.

I hope it is. I'd hate to think of there bein two of em.

Before them in the field there appeared sudden and apparitional a starkly pale set of legs galvanized out of the night like a pair of white flannel drawers.

34

Thow the light to him.

He aint mounted.

Thow it to him.

He was standing in the middle of the patch facing them, blinking, his overalls about his ankles.

Hold it right there, old buddy. Dont move.

But he did. He caught up the bib of his overalls in both hands and turned to run. The voice called out again. He had the straps clenched in his fist, making for the field's edge. The train bawled twice out there in the darkness. Now beg God's mercy, lecher. Unnatural. Finger coiled, blind sight, a shadow. Smooth choked oiled pipe pointing judgment and guilt. Done in a burst of flame. Could I call back that skeltering lead.

He was lying on the ground with his legs trapped in his overalls and he was screaming Oh God, Oh God. The man still holding the smoking gun stood about him like a harried bird. The blood oozing from that tender puckered skin in the gray moonlight undid him. Shit, he said. Aw shit. He knelt, flinging the gun away from him. The other man picked it up and stood by. Hush now, he said. Goddamn. Hush.

Lights from the house limn them and their sorry tableau. The boy is rolling in the rich damp earth screaming and the man keeps saying for him to hush, kneeling there, not touching him.

The deputy held the car door and he climbed out and they entered a building of solid concrete. The first deputy handed Harrogate's papers to a man at a small window. The man looked through the papers and signed them. Harrogate stood in the hall.

Harrogate, the man said.

Yessir.

He looked him over. Goddamn if you aint a sadsack, he said. Walk on down to that door.

Harrogate walked down the corridor to an iron barred door. The other deputy had emerged from a side door with a cup of coffee. He had his thumb stuck in his belt and he blew on the coffee and sipped at it. He did not look at Harrogate.

After a while the man came down the hall with a big brass ring of keys. He opened the gate and pointed for Harrogate to enter. He shut the gate behind them and locked it and turned and went up a flight of concrete stairs. There were two men in striped pants and jumpers sitting there smoking. They scooted against the wall to let the man pass. Harrogate had started up the stairs when one of them spoke to him.

You better not go up there if he aint said to.

He came back down again.

When the man reappeared he had a young black with him. The black wore stripes too. The man opened the door to a large cell and they entered. The black looked at Harrogate and shook his head and went on through to a door at the rear. There was a little window in the wall and Harrogate could see him in there thumbing through stacks of clothing on a shelf.

Strip out of them clothes and take a shower yonder, said the man.

Harrogate looked around. In the center of the room was a stained porcelain trough with a row of dripping taps hung from a pipe. In each corner at the front of the cell was a concrete wall about as high as Harrogate. Behind one wall there were three toilets and behind the other there were two showers. While he was looking at the showers a dry towel hit him in the back of the head and fell to the floor.

You better get on some kind of time, the man said. Harrogate picked up the towel and put it around his neck and undid his shirt and peeled out of it and laid it on a bench by the wall. Then he unbuttoned his trousers and stepped out of them and laid them across the shirt. He looked like a dressed chicken, his skin puckered with the shotwounds still red and fresh looking. He raised his shoes each and slid them from his feet without untying the laces. The concrete floor was cold. He crossed to the showers and peered at them, their valves and spouts.

I aint goin to tell you again, said the man.

I dont know how, said Harrogate.

The black boy at the window turned his face away.

The man looked up at this news with what seemed to be real interest. You dont know how to what? he said.

How to run a shower.

What are you, a fuckin smart-ass?

No sir.

You mean to tell me you aint never took a shower?

I aint never even seen one.

The man turned and looked back down the hall. Hey, George?

Yeah.

Come in here a minute.

A second man looked in. What is it? he said.

Tell him what you just told me.

I aint never even seen one? said Harrogate.

Seen what?

A shower. He dont know how to take a shower.

The second man looked him over. Does he know where he shit last? he said.

I doubt it.

It was down at the county jail, said Harrogate.

I think you got a smart-ass on your hands.

I think I got a dumb-ass is what I got. You see them there handles? These here?

Them there. You turn em and water comes out of that there pipe.

Harrogate stepped into the shower stall and turned the taps. He picked a slab of used soap from a niche in the wall and soaped himself and adjusted the taps, stepping under the shower carefully so as not to wet his hair. When he was done he turned off the shower and took the towel down from where he'd hung it over the top of the partition and dried himself and crossed the floor to where he'd left his clothes. He had one leg in his trousers when the black spoke to him.

Hold it, little buddy.

He paused on one leg.

Bring them over here.

Harrogate collected his clothes and carried them to the window. The black took them and hung them on a hanger gingerly with two fingers. The man was sorting about behind him.

It's hangin on the nail yonder, the black said.

Harrogate was sitting naked on the bench. The man came out with a longhandled spraygun. He stood up.

Raise your arms.

He did. The man pumped the sprayer and squirted his armpit.

Shoo, said Harrogate. What's that for?

Bugs, said the guard. Turn around.

I aint got no bugs.

You aint now, said the man. He sprayed under the other arm and then gave Harrogate a good spraying over his sparse pubic hair. Get them crotch crickets too, he said. When he was done he stepped back. Harrogate stood with his arms aloft like a robbery victim.

Damn if you aint just barely feathered, said the man. How old are you?

Eighteen, said Harrogate.

Eighteen.

Yessir.

You just did get in under the wire, didnt ye?

I reckon.

What's these here?

That's where I's shot.

The man looked from his skinny body to his face again. Shot, eh? he said. He handed the spraygun through the window to the black and the black hung the gun back up behind him and pushed a folded set of stripes through the window at Harrogate.

Harrogate unfolded the suit and looked at it. He held the shirt in his teeth while he flapped the trousers out and started to step into them.

Aint you got no underwear? said the man.

No.

The man shook his head. Harrogate stood on one leg. He took a little hop to capture his balance.

Go on, said the man. If you aint got any you aint got any.

He dressed and stood barefoot. The trousers ran down over his feet and onto the floor and just his fingertips hung from the sleeves of the jumper. He looked at the black in the window.

Dont look at me, said the black. Them's the smallest they come. Roll them sleeves and pants up. You'll be all right.

Harrogate rolled the sleeves back two turns. The clothes were clean and rough against his skin. Do I wear my own shoes? he said.

You wear your own shoes.

The smallest prisoner crossed the floor and stepped into his shoes and clattered back to the window. The man looked him over sadly and handed him a blanket. Let's go, he said.

Harrogate followed him out and up the stairs, shuffling along, a slight limp. At the top of the stairs they turned down a hall past huge barred cages like the one they'd left. At the end of the hall sat a man at a table reading a magazine. He rose smiling and placed the magazine facedown on the table.

The man was sorting through the keys. I think they ought to've thrown thisn back, Ed, what do you think?

Ed looked at Harrogate and smiled.

The man opened the iron door and Harrogate entered alone. A concrete room painted pea green. He walked past the sink, the taps each tied with little tobaccosacks hanging from their mouths. Pale winter light fell through the welded iron windows. The door clanked shut behind him and the guard's footsteps receded in the corridor.

With his blanket he went down the room past rows of iron beds in blocks of four all painted green, some with sacklike mattresses, some with nothing but the woven bare iron straps that served for springs. He went along the aisle looking left and right. A few figures lay motionless in the cots he passed. He went to the end of the room and stood on tiptoe and peered out the window. Rolling hills. Stark winter trees. He came back up the aisle and nudged a sleeper by the foot. Hey, he said.

The man on the pallet opened one eye and looked at Harrogate. What the fuck do you want? he said.

Where am I supposed to sleep?

The man groaned and closed his eyes. Harrogate waited for him to open them again but he did not. After a while he jostled the foot again. Hey, he said.

The man did not open his eyes. He said: If you dont get the fuck away from me I'm going to kick the shit out of you.

I just wanted to know where I'm supposed to sleep.

Anywhere you like you squirrely son of a bitch now get the hell away from here.

39

Harrogate wandered on up the aisle. Some of the bunks had pillows as well as blankets. He picked one out that had only a bare tick and climbed up and spread his blanket and sat in the middle of it. He sat there for a while and then he climbed down again and went to the bars and peered out. Someone in a suit like his was coming backward down the hallway towing a bucket on wheels by a mop submerged in the black froth it held. He glanced at Harrogate as he went past, a cigarette in the corner of his mouth. He didnt look friendly. Across the hall another prisoner was peering from his cage. Harrogate studied him for a minute. Then he gave sort of a crazy little wave at him. Hidy, he said.

Sure, said the other prisoner.

Harrogate turned and went back and climbed into his bunk and lay staring at the ceiling. Concrete beams painted green. A few half blackened lightbulbs screwed into the masonry. It had grown dim within the room, the early winter twilight closing down the day. He slept.

When he woke it was dark out and the bulbs in the ceiling suffused the room with a sulphurous light. Harrogate sat up. Men were filing into the cell with a sort of constrained rowdiness, not quite jostling one another, lighting or rolling cigarettes, speaking only once they were inside. A rising exchange of repartee and shaded insult. One spied Harrogate where he sat up in his cot like a groundsquirrel and pointed him out.

Looky here, new blood.

They filed past. Toward the end came men hobbling with what looked like the heads of pickaxes welded about one ankle. The door clanged, keys rattled. Two men turned in at the bunks beneath Harrogate. One of them lay down and closed his eyes for a minute and then sat up and shucked off his shoes and lay back and closed his eyes again. The other stood with his head bent a few inches from Harrogate's knee and began to unload his pockets of various things. A pencil stub, matchbooks, a beercan opener. A flat black stone. A sack of tobacco. He saw Harrogate watching him and looked up. Hey, he said.

Hcy, said Harrogate.

You dont piss in the bed do you?

No sir.

You smoke?

I used to some. Fore I got thowed in the jailhouse and couldnt get nary.

Here.

He pitched the sack of tobacco up onto Harrogate's blanket.

Harrogate immediately opened the sack and took a paper from the little pocket under the label and began to roll a cigarette.

You get one of those every week, the man said.

When do I get mine?

Next week.

You aint got no match have ye?

Here.

Harrogate lit the cigarette and sucked deeply and blew out the match and put it in his cuff.

Keep em.

He put the matches in his pocket.

How old are you?

Eighteen.

Eighteen?

Yessir.

You just made it didnt you?

That's what they keep tellin me.

What's your name?

Gene Harrogate.

Harrogate, the man said. He had one elbow on the upper bunk and was holding his chin in his fingers, studying the new prisoner with a rather detached air. Well, he said. My name's Suttree.

Howdy Mr Suttree.

Just Suttree. What are you in for?

Stealin watermelons.

That's bullshit. What are you in for.

I got caught in a watermelon patch.

What with, a tractor and trailer? They dont send people to the workhouse for stealing a few watermelons. What else did you do?

Harrogate sucked on his cigarette and looked at the green walls. Well, he said. I got shot.

Got shot?

Yeah.

Whereabouts? Yeah, I know. In the watermelon patch. Where did you get hit.

Pret near all over.

What with, a shotgun?

Yeah.

For stealing watermelons.

Yeah.

Suttree sat down on the lower bunk and put one foot up and began to rub his ankle. After a while he looked up. Harrogate was lying on his stomach looking down over the edge of his bunk.

Let's see where you got shot, said Suttree.

Harrogate knelt up in the bed and lifted his jumper. Little mauve tucks in his pale flesh all down the side of him like pox scars.

I got em all down my leg too. I still caint walk good.

Suttree looked up at the boy's eyes. Bright with a kind of animal cognizance, with incipient good will. Well, he said. It's getting rough out there, isnt it?

Boy I thought I was dead.

I guess you're lucky you're not.

That's what they said at the hospital.

Suttree leaned back in his bunk. What kind of son of a bitch would shoot somebody for stealing a few watermelons? he said.

I dont know. He come out to the hospital and brung me a ice cream. I didnt much blame him. He said hisself he wished he'd not done it.

Didnt keep him from pressing charges though, did it?

Well, I guess seein as he'd done shot me he couldnt back out.

Suttree looked at the boy again with this remark but the boy's face was bland and without device. He wanted to know when supper was served.

Five oclock. Should be in a few minutes.

Do they feed good?

You'll have time to get used to it. What did you draw anyway?

Eleven twenty-nine.

Old eleven twenty-nine.

Boy they feed good in that hospital. Best you ever ate.

Couldnt you have run off from there?

I never had no clothes. I thought about it but I didnt have stitch one nor no way to come by any. I'd rather to be in the workhouse than get caught out wearin one of them old crazy nightshirts they make ye wear. Wouldnt you?

No.

Well. That's you.

That's me.

Harrogate looked down at him but he had his eyes closed. He rolled back over and stared at the ceiling. Someone had written a few sentiments there but they were lost in the glare of the lightbulbs. After a while he heard a bell clang somewhere. A guard came to the door and opened it and when Harrogate sat up he saw that the prisoners were shaping up ready to leave and he hopped from the bunk and shaped up with them.

They marched down the concrete stairs and turned through a door and filed through a messhall where picnic tables ran the length of the room. They were cobbled up out of oak flooring and had the benches bolted to them. At the end of the messhall the prisoners turned into the kitchen where each man got a tin plate and a large spoon. They filed past a steamtable where the kitchen help likewise in stripes ladled up smoking pinto beans, cabbage, potatoes, hot rounds of cornbread. Harrogate had his thumb in his plate and got hot cabbage spooned over it by a smiling black man. He said: Yeeow. Swapped hands and stuck the thumb in his mouth. A guard came over and looked down at him. Was that you? he said.

Yessir.

One more holler out of you and you get no supper.

Yessir.

Nearby prisoners wore pinched faces, apparently in pain, eyes half shut with joy constrained. Harrogate followed on into a messhall like the one they'd come through. The benches and tables were filling up with prisoners. He sought out Suttree and sat next to him and fell to with his spoon. A great clanking and scraping throughout the hall and no word spoke. The table across from them was taken by black prisoners and Harrogate eyed them narrowly from under his brows, his head bent over his plate and the spoon he gripped like a trowel rising and falling woodenly.

When his group had all done eating the guard walked along behind them to the head of the table and rapped and they rose and filed back through the kitchen, scraping their plates into a slopcan and stacking them on a table, dropping their spoons into a bucket. Then they filed out through the other messhall, now partly filled with prisoners eating, and into the hall and up the stairs to their cell again.

They wasnt no meat, said Harrogate.

That's right, said Suttree.

Do they ever have meat?

I dont know.

Have you ever eat any meat here?

You mean other than breakfast bacon?

Yeah. Other than breakfast bacon.

No.

Harrogate leaned against the bunk. After a while he said: How long you been here?

About five months.

They hell fire, said Harrogate.

It was dark when they rose in the morning and dark when they filed into the kitchen to get their plates and spoons and still dark when they turned out in the dewfall and grainy mist of the yard. He stood there with his sleeves and cuffs rolled two turns each and watched the men climb into the trucks. He looked for Suttree but by the time he saw him he was already in a truck and the door was shut. Some of the trucks started to pull away. A guard came over and looked down at him. He stooped with his hands on knees to see into his face. Who the hell are you? he said.

Harrogate.

The guard nodded his head as if this was the right answer.

Did you get your breakfast?

Sure did.

Feel like you're ready for a day's work do you?

I reckon.

Well we have a truck over here for you to ride in if that's all right with you.

Thisn here?

Yeah. You dont care do you?

Harrogate grinned. Shoot, he said. I reckon that's what all I'm here for. I'll do just whatever.

Well we're mighty pleased about that. We like for everbody to be happy.

Shoot, said Harrogate over his shoulder as he slouched toward the waiting truck. I aint hard to get along with.

As he reached the rear of the truck and put up one hand to help himself the guard fetched him a kick from behind that lifted him through the door and dropped him among the boots and shoes of the other prisoners. They looked down at him with crazed grins and someone jerked him forward by the collar in time to keep the door from slamming on his foot. A redheaded man leaned down and said: Get in here, idjit. You make that son of a bitch mad this early of the mornin and I'll kick your ass myself.

I didnt know which truck I was supposed to go to.

Well no truck was the wrong one. Set over here. This son of a bitch drives like a drunk indian goin after more whiskey.

The truck coughed up gouts of white smoke and they lurched off into the fog down the hill and down the winding workhouse road to the highway where the taillights of the other trucks went by twos like eyes before them in the cool October dawn. The prisoners sat in rows facing each other, jiggling and rolling, some trying to sleep. Harrogate crouched on the bench with his hands beneath his thin legs and watched the floor. There was no conversation. The truck gained speed and the tires sang on the black road.

At the first stoplight a young girl was waiting for a bus at the edge of the road. The prisoners shoved and crowded at the wiremesh door of the truck. She turned to stare out over the barren lots toward houses swimming in the mist. A cold light was leaking across the landscape from the east. Harrogate watched two birds come out of the colorless heavens and alight upon a wire and look down into the truck and fly again. They went on, the driver's eyes in a car come up behind them somewhat uneasy at the sight of these striped miscreants.

By good daylight they had crossed the north end of the county and were pulled up at a roadside where sewerpipe lay unjointed along a selvedge of red mud and where riders from the first truck had already descended into ditches and begun to swing picks. The sun rose and warmed them where they stood waiting tools and orders. A man handed Harrogate a pick, stepped back and studied him with it and took it away again. A few cars eased past, faces at the glass. Men bound for work in the city looking out with no expression at all. The prisoners shuffled and milled about until all had tools and Harrogate stood alone. He had started down into the ditch with naked hands when a guard called to him.

Wait here a minute, he said.

The guard went away and returned with another man who looked down at Harrogate suspiciously.

How old are you son?

I'm still eighteen, said Harrogate. He had one black tooth in the front of his mouth and he sucked at it nervously.

The two men looked at each other. The younger one shrugged. I dont know, he said.

Well hell. Take him on back and let Coatney have him. You. You go on back with Mr Williams. You hear?

Yessir.

Get in that pickup over yonder and wait, the other man said.

Harrogate nodded and hobbled up the road to the truck and climbed up into the bed and sat there in his outsized togs watching the men in the ditch. He saw Suttree shoveling dirt up over the rim of the excavation and Suttree looked his way once sitting there alone in the truck but he did not nod or gesture. After a while the guard came up. He motioned to him and opened the door of the truck. Get up front, he said.

Harrogate climbed over the side of the truck and opened the door and got in. There was a speaker hanging by a cord from the dashboard and there was a pumpaction shotgun hung in a rack over the rear window. The guard started the truck, glanced down at Harrogate and pulled away shaking his head.

When Suttree came in that night the smallest prisoner was not in the cell. He saw him at supper. Half obscured behind tottering tiers of pans smoking a homerolled cigarette and firing thin pipes of smoke from his nostrils in disgust. He was moved that night to the kitchen cell. When he came to get his blanket Suttree was lying stretched on his cot with his shoes off. His socks were streaked with red clay.

Guess what, said Harrogate.

What.

They got me warshin fuckin dishes.

I know. I saw you.

Shit, said Harrogate.

Hell, that's no bad shake. It beats swinging a pick all day.

It dont to me. I'd rather to do anything as to warsh dishes.

You'll appreciate it more when the weather turns colder.

Shit.

Harrogate gathered up his blanket in his arms. Someone down the cell called up to Suttree was he through with the newspaper.

Yeah, said Suttree. Come and get it.

Fold it and pitch it here.

Suttree folded the paper and tried to remember how you tucked them in for throwing.

Goddamn Suttree, was you not ever a paperboy?

No.

I guess you was on a allowance.

The man had turned out of his cot and come up the hall.

I used to know how to roll them but I've forgotten.

Here. Let me have it. Fuckin educated pisswillies. He goes to college but he cant roll a newspaper. What do you think of that, little buddy?

The man was standing alongside the bunk. Redheaded, freckled, pumpkintoothed. The nose he talked through spread all over his face.

Howdy Mr Callahan, said Harrogate.

Suttree poked his head out from under the bunk. Mr Callahan? he said.

You heard him.

Oh boy, said Suttree, lying back down.

Callahan grinned his gaptooth grin.

Mr. Callahan's got a lot of pull around here, said Suttree. Ask him if he can do something for you.

Do what?

He wants to get out of the kitchen. He thinks washing dishes is beneath his dignity.

Hell fire little buddy. You got the best job in the joint.

I dont like it, said Harrogate sullenly. They got me workin with a bunch of old crippled fuckers and I dont know what all.

Specially in the guard's mess, said Callahan.

Guard's mess? Goddamn, said Suttree.

That's what they promised him, said Callahan. I guess he dont like steak and gravy. Ham. Eggs ever mornin.

Shit, said Harrogate.

It's true, said Suttree.

Hell Suttree, I dont want to be no goddamned dishwarsher. I got to get up at four oclock in the mornin.

Yeah. We sleep in here till five thirty.

You get to fuck around in the afternoon, said Callahan.

Well we dont get done till seven at night.

Well if you dont want to work in the guard's mess ask if they'll put you back on the trucks.

What if they say no?

Say yes.

What happens then? I guess they beat the shit out of ye.

No they wont. Will they, Red?

Nah. Put ye in the hole. Less you get real shitty. Then you go in the box.

Well that's where they'd put me. What is it?

Just a concrete box about four feet square.

You ever been in there Suttree?

No. You're talking to a man that has though.

What did they put you in there for Mr Callahan?

Aw, slappin a little old guard.

He slapped a vertebra loose in his neck, said Suttree.

Goddamn, said Harrogate. When was this?

When was it Red? Two years ago?

Somethin like that.

They hell fire, how long you been in here Mr. Callahan?

That was another offense, said Suttree. He's been in and out.

They dont give ye nothin to eat but bread and water, said Callahan. In the box they dont.

I believe you'll like the guard's mess better than the box.

I aint warshin no more goddamned dishes.

Well, said Suttree, that's you.

That's me, said Harrogate.

I think you've lost your rabbitassed mind, said Callahan.

Maybe. But I'll tell ye one thing. I ever get out of here I sure to shit aint comin back again.

I think I even heard Bromo say that one time.

Who's Bromo?

The old guy. He's been in and out of here since nineteen thirty-six.

He was in fore that, said Callahan. He was in the other workhouse fore this one was built.

Well, said Harrogate. That's him.

Suttree grinned. That's him, he said.

The crimes of the moonlight melonmounter followed him as crimes will. Truth of his doings came in at the door and up the stairs in the dark. Come morning the prisoners were seeing this half fool in a new light. To his elbows in dishwater and wreathed in steam he watched them file across the kitchen with their plates of biscuits and gravy, nodding, gesturing. He smiled back. They saw him again that night, lost in his stained and shapeless suit. He appeared not to have moved the day long nor the stacked pans diminished. After supper he was returned to them clutching his blanket before him.

Well, said Suttree, you back?

Yep.

What happened.

I told em I was done fuckin with em. They want a dishwarsher they can hunt somebody else cause I aint it.

What did they say.

They asked me did I want to be hallboy. Said you make a few dollars sellin coffee.

A few dollars a year.

That's just what I figured. I told em I didnt want no hallboy bullshit.

So what happened?

Nothin. They just sent me on up.

He stood there with his rat's face in a kind of smug smirk. Suttree shook his head.

Yonder he is, called Callahan.

Watermelon man.

Punkins wasnt it?

Punkins? Godamighty.

Yeah, sang out Callahan, we get out we goin to open a combination fruitstand and whorehouse.

Harrogate smiled nervously.

Callahan was sketching for them a portrait of his brothel. Melons in black negligees.

Watch out the niggers dont hear of it.

The niggers is liable to lynch ye.

Other fruits discussed. A cantaloupe turned queer. Do you buy them a drink.

Worst of it is havin gnats swarm around the head of ye dick.

Fruitflies.

Stealing watermelons eh? said Suttree.

Harrogate grinned uneasily. They tried to get me for beast, beast . . .

Bestiality?

Yeah. But my lawyer told em a watermelon wasnt no beast. He was a smart son of a bitch.

Oh boy, said Suttree.

In the morning he went with them on the trucks. Rising in the rank cold, faint odor of bathless sleepers all about. People stirring in the dull yellow bulblight, stumbling into clothes and shoes. The warmth of the kitchen and the smell of coffee. Cooks and potwashers aged or maimed all hovered by the stove with hot crockery mugs in their hands. Harrogate nodded to them distantly, holding his thumbs wide of his plate.

In the long days of fall they went like dreamers. Watching the sky for rain. When it came it rained for days. They sat in groups and watched the rain fall over the deserted fairgrounds. Pools of mud and dark sawdust and wet trodden papers. The painted canvas funhouse walls and the stark skeletons of amusement rides against a gray and barren sky.

A sad and bitter season. Barrenness of heart and gothic loneliness. Suttree dreamed old dreams of fairgrounds where young girls with flowered hair and wide child's eyes watched by flarelight sequined aerialists aloft. Visions of unspeakable loveliness from a world lost. To make you ache with want. In the afternoon the riggers came and set about taking down a spiderlike centrifuge and loading it on a float. As the prisoners shuffled over the grounds filling their crokersacks with bottles and trash the workers backhanded to them packs of cigarettes. Suttree was given a pack and passed it on to an old man with a goiter who took it without a word. The old man was a smoke-hound, a drinker of shaving lotion, stove fuel, cleaning fluid. Suttree watched him shuffle on. Scowling at the world from under his wild thatched brows. His thin and rimpled mouth working very faintly as he spoke with himself. He took up each paper, each bottle, with something like solicitude, looking about as if he would discover who had put it there. Suttree never heard him speak aloud, this elder child of sorrow. He crouched on the truck bench opposite going home, jostled and nodding. He saw Suttree watching him and lowered his eyes and fell to talking to himself with a kind of secretive viciousness.

Sundays a female evangelist from Knoxville would come out to hold service in the chapel downstairs. Concrete tabernacle, small wooden podium. The prisoners who went seemed stricken nigh insensate by this word of God strained distaff they were hearing. Lounging in the wooden folding chairs, heads lolling. She seemed unaware of their presence. She told old tales from bible days that might have come down orally, so altered were they from their origins. In the afternoon visitors arrived. Family scenes, mothers and fathers, wives, anonymous kinfolk gathered at the long tables in the dining hall. They'd call the names back down the hall and up the stairs and the guard would let them out. To return laden with candy, fruit, cigarettes. No one came for Suttree. None for Harrogate. Callahan's friends from McAnally Flats brought brownlooking apples, sacks of halfspoiled oranges. Callahan would peel these and slice them into a lardpail and cover them with water, adding a little yeast from the kitchen, covering it over with a cloth and storing it under his bed. In a few days a yeasty orange wine would work up and he'd strain it off and invite friends to take a cup with him. They called it julep and it kicked and spewed in the stomach all night. Callahan would get slightly drunk and look about goodnaturedly to see was there thing or body worth destroying.

Byrd Slusser came back, clumping sullenly down the aisle with his blanket, a pick about his ankle. When the workers returned in the evening he was asleep nor did he rise for supper.

In these tranquil evening hours before lights out Harrogate would sit up in his bunk and work on his jailhouse ring. They were made from silver coins and Harrogate had gotten a guard to bore a hole in his and he sat for hours on end with a messhall spoon and beat the coin's rim. The edges of the piece would flare out and come at last to a shape much like a wedding band. Now as he sat tapping Slusser turned in his bunk, raising his leg to clear the rear tine of the pick, and sought out the source of the noise. Harrogate squatted above him in the bunk opposite, bent over his coin, the spoon tapping steadily. Much like a little old cobbler crouched there half lost in his clothes.

Hey, said Slusser.

Harrogate looked down benignly. Hidy, he said.

Knock off that fuckin tappin.

He fixed Harrogate with a fearful look and rolled back over.

Harrogate sat with the coin in one hand and the spoon in the other. He looked down at the man. He took a tentative click at the coinrim. Click. He pulled up the blanket from the edge of the bunk and folded it over his hands, muffling the work between his knees. Click click click. He looked down at the man. The man lay as before. Click click click.

Slusser rose from the bunk slowly like a man bored. He came around the end of the bunk and reached his hand up to Harrogate. Give me that, he said.

Harrogate clutched the blanket to his chest.

You little fistfucker you better hand me that goddamned spoon before I jerk you out of there.

Suttree who'd been half asleep below had a failing sensation in the pit of his stomach. He said: Leave him alone, Byrd.

The boy's tormentor lost interest in him instantly and his eyes swung toward Suttree with a schizoid's alacrity. Well now, he said. I didnt know he was yours.

He's not anybody's.

He's a punk.

I dont believe he is.

Maybe you're one yourself.

Maybe—said Suttree, on whose forehead small beads of sweat had begun to glisten—you've been pulling your pud too much.

Slusser reached and seized him by the front of his jumper and dragged him upright. Suttree gripped his arm, coming out onto the floor. Turn loose of my shirt, Byrd, he said.

Byrd twisted the cloth in his fist. There was no sound in the cell. Suttree could see himself twinned in the cool brown eyes and he didnt like what he saw. He swung at Slusser's face. Immediately a fist crashed against the side of his head. He heard the sea roll. He swung again. His shirt came loose with a loud rip but he did not hear it. He pushed himself forward, his head ducked, and caromed off the side of the bunk. When he looked up he could not see Slusser. Some prisoners were standing between him and the hall and he heard grunts and the meaty sound of fists. Callahan's face went past smiling, beyond the shoulders of the watching men.

Suttree elbowed his way through the spectators. The fight crashed into the bunks and went to the wall and back down the cell, Slusser standing flatfooted because of the pick on his ankle, cursing. Callahan smiling. He was backing Slusser down along the wall in the narrow space behind the bunks. In turning between the bunks Slusser's pick got hung. Callahan stepped forward and slammed him broadside in the head. Slusser lashed out blindly, then kicked out with the pick. It stung a starshaped pock in the concrete and Slusser's eyes rolled with pain. He was still trying to kick Callahan with the pick when the iron door swung and two guards rushed in with slapsticks.

The first person to get clobbered was a country boy from Brown's Mountain named Leithal King. He sat down in the floor holding his head with both hands. Goddamn, he said.

Callahan had leaped back, holding up his hands. He's gone crazy, he said.

Slusser turned. He looked crazy. Eyes wild, a blue swelling at his temple giving his face an asymmetrical twist. The prisoners had fallen away. Slusser turned toward the guards in a half crouch and they fell upon him with slapsticks flailing. Callahan lowered his hands and leaned forward to see better. The slapsticks were going whop whop whop, Slusser on the floor with just the pick sticking out, the guards hammering away from kneeling positions like carpenters on a roof.

When they raised him up he was limp and bleeding from the mouth and ears and his face was his face seen through bad glass. Leithal had risen from the floor and Blackburn pointed his cudgel at him and said: You. Get this man. Callahan you son of a bitch. You get his other side.

I aint done nothin, said Leithal, coming forward uncertainly.

Callahan already had Slusser's arm draped around his neck and was bearing him up. He wiped a thin trickle of blood from his own mouth with a freckled fist and turned and gave the prisoners a pinched grimace of idiotic triumph which sent such a plague of grins among them that the other guard turned at the door. What the hell are you doing, Callahan?

Just holdin this man up. Where you want him?

They followed the guards out the door and Blackburn slammed the gate and locked it and they followed them down the hall and down the stairs, Slusser's pick dragging along behind until the other guard fell back and raised it up and they went on like that, bearing Slusser on toward the box with his hindleg aloft like a wounded iceskater.

The guard returned with Leithal and Callahan and when he unlocked the door Callahan started through it.

Hold it Callahan, said the guard.

Callahan held it.

The guard shut the door behind Leithal and locked it and motioned Callahan down the hall. The prisoners could hear him protesting. Hell fire, what for? I aint done a goddamned thing. Hell fire.

Suttree went back to his bunk, touching his swollen ear with his fingertips. Harrogate was still crouching in the top of his bunk with the spoon in his hand.

Where are they goin with Mr Callahan? he said.

To the hole. Blackburn's wise to his bullshit.

How long will they keep him in there?

I dont know. A week maybe.

Goddamn, said Harrogate. We sure stirred up some shit, didnt we?
Suttree looked at him. Gene, he said.
What.
Nothing. Just Gene.
Yeah. Well . . .
You better hope they keep Slusser in the box.
What about you?
He's already punched me.
Well. As long as they let Mr Callahan out before they do him.
Suttree looked at him. He was not lovable. This adenoidal lep-
tosome that crouched above his bed like a wizened bird, his razorous
shoulderblades jutting in the thin cloth of his striped shirt. Sly, rat-
faced, a convicted pervert of a botanical bent. Who would do worse
when in the world again. Bet on it. But something in him so transparent, something vulnerable. As he looked back at Suttree with his
almost witless equanimity his naked face was suddenly taken away in
darkness.

Some of the prisoners called out complaining. The hall guard told
them to knock it off.

Hell fire, it aint but eight oclock.

Knock it off in there.

Bodies undressing in the dark. The hall light made a puppet show
of them. Suttree sat on his bunk and eased off his clothes and laid them
across the foot of the bed and crawled under the blanket in his
underwear. Voices died in the room. Rustlings. The light from the
yardlamps falling through the windows like a cold blue winter moon
that never waned. He was drifting. He could hear a truck's tires on
the pike a half mile away. He heard the chair leg squeak in the hall
where the guard shifted. He could hear . . . He leaned out of the bunk.
I will be goddamned, he said. Harrogate?

Yeah. Hoarse whisper in the dark.

Will you knock off that goddamned clicking?

There was a brief pause. Okay, said Harrogate.

When they came in from work the next evening Harrogate had a
couple of small jars he'd found in the roadside. Suttree saw him
descend from his bunk after lights out. He seemed to disappear somewhere in the vicinity of the floor. When he reappeared he camped on
the floor at the head of Suttree's bed and Suttree could hear a tin set

down on the concrete and the clink of glass.

What the fuck are you doing? he whispered.

Shhh, said Harrogate.

He heard liquid pouring.

Whew, said a voice in the dark.

A whiff of rank ferment crossed Suttree's nostrils.

Harrogate.

Yeah.

What are you up to?

Shhh. Here.

A hand came toward him from the gloom offering a jar. Suttree sat up and took it and sniffed and tasted. A thick and sourish wine of unknown origins. Where'd you get this? he said.

Shhh. It's Mr Callahan's julep he had workin. You reckon it's ready?

If it'd been ready he'd of drunk it.

That's what I thought.

Why dont you put it up and let it work some more and we'll drink it Saturday night.

You reckon it'll tear your head up?

Suttree reckoned it would tear your head up.

They lay there in the dark.

Hey Sut?

What.

What you aim to do when you get out?

I dont know.

What was you doin fore you got in?

Nothing. Laying drunk.

A deep wheezing of sleepers rose and fell about them.

Hey Sut?

Go to sleep Gene.

By morning a heavy rain had set in and they did not go out. They sat in small groups in the dimly lit cell and played cards. It was cold in the room and some wore their blankets shawled about their shoulders. They looked like detained refugees.

At noon a gimplegged prisoner brought up sandwiches from the kitchen. Thin slices of rat cheese on thin slices of white bread. The prisoners bought matchboxes of coffee from the hallboy for a nickel and he poured hot water in their cups. Harrogate came awake from a deep nap and hopped to the floor to get his lunch. He drank plain water with his sandwich, crouched up there in his bunk, his cheeks jammed. Outside the cold gray winter rain fell across the county. By nightfall it would turn to snow.

He'd finished his sandwiches and was back to tapping at his ring when a new thought changed his face. He put aside his work and climbed down to the floor and crawled under Suttree's bunk. Then he crawled out and back up topside where he fell to work again. In a little while he crawled down again.

Toward dusk a few prisoners looked his way to see what went, the smallest prisoner sitting in the top of his bunk suddenly going whooo whoo like a chimpanzee and lapsing silent again.

When the triangle rang for dinner all fell out save he. Suttree came by from his cardgame and shook him by the shoulder. Hey hotshot. Let's go.

Harrogate raised up with one eye shut, his face matted where it had lain crushed in the blanket. Aaangh? he said.

Let's go to supper.

He swung his legs over the side of the bed and pitched out onto the floor face down.

Suttree had turned to go when he heard the crash. He looked and saw Harrogate struggling in the floor and came back and helped him up. What the fuck's wrong with you?

Yeeegh yeegh, said Harrogate.

Shit, said Suttree. You better stay here. Can you get back in the bunk?

Harrogate fended him away and focused one eye toward the cell door. Sup sup, he said.

You crazy fucker. You cant even walk.

Harrogate started across the tilted floor listing badly. The other prisoners were jammed at the door, filing out by twos and down the stairs. Some looked back.

Look comin here.

What's happened to him?

Looks like one leg's grown longer'n the other one.

Harrogate crashed into the end of a set of bunks and reeled away.

Damned if the country mouse aint drunker'n hell.

Them eyes look like two pissholes in the snow.

He veered toward them like a misfired android. One caught him up by the sleeve.

You goin to supper, Countrymouse?

You fuckin ay, said Countrymouse.

They covered for him in line, holding him erect, shielding him from the guards. The cook's helper who loaded his plate looked at his face probably because it was the only one in the line passing at that diminished altitude. Shit a brick, he said.

Bet your ass, said Harrogate, winking profoundly.

They went on to the messhall. Harrogate stepped over the bench and misbalanced and stepped back. He raised his foot to try again. One of the prisoners grabbed his leg and pulled it down and caught his tilting plate and jerked him into the bench alongside him.

Hee hee, said Harrogate.

Someone kicked him under the table. He peered about at nearby faces for the culprit. The blacks filing in at the table opposite seemed to have wind of him already and were ogling and grinning.

Harrogate spooned up a load of pinto beans and shoved them toward his jaw. Some fell down the front of him. He looked after them. He began to spoon beans from his lap. Several guards were watching. He was having difficulty sitting on the bench. He was tottering about. The guard at the head of the table, a man named Wilson, walked down to get a better look. Harrogate sensed him standing there above him and turned to see, falling against the prisoner at his side as he did so. Wilson looked down into the thin face, now slightly green. Harrogate turned back to his food, holding onto the edge of the table with one hand.

This man's drunk, said Wilson.

Somewhere down the table someone muttered No shit and a ripple of tittering passed through the messhall. Wilson glared. All right, he said. Knock it off. You. Get up.

Harrogate put down his spoon and took another grip on the table and raised himself up. But since the bench would not push back from the table he remained in a sort of crouched position, finally losing his balance and sitting down again. Now he turned in his seat and tried to get one foot over the bench, lifting his leg up by the cuff of his trousers, one elbow resting in his food.

The clanking and scraping of spoons had ceased altogether. The only sound in the messhall was Harrogate struggling to free himself from the table. Wilson standing over him like a faith healer over a paraplegic. Until he actually raised up astraddle the bench, creamed corn dripping from his sleeve. Ick, he said.

What? said Wilson menacingly.

The country mouse closed his eyes, belched, opened them again. Sick, he said. He was trying to raise his other leg. The prisoner alongside looked up at him and leaned away. Harrogate lurched and his neck gave a sort of chickenlike jerk and he vomited on Wilson's shoes.

The prisoners on either side of Harrogate leaped up. Wilson's slapstick was out. He was looking at his shoes. He couldnt believe it. Harrogate wore a look of terror. He seized hold of the table, looking about wildly, his gorge swollen. He spied his plate. He leaned toward it. He vomited on the table.

You nasty little bastard, screamed Wilson. He was doing little kicks, trying to shake the puke from his shoes. The prisoners who'd been sitting opposite Harrogate had risen from the table and were watching the country mouse in awe. Harrogate looked up at them with weeping eyes and managed just the smallest blacktooth grin before he puked again.

They did not see him for ten days. Then one morning as they filed through the kitchen with their plates there he was, grinning sheepishly, ladling up gravy for their biscuits. Beyond him through the steam, on a can with a cigarette in his mouth, sat Red Callahan. No one asked where Slusser was.

That night when they came in he must have been showering in the kitchen cell because when they went past on their way to their own quarters silently in twos, exuding the aura of cold they'd brought in with them, Harrogate suddenly appeared naked at the bars, his thin face, his hands clutching, like a skinned spidermonkey.

Sut, he called out softly. Hey Sut.

Suttree heard his name. As he came abreast of the smallest prisoner he dropped out of the line. When will the phantom puker strike again, he said. What the fuck are you doing bare assed?

Listen Sut, that fuckin Wilson's got it in for me. I got to get out of here.

Out of where?

Here. The joint.

You mean run off?

Yeah.

Suttree shook his head. That's crazy, Gene, he said.

I need you to help me.

Suttree fell back in at the tail of the line. You're nuts, Gene, he said.

He saw him again a week later on Thursday when he was assigned to the indigent food detail. The needy trooping through in rags, their eyes rheumy, snuffling, showing their papers at the desk and going on to where the prisoners unloaded bags of cornmeal from pallets or scooped dried beans into grocery bags. Suttree sought their eyes but few looked up. They took their dole and passed on. Old shapeless women in thin summer dresses, socks collapsed about their pale and naked ankles, shoes opened at the side with knives to ease their feet. The seams of their lower faces stained with snuff, their drawstrung mouths. To Suttree they seemed hardly real. Like pictureshow paupers costumed for a scene. At the noon dinner break he and Harrogate fell in together. They crouched with others among the palleted beans and unwrapped their sandwiches.

What we got?

Baloney.

Anybody got a cheese?

They aint no cheese.

Sut.

Yeah.

Shhh. Do you know where we're at?

Where we're at?

I mean which way is town?

Harrogate speaking in loud hoarse whispers, spewing bits of bread.

Suttree jerked a thumb over his shoulders. It's thataway, he said.

Harrogate motioned his thumb down and looked about. What I figure to do, he said . . .

Gene.

Yeah.

If you run off from here you'll wind up like Slusser.

You mean with a pick on my leg?

I mean you'll be in and out of institutions for the rest of your life.

Save for one thing.

What's that.

They aint goin to catch me.

Where will you go?

Go to Knoxville.

Knoxville.

Hell yes.

What makes you think they wont find you in Knoxville?

Hell fire Sut. Big a place as Knoxville is? They never would find ye there. Why you wouldnt even know where to start huntin somebody.

Suttree looked at Harrogate and shook his head.

How far you reckon it is to town? said Harrogate.

It's six or eight miles. Listen. If you've got to run off why dont you wait and slip off from the county garage some evening?

What for?

Hell, you're practically in town. Besides it would be dark or damn near it.

Harrogate paused from his chewing, his eyes fixed on his shoe. Then he commenced chewing again. You might be right, he said.

Suttree was unwrapping his other sandwich. It dont make all that much difference actually, he said.

Why's that?

Cause they'll catch your skinny ass anyway.

They aint no way.

What do you aim to do about clothes? What do you think people are going to say when they see you wandering around in that outfit?

I'll get me some clothes first thing.

Suttree shook his head.

Hell Sut. I can slip around.

Gene.

Yeah.

You look wrong. You will always look wrong.

Harrogate looked at the floor. He had stopped chewing. No I wont, he said.

The weather turned colder and they did not go out. Wilson put Harrogate to work painting the black borders along the lower hallway walls that served for baseboards. The workhouse smelled of paint and so did the country mouse when he came up in the evening with the smears of black on his face like a guerrilla fighter.

One night Suttree said to him: Dont you have any family?

The lights were out. A few bodies shifted in the dark. Dont you? said the small voice overhead.

Christmas came and some of the married prisoners were furloughed home to holiday with their families. A few were released. Slusser came from solitary, the pick still on his leg. He entered with his blanket and went down the aisle without speaking to anyone.

There was a lighted tree in the recreation room downstairs and on Christmas day they had turkey with all the trimmings. Callahan in the kitchen drunk making pumpkin pies out of old sweet potatoes and carrots. Sots loose from the drunk tank wandering about crazed with thirst. An air of wary joy, like Christmas in some arctic outpost.

The following day was Sunday. Suttree was playing poker when his name was called. He played on.

That's you, Suttree.

He folded his cards. He glanced toward the door and rose heavily, handing the cards down to Harrogate. Dont lose all my money, he said.

The hall guard opened the door and he went out and down the stairs.

The messhall was filled with families. Enormous baskets of fruit. Country people, some bewildered, some in tears. Old men who had been here themselves perhaps.

Over yonder, said Blackburn.

She was sitting at the table at the far end of the hall. Quietly in her good clothes. He turned to go back but Blackburn gripped him by his sleeve and pulled him around. You get your ass over there, he said.

He made his way along the edge of the table. She had her purse in her lap and she was looking down. She was still wearing her hat from church. He sat down on the bench across the table from her and she looked up at him. She looked old, he could not remember her looking so. Her slack and pleated throat, the flesh beneath her jaws. Her eyes paler.

Hello Mother, he said.

Her lower chin began to dimple and quiver. Buddy, she said. Buddy . . .

But the son she addressed was hardly there at all. Numbly he watched himself fold his hands on the table. He heard his voice, remote, adrift. Please dont start crying, he said.

See the hand that nursed the serpent. The fine hasped pipes of her fingerbones. The skin bewenned and speckled. The veins are milkblue and bulby. A thin gold ring set with diamonds. That raised the once child's heart of her to agonies of passion before I was. Here is the anguish of mortality. Hopes wrecked, love sundered. See the mother sorrowing. How everything that I was warned of's come to pass.

Suttree began to cry nor could he stop it. People were looking. He rose. The room swam.

Buddy, she said. Buddy.

I cant, he said. Hot salt strangled him. He wheeled away. Blackburn would have stopped him at the door but when he saw his face he let him go. Suttree jerked his arm away and went through the gate and up the stairs.

He was released a few days later on order from Judge Kelly. The country mouse had run off from a work detail the morning before and as Suttree came from the supply room dressed in the clothes he'd worn through the slam seven months earlier Harrogate was being led clumping along the hall with a pick on his leg. They exchanged glances as they passed but you couldnt say it in words. Suttree was taken back to town in the same car that had brought him out. It was snowing but the roads were clear.

He woke in the logy heat of full summer noon with the sun beating on the tin roof above him and raising a sour smell out of the old wood of the cabin. He could hear the howl of the saws in the lumbermill across the river and he could hear the intermittent scream of swine come under the knacker's hand at the packing company. He turned his face to the wall and opened one eye. Watched through a split in the sunriven boards the slow brown neap of the passing river. After a while he struggled up, blinking in the dusty slats of sunlight that sliced through the hot murk. He tottered erect onto the floor in the trousers he'd slept in and made his way to the door and stepped out, scratching his naked belly, watching the boards for stray fish hooks as he went barefoot toward the rail. He leaned on his elbows and looked out over the river. The skiff had sunk to the gunwales and lay quietly awash in the current. He propped up one foot and studied his toes. He could hear everywhere in the hot summer air the drone of machinery, the lonely industry of the city. He blinked and stretched. A graveldredger was moving upriver, her pipes and tackle slung up in the trucks. He watched it pass. A figure on the pilot deck waved and he waved back.

Suttree took the rope loose from the rail and began to haul the skiff along the side of the houseboat. It yawed and wallowed in the river. He threw the rope ashore and went down the plank and retrieved it from the mud and miring to his anklebones he eased the skiff in. He got hold of the ring in the prow and braced himself and lifted. Mud spurted between his toes. He hoisted the front of the skiff and watched the water sluice heavily over the transom into the river. Tails flared and subsided. He hauled the skiff partly up the bank and lifted it sideways. The trapped fish milled and surged. He tilted with care, their shapes riding up along the overflow and dropping back again. When he lowered the skiff they lay gaping on the boards under a sun that withered them visibly.

Suttree gripped his forepockets, searching. He rose and went to the shanty and returned with a large claspknife. He reached into the bottom of the boat and brought up a catfish by the lower jaw. It quivered slightly and curled its tail. Suttree turned it and sank the point of his knife into its throat and opened its wet and pale blue belly with a clean slicing motion that dumped forth the living viscera down his forearm in a welter of dark blood. He seized these entrails and hauled them from the fish and slung them, a wet anneloid mass writhing brightly in the sun and dropping through the placid face of the river with a light splash that sucked away almost at once. He laid the cleaned fish by and seized the next. They were seven in all and he had them dressed in minutes and aligned in the shade under the skiff's seat. He cut the leaders from the hooks he'd salvaged and he rinsed the blood and mucus from his hands and cleaned the knife and folded the blade away and returned to the shanty.

When he came out again he wore a shirt loosely unbuttoned and he had a towel over one shoulder and he carried a small porcelained basin and a leather shavingbag. He came down the plankwalk and went across the field toward the warehouse still barefoot and stepping carefully, emerging onto the railbed and walking three tentative steps on the hot steel before hopping off again. He did a little hotfoot dance and went on among the cinders and rough ties. Passing through a landscape of old tires and castoff watertanks rusting in the weeds and bottomless buckets and broken slabs of concrete. When he left the roadbed he turned up along the side of the warehouse, the new tin brightly galvanized and reeling in the enormous heat and his shadow wincing blackly across the corrugated glare of it like a crepepaper player in a shadowshow. At the far end of the warehouse was a brass spigot. Beneath it the cracked red clay lay shaped in a basin centered by a dark ocherous eye where the water dripped. Suttree knelt and laid out his things, hung his small mirror from a nail, set his washbasin under the tap and turned on the water. Squinting, he inspected his beard, testing the water idly with one finger. It came hot from the tap in this weather and he laved a palmful over his cheeks and wet his brush and lathered carefully. Then he opened his razor and stropped it briefly on the side of his shavingbag and commenced to shave, pulling the skin taut with his fingers.

When he was finished he flung away the water in a beaded explosion of vapor under the scorching wall of the warehouse, a brief rainbow. He filled the basin again and took off his shirt and splashed himself wet and soaped and rinsed and dried himself with the towel. He put away the razor and brushed his teeth, squatting on his heels there in the raw clay, looking about. A hot silence hung over the riverfront. Over the stained and leaning clapboard shacks, over the barren rubble lots and the fields of wirecolored sedge, over the cratered wastes of hardpan and the railway road. And silence among these broiling colossi of tin and down by the stones and bracken and mud that marked the river shore. Something that looked like a mouse save it had no tail came out of the weeds below him and crossed the open like a windup toy and scuttled from sight beneath the warehouse wall. Suttree spat and rinsed his mouth. A black witch known as Mother She was going along Front Street toward the store, a frail bent shape in black partlet with cane laboring brokenly through the heat. He rose and collected his things and went back down the dry clay gutter by the edge of the warehouse and along the tracks and across the fields.

As he neared the shanty he saw a long gray cat struggling toward the weeds towing its own length of fish. He shouted and waved at it. He scooped and shied a rock. Hobbling along gingerfooted through the stubble. When he came up the cat squared off at him, a starved and snarling thing with the hackles reared along its razorous spine. It did not let go the fish. Suttree threw a rock at it. The cat's ears lay flat along its head and its tail kept jerking. He threw another rock that caromed off its stark ribs. It dropped the fish and yowled at him, still crouched there cocked on its bony elbows.

Why goddamn you, said Suttree. He cast about until he found a huge clod of dried mud and going close he broke it over the animal. It squalled and scrabbled away, shaking its head. Suttree retrieved the fish and looked it over. He rinsed it in the river and gathered up the other fish and piled them in his washbasin, a tottery load, and went on to the shanty. The cat was already back in the skiff, searching.

With the day's sun full on the tin roof the heat in the houseboat was unendurable. He put away his things and got a clean shirt and trousers from his cardboard bureau and dressed and took his shoes and socks and towel and went out onto the deck. There he sat looking out through the rails with his feet hanging in the river. Down near the bridge an old man poled a skiff by the shore. Standing precarious and daring. Wielding a longhandled hook. A fellow worker in these cloacal reaches, plying the trade he has devised for himself. The old man's name was Maggeson and Suttree smiled to see him at his work, going slow, shaded by the fronds of a huge and raveled fiber hatbrim.

He dried his feet and put on his socks and shoes and combed his hair. Inside the shanty he wrapped the fish in a newspaper and tied them with a string and took the coaloil can from its corner. At the door he looked to see had he forgotten anything and then he left.

When he reached the street he walked along until he found a flat place at the paving's edge and under the weeds and here he stopped and poured the kerosene over the warm tar. Then he set the can from sight in the weeds and went on.

Gravely, gravely, small chocolate children nodded or lifted pale brown palms. Hello, Hidy He climbed up from the river and went toward the city with his fish.

Early in his living by the river Suttree had found a shortcut through old gardens on the river bluff, a winding path with cinder paving that angled up behind old homes of blackened boarding and old porches where rusted skeins of screening fell down the rotting facades. But passing under one high window always he heard a dull mutter of invective and sullen oaths and he no longer took the near path but went the longer way round by the streets. The invector however had moved to a new window so large was the house that he shared with his soul and he could still watch for the fisherman to pass. In these later years he had become confined altogether and this was hard for one accustomed to tottering daily abroad and dripping vitriol on passing strangers. He keeps his watch with fidelity. An old man dimly seen in upper windowcorners.

Market Street on Monday morning, Knoxville Tennessee. In this year nineteen fifty-one. Suttree with his parcel of fish going past the rows of derelict trucks piled with produce and flowers, an atmosphere rank with country commerce, a reek of farmgoods in the air tending off into a light surmise of putrefaction and decay. Pariahs adorned the walk and blind singers and organists and psalmists with mouth harps wandered up and down. Past hardware stores and meatmarkets and little tobacco shops. A strong smell of feed in the hot noon like working mash. Mute and roosting pedlars watching from their wagonbeds and flower ladies in their bonnets like cowled gnomes, driftwood hands composed in their apron laps and their underlips swollen with snuff.

He went among vendors and beggars and wild street preachers haranguing a lost world with a vigor unknown to the sane. Suttree admired them with their hot eyes and dogeared bibles, God's barkers gone forth into the world like the prophets of old. He'd often stood along the edges of the crowd for some stray scrap of news from beyond the pale.

He crossed the street, stepping gutters clogged with greenstuff. Coming from behind the trucks a beggarlady's splotched and marcid arm barred his way, a palsied claw that gibbered at his chest. He slid past. Stale nunlike smell of her clothes, dry flesh within. The old almstress's eyes floated by in a mist of bitterness but he had nothing but his fish.

He passed under the shade of the markethouse where brick the color of dried blood rose turreted and cupolaed and crazed into the heat of the day form on form in demented accretion without precedent or counterpart in the annals of architecture. Pigeons bobbed and preened in the high barbicans or shat from the blackened parapets. Suttree pushed through the gray doors below.

He went over the cool tiles, his heels muted by sawdust and wood-shavings. A halfman on a skatecart oared past with leather chocks. Huge fans wheeled slowly in the upper murk and marketers shouldered past with baskets, eyes stunned by the plenty through which they moved, shy women in wrappers of gingham print with the armpits eaten out and trailing small streaked children in tennis shoes. They milled and turned and shuffled by. Suttree wandering among the stalls where little grandmothers offered flowers or berries or eggs. Rows of faded farmers hunched at the lunchcounters. This lazaret of comestibles and flora and maimed humanity. Every other face goitered, twisted, tubered with some excrescence. Teeth black with rot, eyes rheumed and vacuous. Dour and diminutive people framed by paper cones of blossoms, hawkers of esoteric wares, curious electuaries ordered up in jars and elixirs decocted in the moon's dark. He went by stacks of crated pullets, plump hares with ruby eyes. Butter tubbed in ice and brown or alabaster eggs in ordered rows. Along by the meatcounters shuffling up flies out of the bloodstained sawdust. Where a calf's head rested pink and scalded on a tray and butchers honed their knives. Great cleavers and bonesaws hung overhead and truncate beeves in stark abbatoir by cambreled hams blueflocced with mold. At the fishmarket cold gray shapes dimly limned in troughs of powdered ice.

Suttree eased past the cool glass cases with their piscean wares and went on to the rear of the stall.

Hello Mr Turner.

Howdy Suttree, said the old man. What have you got?

Two nice cats and some carp. He unrolled the paper and laid them out on the block. Mr Turner thumbed one of the catfish over. Bits of newsprint clung to it. He felt the flesh, picked up the two fish and laid them in the scales.

Call it seven pounds.

All right. What about the carp?

He regarded the dull placoid shapes with doubt. Well, he said. I could maybe take one of them.

Well.

He lifted out the catfish and selected a small carp. They watched the needle swing. The old jowter twisted up his apron in his hands. Two and a half, he said.

Okay.

He nodded and went to his till and rang open the drawer. He came back with a dollar bill and four cents and handed the money to Suttree.

When are you going to bring me some of them little channel cats?

Suttree had slid the folded dollar into his pocket and was rewrapping the remaining fish. He shrugged. I dont know, he said. When I get a chance.

Turner watched him. Windchimes belled thinly, a flutter of glass above them stirred by the fans. I get people askin all the time, he said.

Well. Maybe later on this week. I have to go up on the French Broad for them. This hot weather is bad.

Well, you bring me some quick as you get a chance.

All right.

He slid the other fish under one arm and nodded.

Mr Turner wiped his hands again. Come back, he said.

Suttree went on through the markethouse and out the double doors to Wall Avenue. A blind black man was fretting a dobro with a broken bottleneck and picking out an old blues run. Suttree let the four pennies into the tin cup taped to the box. Get em, Walter, he said.

Hey Sut, said the player.

He crossed the street toward Moser's to admire the boots in the window. A graylooking cripple sat on the walk with a hatful of pencils trapped in his wasted kneecrooks. His head lay sunken on his chest. As if he were trying to read the sign hung from his neck. I AM A POOR BOY. His grizzled wool tiaraed with smoked glasses worn gogglewise. Suttree went on. He crossed Gay Street with the shoppers and went up the long cool tunnel of the bus station arcade and through the doors.

A nasal voice called out through a megaphone the names of southern cities in this cavern of stale smoke and boredom. Suttree adjusted his fish and went through the doors at the far side of the waiting room and down the concrete steps, along the platform past idling buses and into State Street. He went past the firehouse where the inmates sat tilted in cane chairs along a shaded wall and he went down the hill past dolorous small taverns and cafes and down Vine Avenue by secondhand furniture stores among throngs of blacks and along Central where loud and shoddy commerce erupted out of the dim shops into the streets and packs of scarred dogs wandered. Shouldering his way through dark shoppers in a market ripe with sweat and the incendiary breath of splo drinkers, wide white teeth and laughter and cupshot eyeballs. Beyond the grocery cases a long trestle of beerdrinkers. An old woman thickly mantled in rags mumbled something incoherent at his ear in passing. He leaned on the meatcase and waited.

A pocked black face peered at him over the top of the counter through racks of packaged sausage and porkskins.

I've got four fresh buglemouth, Suttree said.

Lessee.

He handed up the limp package. The dark butcher unrolled it and looked the fish over and placed them in his bloodstained balance. Foteen pound, he said.

All right.

How come you aint never got no catfish?

I'll try and get you some.

Folks astin all the time: Where yo catfish at? Aint none, that's all.

I'll see if I can get you some.

Dollar twelve.

Suttree held out his hand for the money.

Out in the baking street with the bills wadded together in the toe of his pocket he swung along whistling. He went up Vine to Gay Street and along the walk by pawnshop windows. Wares to find a thousand trades. Consulting with his image in the glass he studied a display of knives. Come in, come in. A round and shirtsleeved merchant from the doorway. Suttree moved along. Late noon traffic pushed sluggishly through the heat and trolleys clicked past dimly dragging sparks from the wires overhead.

He cruised the cool wooden dimestore aisles, eyeing the salesgirls. He revolved into the perfumed and airconditioned sanctuary of Miller's. A cool opulence available to the most pauperized. Up the escalator to the second floor. Holt was standing with his hands clasped in the small of his back like an usher at a funeral. He wore a shoehorn in his waistband and a small grin.

He didnt make it today.

Thanks, said Suttree.

He went down the escalator and into the street again.

Jake the rack stood with his hands in the change of his apron, tilling the coins. He spat enormously and dark brown toward a steel spittoon and stepped to a table where the balls were being shucked up from the pockets and a player was pounding the floor with his cue. He called back over his shoulder: He just left, him and Boneyard. I think they went to eat. Jim's drunk.

He saw them in the rear of the Sanitary Lunch, J-Bone and Boneyard and Hoghead all three, bleary figures gesturing beyond the fogged glass. He went in.

Jimmy the Greek speared up meat from his gasping trypots and forked the slabs onto thick white plates. He adjusted salads with his thumb and wiped away drips of gravy with his apronskirt. Suttree waited at the counter. The fans that hung from the stamped tin ceiling labored in a backwash of smoke and steam.

The Greek was blinking at him.

Two hamburgers and a chocolate milk, Suttree said.

He nodded and scratched the order on a pad and Suttree went on to the back of the cafe.

Here's old Suttree.

Come here and set down, Sut.

Scoot over, Hoghead.

Suttree looked them over. What are you all doing?

I'm tryin to get well, said J-Bone.

How do you feel?

I feel like I need a drink.

Suttree looked at Hoghead. A halfcrazed grin spread over Hoghead's freckled face. Suttree looked from one to the other of them. They were all drunk.

You sons of bitches havent been to bed.

Early Times, called out J-Bone.

J-Bone's crazy, Hoghead said.

Boneyard's black eyes darted about from one to the other.

The Greek set down a glass of water and a carton of milk and an empty glass.

Bring us another Coke, Jimmy, J-Bone said.

He nodded, collecting dishes.

Suttree took a drink of the water and poured the water into the empty glass and opened the milk and poured it into the cold glass and sipped it. J-Bone was fumbling around under the seat. When the Greek came back he straightened up and cleared his throat loudly. The Greek set down a plate with two hamburgers and a Coke with a glass of ice and shuffled off again. Suttree lifted the sandwiches open and poured salt and pepper. The meat was seasoned and thinned with meal and there were scoops of coleslaw on top.

J-Bone had come up with a bottle from under the booth and was pouring whiskey over the ice, holding the glass in his lap and looking about cunningly. He slid the bottle partly from the sweatwrinkled bag that held it and checked the level of the contents and slid it back.

We're on that good stuff now, Sut. Here. Have a little drink.

Suttree shook his head, his mouth full of hamburger.

Go on.

No thanks.

J-Bone was looking at him crazily. He leaned a little, as if to lift one leg. His eyes wandered in his head. An enormous fart ripped through the lunchroom, stilling the muted noontime clink of cutlery and cup clatter, stunning the patrons, rattling the cafe to silence. Boneyard rose instantly and took a stool at the counter, looking back wildly. The Greek at his steamtable tottered backwards, one hand to his forehead. Hoghead staggered into the aisle, strangling, his face a mask of anguish and the lady in the next booth rose and looked down at them with a drained face and made her way to the cash register.

Hee, crooned J-Bone into cupped hands.

Goddamn, said Suttree, rising with his plate and glass.

Hurt yourself Jim? called Boneyard past the back of his hand.

Whew, said Hoghead, sitting at the counter. I believe somethin's crawled up in you and died.

The Greek was glaring toward the rear of the cafe. J-Bone, in the booth alone, wrinkled his face. After a minute he climbed out into the aisle. Lordy, he said. I dont believe I can stand it my ownself.

Get away from here.

I'm trying to eat, Jim.

Lord, said J-Bone. I believe it's settled in my hair.

Let's get out of here, said Boneyard.

Suttree looked at the grinning faces. Just a minute and let me finish this, he said.

The interior of the Huddle was cool and dark, the door ajar. They came down the steep street and turned in two by two.

Dont bring no whiskey in here, said Mr Hatmaker, pointing.

J-Bone turned and went out and took the near empty bottle from under his shirt and drained it and threw it across the street where it exploded against the wall of the hotel. A few faces appeared at the windows and J-Bone waved to them and went in again.

The light from the door fell upon the long mahogany bar. A pedestal fan rocked in its cage and huge flies droned back and forth beneath the plumbing hung from the ceiling. Whores lounged in a near booth and light in dim smoked palings sloped in through the dusty windowpanes. Blind Richard was sitting at the corner of the bar with a mug of beer before him and the wet duck end of a cigarette smoldering in his thin lips, his blownout eyeballs shifting behind squint lids, his head tilted for news of these arrivals. J-Bone walloped him on the back.

What say, Richard.

Richard unleashed his wet green teeth in the semidark. Hey Jim. I been lookin for you.

J-Bone pinched his sad dry cheek. You sly rascal, you found me, he said.

Suttree tapped him on the elbow. You want a fishbowl? Give us three, Mr Hatmaker.

At a table in the rear a group of dubious gender watched them with soulful eyes. They tucked their elbows and their hands hung from the upturned stems of their wrists like broken lilies. They stirred and subsided with enormous lassitude. Suttree looked away from their hot eyes. Mr Hatmaker was drawing off beer into frozen bowls. Suttree handed back the first of them beaded and dripping and dolloped with thick foam. Richard's nose twitched.

How are you, Richard?

Richard smiled and fondled the facets of his empty mug. He said that he was only fair.

Well, said Suttree, give us one more. Mr Hatmaker.

Watch old Suttree spring, said Hoghead.

You want a Coca-Cola?

What for? Jim drank all the whiskey didnt he?

Ask Jim.

Here you go Richard.

Looky here, said Jim.

What?

Look what's loose.

They turned. Billy Ray Callahan was standing in the door smiling. Hey Hatmaker, he said.

Mr Hatmaker raised his head, whitehaired and venerable.

Is Worm barred?

The barkeeper nodded dourly that he was.

How about lettin him back in?

He set the last schooner on the bar and wiped his hands and took the money. He stood looking toward the door, weighing the bill in his hand. All right, he said. You can tell him he's not barred no more.

What about Cabbage and Bearhunter?

They aint barred that I know of.

Come on, assholes.

They entered grinning and squinting in the gloom.

Red On The Head like the dick on a dog, sang out J-Bone.

Callahan whacked him in the belly with the back of his hand. Hey Jim, he said. How's your hammer hangin? He glanced about. The whores looked up nervously. He bequeathed upon them collectively his gaptoothed grin. Ladies, he said. He crouched slightly to peer toward the back of the room. Hey, he called. The queers is back. He punched Worm playfully on the shoulder and pointed toward the group at the table. They turned to one another in elaborate indignation, drawing their wandlike arms to their breasts. With the unison of the movement those pale and slender limbs mimed dancing egrets in the gloom. Callahan extended a hand into the air. Hidy queers, he said.

Suttree was standing against the bar watching all this with something like amusement. When Callahan saw him he gathered his head into the crook of his arm. Goddamned old Suttree, he said.

How's it feel to be on the street again?

Feels thirsty. You holdin anything?

Give us another fishbowl, Mr Hatmaker.

Callahan reached past Suttree and gave Blind Richard a great whack on the shoulders. Richard's cigarette hopped from his mouth and expired in his beer. What say Richard old buddy! screamed Callahan.

The blind man raised up coughing. He put one finger to his ear. Goddamn, Red. I aint deaf. He was groping about on the bar with long yellow fingers.

Where'd my cigarette get to, Jim?

Red got it, Richard.

Give me my cigarette, Red.

Suttree passed the mug of beer from the bar and Callahan sucked down about half of it and belched and looked about. Someone had put a coin in the jukebox and pastel lights exchanged within the plastic fascia. Bearhunter and Cabbage composed a light impromptu dance. Boneyard watched, his anthracite eyes shining.

Tell him to give me my cigarette, Jim.

An enormous whore had come to the bar with empty mugs for filling. She stood against Suttree and gave him a sidelong look of porcine lechery.

Watch out, Suttree, called Cabbage.

Your buddy was supposed to of got out with us, said Red.

Harrogate?

Yeah. They couldnt find him no clothes. He says he's comin to the big city to make his fortune.

He's as crazy as a shithouse rat.

That old big gal's after you, called Cabbage, punching buttons at the jukebox.

The whore grinned and took the filled mugs to the table.

J-Bone turned to the room with outspread hands. All right now. Who got Richard's cigarette?

Richard tugged at his sleeve. Here, Jim. Let it go.

Hell no. Nobody leaves the room.

Callahan leaned and called to a thin woman among the whores. Hey Ethel. How's that rabbit hole?

Somebody told me you were a fisherman now, said Bearhunter.

Damn right he is, said Cabbage. Catches them *big ones.*

Piss on you, Cabbage.

Cabbage put one hand to his mouth. That old Suttree, he called. He knows where the good holes is at.

Listen at old Cabbage hammer, said J-Bone.

Old Cabbage, said Red, he beat that morals charge they had him on. They caught him and this girl parked in a car buck naked but old Cabbage, he ate the evidence.

Aw shit, said Richard. Who put a danged old cigarette out in my danged beer?

Who done that? called J-Bone.

A small owlfaced man was trying to get up a game on the bowling machine. Here's my horse, said Boneyard, raising J-Bone's arm aloft.

I'm too drunk. Who was it put a duck out in Richard's beer when he wasnt lookin?

Bill, you and me partners, said Worm.

Here's my horse, said Red, hugging Richard's thin shoulders.

Where's Ethel? She'll play. Get her.

Ethel was at the end of the bar with her empty mug. She snapped her fingers and pointed at her crotch with her thumb. Get this, she said.

Suttree studied her. Her bony sootstreaked arms were bare to the shoulder and one bore a slaverous and blueblack panther. He could see part of a peacock, a wreath with the name Wanda and the words Rest In Peace 1942. He had his head tilted studying the blue runes on her legs when she turned with her beer. She hiked her skirt up around her waist with one hand and cocked her leg forward. A hound was chasing a rabbit down her belly toward her crotch. She said: When you get your eyes full, open your mouth.

Whoops from the drinkers. Hoghead leaning to see. Wait a minute, he said.

But she had flipped her skirt down with an air of contempt and swaggered past with her beer.

I told you about that Suttree, called Cabbage. He's a hole findin fool.

Let's see that rabbit hole Ethel.

Let's see one of you loudmouthed fuckers buy a beer.

Buy her a beer Worm.

Fuck her. She's got a beer.

Give us a fishbowl Mr Hatmaker.

Ever who's playin get your dime up.

What are we playin for?

Make it light on yourself.

Who got my beer. Hey, Red?

Late summer darkness fell and lights came on within the tavern, the beerlamps and plastic clocks with country scenes. Suttree fell in among the winners from the bowling game and they set forth in a huge old Buick.

Idling in an alleyway under a yellow lightbulb by a clapboard wall where a man naked to the waist palmed to them a pint bottle in a paper bag. On to other taverns where in the smoke and the din and the music the night grew heady. At the B & J Suttree became enamored of a ripe young thing with black hair who wrought on the dancefloor an obscene poem, her full pale thighs shining in the dim light where she whirled.

He stood to dance, took two steps sideways and sat again.

He began to grow queasy.

He was looking down into a tin trough filled with wet and colorful gobbets of sick. Scalloped moss wept from a copper pipe. A man sat sleeping on the toilet, his hands hanging between his knees. There was no seat to the toilet and the sleeper was half swallowed up in its stained porcelain maw.

Hey, said Suttree. He shook the man by the shoulder.

The man shook his head in annoyance. A foul odor seeped up between his lardcolored thighs.

Hey there.

The man opened one wet red eye and looked out.

Sick, Suttree said.

They glared at each other.

Yeah, said the man. Sick.

Suttree stood spraddlelegged before him, swaying slightly, one hand on the man's shoulder. The man squinted at him. Do I know you?

Suttree turned away. Two other men come in were standing at the trough. He tottered into the corner and vomited. The men at the trough watched him.

They rolled through the dim shires of McAnally singing rude songs and passing a bottle about in the musty old car.

Wake up, Sut, and take ye a drink.

What's wrong with old Suttree.

Suttree's all right, said J-Bone.

He waved them away, his wheeling skull pressed for coolness against the glass of the quarterwindow.

I believe he's been taken drunk.

Get ye a drink here to sober up on. Hey Bud.

Suttree groaned and fended away with one hand.

At the door of the West Inn they were halted by a shaking head. Suttree hung between friends.

Dont bring him in here.

Callahan pushed past them through the door.

I didnt know that was you, Red. Just bring him on in and set him in the booth yonder.

A group of musicians played with fiddle and guitar a rustic reel and a drunk had taken the floor and begun to waltz like a mummer's bear. One shoesole was pared from its welt and gave to his shuffle a little offbeat slap. In a daring pirouette, vacanteyed and face agrin, he overlisted and careered sideways and crashed among a table of drinkers. They flushed like quail from under the spilled bottles and mugs, wiping at their laps. One had the drunk up by the collar but he saw Callahan smiling at him and grew uncertain and let him go.

Suttree, roused by the commotion, looked up. His friends were drinking at the bar. He reared from the booth and staggered into the center of the floor, looking about wildly.

Where you goin Sut?

He turned. To see who'd spoke. The seeping roachstained walls spun past in a wretched carousel. Two thieves at a table watched him like cats.

J-Bone had him under one arm. Where you goin, Bud?

Sick. Sicky sick.

They staggered toward the washrooms, a shed at the rear of the building and barren save for a toilet bowl. An opaque smoketarred lightbulb that looked like an eggplant screwed into the ceiling. A maze of corroding pipes and conduits.

The walls were papered in old cigarette signs and castoff cardboard up which piss rose wicklike from the floor in dark and flameshaped stains. Suttree stood looking down into the bowl. A beard of dried black shit hung from the porcelain and a clot of stained papers rose and fell with a kind of obscene breathing. J-Bone was holding him by waist and forehead. Hot clotted bile flooded his nostrils.

Walk him around.

Come on Sut.

He looked. They were going toward a dimlit shack. Somewhere beneath him his feet were wandering about.

Fuck it, he said.

Old Sut's all right.

I'm an asshole, he told a wall. He turned, seeking a face. I'm an asshole, J-Bone. A photograph of a family of blacks in some sort of ceremonial robes went past. He raised a hand and fondled the wallpaper's yellowed sleavings.

He was entering a room. Most stately. Nothing to be alarmed. Dark faces watched him through the smoke. Must nods to each. Appear plausible.

He heard voices rising louder. Hoghead's high cackling laugh. Here Sut.

He looked down. He was holding a jellyjar of white whiskey. He raised it and sipped.

I like the hell out of old Suttree, John Clancy said.

He was sitting on the lumpy arm of a stuffed chair. Something was under discussion. A slatshaped negress bent to look at him. He too drunk, she said.

Suttree lifted his glass in mute agreement but she had gone.

Someone rose from the chair. He must have been leaning against them because now he fell into the depths they had vacated, spilling the whiskey on himself. His face lay wedged in a rank corner of the upholstery.

He muttered into the musty springs.

Someone was helping him. He rose from a dream, a ragestrangled face screaming at him. He reeled toward the door. In the corridor he turned and made his way along to the rear of the house, caroming from wall to wall. A black woman stepped from out of the woodwork and came toward him. They feinted. She passed. He clattered into a bureau and fell back and went on. At the rear of the hallway he floundered through a curtain and stood in a small room. Somewhere before him in the dark people were breeding with rhythmic grunts. He backed out. He pulled at a doorknob. His gorge gave way and the foul liquors in his stomach welled and spewed. He tried to catch it in his hands.

God, he said. He was wiping himself on a curtain. He found a door and entered and collapsed in the cool dark. There was a bed there and he tried to crawl under it. It was important that he not be found until he'd had time to rest.

In his stupor he dreamed riots. A window full of glass somewhere collapsed in a crash. He thought he'd heard pistolshots. He struggled to wake but could not. He let his cheek go to a fresh spot on the floor where it was cooler and he slept again.

A dream of shriving came to him. He knelt on the cold stone flags at a chancel gate where the winey light of votive candles cast his querulous shadow behind him. He bent in tears until his forehead touched the stone.

When he woke his head was encoiled by some rank stench. A dull plaque of vomit furred his tongue. Dark faces bent between himself and the dusty bulb burning in the ceiling. Hey boy, hey boy, a voice

78

was saying. He felt himself being jostled from side to side. He closed his eyes. Must ride out this hard weather.

I caint have it. Get him out of here.

He was hauled abruptly erect by his armpits. He looked down. Black hands cupped his chest. Ab? he said. Ab?

She bent to see into his face. Dull moteblown eyeballs webbed with blood. Wheah you buddies at? Hah?

You caint get no sense out of him.

He watched his heels dragging over the linoleum's faded garden.

I see that little white pointedheaded motherfucker he come in with I goin to salivate his ass with a motherfuckin shotgun.

Where are we going?

What he say?

Can you walk? Hey boy.

He caint shit. Get him on out of here.

White motherfucker done puked everwhere.

His feet went banging down some stairs. He closed his eyes. They went through cinders and dirt, his heels gathering small windrows of trash. A dim world receded above his upturned toes, shapes of skewed shacks erupted bluely in the niggard lamplight. The rusting carcass of an automobile passed slowly on his right. Dim scenes pooling in the summer night, wan inkwash of junks tilting against a paper sky, rorschach boatmen poling mutely over a mooncobbled sea. He lay with his head on the moldy upholstery of an old car seat among packingcrates and broken shoes and suncrazed rubber toys in the dark. Something warm was running on his chest. He put up a hand. I am bleeding. Unto my death.

A warm splatter broke across his face, his chest. He twisted his head away, waving one hand. He was wet and he stank. He opened his eyes. A black hand was putting away a limber hosepipe, buttoning, turning. An enormous figure toppled away down the sky toward the mauve and glaucous dawn of the streetlamps.

Sot's skull subsiding, sweet nothingness betide me.

I'd like these shoes soled I dreamt I dreamt. An old bent cobbler looked up from his lasts and lapstone with eyes dim and windowed. Not these, my boy, they are far too far gone, these soles. But I've no others. The old man shook his head. You must forget these and find others now.

Suttree groaned. A switchengine shunted cars in a distant yard, telescoping them in crescendo coupling by coupling to an iron thunder that rattled sashwork all down McAnally Flats. By this clangorous fanfare dull shapes with sidling eyes and pale green teeth congealed with menace out of the dark of the hemisphere. A curtain fell, unspooling in a shock of dust and beetlehusks and dried mousedirt Amorphous clots of fear that took the forms of nightshades, hags or dwarfs or seatrolls green and steaming that skulked down out of the coils of his poisoned brain with black candles and slow chant. He smiled to see these familiars. Not dread but only homologues of dread. They bore a dead child in a glass bier. Sinister abscission, did I see with my seed eyes his thin blue shape lifeless in the world before me? Who comes in dreams, mansized at times and how so? Do shades nurture? As I have seen my image twinned and blown in the smoked glass of a blind man's spectacles I am, I am.

Trades commenced in the hot summer dawn. He rolled his swollen head, drew up his knees. A breeze stirred a child's sedge house nearby.

I am a mouse in a grassbole crouching. But I can hear come whicket and swish the clocklike blade of the cradle.

He woke with the undersides of his eyelids inflamed by the high sun's hammering, looked up to a bland and chinablue sky traversed by lightwires. A big lemoncolored cat watched him from the top of a woodstove. He turned his head to see it better and it elongated itself like hot taffy down the side of the stove and vanished headfirst in the earth without a sound. Suttree lay with his hands palm up at his sides in an attitude of frailty beheld and the stink that fouled the air was he himself. He closed his eyes and moaned. A hot breeze was coming across the barren waste of burnt weeds and rubble like a whiff of battlesmoke. Some starlings had alighted on a wire overhead in perfect progression like a piece of knotted string fallen slantwise. Crooning, hooked wings. Foul yellow mutes came squeezing from under their fanned tails. He sat up slowly, putting a hand over his eyes. The birds flew. His clothes cracked with a thin dry sound and shreds of baked vomit fell from him.

He struggled to his knees, staring down at the packed black earth between his palms with its bedded cinders and bits of crockery. Sweat rolled down his skull and dripped from his jaw. Oh God, he said. He lifted his swollen eyes to the desolation in which he knelt, the ironcolored nettles and sedge in the reeking fields like mock weeds made from wire, a raw landscape where half familiar shapes reared from the slagheaps of trash. Where backlots choked with weeds and glass and the old chalky turds of passing dogs tended away toward a dim shore of stonegray shacks and gutted auto hulks. He looked down at himself, caked in filth, his pockets turned out. He tried to swallow but his throat constricted in agony. Tottering to his feet he stood reeling in that apocalyptic waste like some biblical relict in a world no one would have.

Two bulletskulled black boys watched him come along the path toward the street, lurching out of the jungle with his head in his hands. Through splayed fingers a wild eye fell upon them.

Hey boys.

They regarded each other.

Which way is town?

They fled on bare soundless feet, spinning a lilac dust. He wiped his eyes and looked after them. In that shimmering heat their figures dissolved crazily until all he saw of them were two small twisted gymnasts hung by wires in a quaking haze. Suttree stood there. He turned slowly. To select a landmark. Some known in this garden of sorrow. He wheeled away down the narrow sandy street like the veriest derelict.

These quarters he soon found to be peopled with the blind and deaf. Dark figures in yard chairs. Propped and rocking in the shade of porches. Old black ladies in flowered gowns who watched impassively the farther shapes of the firmament as he went by. Only a few waifs wide eyed and ebonfaced studied at all the passage of this pale victim of turpitude among them.

At the end of the street the earth fell away into a long gut clogged with a maze of shacks and coops, nameless constructions of tarpaper and tin, dwellings composed of actual cardboard and wapsy tilted batboard jakes that reeled with flies. Whole blocks of hovels cut through by no street but goatpaths and little narrow ways paved with black sand where children and graylooking dogs wandered. He turned and started back, staggering under the heat, his stomach curdling. He wandered into a narrow alleyway and fell to his hands and knees and began to vomit. Nothing would come but a thin green bile and then nothing at all, his stomach contracting in dry and vicious spasms that racked him and left him sweaty and shivering and weak when they ceased. He looked up. Tears warped his sight. A small black child with brightly ribboned wool watched him from a bower in a hedge. With the snuffling of her breath she teased in and out of one nostril a creamy gout of yellow snot. Suttree nodded to her and rose and lurched into the street again.

He chanced a slotted eye through his fingers at the boiling sun. It hung directly overhead. He started across the open lots, going carefully with his thin shoes among jagged rings of jarglass and nailstudded slats. From time to time he would pause to rest, leaning forward with his hands on his knees or squatting on one heel and holding his head. He had sweated through his shirt and it stank horrendously. After a while he came out on another street and he went along until he saw in the distance a cutbank that might be a railroad right of way. He set off across the lots again and down alleys and over fences, trying to keep a fix on his destination. He crossed through a row of back yards by battered cans of swill where clouds of fruitflies droned and swung on the wind and dogs slouched away. A fat negress stepped from an outhouse door hauling up her bloomers. He looked away. She bawled out some name. He went on. A man called out behind him but he didnt look back.

He cut down an alley and went past a row of warehouses and at the end he could see the Dale Avenue market sheds and beyond them the gang tracks of the L&N merging toward the yards. He crossed the tracks and climbed the bank on the far side to Grand Avenue. Two boys were throwing rocks at a row of bottles down in the railway cut. Smoke on the water, one called.

Fuck you, said Suttree.

A wave of nausea washed through him and he paused to rest on an old retaining wall. Looking under his hand he saw dimly the prints of trilobites, lime cameos of vanished bivalves and delicate seaferns. In these serried clefts stone armatures on which once hung the flesh of living fish. He lurched on.

He stopped in the middle of the street before the tall frame house on Grand. Paintless boards smoked a bluish color. He called to a woman sitting on the porch. She leaned forward peering.

Is Jimmy there?

No. He's not come in from last night. Who is that?

Cornelius Suttree.

Lord have mercy I didnt know who that was. No, he's not here, Cornelius. I dont know where he's at.

Well. Thank you mam.

You come see us.

I will. He waved a hand. A police car was turning the corner.

They drove past. Before he got to the end of the street they had circled and pulled up alongside him from behind.

Where you goin, boy?

Home, he said.

Where you live?

Down off Front Avenue.

Beefy face, small eyes looking him over. The face turned away. They said something between them. The one turned back. What's happened to you?

Nothing, he said. I'm all right.

I believe you a little drunk aint ye?

No sir.

Where you been?

He looked at his crusted shoes and took a breath. I was visiting some people over here. I'm just on my way home.

What you got all over the front of you there?

He looked down. When he raised his head again he fixed his eyes across the cruiser's roof upon the bleak row of old houses with their cloven hanging clapboards and their cardboard windowpanes. A few blackened trees stood withering in the heat and in this obscure purgatory a thrush was singing. Mavis. Turdus Musicus. The lyrical shitbird.

I spilled something on me, he said.

You smell like you been dipped in shit.

Two boys were coming along the broken walk. When they saw the cruiser they turned and went back.

The door opened and beefy got out.

Maybe you better get in here, he said.

Dont put that stinkin son of a bitch in here. Call the wagon.

Well. You just stand right there.

I'm not going anywhere.

I'll tell you that, you aint.

He listened dreamily to the crackling of the intercom.

The paddywagon came down off Western and Forest avenues and pulled up in front of the cruiser and two policemen got out. They opened the door and Suttree walked toward it.

Boy if he aint a sweet blossom, one said.

There was a drunk inside sitting on the bench that ran the length of the wagon. Suttree sat opposite. The door banged shut. The drunk leaned forward. Hey old buddy, he said. You got a cigarette? Suttree shut his eyes and rested his head against the side of the van.

At the jail he stood before a little window and was asked to empty his pockets. He managed a faint smile.

The officer at his side nudged him with a nightstick. Empty them pockets, boy.

Suttree lifted his caked shirt. His pockets hung like socks.

You got any identification on you.

No sir.

How come you aint.

I've been robbed.

What's your name.

Jerome Johnson.

The officer was writing. We've had trouble with you before aint we Johnson?

No sir.

He looked up. I bet we aint. Get his belt and his shoelaces there.

They took him along the corridor toward the cells.

They opened the door to a large cage and he went in and they shut the door behind him. Someone slept in one corner, his head in a pool of clabbered void. There were no benches, no place to sit. A concrete scupper ran the perimeter of the cage. Suttree shuddered in a seizure of skullpangs. He sat on the floor. It was cool. After a while he knelt and pressed his head against it.

He must have slept. He heard the turnkey rapping along the bars, calling a name. When he came past Suttree spoke to him.

Can you call me a bondsman back here?

What's your name?

Johnson.

How long you been in?

I dont know. I was asleep.

You got to stay in six hours anyway.

I know. I was wondering if you'd check for me.

The turnkey didnt say he would or wouldnt.

After a while Suttree stretched out on the floor and slept again. He woke from time to time to shift a bone where it wore against the concrete. It was evening before the bondsman came.

A small dapper man in mesh shoes. He looked up at the foul enigma caged before him. You Johnson? he said.

Yes.

You want to make bail?

Yes. I dont have any money. You'll have to call.

Okay. Who do I call? He had out a pad and pencil.

Suttree gave him the number.

All right, he said. Wait here.

Sure, said Suttree. Listen.

What?

Tell them Suttree. But to ask for Johnson.

You can get in a lot of trouble that way.

I can get in a lot the other way.

Okay. What was it again?

Suttree.

The bondsman was shaking his head, writing the new name. You people are really something, he said.

He was back in a few minutes. He aint home, he said.

Did she say when he might be in?

Nope.

What time is it?

Around seven. He flicked his cuff back. Ten after.

Goddamn.

Dont you know nobody else?

No. Look, try it again in an hour, will you? You sure you got the right number?

21505. Right?

That's it.

What's the guy's name anyways?

Jim.

I know that. What's his full name.

Jim Long.

The bondsman gave him a funny little look. Jim Long? he said.

Yes.

Got a brother named Junior?

That's him.

The bondsman looked at him sideways.

What is it? said Suttree.

Shit.

What's the matter?

Why hell fire, the bondsman said. Both of em are right behind you in number eight. They been here since this mornin and cant raise bond neither.

He was looking at Suttree more curiously yet. Suttree's face began to wrinkle and go peculiar. A horse snigger leapt from his lips and his eyes wandered.

You're crazy as shit, said the bondsman.

Suttree sat down on the concrete floor and held his stomach. He sat there shaking and holding himself. You're a real nutwagon, aint ye? said the bondsman.

Later he called through the bars to his friends but they didnt answer. A voice somewhere asked why he didnt shut the fuck up. Later still the lights in the corridor ceiling came on. The man in the corner had not moved and Suttree didnt want to look at him if he were dead. He lay on the floor again and drifted in and out of a poor sleep. He dreamt whole rivers of icewater down his parched throatpipe.

At some hour unknown he woke to sounds of commotion. He had half his hand in his mouth. Looking up he saw a man stoop and swing a bucket of water through the bars over him. Sputtering, he got to his knees.

The bucket clanged to the floor. The man studied him there in his cage. Suttree turned away. In the corner his cellmate was standing. When Suttree looked at him the cellmate said: You dont shut up that hollerin I'm goin to knock your dick in your watchpocket.

He closed his eyes. The gray water that dripped from him was rank with caustic. By the side of a dark dream road he'd seen a hawk nailed to a barn door. But what loomed was a flayed man with his brisket tacked open like a cooling beef and his skull peeled, blue and bulbous and palely luminescent, black grots his eyeholes and bloody mouth gaped tongueless. The traveler had seized his fingers in his jaws, but it was not alone this horror that he cried. Beyond the flayed man dimly adumbrate another figure paled, for his surgeons move about the world even as you and I.

He scouted in the weeds until he found a suitable tin before going out to the road. The kerosene had rendered soft a patch of tar in the roadsurface and he knelt and began to dig it up with an old kitchen knife, stringy viscous gobs of pitch, until he had as much as he needed.

When Daddy Watson came by he had the skiff upturned on the bank and was patiently caulking the seams.

Well, you still alive, the old man said.

Suttree looked up, squinting in the sun. He wiped his nose against his forearm, sitting there holding the tarpot in one hand and the knife in the other. Hello Daddy, he said.

I allowed ye'd gone under.

Not yet. Why?

Didnt see ye. Where ye been?

Suttree daubed the rank black mastic along a seam and pressed it home. Jail, he said.

Hey?

I said I've been in jail.

Have? What for?

I fell in with a bad crowd. What brings you over here?

The old man pushed back his striped engineer's cap and readjusted it. Just on my way to town. Thought long as I was this close I'd check on ye. I allowed ye must of gone under.

I'm still in business. How's everything on the railroad?

Just by god awful.

Suttree waited for an enlargement upon this but none seemed coming. He looked up. The old man was rocking on his heels, watching.

What's the problem, Daddy?

Just railroadin is the problem, son. It's the nature of it, I'm convinced. He hauled forth an enormous railroader's timepiece and checked it and put it back.

How's old number seventy-eight?

Lord love her she's old and wore out about like me but she's faithful as a dog. Ort to give her a gold watch and chain.

He was leaning forward watching over Suttree's shoulder as he caulked.

You know, he said. I wish I could get you to come over to my yard with that stuff. I got a leak in my caboose roof needs somethin done about it.

Suttree bent forward and averted his face. Got a what? he shouted, eyes half closed with mirth.

Say I got leaky roof. Caboose roof.

Suttree shook his head. He looked up at the old man. Well, he said. If I've got any left I'll bring it over.

The old man straightened up. That's neighborly of ye and I'd take it as a favor, he said. He was hauling out the watch again.

I'd best get on to town if I'm to get to the store fore it closes.

What time is it, Daddy?

Four nineteen.

Well. Stop again when you can stay longer.

I'll do it, said the railroader. And dont forget to save me some of that there pitch if you've got it to spare.

Okay.

I allowed ye'd gone under when I didnt see ye on the river.

No.

Well.

He watched the old man go across the steaming fields, tottering stiffly in his overalls. When he reached the tracks he turned and lifted one hand farewell. Suttree lifted his chin and turned back to his work.

When he had the underside of the skiff daubed up he set the tar by and turned the skiff over and eased it along the mud into the river. He took the rope and walked out along the gallery of the houseboat and tethered it to the railing. He took the oars from where they stood against the side of the house and lowered them into the skiff. Slouched on the railing he watched the dried silt in the bottom of the skiff darken along the joints where the boards would swell shut in the water. As he stood there the five oclock freight ran out on the trestle downriver. Crossing the high span of black wickered steel like an enormous millipede, balls of smoke coughing from the blowhole in the engine's head and the sootcolored cars clattering after and leaving the air curiously serene behind the racket of their passage.

He pulled a bottle of orange soda from the river by a long cord and uncapped it and sat with his feet propped on the rail taking cool sips. A black woman appeared on the deck of the houseboat upriver and slung two rattling bags of trash overboard and went in again. Suttree leaned his head against the hot boards and watched the river go past.

The shadow of the bridge had begun to lie long oblique and sprawling upstream and pigeons ascending into its concrete understructure evoked upon the water before him shapes of skates rising batwinged from the river floor to feed in the creeping dusk. He closed his eyes and opened them again. Plovers along the shore jerking like wired birds in a shooting gallery. Down there a pipe piping gouts of soap-curd and blue sewage. Dusk deepened. Swifts vanished back over the pewter face of the river toward the city. On thin falcon wings night-hawks dipped and wheeled and a bat fluttered past, circled, returned.

Inside Suttree lit a lamp and adjusted the wick. With the same match he lit the burners of the little kerosene stove, two rosettes of pale blue teeth in the gloom. He set a saucepan of beans to warm and got down his skillet and sliced onions into it. He un-wrapped a packet of hamburger. Small moths kept crossing the mouth of the lampchimney and spinning burntwinged into the hot grease. He picked them out on the tines of the brass fork with which he tended the cookery and flipped them against the wall. When all was ready he scraped the food from the pans onto a plate and took it together with the lamp to the small table by the window and laid everything out on the oilcloth and sat and ate leisurely. A barge passed upriver and he watched through the cracked glass the dip and flicker of her spotlight negotiating the narrows beneath the bridge, the long white taper shifting in quick sidelong sweeps, the shape of the beam breaking upriver over the trees with incredible speed and crossing the water like a comet. A white glare flooded the cabin and passed on. Suttree blinked. The dim shape of the barge came hoving. He watched the red lights slide in the dark. The houseboat rocked easy in the wake, the drums mumbling under the floor and the skiff sidling and bump-ing outside in the night. Suttree wiped his plate with a piece of bread and sat back. He fell to studying the variety of moths pressed to the glass, resting his elbows on the sill and his chin on the back of his hand. Supplicants of light. Here one tinted easter pink along the edges of his white fur belly and wings. Eyes black, triangular, a robber's mask. Furred and wizened face not unlike a monkey's and wearing a windswept ermine shako. Suttree bent to see him better. What do you want?

When the River Queen passed he was in bed, drifting toward sleep. He heard the labored sludging sound of her wheel beyond his window. As if she bore through liquid mud. A party on deck in song. The voices carrying the water's acoustic calm, the old sternwheeler plying upriver with hard liquor and ladies of quality, soft lights above the green baize blackjack tables and the barman polishing the glasses and the danceband musicians leaning on the rail between sets, until the voices waned with distance and the last echoes honed away to a faint murmur of wind.

Right along here anywheres is okay, said Harrogate, pointing languidly out the open truck window.

The driver glanced sidelong and bored. You got to have a address, peckerhead.

What about the Smoky Mountain Market?

That aint a address. It's got to be where people lives.

He looked about, sitting up in the front of the cab like a child. What about the church yonder? he said.

Church?

Yeah.

Well, I dont know.

Do they not hold with goin to church?

The driver cut the wheel and swung left and pulled up in front of the church. All right, he said. Get your ass out.

He hopped down and reached and banged the door shut. Thanks, he called, waving one hand up to the driver. The driver didnt look. He pulled away and the truck disappeared down the street in the noon traffic.

Harrogate came batting his way through the jungle of kudzu that overhung the bluffs above the river until he found a red clay gully of a path going down the slope. He followed along through lush growths of poison ivy and past enormous mummy shapes of vinestrangled trees, banks of honeysuckle dusted in ocher, into a brief cindery wood where grew black sumacs, pokeweeds gorged with sooty drainage whose clustered fruit gleamed small baubles of a poisonous ebon blue.

The path switchbacked and ran out on a cutbank above an abandoned railsiding. He descended into the roadbed and went on. The old right of way lay dim among the weeds, the rails rusted, curving away over rotted ties and dark slag. He trudged along happily in his outland garb, his thin shoes cupping the rails. The river ran below him surly and opaque and shaping itself on the curious forms of limestone that jutted from the bank. By and by he came upon two fishbutchers slick with blood by an old retaining wall, holding a goodsized carp between them. He greeted them with a smile, a curiously attired person emerging from the shrubbery. They stayed their gorestained hands a moment to study him while the fish bowed and shuddered.

Hidy, he said.

These two regarded each other a moment and then looked down

at him. Blood dripped from the fish. Blood lay among the leaves in little jagged grails of bright vermilion. One beckoned with a dripping claw. Hey boy. Come here.

What do you want?

Come here a minute.

I got to get on. He was going along sideways over the ties.

Just come here a minute.

He sidled away and broke into a run. They watched him without expression until he had gone from sight in the weeds and then turned back to their fish.

A half mile down the track he came upon rolling stock on a siding, an old black iron locomotive with inscriptions of faded gilt and wooden cars quietly rotting in the sun. Creepers threaded the wrecked windows of the coaches, ancient and chalky brown with their riveted seams and welted coamings like something proofed for descents into the sea. He walked the aisle between the dusty green and gnawn brocaded seats. A bird flew. He came down the iron steps to the ground. A voice said: All right, young feller, off of them there cars.

Harrogate turned and beheld an overalled railroader coming down the tracks toward him, an oldtimer in a striped cap with a heavy brass watchchain hanging from him.

The country mouse turned to see which way to run but the man had paused to stoop above a rusted truck with his longspouted oilcan. He was shaking his head and muttering. Old black engine oil dripped from a seized journal. He raised himself erect and checked the time by the clocksized watch he wore in his bibpocket. Where's your buddies at today? he said.

Harrogate looked about to see if it was he that was addressed. A cat regarded him dreamily from the domed roof of the coach, belly weighed with pigeon eggs against the warm tar.

It's just me, said Harrogate.

The old man squinted at him. Your daddy aint a railroad man is he?

No.

I allowed maybe I knowed ye.

I'm new around here.

I dont know ye then.

My name's Gene Harrogate, said Harrogate coming forward. But the old man shook his head and waved him away and climbed laboriously over the couplings between the cars. I know all the people I want to know, he said.

You dont know old Suttree do ye? Harrogate called after him, but the old man didnt answer.

Harrogate went on down the line, under the old steel bridge and out from the shadow of the bluff past a lumberyard and a slaughter-house. Rich odors of pinepitch and manure. The siding switched off among the yards and he crossed a field with a ragged camp of shacks sketched into the distance and a weedy sea of auto wrecks washed up on the flank of a hill. He came out upon a narrow road and after a while he came to a gate construed from an old iron bedframe all overgrown with dusty morninglories and hung about with humming-birds like windtoys on strings. In the yard lay a man in greasy overalls with his head resting on a tire.

Hey, said Harrogate

The man reared up wildly and looked about.

I'm a huntin Suttree.

We're closed, said the man. He rose and crossed the yard toward a tarpaper shack covered with hanging hubcaps, no two alike. Bump-ers were stacked against the wall and water dripped from a tap into a gastank halved open with a torch. Beyond in the rank and steamy foliage wrecked cars crouched and everywhere in this lush waste were blooming flowers and shrubs.

Look around if you want, the man called. Dont bother me. Dont steal nothin. He disappeared into the shack and Harrogate pushed open the gate and entered. The gate was weighted with a chainload of gears and closed gently behind him. The air was rich with humus and he could smell the flowers. Wild datura with pale strange trum-pets and harebells among the debris. Great gangly rosebushes covered with dying blooms that collapsed at a touch. Phlox lavender and pink along a leaning wall of cinderblock and loosestrife and columbine among the iron inner works of autos scattered in the grass. He crossed to the shed and peered through the open door. The man was lying stretched out on a car seat.

Hey, Harrogate said.

The man lifted his arm from his face. What in the name of God do you want anyway? he said.

Harrogate was peering about in the gloom of this small hut crammed with the salvage of highway disasters. Faint country music came from a car radio in the floor. Tires rose in black serried pillars and batteries lay everywhere suppurating a dry white foam.

I'm a huntin old Suttree, he said.

He aint here.

Where might I find him at do ye reckon?

Web City.

Where's that at?

Up a spider's ass.

The junkman put his arm back across his eyes. Harrogate watched him. It was incredibly hot in the shack and it reeked of tar. He studied the outlandish collection of autoparts. You a junkman? he said.

What did you need?

Nothin.

What are ye sellin?

I aint sellin nothin.

Well let's buy or sell one.

I thought you was closed.

Now I'm open. I guess you've got a bunch of hubcaps you've stole.

No I aint.

Where are they?

I aint got none. I'm just out of the workhouse now for stealin watermelons.

I aint buyin no watermelons.

Harrogate shifted to the other foot. His clothes did not move. You live here? he said.

Mmm.

It's neat. I bet a feller could fix hisself a place like this for next to little or nothin, couldnt he?

The man's toes were pointed toward the ceiling and they spread and closed again in a gesture of noncommitment.

Boy I wisht I had me a place.

The man lay there.

Hey, Harrogate said.

The man groaned and rolled over and reached under the car seat and pulled out a quart jar of white whiskey and sat erect enough to funnel a drink down his gullet. Harrogate watched. The man deftly reapplied the twopiece lid and laying the half filled jar against his ribs he subsided into rest and silence once again.

Hey, said Harrogate.

He opened one eye. Boy, he said, what's wrong with you?

Nothin. I'm all right.

You want a job?

Doin what?

Doin what, doin what, the man said to the ceiling.

What kind of a job?

The man sat and swung his feet to the clay floor, the jar cradled in his arm. He shook his sweaty head. After a minute he looked up at Harrogate. I aint got time to mess with people too sorry to work, he said.

I'll work.

Okay. You see that frontended forty-eight Ford out there? That ragtop?

I dont know. They's a bunch out there.

This one is like new. I need the upholstery out of it fore it ruins. Seats, carpets, doorpanels. And I need em cleaned.

What are you payin?

What'll you take?

Harrogate looked at the ground. A black swarf packed with small parts in a greasy mosaic. I'll take two dollars, he said.

I'll give ye a dollar.

Dollar and a half.

You're on. They's wrenches in that box yonder and a screwdriver. The seats unbolts from underneath. Them door and winderhandle scutches are spring loaded you push in on em and knock the pins out with a nail. Armrests unscrews. When you get em all out I got some soap and they's a watertap at the side of the house.

Okay.

The man set down the jar and rose and went to the door. He pointed out the car. It was accordioned to half its length. Bring them sunvisors too, he said.

What happened to it?

Run head on into a semi. Froze the speedometer on the peg. You'll see it.

Harrogate looked at the car in some wonder. How many was in it?

Four or five. Bunch of boys. They found one in a field about two days later.

Did it kill em?

The junkman looked down at Harrogate. Did it what? he said.

Did it kill em.

Why no. I think one of em got a skint knee is all.

Boy I dont see how it kept from killin em.

The junkman shook his head wearily and went back in.

Harrogate got the toolbox and went out to the car. He pulled on one crumpled door and pried at it. He went around to the other one but it had no handle.

Hey, he said, standing in the door of the shack again.

What now?

I caint get in. The doors is jammed.

You may have to jack em open. Go in through the top and take one of them jacks yonder and some blocks. And quit botherin me.

He went back out, small apprentice, clambering up on the decklid and climbing down through the bows and stays and rags of canvas into the interior of the car. It smelled richly of leather and mildew and something else. The windshields were broken out and along the jagged jaws of glass in the channels hung cured shreds of matter and small bits of cloth. The upholstery was red and the blood that had dried in spattered shapes over it was a deep burgundy black. He propped his feet against one door and gave it a good kick and it fell open. Some kind of globular material hung down over the steering column. He climbed out of the car and bent down to find the heads of the bolts beneath the seats. The carpeting had been rained on and was lightly furred with pale blue mold. Something small and fat and wet with an umbilical looking tail lying there. A sort of slug. He picked it up. A human eye looked up at him from between his thumb and forefinger.

He set it carefully back where he'd gotten it and looked around. It was hot and very quiet in the little yard. He reached and picked it up again and studied it a minute and set it back and rose from his knees and went toward the gate, holding his hand before him, down the road toward the river.

After he'd washed his hand for a while and squatted and thought about things he started back toward the bridge. There was a lower path that kept to the very brim of the river, winding over roots and along blackened shelves of stone. Fragile mats of trampled growth hanging over the water. Harrogate studied the shape of the city cross-river as he went.

Under the shadow of the bridge the bare red earth lay in a strip of sunless blight. Rusty baitcans, tangled strands of nylon fishline among the rocks. He came out of the weeds and up past the ragpicker's firepit with its stale odor of smoked stones and stopped to study the darkness under the concrete arch. When that ragged troll appeared from behind his painted rock Harrogate nodded affably. Hidy, he said.

The ragpicker scowled.

I guess it's done took in under here, aint it?

The old hermit made no answer but Harrogate seemed not to mind. He came closer, looking things over. Boy, he said. You got it fixed up slick in under here, aint ye?

The ragpicker raised slightly up like a nesting bird disturbed.

I'll bet that there old bed sleeps good, said Harrogate pointing.

You better look out, spoke a voice from the high arches. That old man is mean as a snake.

Harrogate craned his neck to see who'd said it. Fat birds the color of slate crooned among the concrete trusses overhead. Who's that? he called, his voice returning all hollow and strange.

You better run. He's known to carry a pistol.

Harrogate looked at the ragpicker. The ragpicker flapped about and bared his teeth. He looked up again. Hey, he called.

There was no answer. Where's he at? said Harrogate. But the ragpicker just mumbled and withdrew from sight.

Harrogate approached closer and peered into the gloom. The old man was seated in a burst chair at the rear of his quarters. There were odds and ends of furniture standing all around on the rank dirt floor and there was a vaguely eastern carpet with a raw cord warp that was eating away the serried minarets and there were oil lamps and stolen roadlanterns and cracked plaster statuary that stood like ghosts in the semidark and earthen crocks and crates of bottles and bricabrac and mounded troves of shoddy and great tottering sheaves of newsprint and heaps of rags. The bed was old and ornate with crown and finial in cast brass.

Caint you read, boy? the old man's voice piped sepulchral from his lair.

Not real good.

That there sign says to keep out.

They lord, I wouldnt come in without bein asked. You got it fixed up slick in here, I'll say that.

The ragpicker grunted. He had his feet up in the chair with him and his thin polished shins shone like naked bones crossed there.

Dont they nobody bother ye down here?

I get a loose fool or two come by ever now and then, said the ragman.

How long ye been here?

97

About that long, the old man said, spacing a random measure between his palms.

Harrogate grinned and rose to the challenge. You know the difference tween a grocery store fly and a hardware store fly?

The ragman's eyes grew even colder.

Well, the grocery store fly lights on the beans and peas, and the hardware store fly lights on the nails and screws. Harrogate folded suddenly and slapped his thigh and cackled like a stricken fowl.

Boy why dont you get on down the road wherever you come from or was goin to one and leave me the son of a bitching hell alone?

Hell, I just stopped to say Hidy. I didnt mean nothin by it.

The old man closed his eyes.

Say listen. Is they anyone under the far end yonder?

The ragman looked. Across the river down the long aisle of arches lay the distant facing image of his own shelter. Why dont you go see? he said.

Danged if I wont, said Harrogate. If it aint spoke for we'll be neighbors. He waved and started up around the side of the bridge. We'll get along, he called back. I can get along with anybody.

It was midafternoon when he crossed into the city and descended the steep path at the end of the bridge, swinging down through a jungle of small locust trees filled with long spikes and blackened starlings that flew shrieking out over the river and circled and came back. He emerged onto the barren apron of clay beneath the bridge. Small black children playing there in the cool. Below them a black and narrow street. One of the children saw him and then they all looked up, three soft dark faces watching.

Hidy, he said.

They squatted immobile. Small wooden trucks and autos stalled in streets graded out with a broken shingle. Beyond them a brown clapboard house, foreyard a moonscape in clay and coaldust, a few sorry chickens crouched in the shade. A black man swung reposed and prone on a bench hung by chains from the porch ceiling and a line of faded wash steamed in the windless heat.

What are you all doin?

The oldest spoke. We aint done nothin.

You all live over yonder?

They admitted it with solemn nods.

Harrogate looked about. He reckoned he'd not be put to living next door to niggers leastways. He climbed down the bank and came out on the road and went on downriver past rows of shacks. The road was pocked and buckled and after a while it went to sand and dried mud and then nothing. A thin path wandered on through weeds hung with wastepaper. Harrogate followed after.

The path cut through heatstricken lots and fallow land and passed under a high trestle that crossed the river. A tramp's midden among the old stone footings where gray bones lay by rusted tins and a talus of jarshards. A ring of blackened bricks and the remains of a fire. Harrogate wandered about, poking at things with a stick. Pieces of burnt foil sunburst in blue and yellow. Dredging charred relics from the ashy sleech. Melted glass that had reseized in the helical bowl of a bedspring like some vitreous chrysalis or chambered whelk from southern seas. He dusted it on his sleeve and carried it with him. Across a smoking alluvial strewn with refuse to the faint rise of the railtracks and the river beyond.

A row of black fishermen sat along the ties where the tracks crossed the creek, their legs dangling above the oozing sewage. They watched their corks tilt below them in the creek mouth and did not turn to see him teeter past along the rail, his head averted above the sulphurous fart reek that seeped up between the ties.

You all doin any good? he sang out.

A baleful face looked up and looked away again. He stood watching for a while and then went on, tottering in the heat. The sun like a bunghole to a greater hell beyond. On the hill above him he could see the brickwork of the university and a few fine homes among the trees. He came out at length onto a small riverside street. His sneakers lifting from the hot tar with smacking sounds. A sidelong dog receded at a half trot before him down the street toward the shade of some lilac bushes by one of the combustible looking shacks there. Harrogate studied the landscape beyond. A patch of gray corn by the riverside, rigid and brittle. A vision of bleak pastoral that at length turned him back toward the city again.

He wandered Knoxville's sadder regions for the better part of the afternoon, poking in alleys, probing old cellars, the dusty lees or nether dank of public works. Him wide eyed in his juryrigged apparel not unlike some small apostate to the race itself, pausing here at a wall to read what he could of inscriptions in cloudy chalk, the agenda of anonymous societies, assignation dates, personal intelligence on the habits of local females. A row of bottles gone to the wall for stoning lay in brown and green and crystal ruin down a sunlit corridor and one upright severed cone of yellow glass rose from the paving like a flame. Past these gnarled ashcans at the alley's mouth with their crusted rims and tilted gaping maws in and out of which soiled dogs go night and day. An iron stairwell railing shapeless with birdlime like something brought from the sea and small flowers along a wall reared from the fissured stone.

He paused at some trash in a corner where a warfarined rat writhed. Small beast so occupied with the bad news in his belly. It must have been something you ate. Harrogate crouched on his heels and watched with interest. He prodded it gently with a curtainrod he'd found. From a doorway a girl watched him motionless and thin and unkempt. A crude doll dressed in rags with huge eyes darkly dished and guttering in her bird's skull. Harrogate looked up and caught her watching him and she went all squirmy with her hands pulling at the raveled hem of her dress for a moment before her head snapped back and he could see a ropeveined claw clutched in her hair and the girl jerked backward and disappeared through an open door. He looked down at the rat again. It was moving one rear leg in slow circles as if to music. It must have felt some cold pneuma pass for it suddenly shivered and then it let out its feet slowly until they came to rest. Harrogate poked it with the curtainrod but the rat only rolled loosely in its skin. Fleas were running out at the lean gray face.

He rose and nudged the rat with his toe and then went on down the alley. He crossed a tarred street bedded with bottlecaps and bits of metal, scattered patterns in niello and one improbable serpent, the ribbed spine polished by traffic and partly coiled in a pale bone omen he could not read. Overhead the bowls of stoned out polelamps. A lank black slattern stood hipshot in a doorframe. Hey boydove, you gettin any gravel for yo goose? Whoopla laughter scuttling after him and a gold tooth winksome, bawdy dogstar in the ordurous jaws of fellatio major.

He went where torpid blacks crouched or drowsed in doorways, stoops, on corners almost in the traffic. Old men like effigies with fingers laced and capped upon the heads of canes between their knees. In suits thought long extinct, perforated two-tone shoes, socks rolled in obscene tubes about their thin black ankles. A hawkfaced ebon freak importuned him, sussurous, long underlip leaking a clear drool. Flies clove the air like comets. He passed on. Eyes averted. Dark matrons at the upper windows in hot and airless dishabille, chocolate breasts leaning. Dusklovers. Ancillary disciples to the rise of night.

He'd come from the dwellingstreets of whites to those of blacks and no gray middle folk did he see.

Summer dusk had crept long and blue and shadows risen high upon the western building faces when he came up Gay Street. He went along the shopfronts like a misplaced poacher, his eyes squirreling about and his broken clown's sneakers flapping. At Lockett's he paused to admire dusty charlatan's props in the window, small boxes of sneeze powder, cigars laced with cordite, a stamped tin inkstain. Stapled to display cards from which the sun had bleached all message. A china dog bowbacked and grunting. Harrogate filled with admiration at such things. He stepped slightly back to note the merchant's name and then went on. Passing under the Comer's Sport Center sign, a steep stairwell and the muted clack of balls overhead. There it is, he said. Bigger'n life.

He turned up Union Avenue, past the Roxie Theatre, Webfoot Watts and Skinny Green on the bill with all-girl revue. Harrogate stepping around to see the tariffs. The girl looked down from her glass cage like a cat. He smiled and drew back. He went down Walnut Street past hardware stores and beer taverns and ramshackle poultry shops. He swung up Wall Avenue and into Market Square. His small face peering through the windows of the Gold Sun Cafe where supper plates were being sopped clean and rawlooking girls went up and back in their soiled white uniforms.

Down Market Street countrymen sat beneath canopies in canebottomed chairs or on upended peachcrates or perched on the leadcolored fenders of old Fords fitted out with crude truckbeds nailed up out of boards. Folks putting up their stuffs for this day, shops being closed. A few sunfaded awnings winched shut. Two roustabouts collected a beggar from the walkway and set him in a truck. Harrogate went on. An old man seated before a basket of turnips hissed him and gestured with his chin, seeking a buyer, Harrogate to his worn eyes no worse a prospect than others coming along. Harrogate watching the gutters for anything edible fallen from the trucks. By the time he reached the end of the street he had a small bouquet of frazzled greenstuffs and a bruised tomato. He went into the markethouse and washed these things at the drinking fountain marked White and ate them while he wandered down the vast hall with its rich reek of meat and produce and woodchaff. A few vendors squatted yet in their stalls, old women with tawed faces and farmers with their quilted napes. A honeyseller sitting quietly in immaculate blue chambray, his jars on the low table before him arranged faultlessly, the labels marshaled aislewise. Harrogate went by, chewing his lettuce. Past a long glass coffin where a few lean fish leered up with cold and golden eyes from their beds of salted ice. Windchimes tinkled overhead in the slow fanwash. He pushed open the heavy doors at the end of the hall with their hundred years' accretion of navalgray paint and stepped out into the summer night. Standing there wiping his hands on the front of him, his eyes drawn by the cryptic piping of hot neon across the night and by the chittering of goatsuckers aloft in the upflung penumbra of the city's lights. A streetsweeper puttered past with his cart. Harrogate crossed the street and went up the alley. A family of trashpickers were packing flat cartons onto a child's wagon, the children scurrying among the rancid cans like rats and as graylooking. None spoke. They had tied the folded boxes down with twine, a parlous and tottering load that the man steadied with one hand while the woman drew the cart along and the children made forays into trashbins and cellar doors, watching Harrogate the while.

He made his way by alleys and small dark streets to the lights at Henley Street where he'd earlier spied a church lawn. Here he found himself a nest among the curried clumps of phlox and boxwood and curled up like a dog. He had a few things he'd collected in his pocket and he took these out and set them alongside in the edging of mulch and lay back again in the grass. He could feel under his back the rumble of trucks passing in the street. He shifted his hips. He folded his hands behind his head. He must prop his upturned toes together to ease the weight of the enormous shoes from his bird's ankles. After a while he slipped them off and lay back again. Yellow lamplight clung in his lashes. He watched insects rise and wheel there. A hunting bat cut through the cone of light and sucked them scattering. They re-formed slowly. Soon two bats. Veering and rending the placid life that homed to ash in the columnar light. Harrogate awonder at how they did not collide.

He was sitting up in the shrubbery long before good daylight, waiting for the day to come for him to set forth in, watching the glozy headlights come out of the fog on the bridge and draw past him into the town. Shapes evolved out of the gray dawn. What he'd thought to be another indigent hosteled on the grass below him was a newspaper winded up against a bush. He rose and stretched and crossed the lawn to the street and went toward Market where all sorts of country commerce had begun.

Harrogate eased his way among the rotting trucks and carts at the curbside until he had the lay of things and then his scrawny hand darted out and seized a peach from a basket and tucked it down the windsock of a pocket that hung inside his trousers. The next thing he knew an old lady had him by the collar and was beating him over the head with a mealscoop. She was yelling in his face and spraying him with snuffjuice. Shit, said Harrogate, trying to pull away. A long ripping sound ensued.

Quit it. You're tearin my goddamned shirt.

Bong bong bong went the mealscoop on his bony head.

Give it back, she squalled.

Hell fire. Here. He thrust the peach at her and she immediately turned loose of him and took the peach and wobbled back to her truck and restored it to the basket.

He felt his head. It was all knotty. Shit a brick, he said. I didnt want the goddamned thing that bad. A legless beggar mounted on a board like a piece of ghastly taxidermy had come awake to laugh at him. Fuck you, said Harrogate. The beggar shot forward on ballbearing wheels and seized Harrogate's leg and bit it.

Shit! screamed Harrogate. He tried to pull away but the beggar had his teeth locked in the flesh of his calf. They danced and circled, Harrogate holding to the top of the beggar's head. The beggar gave a shake of his head and a tug in a last effort to remove the flesh from Harrogate's legbone and then turned loose and receded smoothly to his place against the wall and took up his pencils again. Harrogate went limping down the street holding his leg. Crazy sons of bitches, he said, hobbling among the shoppers. He was almost in tears.

He crossed through the markethouse and went up the other side of the square. Something was pulling at his shoe. He bent to see. Chewing gum. He sat in the gutter with a stick and scraped at it. Turning a pink blob of it on the end of the stick . . .

Harrogate coasted by the blind man in front of Bower's, watching the crowd. No one watched back. He returned, bent lightly, jabbed with his stick at the cigarbox in the blind man's lap. The blind man raised his head and put one hand over the box and looked about. Harrogate going up the street tilted the stick. A dime clung to the end of it. He swung about and came back. The blind man sat warily. Paleblue and moldgrown grapes caved and wrinkled in his eyesockets. Harrogate executed a fencer's thrust and came up with a nickel.

Hey you cocksucker, called the blind man.

Fuck you, said Harrogate, skipping nimbly on.

He went into the Gold Sun and ordered coffee and doughnuts, sitting at the counter among the morning smells of fried sausage and eggs. He rolled back the folds of his trouserlegs and examined his wound. The beggar's illspaced teeth had printed two little sickle shapes, the flesh blue, small pinlets of blood. Harrogate wet a paper napkin in his water glass and laved it over his queer stigmata. Son of a bitch, he muttered. He drank the coffee and slid his cup forward for more.

In the streets again he rubbed his little belly and set out for Comer's. Climbing the stairs. A small bent person at the landing watched. Who knew every cop in town in or out of uniform. Harrogate pushed open the green door with its wiremesh covered glass and entered. To his surprise the place was nearly empty. A blond youth was practising three rail banks at the second table. The rack was brushing the tables in the rear. A whimsical man with a paunch hanging over his changeapron and jaws knobby with tobacco. At Harrogate's elbow tickertape hung from a glass bell and several old men sat along the benches to the front of the hall and watched the day start in the street below.

Harrogate went to the counter where a man in an eyeshade was counting money. You know Suttree? he said.

What? said the man.

Suttree.

Ask Jake. He tilted his head toward the rear of the hall and went on counting. Harrogate went wobbling down the aisle past the tables, the cues racked up on the walls like weapons in some ancient armory. Hey, said the blond youth.

What?

You want to play some nine ball?

I dont know how to play.

Rotation?

I aint never shot no pool.

The blond youth studied him a moment, chalking his cue with a little rotary motion. He bent to shoot.

You know Suttree?

He stroked. The one ball went down the table, circled the racked balls from rail to rail and returned to drop in the upper corner pocket. Harrogate waited for the shooter to answer but the shooter took the ball from the pocket and set it up and bent again with his cue and did not look up. Harrogate went on to the rear.

You Jake? he said.

Yep.

You know Suttree?

He turned and looked down at Harrogate. He spat into a steel cuspidor on the floor and wiped his mouth with the back of his hand. Yeah, he said. I know him.

You know where he's at?

What'll you take for them britches?

Harrogate looked down. Them's all the ones I got, he said.

Well. He aint here.

I was wonderin if you might know where he's at.

Home I reckon.

Well where's he live?

He lives down on the river. I believe in one of them houseboats.

Houseboat?

Yep. Jake bent, the change in his apronpocket swinging. He began to brush the dust toward the corner pocket. Harrogate had turned to go.

What about that shirt?

What about it?

How would you trade?

Hell fire, said Harrogate. Yourn'd do me for a overcoat.

Jake grinned. Come back, little buddy, he said.

At the bottom of Gay Street he stood leaning on the bridge rail looking down at the waterfront. There's the goddamned houseboats, he said.

Coming down the steep and angled path behind the tall frame houses he thought he heard a voice. He tilted back his head to see. Half out from a housewindow high up the laddered face of soot-caulked clapboards hung some creature. Sprawled against the hot and sunpeeled siding with arms outstretched like a broken puppet. Hah, he called down. Spawn of Cerberus, the devil's close kin.

Harrogate clutched his lower teeth.

A long finger pointed down. Child of darkness, of Clooty's brood, mind me.

Shit, said Harrogate.

The window figure had raised itself to address some other audience.

See him! Does he not offend thee? Does such iniquity not rise stinking to the very heavens?

This viperous evangelist reared up, his elbows cocked and goat's eyes smoking, and thrust a bony finger down. Die! he screamed. Perish a terrible death with thy bowels blown open and black blood boiling from thy nether eye, God save your soul amen.

Shit fire, said Harrogate, scurrying down the path with one hand over his head. When he reached the street he looked back. The figure had wheeled to a new window the better to see the boy past his house and he leaned now with his face pressed to the glass, his dead jaundiced flesh splayed against the pane and one eye walled up in his head, a goggling visage misshapen with hatred. Harrogate went on. Great godamighty, he said.

He went down Front Street past a rickety store where blacks lolled and eyed his advent doubtfully and he took a dogpath across the gray fields toward the shantyboats, emerging onto the railway with his curious trousers striped with sootprints of the weeds he'd forded, the air hot and breathless with the smell of cinders and creosote and the fainter reaches of oil and fish standing off in a sort of haze along the river itself.

He climbed the mudstained cleated plank of the first houseboat and tapped at the door. A small eddy of garbage and empty bottles circled slowly in the water beneath him. When the door opened he was looking into the face of a coalcolored woman who wore an agate taw in one eyesocket. What you wants? she said.

I thought maybe old Suttree lived here but I dont reckon he does. She didnt answer.

You dont know where he lives do ye?

Who you huntin?

Suttree.

What you wants with him.

He's a old buddy of mine.

She looked him up and down. He aint goin to mess with you, she said.

Shit, said Harrogate. We go way back, me and Suttree do.

Suttree was up at first light to run his lines. The gray shape of the city gathering out of the fog, upriver a gull, pale and alien bird in these midlands. On the bridge the lights of the cars crossed like candles in the mist.

Maggeson was already on the river when he set forth, standing like some latterday Charon skulling through the fog. With a long pole he hooked condoms aboard and into a pail of soapy water. Suttree paused to watch him but the old man drifted past without looking up, standing with prurient vigilance, in the cropped shore currents watchful and silent.

Suttree rowed in a sunless underregion of swirling mists, through bowls of cold and seething smoke. The bridgepier loomed and faded. Downriver a dredger. Two men at the rail smoking, stitched out of the fog and gone again, their voices faint above the puckered chug of the engine. The red of the wheelhouse light went watery pale and faded out. He oared slowly, waiting for the fog to lift.

When he ran his lines some of the fish were dead. He cut the droppers and watched them slide and sink. The rising sun dried and warmed him.

He was back by midmorning and sat on the rail and cleaned his catch. Ab's cat came and perched like an owl and watched him. He handed it a fish head and it bared a razorous yawn of teeth and took the head delicately and went back along the rail. Suttree skinned two catfish and wrapped them in newsprint and washed his knife and his hands in the river and rose.

Going up the river path he passed two boys fishing.

Hey boys, he said.

They turned huge eyes up at him.

Doin any good?

Naw.

Their bobbers lay quietly in the scum. Ringent pools of gas kept erupting in oily eyes on the surface. Mauves and yellows from the spectrum guttered and slewed in the dead current.

You boys like to fish?

We dont gots to.

Good for you, said Suttree.

At Ab's place he handed her the fish at the door and she motioned him past into the room. A thick funk of stale beer and smoke. She folded back the paper, old news repeated mirrorwise on the pale ribbed flesh. She poked a black finger in the meat.

Where's the old man? said Suttree.

He's in there. Go on.

In the far corner sat an enormous figure obscured in the gloom. Come in Youngblood.

Hey.

Set down. Bring the man a beer old woman.

I dont want anything.

Bring him a Redtop.

She shuffled past in her ruptured mules through a curtain to the rear. A squalid sunlight fell briefly. Everywhere from cracks or knotholes small hieroglyphs of light lay about in the cabin, on table and floor and across the cardboard beer signs.

When she came back she leaned across Suttree and clicked a wet bottle down on the little stone table. He nodded to her and raised it and drank. The black man now coalesced out of the semidark seemed to fill half the room. Where you from in the world, Youngblood, he said.

Right here. Knoxville.

Knoxville, he said. Old Knoxville town.

She was clattering about in the back room. After a while she came from behind the curtain again and sat in her chair with her feet up. She was instantly asleep, the blind eye half open like a drowsing cat's, her mouth agape. Toes peered from the mules like little clusters of dark mice. On her broad face two intersecting circles, fairy ring or hagstrack, the crescent welts of flesh like a sacerdotal brand on some stone age matriarch. Annular treponema. Read here why he falls in the streets. Another Jena, another time.

Suttree sat in the hot little room with the tombstone tables and sipped his beer. Water dripped constantly from the bottle. In the corner the poker table had been swept and the lamp filled. Flies walked about everywhere.

Get you another beer, Youngblood.

Suttree tilted the bottle and drained it. I got to go, he said.

The black wiped his eyes with one huge hand. Stories of the days and nights writ there, the scars, the teeth, the ear betruncheoned in some old fray that clung in a toadlike node to the side of his shaven head. You come back, he said.

Early afternoon in the city with his fish sold he ate the beef stew at Granny and Hazel's. He walked in the streets, a lonely figure. On Jackson Avenue he saw Maggeson in a dingy white suit and straw boater. The rubber baron, small eyes distorted behind the dished glass lenses.

Someone called to him, he turned. Hoghead Henry's small and jaunty shape was coming from an alleyway heralded by pigeons flapping upward into the sad air with right alarm, immune to Hoghead's huckleberry insouciance. He swept his rumpled linen beneath the band of his trousers with a slice of his flattened hand and gave Suttree a crooked grin. When did you get out?

Tuesday. Brother and Junior got out with me.

Hoghead grinned. They started up the street. Old Junior, the cops brought him in one night and turned him over to Mrs Long, he was about three fourths drunk and been in some kind of trouble, I forget, and Mrs Long told the cops, said: I dont know what's wrong with him. My oldest boy Jimmy never causes me the least trouble. Next night here they come with Jim.

Suttree smiled. I hear that old woman shot at you the other night.

Old crazy nigger woman. She shot about four holes in the wall. Shot a picture down. I ducked behind the sofa and she shot a hole in that and John Clancy said they was a rat the size of a housecat come out from under it just a shittin and a gettin it. He was layin in the floor and he said it run right over the top of him.

What did you do down there anyway?

Aw, you dont have to do nothin to stir up a bunch of old crazy niggers.

You know what she called you?

What'd she call me?

Called you a white pointedheaded motherfucker.

Hoghead grinned. They had me in the paper one time, they're always callin anybody towheaded that's got lightcolored hair, they had me in there and I'd said somethin smart to this juvenile judge and they put: said the twoheaded youth.

Suttree grinned. Where you going?

Just up here with some punchboards. Come go with me.

I pass.

Well, I got to get on. Stay out of the jailhouse, you hear?

I hear, said Suttree.

When he crossed the porch of Howard Clevenger's store on Front Street there was an old woman rummaging through a basket of kale there as if she had lost something in it. Oceanfrog Frazer was standing at the screendoor. He patted Suttree on the ribs. What's shakin, baby.

Hey, said Suttree.

They pushed through the door together. Atop the drink cooler squatted a black and ageless androgyne in fool's silks. A purple shirt with bloused sleeves, striped fuchsia trousers and matching homedyed tennis shoes. A gold leather motorcycle belt about a vespine waist. A hat from the hand of a coked milliner. Hi sweetie, he said.

Hello John.

Trippin Through The Dew, said Oceanfrog.

Hey baby.

Hey Frog, called a black from the rear of the store.

What you want?

Come here baby. I got to talk to you.

I aint got time to mess with you.

Suttree poked among the loaves of bread.

Oceanfrog lifted a carton of milk from the cooler and opened it and drank.

Hey Gatemouth.

Yeah baby.

You hear about B L's old lady catchin him?

No man, what happened?

She come in over there Sunday caught him in bed with this old gal and started warpin him in the head with a shoe. This old gal raised straight up in the bed buck naked and hollered at her, said: Lay it to him honey, said: I was married to a son of a bitch just like him.

A high whinny escaped the painted gaud perched at Oceanfrog's elbow. The mascaraed eyes sidled, the black and languid hands made draping motions about the elbows. Oceanfrog you is a mess, she said.

Old B L's crazy, said Gatemouth.

Suttree smiled among the rusting canisters of food at the back wall. He passed behind the hoglike bulk of Gatemouth in his chair. Hey baby, said Gatemouth. What's the haps?

Hey, said Suttree, moving toward the meatcase.

A discussion on the mating habits of possums ensued. A young black named Jabbo entered the store.

Hey baby, called Gatemouth.

Gate City, said Jabbo. Aint no town and it aint no city. He glared at Trippin Through The Dew. How about gettin your nelly ass off the dopebox.

Ooh, said the invert, sliding to the floor like a neon eel.

Gatemouth says a possum dont have a forked peter, Oceanfrog told the store.

I never, said Gatemouth. I said he dont screw her in the nose.

What's his peter forked for then?

Cause he's a marsuperal, motherfucker.

Oceanfrog laughed deep in the back of his throat. Shiny tombstone teeth, gums coral pink. Shit man, he said. You completely eat up with the dumb-ass.

Ask Suttree.

I dont know, said Suttree.

He dont want the whole river to know what a fuckin dumb-ass you is, said Oceanfrog. He tipped the carton of milk and rifled a long drink down his dark throat.

Who is that crazy motherfucker up in that house hollers at everbody? said Jabbo.

Where at honey? The queen of Front Street was solicitous. Jabbo ignored her. Up here, he said, pointing. Crazy motherfucker hollers the craziest shit I ever heard.

That's just the old crazy reverend up there, said Gatemouth. Hollers all the time: Are you warshed in the blood.

He can talk some shit.

I goin to slap his head sideways he dont get off of me.

He hollers at everbody.

I aint everbody.

He's a cripple.

He'll be crippled.

They has to carry out his slops and everthing.

He trimmed hisself, said Trippin Through The Dew.

Done what?

Trimmed hisself. With a razor. Just sliced em on off honey, what they tell me.

That wouldnt cripple you.

It would smart some, said Oceanfrog.

He was done crippled fore he done it.

I goin to trim his fuckin wig he dont quit that hollerin at me, said Jabbo.

Suttree ducked the yardlong coil of dead flies that hung from the ceiling and came to the counter with his purchases.

What else? said Howard.

That's it.

He totted with pencil on a scrap of paper.

Forty-two cents.

Suttree dredged up coins from his jeans.

Where you goin, Sut?

Home.

Sure you is. Tell me. Slip off up here somewheres and dip your wick in somethin.

Suttree grinned.

Old Suttree, said Oceanfrog. He caint fade nothin.

Why dont you put me on something?

Shit. You got it all locked now.

He aint interested in them nigger gals. Is you Suttree?

Suttree looked at Jabbo but he didnt answer.

Howard dropped the last of the groceries into the sack and slid it toward Suttree. He took it under his arm and nodded toward the dark idlers. See you, he said.

Hang loose, said Oceanfrog.

The screendoor clapped shut.

Ooh that's a pretty thing, said Trippin Through The Dew.

After he'd eaten his supper he snuffed the lamp and sat in the dark and watched the lights on the far shore standing long and wandlike in the trembling river. Down from Ab Jones's sounds of laughter carried over the black water like ghost voices, old dead revelers reminiscing in the night. After a while he rose and went out and up the river path to the door.

He sat in the corner and sipped a beer. Oceanfrog was sitting in for the house in a light poker game and Ab lay sleeping in the back room. Suttree heard him breathing in the dark when he went past his bedroom, going on to the cubicle behind the torn and stained plastic showercurtain, standing there half holding his breath, the boards in the reeking gloom splotched with a greenish phosphorescence, a sinister mold that glowed faintly. A section of galvanized gutterpipe sluiced the urine down to a rathole in the corner and out into the passing river. There was a small lizard of some kind wet and pale that clung to a naked stud and Suttree pissed on it and it wriggled out through a crack in the wall. He buttoned his trousers and spat into the trough. Reassessing the agility of germs in a sequence of them climbing falling water like salmon he wiped his mouth and selected a clean place on the wall and spat again.

He sat with the back of his head against the board wall and his mind drifted. Moths crossed the mouth of the lamp in its scroll iron sconce above his head, the shape of the flame steadfast in the pietin reflector. On the ceiling black curds. Where insect shadows war. The reflection of the lamp's glass chimney like a quaking egg, the zygote dividing. Giant spores addorsed and severing. Yawing toward separate destinies in their blind molecular schism. If a cell can be lefthanded may it not have a will? And a gauche will?

In another part of the room Fred Cash was reciting poetry. Suttree heard the last of the Signifyin Monkey and then the ballad of Jack-Off Jake the poolroom snake who fucked his way north to Duluth. He rose and got another beer. Doll in her slippers collected bottles and shuffled off mutely through the smoke and the gloom. Suttree traced with one hand dim names beneath the table stone. Salvaged from the weathers. Whole families evicted from their graves downriver by the damming of the waters. Hegiras to high ground, carts piled with battered cookware, mattresses, small children. The father drives the cart, the dog runs after. Strapped to the tailboard the rotting boxes stained with earth that hold the bones of the elders. Their names and dates in chalk on the wormscored wood. A dry dust sifts from the seams in the boards as they jostle up the road . . .

The cards whispered along the table, the bottles clinked. Under the floor the muffled bong of a barrel shifting. Doll rocked and snored in her chair with the cat in her lap and beyond the little window the houseboat shadowed by the city lights ran darkly in the river among the tarnished stars.

His subtle obsession with uniqueness troubled all his dreams. He saw his brother in swaddling, hands outheld, a scent of myrrh and lilies. But it was the voice of Gene Harrogate that called to him where he tossed on his bunk in the murmurous noon. Harrogate's hand in supplication from the tailgate of a truck, face waffled in the wire mesh, calling.

Suttree sat up groggily. His hair lay matted on his skull and beads of sweat trickled on his face.

Hey Sut.

Just a minute.

He pulled on his trousers and lurched toward the door and flung it open. Harrogate stood there amuck in his clothes, bright thin face, a frail apparition trembling and conceivably unreal in the heat of the day.

How you doin, Sut?

He leaned against the jamb, one hand over his eyes. God, he said.

Was you asleep?

Suttree retreated a step into shadow. He did not take his hand from his face. When did you get out?

Harrogate entered with his country deference, looking about. I been out, he said.

How did you find me?

I ast around. I went to that yan'n first. They's niggers lives there. She told me where you was at. He looked about the little cabin. They was in bed up yonder too, he said. Boy.

Wait a minute, said Suttree.

What?

He turned him about in the light from the window. What are you wearing? he said.

Harrogate shuffled and flapped his arms. Aw, he said. Just some old clothes.

Did they rig you out in these at the workhouse?

Yeah. They lost my clothes what they give me at the hospital. I dont look funny do I?

No. You look crazy. He pulled at Harrogate. What is this?

Harrogate held his arms aloft. I dont know, he said.

Suttree was turning him around. Good God, he said.

The shirt was fashioned from an enormous pair of striped drawers, his neck stuck through the ripped seam of the crotch, his arms hanging from the capacious legholes like sticks.

What size do you wear?

What size what?

Anything. Shirt to start with.

I take a small.

A small.

Yeah.

Take that damn thing off.

He peeled out of the shirt and stood in a pair of outsize pastrycook's trousers with cuffs that reverted back nearly to his knees.

Why the hell didnt you cut the legs off those?

He spread his feet and looked down. I might not be done growin, he said.

Take them off.

He dropped them to the floor and stood naked save for his shoes. Suttree collected the trousers and hacked a foot or more from the legs with his fishknife and rummaged through his bureau until he found a shirt.

The shoes is mine, Harrogate said.

Suttree looked down at the enormous sneakers. I guess your feet might grow another four or five inches, he said.

I caint stand a tight shoe, said Harrogate.

Here, try this shirt. And turn these trousers up on the inside where it wont show.

Okay.

When he had dressed again he looked less like a clown and more like a refugee. Suttree shook his head.

I got shot in the bottom of my shoe, Harrogate said. He held up one foot.

Gene, said Suttree, what are your plans?

I dont know. Find me a place here in town I reckon.

Why dont you go back home?

I aint goin back out there. I like it uptown.

You could still come in when you took a notion.

Naw. Hell Sut, I'm a city rat now.

Where are you going to live?

Well. I thought you might know a place.

You did.

That old codger up under the bridge has got him a slick place. Nobody never would find ye up in under there.

Why dont you move in at the other end up here?

I looked at it but it's open to the road where you aint got no privacy. Besides they's niggers lives next door.

Oh well, said Suttree. Niggers.

Do you not know of anyplace?

How about the viaduct? Have you looked under there?

Where's it at?

You can see it right here. See?

Harrogate followed his pointing finger, looking out the open door toward the city where a smaller replica of the river bridge stood astraddle of First Creek.

You reckon it's not taken?

I dont know. It may be just crammed with folks. Why dont you go see?

Harrogate rose from the cot where he'd been sitting. He was eager to be off. Hell fire, he said. It'd really be slick if it wasnt took wouldnt it? I mean, bein uptown like it is and all.

You bet, said Suttree

The viaduct spanned a jungly gut filled with rubble and wreckage and a few packingcrate shacks inhabited by transient blacks and down through this puling waste the dark and leprous waters of First Creek threaded the sumac and poison ivy. Highwater marks of oil and sewage and condoms dangling in the branches like stranded leeches. Harrogate made his way through this derelict fairyland toward the final concrete arches of the viaduct where they ran to earth. He entered delicately, his eyes skittering about. There was no one in. The earth was cool and naked and dry. Here some bones. Broken glass. A few stray dogturds. Two bent and mangled parking meters with clots of concrete about their roots.

Boy, whispered Harrogate.

There was a little concrete pillbox filled with pipes and conduits where you could store things and with the weeds grown about outside there was never a retreat so secluded. Harrogate sat on his heels and hugged his knees and looked out. He watched the pigeons come and go up under the high arches and he studied the warren of shacks on the farther bank of the cut where they hung yoked by insubstantial brigades of torn gray wash. Dark and near vertical gardens visible among the tin or tarred rooftops and vast nets of kudzu across the blighted trees.

Come evening he had accumulated some crates and aligned them in a sort of storage wall and he had made a firepit of old bricks and he had his eye on other goods which required but fall of dark to come by. By then he was uptown salvaging tins from trashcans for cookware. Appropriating the mattress from a lounge on a houseporch. All the redglobed lanterns from a ditchside where watermains were under repair.

He sat by the fire a long time after he had boiled and eaten the vegetables pilfered from gardens across the creek. His little grotto glowed with a hellish red from the lanterns and he reclined on the mattress and scratched himself and picked his teeth with a long yellow fingernail.

When Suttree came by next noon on his way to the market the city rat had just returned. He ushered in his guest expansively. How you like it, Sut?

Suttree looked around, shaking his head.

What I like about it is they's plenty of room. Dont you?

You better get rid of those parking meters, Suttree said.

Yeah. I'll haul em off to the creek this evenin.

What's in here? He was peering into the little concrete vault.

I dont know. It's a slick place to keep your stuff though, aint it?

Overhead in the arches there was a dull snap and a violent flapping of wings.

Hot damn, said Harrogate, slapping his thigh.

A pigeon fluttered down brokenly and landed in the dust and wobbled and flopped. It had a rat trap about its neck.

That makes three, said Harrogate, scurrying to secure the bird.

Suttree stared after him. Harrogate removed the trap and climbed up into the vaulted undercarriage of the viaduct and reset it, scooping the scattered grain over it with one hand. Boy, he called down, his voice sepulchral, them sons of bitches is really dumb.

What are you going to do with them?

I got two in the pot yonder stewin up with some taters and stuff but if this keeps up I'm goin to sell em.

Who to?

Harrogate hopped down, the dust pluming from under his sneakers. He gave his trousers a swipe with his hands. Niggers, he said. Shit, they'll buy anything.

Well, said Suttree. I was going to ask you if you wanted some fish but I guess you've got enough to eat for a while.

Hell, come take supper with me this evenin. They's enough for two.

Suttree looked at the limp and downy bird, its pink feet. Thanks, he said, but I guess not. He nodded toward Harrogate's mattress. You need to get your bed up off the ground there, he said.

I wanted to talk to you about that. I got my eye on some springs down here by the creek but I caint get em by myself.

Suttree tucked his fish beneath his arm. I'll stop by later, he said. I've got to get on to town.

I got to figure some way to keep these dogs out of here too.

Well.

I'll have her fixed up slick next time you see it.

Okay.

Livin uptown like this you can find pret near anything you need.

Dont forget about the parking meters.

Yeah. Okay.

Suttree took a final look around and shook his head and went out through the weeds to the world.

Sunday he set forth downriver in the warm midmorning, rowing and drifting by turns. He did not run his trotlines. He crossed below the bridge and swung close under the shadow of the bluffs, the dripping of the oars in the dark of the river like stones in a well. He passed under the last of the bridges and around the bend in the river, through peaceful farmland, high fields tilted on the slopes and rich turned earth in patches of black corrugation among the greening purlieus and small cultivated orchards like scenes of plenitude from picturebooks suddenly pasted over the waste he was a familiar of, the river like a giant trematode curling down out of the city, welling heavy and septic past these fine homes on the north shore. Suttree rested from time to time on the oars, studying from this late vantage old childhood scenes, gardens he knew or had known.

He took the inside of the island, narrow water that once had served as race to the old dutchman's light mill and beneath which now lay its mossgrown ruins, concrete piers and pillowblocks and rusting axletrees. Suttree held to the shallows. Silt ebbed and fell among the reeds and small shoals of harried and brasscolored shad flared away in the murk. He leaned upon the dripping oars, surveying the shore bracken. Little painted turtles tilted from a log one by one like counted coins into the water.

The child buried within him walked here one summer with an old turtlehunter who went catlike among the grasses, gesturing with his left hand for secrecy. He has pointed, first a finger, then the long rifle of iron and applewood. It honked over the river and the echo drifted back in a gray smoke of sulphur and coke ash. The ball flattened on the water and rose and carried the whole of the turtle's skull away in a cloud of brainpulp and bonemeal.

The wrinkled empty skin hung from the neck like a torn sock. He hefted it by the tail and laid it up on the mud of the bank. Green fungus hung from the serried hinder shell. This dull and craggy dreamcreature, dark blood draining.

Do they ever sink?

The turtlehunter charged his rifle from a yellowed horn and slid a fresh ball down the bore. He recapped the lock, cradling the piece in his armcrook.

Some does, some dont. Quiet now, they be anothern directly.

What do you do with them?

Sell em for soup. Or whatever. The boy was watching the dead surface of the river. Turkles and dumplins if ye've a mind to. They's seven kinds of meat in one.

What do turtles eat?

Folks' toes if they dont be watchful wadin. See yan'n?

Where?

Towards them willers yander.

Down there?

Dont pint ye fanger ye'll scare him.

You pointed.

Thatn's eyes was shut. Hush now.

He opened his eyes. Redwings rose from a bower in the sedge with thin cries. He bent to the oars again and came down the narrows and into the main channel, the skiff laying a viscid wake on the river and the bite of the oars sucking away in sluggish coils. He tacked toward the south bank in order to bias the bend in the river, coming through the shadowline into a cooler wind. Sheer limestone cliffs rose cannellate and palewise and laced with caves where small forktailed birds set forth against a sky reaching blue and moteless to the sun itself.

Below here the river began to broaden into backwater. Mudflats spiracled and bored like great slabs of flukey liver and a colony of treestumps like beached squid drying grayly in the sun. A dead selvedge traversed by crows who go sedately stiff and blinking and bright as black glass birds from ort to ort of stranded carrion. Suttree shipped the oars and drifted to the bank and stood rocking and recovering as the prow of the skiff grated up against the mud, stepping ashore easily with the rope and mooring the skiff to a root with a halfhitch. He crossed through the high grass and went up the slope, climbing with handholds in the new turf until he gained the crest and turned to look down on the river and the city beyond, casting a gray glance along that varied world, the pieced plowland, the houses, the odd grady of the small metropolis against the green and blooming hills and the flat bow of the river like a serpentine trench poured with some dull slag save where the wind engrailed its face and it shimmered lightly in the sun. He went along the crest of the bluffs through the windy sedge walking up small birds that flared and hung above the void on locked wings. A toy tractor was going on a field in a plume of dust. Down there the island ringed in mud. Suttree scaled a slate out over the river. Turning, winking, lost. He descended through a heavy swale of grass and went on, fording a thorny wicker patch of blackberries, crossing the face of a hill past the promontory kept by the old mansion, a great empire relic that sat shelled and stripped and rotting in its copse of trees above the river and brooded on the passing world with stark and stoned out window lights.

Suttree went along the high rolling country above the river. Two seagulls tracked their pale shapes in the shadowed calm under the bluff and far downstream he saw an osprey turn very high and hang above the distant thunderheads with the sun parried pure white from underwing and panel. He has seen them fold and fall like stones and he stayed to watch it out of sight.

The path he followed wound along the hills through grass and bramble and cut crosscountry toward the lower reaches of the river. It angled down a long bank of shale, it went through a wood. When he came upon the river again it was upon a dead and swollen backwater of coves and sloughs where slime and froth obscured the shapes of floating jars and bottles and where lightbulbs peered from the slowly heaving jetsam like great barren eyes. He went along the narrow path past fishermen, old women, men and boys. Galvanized minnowpails were tied to stumps at the water's edge and picnic hampers stood in the shade. A little girl squatted with her skirt hiked and watched between spattered shins her water trickle along the packed clay. Old men nodded solemnly to Suttree as he passed. Howdy. Howdy. Doin any good?

He went down a strand of mud and crusted stone strewn with spiderskeins of slender nylon fishline, tangled hooks, dried baitfish and small bones crushed among the rocks. Toeing tins from their molds in the loam where slugs recoiled and flexed mutely under the agony of the sun. The path climbed along a wall of purple sandstone above an embayment and in the sunlit shallows below him he could see the long cataphracted forms of gars lying in a kind of electric repose among the reeds. Bird shadows scuttled past but did not move them. Suttree leaned against the face of crumbling stone and watched them. One of the gars came about slowly, the water stirring and going among the willows. His dull side gave back the light like burnt brass. The other three lay like dogs, heavy shapes of primitive rapacity basking in the sun. Suttree moved on. At the head of the cove a hogsnake snubnosed and bloated lay coiled and sleeping in the dry ruins of a skiff.

The path ran on to a landing and there was a biblecamp bus parked there and people in their clothes were floundering around in the water.

He descended the grassy bank among the watchers and took a seat. A preacher in shirtsleeves stood waistdeep in the water holding a young girl by the nose. He finished intoning his chant and tilted her over backwards into the river and held her there a moment and brought her up again all streaming and embarrassed and wiping the water from her eyes. The preacher was grinning. Suttree moved closer to watch. An old man nodded to him.

Howdy.

Howdy.

The girl had nothing on beneath her thin dress and it clung wet and lascivious across her cold nipples and across her belly and thighs.

You saved? said the old man.

Suttree looked at the old man and the old man looked back with eyes smoky and opaque.

No, he said.

The old man unscrewed a jar of dark brown liquid he held in his lap and spat into it and put the lid back again and wiped his mouth. Say you aint? he said.

No, Suttree said. He was watching the girl clamber out of the river.

The old man nudged another near him. Here's one aint saved. Says it hisself.

This old man looked past the first one's shoulder toward Suttree. Him?

Aye.

Been baptized?

You been baptized?

Just on the head.

Just on the head, he says.

That aint no good. It wont take if you dont get total nursin. That old sprinklin business wont get it, buddy boy.

The first one nudged Suttree. He'll tell ye right, he said. He's a lay preacher hisself.

Sprinklers, said the lay preacher in disgust. I'd rather to just go on and be infidel as that. He turned away. He was dressed in soft blue overalls and he was very clean. The other one eyed Suttree again. Suttree was watching the preacher in the river.

Tell him to get down yonder in the water if he wants to be saved, the second old man said. He put one hand to his mouth, his jaw muscles working.

It aint salvation just to get in the water, the first said. You got to be saved as well.

Suttree turned and looked at him. Can you take your shoes off? he said.

The second old man leaned to see him. Jesus never had no shoes, he said.

The first was motioning for quiet with one flapping hand. He turned to Suttree. Aint no need to damp your shoes, he said. A feller can repent shod or barefoot either one. Jesus dont care.

What do you think about the pope and all that mess over there? Suttree said.

I try my bestest not to think about it atall, the old man said. He suddenly flung one arm upward in a gesture of such violent salutation that people drew back from around him.

That's my grandniece Rosy yonder. Just turned fourteen and saved right as rain. Makes a feller wonder at the ways of the Lord, dont it? How old are you, son?

Pretty old, said Suttree.

Well dont fret. I was seventy-six fore I seen the Lord's light and found the way.

How old are you now?

Seventy-six. I was awful bad about drinkin.

I've done it myself.

The old man glanced again at Suttree. Suttree looked about, then leaned to his ear. You dont have a little drink hid do you?

The old man's eyes careened about in their seamed sockets. Oh lord no, he said. I've plumb quit. Lord I wouldnt have nothin like that.

Well, said Suttree.

He'd scooted away a bit and he turned to watch the ceremonies. The grandniece smiled at those on the bank. Some waved.

The other old man leaned across and jabbed at Suttree with a thick finger. Go on, he said. Get down in that water.

There she goes, said Suttree, pointing.

That's my grandniece, the old man said, waving to the waters beneath which she had subsided.

Two women on the grass in front of them were turning and giving them dark looks. Suttree smiled at them. On down the bank groups were unwrapping sandwiches and opening cold drinks. There was a fat woman spread on the ground with an enormous teat hanging out and a small child fastened to it.

Tell him to come to the meetin tonight, said the second man.

Come to meetin tonight, the first one said.

Where at?

Gospel tent just up off the highway yonder. Did you not see it?

No.

Lord it's big enough. You come to meetin. They havin the reverend Billy Byington and the Sunrise Singers is supposed to be there too.

They are?

Dadjim right. Same as you hear on WNOX.

The women were turning and scowling.

The old man unscrewed and spat into his jar again and leaned forward. You come tonight, he said. I hear tell they might be goin to have May Maude. That does the oldtimey note singin.

There was a man now going into the water like a sleepwalker. He had his hands before him and his eyes were half closed and he was singing some incoherence over and over. The preacher took a step toward him, so unsteady he looked, the preacher smiling with a kind of grave benignity. Friends on the bank seemed to sway with him. This new candidate flailed once, eyes widening in alarm. The preacher lunged toward him with hands out. The man came aright and surged forth, his coattails dipping, reaching for the preacher and then going suddenly sideways with a long moan. The watchers on the bank stiffened. His hands wheeled wildly in the air and this supplicant went from sight like a drunken music conductor.

Suttree shook his head. The old man gave him a little crooked grin, his jawseams grouted with black spittle.

The preacher was blessing the subsiding roil with one hand and with the other was groping about in the water.

Suttree chuckled. The two women rose together and moved away over the grass. A man who was with them but was enjoying himself anyway turned and grinned. Boys, he said, that ought to take if it dont drownd him.

The preacher had the man up by the collar. He was sputtering and reeling about and he looked half crazy. The preacher steadied him by the forehead, intoning the baptismal service.

Suttree rose and dusted the grass from his trousers.

You aint fixin to leave are ye? the old man asked.

I sure as hell am, said Suttree.

You better get in that river is where you better get to, said the one in overalls. But Suttree knew the river well already and he turned his back to these malingerers and went on.

He went up the river path, swinging along in the sunshine, crossing a slough by a driftwood bridge and following the backwater of the smaller river that flowed in on the left. An upcountry river that grew more green as he went until it was a clouded jade. He sat to rest on a dusty log and watched it pass. A bittern stood in singlefooted siege among the cattails and small waterserpents swam. A dog came upstream on the far side tongue lolled with the heat and at a listless trot that told a weary way to go. He whistled at it and it looked at him and went on. Passing upstream it set the halms of marshweed quivering where nesting fish moved out unseen.

Suttree rose. The bittern flew. He went on until he came to a country road. It was hot walking and he didnt hurry. By and by he came to a small house.

He crossed to the front porch and tapped at the door. There were freshly painted boxes on the porch with new flowers cracking the loam of their beds and wasps were hanging about the eaves. The door opened and a small old woman peeped out. Yes, she said.

Hello Aunt Martha.

She pushed open the screendoor. Lord have mercy, she said. Buddy? Why Buddy.

How are you?

Oh lord, she said. She was tiny and frail and the hand that tucked at him trembled like a bird. Come in, she said.

Where's Clayton?

He's asleep. He eat a big dinner and he's asleep. Oh my lord he'll just be so tickled.

They entered the cool semidark of the front room with her taking his elbow like one might a blind man or like a blind man might. He could smell the rich cookery of their Sunday noon meal. She did not take her eyes from him. Have you eat? she said.

I had breakfast late.

They went into the kitchen where dishes still sat at table. Beyond was a sunporch rife with plantlife and the sun fell warmly through the glass and across the floor and table.

Set down, Buddy, she said, her doll's hands fussing at him. Let me just warm you up some dinner.

Dont bother with that, Aunt Martha. I just stopped by for a minute.

It's not any bother. You just set there. You want a glass of cold sweetmilk?

Yes mam, I'd love one.

I'll have some ice tea in just a minute. Lord I was thinkin about you all this mornin.

Suttree stretched his feet beneath the table. She brought a jar of milk from the refrigerator and a tall glass, pouring as she went, talking.

I was sortin out some old things and got to lookin through them old albums and pictures and I thought about you.

He set the halfdrained glass of milk on the table and blew and wiped his forehead with the back of his hand. She poured it full again. I wish you'd come see us more, Buddy. What do you want to be so mean for?

Where are the pictures?

They're right here. Did you want to look at them?

If they're handy. If you dont care.

Why they're just right here.

He drank the rest of the milk and looked out at the flowers and the sun. She came in with two old leather photo albums and a blue shoebox. She laid these on the table and pushing the box to one side to make room she opened the first album. Just go ahead and look while I warm this dinner up.

He took her hand. It was thin and finely boned and cool. I couldnt eat anything, he said.

I wish you would.

He looked around. Just let me have a piece of that cake, he said.

You better eat somethin.

No.

She lifted a cracked cakebell and sliced away a heavy wedge of the chocolate cake it contained and laid it on a plate and set it by him.

He was bent over the album, confronting figures out of his genealogy. Who's this? he said.

She rested her hand on his shoulder and peered with him. Lord, she said, let me get my glasses, I caint make it out.

An ancient woman spreadeagled in a bed, dried hands at her sides, a cured looking face. She is bald save for sheaves of hair on either side her head and they lie opposed and extended upon the pillow like pale horns.

She came back with her spectacles and bent over the photo. That's

Aunt Liz just afore she died. She was bald pret near. This here's Roy's baby picture.

A tintype picked from the wedge of the pages. Sailorsuited poppet a fiend's caricature of old childhoods, a gross cartoon.

The old woman's slow hands sorted a loose packet of brown faded photographs, glasses riding down the bridge of her nose as she nods in recognition. She must set them back again with her finger, shuffling these imaged bits of cardboard, paper, tin. They have a burnt look to them, as if dried in a flue. Dark and haggard eyes peer out. In the photographs the children appear sinister, like the fruit of forbidden liaisons.

Who's that?

That's Uncle Carter. He was a goodlookin somethin, wasnt he?

Who's this little boy here?

That's John.

He leaned closer to see was there anything left of that face in the face he knew.

This must be about nineteen ten.

Lord, I guess. I dont know. Here's Helen.

How long has Uncle Carter been dead?

She looked high on the far wall of the kitchen as if perhaps it were written there. He died in nineteen twenty-six. Guess who that is, she said, pointing.

He looked at the darkeyed girl. It was a very old picture. Aunt Martha when he looked at her had one hand to her mouth and was regarding the photograph with a shy and wistful look. Suttree said: That's you, Aunt Martha.

She pushed at his shoulder. Shoo, she said. How did you know that was me?

Why it looks just like you.

Go on, she said. She shook her head slowly. I just loved that dress. Look here. Here's E C.

He looks good in a hat, Suttree said.

Lord, she said, laughing, you remember that?

Sure, he said.

This is Grandma Cameron. She was ninety-two when she died.

This is Uncle Milo.

He was a merchant seaman you know.

Suttree nodded. I remember you Uncle Milo. Lost under Capricorn all hands aboard a bargeload of birdshit one foggy night off the limeslaked coast of Chile. Souls commended to the sea's salt clemency.

He'd not been home for thirteen year.

Foreign stars in the nights down there. A whole new astronomy. Mensa, Musca, the Chameleon. Austral constellations nigh unknown to northern folk. Wrinkling, fading, through the cold black waters. As he rocks in his rusty pannier to the sea's floor in a drifting stain of guano. What family has no mariner in its tree? No fool, no felon. No fisherman.

Who is this, Aunt Martha?

Do you not know who that is?

He seized the faded picture and scrutinized the girl. She looked out at the void with one cast eye and a slack uncertain smile.

It's not Mama is it?

Why sure.

He turned the page. It doesnt look like her, he said.

The old lady turned back the leaf and regarded the picture. Well, she said, it's not a good likeness. She was a whole lot prettier than that. Here's Carol Beth.

How old was she when she died?

Nineteen. Lord that was a sad time.

This is a dog. He is dead too.

This is the house where the dead lived. It is gone, lost and gone.

What was the dog's name?

She bent to see. I disremember, she said. They had one one time named John L Sullivan cause it was the fightinest little thing you ever seen.

We had one named Jose Iturbi. Because it was the peeinest dog.

Oh Buddy, she said, slapping his arm. I'd be ashamed.

Suttree turned the page, grinning. Bits of ribbon, hairlocks fell slowly down over the photos. She reached past him to adjust these from obstruction. An old man came to light holding a baby in his arms. Proposing it stiffly before him like an offering, old lace and swaddled windings that hung from a small bald and squinting face.

That's you, she said, after a silence.

This is me, he said.

Cold eyes bored at him out of the cowled coverlet. The congenitally disaffected.

Lord you were such a angel your mother wished she had all boys.

Suttree's spine convulsed in a long cold shunting of vertebrae. He looked up at the old woman. She gazed at the photograph through her delicately wired eyeglasses with that constrained serenity of the aged remembering and nothing more. Let me fix some tea, she said.

He lifted the slice of cake and bit into it and turned the page. The old musty album with its foxed and crumbling paper seemed to breathe a reek of the vault, turning up one by one these dead faces with their wan and loveless gaze out toward the spinning world, masks of incertitude before the cold glass eye of the camera or recoiling before this celluloid immortality or faces simply staggered into gaga by the sheer velocity of time. Old distaff kin coughed up out of the vortex, thin and cracked and macled and a bit redundant. The landscapes, old backdrops, redundant too, recurring unchanged as if they inhabited another medium than the dry pilgrims shored up on them. Blind moil in the earth's nap cast up in an eyeblink between becoming and done. I am, I am. An artifact of prior races.

Some curious person in the past with a penchant for deathbed studies has remembered to us this old man upreared among his stained coverlets, stale smell of death, wild arms and acrimony, addressing as he did kin long parted in a fevered apostrophe of invective. The nurse swore they spoke back. He listened, no ranting fool. Commend him gently, whom the wrath he suckled at his heart has wasted more than years. Suttree remembered the blue pools of his dead eyes. He and his sisters filing past the tall old bed. Lifted up to see. Waxen flesh obscenely wrinkled. In the picture this old grandfather sat up in his yellowed bedding like a storybook rat, spectacles and nightcap and eyes blind behind the glass. And pictures. The old picnics, family groups, the women bonneted and with flowers, men booted and pistoled. The patriot in his sam browne belt and puttees, one of the all but nameless who arrived home in wooden boxes on wintry railway platforms. Tender him down alongside the smoking trucks. Lading bills fluttering in the bitter wind. Here. And here. We could not believe he was inside. Cold and dry it was, our shoes cried in the snow all the way home. The least of us tricked out in black like small monks mourning, a clutch of vultures hobbling in stiff black shoes with musty hymnals in our hands and eyes to the ground. Someone to be thanked for digging in such frozen ground. Weary chant told from an old psalter. The leaves clap shut dully. Pulley squeak, the mounded flowers sucked slowly into the earth. A soldier held the folded flag to Mamaw but she could not look. She pushed gently at it with one hand, a gorgon's mask of grief behind her black glove. Scoop of dirt rattling, this sobbing, these wails in the quiet winter twilight. Blue streetlights came up beyond the wall as we turned to go.

She came with the tea, a tall vase full, chocked with ice, a curl of lemon. He ladled sugar in.

That's Elizabeth again, said the old lady. That's as old a picture as there is, I reckon.

Between the mad hag's face and this young girl a vague stellar drift, the wheeling of planets on their ether trunnions. Likenesses of lost souls haunt us from old chromos and tintypes brown with age. Bloodless skull and dry white hair, matriarchal meat drawn lean and dry on frail bone, a bitter refund ashen among silk and lilies by candlelight in a cold hall, black lacquered bier on sawhorses wound with crepe. I would not cry. My sisters cried.

This here's Uncle Will. You might not remember him. He was like me, he couldnt turn his head to do no good. She turned her head stiffly to show.

Yes.

He was a blacksmith. They all had trades.

He was a drunk, he a grifter.

Suttree turned up a tinted photograph of a satin lined wickerbound casket with flower surrounds. In the casket a fat dead baby, garishly painted, bright fuchsia cheeks. Never ask whose. He closed the cover on this picturebook of the afflicted. A soft yellow dust bloomed. Put away these frozenjawed primates and their annals of ways beset and ultimate dark. What deity in the realms of dementia, what rabid god decocted out of the smoking lobes of hydrophobia could have devised a keeping place for souls so poor as is this flesh. This mawky wormbent tabernacle.

What say boy?

Suttree turned. Clayton was standing in the door scratching his stomach and grinning.

Hey, Suttree said.

They shook hands and Clayton patted him on the back.

Mama you know better than to let this fool in the kitchen. He'll eat us out of house and home.

Now you hush, Clayton.

What are you boring him with them old pictures for? You want a drink, Buddy?

Why I'll bet Buddy dont even drink, do you Buddy?

Oh no, Clayton said. Buddy wouldnt take a drink.

Suttree grinned.

Lord I raised some that will, said the old lady. I dont know where they get it at.

At Ab Franklin's, said Clayton, grinning and pouring at the sink.

I mean where they take after it from.

Clayton pointed with the bottle toward the albums. Take a look at a few of them old hard assed sons of bitches in there and tell me if you think any of em ever took a drink.

Why Clayton, said the old lady.

You sure you dont want a drink, Bud?

No thanks.

Put them old moldy pictures up and come out in the back here.

Suttree slid back his chair and rose and followed him out through the sunporch and into the yard, holding for a moment the cold glass of tea against his forehead. Clayton grinned at him.

You better have a little hair of the dog, Bud.

No, I'm all right.

Clayton lowered himself into a lawnchair and stretched his naked feet in the grass. Damn if I didnt tie one on last night, he said. The last thing I remember was somebody sayin did he have a hat.

Suttree held a folded bill toward him.

What's that?

Here. That twenty I owe you.

Hell, that's all right.

No. Here.

Hell, I dont need it.

Go on. He pushed it toward him.

You sure you cant use it?

No. Thanks a lot.

Clayton took the bill and tucked it into his shirtpocket. Well, he said. That old crossbar hotel has got some pretty high rates, aint it?

Suttree took a long drink of iced tea. It had mint in it. He liked the rough leaves against his lip and their rich smell. It does, he said.

Are you still fishin?

Yep.

You want a job?

Nope.

Clayton shook the ice in his glass. You're a funny son of a bitch, he said.

Suttree stood looking out across the fields behind the house toward the mountains. He raised his glass and drained it.

Set down, said Clayton, patting the arm of the other chair.

Suttree propped one foot in the seat of the chair and rested his elbow on his knee. A cool breeze swung the kettled creepers hung from the porchjoists.

I believe it's fixin to cloud up and rain, Clayton said.

Paper said it was supposed to.

How'd you come out?

I just walked.

Where from? You didnt walk out from town did you?

Well, I cut across from the river. I didnt have anything else to do.

I'll give you a ride back this evenin anytime you get ready.

That's all right, Suttree said.

Aunt Martha came from the kitchen with a fresh pitcher of tea.

You'll stay and take supper with us wont you?

I better get on back.

The old lady filled his empty glass. Why Buddy, she said, you stay and eat with us.

Thank you, but I better not.

Hell, just stay with us. You dont have anything to do.

The old lady bent and poured Clayton's half filled glass full. He sat looking down at it. Goddamn, he said. He pitched it out across the grass.

Why Clayton.

Clayton rose and went into the house muttering to himself.

Buddy, I do wish you'd eat with us.

I appreciate it, Aunt Martha, but I need to get back.

Let me bring you another piece of cake.

No thank you. Really.

She came no higher than his shoulder. He almost reached down to touch her.

Clayton called to him from the door: You sure you couldnt use a drink?

Suttree shook his head.

Clayton came out with his drink, one hand in his hippocket. They stood there in the shade, the three of them. Suttree drained his glass and handed it to the woman. I've got to go, he said.

They followed him into the kitchen and through the house. The aunt would have taken his elbow save that her hands were full. She set the glass and pitcher hastily on the table and caught him up. Suttree turned and was surprised to hear her talking of the weather. You let Clayton take you, she said. They will come a storm this evenin long fore you get back to town.

I wont melt, he said.

He got out the door. Clayton was looking past the top of her head. Take care Bud.

Buddy you come see us, you hear?

He went on down the path into the road. He turned and raised one hand. The old lady waved timidly with just her fingers and Clayton saluted with his glass. It was much cooler and the wind was rising. Coils of dust rose in the road and spun off like smoke and the sky to the west lay banked in a discolored mass of thunderheads.

When he reached the highway large drops of rain were falling. They made hot slapping sounds on the macadam. He could see the rain coming across the fields where the darkly overtaken blooms buckled and dipped. He pocketed his hands and slumped and countrylooking he went down the edge of the black highway in the advancing downpour.

Before he had gone far an old Hudson pulled alongside him and sat there rocking and smoking and chattering while a man leaned across and lowered the glass just enough to let his voice out.

Hop in, old buddy.

I hate to get in your car wet as I am.

Caint hurt this old car.

Suttree climbed in and they pulled away. He watched the steamy green landscape fade beyond the dance of water on the hood.

Boy it's come a clodbuster aint it, the man said.

It is that.

The man was leaning over the wheel to see. He nodded toward the dashboard where the radio was glowing. Listen at that there, he said.

Suttree inclined one ear. A dim voice in the dashboard had a story to tell.

Well he come down from there and he said: See ary raincloud up there? and he said: Nary one. And he said: Better go on up there and look again, and he went on up there neighbors and he come back down again and he ast him again, said did he see ary sign of a raincloud and he told em no, said he'd not saw sign one, and he said: Well, better go on up there one more time, and he done it, went up there, and directly he come down again and he ast him, said: Is they ary raincloud up there now? and he said yes, said: They's one up there about the size of ye hat, and he said: Well boy you better get off the mountain cause it's a fixin to rain.

The driver smiled. He can lay it down, caint he.

Suttree nodded.

I like to hear old J Basil. He's all the time sayin: Aint that right Mrs Mull. Old deep voice. And she'll say: That's right Mr Mull. You like to hear him?

He's all right, Suttree said.

Small birds were crossing the road in the windy sheets of rain. Going up a grade the wipers died and the glass peened over with rainwater. Suttree could not see out. Beyond radio and exhaust and valvechatter he could hear thunder rumbling away over the bewept hills.

They topped the hill and the glass cleared in a slow arc. Around a curve and Suttree pointed. I get out here, he said.

The man looked. Where? he said.

Here. Anywhere along here.

You not goin to town?

No. Just right here.

The driver looked about and he looked at Suttree. They aint nothin here, he said.

Just anywhere along here, Suttree said. This is where I get out.

The driver pulled up along the graveled shoulder and stopped. He watched Suttree. Suttree climbed out into the downpour.

I sure thank you, Suttree said.

You welcome, the man said.

Suttree banged the door shut and stood back. The car moved out onto the highway. Through the runneled glass he could see the man's face turn again, as if to fix him there.

Suttree crossed the road in the rain and blue motor smoke and descended an embankment into the fields. He went crosscountry among easy hills and sometime pastureland, through a copse of dark cedars where the ground was almost dry, down a long and narrow limestone draw where small flat cactus clung to the south walls and the rain swept grayly across the ledges and swirled away before him.

He came out on the bluff and went on up the hill toward the house. Came through the weeds upon a walkway of herringboned brick all but overgrown. Past cracked urns bedight with concrete flora, broad steps, tall fluted columns with their shattered paint. The immense and stark facade seemed to recoil before his footfalls.

As he entered the foyer three young boys dropped like stricken bats from a balcony above the main reception room to his right and lit soundless on the dusty floor and passed out through a window in the opposite wall.

A chandelier lay burst in the floor. He stepped around it and ascended the lefthand stairway, slowly curving into the dusky upper chambers, keeping to the wall because save random jagged spindles the balustrade was gone. At the top of the stairs stood newel and finial intact and solitary like a rococo hitchingpost.

He wandered dripping through the high rooms with their ruined plaster, the buckled wainscot, the wallpaper hanging in great deciduous fronds. Small mounds of human stool with stained shreds of newsprint. From an upper window he watched the three boys go along the brow of the hill in the rain. Wedges of dry cracked glazing lay among the broken panes of glass in the floor. Below the window a mossy courtyard where old concrete dolphins rusted in a dry fountain and the dark handkilned bricks of the walkways lay grown with moss and lichens. Black ivy crept the garden walls and small mute birds peeped out. Across the river, the rainy hodden landscape, he could see traffic going along the boulevard, locked in another age of which some dread vision had afforded him this lonely cognizance.

He emerged from the narrow back stairwell and came up the hall with slow tread over the weathersprung parquetry, past great doors of solid cherry split open in long fibrous cracks and plundered of their knobs and hardware. Into this drawing room with high plaster frieze and foliate scrollwork. Prolapsed and waterstained ceiling, the sagging coffers. He turned, a vain figure in the ruins. Blind parget cherubs watched from the high corners.

Hello, he called. A voice that went from room to room and back again.

Gods and fathers what has happened here, good friends where is there clemency?

One spring morning timing the lean near-liquid progress of a horse on a track, the dust exploding, the rapid hasping of his hocks, coming up the straight foreshortened and awobble and passing elongate and birdlike with harsh breath and slatted brisket heaving and the muscles sliding and bunching in clocklike flexion under the wet black hide and a gout of foam hung from the long jaw and then gone in a muted hoofclatter, the aging magistrate snapped his thumb from the keep of the stopwatch he held and palmed it into his waistcoat pocket and looking at nothing, nor child nor horse, said anent that simple comparison of rotary motions and in the oratory to which he was prone that they had witnessed a thing against which time would not prevail.

He meant a thing to be remembered, but the young apostate by the rail at his elbow had already begun to sicken at the slow seeping of life. He could see the shape of the skull through the old man's flesh. Hear sand in the glass. Lives running out like something foul, night-soil from a cesspipe, a measured dripping in the dark. The clock has run, the horse has run, and which has measured which?

He moved along the hall toward the dining room. Paint on these old paneled doors crazed and yellowed like old porcelain. Something more than time has passed here. In this banquet hall. Scene of old heraldic feasts. Suttree in silent recognition of the somewhat illustrious dead. Large companies seated. A fat marcassin to adorn the board. The male bonecoupling rearing white and steaming up from the broken meat. Eyes watch. A malediction for those belated on the road and now commence. Mad trenchermen in armed sortees above the platters, the clang of steel, the stained and dripping chops, the eyes sidling. Yard dogs and starving palliards contest the scraps among the straw. There is nothing laid to table save meat and water. There is no sound of human speech. Beyond the muted clamor at the board there is a faint echo of another chase. Far hue and cry and distant horns and hounds in pain with eagerness. The master of the table has looked up. Down murrey fields another hunt has cried the stag. A shield crashes to the floor and three white birds ascend to the rafters and roost uncertainly. The master wipes his fingers in his hair and his rising says that the feast is done. Outside darkness has begun and the hounds' voices are chimes in the distance that toll seven and cease. They wait for the waterbearer to come but he does not come, and does not come.

Suttree went out through the kitchen and through the ruined garden to the old road. Reprobate scion of doomed Saxon clans, out of a rainy day dream surmised. Old paint on an old sign said dimly to keep out. Someone must have turned it around because it posted the outer world. He went on anyway. He said that he was only passing through.

At night he could hear the sewage gurgling and shuttling along through the pipes hung from the bridge's underbelly overhead. The hum of tires. Faint streetlight fell beyond the dark palings of sumac and blackberry. He rubbed his stomach and belched in his crepuscular solitude, the lamp at his elbow turned down so that the small flame burned in the glass bell ruby black. He has eaten for his supper an entire chicken boiled in a lardpail he, and he himself is the batfowler who crossed like smoke the dark garden patches above First Creek, something out of the night that drifted bedraped with dead hens down toward the moonlit miasma whitening the cleft of the glen, the ragged trees that seemed to be breathing cold, crossing this small and wretched estuary by a fallen truckdoor and climbing rapidly the far side toward the arches of the viaduct.

Suttree came, each day new marvels. They sat in purloined lawnchairs and watched a pigeon ringing down, standing off with backing wings and neck hooked while his pink pettysingles reached to grasp the pole and then like the Dove itself descending the bird limned in blue flame and a hot crackle of burnt feathers and the thing pitching backward to fall blackened to the ground in a plume of acrid smoke.

Gene, Suttree said.

Slick aint it?

Gene.

Yeah.

What have you got that pole wired to?

Harrogate pointed. Them lightwires yonder. What I done, I got me some copper wire and wired it and tied one end to a rock and thowed it . . .

Gene.

Yeah.

What the hell do you reckon is going to happen when somebody touches that pole?

Harrogate had not even risen to secure the bird. He sat there squatting in the lawnchair with his arms wrapped around his knees, smoked odor of his ragged clothes, looking up at the pole and then at Suttree. Well, he said. I'd say it would knock em on their ass.

It would kill them.

Harrogate looked mildly speculative. You reckon it would? he said.

Another day pigs. A whole covey of red shoats loose from some hillside hogpen that crossed a clearing in the blackened vines and went on downcreek toward the river. Harrogate watched them and then suddenly sat very erect, looking around.

If them niggers catches you eatin one of their hogs they will have your ass, he said.

But they got to catch me.

He rose and started down the hill toward the road and toward the creekside jungle where the pigs had gone. As he went he studied the pens scattered among the trees on the hillside above him, eclectic shelters hammered up out of snuff signs and boards and odds of fencing all hung in plumbless suspension down the bald and raingutted slope. He could see no one hunting hogs. When he struck the path along the creek he could see the tracks of the pigs here and there in the patches of black mire like the delicately pointed prints of small deer. Coming past a collection of old waterheaters he started them and they flushed into the wall of ivy with high raspy snorts. He picked one out and dove after it. It went through a mass of vines and over a mound of broken fruitjars and disappeared with an agonized squall. Harrogate fetched up in a small clearing. He had tilted himself into a locust tree and was bleeding in several places. He could hear the pigs diminishing in the distance.

When they came out on the riverbank at the point they paused to test the air. They started downstream at about the time that Harrogate emerged from the brush and they checked and swung back along the creek, their noses dishing and their eyes white. They defiled down a gully to the water and bunched and jerked their noses at it and came back. Harrogate was closing on them like a gangly tiptoe spider. They veered with new alarm and snuffled and went on down the point.

Looky here at these pigs daddy.

A man rose up from the tall grass where he'd been sitting and put his hand on top of his hat and turned around. The pigs flared like quail. They passed Harrogate some to the left and some to the right all screaming and he looked about and threw himself finally in the general direction of the pigs and landed full length with a grunt.

When he came upon them next they were feeding in a bower of honeysuckle, turning up the black earth and devouring worms and grubs and roots with subdued hoggish joy. Harrogate watched them through the vines, admiring them for plumpness, salivating slightly. He had resolved upon a rush, the pigs being too wary for stealth. He came headlong through the honeysuckle, his eye on one pig and one

pig only. They squealed and went rocketing away through the under-
brush, his the fleetest of the pack. In no time they were gone. He stood
leaning against a tree, his hand on his chest, panting. He turned
around. There was a sustained muffled screeching coming from behind him. He retraced his steps and crossed the chopped ground of
the clearing. Following the sound he came upon a pig with its head
in a bucket. As he approached it went running. It crashed into a tree
and fell back and lay there squealing. He ran to it and seized it by a
hindleg. It kicked and peeled back a long flap of hide from his forearm. He dropped it again and tried to push the skin back over the
wound. Goddamn, he said. The pig went on through the bushes.

He could hear it caroming about, the bucket banging and the pig
screeching. He plunged after it. It ran head on into the creek and
floundered there in the filthy water with gurgling screams. Harrogate
launched out birdlike and fell upon the shoat with an enormous
splash.

He came bedraggled and wet and filthy up through the woods
dragging the pig by the hindlegs. Casting about for something to
knock it in the head with. He finally selected a stick and laid the pig
down, pinning the rear feet to the ground with one hand. He began
to beat the back of the pig's head what of it showed above the bucket
rim, knocking the bail off, denting in the bucket, raising bloody weals
along the pig's neck and the pig shrieking until finally the stick broke
and he flung it away. The pig gave a great jerk and he fell upon it to
hold it down. Shit amighty, he said.

He came up with the pig holding it about the waist, the bucket
against the side of his face and blood running all down the front of
him, hugging it while it kicked and shat. Coming up the creek walking
spraddlelegged and half staggering until finally he must stop to rest.
He and the pig sitting in a copse of kudzu quietly getting their strength
back like a pair of spent degenerates. Every time the pig squirmed
Harrogate would call down into the bucket for it to quit. His arms
were getting tired and the one that had been peeled was hurting. He
struggled up again with the pig and got as far as the garden of
waterheaters when his eye fell on a piece of pipe lying naked and
unattached upon the ground. He picked it up and hefted it, the pig
sagging in his arm, its forefeet sticking out. He laid the pig down,
kneeling on it until he could get both hindfeet in a good grip, and then
he raised the pipe and swung with all his strength. Blood spewed from
under the edge of the bucket. The pig screamed and gave a mighty

surge and began to run sideways in a circle, dragging through the black leaves and rubbish. Harrogate swung again. The bucket went skittering off and the pig's fearcrazed eye looked up at him. A whitish matter was seeping from its head and one ear hung down half off. He brought the pipe down again over its skull, starting the eye from its socket. The pig had not stopped screaming. Die goddamn you, panted Harrogate, swinging the pipe. The pig humped and stiffened. He bashed it again, spattering brains over the ground. It stretched out, trembled and quit.

Harrogate stood over his victim with a heaving chest and cursed it. He pitched the pipe away and hefted the pig by its hindlegs and got it over his shoulder, its bloody head flopping, the brains bulging soft and wet from one side of its broken skull. He labored up to the edge of the road and laid the pig in the dusty bushes and rested. Before starting across the road he checked to see that no one was about. Strange urchin dragging a dead pig. A trail of blood. Twigs, small stones clung to the clot of brains. He dragged it up the path and under the viaduct and laid it out on the cool earth and sat looking at it.

He honed his shoplifted pocketknife on a small stone and knelt down by the dead pig and took it by one leg and held it so for a minute and then let the leg go. He squatted on his heels and flipped the knife into the dirt two or three times, his forehead wrinkled. Finally he raised the pig's leg and stuck the blade into the pig's stomach. Then he had another thought and seized one ear and wrested the head up and hacked open the throat. Blood poured out and ran over the dirt.

Now he sliced the pig open and hauled forth the guts, great arm-loads of them, he'd never seen so many. What to do with them. He lugged them down the path and flung them into the bushes and came back. As he had no way of scalding the pig he had decided upon skinning it.

When the owner of the pig arrived he found a scrawny and blood-covered white boychild standing on what was left of his property sawing at it with a knife and hauling on the skin and cursing. The dirty half flayed pig looked like something recovered from a shallow grave.

He was a black of a contemplative nature and he was just slightly drunk and he stood leaning there against the abutment of the viaduct and took a sip from a halfpint bottle and slipped it back into his hip pocket and wiped his mouth and watched this spectacle of frenzied mayhem with a troubled gaze.

Ahhg, said Harrogate when he glimpsed him leaning there.

The owner nodded his head. Mmm-hmm, he said.

Hidy.

He turned his head and spat and regarded Harrogate with one eye slightly veiled. You aint seed a stray shoat abouts have ye?

A what?

Little old hog. A young, young hog.

Harrogate tittered nervously. Hog? he said in a high voice.

Hog.

Well. I got this one here. He pointed at it with the knife. The black craned his head to peer. Oh, he said. I thought that was somebody.

Somebody?

Yes. You say that's a hog?

Yes, said Harrogate. It's a hog.

You wouldnt care for me to look at it would ye?

No. No no. He gestured at it. Go ahead.

The black man came forward and bent and studied the pig's ruined head. He took hold of the tip of the ear and turned it slightly. This hog's dead, he said.

Yessir.

I swear if it dont look almost exactly like one I had up at my place.

It was just sort of runnin around.

What was your plans for this here hog if you dont care for my askin?

Well. I'd sort of figured on eatin it.

Unh hunh.

Did you mean to say it was yourn?

If I'm not mistook.

Well foot fire, if it's yourn why then just go on and take it.

The owner was looking about the little camp for the first time. You live here? he said.

Yessir.

I see lights over here of the night.

I generally keep a lantern goin.

I guess it's cold in under here. In the winter.

Well, I aint been here in the winter yet.

I see.

You say you live up on the hill yonder?

Yes. You can see my place from just out here.

Boy I like it down here dont you? I mean you're close to town and all. And they dont nobody bother ye.

The owner looked at Harrogate and he looked at the pig. Boy, he said, what do you reckon I'm goin to do with that there mess?

I dont know, said Harrogate in a quick nervous voice.

Well you better think of somethin.

I'd take it if you didnt want it.

Take it?

Yessir.

Is you prepared to compensate me for that there hog?

Do what?

Pay me.

Pay ye.

Now you got it right.

Harrogate was still standing astraddle the deceased animal and now he unstood himself from over it and wiped his bloody hands down the side of his trouserlegs and looked up at the owner. How much? he said.

Ten dollar.

Ten dollar?

It'd of brung ever cent of it.

I aint got no ten dollars.

Then I reckon you'll have to work it out.

Work it out?

Work. It's how most folks gets they livin. Them what aint prowlin other folks' hogpens.

What if I dont?

I'll law ye.

Oh.

You can start in the mornin.

What you want me to do with this?

The owner had already started out through the weeds. He turned and looked back at Harrogate and at the hog. You can do whatever you want with it, he said. It's yourn.

How do I find you up yonder?

You ast for Rufus Wiley. You'll find me.

How much a hour do I get? To work it out at? Harrogate was fairly shouting across the space between them there under the viaduct although Rufus was not yet thirty feet away.

Fifty cents a hour.

I'll take seventy-five, called Harrogate.

But Rufus didnt even answer this.

All that night cats moaned in the dark like cats in rut and circled and spat. Lean dogs came from the weeds highhackled and tailtucked with their lips crimpt and teeth bright red in the light of the roadlanterns. Beyond in the dark where the guts lay they circled and snapped and glided in like sharks.

He lay by a dying fire in the creeping damp and listened to the snarling and rending out there until some hour toward dawn when these windfall innards had been divided and consumed and even the most brazen cur had decided not to risk the red hell of lanterns surrounding Harrogate's hog where it hung. The spoilers all slunk away to silence one by one and only a thin cat squall came back, far, now farther, from the hill beyond the creek.

When Harrogate went down the little path toward the hoglot lugging the pail of slops before him in two hands all the small pigs had been returned to the pen and they greeted him with squeals and snorts, jostling along the fence, their pale hammershaped snouts working in the mesh. He looked back over his shoulder toward the house and then fetched the nearest a good kick in the head.

He poured the curdled stinking mess down a rough board chute and stepped back. The pigs grunted and shoved and slurped at the swill and Harrogate shook his head. In the adjoining pen the sow lay sleeping in mud. He moved along the fence and bent to study her. Striped lice the size of lizards traversed the pink nigh hairless swine's hide. He picked up a piece of coal and threw it and it made a dull thump against the fat barrel of her bulk. Her ears twitched and she raised up and snuffed about. The chunk of coal lay just behind her foreleg and she found it and set to eating it, grinding it up with great crunching sounds, a black drool swinging from her jowls. When it was gone she looked up at Harrogate to see if there were more. Harrogate pursed his lips and spat between her eyes but she seemed not to notice. You're crazier'n shit, he said. The hog tested the air with her snout and Harrogate turned and went back to the house.

Dont set that bucket in here, she said. This aint no hogpen.

Harrogate gave her a malignant look and went back out again.

When's dinner? he said, his face at the screendoor.

When it's done.

Shit, he said.

What you say?

Nothin.

I hear him say for you to cut some wood?

Harrogate spat and made his way across the small scrabbled lot to the woodpile. Pullets trotted off before him, a patchy band of birds in moult, small leprous fowl that scudded across the mud with bald pinshaft rumps. He picked up a handaxe used for splitting kindling and set about chopping ants in two as they crossed a pine log. Niggers, he said. Shit.

On the other hand he was eating pretty good. Long after he'd worked out the price of the shoat he was still around to fetch and carry or lie these last warm days in a den in the honeysuckle and read comicbooks he'd stolen, risible picturetales of walking green cadavers and drooling ghouls.

Next door but one lived a pair of nubile young black girls and he used to hang from a treelimb outside their window at night in hopes of seeing them undress. Mostly they just stepped out of their cotton dresses and went to bed in their undershifts. He tried to lure the younger one to his bower in the honeysuckle with promises of comicbooks. She said: Me and Marfa come down there directly she gets in.

They came sidling and giggling after supper and carried off his whole supply. Visions of plump young midnight tits, long dusky legs. It was September now, a season of rains. The gray sky above the city washed with darker scud like ink curling in a squid's wake. The blacks can see the boy's fire at night and glimpses of his veering silhouette slotted in the high nave, outsized among the arches. All night a ruby glow suffuses the underbridge from his garish chancel lamps. The city's bridges all betrolled now what with old ventriloquists and young melonfanciers. The smoke from their fires issues up unseen among the soot and dust of the city's right commerce.

Sometimes in the evening Suttree would bring beers and they'd sit there under the viaduct and drink them. Harrogate with questions of city life.

You ever get so drunk you kissed a nigger?

Suttree looked at him. Harrogate with one eye narrowed on him to tell the truth. I've been a whole lot drunker than that, he said.

Worst thing I ever done was to burn down old lady Arwood's house.

You burned down an old lady's house?

Like to of burnt her down in it. I was put up to it. I wasnt but ten year old.

Not old enough to know what you were doing.

Yeah.—Hell no that's a lie. I knowed it and done it anyways.

Did it burn completely down?

Plumb to the ground. Left the chimbley standin was all. It burnt for a long time fore she come out.

Did you not know she was in there?

I disremember. I dont know what I was thinkin. She come out and run to the well and drawed a bucket of water and thowed it at the side of the house and then just walked on off towards the road. I never got such a whippin in my life. The old man like to of killed me.

Your daddy?

Yeah. He was alive then. My sister told them deputies when they come out to the house, they come out there to tell her I was in the hospital over them watermelons, she told em I didnt have no daddy was how come I got in trouble. But shit fire I was mean when I did have one. It didnt make no difference.

Were you sorry about it? The old lady's house I mean.

Sorry I got caught.

Suttree nodded and tilted his beer. It occurred to him that other than the melon caper he'd never heard the city rat tell anything but naked truth.

In the long windy days of fall Harrogate joined the blacks to fish for carp at the point, smiling and incompetent. A pale arm among darker waving from the shore to Suttree as he set forth in the cool mornings.

Suttree busy caulking up the batboards of his shanty with old newsprint. The cooler days have brought a wistful mood upon him. The smell of coalsmoke in the air at night. Old times, dead years. For him such memories are bitter ones.

Trippin Through The Dew has a muskrat coat bought in a junkshop on Central Avenue which he has dyed purple.

Mother She has come from upcountry with sacks and jars of the season's herbs. Her little yard lies deep with sere brown locust pods. In the trees small victims struggle, toad or shrewlet among the thorns where they have been impaled and the shrike who put them there trills from a nearby lightwire and it has begun to rain again.

And from his fleerglass window the shut-in watches for idle travelers on the path below, gripping the worn oak arms of his wheelchair, wishing all on to a worse hell yet.

The ragman hurried home with dark hard at his heels. When he reached the end of the bridge the lights went up behind him and he turned to look back for a moment before he ducked past the railing and down the red clay path to his home. Crouched before his fire he could see the stars come out in the darkening river. He kneaded his bony hands and watched the shapes flame took among the sticks of wood as if some portent might be read there. He smacked his gums and spat and gestured with his hands. He'd stood off a family of trashpickers in the alley that morning. There under the deepwalled shadows where the windows were barred and iron firestairs hung in chains overhead. Setting the dark brick corridor full of voices, aged but spoken with authority. Run them off like rats. And out of there you. And dont come back. Suttree rose from the rock where he'd been sitting and shook the stiffness from one knee. The old man looked up at him. From under the whites of his eyeballs peeked a rim of the red flame that raged in his head. You come back and find me dead, he began. Find me layin here dead, you just thow some coaloil on me and set me alight. You hear?

Suttree looked off toward the river and the lights and then he looked at the ragman again. You'll outlive me, he said.

No I wont neither. Will ye do it?

Suttree wiped his mouth.

I'll pay ye.

Pay me?

What will ye take? I'll give ye a dollar.

Good God, I dont want a dollar.

What would you have to have?

You wouldnt burn. He gestured with his hands. You wouldnt burn up with just coaloil thrown on you. It'd just make a big stink.

I'll get some by god gasoline then. I'll get five gallon and have it settin here at all times.

They'd send out the firetrucks when they saw that.

I dont give a good shit what they send. Will ye?

All right.

You wont take no dollar?

No.

I hold ye to your word now.

Whatever's right, said Suttree.

I aint no infidel. Dont pay no mind to what they say.

No.

I always figured they was a God.

Yes.

I just never did like him.

As he was going up Gay Street J-Bone stepped from a door and took his arm. Hey Bud, he said.

How you doin?

I was just started down to see you. Come in and have a cup of coffee.

They sat at the counter at Helm's. J-Bone kept tapping his spoon. When the coffee was set before them he turned to Suttree. Your old man called me, he said. He wanted you to call home.

People in hell want ice water.

Hell Bud, it might be something important.

Suttree tested the cup rim against his lower lip and blew. Like what? he said.

Well. Something in the family. You know. I think you ought to call.

He put the cup down. All right, he said. What was it?

Why dont you call him.

Why dont you tell me.

Will you not call?

No.

J-Bone was looking at the spoon in his hand. He blew on it and shook his head, the distort image of him upside down in the spoon's bowl misting away and returning. Well, he said.

Who's dead, Jim?

He didnt look up. Your little boy, he said.

Suttree set his cup down and looked out the window. There was a small pool of spilled cream on the marble countertop at his elbow and flies were crouched about it lapping like cats. He got up and went out.

It was dark when the train left the station. He tried to sleep, his head rolling about on the musty headrest. There was no longer a club car or dining car. No service anymore. An old black came through with his zinc sandwichtray and drink cooler. He passed down the corridor of the semidarkened car crying his wares softly and disappeared through the door at the far end. A racket of wheels from the roadway and a slip of cool air. The sleepers slept. The sad and dimly lit back side of a town went down the windows. Fencerails, weedlots, barren autumn fields sliding blackly off under the stars. They went across the flatland toward the Cumberlands, the old car rocking down the rails and the polewires sewing tirelessly the night beyond the cold windowglass.

He woke in various small mountain towns through the early hours of the morning, old people with baskets laboring up the aisle, black families with sleepy children clumping past, whispering, the rusty coaches wheezing and steaming and then the slow accumulate creaking and grating of iron as they pulled out again. It had grown cold in the night but he was numb with other weathers. An equinox in the heart, ill change, unluck. Suttree held his face in his hands. Child of darkness and familiar of small dooms. He himself used to wake in terror to find whole congregations of the uninvited attending his bed, protean figures slouched among the room's dark corners in all multiplicity of shapes, gibbons and gargoyles, arachnids of outrageous size, a batshaped creature hung by some cunning in a high corner from whence clicked and winked like bone chimes its incandescent teeth.

In the cold autumn dawn that crept the fields he woke and watched the passing countryside through the glass. Light rain or mist, small beads of water racing on the pane. They crossed a creek by an old trestle, black creosoted timbers flicking past. On the gray water two boys in a skiff, motionless, watching the faces pass like a filmstrip above them. One raised a hand, a solemn gesture. In the distance smoking millstacks arranged upon a gray and barren plain. Somewhere beyond them the cold rain falling in a new dug grave.

The train lurched and rumbled. Went pounding down a long levee with marsh and swampland smoking in the bluish light, a white egret onelegged and livid in the water quartered to a darker antipode and rigid as a plaster lawnbird. Stark woods beyond, a few leaves falling. Suttree wiped his eyes with his shoulders and rose and went down the aisle past the stale and empty seats.

He stood between cars, the upper half of the door latched back and the cool morning wind blowing in. Leaning with his elbows propped, the car rocking and swaying as they came into the yards. Staccato lights tracking in the gray frieze out there. In an upper window a man in his undershirt with his braces hanging. Across the narrow space he and Suttree looked at each other for just a moment before he was snapped away. The gray steel trusses of a bridge went past, went past, went past. In the sidelong morning light he saw the shadowed halfshapes of auto shells crouched in dying ivy down a long and barren gut.

In the station Suttree stood bending to deal with a small man in a cage. Polished blue suit, a lapel badge. Ten oclock, the man said.

He nodded. There's no other transportation out there I dont guess.

The little man was stamping long rolls of ticket. He pouched his lower lip and shook his head.

Thanks.

Less you wanted to take a cab. Costs right smart.

Thanks, Suttree said.

He found a Krystal near the bus station and had scrambled eggs and toast and he looked through the newspaper but could see no news for him. At ten oclock he boarded the bus and leaned back and closed his eyes. Remorse lodged in his gorge like a great salt cinder.

What will she say?

What will her mother say?

Her father.

Suttree got up and swung down toward the door but the bus had already started. He hung by one hand swaying. All night he'd tried to see the child's face in his mind but he could not. All he could remember was the tiny hand in his as they went to the carnival fair and a fleeting image of elf's eyes wonderstruck at the wide world in its wheeling. Where a ferriswheel swung in the night and painted girls were dancing and skyrockets went aloft and broke to shed a harlequin light above the fairgrounds and the upturned faces.

They watched him from the porch, gathered there like a sitting for some old sepia tintype, the mother's hand on the seated patriarch's shoulder. Watched him coming up the walk with his empty hands and burntlooking eyes. Suttree's abandoned wife.

She came down the steps slowly, madonna bereaved, so grief-stunned and wooden pieta of perpetual dawn, the birds were hushed in the presence of this gravity and the derelict that she had taken for the son of light himself was consumed in shame like a torch. She touched him as a blind person might. Deep in the floor of her welling eyes dead leaves scudding. Please go away, she said.

When is the funeral?

Three oclock. Please Buddy.

I wont . . .

Dont say anything please I cant bear it.

By now the mother had come from the porch. She was dressed in black and closed upon them soundless as a plague, her bitter twisted face looming, axemark for a mouth and eyes crazed with hatred. She tried to speak but only a half strangled scream came out. The girl was thrown aside and this demented harridan was at him clawing, kicking, gurgling with rage.

The girl tried to pull her away. Mother, she wailed, Mother . . .

The old lady had gotten Suttree's finger in her mouth and was gnawing on it like a famished ghoul. He seized her by the throat. The three of them went to the ground. Suttree could feel something thudding at the base of his skull. The old man had come from the porch and was hitting him with his shoe. He tried to get to his feet. The girl was screaming. Stop it you all! Oh God, stop it!

Get the police, Leon, screamed the old lady. I'll hold him.

Suttree staggered erect in the midst of this sorry spectacle groaning like a bear. The old man had fallen back. The girl was pulling at the old lady but she was hanging onto his leg with a maniac's strength and gibbering the while. You ghastly bitch, he said, and fetched her a kick in the side of the head which stretched her out. With this the girl fell upon him in much the same manner. He flung her back and tottered away a few steps to get his breath. The old man was coming from the house loading a shotgun as he ran. Suttree vaulted through the hedge. He crossed a lawn and went through another hedge and down a small lane past some chickens in a foulsmelling pen, the birds flaring and squawking, Suttree crossing through another yard and coming out alongside a house where a man in a lawnchair looked up from the nothing he was contemplating and smiled curiously. Suttree nodded to him and went on down the drive into the road. He looked back but no one was coming. He walked on out to the highway and squatted by the side of the road to rest and when a car came down the pike he rose to flag it with his thumb.

In a few minutes another car came along and this one stopped. Suttree climbed in and said hello. The man looked at him once or twice with alarm. Suttree looked down at himself. The front of his shirt was ripped open and his left hand was covered with blood. He zipped up his jacket and they rode on in silence.

A small town in the flatlands. He had been here once but remembered it little. A fresh breeze was herding leaves along the walkways and little shopsigns swung and creaked in the smoky air. He pointed toward the curb and the man pulled over to let him out. Much obliged. The man nodding. Suttree could see him looking over the seat for bloodstains as he pulled away.

He went to the poolhall and washed up and looked at his hand. Four bright slashes on his jaw. He plucked small bits of harrowed flesh from the edges of the wounds and daubed at them with a wet paper towel. The face in the mirror that watched was gray and the eyes sunken. He put on his jacket and went to the front counter and asked to use the telephone. The man nodded toward it. There was a directory hanging from a chain. He opened to the back and found two listings under Funeral Parlors, dialed the first and spoke with a soft-voiced girl.

Are you people in charge of the Suttree funeral?

Yessir. That's at three oclock this afternoon.

Suttree didnt hear. The words *Suttree funeral* had caused him to let the receiver fall away from his ear.

Hello, said the girl.

Yes, said Suttree. Where is the burial to be?

At McAmon Cemetery.

Where is that?

The girl didnt answer for a moment. Then she said: The cortege will be going directly to the cemetery after the services. If you cared to join, or if you . . .

Thank you, Suttree said, but if you could just give me directions.

He walked about in the town. Peaceful and sunny in the mid Americas on an autumn day. The dread in his heart was a thing he'd not felt since he feared his father in the aftermath of some child's transgression.

He ate a sandwich in the drugstore and in the afternoon he started out toward the cemetery. Along a little country road where leaves lay in yellow windrows through the woods or tumbled over the dark macadam. It was an hour's walk and few cars passed.

Two stonework columns marked the entrance, the chain down and heaped in the grass. He went down the little gravel road among the stones until he saw on a hill a green canopy. Two men were sitting in the grass eating their lunch. Suttree nodded to them as he passed. Beneath the canopy were folding chairs in rows, a green canvas mound with flowers arranged.

He could not bring himself to ask if this were the place where his dead son was going and he walked on. If there were other burials in preparation he would see them.

In an older part of the cemetery he saw some people strolling. Elderly gent with a cane, his wife on his arm. They did not see him.

They went on among the tilted stones and rough grass, the wind coming from the woods cold in the sunlight. A stone angel in her weathered marble robes, the downcast eyes. The old people's voices drift across the lonely space, murmurous above these places of the dead. The lichens on the crumbling stones like a strange green light. The voices fade. Beyond the gentle clash of weeds. He sees them stoop to read some quaint inscription and he pauses by an old vault that a tree has half dismantled with its growing. Inside there is nothing. No bones, no dust. How surely are the dead beyond death. Death is what the living carry with them. A state of dread, like some uncanny foretaste of a bitter memory. But the dead do not remember and nothingness is not a curse. Far from it.

He sat in the dappled light among the stones. A bird sang. Some leaves were falling. He sat with his hands palm up on the grass beside him like a stricken puppet and he thought no thoughts at all.

In midafternoon an old Packard hearse came wending through the woods leading a few cars and circled the canopy on the hill and parked on the far side. The cars came quietly to rest and people in black emerged. Steel doors dropped shut softly one by one. The mourners moved graveward. Four pallbearers lifted the small coffin from the funeral car and carried it to the tent. Suttree came up over the hill in time to see it go. Some flowers fell. He walked up the hill above the gravesite and stood numbly. The little bier with its floral offerings had come to rest on a pair of straps across the mouth of the grave. A preacher stood at the ready. The light in this little glade where they stood seemed suffused with immense clarity and the figures appeared to burn. Suttree stood by a tree but no one noticed him. The preacher had begun. Suttree heard no word of what he said until his own name was spoken. Then everything became quite clear. He turned and laid his head against the tree, choked with a sorrow he had never known.

When all the words were done a few stepped forth and placed a flower and the straps began to lower, the casket and child sinking into the grave. A group of strangers commending Suttree's son to earth. The mother cried out and sank to the ground and was lifted up and helped away wailing. Stabat Mater Dolorosa. Remember her hair in the morning before it was pinned, black, rampant, savage with loveliness. As if she slept in perpetual storm. Suttree went to his knees in the grass, his hands cupped over his ears.

Someone touched his shoulder. When he looked up there was no one there. The last of the motorcade was moving down the little drive toward the gate and save the two sextons crouched in the hillside grass like jackals he was alone. He rose and went down to the grave.

There among flowers and the perfume of the departed ladies and the faint iron smell of the earth to stand looking down into a full size six foot grave with this small box resting in the bottom of it. Pale manchild were there last agonies? Were you in terror, did you know? Could you feel the claw that claimed you? And who is this fool kneeling over your bones, choked with bitterness? And what could a child know of the darkness of God's plan? Or how flesh is so frail it is hardly more than a dream.

When he looked up the gravediggers were watching him from the side of the hill. He called to them but they did not answer. Thinking him mad with grief perhaps. Perhaps he addressed his God.

You two. Hey.

They looked at each other and after a time rose slowly and came shambling down across the green like ordinaries in a teutonic drama. Suttree was sitting in one of the folding chairs. He gestured loosely at the grave. Can you fill this in now?

They looked at each other and then one of them folded his arms and looked down. Orville's comin with the tractor, he said.

We was just supposed to fold these here chairs and stack em, the other said. They got to come out and take the tent down.

Suttree stared at them. The one with his arms crossed began to rock up and down on his heels and look about.

Orville and them be here directly, the other one said.

Suttree rose from the chair and pulled back the canvas drop where it was thrown over the mound of earth. A few racks of flowers toppled. A pick and two spades lay there and he took up one of the spades and sank it into the loose dirt and hefted it and sent a load of clods rattling over the little coffin.

The two men looked at each other.

We got to get them straps, the one said.

You better get em then, said Suttree, swinging a spadeload of clay.

Well hold up a minute.

The smaller man stepped down into the grave to free the straps and the other one hauled them up.

You want this here wreath? said the man in the grave, raising up, just his head sticking out. He shook it. It's got dirty, he said.

Get out of there, said Suttree.

He climbed out and stood back. Orville and them'll be here in a minute, he said.

Suttree didnt answer. He labored on, shoveling the dirt, the two men watching. After a while they began to stir about, folding shut the chairs and stacking them against the corner pole of the canopy. Suttree stopped and took off his jacket and then bent to work again.

Before the grave was half filled a truck entered the cemetery gates towing a lowboy with a tractor chained to the bed. The tractor was rigged with a frontloader. They came up the hill and swung down alongside the tent. The driver of the truck looked down at Suttree, his chin on his arm. He spat and looked out over the cemetery grounds and opened the door and climbed down. I allowed you'd have this thing down, he called out.

Suttree looked. The other two men were smoking and grinning and shuffling their feet. The three of them looked over at him. He shoveled on. The driver in the lowboy climbed out and the four of them stood around talking and smoking. I dont know, one of them said. He just jumped up and went to shovelin.

I reckon he was. I dont know. No, he was settin up here on the side of the hill.

Hey, called one of the new men.

Suttree looked up.

We got a tractor here to do that with if you want to wait a minute.

Suttree wiped his brow with the back of his sleeve and kept on shoveling. The men trod out their cigarettes in the grass and set about uncleating ropes, gouging stakes from the ground. They hauled down the canopy and folded it out on the ground and Suttree worked on in the open air. They disjointed the pipework frame and loaded poles and ropes and canvas in the truck and passed the folded chairs in after.

We might as well leave the tractor on the float, one of the men said.

We goin to do them sods in the mornin?

We'll have to. It's done past quittin time now.

They sat in the grass watching him. Already it was evening and overcast and before he was done a small rain came cold and slowly falling out of the south autumn sky. Suttree pitched a final shovelful of clods over the little mound and dropped the spade and picked up his jacket and turned to go.

You can ride in with us if you want, one of the men said.

He looked up. They were squatting in the rear of the truck watching the rain. He went on.

Before he reached the cemetery gates a gray car with a gold escutcheon on the door came down the little gravel road and stopped alongside him. A paunchy man in tan gabardines looked up at him.

Your name Suttree?

Suttree said it was.

The man climbed out of the car. He wore a tooled belt and holster and his clothes were neatly pressed. He opened the rear door of the car. Get in, he said.

Suttree climbed into the back of the car and the door shut after him. There was a heavy screen mesh separating him from the front seat. As if the car were used for hauling mad dogs about. There were no door handles or window cranks. The driver looked at him in the mirror and the man in the gabardines looked straight ahead. Suttree leaned back and passed his hand over his eyes. As they came into town people watched him from the street.

Pull over here, Pinky, the man said.

They came to a stop at the curb.

Go get yourself a Coke.

I'm all right.

Go get yourself a Coke.

The driver looked back at Suttree and climbed out and shut the door. The sheriff leaned one arm across the back of the seat and regarded Suttree through the wire. Then he climbed out and opened the back door.

Get up here, he said.

Suttree climbed out and got into the front of the car. The sheriff walked around and climbed into the driver's seat. He studied Suttree for a minute and then he said: Let me tell you something.

All right, said Suttree.

He reached down and tapped Suttree's knee with his forefinger. You, my good buddy, are a fourteen carat gold plated son of a bitch. That's what your problem is. And that being your problem, there's not a whole lot of people in sympathy with you. Or with your problem. Now I'm goin to do you a favor. Against my better judgment. And it's not goin to make me no friends. I'm goin to drive your stinkin ass to the bus station and give you an opportunity to get out of here.

I dont have any money.

I never reckoned that you did. I intend to put up five dollars cash money out of my own pocket to get you started. I aint interested in where you go, but I aim to see to it that you go five dollars' worth in some direction and you and me both are goin to hope that you dont never come back. Now do you want to know why?

Why what?

Why I'm puttin up the five dollars.

No.

I thought maybe the economics of it might interest you. I hear tell you're supposed to be real smart.

I dont care.

The reason I'm investin five dollars in your absence is because the man whose daughter's life you ruined happens to be a friend of mine and a man I not only like but respect. And I'd like to see him have some peace of mind. I know he aint goin to thank me for this. What he'd like is to see you hung. But I know him for a fairminded man and a peacelovin man and I know that he'll be happier in his mind if he just gets you out of his sight. He might even come to forget there ever was a lowlife like you although I doubt it.

What do you get out of it?

Not a thing, good buddy.

You said I ought to be interested in the economics of it.

I said it but I dont believe it. It's not much economics anyway. About the only thing to be said for gettin fucked out of five dollars this way is that you wont catch the clap. I never expected you to understand.

No one cares. It's not important.

That's where you're wrong my friend. Everything's important. A man lives his life, he has to make that important. Whether he's a small town county sheriff or the president. Or a busted out bum. You might even understand that some day. I dont say you will. You might.

The sheriff turned in the seat and reached for the key and turned it. But the motor was already running and the starter made a sudden wild screeching sound. He muttered to himself and shifted the gears and they went on down the street.

The bus station was in the back of a cafe and when they pulled up in front there were two buses idling in the alley. The sheriff shifted and took out his billfold and lifted a five dollar bill from it and handed it across.

I suppose I have to take it, Suttree said.

You suppose correctly.

Suttree took the bill and looked at it.

Now, the sheriff said, I want you to take whichever bus out of here best pleases you and I want you to ride five dollars in that direction and I dont want you back. You got that?

I've got it.

Suttree was holding the money in his hand. The sheriff looked at him. You all right? he said.

Yeah. I'm all right.

I'm puzzled that you'd have the face to come here.

Well. You're puzzled.

I will say one thing: you've opened my eyes. I've got two daughters, oldest fourteen, and I'd see them both in hell fore I'd send them up to that university. I'm damned if I wouldnt.

How many sons have you got?

Not any. Look Suttree, I'm sorry as far as that goes. These people did want me to put you in jail.

I know.

Well. You get your ticket right in there. Dont let me see you on the street. You stay in there till your bus runs. You hear?

Suttree opened the door and climbed out. He looked down at the sheriff and then he shut the door.

You take care, the sheriff said.

Okay.

The sheriff had bent forward to see his face. Suttree turned and walked into the cafe.

He left the bus in Stanton Tennessee with three dollars still in his pocket. It was ten oclock at night. He walked down to a cabstand and bought a pint of whiskey from a driver and put it in his shirt and hiked out to the edge of town and stood in the road holding his thumb up at the lights that passed. None stopped. After an hour he walked on. It had turned cool. He could see lights far up the highway, a roadhouse or cafe.

The sign said it was a truck stop and there was a diesel rig pulled over on the gravel with the motor running. Suttree peered in through the plateglass window. A cold hall of a place. Plastic tables. Two boys playing a pinball machine. The driver sat at the counter drinking coffee. Suttree searched his pockets for a dime but he had none. He went in anyway.

An ancient waitress was cleaning out the coffee urn with a short-handled mop. When she saw Suttree she climbed down off the chair she was standing on and came shuffling up the aisle behind the counter. Suttree leaned on the counter next to the driver. The driver looked at him.

Is that your rig? said Suttree.

The driver set his cup down. Yeah, he said. That's my rig.

You reckon I could get a ride with you?

Where you goin?

To Knoxville.

I aint goin to Knoxville.

Well where are you going?

I aint goin to Knoxville.

The driver bent and sipped his coffee and Suttree stood looking down at him and then turned and left the cafe. He started back down the highway toward the town. The lights had dimmed, the town seemed farther at this midnight hour. Partway down the road he stopped and opened the bottle and drank.

The first building he came to was a church. There was a small illuminated glass case standing in the yard, white letters on a black plastic board within. Insects were swarming over the dimly lit church news. Suttree turned across the lawn and went to the back of the church and sat in the grass and drank the whiskey. After he had drunk a little of it he began to cry. He began to cry harder and harder until he was sitting there in the grass with the bottle upright between his knees, wailing aloud.

He must have slept. When he woke he was lying in the grass looking up at the heavens. A cloudless night strewn with stars. Salt taste of sorrow in his throat. He saw a star spill across the sky, a light trail of fire and then nothing. Hot spalls of matter rifling through the icy ether. Misshapen globs of iron slag.

The night had grown much colder. He lay in the grass shivering and he tried to sleep but he could not. After a while he rose and took the whiskey and went to the rear door of the church and tried it and it opened.

He was in a cellar. There were stacks of old newspapers and magazines along one wall and he stretched out on these and lay there. Then he sat up and took some to spread over him and lay down again. Then he started to cry again, lying there in the dark of the church cellar under the old newspapers.

It was midmorning when he woke. A truck gone out the pike had rattled the cellar door. He sat up in a flurry of newsprint and looked about. Light fell from a high window. Some kind of small bird was pecking in the grass there. Suttree rose and ran his hand through his hair. His throat was dry and his head hurt. The rest of the whiskey stood in the bottle on the floor and he fetched it up and held it to the light. It was about a third full and he unscrewed the cap and took a drink and shuddered and shook himself and then took another drink. Then he went out.

It took him all day to cross the state. He was unshaven and he looked bad. Toward evening he was in a nameless crossroads high in the Cumberland Mountains. A quarter mile down the road in the dusk stood a figure like his own, a wanderer longmirrored in the black asphalt, one arm aloft. Suttree walked on. It was a husky young boy and he had stationed himself in front of a small country store to try for a ride. Suttree walked on past. The store was closed and the windows boarded up and some twisted pipes grew from the concrete apron in front where a gaspump had been ripped up.

Hey, the boy said.

Hey, said Suttree.

You live around here?

No.

You aint got a cigarette on you have you?

The boy was walking down toward him, studying him with a kind of sly intensity that drifters seem to come by. No, Suttree said.

I saw you thumbin down there. Where you headed?

Knoxville.

I'm goin to Florida. I got a sister in Fort Lauderdale. He turned and spat. He had on a shortsleeved shirt and Suttree in his jacket was already cold. Dark as it was he could see him but poorly. Tattoos along one arm.

I'll go on down, said Suttree.

The boy changed his tone. Listen, he said. Why dont we hitch together. We might have a better chance.

Suttree looked at him. He was dressed in jeans and his hair was wild and he wore a general look of dangerous filth. A big meanlooking kid. I'll go on down, said Suttree. Let you have first shot.

You reckon anybody might stop along here after dark?

I dont know. Your guess is as good as mine.

Yeah?

Where did you come from?

The kid's eyes shifted. St Louis, he said.

St Louis, said Suttree. I've been through there.

Aint this a hell of a place to get stuck?

Yeah. Good luck.

Listen. How far is it to the next town?

I dont know.

Suttree had started off. Listen, the kid called again.

What?

You got a quarter you could let me have?

Suttree shook his head no.

The kid was walking down toward him. Come on, man, he said. I aint eat in two goddamned days. Hell, fifteen cents. Somethin.

I aint got a dime, Suttree said.

Let's see.

Suttree watched him. He was standing on the balls of his feet and he looked hungry. What? he said.

I said let's see. Let's see you turn your pockets out.

I told you I'm not holding anything.

The kid moved slightly to his left. That's what you say, he said. I'd like to see.

That's your problem, Suttree said. He stepped back and turned to go. As he did so the kid jumped him. Suttree ducked. They went to the ground together. Suttree could smell the stale sweat of him. The kid was trying to hit him, short chops with his big fists. Suttree pushed his face against his chest. Fear and nausea. The kid quit punching and tried to get him by the throat. Suttree rolled. They came up. The kid had hold of his jacket. Suttree swung at him. They closed, feet scrabbling in the gravel there in the near dark in front of the abandoned store. The kid turned loose of Suttree to hit him and Suttree dropped to one knee and seized the kid behind the calves and pulled him down hard on his rump. Then he was running down the highway. The kid's shoes slapping after him. Taste of blood in his mouth. But the footsteps faded and when Suttree looked back he could see in the deeper dusk by the roadside the kid crouched to get his breath.

You yellow cocksucker, the voice came drifting up the highway.

Suttree put his hand to his heart where it boomed in the otherwise silence of the wilderness. He went on up the road in the dark.

It is little more than dawn when the general comes down Front Street slumped on the box of his coalwagon, the horse named Golgotha hung between the trees and stumbling along in the cold with his doublejointed knees and his feet clopping and the bright worn quoits winking feebly among the clattering spokes. In the whipsocket rides a bent cane. There is a gap in the iron of one tire and above the meaningless grumbling of the wagon it clicks, clicks, with a clocklike persistence that tolls progress, purpose, the passage of time. When they stop it is in a violent shudder, as if something has given way. The general climbs and climbs down from his seat and goes to the rear and takes up his blackened basket and sets it in the street. He levers up the lantern glass and blows out the tiny flame. He hands down coal lump by lump until the basket is filled and with pain he hefts and carries it toward the dim house, through the chill fog bent and muttering, returning lightened but with no better speed or humor to where the horse stands sleeping in the traces.

They come trundling and slowly aclatter up the empty street, pass under the bridge and take the bitter and frozen fields toward the river. In the hoarcolored dawn they seem to be drifting, closed away in the cold smoke until just the general's shoulders and the slouched back of him with his hat perched on the shoulders of his clothes and the hat the horse wore float over the cold gray void like transient artifacts from a polar dream.

> Ooh coal, kindlin wood
> Would if I could
> Hep me get sold
> Coal now.

It was six degrees above zero. Suttree crawled from his bed, pulled on his coat and got his trousers and climbed up onto the bed to don them so cold the floor was. He squatted and fished his socks out from beneath the cot and shook out the dust and pulled them on and stepped into his shoes and went to the door. Mist swirled about him. The old black coalpedlar sat his cart, the horse sidled and stamped.

Couldnt you just leave a basket and go on?

I see you aint froze, said the general, climbing down.

Suttree got the basket from beside the door and came down the walk. The river was frozen between the houseboat and the bank, a thin skim of wrinkled ice through which fell chunks of frozen mud from the underside of the flexing plank. He threw the empty basket up on the wagon and took the full one from the old man.

I gots to have me some money today, the general said.

How much?

You owes me eighty-five cents.

How do you know?

The old man patted his gloved hands together. His head was wrapped in rags. I keeps it all in my counts, he said. You keep you own if'n you dont like mine.

Where do you keep them?

That's all right where I keeps em.

How much will you take?

What all I can get, I reckon.

Suttree set the basket on the frozen ground and reached in his trouser pocket. He had thirty-five cents. He gave it to the old man and the old man looked at it a minute and nodded and pulled a cord that went down into his clothing. A long gray sock appeared. The top of it had been fitted with an old brass pursecatch and he unsnapped it and dropped in the coins and lowered it back where it had come from and climbed up onto the wagon box.

Hump sleepyhead, he said.

The horse lurched forward. Suttree watched them cross the field, fording the pale vapors, the dead lamp hung by its bail from the tailboard, the cart tilting up at the tracks and tilting back again and descending from sight. Upriver he could see a hazy swatch of cold blue light where the sun was rising through the river fog but it was no light much and no warmth at all. He took the basket of coal and toted it back up the plank and went in. He didnt even bother to shut the door. He put the basket by the stove and took up the coalscuttle and shook it. Jacking open the cold stove door with his foot he tipped the scuttle, the coal clunking in, dry ash stirring upward. Suttree peered down the iron gullet, prying at the slag in the stove's belly with the poker. He crumpled a newspaper and dropped it down alight and held his hands to the fleeting warmth. The newspaper curled up in a tortured ash that rose in the stove's mouth, a charred gravure whereon lay gray news, gray faces. Suttree hugged himself and swore. An icy wind was singing in the cracks. He fetched the lamp from the table, removed the chimney and unscrewed the brass wickpiece and emptied the lamp oil into the stove. A white smoke rose. He struck a match and dropped it in but nothing occurred. He snatched up a piece of newspaper and lit it and poked it in. A ball of flame belched up. He did a few stiff dancesteps and went out to relieve himself.

Ice lay along the shore, frangible plates skewed up and broken on the mud and small icegardens whitely all down the drained and frozen flats where delicate crystal columns sprouted from the mire. He hauled forth his shriveled giblet and pissed a long and smoking piss into the river and spat and buttoned and went in again. He kicked the door shut and stood before the stove in a gesture of enormous exhortation. A frozen hermit. His lower jaw in a seizure. He cast about and got his cup and looked into it. He turned it up and tapped it and an amber lens of frozen coffee slid forth and went rocking and clattering around the basin. He took down the frying pan and set it on the stove and spooned the stiff gray grease. From his packingcrate pantry he selected two eggs and tapped one smartly on the rim of the pan. It rang like stone. He threw it against the wall and it dropped to the floor and rolled oblong and woodenly beneath the bunk. He hung the pan back on the wall and stared out the window. Frost ferns arched from the sashcorners over the glass and the river slouched past like some drear drainage from the earth's bowels. Suttree buttoned his coat and went out.

All the weeds were frozen up in little ice pipettes, dry husks of seedpods, burdock hulls, all sheathed in glass and vanes and shells of ice that webbed old leaves and held in frozen colloid specks of grit or soot or blacking. Wonky sheets of ice spanned the ditches and the ironcolored trees along the wintry desolate and bitter littoral were seized with gray hoarfrost. Suttree crossed the brittle fields to the road and went up Front Street. A parcel of black children came by from the store towing a child's wagonload of coal, chips and dust scavenged from a railsiding, going along quietly and barely clothed and seemingly dumb to the elements. Suttree's underjaw chattered till he had thought for his teethfillings. He crossed the street and crossing the store porch read the tin thermometer on the wall at zero or near it. He entered and went directly to the back without answering Howard Clevinger's courtly matin greeting. An old black widow was crouched by the grocer's stove on an upturned basket watching the fire through a jagged crack in the hot iron. She seemed to be in tears, so thick dripped the rheum from the red underlips of her eyeholes. She had a club foot and wore boots sewn up from an old carpet, blue balding pile with mongrel flowers, an eastern look about her, mute and shawled. She kneaded her hands each in each in their cropfingered army gloves and mumbled a ceaseless monologue. Suttree standing there inclined his head to hear, wondering what the aged dispossessed discuss, but she spoke some other tongue and the only word he knew was Lord.

Jabbo and Bungalow came in out of the weather in a bathless reek of cold wool and splo whiskey. They stood by the stove and nodded and spread their hands.

Cold enough for ye?

I'm frozen.

You needs you a good drink, Suttree.

Go on and give him one then, big time.

Bungalow looking at Jabbo with question.

Go on. Suttree aint too proud to drink after a nigger. Is you, Suttree?

The old woman vacated her basket and moved away to the wall.

I pass.

Where's the bottle.

Bungalow, lifting the front of his jersey, drew a pint bottle partly filled with a clear liquid from his waistband. The blacks looked warily toward the storekeeper. Jabbo took the bottle and unscrewed the cap and handed it toward Suttree.

Here go, man.

I cant use it.

Go ahead.

No.

I thought you said old Suttree didnt care to drink after a black man.

Why dont you come off that shit.

Jabbo was weaving very slightly like a krait just faintly disturbed. His sullen lip hung loose. He shook the bottle slowly. It's good whiskey man. Good enough for me and Bungalow.

I said I didnt want one.

Jabbo pressed the bottle against his chest.

Suttree raised his hand and gently put the bottle from him. The only sound in the store was the rusty creak of the damper swinging in the tin flue with the wind's suck.

It's Thanksgiving man. Have a little drink.

The bottle was at his chest again.

You better get that bottle out of my face, Suttree said.

You askin or tellin.

I said get it out of my face.

This aint Gay Street, motherfucker.

I know what street I'm on. Maybe you better get off those red devils. Why dont you offer Howard a drink?

He dont drink, said Bungalow.

Shut up, Bungalow. Come on, Mr Suttree, please suh, take a little drink with us poor old niggers.

Oceanfrog Frazer had entered the store. The members by the stove felt his presence, or perhaps it was the cold draft of air from outside or the way the damper fluttered. The old lady had moved off to a corner where she mumbled among the canned goods. Oceanfrog came from the cold to the stove, palms gesturing benison, an easy smile. He looked at the blacks and he looked at Suttree. Jabbo held the bottle uncertainly.

Friends and neighbors, said Oceanfrog.

Old Suttree wont take a drink, said Bungalow.

Shut up, Bungalow.

Oceanfrog'll take a drink, said Oceanfrog.

Jabbo looked at the bottle. Oceanfrog took it gently and held it to the light in spite of Howard Clevinger who was now looking toward the rear. The bottle was about two thirds dry. Oceanfrog tilted it. Bubbles shot upward through the liquid and a great boiling and churning occurred within the glass, the liquor scuttling down the neck of the bottle. Frazer's black cheeks ballooned. He leaned and spewed a long clear pisslike stream through the standing door of the stove and a ball of bluish flame leaped. Bungalow stepped back. Oceanfrog eyed the bottle sadly, his brows scorched up in little owlish tufts over the cold eyes.

That's awful whiskey, Jabbo, he said.

Are you all drinkin whiskey back there?

Aint nobody got any whiskey, Howard.

I better not hear of no whiskey drinkin in my store.

You all didnt ought to drink that old shit, Jabbo. Here.

What I want with that, motherfucker?

Oceanfrog, shrugging, dropped the bottle in the stove, Bungalow stepped back again. A whooshing disturbance occurred in the stove's bowels. What say, Suttree, said Oceanfrog.

Not much. How you?

Just tiptoein.

Feylovin motherfucker, said Jabbo.

I guess I goin to have to slap a black pumpknot on somebody's old bony head, said Oceanfrog. He didnt even look at Jabbo.

Shit, said Jabbo. He jerked his jacket up on his shoulders and reeled toward the door. Bungalow looked after him. To go or stay? He spread his feet and held his hands to the warmth while he thought about it.

What's wrong with him? said Suttree.

He thinks he's bad. Gets on them reds. Old Bungalow here, he dont do that shit. Do you, Bunghole?

Bungalow looked shyly at the floor. Naw, he said.

You look like you been hit with a blivet, Bunghole.

Bungalow didnt answer. He stepped back to make room for the old lady who had come to the stove again and was pulling at the basket and adjusting her skirts to sit. Suttree looked down at her as she refolded the shawl, at the thinly grizzled crown of her small skull. A few graybacks retreated in the rancid wool.

You aint got a turkey staked out somewheres today have you Bungalow?

I wisht I did.

I bet old Suttree does.

Not yet I dont.

Shit, said Bungalow. You know he is.

I guess in a bind we can eat at Bungalow's, said Suttree.

Shit. Aint nothin to eat at my house.

Oceanfrog had turned around to warm his backside. Suttree heard a little choking sob and looking down he saw that the old woman was crying to herself, dabbing at her nose with a bony knuckle.

That old Suttree, said Oceanfrog. You got to watch him. He's a rathole artist. Tell him open his coat there Bungalow, see if he aint got a turkey under it. He looked at Suttree, then he looked down at the dollshaped pile of sticks at his feet. He stooped. Hey, he said. What's wrong with you, little mama?

She was muttering and talking and sobbing to herself and she didnt seem to notice she'd been spoken to.

Hey Howard, said Oceanfrog. Who is this old woman?

How would I know.

How would Howard know? said Oceanfrog. He went to the box and lifted the lid and poked around and came back with a half pint of milk and opened it and bent and put it in the old woman's hands. When

Suttree left she was still holding it and she was still talking but she wasnt crying anymore.

He went on up the street. Two small boys were coming along. Hey boys, he said.

What's your name? said one.

Suttree. What's yours?

No answer. The other one said: His name's Randy. He's my brother.

Suttree looked at them. They were wreathed in steam and small sacs of mucus hung from their nostrils. Who's the oldest?

Randy's brother looked at the ground a minute. Allen is, he said.

Suttree grinned. How many of you are there?

I dont know.

You better come on, said Randy.

We'll see you, Suttree said.

He watched them. Skipping down the street, one look back. Ashcolored children hobbling down the gloom. This winter come, gray season here in the welter of sootstained fog hanging over the city like a biblical curse, cheerless medium in which the landscape blears like Atlantis on her lightless seafloor dimly through eel's eyes. Bell toll in the courthouse tower like a fogwarning on some shrouded coast. A burnt smell in the air compounded of coalsoot and roast coffee. Small birds move through the glazed atmosphere with effort.

He crossed the street at the top of the hill and went through the rimey grass toward the post office. Down the long marble corridor and out the far side. Up this alley. Sheer brick walls the color of frozen iodine. Slow commence of traffic, pitch and clang of trolleys. Newsmen stamping at their corners, fingers stirring the coinage in their soiled changeaprons. On Market Street beggars being set out like little misshapen vending machines. Whole legions of the maimed and mute and crooked deployed over the streets in a limboid vapor of smoke and fog. The carlights seemed to tunnel through gauze. Pigeons gurgled and gaped from their ledges on the markethouse, winged shapes flapped forth through the gray haze. Shivering, he made his way toward the dewy neon windowlight that bears the painted ham.

Suttree studied the breakfast through the glass, stroking the lavender lunule on the side of his jaw. None there he knew save one, Blind Richard at coffee. He shrugged up his coat about his shoulders and entered.

A few heads turned. Old codgers bent above their gruel. A clack of china teeth. In a shroud of cold he stood within the door, then made his way down the counter.

Richard, he said.

Gray head goggling fowlwise on a scarious neck, turning. The soapfilled eyesockets.

Hey Suttree. How you doin?

Okay. How are you.

Other'n bein froze I caint complain. The blind man cracked a squaloid smile all full of toothblack and breakfast scraps.

Are you holding anything?

Smile draining. Aye, gape those barren lightshorn eyeballs.

What did you need, Sut?

Let me have a dime.

Richard sought about in a gray pocket. Here you go.

Thanks Richard. He moved down the counter to an empty stool and ordered coffee. Steaming cup of morning purgative. Ponderous white chipped cup with the sandy rim. Spectra winking, pinlets of oil atop impotable tarleachings. He brimmed the cup with cream. Beyond the steambleared windowpanes warped figures shrouded up in overcoats went wobbling past. He sipped the coffee. Ulysses entered. He hung his hat carefully and eased himself down on the stool by Suttree and laid his paper by and took up the menu. You still glutting the labor market, I see, he said.

Morning Ulyss.

Been anyone in here this morning hiring?

Not yet. Let's see a piece of the paper.

Ulysses separated the sheets and passed him a section. He folded the menu and replaced it in the rack and looked up. Two scrambled with ham and coffee, he said. The Greek nodded. Suttree thumbed forward his cup for a refill.

Turned off a bit chill hasnt it? said Ulysses.

They spread their papers. Two cups of coffee clattered to. They were at passing cream and sugar, stirring idly.

Jo Jo says it went down to six above, said Suttree.

Mmm, said Ulysses.

The ham and eggs arrived on an oblong platter of gray crockery. Suttree folded the paper and laid it on the counter at Ulysses' elbow.

You want to see this piece? said Ulysses.

No thanks. I've got to go.

Dont rush off.

Suttree drained his cup and rose. The Greek looked up from turning rashers of brains at the grill. Suttree pitched the dime on the counter and buttoned his coat.

How's J-Bone these days, said Ulysses.

About the same.

He doesnt come around much anymore.

He's working now.

Ulysses smiled. Another victim fallen to employment, eh?

All these good men, said Suttree.

He went by Gay Street to the lower end of the town, down Hill Avenue past the Andrew Johnson and Blount Mansion to the viaduct. A little stone stairway descended from the street. No sign of life in the cold clay warren below.

Gene.

Voice croupy in the cavern. He looked about. After a while he called again. From the little concrete vault that housed sheathed pipes and strange gray vats of electricity came a muffled answer.

It's me, said Suttree.

Pinched face at the door. Harrogate crawled out and squatted on the ground. He wrapped his arms about the folded bones within his denim trouser legs and looked up at Suttree. He was a pale blue color.

Well, said Suttree.

Shit, said Harrogate.

What happened to your bed?

Harrogate gestured over his shoulder. I pulled the mattress in yonder. I've never knowed such cold as this.

Well get off your ass and let's go uptown.

I went up to the hotel a while back. This nigger come over ast me what it was I wanted and I had to leave again.

You got any money?

Not a cryin dime.

Well come on let's go. You'll freeze down here.

I done already am. Shit.

Harrogate rose and spat and heisted up his shoulders in a shuddering gesture of despair and crossed the frozen ground toward the stairs. You could see the shape of his shoulderblades through the army jacket he wore. They climbed to the street above, hands in pockets.

Have you eaten anything?

Harrogate shook his head. Shit no. I'm a mere shadder.

Well, let's see about getting some groceries in your skinny gut.

You got any money?

Not yet.

Shit, said Harrogate.

They hiked up the cold and desolate street. A bitter wind had risen and little balls of soot hobbled along the walks. Old papers rose and rattled in an alleyway and a paper cup went scuttling. These lone figures going through the naked streets swore at the cold and something like the sun struggled at ten oclock sleazy and heatless beyond the frozen pestilential miasma that cloaked the town.

At Lane's Drugs they peered in.

They're closed.

It's Thanksgiving.

Harrogate looked about. Well hell, he said.

We'll go down to Walgreen's. They always have a turkey dinner.

Large posters hung within the glass facade. A steaming plate of turkey meat with dressing and potatoes and peas and cranberry sauce. The price was fifty-nine cents.

How does that look? said Suttree.

Harrogate just shook his head.

They filed through the door and Suttree went to the cash register. A blond girl in glasses raised up from below the counter with cartons of cigarettes to fill the little shelves. Hey good-lookin, she said.

Hi Mary Lou.

What are you doin?

I came to eat.

She looked past him and around. Okay, she said.

I brought a friend.

Okay, she said.

He smiled and pursed his lips in a kiss and he and Harrogate made their way down along the counter and climbed onto stools.

Two turkey dinners, Suttree said.

She wrote on the green ticket. You all want coffee?

You want coffee, Gene?

Hell yes.

Two coffees.

They sipped water from little paper cones in openwork holders.

Quit looking so nervous, Gene.

Yeah yeah, sure sure, said Harrogate. He was staring at the gaudy cardboard placards above the fountain with their icecream sundaes and model sandwiches. He looked about and he leaned toward Suttree. I thought you said you didnt have no money, he whispered.

I thought you said you had some.

I'm gettin the fuck out of here.

Suttree took hold of his sleeve. I was just kidding, he said.

You sure?

Sure.

Harrogate unbuttoned his jacket and began to look about more easily. Coffee arrived.

How did you sleep last night?

He spooned great lavings of sugar. Not worth a shit, he said. You?

Suttree just shook his head. The stripling on the stool beside him with his heron's legs dangling smelled like a smoked jockstrap. Even the waitress's eyes went a little funny when she passed and she herself no rosegarden.

Looky here, said Harrogate.

She set before them each a white platter. Sliced turkey and dressing pooled over in thick gravy and steaming creamed potatoes and peas and a claretcolored dollop of cranberry sauce and hot rolls with pats of creamery butter. Harrogate's eyes were enormous.

You all want some more coffee?

Yes mam.

Harrogate had his mouth so crammed with food his eyes bulged.

Take it easy, Gene. There's no prize at the bottom of the plate.

Harrogate nodded, slumped over the plate and encircling it with one arm while he scooped falling forkfuls toward his underjaw. There was no conversation. Down the counter a man sat reading the newspaper. The waitresses lollygagged about, dragging foul dishclouts across the stainless steel equipment. Suttree took in this scene of stone eyed boredom while he ate. He'd have ordered second plates around had it not been for attracting attention.

With his belly full Harrogate's countenance grew cute and his eyes began to sidle. They drank more coffee. He leaned toward Suttree.

Listen Sut. Let me have the checks and we'll slip on around to the other side and look at the magazines till we see the coast is clear and then we'll ease on out.

It's all right.

Hell, save your money. We may need it. Listen, they're easy here.

Suttree shook his head. They're watching you, he said.

What all do you mean, watching me?

You look suspicious.

I look like it? What about you?

They can tell I'm all right just by looking.

Why you shit-ass.

Suttree was laughing with his mouth full of coffee.

Come on Suttree. Hell, you can go out first if you want and I'll foller ye.

Suttree wiped his chin and looked down at the sharp and strangely wizened childsface rapt with larceny. Gene?

Yeah?

You waste me.

Yeah. Well.

In the street they stood facing downwind, picking their teeth.

What are you going to do?

I dont know. Freeze.

Dont you know anybody over on the hill you could sort of visit?

I dont know. I could go up to Rufus's maybe.

Well get somewhere. I'm going over to see how the old man is. We'll figure something out.

I believe it's the end of the world.

What?

Harrogate was looking at the pavement. He said it again.

Look at me, Suttree said.

He looked up. Sad pinched face, streaked with grime.

Are you serious?

Well what do you think about it?

Suttree laughed.

It aint funny, said Harrogate.

You're funny, you squirrely son of a bitch. Do you think the world will end just because you're cold?

It aint just me. It's cold all over.

It's not cold by Rufus's stove. Now get your ass up there. I'll see you later.

A colder wind was coming upriver across the bridge. Suttree scurried along like a hunchback. When he got to the other side he scrambled down the frozen mudbank and ducked under the bridge. There was no fire.

Ho, he called.

Oh, said a voice from the arches.

He entered and looked about. The old man's bed and the old man's cart and the mounds of junk and rags and furniture. Frozen seepage hung from the bell joints of cesspipes overhead. Suttree turned and went back up the bank to the street and crossed the bridge again.

He went up Market and up the hill to Vine Avenue and the halfdollar dosshouse there, old darkened brick and gabley mansard roof shingled up in slates the shape of fishscales. He looked for a bell but there were just the wires hanging from a hole so he tapped on the glass of the sidelights. They gave soft and soundless in their lead muntins. He tapped on the door. After a while he tried the knob. The door was unlocked and he entered. Into a cold and narrow hallway. He shut the door and went down in the semidark calling out hello. No one was about. He paused at the coiled banister finial and gazed up the cold black stairwell. He listened. A sound of snuffling. Someone spat. He came back along the hall and opened a door. Upon a drawing room full of derelicts. It looked like the hatching of some geriatric uprising, this congregation of the ravaged on their rickety chairs all gathered about a patent iron stove, old graylooking men crouched by the warmth in the barren room, nodding and muttering and hawking gobbets of spit clogged with dust and blood against the hot iron to sizzle and stink. The ragpicker was crouched in the corner on the old hearth almost behind the stove. Suttree saw him look up, eyes that could not see far. The ragpicker didnt know who had come in until Suttree said his name.

Who's that? he said, craning his neck and looking up.

Suttree.

Ah, said the ragpicker.

Suttree smiled. A warm odor of filth hung in the room cut through with a reek of urine.

What are you doing?

Mildewing. You?

I'm freezing.

This is just the commence of it. I look for the river to freeze over. You better draw your lines. The ice'll cut em. You never will find em. I've seen it to happen. Bet me.

Suttree squatted and held his hands to the fire. A man with a mauve face like the faces of the dead was looking down at him.

How long have you been up here? said Suttree.

Since two days ago.

Suttree looked around. Mauve man was looking at a hole in the floor. A quivering string of drool hung from his lower lip halfway to his shoe.

How long do you plan on staying?

The ragpicker shrugged up his buzzard's shoulders. For however long it stays cold. I dont care. I just wisht I could die and I'd be better off.

Suttree ignored this. He'd heard it all before. How many do they have staying here? he said.

The ragpicker waved his hand. I dont know. What all's here, I reckon. Aint no other place in the house warm that I know of.

Where are the rooms, upstairs?

Yeah, upstairs. The beds is all took.

Mauve man had been listening. Cecil's aint took, he said.

Well. Cecil's aint took.

Who's Cecil?

Just old Cecil. He died.

Oh.

He never died in the bed though.

Where'd he die?

Uptown. He got too drunk to come in and I reckon he passed out. He was froze, they said. I dont know.

He froze, said Mauve man. Old Cecil did.

Cecil froze.

Old Cecil froze from head to toes

And stiffer than a tortoise

In spite of drinking strained canned heat

And dilute Aqua Fortis

Suttree waved away these things from his ears. Cecil was being discussed by the company. All agreed that the day of his death was a cold one. Today even colder. It's colder than a welldigger's ass said one, another said A witch's tit. A nun's cunt said a third. On Good Friday.

Suttree leaned and touched the old man's arm. His coat with the eaten elbows. The ragpicker jerked awake and turned a baleful red eye on him.

Who do you see about a room here?

He aint here.

It's fifty cents isnt it?

By the night it is. You can rent by the week and beat them rates. Two fifty. If you've got it. What's wrong with your place? You've not got thowed out have ye?

It's for somebody else.

Well you better tell him to come on. With this weather. You caint look for somebody to die just ever day.

When is whatsit due back?

I caint say.

Can I look upstairs?

You can look anyplace you take a notion because he aint here.

Do you need anything?

I need everthing.

Suttree rose.

Bring something for the pot, said the ragman, and you can sit in. He gestured upward with a gray hand webbed in part of a sock. A lardpail simmered on the one eye of the iron stove and a pieplate with a rock in it lifted along one edge like a thin frogjaw and belched forth a gout of steam and clapped shut again.

I'll see what I can do, said Suttree. He eased his way around the edge of these half addled aged and rumsoaked dotards and ascended the stairs.

Muted light fell through a window at the end of the hall. The doors had all been unpinned from their hinges and taken away. Suttree peered into an old boudoir with mattresses along the walls. Tattered gray army blankets. A thin little man was squatting by the window masturbating. He did not take his eyes from Suttree nor did he cease pulling at his limp and wattled cock. It was deadly cold in the room. Suttree turned and went back and down the stairs.

Mrs Rufus opened the door.

Cold enough for you? said Suttree.

She motioned him in.

Harrogate was sitting by the stove with a parcel of blacks all of whom were drunk or working at it. When Harrogate turned and raised his head Suttree saw that the city rat himself was reeling.

How the hell did you manage to get drunk this quick? he said.

Drinkin whiskey is how. Have a goddamn drink Sut. Give him a drink Cleo.

An angular black with splaycd teeth held forth a quart picklejar half full of splo. Suttree waved it away.

Where's Rufus?

He aint here.

I can see that.

I told that fool not to give him none of that whiskey, said Mrs Rufus from behind him in a muted shriek.

I never poured it down his thoat, said a dark dwarf by the stove-door.

Suttree looked around. Well fuck it, he said.

Who is this cat? said a tawny freckled halfbreed. Small skull covered with snips of copper wire.

He's cool man, he's cool, said Harrogate, having fallen easily into the way of things.

Suttree turned and went out. He pulled the door to behind him and went on along the little cinder path past the hoglot, a pair of snouts working in the fence mesh to get the wind of him. Long ears tilting, pale eyes watching from their purlieu of frozen mire. He went out to the road and across the viaduct toward town. The lightest rain of soot was falling and a handful of small birds flared suddenly about him, moving through the bitter air with a faint rasping sound. Suttree looked down at the blackwater creek swirling below, the gray panes of scalloped ice. He went on toward the town, a colorless world this winter afternoon where all things bear that grainy look of old films and the buildings rise into an obscurity prophetic and profound.

He went up Central, slumped and hands deeply pocketed. An eyeless beggar addled with the cold sat in the empty feastday street singing a canticle to his eternal night and holding out a simple frozen claw for whatever might fall almswise. Suttree hawked up and thooked forth a clot of phlegm against a boarded storewindow and started across the street. As he did so his eye fell on a cartoken in the gutter. He bent to claim it. Small brass coin stamped through with a K. He crossed the street and swung up through the open door of a standing trolley and dropped the coin in the glass cage and went down the aisle. The driver watched him in the mirror. Suttree eased himself into the cold leather seat and looked out.

Lights came on above the shops, a neon sign here, sudden paltry spanglements against the bluegray dusk. A fabled miscellany in this pawnshop window. The door clattered and hushed shut and the trolley lurched forward. The pale domes of light in the clerestory waxed more yellow. The seats to the front of the streetcar were vacant yet two blacks hung by one arm each like gibbons from the chrome rail overhead and swayed with the gathering speed. With the heel of his hand Suttree cleared a small window in the frosted glass and peered out at the few figures receding along the walks. Fellow citizens in this bewintered city. A passing rack of hot neon washed his own sad countenance from the glass. He leaned his head against the cold pane, watching pedestrians toil from pool to pool of lamplight, trailing wisps of vapor, bent figures, homebound. He could smell the old varnished wood of the sash and the brass of the catches. The trolley slowed, surged forth again. Cars passed below, a rumpling sound of tires over the bricks. The buildings dropped away. They were going by a frozen mudflat, lunar, naked, spoored with fossil dogtracks. Under the billboard lights small sprawling mica constellations.

The lightwires slung past in shallow convections pole to pole and the loneliness rode in his stomach like an egg.

Bell ching. This archaic craft grinding to a halt. People shuffling out through the folding door. A wet pneumatic hiss, clanking into motion once again. Your face among the brown bags old lady. Waiting to cross. Blinking at the transit of these half empty frames slapping past. Beyond in a yellowlit housewindow two faces fixed aspectant and forever in some domestic vagary. Rapid his progress who petrifies these innocents into stony history.

They swung past the deserted park, the midway, the ferriswheel like a burntout armature standing black and cold against the farther streetlamps. The trolley heeled hard by a brick wall and went rattling down an alleyway where scrawled fucks in rainwashed chalk flashed past the window under the crackling blue stroboscope of the antenna. They wheeled through a long carbarn and pulled to a stop with dimming lights.

End of the line, buddy, the driver called back.

I'll just ride on back to town with you, Suttree said.

Well you'll have to come up here and put a token in the box.

I thought you could ride as far as you wanted on one token.

Not on this streetcar.

Suttree rose and made his way down the aisle, his eye studying the floor for a chance of coin or token among the matchstems and gumwrappers. Listen, he said, cant I just ride on back?

Fares is one way, said the driver.

I dont have another token.

They're five for thirty cents. Or you can put in a dime.

I dont have any money.

Oh well, said the driver. He reached and got his little leather bag and rose. This would be a pleasant world if everybody could just ride and ride.

He descended the steps with his satchel and crossed through the dim electric gloom of the terminal toward the dispatch office. Suttree went out to the street.

A few carlights came owllike from the murk and receded. He stood beneath a streetlamp with his thumb out. In his thin coat he was cold to the bone in moments. The streetcar hove from the carbarn and sucked by the soft yellow bore of the headlamp went trundling past. Blacks nodding in their windowstrips. A trolley of dolls or frozen dead.

Suttree with one foot in the gutter glared numbly after the helmless driver and the springworn trucks moaned and lolled on their shackles and a blue tailstar clicked along the wires and the trolley drew away into the night. He gripped his thighs through his threadbare pockets and set off along the weedy walkway. The lights of Knoxville quaked in a faint penumbra to the west as must the ruins of many an older city seen by herders in the hills, by barbaric tribesmen shuffling along the roads. Suttree with his miles to go kept his eyes to the ground, maudlin and muttersome in the bitter chill, under the lonely lamplight.

The old railroader had a fire going in the little iron stove and he'd pulled his bed crosswise before it for warmth. Suttree slid the door shut. Back down the tracks the gray ruins of summer weeds looked wrinkled and very old.

Come set by the fire, the old man said. I didnt know it was so cold.

I've brought it all inside with me. How have you been?

Mean as ever. How you makin it?

I'm about froze out. Thought I'd better check on you to see were you still living.

The old man chuckled to himself. Well lord, he said. A little cold wont kill me I dont reckon. Set down.

He raised himself up slightly and rocked to one side as if he would make room and then subsided in the same place. Suttree sat on the edge of the bunk. Strangely like his own. The rough army blanket. The old man had been reading a coverless book and he laid it down and removed his glasses and pinched the bridge of his nose. A small desk stood against the wall and in the pigeonholes were yellowed timetables, waybills and tare sheets. In the far corner a great stack of old newsprint and magazines. The old man's eyes must have followed his.

I give up on the newspapers, he said.

Why's that?

I never read one but what somebody aint been murdered or shot or somethin such as that. I never knowed such a place for meanness.

Was it ever any different?

How's that?

I said was it ever any different.

No. I reckon not.

Well it's always been in the papers hasnt it?

Yes. I just give up on it is all. I get older I dont want to hear about it. People are funny. They dont want to hear about how nice everthing is. No no. They aint somebody murdered in the papers their day is a waste of time. I give it up myself. Seen it all. It's all the same. Train wrecks of course. Natural catastrophe. A train wreck'll make ye think about things.

Did you ever see a train wreck?

Oh yes.

What's the worst one you ever saw?

Seen or heard tell of?

Either one.

I dont know. I seen a boiler cut loose in Letohatchie Alabama blowed the whole locomotive cab and all up onto a overpass and just left the trucks settin on the track. They'd stopped to take on water but fore they could fill her the crown sheet went. I seen that. But they was one blew up in the roundhouse in San Antonio Texas in the year nineteen and twelve that blowed the whole roundhouse down and a lot of other buildins besides. They found one chunk of the boiler that weighed eight ton a quarter mile from the wreck. Another piece weighed almost a thousand pound tore a man's house down a half mile away. I was just a young man at the time but I remember readin it like it was yesterday. Had all the pitchers in the paper. I think they was twenty-eight killed and I dont know how many maimed for life.

Suttree looked at the old man. A thousand pound piece of iron went a half mile? he said.

Oh yes. Hadnt hit this feller's house it might still be goin.

Would you have liked to have seen it, Daddy?

The old man looked at Suttree in alarm. Seen it? he said. Where from?

I see, said Suttree.

Course they's been a lot worse wrecks than them. They was a Pennsy engine left the track in Philadelphia about ten year ago, hotbox caused the axle to break, thowed some cars into a bridge and killed eighty people all told. Your worst wrecks was the telescopes. One car would run inside another and just gather everbody up out of their seats and make a big mud pie out of em at the end. Then of course they was bridges and trestles. I remember two trains run out on a doubletrack trestle up in Kentucky goin in opposite directions, about the time they got abreast of one another the whole thing just folded up and dropped into the river. Trestle, locomotives, tenders, cars, folks. All of it. Kaploosh. Back then most of ye trestles was just wood. The coaches was wood too and they had stoves in em about like thisn here and when they'd wreck they'd tip over and set the coaches afire and burn up everbody inside. I tell ye, ridin a train back in them days was a thing you give some thought to.

The old man rose heavily from the bed and opened the stove door and dumped in coal from the scuttle and sat back down again. He dabbed with the back of one knuckle at his nose. Outside it had grown almost dark and a cat appeared at the clerestory window and whined.

You caint get in that way, idjit, the old man called. You come to the door like everbody else.

When I was young I didnt care for nothin, he continued. I was always easy in the world. Saw a right smart of it. Never cared to go just wherever.

How did you happen to end up here?

I aint ended yet. Used to hobo a right smart. Back in the thirties. They wasnt no work I dont care what you could do. I was ridin through the mountains one night, state of Colorado. Dead of winter it was and bitter cold. I had just a smidgin of tobacco, bout enough for one or two smokes. I was in one of them old slatsided cars and I'd been up and down in it like a dog tryin to find some place where the wind wouldnt blow. Directly I scrunched up in a corner and rolled me a smoke and lit it and thowed the match down. Well, they was some sort of stuff in the floor about like tinder and it caught fire. I jumped up and stomped on it and it aint done nothin but burn faster. Wasnt two minutes the whole car was afire. I run to the door and got it open and we was goin up this grade through the mountains in the snow with the moon on it and it was just blue lookin and dead quiet out there and them big old black pine trees goin by. I jumped for it and lit in a snowbank and what I'm goin to tell you you'll think peculiar but it's the god's truth. That was in nineteen and thirty-one and if I live to be a hunnerd year old I dont think I'll ever see anything as pretty as that train on fire goin up that mountain and around the bend and them flames lightin up the snow and the trees and the night.

They nodded and shivered in the fogged car while the gray dawn hovered without. They groaned and stirred and slept. Sometime in the night Sharpe had come awake freezing, coatless, and climbed out to stir about in the alleyway, gathering pieces of cratewood and paper. J-Bone reared up in the front seat. What's that? he said.

What time is it Jim?

I dont have a watch. Where's that smoke coming from?

This fire here.

J-Bone raised himself and looked over the back of the seat. Sharpe had a small fire going in the floor of the car and he was holding his hands over it. J-Bone leaned over the seat and held his own hands out for warmth. Watch Cabbage's leg there, he said.

Sharpe jostled the bony knee.

Hey Cabbage, get your leg out of the fire.

Cabbage reared up wildly and subsided.

Better crack that window hadnt we? said J-Bone.

They grinned at each other across the smoke and the flames.

I'm about to freeze my ass off. What time do you reckon it is?

I dont know. What time's it get light?

Shit if I know. You sure they open at five?

Yeah. Have for years.

Sharpe was peering out across the blueblack night, the buildings stark and tall, the few streetlamps encoiled in fog.

It's gettin smoky in here, said J-Bone.

Does Suttree have a watch?

No. I dont think so. He bent to see. Suttree lay slumped under the wheel with his folded hands between his knees.

Sharpe cranked down the rear window. Smoke was rolling blackly through the car.

Cabbage raised up and looked at Sharpe with drunken sleepshot eyes. What's happening? he said.

We're waiting on that five oclock beer.

The fucking car's on fire.

We're tryin to get warm, Cabbage, said J-Bone.

Cabbage looked from one to the other of them. You sons of bitches are crazy, he said. He opened the door and lurched out into the alley.

J-Bone got out on the other side. Come on Sharpe. Let's walk around some fore we freeze.

See if you can see some more wood out there.

Suttree woke and looked out the window. A garbage truck had gone down the alley. He sat up. He was alone in the car. He opened the glovebox and reached around inside and shut it again. He felt under the seat and he looked in the back. The remains of the fire lay in a blackened crust of burnt rubber on the floor. He looked out down the alley. He was shaking with the cold.

He climbed stiffly from the car and shut the door. Traffic was commencing in the murk, headlamps boring past in pale shrouds. A dog crossed in the hobbled lights. Suttree stove his hands deep in his pockets and hunched his shoulders and went toward the street.

They were seated in a row on stools within the watered windows of the Signal Cafe and they were drinking beer. An old newspedlar sat at the front of the counter humped over his coffee. Suttree swung through the door blowing on his hands and took a stool.

This goddamn Suttree is a five oclock alarm clock, said Sharpe.

Wasnt no danger of sleepin over with Sut along.

Let me have a Redtop, said Suttree to the counterman.

You rest well Sut?

You sons of bitches would let a man lay out there and freeze to death.

I was goin to come out there and get you, Bud.

We run out of firewood.

How long you all been in here?

This is our first one. Hell, he just opened this minute.

Suttree seized the bottle before him and drank and hiked his shoulders up and drank again. Across the street a neon sign that once said Earle Hotel said le Ho. Two workers with their lunchboxes in their armpits stamped and smoked on the corner. Suttree looked at his companions. Their bottles rose and fell like counterweights. I thought five oclock never would get here, said J-Bone.

By nine oclock that night they were twelve or more, all good hearts from McAnally. An hour later they were at a roadhouse called the Indian Rock.

They threaded their way among the tables, Billy Ray Callahan stopping where girls had gone to dance and left purses among the drinks. Callahan draining the glasses and taking the money from the purses and moving on, smiling and nodding to friends and strangers, past a table where a big boy was sitting, Callahan smiling at him invitingly.

What say, big boy.

Big boy looked away.

They pulled tables together and ordered Cokes and set out pints of whiskey. Under the tilting smoke the dancers whirled and the music with its upbeat country tempo scored like an overture the gatherings of violence just beneath the surface, the subtle exchanges in the heated air. Suttree and J-Bone made their way toward the men's room. Cabbage on the floor already dancing mightily, the girl laughing. Kenneth Tipton at a nearby table holding out his hand.

We've got to get these cunts, said J-Bone.

Let's not get too drunk.

When they got back their table was gone. The drinks lay in a pile of glass and icecubes on the wet concrete floor and the table lay caved in a corner. Suttree saw one of the legs in someone's hand. The area was clearing fast, people moving along the walls. Suttree saw Hoghead move with stealth along the rear of a phalanx of battlers and draw back and hit a boy behind the ear and move on. Earl Solomon came pedaling backwards out of the line and slammed up against the wall. Paul McCulley was trading punches with three boys all by himself down by the ladies' room door and the door kept opening and closing and girls looking out by turns.

We better get some of them off of Hulley Babe, said J-Bone.

They started down the room but before they'd gone far someone fell into J-Bone. J-Bone shoved him and he turned around and took a swing and at it they went. Suttree made his way on to where Paul was and grabbed a boy by the wrist and whipsawed and flung him into a table full of half empty drinks. He screamed something at Suttree but it was lost in the melee. Paul hit one of the other boys and he went down and got up and walked off. The third one hit Suttree in the side of the head. Suttree squared off and ducked and the boy looked and saw McCulley coming for him and said: I aint fightin the two of ye.

Why you crawfishin son of a bitch, McCulley said. You didnt mind it the other way around. He shoved the boy back against the wall but the boy turned and ran.

Get that little fucker, Red, called McCulley.

Callahan was standing bloodyheaded in the middle of a pile of fallen bodies looking about. He reached and took the boy by the shoulder almost gently. Pow, he said. Suttree turned his head. McCulley had his arm around him hugging him and laughing and taking him directly into the thick of it.

Who the fuck are we fighting? said Suttree.

Who the fuck cares? If he aint from McAnally bust him.

And they are whelmed in dark riot, the smoking hall a no man's land filled with lethal looking drunks reeling about with bleeding eyes and reeking of homemade whiskey. A scuffling of feet, fists thudding. Long endless crash of glass and chairs and overhead the intermittent whoosh of whiskey bottles crossing the room like mortar shells to explode on the block walls. A wave of bodies swept over Suttree. He struggled up. In the midst of it all he found Kenneth Tipton seemingly encased in a nimbus of peace, holding his wrist and working his hand open and shut. I've fucked up my hand, he said. Then he was swept away.

The floor was slick with blood and whiskey. Someone hit him under the eye. He tried to see J-Bone but he could not. He saw Callahan go by, one eye blue shiny, smiling, his teeth in a grout of blood. His busy freckled fists ferrying folks to sleep. He saw a bottle in a fist rise above the melee, saw it powdered on an unknown skull.

The fight washed up against the ladies' room wall and the structure groaned and slewed. Suttree saw a head snap back and cave a cracked dish shape in the wallboard. Somebody had an old boy in the corner with handkerchiefs trying to stop his ear from bleeding and the old boy was ready to whip his nurse to get back into it. Slapping away the hand attending him, his ear hanging half off. The bouncer was working his way like a reaper through the crowd by the wall, flattening people with a slapstick. When he came upon McCulley, McCulley hit him solidly in the jaw. The bouncer reeled back and shook his head and came on again and swung with the slapstick. It made an ugly sound on the side of McCulley's head. McCulley swung again and caught the bouncer in the face. Blood flew. The bouncer fell back and recovered. Both were preparing to swing together when McCulley's knees gave way and he knelt in the glass and the blood. The bouncer moved on, making his way toward Callahan. Behind him came a man lugging a floorbuffer.

A heavy machine, he could just by main strength raise it. When he hit the bouncer with it the bouncer disappeared.

Suttree tried to work his way toward the wall but a heavy arm came athwart his eyes. He spun. Surrounded now by strangers. The man with the floorbuffer washed up nearby. The buffer rose trembling above the crowd. It came down on no head but Suttree's.

He felt the vertebrae in his neck crack. The room and all in it turned white as noon. His eyes rolled up in his head and his bowels gave way. He distinctly heard his mother say his name.

He was standing with his knees locked and his hands dangling and the blood pouring down into his eyes. He could not see. He said: Do not go down.

He swayed. He took a small step, stiffly fending. What waited was not the black of nothing but a foul hag with naked gums smiling and there was no madonna of desire or mother of eternal attendance beyond the dark rain with lamps against the night, the softly cloven powdered breasts and the fragile claviclebones alabastrine above the rich velvet of her gown. The old crone swayed as if to mock him. What man is such a coward he would not rather fall once than remain forever tottering?

He dropped like a zombie among the din and the flailing, his face drained, his eyes platelike with the enormity of the pain behind them. Someone stepped on his hand as he was crawling across the floor. He tried to rise again but the room had composed itself into a tunnel down which he kept falling. He did not know what had happened to him and his eyes kept filling up with blood. He thought he'd been shot and he kept telling himself that the damage could be repaired if nothing else befell him dear God to be out of this place forever.

He pulled himself up a swaying wall and tried to see. All that frantic bedlam before him seemed to have slowed and each whirling face swam off in perfect parallax like warriors and their mentors twinned, a roomful of hostile and manic siamese. Ahhh, said Suttree. Making his way toward the door he realized with a faint surge of that fairyland feeling from childhood wonders that the face he passed wide eyed by the side of an upturned table was a dead man. Someone going with him saw him see. That's fucking awful, he said. Suttree was bleeding from the ears and couldnt hear well but he thought so too. They stumbled on like the damned in off the plains of Gomorrah. Before they reached the door someone hit him in the head with a bottle.

He must have fallen foul of yet other hands afterwards because when he woke in the hospital he had a broken finger, three broken ribs, a mouthful of loose teeth and one missing. He tried to move but the jagged ends of bone in his chest were like scissors. His head was pounding and his vision skewed in some way and he was vaguely amazed at being alive and not sure that it was worth it. He raised his eyes and felt the dried blood crack across his forehead. Lights kept rising one by one and after a while he realized that they were bulbs in a corridor ceiling and that the periodic squeaking sound was a caster on the cart that was wheeling him. The emergency room was filled with people bleeding. Grumous battlers with misshapen heads. All watched over by hordes of police. They wheeled Suttree on. Bearing his pained bones in their boat of flesh. To where the deadcarriage waits in the dark. Perhaps the wrath of God after all.

Friends row by row watched his passing and waved at him with their fingers and whispered among themselves. Who'd spoke of disorders of the soul and news of night. When you asked for the shop of the heart's apothecary we thought you mad. We saw you took down to the brainsurgeon's keep, deep in the cellar, under the street. Where saws sang in stoven skulls and wet bonemeal blew from an airshaft in the alleyway. Out there in the blue moonlight a gray shecorpse being loaded into a truck. It pulled away into the night. Horned minstrels, small dancing dogs in harlequin garb hobbled after.

The night is cold and colder, a fog moves with menace in the streets. Malefic stirrings underfoot, a foul breath rising visibly from the pierced sewerlids. The watertruck goes by like a nightbeast, its drumshaped brush clanking. Water wells inkblack in the streets repeating the polelamps in glozy rosettes that dish and slide in the wash like radiolarians pale with phosphorous on a midnight sea. The sweepers broom the trash along the flooded gutters, their yellow slickers bright with wet. They leap to the truck and ride with brooms aloft like figures done in lacquered wax, like hortatory gnomes. The hotel nightlights shine behind the drawn venetian blinds and the slatted patterns on the curbside cars give them the look of anchored smallcraft with lapstrake hulls. Out there in the winter streets a few ashen anthroparians scuttling yet through the falling soot. Above them the shape of the city a colossal horde of retorts and alembics ranged against a starless sky. Uneasy sleeper you will live to see the city of your birth pulled down to the last stone.

Suttree heard people discussing his skull. Could he but see himself. His head half shaved and gray and numb with novocaine. An old doctor with a mosquitoclamp and a needle stitched his scalp. Suttree still in his street clothes, one sleeve cut away, stained and stinking with blood and beer and shit. A nurse sat with his elbow in her lap, picking out pieces of glass with a pair of forceps and placing them in a steel tray.

He woke in a small white room. Late evening. Bird shadows oblique upon the wall. He raised his head and looked about. Two pigeons on the windowsill ruffled their feathers. A westerly view, cold winter sunlight. Constant beyond the sounds of traffic in the streets there boomed a slow roll of surf. His head was swathed in bandages and his hand hurt. He held it up. One finger wrapped and resting in an aluminum holder. His hand separated into two hands side by side both injured. He blinked his eyes and they rejoined. Callahan, you bastard, he said. He lay back and slept.

When he woke again he saw that he was not in a room but in a ward. The screen had been pushed away from his bed and he could see down a long hall many men in beds like his. Night time, yellow bulbs burning in the ceiling. A nurse was going down the ward with a cart collecting the dinner trays. He had to keep blinking his eyes to keep things ordered and discrete. He seemed to be in an old folks' home. Iron beds filled with gray octogenarians propped upright in nightshirts, humped and hawking and leering beadily at one another like paranoids.

Suttree tried to raise himself onto one elbow but his chest hurt. He was wrapped in tape to his armpits and he had an image of burial windings here in this room among the dying. He tried to focus his eyes. To see one person in the ward who looked as if he might have more than days to live. A cold sweat broke out upon him. He felt his head. Terminal brain damage under the towels? He tried to recite the multiplication tables and this filled him with sexual memories and caused him to lie back smiling. He slept and in his sleep he saw his friends again and they were coming downriver on muddy floodwaters, Hoghead and the City Mouse and J-Bone and Bearhunter and Bucket and Boneyard and J D Davis and Earl Solomon, all watching him where he stood on the shore. They turned gently in their rubber bullboat, bobbing slightly on the broad and ropy waters, their feet impinging in the floor of the thing with membraneous yellow tracks.

They glided past somberly. Out of a lightless dawn receding, past the pale daystar. A fog more obscure closed away their figures gone a sadder way by psychic seas across the Tarn of Acheron. From a rock in the river he waved them farewell but they did not wave back.

In the morning the old men were upright and drooling with the first light. Two nurses came down the ward with breakfast trays. The one named Miss Aldrich bent above him smiling and went away again. An enameled namepin. Her white starched frock crackled like sheetiron and her crepesoled shoes went silently as mice.

Suttree had been taken from his bloodied clothes and bathed and laid out in clean coarse linen. Miss Aldrich helped him down the long corridor, the old men watching furiously from their rows of beds on either side. Her soft breast against his elbow, crossing from band to latticed band of morning sunlight where it fell through the barred windows. He stood in a concrete room painted white and pissed painfully a few drops into an oldfashioned urinal and came out again. She was waiting for him. Did you do your business? she said, smiling.

Just a little.

Number one or number two?

Suttree couldnt remember what the numbers corresponded to. Wee wee, he said. He felt completely stupid.

She took his elbow to help him back to his bed.

I can make it all right, he said.

I know.

Oh.

Arent you ashamed?

Of what?

Getting into such a terrible fight. You havent seen yourself in a mirror, have you?

Suttree didnt answer. What's wrong with my head? he said.

You broke it.

Broke it?

Yes.

Is it bad?

No. Well, it's not good. It is fractured.

I keep seeing double.

It'll go away. Here.

Suttree tried to get into the bed painlessly. Shit, he said. He sat with care. How many ribs?

Three.

Who else is here?

You mean your little friends?

Yes.

None. Most of them were treated and taken to jail. A few escaped I think. Are you ready for some breakfast?

I guess so. Am I?

Why not.

She brought him a tray with a bowl of oatmeal and milk and a cup of watered coffee.

Is that it? he said.

That's it.

She fluffed his pillows, helped him to sit. Soap scent of her hair and her breast brushing across his eye.

I suppose this is Knoxville General? he said, sniffing the porridge.

She smiled. So you dont even know where you are.

Isnt it?

What makes you think you're in Knoxville?

Come on.

Yes. At St Mary's you get poached eggs. But you have to say your prayers first.

She put her hand to her mouth. Oh, she said. You're not a Catholic are you?

I've been defrocked. This tastes like wet mattress stuffing.

But do you like it?

Just so so. Listen, what is this ward? It looks like where they lock up dangerous incurables.

It's just a ward. Most of our patients are older people.

Older? There's no one in here under ninety. What do they do, unload them here to die?

Yes.

I see.

They're all indigents. Some of them they bring down here from the nursing home when they get too sick. It's an experience.

I'll bet.

You created quite a sensation.

What, among the inmates?

No, silly. Among the nurses.

She brought him the morning paper but he couldnt focus on the print. She cranked up the old metal bed, moving about, flirting with him and smelling good. She told him of her life in the nurses' home, her wide face full of humor. She roomed in the old morgue along with the other nurses in training. Their beds all leveled under two legs with bricks where the concrete floor sloped toward the drain. At supper she brought her girlfriend, a short heavyset nurse, with instructions to take care of him.

Just remember I saw him first, she said. She winked at Suttree. I'll see you tomorrow.

But he was afoot and gone with fall of dark. Hobbling down the corridor in his nightshirt past the snoring elders and through the door at the end. A little vestibule. Through the wired glass he could see out into the lobby where the night nurse sat at her desk. Suttree turned and went back through the ward to the doors at the other end. A further corridor, dimly lit. He came upon a washroom and a closet where white orderly coats and jackets hung from pegs above the mopbuckets and jugs of chemicals. He dressed quickly in the first clothes to hand and he looked at himself in the glass. A wounded peon.

He found a door that opened onto the main hall of the hospital and he walked toward the light at the entrance and out into the night. He went down the street toward Central Avenue and crossed to the Corner Grill. His toes were so folded in the old black shoes he'd found that he could hardly walk.

Strange apparition to enter the dim of the little tavern on a quiet Saturday night. Big Frig rose to help him to a booth with elaborate solicitousness and he and the brothers Clancy reckoned him sole survivor of a madhouse rising, an icecream rebellion, before leaning to hear of his trials.

He got a quart of milk from the store and with the bottle under his arm crossed through the winter twilight the littered benchland to the river and home. He had not been asleep long before someone tapped at his door.

What is it?

Aint dead in there are ye?

No.

Aint seen ye about. Allowed ye was dead.

I'm all right.

He lay in the dark listening to the crazed railroader breathing beyond the door. The old man muttered something but Suttree could not make it out.

What? he called.

He was blowing his nose.

Suttree got up and scratched about on the table for a match and lit the lamp and came to the door in the shorts and sweater he'd worn to bed.

Hidy, said the old man.

Come on in.

Was you in bed?

It's all right. Come on in.

The old man entered stiffly in his striped overalls, his shadow bobbing and looming anxiously behind him. Cold in here, he said.

Suttree set the lamp on the table and went to the stove to poke the fire up.

What happent to your head?

I got hit with a floorbuffer.

Say you did?

What time is it?

Could you not hear it comin?

No. What time is it?

He was hauling at the chain, looking about the dim little cabin.

What are you up to?

I was just on my way in. Thought I better check on ye, aint seen ye and all. I thought ye'd died on me.

You and old Hooper are just alike. All you either one talk about is dying. What do you do, sit around and cheer one another up?

Oh no. I see him seldomer and seldomer. A man gets to my age he thinks about dyin some. It's only natural.

What, dying or thinking about it?

Do what?

I thought you were going to tell me what time it was.

The old man tilted the watch in his hand toward the lamp. I caint see good in here, he said.

You want a glass of milk?

I dont use it thank ye.

Suttree poured his tumbler full and drank and regarded the old man. I make it eight forty-six, the old man said.

Suttree rubbed his eyes.

We all got to go sometime.

He looked at the old man.

I said we all got to go sometime. You get older you think about it. Young feller like you.

The old man gestured in the air with his hand, you couldnt tell what it meant. He sat in the chair by the table, still holding the watch in the palm of his hand.

You want a cup of coffee?

No, no. I'm just on my way in.

Suttree leaned back against the wall and sipped the milk. He could feel the air in the cracks like cold wires. The old man sat there, seemed transfixed by the lampflame like a ponderous cat. After a while he heaved up his shoulders and sighed and put away his watch. He rose and adjusted his cap. Well, he said. If I'm goin to cross that river tonight I'd as well start now.

You take care.

He looked about the little cabin. Well, he said. I'm satisfied you aint dead anyways. I'll look for ye on the river.

Okay.

Suttree didnt get up from the bed and the old man raised his hand and went out into the night. A few minutes later Suttree heard the dogs start up along Front Street and later still when he wiped the water from the glass and peered out he could see the old man on the bridge, or rather he could see the faintest figure disturb the globes of light one by one slowly until the farther dark had taken him.

In the morning he went down the river again to run his lines. Two boys from the riverfront down off the foot of Fifteenth Street had just come in. When Suttree passed they were handing up a string of carp wet and yellow with rubber mouths sucking. One of them chained the boat with an old bicycle lock and they moved up the bank in their cheap black shoes, stopping now and again to pluck the winter nettles from their trouserlegs. Suttree raised his hand and they nodded, tossing their heads like small vicious horses and going on across the tracks.

His own lines came up heavy with dead fish. He cut the droppers one by one and watched the pale shapes flare and rock and sink from sight. He tied on new baited snells and recovered the current with the oars. He looked at the gray sky but it did not change and the river was always the same.

In just spring the goatman came over the bridge, a stout old man in overalls, long gray hair and beard. Sunday morning before anyone was about. A clicking of little cleft hooves on the concrete and the goats in their homemade harness drawing tandem carts cobbled up out of old signs and kindlingwood and topped with tattered canvas, horned goatskulls, biblical messages, the whole thing rattling along on elliptical wheels like a whimsical pulltoy for children. Loose goats flowed around the man and the wagon. A lantern swung from the hinder axletree and a small goat face peered from the tailboard, a young goat who is wearied and must ride. The goatman strode in his heavy shoes and raised his nose to test the air, the cart rumbled and clanked on its iron wheels and they entered the town.

Goats fanned over the post office lawn on Main Street and began to graze, the goatman watching them paternally, hiking along at the head of his curious circus. An officer of the law spoke to him:

Get them damned goats off the grass.

The goatman located the voice with narrowed eyes.

Let's go, oldtimer.

Them's mulish goats at times, said the goatman.

Off, said the lawman, pointing.

You Suzy. Get off that there grass now. It aint for you. All of you now.

The goats grazed on with soft goat bells, with goat's ears tilting.

Them goats needs to be on a lead or somethin you want to bring em thew here.

You caint do nothin with em.

This aint no place for a bunch of damned goats.

We just passin thew, said the goatman.

One of the goats defecated copiously on the paving. Dry round turds that rolled like buckshot. She moved on to the green with grace, the ambling tolerance of goathood, fat teats winking from between her legs. The policeman looked at the goatman.

I want them goats out of here.

They goin.

This aint Sevierville or some damned place where you can bring a bunch of goats through the middle of town any time you've a notion and let em shit all over the place.

I came thew there but I never stayed over.

Well let's be for goin thew here and not stayin over.

Come on honey, the goatman said to the nanny that stood sleeping in the traces. She opened one eye, a cracked agate filled with sly goat sapience. The goatman patted her rump where bones reared up beneath the hide that you could hang a hat on. A puff of dust. She moved. They passed the policeman in a sedate trundling. Little goat peering from the wagon. The goatman calling. Hoo now. The tiny clatter of goathooves in the silent Sunday morning and the goats and the cart and the goatman going on in a penumbra of sunlight, a cartwheel trapped and squealing in the trolleytrack till he stoops to lift it out, stout goatman, strange hat in one hand, the company swinging out and down Market Street toward the river, a bunched and sidling halfcircle of goats starting and checking and wheeling past the goatman down the steep hill and the goatman himself with his back to the cart to check its descent.

Suttree woke in late morning with the cabin filled with sunlight, light lapping on the farther wall where it played off the water, a faint bleating of goats. He rose and went out to the deck in his shorts, stretching in the sabbath noon, a dreamy tranquillity. The river lay empty of traffic and the sawmill's small skylights winked in the sun crossriver with their crooked glass. He propped himself on the rail and looked about. The field between the railroad and the river was filled with grazing goats and there was a small strange hooded wagon there and a rigid windless spire of smoke standing in the bright air.

Goats, he said, scratching his chin.

He looked upriver, Jones's tavernboat, the marble company, the curve of the river toward Island Home. The stand of canes tilting at the point and the dark folk fishing there in overalls and faded floral wear. He looked toward the field again.

He counted as many as two dozen. A small one tethered to the wagonwheel stood on buckling legs. A bearded man in overalls came to the rear of the wagon and got something from within and disappeared again. Suttree went in and dressed.

The goatman looked up at his approach. He was wearing little wire eyeglasses and he was reading from the bible. He went back to his reading and Suttree squatted by the fire and watched him, the old man's finger moving on the page, his lips forming the words. After a few minutes he laid the book aside and took off the spectacles and folded them and placed them in the bib pocket of his overalls. He looked up at Suttree, one eye lightly squinted.

Morning, said Suttree.

And a good day to you, said the goatman. Aint the law I dont reckon are you?

No. I live in that houseboat yonder.

The goatman nodded.

Suttree looked up at the wagon. A large blue sign atop it read

JESUS WEPT

Pretty day, aint it? said the goatman.

It is. How many goats have you got?

Thirty-four.

Thirty-four.

Sally died.

Oh.

She never was real stout.

I guess you like goats pretty well.

Well, I've got used to em. We been on the road fourteen year now.

How come you to have so many?

Had nothin to do with it. Goats will be goats. I used to have more'n what I got now. Didnt have but one kid this spring. I think old Billy yonder's gettin too old to cut the mustard.

Suttree looked out over the field at the goats grazing. Three small black boys had come across from the road and stood now uncertainly just outside the goatman's camp and regarded him with wide eyes.

Come up boys, he said.

They made their way to the head of the wagon where a huge old billy goat was tethered. They stood around looking at him.

Can you touch him? one said.

Why sure. Just go on and rub his head.

He wont bite?

Naw. Scratch his old head there. He likes that.

One reached out tentatively and began to rub the goat's nose. The goat sniffed at the boy's sleeve and began to nibble at it.

He's eatin your sweater Loftis.

I dont care.

He stroked the huge whelked horns.

Where you goin with these here goats?

Down the road, said the goatman.

What you wants with these goats anyway?

Little or nothin. Good fresh milk. God's best cheese.

You have any other animals? said Suttree. Dog or anything?

No. Just goats. I think a feller gets started with goats he just more or less sticks to goats.

I guess so, said Suttree. He had squatted in the grass. The goatman's fire puttered gently among the stones. By the river goat bells clanked thinly in the soft forenoon.

Say you live right yonder? said the goatman.

Yes.

What, live by yourself do ye?

Yes.

Well, it's got a lot to recommend it. Aint never been married?

Once, said Suttree.

I had three and it was three too many. He squinted his eyes and pinched the bridge of his nose. The good book says that there'll be seven women for every man. Well somebody else can have my other four what about you?

Suttree smiled and shook his head noncommittally. He was making a little noose from a weedstem. One of the black boys had come to the rear of the wagon where the young goat was tied and the young goat reared and tugged at his rope.

He aint used to folks yet, said the goatman.

When will he be?

I dont know. Talk to him some there. He'll come around.

Here goat, said the black boy.

The other two had come to the edge of the fire and stood looking at the men squatting there. The goatman eyed them critically. What's your name? he said.

Lonnie.

Lonnie you need you some goat's milk to chink up the slats in them ribs what do you think?

I aint never had none.

Be watchful of them elbows you dont knife somebody. Who's your buddy there?

He aint my buddy, he's my brother.

He dont talk much I guess.

He wont say nothin lessen he knows ye.

You know this feller here? He nodded toward Suttree.

He's a fisherman, said Lonnie's brother.

Thought you said he didnt talk.

Lonnie looked at his brother and his brother looked at the ground.

Is that right? said the goatman, turning to Suttree. You a fisherman?

Suttree nodded.

Make a livin at it do you?

A poor one.

It's a honorable trade. What do you fish for?

Carp, catfish.

What do you catch?

Suttree smiled. Carp and catfish, he said. Might catch a drum now and then. Or a gar.

Man dont always catch what he fishes for.

No.

You aint got any catfish today have you?

I might. You want some?

I wouldnt care to have just a mess for myself.

I'll see what I can do. It'll be this evening. I usually run my lines late on Sundays.

The goatman turned to him. On the sabbath?

The fish dont know the difference.

The goatman shook his head. Cant say as I hold with that.

They sat silently for a moment. The old man smelled of goats and woodsmoke. The boys were going from goat to goat down the field by the river.

Why did Jesus weep? said Suttree.

Eh?

He pointed up at the sign. Why did Jesus weep?

Dont know scriptures?

Some.

He wept over folks workin on Sundays.

Suttree smiled.

Jesus wept over Lazarus, said the goatman. It dont say it, but I reckon Lazarus might of wept back when he seen himself back in this vale of tears after he'd done been safe and dead four days. He must of been in heaven. Jesus wouldnt of brought one back from hell would he? I'd hate to get to heaven and then get recalled what about you?

I guess so.

You can bet I intend to ask him when I see him.

Ask who?

Jesus.

You're going to ask Jesus about Lazarus?

Sure. Wouldnt you? Oh I intend to have some questions for him. I'm goin to be talkin to him some day just like I'm talkin to you. I'd better have somethin to say.

Suttree rose and swiped at the seat of his trousers and looked off down the river. Well, he said. I'll bring you a catfish if I get one.

I dont require a big one.

No. It's okay if it's caught on Sunday?

Just dont tell me about it.

All right.

I wouldnt want to aid and abet.

No. Here come some more fans.

A group of people were picking their way across the pitted lot toward the goatman's camp.

I preach at four, said the goatman. Ought to be a good crowd here by then.

Preach?

I preach ever Sunday at four oclock rain or shine. Just straight preachin. No cures, no predictions. Folks ask me about the second comin. Most aint heard of the first one yet. You be here?

Suttree looked down at the goatman. Well, he said. If I'm not, just go ahead and start without me.

He went up the river path toward Ab Jones's. The three black boys had one of the goats by the horns and were going around in circles with it while one of them attempted to climb on its back.

A white derelict named Smokehouse opened the door. He recalled Suttree dimly through drinkgalled eyes and stood aside for him to enter.

How's Tom, said Suttree.

Tom's okay, said the derelict.

Suttree entered the dim room with its odor of stale beer and the urinous smell of chitlins cooking in the back. The derelict shut the door and hobbled on his twisted legs to the wall where he'd left his broom leaning.

Where's Ab? said Suttree.

Aint seen him.

Where's Doll?

She's back in the back.

What happened to your head?

What happened to yours?

Suttree smiled and rubbed the patch of stubble hair at the back of his head. The derelict had a massive bandage taped across the left side of his forehead.

I got hit with a floorbuffer, Suttree said.

I got hit by a bus.

Again?

Smokehouse nodded, looking down at the floor, sweeping futilely at the trash.

Doesnt it hurt? said Suttree.

Some.

Some?

I got drunk first.

Oh.

I wouldnt do it without I got drunk first. I got more sense than that.

Well how do you manage to keep from getting killed if you're drunk?

It aint easy. That's how come that bus run over my legs that time is cause I got too drunk. You got to keep your head about you.

How much will you get this time?

I dont know. They dont want to settle. I may have to get me another lawyer.

What will you do with the money if you get it?

Smokehouse looked up from the floor. He seemed surprised by the question. Well, he said. Get drunk, I reckon. Least I wont have to sweep the floor for no niggers.

For a while.

The derelict pushed at the trash. The sun dont shine up the same dog's ass ever day, he said.

I hope not, said Suttree.

Things is come to a sorry pass when a white man has to look to a nigger for work.

Hard times on the land. Suttree agreed.

You dont have a little drink on ye anywheres do ye?

Suttree had not. Smokehouse had started a new tack when the curtain flipped back and Doll in her disheveled housecoat held out a halfdollar coin.

Run get me two packs of Luckies, she said.

He stood his broom carefully against the wall and took the coin and got his hat from the back of a chair where he'd hung it and shuffled out the door, his racked body like something disjointed and put back by drunken surgeons, the elbows hiked out, the feet bent wrong. Doll watched him with her one watery eye. Mornin, she said.

Morning, said Suttree. How's the old man?

I dont know. He laid up in the bed. Go on back.

I dont want to bother him.

He aint asleep. Go on. She held the curtain back for him.

Suttree entered a room darker yet, some sort of heavy material curtaining the window on the river, a rich funk of nameless odors. There was a radio playing so softly that he just could hear it.

The footrail of the bed came right to the door and Jones lay in the bed like a tree. Who that? he said.

Suttree.

Youngblood. Come in.

You not asleep?

No. I just restin. Come on in.

He raised himself up slightly in the bed and Suttree heard him catch his breath.

I just stopped by.

Set down. Where your beer?

I didnt want one.

Hey old woman. He was groping around in the near dark for something and finally came up with a bottle and unscrewed the cap and drank and put it back. He wiped his mouth with the heel of his hand. Hey, he called out.

She appeared at the curtain.

Bring this man a beer. Set down Youngblood.

Suttree could see him better. He shifted his huge frame and so clearly was he in pain that the fisherman sat at the foot of the bed and asked him what was wrong.

Dont say nothin to her.

What happened?

Same old shit. Your little blue friends. Hush.

She came to the curtain and handed a bottle of beer into the room. Suttree took it and thanked her and she went out again, no word.

Did they put you in jail?

Yeah. I got out about eight oclock this mornin. Made bond. She think I been out whorin I reckon.

Suttree smiled. Werent you? he said.

The scarred black face looked grieved. No man. I too old for that shit. Dont let her know it of course.

Are you all right?

Aint nothin. I got to keep my shirt on she dont see the tape.

Who taped you?

Me.

You know how to do that?

I done it a few times fore this.

I guess you have.

Bein a nigger is a interestin life.

You make it that way.

Maybe.

Suttree sipped the beer. It was very quiet in the cabin.

They dont like no nigger walkin around like a man, Jones said. He had drawn his bottle forth and unscrewed the cap and was taking a drink.

Can you get up and around.

Yeah. I aint down, just restin.

If you need anything I can get it for you. If you need some whiskey.

I know you would. I'm okay.

Well.

You got a good heart, Youngblood. Look out for you own.

I dont have any own.

Yes you do.

Where are they?

Jones wiped his mouth. Let me tell you about some people, he said. Some people aint worth a shit rich or poor and that's all you can say about em. But I never knowed a man that had it all but what he didnt forget where he come from. I dont know what it does. I had a friend in this town I stood up for him when he got married. I'd give him money when he was comin up. Used to take him to the wrestlin matches, he was just a kid. He's a big man now. Drives a Cadillac. He dont know me. I got no use for a man piss backwards on his friends.

Suttree was sitting at the foot of the bed. He took a sip of the beer and held the bottle between his hands.

You see a man, he scratchin to make it. Think once he got it made everthing be all right. But you dont never have it made. Dont care who you are. Look up one mornin and you a old man. You aint got nothin to say to your brother. Dont know no more'n when you started.

Suttree could see the huge veined hands in the gloom, black mannequin's hands, an ebon last for a glovemaker's outsize advertisement.

They were moving as if to shape the dark to some purpose.

I used to work on the river. The Cherokee. Then I was on the Hugh Martin. The H C Murry. It had a better store than them uptown. After the first war they wasnt no more packetboat trade. I was born in nineteen and hundred. Of a night you could hear them boats howlin on the river like souls. The old Martin had a steamhorn could and used to did bring the glass out of folks' sashes. I went on the river when I was twelve. I weighed a hunnerd and eighty pound then. This white man shot me cause I whipped him. I didnt know no better. I was older then, must of been fourteen. Dumb as shit. I went home and got better and fore I could see him to kill him somebody had done done it. Cut his head off. Wasnt no friend of mine. Thowed my black ass in the jailhouse. Went up the side of my head with they old clubs and shit. I laid there in the dark, they aint give me nothin to eat yet. That was my first acquaintance of the wrath of the path. That's goin on forty year now and it dont signify a goddamn thing. These bloods down here think it's somethin to whip up on some police. They think that's really somethin. Shit. You aint got nothin for it but a busted head. You caint do nothin with them motherfuckers. I wouldnt fight em at all if I could keep from it.

Suttree bent to see his face. Jones blinked, eyeballs like eggs in the mammoth black skull. He must have read his pale friend's look because he said almost to himself: That's the truth.

How did you get out?

They found his head. Man had it in a shoebox.

He was unscrewing the bottlecap, taking a drink. His eyes closed and opened slowly in the gloom. This man was a gambler and a whoremaster. He never drunk nor smoked. Run a whorehouse on Front Street that was well known in them days. Boats come in, the hands would all turn out for his place. Streets full of whores, queers any color. Thieves. They come out like roaches whenever you had a dockin. Then this feller cut his head off and carried it around in a shoebox with him. He got drunk one night down on Central Avenue and started showin the old head around. Folks runnin screamin into the streets. Next day I's out.

Was he crazy?

Who?

The murderer.

I dont know. He didnt kill him to rob him. I guess he was a little bit crazy.

Would you have killed him?

I dont know. I reckon I would if that was how he'd of wanted it.

Suttree took a sip of his beer. He could hear Smokehouse in the outer room again, puttering about, glass clinking. He looked at Jones. Have you ever killed anyone? he said.

Not on purpose, said Jones.

It was dark when he came in from running his lines. The nose of the skiff broaching rafts of drifted trash and skeins of shorelight in the black river. Radio music from a shack on Front Street carrying clearly over the night waters. The slamming of a door. He could see the lights at Ab Jones's and downriver he could see the fire at the goatman's camp with the goatman's cart in silhouette and dark goat shadows shifting in the forward reach of light. He boated the oars and stalled against the tirecasings alongside his houseboat and stood up in the skiff and made fast.

He had a livebox made from angleiron and chickenwire hanging in the river by a rope and he hauled this up and opened the top and transferred the fish from the boat to the box and lowered it into the river again. Then he hefted a small catfish up from the floor of the skiff, holding it by the gills, and climbed over the rail and went down the walk to the river path and down to the goatman's camp.

A few people were gathered at the fire. When Suttree came up the goatman turned as if he'd sensed him there and he smiled and nodded.

I thought you'd forgot me.

I brought your fish.

I see you did.

You've not eaten supper have you?

No no. You?

Suttree shrugged.

You welcome to share with me if you like.

I dont much like fish.

That there is a nice one.

Suttree handed down the fish and the goatman took it and held it to the fire to see.

What do I owe you?

I dont know, said Suttree. We can trade it out if you like.

Trade it out, said the goatman. I dont know what I'd trade. Aint got nothin but some picture postcards I sell.

That'll be okay.

Postcards?

Sure. Why not?

The goatman looked at Suttree, then rose and turned toward the wagon. The eyes of the visitors at his fire followed him. He rummaged through his duffel and called out to Suttree. How many you want?

I dont know. What do you get for them?

Ten cents.

Well, what about a half dozen?

He came from the wagon with the cards. The fish bowed and shivered in the firelight.

Take these, he said.

Suttree took the cards. The cards were old but the goatman by the fire was not changed from him that posed upon them.

Okay, said Suttree.

Aint no need to rush off.

What makes you think I was rushing off?

I dont know. But you welcome to stay.

I'd better get on.

The goatman watched him. He was trudging out across the field with his chin down so that withdrawing in the firelight he looked like a headless revenant turned away from the warmth of men's gatherings.

Say, called the goatman.

Suttree turned.

You know if you had you a goat or two down here they'd be good company. You never would be lonely.

What makes you think I'm lonely? said Suttree.

The goatman smiled. I dont know, he said. I aint wrong.

It is told first by Oceanfrog Frazer to idlers at the store. How a madman came down from the town and through the steep and vacant lots above the river. Frazer saw him plunging past in a drunken run, fording a briarbush with no regard and on across the stony yard until he was capsized by a clotheswire.

He's murdered someone, Oceanfrog said.

The fallen man mauled at the earth like a child, not even putting a hand to his throat where the wire had all but garroted him. He scrabbled off on hands and knees across the dirt and soon he was running again. He ran fulltilt into the barbedwire fence at the lower end of the lot.

He's crazy, said Oceanfrog. He stepped to the door and called to him.

The man turned. His clothing was ripped and the shreds of his shirtfront lifted about him like confetti in the breeze and he was covered with blood.

What are you doing? called Oceanfrog.

The man screamed. A high parched gurgle like a rutting cat. Then he turned and ran again, following the fence, out of the lot, crashing through the crude pole gate and crossing the road and disappearing in the fields by the river.

A few dead bats or dying appeared in the streets. Roving bands of unclaimed dogs were herded off to the gas chamber. Harrogate kept himself attuned, somehow fearing that he might be next. One day by Suttree's he said he'd seen a bat.

A dead one?

Just up yander.

You'd better go get it, said Suttree. It's worth a dollar.

It's worth what?

A dollar. You have to take it to the Board of Health. It was in the paper.

You're shittin me.

No, it's worth a dollar.

Why would anybody want to give a dollar for a old dead bat?

They think they've got rabies. It says not to touch them, just scoop them up and put them in a bag.

Harrogate had already started out the door.

Hey Gene.

Yeah.

Do you know where to take it?

No, where do I go?

General Hospital. Out Central.

Yeah. I know where it's at. That's where they took me.

It was true. Legal tender for all debts public and private. He had the bill changed at Comer's, dropping it with a careless flourish onto the glass countertop. He took the change downstairs to Helm's and got a dollar for it and changed the dollar at the Sanitary Lunch but no one seemed to notice. Already schemes were clambering through his head. He bought a chocolate milk and sat wedged in the row of theatre seats at Comer's before a twodollar check game and pondered and sipped the milk.

Fucking rat poison, he said, suddenly looking up through the smoke and the din toward a far wall with wide eyes.

People turned to look at him. Cocky paused in midstroke at the table, the cue quivering in his old palsied hands. Harrogate rose and drained the carton of milk and dropped it in a spittoon and went out.

Ratlike himself, quietly in the dimestore aisles. A small box of pellets slid between the lowermost shirtbuttons to lay against his skin. Things to be done. The Ford hood that he portaged on his shoulders up the river path had sheltered chickens. He stopped often to rest. It had rained in the night and his clothes were soaked from the bushes.

Scarlet trumpets of cowitch overhung the little house and wildflowers bloomed up through the twisted shapes of steel by whatever miracle renders grease and cinders arable and the junkman's lot was a garden more lovely for the phantasm from which it sprang. Harrogate paused at the fence and leaned his hood there. He pushed open the weighted gate, starting a hummingbird from the flowers in the dooryard. Rainwater still dripped from the tarpaper eaves and it lay in bright pools and slashes on the gray and steaming backs of the autos where they reared above the grass and fronds like feeding bovines. He rapped at the open door. The cane at the corner of the shack rattled gently in the wind. Everything lay quiet and sundabbled in this quaint garden by the river.

What can I do for ye? said the junkman.

Harrogate stepped back and looked. The junkman was hanging half drunk from the one small window.

You remember me dont ye? said Harrogate.

No.

Well, listen. I need a car hood.

Just a minute.

He appeared at the door. With splayed fingers attacking the matter that webbed his eyes.

What kind? he said.

It's a Ford.

Any particular year?

I dont know. I got it out here if you could match it up.

The junkman spat and looked at him and started down the stoop past him.

Where's it at? He was standing in the yard with his palms in the small of his back, squinting about.

Right yonder leanin against the fence.

The junkman followed his pointing finger. I hope it dont lean too hard, he said. He sauntered over to the fence and looked down. He gave the hood a shove and it fell over in the dust with a sad bong. The junkman looked it over and he looked at Harrogate. Hell son, he said. What's the matter with thisn?

I hope they aint nothin the matter with it. I just need me one more.

The junkman looked at him for several minutes and then he went back across the little yard and entered the shack again.

When Harrogate peered in he was lying on the cot with one arm across his eyes.

Hey, said Harrogate.

I aint got time to mess with you, the junkman mumbled.

Listen, said Harrogate. I need two alike to make a boat out of.

The junkman removed his arm from his face and looked at the ceiling.

I wanted to get em welded together and tar up the holes so I could have me a boat.

A boat?

Yessir.

How do you sons of bitches find me?

It aint but just me.

All you crazy sons of bitches. I wish I could catch whoever it is keeps sendin em down here.

I just come by myself.

Yeah. Yeah.

Have you not got a hood to match thatn?

I got a forty-six, it's the same cept for the chrome, you can have it for six dollars if you want it.

Well I wanted to talk to you about that.

He looked like an enormous turtle going to the river, staggering under the weight of the welded car hoods, the aft one dragging a trail in the summer dust. He hadn't found any way to take the pot of tar so he'd tied it to one ankle and it scuttled along after him.

He put in above the packing company, sliding his boat through the grass and down the mud of the bank. The water that trickled in looked like ink beading over the tarred floor. He bent and untied the tarpot and set it in the boat and then stepped in cautiously. The steel flexed with a little dead buckling sound somewhere. He gripped the sides, going along on his knees. The back end lifted from the mud and he was adrift in the river.

Shit a brick, said Harrogate with cautious enthusiasm. He pulled off his shirt and sponged up the water to better see where the leaks were. Drifting past the packing company, the lumberyard.

What is that? called a watcher from the shore.

Boat, called Harrogate back.

By the time he reached the bridge he was sitting in the center with his feet spread before him, taking the sun and enjoying the river breeze. He came in at Goose Creek, paddling with his fingers. Up the small estuary, under the low bridge of the railway, lying on his back, muddobber nests overhead and lizards in little suctioncup shoes sliding past his face, easing himself along the wall with one hand. And under Scottish Pike and up the creek, standing in the stern of his new boat and poling with a stick he'd found, the rounded prow browsing through the rippled sludge that lay thick on the backwater.

He spent the night under the boat, it upturned like a canoe and propped with sticks, a small fire before him. Vestal boys came down to visit and to envy. One among the younger was sent for a chicken from his mother's yard and they plucked it and roasted it on a wire and passed about a warm RC Cola and told lies.

He came out of the creek into the river the next morning rowing with a board and a split paddle in oarlocks made from a dogchain. An eerie rattling apparition stroking through the fog. He'd not gone far before he was near run down by the dredger from the gravel company just set out downriver. A face passed high up the bank of fog, not even looking down from the floating wheelhouse. Harrogate had stood in his boat and raised a fist but the first bowwave almost tilted him out into the river and he sat quickly in the floor again and called a few round oaths.

He rowed upriver with his back to the rising sun, envisioning a penthouse among the arches and spans of the bridge he passed beneath, a retractable ropeladder, his boat at anchor by a stanchion, the consternation of a marveling citizenry. At Suttree's he pulled in and rapped on the floor of the deck with his knuckles. Hey Sut, he called.

Suttree raised up in his bunk and looked out. He saw a hand from the river holding onto the houseboat deck. He rolled out and went to the door and around and stood there in his shorts looking down at the city rat.

Slick aint it? said Harrogate.

Can you swim?

This time tomorrow you will be talkin to a wealthy man.

Or a drowned one. Where the hell did you get that thing?

Made it. Me and old drunk Harvey.

Good God, said Suttree.

What do you think of it?

I think you're fucking crazy.

You want to go for a ride?

No.

Come on, I'll ride ye.

Gene, I wouldnt get in that thing and it on dry land.

Well, I got to get on.

Harrogate pushed off and took up his trailing oars. I got a lot to do, he said.

Suttree watched him go on up the river, the little keelless contraption skittering and jerking along. It went pretty good.

Harrogate turned up First Creek and rowed beneath the railway trestle and continued on until he came to a narrows composed of abandoned machinery and high tiered tailings of garbage. He wired his boat to a small tree and went backwards up the bank admiring it.

He tried to nap but lying there in the heat beneath the viaduct with the traffic overhead he had such fantasies of plenitude that his feet made little involuntary trotting motions. By late afternoon he was up and about, flexing his sling with its new red rubbers and firing a few flat stones through the lightwires where they caromed and sang enormous lyrenotes in the budding tranquillity of evening. An addled cock crowed from the black hillside. He looked to his appurtenances and set forth.

He emerged from the creek mouth past the curious dark fishermen, oaring slowly and studying the sky. He stroked his way upstream, past the last of the shacks and as far as the marble company. Coming about on the placid evening calm and easing back the oars alongside and taking up his sling. Pinching up the leather in his fingers. Pouring the pellets. One flew. And there. A goatsucker wheeled and croaked. He hove back on the sling bands nearly to the floor and let go. And again. Random among the summer trees houselights came on along the southern shore. The neon nightshapes of the city bloomed, their replicas in the water like discolored sores. Across the watered sky the bats crossed and checked and flared. Dark fell but that was all. He was drifting beneath the bridge. He laid down the sling and took up the oars and came back.

It was a hot night for heavy thinking. He lay with his hands composed upon his chest. Beyond the bridge's arching brow drifting fireflies guttered against the night and the wind bore a heady scent of honeysuckle.

It was a grayhaired and avuncular apothecary who leaned not unkindly down from his high pulpit. Enormous fans stirred overhead, shifting the reek of nostrums and purgatives. Beyond the counter ranged carboys and galleypots and stainedglass jars of chemic and cottonmouthed bottles cold and replete with their particolored pills. Harrogate's chin rested just at the cool stone trestle and his eyes took in this alchemical scene with a twinge of old familiarity for which he could not account.

May I help you? said the scientist, his hands holding each other.
I need me some strychnine, said Harrogate.
You need some what?
Strychnine. You know what it is dont ye?
Yes, said the chemist.
I need me about a good cupful I reckon.
Are you going to drink it here or take it with you?
Shit fire I aint goin to drink it. It's poisoner'n hell.
It's for your grandmother.
No, said Harrogate, craning his neck suspectly. She's done dead.

The chemist tore off a piece of paper from a pad and poised with his pen. Just let me have the name of the person or persons you intend to poison, he said. We're required to keep records.

Suspecting japery, Harrogate grinned an uneasy grin. Listen, he said. You know about these here bats?

Oh yes indeed.

Well, that's what it's for. I dont care to tell you because they aint nobody else but me could figure out the rest of it.

I'm sure that's true, the chemist said.

I didnt bring nothin to fetch it in. You got a jar of some kind?

How old are you? said the chemist.

I'm twenty-one.

No you're not.

What'd you ast me for then?

The chemist removed his glasses and closed his eyes and pinched the bridge of his nose between his thumb and forefinger. He donned the spectacles again and looked down at Harrogate. He was still there. I can't sell strychnine to minors, he said. Nor to folk of other than right mind. It's against the law.

Well, said Harrogate. That's up to you.

Yes, said the chemist.

Harrogate backed sidling down the pale medicinal corridor, past ordered rows of canisters and jars. The rotors overhead sliced through the antiseptic air slow and constant. He pushed back the door with one hand. Bell ching. A slender rod came sucking out of a little piston. The chemist had not moved.

You're just a old fart, called Harrogate, and ran.

Suttree just shook his head. He was sitting with his trousers rolled and his bare feet hanging in the river.

Come on, Sut.

Gene.

Yeah.

I am not going in no goddamned drugstore and buy strychnine. Not for you. Not for anybody.

Hell Sut, they'd sell it to you. If I tell you what I want with it will you?

No.

They sat there watching Suttree's toes resting on the river.

Listen, Sut . . .

Suttree put his forefingers in his ears.

Harrogate leaned more closely. Listen, he said.

He waited down on Stinky Point, one eye for measuring the sun's decline, the other weathered out for his friend's coming. He had a pieplate with a piece of high and wormy hog's liver in it and he was cutting this up in small gobbets with his pocketknife. Suttree came through the weeds hot and perspiring and squatted on the bank and drew a small package from the hippocket of his jeans. Here, you crazy son of a bitch, he said.

Harrogate's black rat's eyes glazed over with joy. He untied the string and lifted a glass vial from the paper and examined it. A pale label with a green skull and bones. Shithouse mouse, he said. Thanks Sut. I sure as shit appreciate it.

You owe me two dollars.

Old buddy, that kind of money aint nothin now. You'll have it in the mornin.

Suttree watched him go on through the weeds to the river where his boat rode tethered to a cinderblock by a length of wire. He turned and smiled back and stepped neatly into the boat, holding the bottle in one hand, the tin of liver in the other. He sat carefully and laid his things out before him and leaned slightly forward and unpocketed the small catapult he'd fashioned from a treefork. Unwiring himself from the land he took up his makeshift oars and feathered gently into the current and away.

From the deck of his houseboat Suttree watched the antics of this half daft adolescent with a mild disgust. Standing amidships in his cocklecraft Harrogate tacked here and there. In the quiet evening the face of the river grew glassy. Suttree muttered to himself. He'd not muttered long before a bat came boring crazily askew out of the sky and fell with a plop onto the surface of the river and fluttered briefly and was still. Suttree sat up in his folding chair. Bats had begun to drop everywhere from the heavens. Little leatherwinged creatures struggling in the river. Harrogate oaring among them. One dropped with a mild and vesperal bong on the tin of Suttree's roof. Another close by in the water. Lying there on the dark current it seemed surprised and pitiful.

Harrogate in his tin coracle was hefting them aboard with a dipnet of his own devising. A bullbat fell bandywinged. A swift, a swallow. Along the dimming shore of broken fence and rubble and over the sparse colonies of jakelike dwellings a new curse falling, a plague of bats, small basilisks pugnosed with epicanthic eyes and upreared dogs' ears filled with hair and bellies filled with agony. In the smoke and burgundy dusk they dimpled the face of the river like lemmings. Two small black boys had packed a halfgallon picklejar with ones they found and screwed down the lid to keep them until needed. In the floor of Harrogate's boat the brown and hairy mound grew, strange cargo, such small replicas of the diabolic with their razorous teeth bared in fiends' grins. By dark he had a half a boatload and by the warehouse lights he struck a landfall just below the creek and tied up. He sat on the bank and drank in the evening calm and the winey honeysuckle air and waited for the last of the crawling pile of bats to die. When they had done so he loaded them in his sack and staggered up the bank and home.

In the morning he set out with them. A light heart and deep rejoicing for the fortune of it made the load less heavy yet he still must rest here and there by the streetside. By such stages he labored out Central Avenue small and bowed and wildlooking.

What you got in the sack son?

He peered from under the load at his inquisitor lounging in the open window of the halted cruiser. He shifted the weight a little higher on his shoulder. Bats, he said.

Bats.

Yessir.

What, ballbats?

No, them little'ns. Flittermouses.

The policeman's face bore a constant look of tolerant interest. Set the sack down son and let's see what all you got there.

Harrogate rolled the sack from his shoulder and lowered it to the paving and spread the drawstrung mouth with his thumbs. A musky smell rose. He tilted it slightly policeward. The officer thumbed his cap back on his head and bent to see. A prefiguration of the pit. Vouchsafed a crokersack vision of hell's floor deep with the hairy damned screaming mute and toothy toward the far and heedless city of God. He raised his head and looked at the waiting Harrogate and he looked at the bright sky above Knoxville and he turned to the driver.

You know what he's got in that sack?

What's he got?

Dead bats.

Dead bats.

Right.

Well.

What do you think?

I dont know. Ask him where he's goin with em.

Where you goin with em?

Up here to the hospital.

The officer had his chin resting on his shoulder. His face went blank. Rabies, he said. He turned to the driver and said something and they pulled away. Harrogate shouldered the bats and set forth again.

He climbed the marble stairs and went past the old columns of the portico and down the hall to a desk. Howdy, he said.

A nurse looked up.

I got some more.

What?

Some more. Bats.

I dont know what you're talking about.

Bats. I got a whole damn . . . I got a whole sackful.

She stared at him warily.

Looky here, he said, pointing.

She stood up and leaned over and looked down. Harrogate fumbled with the sack, trying to see her tits. She put her hand to her collarbone. He spread the sack open and she leaped back.

It's a mess of em, aint it?

Get those things out of here, she whispered.

Where do I take em?

But she had gone down the hall on her white crepe shoes. She came back with a man in a white tunic. Him? said the man.

Harrogate stood his ground.

Let me see what you've got there.

He held open the mouth of the sack.

The man turned pale. He gestured at the nurse. Call the clinic, he said. Tell them we've got about a bushel of dead bats up here.

She was dialing.

Where did you get them? said the man.

Just here and there, said Harrogate.

A woman was coming down the hall. The man went to her and ushered her back toward the door.

Dr Hauser says to bring them on, said the nurse, holding one hand over the mouthpiece of the telephone.

Tell him we're on our way.

I guess you aint used to gettin this many at a time, said Harrogate.

They sat him in a little white room and gave him a box of vanilla icecream. He watched the sunlight on the walls with dreamy content. After a while a nurse brought him a little metal tray with a hot lunch.

You can just take it out of what all you owe me, Harrogate told her.

The afternoon set in and he grew bored. He went to the door and looked out. An empty corridor. He sat some more. It grew warmer. He lay on the tile floor with his hands cradling his head. His mind roved over storewindows. He saw himself ascending the stairs at Comer's in pressed gabardines and zipper shoes, a slender cigar in his mouth, an italian switchblade knife silver bound with ebony handles in one pocket, a gold watchchain draped across the pleats of his slacks. Greeted by all. Pulling the roll of bills from his pocket. He went back down the stairs and came up again in different attire, a pullover shirt like Feezel's. Dark blue. With pale gray trousers and blue suede shoes. Belt to match. The door opened. He sat up.

Mr Harrogate.

Yes mam.

Dr Hauser would like to see you.

They went through three doors. The doctor was standing at a bench among bottles and jars. The nurse closed the door behind him. Harrogate stood there with his hands hanging down inside the pockets of his capacious trousers. The doctor turned and looked dourly across the upper rims of his glasses at him.

Mr Harrogate?

Yessir.

Yes. Would you just come with me a minute?

Harrogate followed him into a tiny office. A little white cubicle with glass bricks in the ceiling. Occasional pedestrians walked overhead, muted heels and sunlight. The pipes that hung from the ceiling were painted white. He looked everything over.

That was quite a collection of bats, said the doctor.

They's forty-two of em.

Yes. None rabid at all. We were curious. We couldn't find any marks on them.

Harrogate grinned. I figured you might reckon they'd been shot or somethin. Many of em as they was.

Yes. We examined one.

Mm-hmm.

Strychnine.

Harrogate's face gave a funny little twitch. What? he said.

How did you do it?

Do what?

How did you do it? Poison forty-two bats. They only feed on the wing.

I dont know nothin about it. They was dead. Listen. I brought one down here before and nobody never said nothin. They never said they was a limit on how many you could collect on.

Mr Harrogate, the city is offering a reward for any dead bats found in the streets. We have what could become a critical situation here with rabies. That's the purpose of the reward. We have not authorized the wholesale slaughter of bats.

Do I get the money or not?

You do not.

Shit.

I'm sorry.

Well.

I would like to know how you managed to poison them.

Harrogate sucked at his black foretooth. What will you give me? he said.

The doctor leaned back in his chair and studied him all over again. Well, he said, feeling the spirit of things, what will you take?

I'll take two dollars.

That's too high. I'll give a dollar.

Make it a dollar and a quarter.

All right.

That includes the dinner and the icecream.

Okay.

I done it with a flipper.

With a flipper?

Yessir.

The doctor looked at the ceiling. Ah, he said. I see. What? Did you poison scraps of meat and then shoot them in the air?

Yeah. Them sons of bitches like to never quit fallin.

Very ingenious. Damned ingenious.

I can figure out anything.

Well, I'm sorry your efforts were for nothing.

Maybe a dollar and a quarter aint nothin to you but it is to me.

When Suttree called on him he found a shrunken djinn hulked over an applebox tracing with a chewed pencil stub a route beneath the city on a map of it. A sanguine scene, there by the bloodcolored light of the construction lantern. At Suttree's approach a bright red cat rose from before the lamp and moved away into the dark. Harrogate looked up, feet tucked and bright smile, a diabolic figure across which the shadow of a moth passed and repassed like a portent.

How did you make out?

Set down Sut. Not worth a shit.

Wouldn't they pay?

Naw. I got to hand it to em. They're smart.

Well.

I'm glad you come. Looky here at this map.

Suttree glanced at it.

It shows where all the buildings is and you can measure it on here, see, on this here scale?

Yeah?

Well shit. I mean, what with them caves down there and it all holler and everthing?

So?

Lord, Sut, it's tailormade. They're just askin for it.

Suttree rose. Gene, he said, you're crazy.

Set down Sut. Looky here. The goddamned bank is only . . .

I dont want to look. I dont want to hear.

Harrogate watched him wane from the gory light toward darkness.

It's a dead lock, Sut, he called. I need you to help me.

Beyond in the dark of the town late traffic passed.

Sut?

A chained dog yapped from the shackstrewn hillside across the creek.

I need you to help me, he called.

In the early months of that summer a new fisherman appeared on the river. Suttree saw him humped over the oars in a skiff composed of actual driftwood, old boxes and stenciled crateslats and parts of furniture patched up with tin storesigns and rags of canvas and spattered over with daubs of tar. A crazyquilt boat sculled through the loose fog by a sullen oarsman who looked not right nor left.

Standing at Turner's stall Suttree stared down into the long glass bier. Little beads of water ran on the heavy slant panes in their nickel and porcelain mortises. Inside on a bed of crushed ice dimly lit and lightly garlanded with parsley sprigs lay a catfish with a nine inch dinnerplate in its mouth. Old men kept drifting by to peer in and comment. A little card rested against the broad yellow flank. It said: Caught in the Tennessee River June 9 1952. Wt. 87 lbs.

Mornin Suttree, said the fishmonger.

Where the hell did you get this?

Some Indian brought it in here this mornin. Aint that a fish?

It's the biggest catfish I ever saw.

Old Bert Vincent was by a little while ago, said it was the biggest he ever seen personally.

I dont guess you'll be needing any fish this morning.

Not this morning.

Suttree crossed through the markethouse and went on toward niggertown with his fish.

In the evening he watched the Indian set out again on his one line below the railway trestle. And back. He hove to in the blue shadow under the bluff and drifted from sight. Eighty-seven pounds, Suttree muttered.

On his run downriver in the morning he watched for the Indian's skiff. He saw it swinging loosely below the sheer rock of the south shore. Trash hung in the vines all down the face of the bluff and a thin faultline angled up and switched back until it gained the rim of a cave a hundred feet above the river. Up there watching was the fisherman. Suttree raised his hand. The figure on the cliff gestured back. Suttree eased the oars into the river and went on.

When he came back upriver the Indian was cleaning fish on a rock at the foot of the bluff. When he saw Suttree he stood up and looked up at the cave and wiped his hands on the sides of his jeans.

Suttree eased the skiff alongside the rock and shipped the inside oar.

There was a shallow pool among the rocks and from the bottom countless fish heads stared up through the silty water to the streaked sunlight of a world dead to them. Coiled viscera ebbed in the murk and a few tins gave back a baleful light. Howdy, he said.

Hey, said the Indian.

How's it going?

Okay.

I saw that blue cat down at Turner's. I dont see how you got it in the boat.

Yeah, said the Indian.

Suttree looked out over the water and he looked up at the Indian again. A tall and ocherskinned stranger in a pair of busted out brogans, the sorry clothes, the stove knees and elbows not patched but simply puckered shut with crude stitching. Pinned to his shirt and joined by their weighted wire he wore a pair of china eyes that had once swung in a doll's skull.

I live up the river yonder, said Suttree. Just above the bridge in that first houseboat.

The Indian nodded. I seen you, he said. In the sun his homecut hair looked blue and his eyes were black. Suttree couldnt tell if he was looking at him or just down at his shoes.

There's the size I catch. Suttree held up the smallest catfish in the boat.

You want some bait?

Bait?

Sure.

What kind you got?

Wait on me till I get you some.

Suttree watched him, sculling to recover the current. He went up the bluff like a goat.

When he came back he handed down a jar to Suttree. Suttree took it and looked at it and turned it against the sun and unscrewed the cap and sniffed at it. Goddamn, he said.

The Indian had squatted on the rock to watch him more closely and now he slapped his thigh and laughed.

Shit, said Suttree. He clapped the lid back over the mess.

Dont smell it, said the Indian, grinning.

Now you tell me. He tilted the jar at arm's length. Will it stay on the hook?

Sure.

Well. Thanks. Maybe I'll catch one of those big mammyjammers. Sure, said the Indian.

Suttree set the jar on the seat and pushed off from the rocks. Thanks again, he said. Come see me.

The Indian stood and put his hands in his pockets and gave a little toss of his chin. Okay, he said.

The next week he didnt see him. The crazy boat was gone. Suttree tried the bait but the odor of it, the gagging vomit reek, was more than he could stand. He'd wash his hands again and again after molding it on the hooks. The third morning he caught two turtles and he let the jar descend down through the duncolored water behind the last flaring dropper and went back to his cutbait and doughballs.

Monday morning someone rapped at his door and he turned out in the dawn chill to find the Indian there. He wore the same clothes, the same shoes. The tandem eyeballs still pinned to his pocket. Hey, he said.

Come on in, said Suttree.

How you do with the bait?

Okay. Kept catching turtles.

Hey. Turtles. Snappers, hey?

Yeah. Watch your head.

The Indian stooped and entered and turned.

Sit down. Suttree motioned loosely toward the dim interior.

Them is good to eat, said the Indian. Best meat there is.

Yeah, well. They're a lot of trouble to fix.

You bring him to me. I show you how to fix him.

You want a cup of coffee?

Sure.

Have it in a minute. Go on, sit down.

The Indian sat on the bunk and crossed his legs.

I didnt see you for a couple of days.

No.

Suttree ladled water out of a lardpail into the coffeepot and lit the burner. He measured in the coffee. I used to know an old guy who shot turtles down on the river. I never see the meat for sale though.

Yeah, well. I sell em sometime.

Suttree set the pot on the burner and put the lid on and turned the flame up. He got down the spare cup. It had a dead spider curled in it and he pitched the spider into the trash and rinsed both cups. When the coffee perked he poured the cups full and turned and handed one to the Indian.

He took the cup gravely and blew on it. He gave off a rich acidic smell of woodsmoke and grease and fish. Sparse whiskers on his fine skin. His arms lean, longmuscled, blueveined.

I never ate one, Suttree said.

One what?

Turtle.

You come to my place sometime I fix him for you.

Okay, said Suttree.

The Indian sipped the coffee and regarded him above the cuprim with grave black eyes. I got thowed in jail, he said.

When?

Last week. I just got out.

What did they have you for?

Vag. You know. They got me once before.

How did you get out?

They let me sweep up. They let me clean up and then they let me out. I come down this mornin and my boat was gone.

Where did you leave it?

Just down here. I reckon some boys took it.

Have you looked for it?

Yeah.

Suttree watched him. Well, he said. Why dont we go in my boat and see if we can see it.

I'll pay you.

It's all right.

He got his shoes and socks. These river rats will steal anything that's not nailed down.

They might of sunk it.

Would it sink?

Put enough rocks in it.

Suttree shook his head.

They went downriver with Suttree rowing and the Indian bailing, bending toward each other at their tasks.

They had a hell of a nigger in there, the Indian said.

Where's that?

In the jail. They had this great big nigger. They fought all over the jailhouse. They'd go in there and bust his head with slapsticks. He'd come around after a while and start cussin em all over again.

Suttree stayed the oars.

He raised some knots on a few of them jailers, the Indian said.

Did he get out?

Yeah. Somebody come and got him yesterday.

Suttree rowed on.

They went past the last bridge and down the bend in the river. They watched the shore.

That's not it is it? said Suttree, pointing.

The Indian shaded his eyes. No, he said. It's just some trash.

Suttree dabbed his eye against his shoulder with a shrugging motion and went on.

You want me to row awhile?

No. It's okay.

They found the skiff awash in shallow water near the head of the island. Suttree eased alongside and laid back the oars. The Indian stood.

Is it stove? said Suttree.

No. I dont think so.

They must still be here on the island.

The Indian scanned the steaming reaches of reed and willow. A plover was crossing the siltbar like a gallery bird. Suttree stepped out with the rope and they pulled the skiff ashore.

There was a little path going up the island through the weeds. They went with caution. Redwings circled and cried.

They entered a clearing where charred sticks and blackened stones marked a fire. A few empty bean tins. They walked around the glade.

Looks like they skedaddled, Suttree said.

Yeah.

They cant be far.

Let em go, the Indian said.

Yeah?

Sure.

Okay.

They turned and defiled out of the glade, Suttree behind the Indian. Dragonflies kept lifting from the tops of the reeds like little chinese kites.

What's your name? said Suttree.

The Indian turned and looked back. Michael, he said.

Is that what they call you?

He turned again. No, he said. They call me Tonto or Wahoo or Chief. But my name is Michael.

My name's Suttree.

The Indian smiled. Suttree thought maybe he was going to stop and shake hands but he didnt.

They got the boat bailed and afloat and Suttree shoved it out onto the pale brown waters. The Indian took up the oars and brought it about headed upriver. What do I owe you? he said.

Not anything.

Well. Come see me and I'll fix you that turtle.

Suttree raised his hand. Okay, he said. Watch out for the cops.

The Indian dipped the oars into the river and pulled away.

Suttree stepped into his skiff and walked to the rear of it and shoved off from the flats with one oar. The Indian's patchwork boat was soon far upriver, light winking off the sweeps where they'd been broken and pieced back with tacked and flattened foodtins. He eased his own oars into the water and started up the inside of the island. He watched for sign of the thieves along the shore and he saw a muskrat nose among the willows and he saw a clutch of heronshaws gawping from their down nest in the reeds, spikelet bills and stringy gullets, pink flesh and pinfeathers and boneless legs spindled about. He tacked more shoreward to see. So curious narrow beasties. As he pulled abreast of them a rock sang past his ears. He ducked and looked toward the shore bracken but before he could collect himself another rock came whistling out of the willows and caught him in the forehead and he fell back in the boat. The sky was red and soaring and whorled like the ball of an enormous thumb and a numb gritty feeling came up against the back of his teeth. One oar slid from its lock and floated off.

The skiff drifted down past the landing and down past the end of the island. Suttree lay sprawled in the floor with blood running in his eyes. A tree branch turned against the sky. He pulled himself up, gripping the side of the skiff. He could taste a tincture of iron in his throat and he spat a bloody mucus into the water. He knelt over the side and palmed water at his face and his face was slippery with blood and blood lay in the water in coagulate strings. He touched gently an eggshaped swelling. His whole skull was throbbing and even his eyes hurt. He looked upriver toward the island and swore murderously. The other oar was floating a few yards downriver and he sculled after it. Light kept winking up on the riffles and blood was dripping from his forehead and he felt half nauseous. He recovered the drift oar and rowed back upriver in the main channel. He watched along the shoreline of the island but he saw nothing. After a while his head quit bleeding.

Doll came to the door at Ab's and looked him up and down. Hunh, she said. What happen to you?

Some son of a bitch hit me with a rock.

Mm-mmm, she said, shaking her head. Come in.

How's Ab?

She shut the door behind him.

Suttree turned in the stale and darkened room. Why didnt you tell me he was all screwed up?

I caint do nothin with him.

Where is he, in the back?

She gestured him on with one hand and he pushed back the curtain. At first he could not see him well but gradually the black's half closed and swollen eyes appeared, his glistening misshapen face. His broken mouth moved painfully. He said: Hey Youngblood.

Suttree heard his breath suck in the quiet. Hey Ab, he said. How are you.

I'm okay. I's just slippin me a nap. What you up to in the heat of the day? You catchin any fish?

Not to amount to anything. Have you had a doctor?

A throaty laugh shook the sagging bedsprings. He moved his head on the pillows as if he'd seek a darker place to rest it. What I needs with a doctor?

I think you need some help.

That may be. But I aint in need of bein patched up and prayed over.

What can I get you?

Ah Youngblood. I dont need nothin.

Somebody told me you tried to whip everybody at city jail.

You caint do nothin with them crackers. They needs they wigs tightened ever little bit.

I remember the last time they picked up Byrd and Sam Slusser you saw cops for weeks all over Knoxville with bandages and black eyes limping around.

Jones chuckled.

I guess far as that goes we might look for some this week.

Ah, said Jones. Aint but one of em I wants.

Who's that, Quinn?

Jones didnt answer. How's you little buddy? he said. He aint drownded hisself in that boat yet is he?

Not yet.

He come by here other day tryin to sell the old woman what he call scobs.

Scobs?

What he call em. Look like old pigeons to me. He had em all dressed and everthing. He some kind of a mess, aint he?

He's crazy as a mouse in a milkcan.

Jones chuckled.

I'm going uptown. You want me to bring you anything?

Naw.

You sure you okay?

He turned his battered face. Do somethin for me, Youngblood.

Name it.

Go see Miss Mother for me. Tell her I needs to see her.

Wouldnt Doll go for you?

Doll dont want me to have no truck with her. She wont run her off if she comes down here. You tell her.

What else?

That's all. I'd be much obliged.

Okay. Take care and I'll see you later.

Yeah, said the black.

He crossed the fields and went up Front Avenue and turned down a steep cinderpath past a run of chickens, a sleeping dog. The path went through a locust wood and the huge beanpods hung everywhere in a sunlight stained and made obscure by windblown papers staked out among the blackened upper branches, tents of newsprint and trash and the ruins of kites all tattered and rainleached and impaled upon the locust spikes. He crossed an iron sewer main half out of the ground and he descended into an old limestone sink that had been filled back as a city dump and graded over years ago. Now it was a small glade and there was a raw board shack in the center of it. Suttree came down the path and out from the last of the trees. The ninekiller flew. A few garish outland birds leaned from the limbs to watch him, gaudy longtailed fowl, he didnt know what kind. Their moult feathers lay about in the dust of the yard. He crossed to the door and tapped with his knuckles.

It opened on a female dwarf coalblack in widow's weeds who wore little goldwire spectacles on a chain about her neck. Scarce four feet tall she was, her hand on the doorknob at her ear like a child or a trained house ape. She looked up at Suttree and she said: Well, you aint come for yourself I dont reckon.

No mam, he said. She turned her head and cocked it slightly. He said: I came for Ab Jones. He wanted to know if you could come over to his place.

Come in here, she said, stepping back.

He entered with a peculiar feeling of deference. When she shut the door behind them they were in almost total dark. She led the way along a hall and through a curtained doorway. Black drapes were tacked to the window sashes. He could make out a table and some chairs and a small cot.

Set down, she said.

He sat at the table and looked about. She had left the room. Strange effects began to accrue out of the semidark like figures in a dream. On the table was an assortment of silver vases and candlesticks and porringers and bowls all covered over with sheets of yellow cellophane. There was a fireplace that held a broken coalgrate propped on bricks and there was a beveled lookinglass above the mantel. On the mantel a lamp, a vase, a marble clock. What appeared to be a stuffed bird. Smaller objects harbored in the gloom. An electric fan on the table kept turning from side to side and washing him with periodic gusts of fetid air. Flowered wallpaper had been glued over the shack's naked boards and the joints had laddered and split the paper. Everywhere hung portraits of blacks, strange family groups where the faces watched gravely from out of their paper past. Hanging in the dark like galleries of condemned. Their homemade clothes.

He heard the creak of a cellar door. On the hearth cut flowers in a blue coalscuttle stirred and trembled.

He could hear her coming from outside, doorlatch and the scuffle of her soft shoes. She entered and closed the door behind her. In the light of its closing he saw a coatrack hung with little fairground birds that swung or turned on their wires in the wind. She came to him and took his head in her hand and held up something small and oddly shaped and wrapped in an old socktoe. Suttree fended it off. Wait a minute, he said. What is that?

Hold still, she said.

He reared back. In his hand her forearm felt like a thin piece of kindling.

Aint a fool a wonderful thing? she said. It's ice, boy. Now set still.

He subsided into the chair and she laid the cold wet rag against the knot on his forehead and took his hand in her own, a thin little thing you'd remember from touching hands with a monkey through the bars or having a pet coon. She guided his hand to the ice and he held it there. A small rill of water ran down his nose. His head began to feel nicely numb.

You'd better bring some of this for Jones, he said.

What's got with him?

He got beat up pretty bad down at the jail last week. I guess that's why he wants to see you.

He dont care nothin about that. He want to kill his enemies is what he want.

Kill his enemies? Suttree had his head bent forward to let the water drip.

Mm-hmm.

Which enemies?

Standing there by the chair where he sat her eyes were level with his. She looked at him. A face wherein lay everything and nothing. A visage hacked from cold black wax. She gestured with one hand, extending her arm and suggesting the world that stood beyond the thin board walls and beyond the locust forest, a gesture both grave and gracious that acknowledged endless armies of the unbending pale. That was all. She put a finger in her mouth to adjust her teeth.

Suttree stood and said that he must go.

She held back the curtain and he went through and made his way to the door. He paused there with his hand on the knob. What should I tell Jones? he said.

I caint make no call down there.

He really wants you to come.

Mm-hmm.

He needs you to come.

I knows that.

Can I bring him up here?

He knows where I'm at.

Well.

He opened the door. White sunlight blinded him. Thank you for the ice, he said.

Mm-hmm, she said.

By the time he reached the street the ice was gone and he stopped in Howard Clevinger's to get another piece. Lifting the rusty lid of the drinkbox and sorting through the cold water for a rightsized chunk, the smooth shapes sliding about among the bottlenecks with bits of paper and flakes of fallen paint. Gatemouth was watching him from the rocker and when he raised up from behind the lid and clapped the piece of ice to his forehead he laughed and wheezed and rocked and shook his head.

Ho ho, said Suttree.

Who went up the side of yo head, baby?

Suttree leaned back. On the cardboard ceiling were tacked odd-shaped bits of paper.

Who you jump salty with, Sut?

I ran into a door.

Hee hee, chuckled Gatemouth.

Where's all your nutwagon friends today?

Out amongst em.

Good, said Suttree. He held the ice to his head and went out. Clevinger, slouched in his chair with his arms crossed, opened one eye when he passed the counter and closed it again. Suttree went up the hill toward town.

It was late afternoon when he returned. He sat on the porch and watched the river pass. Before dark fell he rose and went up the river to Ab Jones's.

Two white men were drinking beer in the corner and Doll was frying hamburgers on the little burner in the galley. He went through the room and pushed back the curtain. The bed was empty. He pushed back the plastic shower curtain on the other side. Jones was standing at the urinal, bracing himself up with one hand against the wall. He was wearing a pair of khaki undershorts and even in the dim light from the small window on the river Suttree saw such galaxies of scars and old rendings mended and slick and livid suture marks as made him gasp. He looked like some dusky movie monster patched up out of graveyard parts and stitched by an indifferent hand. Suttree let the curtain fall.

What did she say, Youngblood?

She said for you to come up there.

He was looking at the floor, waiting for an answer. Jones didnt answer.

I told her you needed her to come but she wouldnt have any part of it.

Well.

You want me to try again?

Naw. Go on out there and get you a beer.

Do you think you could make it up there?

I'll get up there one of these days.

Suttree went back to the front room.

You want a hamburger? Doll said.

Suttree said he would.

He got a beer from the cooler and crossed to the far corner and sat down. The two men watched him. Suttree took a long pull from the bottle and set it on the marble at his elbow. She came shuffling over in her houseshoes and set a thick plate before him with a hamburger and some pickles and went back.

Hey, said one of the men.

Suttree looked at them.

How come he gets his first? He come in after us.

She looked up from behind the plywood counter. Her one eye blinked. She looked enormously tired. He work here, she said.

They looked at Suttree. He raised the hamburger and took a good bite. It was heavily seasoned with pepper. Rich grease and mayonnaise dripped to the plate.

Hey buddy, you work here?

Suttree looked at them. They didnt look good.

How about bringin us a couple more beers, good buddy.

He pointed toward Doll. Tell her, he said.

Hell, she said you worked here. Do you not wait tables?

Shit boy, we might be heavy tippers and you not know it.

Suttree set the beer down and leaned forward in his chair. I'm going to tell you goofy pricks something, he said. If you cause that big son of a bitch to come out here as bad as he feels he is going to kill you where you sit.

They looked toward the rear where he'd pointed. One turned to the other. Is he back there? he said.

Shit if I know.

I thought he was in jail.

Suttree looked at Doll. She was turning the pats of meat, her sullen face shining with grease and steam.

We'll see you outside, motherfucker, said the man at the table.

Sure, said Suttree. He finished his hamburger and drained the beer bottle and rose. He set the plate and bottle on the counter and wiped his mouth with his sleeve.

What do I owe?

You dont owe nothin.

Thanks Doll.

Dont you bring that witch down here.

Suttree grinned. She wouldnt come, he said.

Mm-hmm. She came from behind the counter with the plates and Suttree went on to the door. He listened for the men to say something but they didnt.

He crawled into bed without lighting the lamp and he was up not much past daybreak and out to run his lines.

When he came back upriver with his catch the Indian's skiff was moored to the rocks under the bluff and the Indian hailed him from the top with a piercing whistle.

Suttree waved.

The Indian cupped his hands and called for him to pull in. Suttree feathered the left oar and came up under the shadow of the rocks. The Indian was working his way down the path. Suttree sat the oars and waited.

I got us a turtle, the Indian said. He bent to look at Suttree. What happened to you?

What?

He pointed at Suttree's head. Suttree put a finger gently to his wound. I got that yesterday. Your buddies.

My buddies?

When I was coming back up after I left you somebody cut loose at me with a flipper.

He was a hell of a shot.

Suttree looked up to see if he was smiling but he wasnt. He rose and went down the rocks. Come on, he said. I'll show you your supper.

Suttree climbed from his skiff with the rope and made fast. The Indian had taken up a cord from among the rocks and was hauling it in hand over hand. A hulking shape loomed and subsided. It entered the shadowline of the rock pool and scuttled slowly among the ebbing fish heads. Suttree shaded his eyes. It rose up, dragged by its head, a mosscolored shadow taking shape, a craggy leathercovered skull. The Indian braced his feet and swung it up dripping from the river and onto the rocks and it squatted there watching them, its baleful pig's eyes blinking. It was tied through the lower jaw with a section of wire and the Indian took hold of the wire and tugged at it. The turtle bated and hissed, its jaws gaped. The Indian had out his pocketknife and now he opened it and he pulled the turtle's obscene neck out taut and with a quick upward motion of the blade severed the head. Suttree involuntarily drew back. The turtle's craggy head swung from the wire and what lay between the braced forefeet was a black and wrinkled dog's cunt slowly pumping gouts of near black blood. The blood ran down over the stones and dripped in the water and the turtle shifted slowly on the rock and started toward the river.

The Indian undid the wire and flung the head into the river and reached up the turtle by its tail and swung it trailing blood toward Suttree for him to heft.

Suttree reached to take it by one hindfoot but when he touched the foot it withdrew beneath the scaly eaves of the shell.

Here, you can get him by the tail.

He reached past the Indian's grip and took the headless turtle. Blood dripped and spattered on the stones.

What do you think he'll weigh?

I dont know, said Suttree. He's a big son of a bitch. Thirty pounds maybe?

May be. Lay him down here and we'll dress him.

Suttree laid the turtle on the rock and the Indian scouted about until he came up with a goodsized stone.

Watch out, he said.

Suttree stepped back.

The Indian raised the stone and brought it down upon the turtle's back. The shell collapsed with a pulpy buckling sound.

I never saw a turtle dressed before, said Suttree. But the Indian had knelt and was cutting away the broken plates of shell with his pocketknife and pitching them into the river. He pulled the turtle's meat up off the plastron and gouged away the scant bowels with his thumb. He skinned out the feet. What hung headless in his grip as he raised it aloft was a wet gray foetal mass, a dim atavism limp and dripping.

Plenty of meat there, said the Indian. He laid it out on the rock and bent and swished the blade of his knife in the river.

How do you fix it, said Suttree.

Put him in a pot and cook him slow. Lots of vegetables. Lots of onions. I got my own things I put in. Come on I show you.

I've got to get on to town with these fish. How long does it take to cook.

Three, four hours.

Well why dont I come back this evening?

Okay.

Suttree looked at the saclike shape of the shucked turtle dripping from the Indian's hand.

You be sure and come, the Indian said.

I'll be here.

He pushed off in the skiff and took up the oars. The Indian raised the turtle and swung it before him like a censer.

As he left the markethouse it was beginning to rain. Merchants were out with poles winching down their awnings. The vendors scurried among their trucks, stowing their produce more inboard and a crazed prophet in biblical sandwichboards tottered past muttering darkly at the heavens. Suttree went up the alley and up the back stairs at Comer's.

A company of mutes were playing check at the rear table and some raised their hands in greeting. Suttree raised back, going to the washbasin for paper towels. One of the mutes gestured at him, carving words with a dexter hand in the smoky air. Suttree was drying his face. He thought he had the gist of it and nodded and formed words with his own fingers, puzzled, erased, began again. They nodded encouragement. He fashioned his phrase for them and they laughed their croaky mute's laughter and elbowed one another. Suttree grinned and went on to the lunchcounter.

Eddie Taylor was playing bank pool in the sideroom onehanded against a stranger and spotting him two balls. Suttree sat at the counter and turned his stool to watch. The balls rifled across the felt and whacked viciously into the pockets, Taylor laughing, joking, chalking his cue. Bending, stroking. The ball smoking back down from the end rail. Whop.

The Knoxville Bear, called out Harry the Horse on his way to the cashregister.

Stud was wiping the counter at Suttree's elbow. What for ye, Sut, he said.

Let me have a chocolate milk.

Buddy boy, said Jake.

Hey Jake.

Jake spat into the stainless steel spittoon and wiped his mouth. The bear can walk the balls to the pockets caint he.

Yes he can, said Suttree.

While he was drinking his milk small weird Leonard took a seat beside him and leaned to case the game at the table and leaned back. Hey Sut?

Hey Leonard.

What the fuck is a yegg?

A yegg?

Y E doubleG.

Suttree looked at Leonard. Who called you that?

What is one?

Well. I dont know. A yegg is a . . . I guess a hoodlum.

Hoodlum huh?

More or less.

Yeah. Okay.

I never heard the word except in this crazy newspaper.

Yeah, well. Leonard looked about nervously and rose. I'll see ye, Sut.

Suttree watched him go out toward the front and the stairs. Stud, he said. Hand me that paper.

He found the story on page two. Yeggs last night boarded the River Queen, popular Knoxville excursion boat, in what was apparently an unsuccessful robbery attempt. He smiled and finished the milk and laid his dime on the counter and pushed back the paper.

The Jellyroll Kid was in a check game at the front table and when Suttree sat in one of the lopsided theatre seats the kid sidled to him and turned down his cupped hand for Suttree to read his pills. He had the one and the twelve. Suttree noted them with a poker face. You shoot up here with the big dogs do you? he said.

It's just a dollar. The kid was watching the table. He'd broken the rack and the twelveball was hung in the corner pocket. Flop set his cue crutch up on the felt and laid the cue in it and stroked and sighted, sawing the cue smoothly, holding the crutch under his stump. He shot the eight in the side pocket and the cueball kissed its way along the balls on the rail and tore out the oneball and nudged a ball up against the twelve. The twelve dropped into the pocket.

Check, called Jellyroll, taking the pill from his pocket and wedging it under the rail at the head of the table. Flop looked up at him and chalked his cue and laid by the crutch and set the cue on the rail and began to stroke back and forth and sight. Jellyroll looked off down the hall. Jerome Jernigan turned his eyes up in disgust. Flop stroked the oneball into the corner.

Double, said Jellyroll, throwing his pill on the table.

Shit, said Jerome.

Rack, said Jelly.

The Jellyroll Kid, said Jake, shucking the balls up out of the pockets and rounding them up with the rack.

Jelly threw a quarter on the table and collected his dollars from the other players and funneled the pills back into the leather bottle and shook it and handed it to Suttree. Suttree tipped it and let two pills fall into his palm and passed the bottle to Flop.

That's the luckiest son of a bitch in the world, Flop said.

Jellyroll broke the balls on the table. Suttree turned up the pills and looked at them. He had the one and the fifteen.

Which way can I go, Sut?

Suttree looked at the table. The eightball was sewn up.

You can go any way you want.

I dont even want to know what I've got, said Jelly. He shot the fifteen into the corner and chalked his cue.

Check, said Suttree, rising and putting the fifteen pill under the rail.

How's that fourteen look, Sut?

That's too hard a shot, Jelly.

Jelly walked around the table and sighted on the oneball and banked it across the side.

Double, said Suttree.

No shit? said Jelly, raising up and grinning.

Rack, said Jerome.

Flop shook his head. The other man stood up and threw his pills on the table and took the pillbottle and emptied the pills out onto the felt. Let him draw his own fuckin pills, he said.

Yes, said Jelly. I aint had the eightball a time.

How sweet it is on the Jellyroll Kid, said Jake, racking up the balls.

The stranger was counting the pills back into the bottle. Jellyroll grinned and winked at Suttree. Kenneth Tipton told me he got in a check game up here last week with four highschool boys. He was the last to draw pills and when he went to draw them there wasnt but one left in the jug. He held it up and asked could he borrow one from somebody.

Suttree grinned. Jimmy Long got in a bank game up here with a hustler one time, they butted heads for about an hour, finally this hustler says: Let's play one game lefthanded for ten. Old J-Bone says okay and this hustler *was* lefthanded.

Jelly laughed and bent and broke the balls and reached for the pillbottle. Suttree rose.

Where you goin Sut?

I've got to go.

Shit, dont leave now. We'll go drink a beer here in a minute.

I'll see you later.

Jelly was looking at his pills. Drink some mash and talk some trash, he called out.

Suttree went past the counter. Hey Fred, he said.

Buddy boy, said Fred.

He pushed open the door and nodded to the sentry at the top of the stairs and went down the stairwell to the street.

In the evening he rowed back across the river with six bottles of cold beer under the seat. The shadow of the bluff lay deep and cool along the south shore of the river. He swung in alongside the Indian's patched skiff and tethered his rope and tucked the sack of beer under his arm and started up the bluff.

The path wound up by a steep and narrow way and near the top of the rise came out upon a natural terrace in the rock and a cave. The Indian did not seem to be about. A soapkettle was lodged on a rock hob and the gray flaky ashes when he toed them broke open to an orange heart of burning wood.

Hey Michael, he called.

A lizard crossed the stone floor and slithered into the weeds.

Suttree tipped up the rim of the kettle's lid with a stick. A wafted breath of fragrant steam slid out. The stew simmered gently. He let the lid drop and went to the mouth of the cave and looked in. A red clay floor that shaped itself among the rocks. On the right was a table made from a plank propped on stones. He ducked under the low limestone ledge and entered and set the beer down. Just within the last reaches of daylight he could make out the footrail of an old iron bed.

It was damp in the cave and it smelled of earth and woodsmoke. Suttree went back out. He called again but there was no answer. He walked to the edge of the bluff and looked out. The city lay quiet in the evening sun and innocent. Far downstream the river narrowed with distance where the pieced fields lay pale and hazy and the water placid much like those misty landscapes in which Audubon posed his birds. He sat in a tattered lawnchair and watched the traffic on the bridge below. There was no sound save for a bird that conjured up forbidden jungles with its medley of whoops and croaks. Suttree saw it put forth from the bluff and flutter in midair and go back. He leaned his head back. A mayfly, delicate and pale green, drifted past. Lost ephemera, wandered surely from some upland pastoral. The chat came from its bower on the bluffside and fluttered and snatched the mayfly and returned. After a while it sang again. It sang grok, wheet, erk. Suttree got up and went into the cave and got one of the beers. He returned to the chair and sat and wiped the mouth of the bottle with the web of his thumb and held it up and toasted mutely the city below and drank.

It was almost dark when the Indian returned. He came down the slope above the cave and dropped to the stone floor and crossed to where Suttree sat.

Hey, said Suttree.

How you doin?

Okay. Get yourself a beer there. I set them inside on that table.

You want one?

Yeah.

The Indian crossed the little terrace and lifted the lid from the pot and sniffed. How's it doin?

Okay.

He stirred the mixture with a peeled stick and clapped the lid back over it and pushed more wood into the fire. He came from the cave with the beers and handed one to Suttree and squatted on his heels at the edge of the bluff. The John Agee was coming downriver, her stern paddles trudging the brown waters. They sipped their beers. The lights of the city were beginning to come up across the river. The lamps along the bridge winked on. Cryptic shapes of neon gas bloomed on the wall of the night and the city reached light by light across the plain, the evening land, the lights in their gaudy penumbra shoring up the dark of the heavens, the stars set back in their sockets. Bats came from flues and cellars to flutter over the water like rough shapes of ash tumbled on the wind and the air was clean and fresh after the rain.

You're not from Knoxville, Suttree said.

No.

How long you been here?

Just this summer.

Suttree looked out over the lights of the city. What will you do in the winter?

I dont know.

You'll freeze your ass off up here.

How cold does it get.

Got down to zero last winter.

The Indian turned his head and laid the flat of his chin on his shoulder and spat and turned back to watch the river.

I almost froze in that shantyboat. Stove and all.

The Indian nodded.

What do those signify?

The Indian looked down. He touched the doll's eyes. Them? I dont know. Good luck.

I guess they must work. Judging by that catfish.

Dont you have nothin?

A good luck piece?

Yeah.

No. I guess not.

The Indian rose. Wait a minute, he said. I'll get you something.

When he came back from the cave he handed Suttree a small lozenge of yellowed bone. Suttree held it up and looked at it. It had a hole bored in one end and he turned it in his hand to feel if there were not some carving on it but there wasnt. A few hairline cracks. A tooth? He rubbed its polished surface.

What is it?

The Indian shrugged.

Where did you get it?

I found it.

Do I have to wear it or can I just carry it in my pocket.

You can just carry it if you want to.

Okay.

Dont forget about it.

No. He held it up.

You cant just put it away and forget about it. said the Indian. He

drained his bottle and rose and crossed the terrace to the fire. He
ladled the stew up into heavy white china bowls and came and handed
one to Suttree. Suttree took it in both hands and balanced it and
stirred. He spooned up a piece of the meat and cradled it in his mouth
to cool it. He chewed it. It was succulent and rich, a flavor like no
other.

The Indian came from the cave with two more beers and a lighted
lamp. He set the beers down and he set the lamp on the stone and
crouched like an icon and began to ladle the stew into his jaws. Suttree
watched him eat, his eyes dark and trancelike in the soft orange light,
his jaws moving in a slow rotary motion and the veins in his temple
pulsing. Solemn, mute, decorous. In his crude clothes crudely
mended, wearing not only the outlandish eyes but small lead medallions that bore the names of whiskeys. Sitting solemn and unaccountable and bizarre. He reached and took up his beer and drank. He
rocked the bottle and studied the foam within the brown glass. I found
them in a fish, he said.

The eyes?

Yeah.

What about my piece?

It was in the cave yonder. How you like the turtle?

It's damned good.

The Indian set the bottle down and took up his spoon. How long
you been on the river? he said.

This is my second year.

The Indian shook his head. You wont stay.

Maybe not.

What got you fishin?

I dont know. I sort of inherited my line from another man. Suttree
reached down and got his beer and drank. Dry weeds at the edge of
the rock rattled and hissed in the wind.

What happened to the other man?

I dont know, said Suttree. All he said was not to look for him back.

There was no one in the Huddle save a few whores and weird Leonard, pale and pimpled part-time catamite. They were sitting at the black table drinking beer and sharing ribald tales oft told and partly true of johns and tricks. When he saw Suttree at the bar he rose up and came over.

Hey Leonard, said Suttree.

Listen Sut. I got somethin to ast you.

I've got something to ask you.

He looked about. Come on back in the back, he said. Get ye a beer. Mr Hatmaker, give us a fishbowl over here.

Fat city, said Suttree. Where'd you score?

I got me a little walkabout off old crazy Larry this mornin. Here. Come on back in the back.

They eased into the booth and Suttree cocked his feet up and took a sip of the beer and leaned back. Leonard did the same. After a while Suttree said: Well?

Well.

Well go on.

You ask yourn first.

You know what mine is.

No I dont. What is it.

I'd like to hear the true story. The paper said you finally jumped overboard.

What the fuck, Sut. What are you talkin about?

The River Queen.

Leonard looked around. Hell fire, he whispered hoarsely. That wasnt me.

Then what are you whispering about?

I didnt do it. May God strike me . . .

Suttree seized his upraised hand. Not with me sitting this close.

Leonard grinned.

Did you really have to swim for it?

I dont know nothin about it Sut. I keep tellin ye.

Okay. What was it you wanted to ask me.

Well.

Go ahead.

Shit, I dont know where to start.

Start at the beginning.

Well you know the old man's been sick a long time.

Okay.

And you know the old lady draws that welfare.

All right.

Well she draws so much for everbody. I mean she wouldnt let Sue move out on account of it would cut it down and she gets medical for the old man and he draws unemployment on top of that so she draws good money.

All right.

Well if the old man was to die she wouldnt get but about half what all she's gettin.

Suttree sipped from his bowl again and nodded.

Well . . .

Go on.

Well he's done died.

Suttree looked up. I'm sorry to hear that, he said. When was it?

Leonard passed the top of his closed fist across his forehead and looked around uneasily. That was what I wanted to talk to you about.

Okay. Go ahead.

Well. Shit.

Hell Leonard, go on.

Well. He died see?

I do see.

And Mama stands to lose about half her check.

Well, she wont have the expense of him.

He aint been no expense. She's been savin to get her some things she needs. She done got a steamiron.

Well Leonard if he's dead he's dead. You cant keep him in the back room and make out like . . .

Leonard's finger traced along the top of the table through the water pooled off the frozen mug. He didnt look up.

I mean he wont keep with hot weather coming on. Suttree smiling, smile slowly fading. Leonard gave him a funny little look and went back to scribbling in the water.

Leonard.

Yeah.

When did he die?

Well. He sat erect and rolled his shoulders. Well, he died . . .

Yeah, you said. When?

Last December.

They sat in silence, looking at their mugs of beer. Suttree passed his hand over his face. After a while he said: Did you ever get her refrigerator back?

Naw. She got her anothern.

What did you do, run an ad in the paper?

You mean on her old one?

On her old one.

Naw. Hell fire Sut, I never meant to sell it. This old guy stopped me in the street ast me did I know anybody had one for sale. I told him no but I kept thinkin about it and I got to drinkin whiskey with Hoghead and them and we run out of whiskey and I knowed where the old guy lived and went on over there and then we went to the house on account of she was at work and he offered to give me fifteen dollars for the refrigerator and I said twenty and he said okay. Fore I knowed what happened he had it dollied up and out the door and loaded and gone. I wouldnt of done it had I not been drinkin.

Leonard?

Yeah?

What the fuck are you going to do about your old man?

I wanted to talk to you about it. If we could just get him out of there without anybody bein the wiser we could still draw on him.

You're crazy.

Listen Sut. We're painted into a corner anyways. I mean what if we was to just call up and say he died? I mean hell fire, you caint fool them guys. Them guys is doctors. They take one look at him and know for a fact he's been dead six months.

How does it smell in there?

It smells fuckin awful.

Leonard took Suttree's empty bowl to the bar and refilled it. When he came back they sat in silence, Leonard watching Suttree. Suttree shrugged his shoulders up. Well, he said. He couldnt think of anything to say about it.

Leonard leaned forward. Listen, he said. I just need somebody to help me with him. I can get a car . . .

Suttree leveled up a pair of cold gray eyes at him. No, he said.

If I could just get you to help me load him, Sut. Hell, it wouldnt be no risk to you.

Suttree looked across the table at that earnest little face, the blond hair, the pimples, the eyes too close together. Strange scenes of midnight stealth and mummied corpses by torchlight, old snips from horror movies, flickered through his head. Listen Leonard, he said.

I'm listening.

What does your mother think about all this? I mean, I cant see her going for this crazy hustle.

She aint got no choice. See, what it was, it got out of hand Sut. We left him in there just to finish out the week. You know. So we could draw on him for the full week? Well, the week ended and I said hell, wont hurt nothin to let it go a few more days. You know. And draw that. Well. It just went on from there.

Aint that the way though? Suttree said.

It wasnt nobody's fault Sut. It just got out of hand.

Suttree lifted his beer and sipped it and set it back and looked at Leonard. You're not shitting me are you? he said.

About what?

This whole thing. Are you telling me the truth?

Goddamn Sut. You think I'd kid about a thing like this? Hell, even Lorina dont know he's dead.

What does she think is going on in the back bedroom?

She just thinks he's sick and she caint see him. That's all.

How old is she?

I dont know. Six I guess. She starts school this year. Maybe seven. Look Sut, we can get him out while she's in bed of a night. The old lady'll help us. We'll just haul him out and put him in the trunk. I got some wheelrims and some chains we can use.

What the fuck are you talking about?

Some old rims and stuff. To weight him with.

Weight him with?

Yeah. We'll have that old fucker so loaded down he wont even show up for judgment day.

Where the hell are you going to put him?

Leonard straightened up and looked around. We got to hold it down, he whispered.

Okay.

We'll dump him in the fuckin river of course. You got a better idea?

I sure do.

Okay. Let's hear it.

Forget this goofy goddamned notion and just call the police or whatever and tell them to come and get his stinking ass.

Leonard looked at Suttree. He shook his head. You dont understand, he said.

I understand I'm not getting mixed up in it.

Listen . . .

Get Harrogate to help you. Loonies ought to stick together.

He aint got a boat. Listen Sut . . .

The hell he aint got a boat.

You got to be shittin me Sut. I wouldnt set foot in that fuckin thing.

Suttree drained his mug and stood. I've got to go, he said. You do what you want but count me out.

In the cool of the mornings he'd run his lines, out with the sun on the foggy river. Afternoons he'd walk in the city but he kept much to himself. He came upon Smokehouse uptown and the old derelict pawed him and begged for a coin. Suttree was holding his pocket with one hand while he reached in with the other but then he looked at Smokehouse and said no. He moved past the old cripple but found him fallen in at his elbow, hobbling along on his twisted legs like a broken disciple. Hey, called Smokehouse, though he wasnt a foot away.

Hey yourself, said Suttree.

Hell fire, let me have somethin. A dime. Goddamn, Bud, you got a dime aint ye?

Mine's the greater need, said Suttree.

This brought the old man up short. He watched Suttree go on up Market Street. He called out again but Suttree didnt turn. That's right, called the derelict. That's the way to treat a old cripple man never done nothin but favors for ye.

He made his way down Vine among blacker mendicants but he kept his silver to himself such as he had of it. An old negress in rags washed up on the paving beneath the Human Furniture Company like a piece of dark and horrid flora ran her wasted leg over the walkway before her and invited whomever to walk upon it. It lay there like a charred treelimb. Whomever smile wanly and look away and she calls down upon them the darker curses of a harried god. Her eyes are red with drink, her geography is immutable. Whereas the quick are subject to the weathers of a varied fate and know not where a newer day will find them she is fixed in perpetuity, steadfast, a paradigm of black anathema impaled upon the floor of the city like a medieval felon.

Suttree passed by, in these days moving through the streets like a dog at large. Such old things strangely new, the city seen through eyes unscaled. The repetition of its own images had washed out and leveled it and he saw upright and arrant on the dead alluvial grimmer shapes, the city of his remembrance a ghost like him and he himself a shape among the ruins, prodding dried artifacts like some dim paleontrope among the bones of fallen settlements where no soul's left to utter voice at what has passed. A garrulous jocko was miming buggery behind a young black girl passing on the walk and she turned on him with hot eyes and he fled laughing. The gallery of indolents draped among trashcans and curbstones pointed and croaked. Give it to you mammy, she told them, and the black mummer mimed masturbation at her, two hands holding an imagined phallus the size of a lightpole while the watchers hooted and slapped their knees. To Suttree they appeared more sinister and their acts a withershins allegory of anger and despair, clutches of the iniquitous and unshriven howling curses at the gates and calling aloud for redress of their right damnation to a god who need be interceded with bassackwards or obliquely. Some knew him to nod to and nodded but the hand he raised to greet them with seemed held in a gesture of dread. He moved on in the accomplished dusk. Night found him in the B&J with Bucket and J-Bone and he danced with a young girl who slewed against him shamelessly. Blackhaired, her grimestreaked legs fullthighed under the thin dress, she moved with a kind of lyrical obscenity. She had a tooth out in the front and when she smiled she'd poke the tip of her tongue in the gap. When the place closed they rode through the streets in the back of a cab and he cupped her breast in his palm and she put her tongue in his mouth. He clove her damp and naked thighs with his hand, the moist warm pouched everything tucked under his finger in the silk-crotched crevice there. He took her to Ab Jones's first. An after-hours place, he told her. He'd had them leap from the cab at the sight of his own dark houseboat there on the deserted riverfront. They drank in a corner and he took her down to his shack and lit the lamp and turned the wick low in the glass.

She sat there on the cot in her pale blue drawers while he ran his tongue in her ear. Her drinking her beer, quivering a little. Bitter taste of wax and the weight of her plump young tit naked in his hand. As she lay back he could see her dull hypoplastic doll's face and her full vapid look for a moment before her head went under the dark of the wall. He fell asleep sprawled against her.

He'd been sleeping he knew not how long when a light flared somewhere and the joints in the shanty wall were lit like a bead curtain. He thought it was the sweep of a barge's shorelight but he heard a motor running just beyond his door. He thought police. The motor ceased and the lights dimmed to nothing. He heard a car door slam. He sat up in the cot.

What is it? she said.

I dont know.

Steps on the catwalk, a knock at the door.

Who is it? said Suttree.

It's me.

Who?

Me. Leonard.

Mother of God, said Suttree.

Who is it? said the girl.

Suttree rose from the cot and scrabbled about for his breeches. He got them on and went to the table and turned up the wick in the lampchimney. The girl sat up in the bed with her arms folded across her breasts. Who is it? she said. She was pulling the sheet over herself.

Suttree opened the door. Leonard had not lied. It was himself. Eyes huge and earnest. He spoke in an excited whisper. I got him, he said.

You what?

I got him. He's in the trunk.

Suttree tried to shut the door.

You're breakin my goddamned foot, Sut.

Get it out of the fucking door then.

Listen Sut . . .

I said no, goddamnit.

It's too late Sut. I got him out here I'm tellin you.

You're crazy Leonard. You hear me?

I'll pay ye, Sut.

Get away. Go get one of your faggot friends to do it.

You caint get them motherfuckers to do nothin. Listen, the old lady told me to tell you she never would forget you for it. Listen . . .

You tell him to watch his mouth, the girl called out. There's ladies in here if he dont know it.

Who the fuck is that? said Leonard.

Suttree sagged against the jamb. The lamp on the table behind him was smoking and he stood away from the door and adjusted the wick. You son of a bitch, he said.

Leonard came in and shut the door behind him and leaned against it. He smelled peculiar. Whew, he said. I was afraid you might not be home.

Would to God I wasnt, said Suttree. He pushed back a chair and slumped wearily at the table.

Why didnt you tell me they was someone in here? said Leonard. He nodded affably toward the girl in the bed. Hidy, he said.

Why dont you just go away, said Suttree.

Listen. Come on outside where we can talk.

No.

He glanced impatiently at the girl. We caint talk in here, he whispered hoarsely.

I want to go home, the girl said.

Suttree laid his head on the table. Leonard tugged at his elbow. Sut? he said. Hey Sut.

He got up and got his shoes and put them on. He pulled on his shirt.

Where you goin? the girl wanted to know.

I'll be right back.

I want to go home.

Just wait a minute, will you?

They walked down the plank and out through the weeds and Suttree sat down. It was a warm night and the city behind them drawn upon the dark with its neon geometry seemed somehow truer than the shape it wore by day. The lights on the far side of the river stood recast in the water like torches shimmering inexplicably just beneath the surface.

Leonard.

Yeah Sut.

Sit down.

He sat. We better get started, he said.

Leonard do you really have your father in the trunk of that car there?

Hell Sut. You dont think I'd kid about a thing like that do you?

Suttree shook his head sadly. He groped about and plucked a handful of weeds and let them fall again. After a while he said: Whose car is it?

Whose car?

Yes.

I dont know. Hell Sut, it dont make no difference whose car it is. The car is stolen.

Well, shit. I aint goin to sell it or nothin. I just borrowed it is all. Hell Sut, they'll get their car back. There wont be no heat about the fuckin car.

I see.

There aint nothin to worry about.

No. Of course not.

They sat in silence. Leonard stirred uneasily. After a while he said: Are you ready?

Am I ready?

Yeah.

No. I'm not ready.

Well listen Sut . . .

I sure as fuck am not ready.

Well it aint gettin no earlier.

I will never be ready.

We caint just leave him in the goddamned car. You know that, Sut.

I know that?

Well what the hell.

You crazy bastard. Why me?

You got a . . .

A boat. I know. Mother of God.

Hell fire Sut, I've done done the worst of it. Gettin the car and the chains and all. It wont take no time.

But Suttree had risen from the weeds. Just dont say another word, he said. Just be quiet.

What about her?

You get in the car and go down to just above that tree there. There's a landing. I'll get the boat.

When he went back in she was dressed. I want to go home, she said, and I mean it.

Suttree took up the lamp from the table. You can wait or you walk, he said. It's strictly up to you.

I dont know where I'm at, she said petulantly.

I'm sure of that, said Suttree. You're not alone, either.

You aint goin to leave me in the dark, she called. But Suttree was gone.

He got the boat and rowed down to the landing and pulled in

sideways. When they raised the trunklid of the car a vile stench came flooding out. He stepped back half gagging. Great God, he said.

Bad aint it?

Bad? Suttree looked at the stars. That's the awfullest stink I ever smelled.

That's the biggest reason we had to get him out of the house.

God you're a sick bastard.

Well give me a hand with him.

Just a minute.

Suttree pulled off the cotton undershirt he wore and tied it around his lower face.

Okay, said Leonard.

Leonard's father was wrapped in the sheets he'd died in months before. Leonard was setting out wheelrims and a pile of chain. He got hold of the body and wrestled part of it over the car bumper. Suttree held the lamp.

Get his feet there, Sut, and I'll haul on his arms.

How did you get him in there?

What?

Suttree freed his mouth from the shirt. I said how did you get him in there?

Me and the old lady done it. He aint all that heavy.

Suttree took hold of the limbs beneath the sheet with sick loathing. They dragged the body out and it slumped to the ground with a nauseating limberness. Leonard's father lay like a dead klansman. By the light of the lamp on the bare ground they could see strange brown stains seeping through the sheets. Suttree turned away and went to sit on the bank for a while.

They dragged the remains down to the boat and Suttree stood in the transom and hauled the thing aboard, goggleheaded under the thin cotton, against his naked chest. Leonard bearing up behind with the lamp, chains clanking.

They rowed far downstream. Leonard saying Hell, Sut, any place is good and Suttree rowing on. They looked like old jacklight poachers, their faces yellow masks in the night. The corpse lay slumped in the floor of the skiff. The lamp standing on the stern seat with its thin spout of insects caught in its light the wet sweep of the oars, the beads of water running on the underblades like liquid glass and the dimples of the oarstrokes coiled out through the city lights where they lay fixed among the deeper shapes of stars and galaxies fast in the silent river.

Coming about below the railway bridge Suttree shipped the oars. Leonard was at wrapping his father in chains, fastening them with dimestore locks, chaining up the wheelrims through the center holes. One of the old man's legs lay twisted in the floor of the skiff and Suttree could see the stained flannel pajamas that he wore.

I think that'll get it, Sut, said Leonard.

Think it will?

Yeah. Shit, this'll take his ass to the bottom like a fucking rocket.

Are you going to say a few words?

Do what?

Say a few words.

Leonard gave a sort of nervous little grin. Say a few words?

Arent you? I mean you're not going to bury your father without anything at all.

I aint burying him.

The hell you're not.

I'm just puttin him in the river.

It's the same thing. It's the same as burial at sea.

Well goddamn, Suttree.

Well?

This old son of a bitch never went to church in his life.

All the more reason.

Well I dont know no goddamned service nor nothin. Shit. You say it.

The only words I know are the Catholic ones.

Catholic?

Catholic.

Leonard regarded his chained and hooded father in the floor of the skiff. Hell fire. He sure wasnt no Catholic. What about that part that goes through the shadow of the valley of death. You know any of that?

Suttree stood up in the skiff. The river about them was black and calm and the bridgelights rigid where they lay upstream in the water.

Give me a hand with him.

Leonard looked up, one side of him softly lit by the lamp at his elbow, his shadow in the night enormous. He leaned and took hold of the cadaver and together they raised him. They laid him across the seat, one leg already reaching over the side into the river as if the old man couldnt wait. Suttree put his foot against the thing and shoved it. It made a dull splash and the white sheets flared in the lamplight and it was gone. Leonard sat back down in the stern of the skiff. Whew, he said.

Suttree washed his hands in the river and dried them on his trousers and took up the oars again. Leonard tried him in conversation on several topics as they came back up the river but Suttree rowing said no word.

Suttree drunk negotiated with a drunk's meticulousness the wide stone steps of the Church of the Immaculate Conception. The virtues of a stainless birth were not lost on him, no not on him. The moon's horn rode in the dark hard by the steeple. An older sot wobbled in the street without, caroming along a wall like a mechanical duck in a carnival. Suttree entered the vestibule and paused by a concrete seashell filled with sacred waters. He stood in the open door. He entered.

Down the long linoleum aisle he went, and with care, tottered not once. A musty aftertaste of incense hung in the air. A thousand hours or more he's spent in this sad chapel he. Spurious acolyte, dreamer impenitent. Before this tabernacle where the wise high God himself lies sleeping in his golden cup.

He eased himself into the frontmost pew and sat. By his knee on the pewback a small brass clasp springloaded for the gripping of hatbrims. A little bracket containing literature. Long leatherpadded kneebenches underfoot. Where rows of hemorrhoidal dwarfs convene by night.

He looked about. Beyond the chancel gate three garish altars rose like gothic wedding cakes in carven marble. Crocketed and gargoyled, the steeples iced with rows of marble frogs ascending. Here a sallow plaster Christ. Agonized beneath his muricate crown. Spiked palms and riven belly, there beneath the stark ribs the cleanlipped spear-wound. His caved haunches loosely girdled, feet crossed and fastened by a single nail. To the left his mother. Mater alchimia in skyblue robes, she treads a snake with her chipped and naked feet. Before her on the altar gutter two small licks of flame in burgundy lampions. In the sculptor's art there always remains something unsaid, something waiting. This statuary will pass. This kingdom of fear and ashes. Like the child that sat in these selfsame bones so many black Fridays in terror of his sins. Viceridden child, heart rotten with fear. Listening to the slide shoot back in the confessional, waiting his turn. Light pierced, light fell from the pieced and leaded glass of the windows in the western wall, light moteless and oblique, wine colors, rose magenta, leached cobalt, cinnabar and delicate citrine. The stained-glass saints lay broken in their panes of light among the pews and in the summer afternoon quietude a smell of old varnish and the distant cries of children in a playground. Memories of May processions, a priest in a black biretta rising from his carved oak faldstool to shuffle heavyfooted down the aisle attended by churlish and acnefaced striplings. The censer swings in chains, clinks back and forth, at the apex of each arc coughing up a quick gout of smoke. The priest dips the aspergillum in a gold bucket. He casts left and right, holy water upon the congregation. They pass out the door where two scullery nuns stand bowed in fouled habits. There follows a troop of small christians in little white fitted frocks. They bear candles. They are singing. Cornelius has set Danny Yike's hair on fire. An acrid stench. A flailing about the boy's head by a dracular nun. Patch of blackened stubble at the base of his skull. The boys laughing. The girls in white veils, white patentleather shoes with little straps. Snickering into the roses they hold in their prayerclasped hands. Small specters of fraudulent piety. At the foot of the steps a pale child collapses. Her rose lies dwindled on the stone. Some others taking cue drop about her. They lie on the pavement like patches of melting snow. Folk rush about these spent ones, fanning with folded copies of the *Sunday Messenger.*

Or cold mornings in the Market Lunch after serving early Mass with J-Bone. Coffee at the counter. Rich smell of brains and eggs frying. Old men in smoky coats and broken boots hunkered over plates. A dead roach beneath a plastic cakebell. Lives proscribed and doom in store, doom's adumbration in the smoky censer, the faint creak of the tabernacle door, the tasteless bread and draining the last of the wine from the cruet in a corner and counting the money in the box. This venture into the world of men rich with vitality, these unwilling churched ladling cream into their cups and watching the dawn in the city, enjoying the respite from their black clad keepers with their neat little boots, their spectacles, the deathreek of the dark and half scorched muslin that they wore. Grim and tireless in their orthopedic moralizing. Filled with tales of sin and unrepentant deaths and visions of hell and stories of levitation and possession and dogmas of semitic damnation for the tacking up of the paraclete. After eight years a few of their charges could read and write in primitive fashion and that was all.

Suttree looked up at the ceiling where a patriarchal deity in robes and beard lurched across the cracking plaster. Attended by thunder, by fat infants with dovewings grown from their shoulderbones. He lowered his head to his chest. He slept.

A priest shook him gently. He looked up into a bland scented face. Were you waiting for confession?

No.

The priest looked at him. Do I know you? he said.

Suttree placed one hand on the pew in front of him. An old woman was going along the altar rail with a dusting rag. He struggled to his feet. No, he said. You dont know me.

The priest stepped back, inspecting his clothes, his fishstained shoes.

I just fell asleep a minute. I was resting.

The priest gave a little smile, lightly touched with censure, remonstrance gentled. God's house is not exactly the place to take a nap, he said.

It's not God's house.

I beg your pardon?

It's not God's house.

Oh?

Suttree waved his hand vaguely and stepped past the priest and went down the aisle. The priest watched him. He smiled sadly, but a smile for that.

The ragman laboring up beneath the mound of ripe bedding in which he had entombed himself for sleep looked like a melted candle. He sat cowled and scowling out upon the new day. A draft of dank air went among his silken chinwhiskers and a faint miasma rose off of him like heat from a summer road.

Now he hobbled about in his ragged underwear with his withered and rickety shanks trembling, gathering his clothes in one hand and poking among the mounds of paper for dry ones with which to start his fire. The sound of morning traffic upon the bridge beat with the dull echo of a dream in his cavern and the ragman would have wanted a sager soul than his to read in their endless advent auguries of things to come, the specter of mechanical proliferation and universal blight. Two fishermen passed along the river path, misty figures going silently save for the fragile rattling of their canes, lifting hands toward him where he stood with his palms spread above a thin and heatless spire of smoke, the rank earthy smell of the barren mud beneath the bridge rife with the morning damp, the river passing smoky and silent and overhead in the arches of the bridge the inane and sporadic clapping of pigeons setting forth into the day.

He mumbled and massaged his hands above the fire. He took his kettle to the river and dipped it full of water and came back. The mist was running off the river in little tongues and lapping eddyplaces and there was hope of sunlight somewhere beyond the eastern murk.

He went with his despair through the warrens of the city towing his kindlingwood cart with a sound in those lightless corridors like guts rumbling.

In the belly of an iron trashbin big enough to hold a pokergame he sorted out mementos all the morning long. Indemnified bottles cast off by the idle rich. Redeemable at two cents per. Newsprint for baling. Useless bones. A dead rat, a broken broom, part of an inkpen. A side of gangrenous bacon filled with skippers. The wreck of a fruitcrate which his eyes saw as kindling, salvageable, saleable. A passing truck muted out the footsteps of the kitchen boy from the Sanitary Lunch. The old man felt the door above him darken and looked up with eyes terrible to see the round mouth of a swillcan tipping. He leaped back flailing and was upended by a turtling box. A lapful of lettuce and old bread, nothing worse. The can rattled and clanged. In the distance a trolley answered. The old man appeared in the door of the bin like some queer revenant rising in smokeless athanasia from the refuse to croak a slew of bitter curses out upon the world but the kitchen boy didnt even look back.

I went down this river in the fall of ought one with a carnival dont ast me why. I followed it two year. I seen street preachers come off the circuit in the early summer and bark and shill with the best of em and go back to preachin in the fall. We went to Tallahassee Florida. They was a bunch of loggers come off the river at Chattanooga with us went into town and got drunk we had to wait the train on em. They'd done chained the locomotive to the rails with logchains. We never left out of there till five in the mornin. Had two boxcars loaded with old carny gear. We seen a feller hung in Rome Georgia stood up there on the back of a springwagon and told em all to go to hell he never done it. They drove that wagon out from under him he turned black in the face as a nigger.

Suttree smiled. Is that where you learned ventriloquism?

Where's that?

In the carnival.

No.

I see, said Suttree.

I seen strange things in my time. I seen that cyclome come through here where it went down in the river it dipped it dry you could see the mud and stones in the bottom of it naked and fishes layin there. It picked up folks' houses and set em down again in places where they'd never meant to live. They was mail addressed to Knoxville fell in the streets of Ringgold Georgia. I've seen all I want to see and I know all I want to know. I just look forward to death.

He might hear you, Suttree said.

I wisht he would, said the ragpicker. He glared out across the river with his redrimmed eyes at the town where dusk was settling in. As if death might be hiding in that quarter.

No one wants to die.

Shit, said the ragpicker. Here's one that's sick of livin.

Would you give all you own?

The ragman eyed him suspiciously but he did not smile. It wont be long, he said. An old man's days are hours.

And what happens then?

When?

After you're dead.

Dont nothin happen. You're dead.

You told me once you believed in God.

The old man waved his hand. Maybe, he said. I got no reason to think he believes in me. Oh I'd like to see him for a minute if I could.

What would you say to him?

Well, I think I'd just tell him. I'd say: Wait a minute. Wait just one minute before you start in on me. Before you say anything, there's just one thing I'd like to know. And he'll say: What's that? And then I'm goin to ast him: What did you have me in that crapgame down there for anyway? I couldnt put any part of it together.

Suttree smiled. What do you think he'll say?

The ragpicker spat and wiped his mouth. I dont believe he can answer it, he said. I dont believe there is a answer.

In the summer of his second year in the city Harrogate began to tunnel toward the vaults underground where the city's wealth was kept. By day in the dark of dripping caverns, stone bowels whereon was founded the city itself, holding his lantern before him, a bloodcolored troglodyte stooped and muttering down foul corridors, assaying vectors by a stolen scout compass that spun inanely in this nether region so gravid with seam and lode. Coming from his day's labors slavered over with a gray paste that on contact with the outer air began to cure up and flake away leaving on his skin and on his clothing a dull cast of claydust so that he looked like something that had been smoked, his eyes collared up in cups of grime, the red rims raw as wounds.

Summer was full on and the nights hot. It was like lying in warm syrup there in the dark under the viaduct, in the steady whine of gnats and nightbugs. Coming up Henley Street one morning he was amazed to see a truck fallen through the paving. Settled on an enormous cracked asphalt plate some five feet below grade with a ring of spectators gathered about it and the driver climbing from the hole swearing and laughing.

I reckon once a feller got in under there he could go anywheres he took a notion right in under the ground there couldnt he?

I dont know, Gene. There's lots of cave under there. Suttree was pulling a wire minnowbucket from the bottom of the river by a long cord. He swung it dripping to the rail and opened the top and lifted out two beers and let the cage back down. He opened the beers and handed one to Harrogate and leaned back against the houseboat wall.

That goddamned truck like to of fell plumb out of sight.

I saw it.

What if a whole goddamned building was to just up and sink?

What about two or three buildings?

What about a whole block? Harrogate was waving his bottle about. Goddamn, he said. What if the whole fuckin city was to cave in?

That's the spirit, said Suttree.

He'd sit by night in the light of his red roadlanterns while honeysuckle bloomed in the creek gut. Poring over obsolete city maps, tracing out a course on paper scrawled with incomprehensible runes, strange symbols, squatting, a cherrycolored troll or demon cartographer in the hellish light charting the progress of souls in the darkness below. When Suttree came up the little path through the weeds the city mouse's cat rose and stretched and went out the other side. Harrogate looked up from his work.

How's it going? said Suttree.

Hey Sut. Come on in.

He approached, not without a certain wariness here where enormities proliferated. Harrogate was dragging an old chair over the clay and dusting it off for Suttree to sit in. Suttree bent over the charts laid out on the applebox.

How's it look? said Harrogate.

How's what look?

My deal there. He gestured with one hand at the maps.

Suttree looked down at the thin pink face, teeth pink and black in the red light. He shook his head and sat in the chair and crossed his legs. Harrogate had taken up one of the charts from the table and was looking at it. I aint got no way of knowin how deep I am, he said.

You've got no way of knowing how crazy you are.

I'm goin to have to have some help.

You sure are.

I need somebody to tap or somethin. Where they think I'm at.

Where they think you're at.

Yeah.

Suttree closed his eyes. He pinched the bridge of his nose and shook his head slowly. Harrogate had bent himself once more to the work. Wielding a plastic protractor, his tongue out at the corner of his mouth, reinventing plane geometry. Suttree soon enough found himself watching over the city mouse's shoulder. By the time the cat came back he was sitting at the little crate himself, describing angles, formulas, the small face of the apprentice felon nodding at his elbow.

In the damp and alveolar deeps beneath the city he probed with a torch he'd stolen, sighting courses from stone to stone to reckon by and charting with his crazed compass a fix of compounded errors.

Down old caverns where carboncolored water leaked from overhead or treacly sipes of sewage. Through a region of ruptured ducting and old clay drains and into a dark stone gullet skewered by a jointed cesspipe. Everywhere a liquid dripping, something gone awry in the earth's organs to which this measured bleeding clocked a constantly eluded doom.

One afternoon he entered a large vault in which stood from floor to dome and slightly tilted a slender flue of cold white light. Harrogate drew back. There was a scrabbling sound overhead, dirt sifted down. A shadow stained the little figure of light on the stone floor and was snatched away. He advanced cautiously. With the beam of his flashlight he severed the shaft and watched it knit back again. It was only light, a cool bore of it standing moteless in the dark like a phosphorescent rope taut in the black of the sea's deeps. He balanced it on his palm. Through a small hole in the roof he could see the sky.

Harrogate rose by faults and ledges, the torch in his teeth. He hung by his nails from a seam in the rock, he peered out with a cautious eye. A spray of pine needles stirred against the depthless blue. A lizard scuttled, a bird. He listened. Beyond the drone of insects and the sound of the wind he thought he heard distant traffic but he was not sure. He made his way back down to the floor of the vault and squatted there tapping his fingers against his knee, the shaft of light terminating in the top of his head without apparent pain or power of inspiration.

He unfolded from his pocket the damp and thumblacked map of the city whereon he'd traced with grocer's crayon deadreckoned reaches, corrected tangents, notes on distance. He held the light above his head and fastened down a mark with his finger.

Shit if I know where I'm at, he said to the silence.

Am at, said a soft stone echo.

He folded his chart and rose. He studied the pale thin probe from the outer world and he finally climbed up and stopped the hole with his rolled map.

He never found it from the outside. After wandering about for days he came back and took the map down again. He'd brought some oily rags filched from a can at the gas station on Henley Street and he lit these in the chamber and went out. All day he looked along the edge of the city and down by the river and anywhere he could see or hope to see a pine tree. He began to suspect some dimensional displacement in these descents to the underworld, some disparity unaccountable between the above and the below. He destroyed his charts and began again.

That year there were locusts. They howled in the green trees like panthers, struggled in their fallen hundreds on the river's face.

He fell listless and enervated from histoplasmosis.

He feared in the lightless depths great rats, beveltoothed and bare of tail, spiders hairy or naked or lightly downed or partly bald, rope-shaped reptiles, their fangs, their tuningfork tongues. Their memberless economy of design. Bats hung in clusters like bunches of dark and furry fruit and the incessant drip of water echoed everywhere through the spelaean dark like dull chimes. In the pools lay salamanders cold and prone and motionless as terracotta figurines.

The matches that he struck periodically to test the air burned with an acetylene blue and he'd watch the flame draw down the matchstem and wink out and the darkness would hood him almost audibly. Sitting there with his thumb on the button of the flashlight and listening until the terror rose up in his throat and then pushing the button and creating again the filthy basilica in which he sat, the batclotted arches, the high amorphous convolutions of limestone from which scum dripped. Gray sewage percolating down through faults and bedding planes. Dark leachings from the city's undersides and speleothems accresced out of some grim slime quietly oozing in the dark.

Harrogate stepping from pool to pool of blue sludge in a tunnel where the light of his torch found trace of human work. A few old timbers black with rot, a bucket, a bone. He turned the bone in his hand, inspecting the minute chamfering of miceteeth, vermiculate scrimshaw, the brown and corallike fluting of the marrowed bore. Wherein lay a slick millipede. He dropped it clattering on the rock. The millipede ran like a train. He retrieved the bone and looked it over, holding it for size against various parts of his anatomy. Bet me, he said softly. They's somebody down here murdered.

He loaded it into a hindpocket and set forth again, his light in one hand and a clawhammer in the other, the channel narrowing, turning. A region of old timbers crossed with chalk, boards laid over the wet red clay of the cave's floor.

He was brought up by a wooden wall against which the corridor terminated neat and flush. Harrogate studied this barricade with his flashlight and he studied the wet stone ceiling and the walls. With the hammer he prized away a chunk of pulpy wood until he got the board levered up. He took it in both hands, dropping the hammer, the flashlight in his armpit illuminating odd points above his head. The board gave with a gradual springy feeling and fell at his feet. He trained the flashlight on the place. Behind the boards was a wall of solid concrete. Knotty grain and the marks of a circlesaw in the masonry. He set the claws of the hammer under the next board and pried it up and ripped it away. With the hammer he went tapping across the face of the barricade listening. The tapping went down the chamber and returned. He sat in a pile of slag and studied what to do. And were they walling in or walling out? He tapped at the empty rubber toecap of his outsize sneaker with the hammer. After a while he raised his head. Dynamite, he said.

The times that Suttree called on him now he found him deeper yet in his plottings, frowning over his charts, composing campaigns to entrap the phantoms with which he was beset.

How are you doin? he said.

Okay.

You breached the bank vaults yet?

Nope. But come here and look.

Harrogate rose from his table and went back toward the darker arches to the little concrete bunker. He beckoned with one finger.

What is it?

Come see.

Suttree approached and looked in.

Looky here, said the city mouse.

What is it?

Suttree was kneeling. He reached into the dark and felt a wooden box where cold waxed shapes like candles lay. He lifted one out and turned it to the light.

Gene, you're crazy.

That's the real shit there. Buddy boy that'll get it when Bruton Snuff wont.

You cant blow it. You dont have a detonator.

I can blow it with a shotgun shell.

I doubt it.

You keep your old ear to the ground.

Gene, you'll blow yourself up with this shit.

I thought you said I couldnt blow it?

Suttree shook his head sadly.

Hot summer nights along the river and drunkenness and tales of violence. Steps in the dead of night, hollow as the clop of hooves on the shantyporch boards where Suttree lay silent within, breathing in the dark. He heard his name said.

He lit the lamp and held it up to see the junkman at the window like a drunken burglar. He rose from the cot to let him in, steering him as he crossed the floor in his reeling step like a strange and midnight dance lesson there in the little shack.

The junkman sat, he looked up. Was you asleep?

No.

He nodded enormously, his head rising and falling a foot or more. Didnt allow ye was. I knowed ye for a night owl. You got a smoke? I'm give out.

I dont have any.

The junkman was patting his pockets.

You didnt walk all the way over here for a cigarette did you?

No.

Wasnt the Smoky Mountain open?

I dont know. You aint got a little drink laid back anywheres have ye?

I may have a beer about half warm. You want that?

Be better'n a poke in the eye with a stick.

Suttree rose and went out and took up the minnowbucket and got a beer out of it. He carried it back in the shanty and got the opener and uncapped the beer and handed it to the junkman. Harvey stalked the bottle with a veering hand and seized it and blinked and drank.

Where'd you get in the mud at?

He looked down. He appeared to be wearing puttees, slavered with mud as he was to his knees. I mired up, he said. Like to never found your place dark as it is. Like to of fell in the fuckin. He paused to belch. Fuckin river.

Do you want me to row you back over?

Harvey took a drink of the beer and eyed Suttree blearily. His face was very white and the wrinkled pouches of skin beneath his eyes looked translucent. Goin to see Dubyedee, he said. No good son of a bitch.

You dont need to see him at this hour of the night. Why dont you let me run you home.

The junkman shook his head testily. See my no good shitass brother.

If you start across that bridge the cops'll get you.

They never got me comin over.

You better wait till tomorrow.

Harvey was holding the bottle in his hands between his knees. I'll get me a goddamned pistol, he said, nodding his head.

Pistol?

Goddamn right.

You going to shoot your brother?

Fuck no. Shoot them goddamn thieves.

What, over at your lot?

Goddamned right.

Hell, they're just kids.

They're fuckin thieves. Steal anything they can get their hands on.

Why dont you just run them off?

Might as well shoot em now. Fore they get any bigger.

He took a drink of the beer and wiped his mouth with the palm of his hand. Just like girls, he said. They grow up and hit in along about thirteen or fourteen and they's a few of em start screwin everbody in town. That's ye whores. It aint that they're young. All whores is young sometime just like all thieves is. You dont wait till you're old to start peddlin your ass or stealin either one. Nip em. He paused. Nip em in the bud.

Why dont you get a watchdog?

I done had one of them.

What happened to it?

I dont know. I believe they stole it.

You better let me run you across the river.

You can run me up to Goose Creek if you want to. He was looking up and regarding Suttree in the dim lamplight with one eye squint.

You dont need to go up there.

Fuck I dont.

You can see him tomorrow.

You know what he ast me?

What?

Ast me how come it was that I was always sober enough to buy a wreck but too drunk to sell one.

Well?

Well what?

Well what's the answer?

The junkman glared at Suttree for a moment and then shook the empty bottle. You aint got another one of them have ye? he said.

I'm afraid that's it.

You reckon old Jones'd find a man a drink at this hour?

I reckon old Jones'd find a man a pumpknot on his bony head if he banged on that door after the lights were out.

Somebody'll kill that nigger one of these days.

Yes, they will.

Wonder what about Jimmy Smith?

Jimmy Smith will shoot you.

The junkman shook his head sadly at the utter truth of this. He rose unsteadily. He smiled. Well, he said. Maybe old Dubyedee will have a little drink.

You can stay here if you want.

The junkman waved a hand about. I thank ye, he said, but I best be huntin that drink. I believe a little drink'd do me more good right now than just about anything I can think of.

Suttree watched him totter down the planks in the band of yellow light. He veered, he stood with one foot, he went on. When he reached the shore he raised one hand.

Come back, called Suttree.

The junkman raised the hand again and kept going.

It was a full two miles out Blount Avenue to his brother's junklot and the junkman reeled along in the lamplight through a floating world of honeysuckle nectar and nightbird cries and distant dogs that yapped at their moorings.

He made his way across the little wooden bridge and past the dim shapes of the cars and stood before the housetrailer.

Dubyedee!

The waters of Goose Creek purled past the tirecasings and body-panels in the farther dark of the yard.

Come out you old fart.

He stumbled among the articles of their common trade. Blood black and crusted in these broken carriages. A shoe.

Dubyedee! Come out, goddamnit.

He had ceased calling and was sat within a truck when a light came on in the trailer. The door opened and light fell across the yard among the cluttered shapes and Clifford stood looking out. What do you want? he said.

Want Dubyedee. Harvey spoke through the steeringwheel spokes in which his head lay cradled.

What? said Clifford.

He raised his head. Clifford hung in the white web of the broken windshield. I want Dubyedee, he said.

He aint here.

Where's he at?

He aint here. He dont live here now.

It's just old drunk Uncle Harvey aint it?

You said it, I never.

No, you never. You smug sack of shit.

What?

I said you're a smug sack of shit.

Clifford's head turned in silhouette in the doorframe as if he'd turned to spit. He aint here, Harvey. Go on home.

He aint here Harvey. Go home Harvey. Where's he live at now?

You caint get out there. It's too far.

I'll be the judge of that. Where's he live at?

Why dont you come up and I'll give ye a cup of coffee.

Harvey shook his head. Aint you somethin, he said.

What?

I said you sure are somethin. Clifford old buddy. You sure are. Get some coffee in him. Clifford you favor your old man more than a little, did you know that?

You want some coffee I'll fix ye some. Otherwise I'm goin to bed.

Lord God, Clifford, dont let me keep ye from your sleep. I'd not do it for the world.

The figure shored up in the doorway shifted. You can sleep in the shed if you want. I'll give you the key.

You aint got a drink in there have ye?

No.

Then you aint got nothin in there I want.

The light withdrew up the path. Then it vanished from the small-paned window in the door. Harvey smiled and leaned back in the truck.

Clifford!

Dogs hereto sleeping woke with howls all down the creek.

Clifford!

The light snapped on again. The door opened.

What now, goddamnit?

You wasnt asleep was ye?

I got to work tomorrow Harvey. Some of us is got to work for a livin yet.

Is he payin ye now Clifford? Or you still just gettin your keep.

He pays me.

Big boy like you.

If you dont want nothin I'm goin to bed.

I'll tell you what I'm makin if you'll tell me what you are.

You aint makin nothin is what you're makin. Cause you dont do nothin but lay drunk.

What you are, what you are, said Harvey aimlessly.

You dont need to know.

Dont need to know, dont need to know. You sure you aint got a little drink in yonder?

I told you I'd fix you some coffee if you want it.

Let me tell you about your coffee, Clifford. You want to hear about your coffee?

Clifford didnt want to hear. He shut the door again and the lights went out.

What about your daddy, called Harvey. Want to hear about that thievin son of a bitch? Want to hear how he robbed his own brother blind? Clifford?

Lying in his cot in the early hours Suttree half asleep heard a dull concussion somewhere in the city. He opened his eyes and looked out through his small window at the paling stars, the sparse electric jewelry of the bridgelights hung above the river. Perhaps an earthquake, seams shifting deep in the earth, sand sifting for miles down blind faults in eternal dark. It did not come again and after a while he slept.

Coming back upriver in the hot noon he kept to the south shore and passed under the bridge and passed the lumber company and the packinghouse and moored the skiff at the foot of the path that led to the junkman's lot and the road beyond. A brief spate of summer rain had fallen in the morning and the smell of it in the shoreland woods rose rank and steamy like the air in a hothouse. On the narrow path he met a cluster of deferential blacks who passed sidling, their eyes cutting to and back like horses. A light clank of baitbuckets and a bristling of canes. The cars in Harvey's lot lay humped and black in the sun with visible heat rising from them in the wrinkled air. Suttree passed through a reek of milkweed and oil and hot tin toward the little bedstead gate.

He found him senseless and hanging half off the ragged army cot. The little shack smelled of grease and tarpaper and filth. Suttree took the junkman up by arm and elbow and eased him back onto the bed, solicitous yet somewhat loath to touch him in his leprous rags. Harvey rolled a whited eye and muttered and fell back. Suttree looked around the little cabin. Floor strewn with gears, axleshafts, batteries. Tottering columns of tires. A cupboard of hubcaps like curious silver, mangled and banged, painted or stamped with loutish new world crests.

He stood in the door and looked out over the junkman's lot. Tall hollyhocks by the weighted gate and dockweed blooming and begonias down along the remnants of the fence. In the corner of the lot a stand of sunflowers like some floral enormity in a child's garden. Suttree sat on the cinderblock steps. The flowers moved in the wind. He could not see the river but there was a barge going upstream through the trees like a great train of wares ferrying soundlessly by means unknown up the valley floor. On the far shore a riprap of broken marble. Rough shapes of iron rusting in the sun. In the gloom of the shack the junkman groaned and turned. One among a mass of twisted shapes discarded here by the river. Suttree turned and saw him fend with his arm some phantom, a gesture of dread such as the mad favor, his anguish no less real. Suttree rose and went out through the gate and the gate clanged gently shut behind him.

When Harrogate pulled the string on his homemade detonator he had one finger in his ear. The explosion blew him twenty feet up the tunnel and slammed him against a wall where he sat in the darkness with chunks of stone clattering everywhere about him and his eyes enormous against the unbelievable noise in which he found himself. Then he was sucked back down the tunnel in a howling rush of air, his clothes scrubbing away and peelings of hide until he found himself lying on his face in the passage with a shrieking in his ears. Before he could rise it returned and snatched him up again and scuttled him back along the floor in a cloud of dust and ash and debris and left him bleeding and halfnaked and choked and groping for something to hold to. Dont come no more, he cried aloud in the ringing vault. I done had enough. Far back through the broken wall he could hear the echoes of the blast shunting row on row down the cavern to ultimate nothingness.

He lay very quietly. He was bruised and bleeding and numb all over and he began to cry. His head was ringing and he was half deaf yet he could hear in the horrid darkness shapes emerge from the reeks and crannies, features stained with boneblack, jaws adrip. He could hear the blood running in his body and he could hear the organs working, the lungs filling and collapsing. Little girls in flowered frocks went tripping out through stiles of sunlight and their destination was darkness as is each soul's. Coming toward him was a soft near soundless mass. Sucking over the stones. Seeking him out. He pulled himself up and listened. Coming down the tunnel. Something nearing in the night. A sluggish monster freed from what centuries of stony fastness under the city. Its breath washed over him in a putrid stench. He tried to crawl. He scrabbled blindly among the stones in the dark. He was engulfed feet first in a slowly moving wall of sewage, a lava neap of liquid shit and soapcurd and toiletpaper from a breached main.

When Suttree saw the piece in the paper that said: *Earthquake?* he read and knew. He folded the paper and rose and went out the door and down the steps.

At Harrogate's there was no one home, not even the cat. He stirred the cold ashes in the firepit, he poked among the city rat's belongings.

In the afternoon he went about where the rat was known but no one knew where he could be.

It was evening when he came upon Rufus down on Front Street. He was sat in a gutterful of lamplight before the store as if he were waiting for it to open. He raised up when he saw who it was. Hey Sut, he said. How you makin it?

Just slidin, said Suttree. What are you doing?

Aw just settin. He pushed back his cap with his thumb and rubbed his head and smiled.

Suttree sat beside him on the little stone curb.

You want a drink? He canted the bottle he held to one side for the light to follow the label. They looked at the bottle together in silence. Get ye a sup. Tastes pretty good.

Suttree took the bottle and twirled off the little fluted plastic cap and hooked a good shot of it back.

Smoke rose from his noseholes.

Agh gie gie, he said.

Oh yes, said Rufus, shaking his head profoundly. It'll talk to ye. Great God.

Rufus took the bottle from him gently and supped a good sup and stood it carefully in the road before them. Suttree wiped his eyes with the balls of his fingers. The vapors seemed to have risen to his brain. Even the smell of honeysuckle that had choked the air with its hot and winey perfume and memories of summer eve was burned away. He looked at Rufus with watery eyes. Have you seen Harrogate? he said.

Harrogate? Rufus turned and jerked his head back and frowned at Suttree across his shoulder. The city mouse? Naw. He aint been round. What you wants with him?

I think he's all fucked up somewhere.

Wherever he at he's fucked up. Aint no news in that.

Did you hear that earthquake last night?

I did. Rattled the glass in my windersashes. Woke my old lady up. You hear it?

Suttree nodded.

Get ye a little old drink there, Sut.

I dont believe I can stand it.

Why that there's a nice little whiskey.

The whiskey stood in the road.

I got a old dog stobbed up in my slopbarrel, said Rufus.

Suttree nodded. His lips moved as if he were repeating this to himself.

I caint get near him to fetch him out. He keeps wantin to bite me.

How did he get in there?

Fell in I reckon. Eatin my slops. I aint tippin out my slops for no fool ass dog.

No.

I remember from when I was a boy down in Loudon County and I had this uncle used to make whiskey all the time. We went up to his still one evenin and he had five barrel of mash settin around on the ground workin and we got up there and in ever barrel one they was a old hound. They was stobbed up in them mashbarrels to they neck and they was drunk and just a singing to beat the band. You never seen a more pleasant sight. We set on the ground and laughed and the more we laughed the louder they'd sing and the more they sung the louder we'd laugh.

How did you get them out?

We cut us a green hickory and run it through they collars and got one either end and snaked em out. They was some might too drunk to walk hardly.

Well why dont we get this one out of your mashbarrel like that?

He aint got no collar on.

I see. Well why dont we get a rope on him and haul him out?

We might could try it. I hate to go up there at all.

Why is that?

Old lady's put out with me.

Well you got to go sometime.

I know it. But sometimes I just purely hate it.

Come on. You cant sit down here all night.

Suttree stood up and Rufus rose and dusted the sag of his trouserseat with two handswipes and stooped, tilted, recovered, seized the bottle and reared upright. Beat no drink atall, dont ye? he said to the bottle.

They labored up the switchback path through the kudzu and came out in a dark little lane. It was a clear night and they walked slowly and the black man would pause again before they reached the house to take another drink and restore the bottle to the pocket of his ample trousers. Suttree could smell above the honeysuckle a sour reek from the hoglot like the smell of vomit. Through the vines stood a windowlight. Rufus held up one finger and they paused and consulted.

Let me get my lannern.

Okay.

Suttree crouched in the lane. He heard a door open and close and then in a moment he heard a high shrieking voice that seemed to speak in a tongue unknown to him. The door opened and Rufus came from the porch holding up the lantern and adjusting the wick.

They walked out past the shed and Rufus lifted a nail out of the hasp-staple on the smokehouse door and entered and reappeared with a hank of coarse rope. They went on along a fence patched up from scraps of board and tin. Something scuttled off among the weeds. A hog grunted in the dark. Rufus held the lantern up and in the light Suttree saw the dog's eyes.

Yonder he is.

Suttree took the lantern and approached the dog. A sodden hound with wet bread hanging from his head, stogged to the neck in a slopdrum. He had his forepaws on the rim of the drum and as Suttree approached he bared his teeth in the lamplight.

Cant he get out? said Suttree.

He dont appear able. I see him rear up a time or two but he caint get pulled loose enough from that slop to jump.

Well hand me that rope.

Watch you dont get too close. He'll growl and make at ye.

Hold the lantern.

You watch him now.

Suttree fetched an empty drum and stood it bottom up alongside the dog and stood on it. The dog turned to face him. He made a noose in the rope and dropped it over the dog's head and the dog's teeth closed on the air with a dull wet chop. When he felt the rope tighten about his neck he began to moan.

Suttree doubled the rope in his fist and began to haul on the dog. The dog's eyes rolled wildly and it began to scrabble at the drum.

Great God this son of a bitch is heavy.

It rose strangled and dripping from the barrel and slid over the side and collapsed in a foul wet mass on the ground.

They stood watching it, Suttree on the drum holding the lantern. It looked like some strange medieval beast lying there gasping and stinking. Suttree steered the rope off the hound's neck and after a while it rose and shook itself and staggered off heavily through the honeysuckles.

Suttree coiled the rope save for the fouled noose of it and dragging this behind they went back up the path and sat on the porch. Rufus snuffed the lantern and leaned back against the post and closed his eyes. Then he opened them and patted his pocket where the bottle lay and then he closed them again. You caint see his lights now, growed up like it is, he said.

Whose lights?

The city mouse. When it's growed up thisaway you caint see over yonder. I dont know if he been there or not.

I dont believe he was there last night.

He might of got off drunk with Cleo and them. They gives him whiskey all the time.

Suttree nodded. Across the gut the lights of the city lay staggered on the night. You know any caves around here? he said.

Rufus opened his eyes. Caves? he said.

Do you know any?

They's a big cave yon side of the river. Cherokee cave.

I mean on this side.

They's caves all in under Knoxville.

Do you know how to get into them?

You dont want to mess around in no caves. What you wants to mess around down in under the ground for?

If you dont tell me how to get in those caves I'm going to get that dog and put him back in your slopbarrel.

Rufus grinned. He straightened out one leg across the porch and reached in his pocket for the bottle. Sheeit, he said.

I may get two dogs.

Harrogate wounded and covered in shit found in his pocket a pennybox of matches and a candlestub and made a light. The slender flame leaned and fluttered. He groped in the sewage for his flashlight, up and down the passage. When he found it he fetched it up and shook it and worked the button back and forth but it would not light. He knelt there looking about at the stone walls surrounding. Hot wax ran on his hand and he scratched at it absently. He began to clamber back up the tunnel toward higher ground.

He bathed himself in a black pool while the candle grew squat. Checked his injuries. Dismantled and put back the flashlight and tried it. Unscrewed the bezel that held the lens, took out the bulb and held it to the candlelight but he could not see wires or no wires. He watched the candle. It wasnt dripping. It just looked as if it were being sucked down through the stone.

He left it burning there and went as far as the edge of the light, his small shadow swallowed up finally in the greater dark beyond. He turned and came back. He squatted and watched the flame totter. The dank stone room grew smaller, drew in about him. He crouched in the smallest cup of light with his hands joined at the back of the flame as if he would gather it to him. Hot oil ran on the stones. The wick toppled and dropped with a thin hiss and dark closed over him so absolute that he became without boundary to himself, as large as all the universe and small as anything that was.

Suttree went by a wellrope down a dry brick cistern. Odor of earth and moss, the old brick dark and crumblesome. The floor of the cistern had fallen in and he went down a tailing of rubble and broken brick into a hole in the earth. He turned on the flashlight he carried and stepped down into the darkness.

He followed a narrow passage where the floor was mud and strewn with old bottleglass. The walls inscribed with names and dates scratched in the soft wet stone. The corridor narrowed and gave onto a drafty blackness where his light went from wall to far wall, an enormous and slaggy tureen traversed by plumbing. Great jointed runs of sewerpipe and tubes of cable cold and wet. He entered warily. No sound but a distant timeless dripping. He listened for any faint sound of traffic in the streets above but that world seemed gone altogether. The grotto lay like a sea cave, smooth and curving, a thing shaped to hold the wind where no wind was. He turned, his light going along the walls, the muddy flowstone and the high domed roof where hung stone teeth and tongues of wet black slag. He crossed the room, patches of dark sludge in the floor like pools of tar. At the far side a round tunnel went on through the rock and Suttree stooping followed after.

He searched the underground until he thought it must be evening and when he emerged again at the foot of the cistern he was surprised to find the day hardly half spent. He looked back down the cistern but he had no heart for going there again.

That evening he visited Harrogate's diggings under the bridge but there was no sign he'd been there. He ran his trotlines before daybreak in the morning and went again to search for him.

He checked out narrow side passages and he watched the little mudspits in the cave's stone floors for footprints but there seemed to have been no travelers here for years. The names and dates on the stone grew old. Cimmerians passed on without progeny. Some lack of adventure in the souls of newer folk or want of the love of darkness. His light ran over the ceilings, the carinated domes, stone scallopings and random hanging spires. The ribbed palate of a stone monster comatose, a great uvula dripping rust. Blades of false cuspidine. Hematite deep burgundy and loded with iron, clotted in the shape of stone offal. Or malachite in green coprolitic stools like small stone turds becrept a brassy green.

He found pale newts with enormous eyes and held them cold and quailing in his palm and watched their tiny hearts hammer under the blue and visible bones of their thimblesized briskets. They gripped his finger childlike with their tiny spatulate palps.

At the end of the day he came upon pieces of light in an upper wall of the tunnel and he squatted and listened and he thought he heard very faint and far the cries of children. He switched off the light and sat in the dark. He sat there for some time. The children's voices went away. The three shapes of light on the floor of the cavern began to climb the farther wall. After a while he rose and went with his own light back the way he'd come.

On the fourth day he found footprints in a patch of gray loam. Tennis shoe tracks and big ones at that. He set his own shoe inside. A little further he found a fresh candybar wrapper. He passed through a large cavern where bats lined the roof, their leather elbows jostling in their sleep, a constant reedy murmuring of squeaks like those numberless cries that Bishop Hatto must have heard in his tower prior to being consumed by mice. Suttree pressed on, down the carious undersides of the city, through black and slaverous cavities where foul liquors seeped. He had not known how hollow the city was.

The air was becoming more tainted, a rising sulphur reek of sewage. Where this smell thickened worst he found the city mouse crouching. He was leaning against a wall and looking back down the tunnel toward the beam of light approaching. He looked like something that might leap up and scurry off down a hole. Suttree squatted in front of him and looked him over.

How about gettin that light out of my eyes, said Harrogate.

Suttree lowered the light. Their faces were blackened like miners or minstrels and the city mouse wore only shreds of clothing and he was covered with dried sewage. True news of man here below. He was looking down at the pool of light.

I thought I was dead. I thought I'd die in this place.

Are you all right?

There was people down here.

What?

There was people down here.

You were seeing things.

I talked to em.

Let's go.

I hate for anybody to see me like this.

Suttree shook his head.

I'd give ten dollars for a glass of icewater, said the city mouse. Cash money.

Suttree would see her in the street, dawn hours before the world's about. A hookbacked crone going darkly and bent in a shapeless frock of sacking dyed dead black with logwood chips and fustic mordant. Her spider hands clutching up a shawl of morling lamb. Gimpen granddam hobbling through the gloom with your knobbly cane go by, go by. Over the bridge in the last hours of night to gather herbs from the bluff on the river's south shore.

He saw Jones all these summer evenings. Sat with friends under a caged windscrew the size of a plane's prop and in the howling wind drank dripping beers and watched the cardplayers in their wet shirts mutter and smoke and deal. Jones spoke no more of the witch. Then one evening he leaned toward Suttree where he sat at the small marble table. Say she wont come down here? He said.

Who.

He snuffled. His eyes shifted but he seemed to be watching the cardtable. That old nigger witch, he said.

Ah, said Suttree. That's what she says.

The black nodded.

Why dont you go up and see her?

He shrugged.

She said it wasnt yourself you wanted to see her about.

He looked at Suttree and looked back to the table again. Who she say I want to see her about.

Your enemies.

Ah, said Jones.

They went in the evening through the locust wood, insects so named screaming in the greenery, beneath great blooms of newsprint and into the steaming sink.

She was tending her garden, stooped with a hoe, a figure the size of a child. The homedyed black of her gown fugitive at back and shoulders from the sun. When she saw them she raised up and went into the house. They crossed the yard. Past the little rows of tomato plants and late runner beans. Suttree tapped at the door and they stood looking out at the little glade. After a while he tapped again.

When she came to the door she was bareheaded and she wore her spectacles. She stood aside for them to enter as if they'd been expected.

They followed her down the little hall in all but darkness toward an open door beyond which stood a table and a lamp burning. Jones stooped to enter, Suttree followed. They stood in the kitchen. Suttree looked about. The walls were hung with pictures, the pictureglass all dull with grease. He bent to study a clan of blacks, some thirty or more all formally aligned, old patriarchs and men and women and small children peering out and in the center seated and shawled what appeared to be a scorched rhesus monkey.

She was standing across the room and the light was poor and she could not have rightly known which photograph among the many he was looking at and yet she said: She was born in seventeen and eighty-seven.

Who is she?

My grandmama. She was a hunnerd and two when she died.

She looks almost that old in the picture.

She's dead in the picture.

Suttree looked at her. The goldwire frames catching the light, the little round panes of glass. He leaned to see the picture again. Someone in the photograph behind the grandmother was holding her head up and her eyes were glazed and sightless. Suttree could not stop looking at this cracked and lacquered scene from times so fabled. The hands at the neck of the creature seemed to be forcing her to look at something she had rather not see and was it Suttree himself these sixty-odd years hence?

Are you in the picture? he said.

I aint in it. That was in Fayette County Kentucky. They kep her in a rootcellar till they could fetch the man to come and take the picture. Her children set with her down there of a night with candles.

Was that before you were born?

No. I was there. I never come out in the picture. I was there when it was took but I never come out.

Where were you in the picture?

Right yonder in that dead place.

He bent to see. On the far right there was a grayed-out patch, a ghost in the photo among her pellagrous predecessors. Here? he said.

She nodded, the little spectacles winking in the lamplight. Set down, she said.

Suttree sat beneath the picture. Jones was still standing almost in the middle of the little room and he seemed suddenly mindless, a great tottering zombie that she must take by one elbow and steer to the table although he has been here before. She's sewn him up like a hound with carpetthread and the blood beading very fine and bright from the pursings of black flesh, stanching lesser holes with cataplasms of cobweb, binding him in bedlinen. With him drunk at the door two days later demanding to be undone and sewn looser because he could not bend. Eyes raddled with blood, reeking of splo whiskey.

He sat. The crowned tooth of flame shifted and reshaped within the glass. Her neckware winked, tin amulets, a toadstone, an ebon baal that hung from a necklace of braided hair. She spread her hands. Under the black and dusky skin you could see how the fingerhinges were fashioned, the lean and jointed bonepipes. She said: I dont know which of these two souls is the worst troubled. Let me see your hand.

Jones laid his hand on the table. Fingers like old bananas, that fat, that brown. She sat slowly and took the hand palm up in her dark little claws and shut her eyes. Then she looked down at it. She bent closer. What's that? she said.

Jones looked. That aint nothin. Just where I took a knife off of some fool.

She pressed his seamy palm with her fingertips. She leaned back. Suttree was studying a photograph above the table to his right. A black boy in uniform who has watched the camera with some suspicion of his own expendability. The old woman said: You wants him here?

The youngblood? The youngblood can stay.

She bent forward and her eyes opened and her mouth made a little popping noise like a turtle's. Gimme five dollah, she said.

Jones raised one hip and reached into his pocket. He brought out a large roll of bills fastened with a rubber band and he dealt a five onto the tabletop. She took it and folded it and it disappeared somewhere about her person and she took his hand again. She began to recount for him aspects of his past. Legends of violence, affrays with police, bleeding in concrete rooms and anonymous coughing and groans and delirium in the dark.

Jones looked up. I aint interested in all that, he said. I just dont want to leave Quinn here and me gone.

You caint buy that.

I caint buy it with five dollar.

A flickering look of impatience in her blueblack face. She told a tale of retribution, silver seals but cannot buy such powers.

She has bored a keep in a treebole and hid therein the dung of her enemy and plugged it shut with an oakwood bung. She leans to them in terrible confidence: His guts swoll like a blowed dog. He couldnt get no relief. His stool riz up in his neck till he choken on it and he turn black in the face and his guts bust open and he die a horrible death a screamin and floppin in his own mess.

Jones nodded. He said that that would suit him fine. Suttree smiled against the back of his hand but the ogress waggled a finger before them both. She rose and went to a cupboard above the cookstove, climbing with surprising agility from a chair to the top of the stove and reaching up and taking down a small and moldy leather poke. She brought it with her to the table and she spread over the naked boards a cloth of black damask, smoothing the creases with hands as black, more deeply creased. She sat with her hands folded so and she rolled her soapy old eyes at them. She took up the pouch and held it and closed her eyes. Her fingers undid the mouth of the little bag and when the strings hung loose she held it clenched by the neck as if what crouched inside might otherwise out. She began to sway lightly back and forth and she was holding her head up very stiffly and something was moving in the black folds of her throatskin as if she were swallowing repeatedly. Suddenly she opened her eyes and looked about and with a motion almost violent raised the leather bag and upended it over the table. Out clattered toad and bird bones, yellow teeth, frail shapes of ivory strange or nameless, a small black heart dried hard as stone. A joint from a snake's spine, the ribs curved like claws. A bat's skull with needleteeth agrin, the little pterodactyl wingbones. Tiny pestles of polished riverstone. These things lay shapen still and final upon the black damask and the dark gospeler of their constellation who would in moments now postulate the denial of the old lie that beholder and beheld are ever more than one, this dusky fugitive of the pyre with whom they trafficked studied the figures briefly and looked away. Looked away, let shut the seamy doors of her eyes. They sat in silence.

Jones spoke. He said: What do it say?

About you it dont.

About Quinn then.

It dont say. It aint you nor Quinn neither. It's him.

Suttree felt the skin on his scalp pucker.

Why aint it me? said Jones.

I caint make it be if it aint.

Do it again.

No.

Jones blinked heavily.

You should of come alone, she said. She still had her eyes shut and Suttree thought that she was talking to Jones but when she opened them she was looking at him.

He did not go back. He passed her in the street one evening toward the summer's end but she might have been any black crone at all, stooped and shawled and silent save for the shuffling of her feet in the gutter. She did not look up nor did she speak and he could smell her on the night wind, lank harridan, a stale musty odor, dust dry. She passed in a light creaking of bones, dried bulb ends grating in their cups. Stranger yet he saw her a final time that year in the streets uptown in the full light of noon and she did look at him. Suttree shunned those adder's eyes in which the sun lay split. She has borne her wares in a catskin bag through the brick alleyways and tarpaper lanes. Something moved her mouth very like a smile. The antique teeth like seedcorn. An odor of violated graves. Her small shadow fell against him like a bird and she passed on. He stood looking after. Five fingers to five pressing he constructed a tactile plate of glass between his fingertips. Then he turned and went on. Give over, Graymalkin, there are horsemen on the road with horns of fire, with withy roods. He ran among the crowds dodging and veering. The jar of his heels on the pavement kept stopping the fans that spun above the shop-doors.

In late October he pulled his lines. Leaves were falling in the river and the days of windy rain and woodsmoke took him back to other times more than he would have liked. He made himself up a pack from old sacking and rolled his blanket and with some rice and dried fruit and a fishline he took a bus to Gatlinburg.

He hiked up into the mountains. The season had gone before, some trees gone barren, none still green. He spent the night on a ledge above the river and all night he could hear the ghosts of lumber trains, a liquid clicking and long shunt and clatter and the jargon of old rusted trucks on rails long gone. The first few dawns half made him nauseous, he'd not seen one dead sober for so long. He sat in the cold gray light and watched, mummied up in his blanket. A small wind blew. A rack of clouds troweled across the east grew mauve and yellow and the sun came boring up. He was moved by the utter silence of it. He turned his back to the warmth. Yellow leaves were falling all through the forest and the river was filled with them, shuttling and winking, golden leaves that rushed like poured coins in the tailwater. A perishable currency, forever renewed. In an old grandfather time a ballad transpired here, some love gone wrong and a sabletressed girl drowned in an icegreen pool where she was found with her hair spreading like ink on the cold and cobbled river floor. Ebbing in her bindings, languorous as a sea dream. Looking up with eyes made huge by the water at the bellies of trout and the well of the rimpled world beyond.

Suttree lay on a warm rock above the river and watched the trout drift and quarter over the cold gray stones. He had baited his small hook with ricegrains. The trout stood or sidled or turned among the pouring leaves. Bulltrout with rutwarped snouts, pale trout with velvet fins. They would not bite.

First he left the roads, then the trails. Small creeks half dry in this late season now the rains have gone. Scrambling up a stone throat pool to pool he saw a mink go black and bowbacked limping over the rocks. Dark mucronate droppings steaming on a shalepane replete with bones, scales, shellshards. At night a high cold wind sucked the fire he squatted by in the eye of the dark. A thin wind, thin air, hard to breathe and bitter cold.

In the morning turning up the frostveined stones for bait he uncovered a snake. Soporific, sleek viper with flanged jawhinges. Fate ridden snake, of all stones in the forest this one to sleep beneath. Suttree could not tell if it watched him or not, little brother death with his quartz goat's eyes. He lowered the stone with care.

That afternoon he crossed the watershed and started down through a dark spruce forest. Ravens flew over the vast high country, the slopes falling away all heather and gray weather wood into the clouds below. He made a fire beneath a shelf of rock and watched a storm close over the valley down there, ragged hot wires of lightning quaking in the dusk like voltage in some mad chemist's chambers. Rain fell, leaves fell, slantwise and wild, a silver storm blowing down the eaves of the world. He'd found a few wild chestnuts and he watched them blacken in the coals. He cracked and cooled them. All things contained of tree therein, leaf and root. He ate. He'd no food other and he thought his hunger would keep him awake but it didnt. He could hear the long wild sough of the wind in the high forest as he lay there in his blanket staring up at the heavens. The cold indifferent dark, the blind stars beaded on their tracks and mitered satellites and geared and pinioned planets all reeling through the black of space.

In the morning there was snow at the higher elevations, a fairyland dust on the peaks. He had bound up his feet with the crokersack and now he simply wrapped the blanket about his shoulders and went down along the ridge, a hermetic figure, already gaunted and sunken at the eyes, a week's beard. Going shrouded in his blanket through the forest beswirled about by cold gray mist, gray weather, cold dày, moss the color of stone. The wind sharp in the dry bores of his nostrils. Down through the pale bare bones of a birch forest where the claw-shaped leaves he trod held little ferns of ice.

Below him ravens rode up like things of wire and crepe weightless on the updrafts. They rocked and wheeled and slid away over the high vast emptiness with lost windmuted croaks.

Suttree in the woods was surprised to find small flowers still. He fell into silent studies over the delicate loomwork in the moss. Annular forms of lichens fiery green that sprawled across the stones like tiny jade volcanoes. The scalloped fungus that ledged old rotted logs, flangeous mammary growths with a visceral consistency and pale indianpipes in pulpy clusters among the debris of humus and rich decay and mushrooms with serrate and membraneous soffits whereunder toads are reckoned to siesta. Or elves, he said. In breeks of kingscord, shirts paned up of silk tailings, no color like the rest. A curious light lay in the forest. He was squatting in the rich and murky earth, the blanket about his shoulders. He wondered could you eat the mushrooms, would you die, do you care. He broke one in his hands, frangible, mauvebrown and kidneycolored. He'd forgotten he was hungry.

He came down an old logging road past the ruins of a CCC camp and swung through the woods toward a stone bridge beyond the sere or barren trees. The road crossed above. The river path went through the low stone arch along a bar of silt where blackened turds lay by pale wet clots of tissuepaper.

When they were building the highway through the mountains a horseman came this way along the river, the gravel peppering the water behind the horse's heels and the horse lined out lean and flat and the rider wide-eyed with the reins clutched. Two boys fishing from the bridge watched him clatter down and pass beneath. They crossed to the other side of the bridge to see him go but the horse was downriver with the stirrups kicking out loose and it ran riderless out on the gravel bar and into the river in an explosion of steam. A pale breadth of buckskin flank turning in the cold green pool.

The rider did not appear. They found him dangling by his skull from a steel rod that jutted from the new masonry, swinging slightly, his hands at his sides and his eyes slightly crossed as if he would see what was the nature of this thing that had skewered his brains.

Suttree went up the narrow valley and deeper into the mountains. Over old dry riverbeds of watershapen stones that lay in the floor of the wood. His beard grew long and his clothes fell from him like the leaves. At these high altitudes the trees were stunted spruce and dark and twisted and nothing moved save he and the wind and the ravens. The spruce trees stood black and bereaved of dimension in the shadow of the high cloven draws, against the sky processional and nunlike ascending in the dusk.

He'd taken to sleeping more and the walking made him dizzy. He'd watch the fire for hours, the curious incandescent world of settling embers, small orange grottoes and the way the wood looked molten there or half translucent. He had begun to become accompanied.

First in dreams and then in states half wakeful. One day in the full light of autumn noon he saw an elvish apparition come from the woods and go down the trail before him half ajog and worried of aspect. Suttree sat in the moss and rested. The woods looked too green for the season. Before two days more had gone he hardly knew if he dreamt or not. Lying on a gravel bar with the tips of his fingers in the icy water he could see his face above the sandy creek floor, a shifting visage hard by its own dark shadow. He stretched himself and bowed his lips and sucked from the passing water. Taste of iron and moss and a silken weight on his tongue. A newt, small, olive, paintspattered, arrowed off downside a rock toward the bubbled green of the deeper pool. The water sang in his head like wine. He sat up. A green and reeling wall of laurel and the stark trees rising. Articulating in the slight lift of the forest wind some arboreal mute's alphabet. Pins of light near blue were coming off the stones. Suttree felt a deep and chilling lassitude go by nape and shoulderblades. He slumped and crossed his wrists in his lap. He looked at a world of incredible loveliness. Old distaff Celt's blood in some back chamber of his brain moved him to discourse with the birches, with the oaks. A cool green fire kept breaking in the woods and he could hear the footsteps of the dead. Everything had fallen from him. He scarce could tell where his being ended or the world began nor did he care. He lay on his back in the gravel, the earth's core sucking his bones, a moment's giddy vertigo with this illusion of falling outward through blue and windy space, over the offside of the planet, hurtling through the high thin cirrus. His fingers clutched up wet handfuls from the bar, polished lozenges of slate, small cold and mascled granite teardrops. He let them fall through his fingers in a smooth clatter. He could feel the oilless turning of the earth beneath him and the cup of water lay in his stomach as cold as when he drank it.

That evening he passed through a children's cemetery set in a bench of a hillside and forlorn save by weeds. The stone footings of a church nearby was all the church there was and leaves fell few and slowly, here and here, him reading the names, the naked headboards all but perished in the weathers of seasons past, these tablets tilted or fallen, titles to small plots of earth against all claiming. A storm had followed him for days. He turned in an ashen twilight, crossing this garden of the early dead by weeds the wind has sown. Brown jasmine among the nettles. He saw small figurines composed of dust and light turn in the broken end of a bottle, spidersized marionettes in some minute ballet there in the purple glass so lightly strung with strands of cobweb floss. A drop of rain sang on a stone. Bell loud in the wild silence. Harried mute and protestant over the darkening windy fields he saw go with no surprise mauve monks in cobwebbed cowls and sandals hacked from ruined boots clapping along in a rude shuffle down small cobbled ways into an old stone town. Storm birds rode up dark and chattering and burst away like ash and mice were going down their homeward furrows like tailed shot.

He crossed in the twilight a pitchgreen wood grown murk with ferns, with rank and steaming plants. An owl flew, bow winged and soundless. He came upon the bones of a horse, the polished ribcradle standing among the ferns pale and greenly phosphorescent and the wedgeshaped skull grinning in the grass. In these silent sunless galleries he'd come to feel that another went before him and each glade he entered seemed just quit by a figure who'd been sitting there and risen and gone on. Some doublegoer, some othersuttree eluded him in these woods and he feared that should that figure fail to rise and steal away and were he therefore to come to himself in this obscure wood he'd be neither mended nor made whole but rather set mindless to dodder drooling with his ghosty clone from sun to sun across a hostile hemisphere forever.

That night he did not even make a fire. He crouched like an ape in the dark under the eaves of a slate bluff and watched the lightning. Down there in the wood the birchtrunks shone palely and troops of ghost cavalry clashed in an outraged sky, old spectral revenants armed with rusted tools of war colliding parallactically upon each other like figures from a mass grave shorn up and girdled and cast with dread import across the clanging night and down remoter slopes between the dark and darkness yet to come. A vision in lightning and smoke more palpable than wortled bone or plate or pauldron shelled with rot.

The storm moved off to the north. Suttree heard laughter and sounds of carnival. He saw with a madman's clarity the perishability of his flesh. Illbedowered harlots were calling from small porches in the night, in their gaudy rags like dolls panoplied out of a dirty dream. And along the little ways in the rain and lightning came a troupe of squalid merrymakers bearing a caged wivern on shoulderpoles and other alchemical game, chimeras and cacodemons skewered up on boarspears and a pharmacopoeia of hellish condiments adorning a trestle and toted by trolls with an eldern gnome for guidon who shouted foul oaths from his mouthhole and a piper who piped a pipe of ploverbone and wore on his hip a glass flasket of some smoking fuel that yawed within viscid as quicksilver. A mesosaur followed above on a string like a fourlegged garfish heliumfilled. A tattered gonfalon embroidered with stars now extinct. Nemoral halfworld inhabitants, figures in buffoon's motley, a gross and blueblack foetus clopping along in brogues and toga. Attendants attend. Suttree watched these puckish revelers pass with a half grin of wry doubt. Dark closed about him. The lightning lapsed away and he could hear the grass kneeling in the wind. He raked leaves to him in his arms and struck a match with fingers stiff and fumblesome. They crackled along the edges and small hot sparks went singing down the wind. He tried again and gave it up. He curled into his blanket there on the high cold ground and he knew he should be cold but he had not been so for days.

In this condition the next morning he passed a deerstand where a small man in overalls crouched with a crossbow. Suttree paid him no more mind than any other apparition and would go on but that the man spoke to him. Hey, he said.

Hey, said Suttree.

The hunter had the crossbow pointed Suttree's way and he cocked his head. What are you? he said.

Suttree began to laugh. He let his blanket fall from his shoulders and he bent from the waist laughing.

The hunter looked anxious at this. Hush, he said. Quit that.

Okay.

The man spat. It dont make no difference noway, he said. You've done run everthing off.

Are you real? said Suttree.

I didnt mean to thow down on ye thataway, said the crossbowman vailing his piece. He looked the traveler over. Not that I aint proud to be heeled and such a crazy thing as you look run loose in these woods. How long ye been scoutin thisaway?

I dont know.

Are ye lost?

I think I know what state I'm in. I doubt you can direct me out of it.

You're lost or crazy or both.

Quite so.

You wouldnt tell on a feller for poachin him a little deermeat would ye?

I dont dine at the king's table, said Suttree.

The hunter spat to one side and shook his head at Suttree. You're loony as a didapper, he said.

At least I exist, said the wanderer. He wafted up the hem of his blanket and gestured at the hunter with it. Begone, he said.

The hunter recoiled and brought his crossbow up again.

Begone I say, said Suttree, shucking the tattered blanket at him.

Why you dipshit idjit if anybody begones anywhere it'll be you with a arrowbolt up your skinny ass.

Suttree batted his eyes. Are you real? he said.

Damned if you aint beyond the bend in a queer road. Where'd you up from anyways?

From over the mountain.

What are you, a yankee or somethin?

I'll tell you what I'm not.

What's that?

A figment. I'm not a figment.

A what?

A figment. A frigging figment. He crooned a weird laugh. The hunter stared at him.

What have you there? said Suttree.

A little sense for one thing.

Is that a crossbow?

I've heard it called that.

How many crosses have you killed with it?

It's killed more meat than you could bear.

Shoot it.

What for?

I want to see. You shoot it.

I think I'll just keep it strung and handy.

Suttree rose from where he'd squatted. Pale liver spots listed across his vision. The woods had grown dim.

It's snowing, he said.

A delicate host expired on his filthy cuff. He pulled the blanket closer. He looked down at himself, at the rags of crokersack, the spats of knitting that had been his socks, at the twill trousers black with woodash, the bulbed green knees of them hanging. He had a beard an inch long and his hair was wild and matted with leaves and the eyes the hunter watched were black and crazed and smoking.

How do I get out of here? he said.

Where is it you're headed?

Out of these mountains.

Well, you're about nine mile from Cherokee.

Which way?

Right yon way. You'll come to the road about two mile.

Thank you.

You run crazy in these woods regular do ye?

No, said Suttree. This is my first time.

He did not come to the road. Coming down a stony draw through green and well nigh lightless grottoes where lay stones and windfall trees alike anonymous beneath the mantled moss he saw cross through a bosky glen two equine phantoms pale with purpose: one, the next, and gone in the dark of the forest. Suttree stumbled out of the woods onto a bridlepath. Faint smell of stables. Broken green horseturds steamed in the cold of the humus earth. He followed the path until it began to veer back toward the mountains and then he entered the woods again.

Nor was he out of them that evening. The snow had not stopped falling and he sat in the feathered darkness and heard it sifting through the woods with just the faintest whisper. He drowsed and woke and nodded off again. He wondered would he freeze, sitting there under a balsam tree watching the snow encroach toward his toes. The rich smell of the branches and the needles in which he sat carried him back to old Christmases, those sad seasons. He dreamed sad dreams and woke bitter and rueful. The snow had stopped and the trees stood stark against a paler sky. With first light he rose and went on.

All day this halfmad outcast staggered through the snow and what a baleful heart he harbored and how dear to him. In midafternoon he came upon a freshet and he turned downstream, his breath pluming. He could smell the water. Going down through the snow where ice tines hung from boughs above their replicas in graygreen pools like jaws from fierce jurassic carnivores. Until late in the day he came out of the snow and crossed through a broad bottomland where the ground gave wet and spongy underneath. In his darker heart a nether self hulked above cruets of ratsbane, a crumbling old grimoire to hand, androleptic vengeances afoot for the wrongs of the world. Suttree muttering along half mindless, an aberrant journeyman to the trade of wonder.

He was wandering in a swampy wood, a landscape of cane and alder where gray reeks swirled. Cognate shapes among the vapors urged him on and in this sad glen under a pale sun he felt he'd grown improbable of succor and he began to run. Headlong through the bracken and briers in whose crushed wake he left small tattered stars of the rags he wore. Until at last he washed up in a little glade and fell to his knees gasping. Clouds lay remote and motionless across the evening sky like milt awash in some backwater of the planet's seas and a white woodcock rose from the ferns before him and dissolved in smoke.

A curling bit of down cradled in this green light for the sake of my sanity. Unreal and silent bird albified between the sun and my broken mind godspeed.

He woke in full daylight by the side of a road. A truck had passed. Leaves stirred about him. He struggled up. His blanket lay in the ditch. His head was curiously clear.

The town that he came to was Bryson City North Carolina. He passed a shabby tourist court and went down the sidewalk in his blanket peering about at the sudden tawdry garishness in which he found himself. At the maze of small town mercenary legend, the dusty shopwindows, the glass bulb of a gaspump. Cars slowed in passing him. He entered the first cafe he came to and sat slowly in a booth. Some stark and darker bearded visage peered him back from the shiny black formica of the tabletop. Some alien Suttree there among the carven names and rings and smears of other men's meals.

What for ye? said a leery matron.

The menu. I dont have a menu.

The old bird's eyes honed by past injustices to a glint just between suspicion and outrage swept over him and to the wall.

Yonder it is.

He looked. Chalk script on a slate. Country steak, he said. Mashed potatoes and beans. Cornbread. And bring me a cup of coffee.

You get three vegetables.

He looked again. Let me have the apples, he said.

She finished writing and padded off on her white wedgeheeled shoes to the rear of the place. In the cameral shutting of the kitchen door he saw a black hand picking at the seat of a pair of greasy jeans. A dark wood clock above the door told a time of two twenty. Suttree seized the water tumbler she'd left and drank. A long cold drink laced with chlorine. His head swam. A pall of fried grease hung in the room. He rose from the booth and went to the counter and got a newspaper and came back. He looked in the upper corner for the date but there was none.

Whoever heard of a newspaper with no date, he said aloud, tearing open the sheets. Here. December third. How long is that?

He stared blankly across the empty dining hall. A huge and blackened trout hung bowed on a board above the counter and knew not. Nor the naked leather squirrel with the vitreous eyebulbs. A dull wooden clicking he'd thought some long coiled component of his forelobe together with the fading colored pictures and the receding attendance of horribles segued into a shrunken indian passing across the glass of the cafe front and the dull tocking of applewood clockworks from above the door. He turned to the paper. A rash of incomprehensible events. He could put no part of it together.

The kitchen door swung out and she came bearing coffee. A thick rimmed cup of sepia crockery. Beads of grease veered on the dishing meniscus of inky fluid it held. He poured cream copiously from a tin pitcher and laced in sugar and stirred. The smell of it flooded his brain and when he sipped it it seemed like an odd thing to drink. He sipped again. The waitress reared above the rim of the cup. He leaned back. A plate of corn muffins fell before him. A small oblong platter with thick flour gravy wherein lay a slab of waffled beef and the vegetables. Suttree could hardly lift his fork. He buttered one of the muffins and bit into it. His mouth was filled with a soft dry sawdust. He tried to chew. His jaws worked the mass slowly. He tried to spit it out and could not. He reached in his mouth and fished it forth with his fingers in thick clogs of paste which he raked off on the side of the platter. He cut away a section of the steak with his fork and eased it past his teeth. His eyes closed. He could taste nothing. His throatpipe seemed grown shut.

He mouthed the piece of meat like an old gummy man, dry smacking sounds. The waitress moved about the room refilling saltcellars, her eyes on him. He caught her watching from the sideboard. He spat in the plate.

Is there something wrong with me? he demanded.

She looked away.

What is this crap?

Other people eat it, she said.

He stabbed at the potatoes with his fork. The imago does not eat, he told the plate mutteringly. Fuck it. He let the fork fall and looked up at the waitress.

Will you take this away and bring me some soup.

You'll have to pay for it.

Suttree watched her with his fevery eyes.

If you didnt want it you ought not to of ordered it, she said.

Will you please bring me some goddamned soup like I asked?

She turned and stalked off to the kitchen. He pushed the plate from him and laid his head on the table.

A hand jostled his elbow. Suttree jerked upright.

What's the matter here? said a man in cook's whites. The waitress hovered behind.

What do you mean what's the matter?

Did you cuss her?

No.

He's a damned liar. He did too do it.

I asked her to bring me some soup.

He cussed me and his dinner and everthing else.

We dont allow no cussin in here and we dont allow no trouble. Now let's go.

He had stood back for Suttree to rise, to pass. He did. He and his blanket. He was shaking with rage and frustration.

He aint paid, said the waitress.

Suttree glared at her.

Just get on out, the man said. I dont need your money.

He stood in the street. He could hear doors closing all back through his head like enormous dominoes toppling in a corridor. He shouldered the blanket and went on. A black man he passed looked him over and called back to him. Suttree turned.

They'll vag you here, said the black.

Suttree didnt answer.

I'm just tellin you. You do what you want.

He was gone. Somewhat jaunty, coatless in the cold. Suttree eyed the sun, cold worn and bonecolored above the chill overcast. He shuffled on. His knees kept grasshoppering out sideways and this way. He passed a storewindow and backed up. The glass was printed with the first three letters of the alphabet and in the hall beyond was a long counter and behind that were shelves ranked with bottles.

He wheeled in through the door, adjusting the blanket as he went. Two men at the counter watched him come. One turned and found something to do and the other rose up from his elbows and stood in charge.

I cant serve you, he said.

Suttree still had his mouth open. He closed it and opened it again. He looked at the bottles. He looked at the counterman.

You better go on, said the counterman.

Where's the bus station, said Suttree.

Where you left it, I reckon.

Suttree suddenly began to cry. He didn't know that he was going to and he was ashamed. The counterman looked away. Suttree turned and went out. In the street the cold wind on his wet face brought back such old winter griefs that he began to cry still harder. Walking along the mean little streets in his rags convulsed with sobs, half blind with a sorrow for which there was neither name nor help.

At the bus station he bought his ticket, smoothing out the crumpled bill on the counter, the grave face of the emancipator looking back from the currency. With the change he bought a candy bar and he sat alone on a bench in the empty waiting room in his blanket eating the candy in micesized bites and reading from a black leatherette copy of the Book of Mormon he found in a pamphlet rack. The candy he managed to get down but the words of the book swam off the page eerily and he thought he'd never read a stranger tale.

The hands on the bald white clockface above the ticket office went by fits and starts. At ten till four he rose and went out, the book in his hand and his hand at his breast and the blanket about him like an itinerant simonist. The baggageman watched warily the shuffling exit of this latterday crazyman.

A driver in a shiny blue suit looked him up and down.

Is this the bus to Knoxville? Suttree said.

He said that it was. Suttree offered his ticket and the driver drew a punch from its holster and punched the ticket and handed it back and Suttree mounted the steps into the bus.

All the faces that he passed were watching out the windows but as he went by they turned and followed him with their eyes. A parcel of old ladies. A young man in pressed twill. At the rear of the bus Suttree swung around and the faces all turned back. He lay down on the rear seat.

When he woke they were swinging through the mountains and he was being shifted up and back on the seat as the rear of the bus followed. He sat up. His blanket had fallen to the floor and he got it and tucked it around him. The coach was filled with stale cigarette smoke and the windows were weeping. A few small domelights shone on magazines up the aisle. Beyond the windshield a pair of red taillights slid away and reappeared and swung back across the front of the bus again. Suttree slept, tottering upright on the seat.

It was after nine oclock when they reached Knoxville. He clambered down on queasy legs and climbed the steps to the terminal. In the men's room he studied himself. An unshorn ghost in a black beard peered back from the glass with eyes like old furnace flues. He pulled the blanket from his shoulders and rolled it and tucked it beneath his arm. His jacket hung in ribbons. He touched the sharpened bones of his face. He raked back his hair with his hands. When he glanced down at his shoes the tiles of the floor seemed to be undulating like the scales of some cold enormous fish. An eye watched from a partly open toilet door. He staggered out. His feet made no sound in the empty arcade and he seemed to go for miles toward the lights of the street.

At night in the bed high in the old frame house on Grand he listened to the engines switching in the yard, the long iron collision of couplings running out in the dark by the warehouse walls until the lamplit night echoed with their hammerings like some great forge where arms for a giants' tournament were being beaten out against the sun's rising and in the light of passing locomotives the shadows of trees and powerpoles raced within the cocked sash of the window across the peeling walls to blackness. He slept and slept. All day the house was empty. She'd come at noon and fix him soup and a sandwich until he felt like a child in some winter illness. Recurrences of dreams he'd had in the mountains came and went and the second night he woke from uneasy sleep and lay in the world alone. A dark hand had scooped the spirit from his breast and a cold wind circled in the hollow there. He sat up. Even the community of the dead had disbanded into ashes, those shapes wheeling in the earth's crust through a nameless ether no more men than were the ruins of any other thing once living. Suttree felt the terror coming through the walls. He was seized with a thing he'd never known, a sudden understanding of the mathematical certainty of death. He felt his heart pumping down there under the palm of his hand. Who tells it so? Could a whole man not author his own death with a thought? Shut down the ventricle like the closing of an eye?

He got up and went to the window and looked out. The houses stood above the railyard with a kind of doomed austerity, locked in a sad frieze against the gray midwinter sky. From each chimney like a tattered rag a tongue of coalsmoke swirled. Beyond the tracks lay the market warehouses and beyond these the shapeless warrens of

McAnally with its complement of pariahs and endless poverty.

He woke in the paler gray of noon to find Blind Richard groping toward him from the door.

Bud? he said, standing there on the boards in the barren room like a medicineshow clown, casting about in the dead air with his frozen grin.

Hello Richard.

The blind man sat on the bed and lit a cigarette and toyed at the ash with the tip of his little finger. Well, he said. I heard you was sick.

I'm all right.

What was it you had?

Suttree eased himself among the sooty sheets. I dont know, he said. Something or other.

Mrs Long look after ye good?

Oh yeah. She's good.

Good a woman as ever walked. Ast anybody. Dont take my word for it.

How are you getting along?

I wisht McAnally was full of em like her. Me? I aint braggin much. Well.

The blind man looked about. Dark sockets clogged with bluish jissom. Smoke drawing upward alongside his thin nose. He knit his yellowed fingers in a mime of anxiety and leaned toward Suttree. You dont have a little drink hid away do ye? he said.

No I dont.

Didnt much allow ye did.

Suttree watched him. How long have you been blind, Richard?

What?

I said how long have you been blind. Were you always blind?

The blind man grinned sheepishly and fingered his chin. Oh, he said. No. I dont remember. I've forgot.

Where did you get that lump?

He touched a faint yellow swelling above his eye. Red done that, he said.

Red did?

Yeah. He comes over you know. Comes over to the house. He sets all the doors about halfway shut. I got in a hurry or I never would of run into it. I know him.

How's everything down at the Huddle?

It's about like you left it.

They sat there in silence on the bed. Beyond the baywindow lay a deadly and leaden sky. Dimpled by the motewenned glass. A small gray rain had begun.

Well, said Richard. I better get on.

Dont rush off.

I've got to get on home.

Come back.

You get well now, said the blind man. You do what Mrs Long tells ye.

I will.

He went down the stairwell holding to the wall. Suttree heard the door close. A few sad birds along the wires watched the rain fall. One had a crooked leg. Gray water was leaking from a rotted length of gutterpipe. As he lay there the water grew more pale and the rain fell and the water grew quite clear and the water beaded on the lacquered leaves of the old magnolia tree in the yard looked bright and clean.

Late Saturday and all day Sunday drunks would come and sit on the bed and talk and sneak him whiskey. None asked if what he had were catching. Mrs Long on her duckshaped shoes came to the top of the landing to complain in her shrill voice and groggy sots clung halfway up the spindleshorn balustrade while ribald laughter rocked in the barren upper rooms of the rotting house.

He came down to dinner, good plain food served in the shambles of patched and tacked furniture destroyed in drunken rages over the years. Another week and he was on the streets again.

His first day uptown he weighed himself on the free scales in front of Woodruff's. He looked at the face in the glass.

He went to Miller's Annex and called on J-Bone.

Up and about eh? Did they run you off at the house?

No. I slipped off after your mama went back to work.

How do you feel?

I feel okay. I feel pretty good.

Where will you be later on?

I dont know. I'm going up to Comer's.

You think you feel well enough to drink a beer?

I might get well.

J-Bone grinned. Old Suttree, he said. He's hell when he's well.

What time you get off? Five thirty?

Yeah.

I'll see you then.

Okay Bud.

When he came through the door at Comer's Dick winked at him and raised his hand. Hey Buddy, he said. Got a letter for you.

Suttree leaned on the counter.

You've lost a little weight havent you?

Some.

Where you been?

I was over in North Carolina for a while.

Dick turned the letter in his hand and looked at it and handed it over. It's been here about two weeks, he said.

Suttree tapped the letter on the counter. Thanks Dick, he said.

He sat among the watchers by the wall and crossed his legs the way the old men do and opened the envelope. It was postmarked Knoxville and there was a letter from his mother and a check from his Uncle

Ben newly dead. He looked at the check. It was for three hundred dollars. He tapped it in his hand and got up and went to the watercooler for a drink and came back. He wadded the letter and dropped it into the spittoon.

Where you been Buddy boy? called Harry the Horse.

Hey Harry, said Suttree.

Harry stood shapeless in his shirt and changeapron by the cashregister. Bill Tilson made a few slow judo feints and laid the edge of his hand athwart Harry's ear. Ah, said Harry. That was on the bone.

On the bone, called Tilson dementedly, passing on along the tables.

Suttree looked up from the check to the racked cues along the wall, the old photos of ballplayers. A quiet figure there in the bedlam of ballclack and calling and telephones, the tickertape unspooling the sportsnews. Fuck it, he said. He rose and went to the front counter.

Can you cash a check for me, Dick?

Sure Bud. He laid the check on the sill of the cashregister and rang open the drawer. He read the check. Fat city, he said. How do you want it?

A couple of hundreds and some twenties.

With the money folded in his front pocket he went down the stairs to the street again.

He went to Miller's and bought underwear and socks and went out through the Annex and crossed through the markethouse. Old Lippner akimbo in his abbatoir. By the side door blind Walter stood sleeping with his dobro and Suttree touched his sleeve. The blind eyes opened and rolled up. Suttree pressed a folded bill into his palm.

You the only man I ever saw could sleep standing up.

An enormous set of teeth appeared and a strong black hand gripped his forearm. Hey fish man. Naw you wrong. Black man taught it to the mule.

You think I could learn it?

You might if they wouldnt let you set down nowheres.

Suttree smiled. I'll see you later.

The blind man pocketed the bill. I hope you catches the river out, he said.

Suttree crossed the street to Watson's. There in the basement he found his size in a rack of sportcoats and selected a pale camelhair and tried it. Faint lines of dirt along the shoulder seams where it had hung. He looked at himself in the mirror. He took a comb from his pocket and combed his hair.

He found a pair of black mohair trousers that had a small tricornered tear at the rear pocket. Couldnt see it with the jacket on. The slacks and the jacket came to thirteen dollars and ninety cents and he paid and went upstairs and bought a yellow gabardine shirt with handstitched collar and pockets.

In a window above Market Street the old tailor stood peering out through the lettered glass, the dusty ells and bolts of cloth spooled out in the window easing the repose of dead flies and roaches. Suttree came up the dark and musty wooden stairwell and swung through the door with his package.

Nice trousers them, said the old man as he measured the inseam with a tattered yellow tape. He gripped the waistband and tugged at them. He put his arms around Suttree's waist and brought the tape together at his navel. The old man barely came to Suttree's shoulder.

You want some out of the seat too.

I think they'll be all right, Mr Brannam. I've lost some weight.

The tailor tugged at the seat of Suttree's new trousers and looked dubious. You going to carry your lunch here? he said.

Suttree smiled. They're really my size, he said. I'll fill back out.

How much you going to fill?

About twenty pounds.

The tailor pulled again at Suttree's waist and shook his head.

They're okay. Let's just do the cuffs.

When you dont get fat you bring em back, okay?

Okay. There's a little tear there in the back too.

I see him, said the tailor, marking with his chalk.

Suttree waited in a wooden folding chair while the trousers were cuffed and he paid the old man and thanked him and went down the stairs again.

He bought a pair of shoes at Thom McAn's that had zippers up the side and were the color of blood. With his packages he climbed the stairs to Comer's and at the rear of the premises he stripped and washed and put on his new clothes. His old ones he wrapped in the paper and he left them with Stud at the lunchcounter. Stud took the package and looked back again and whistled and Jake took hold of him by the shoulder and turned him around and looked him over and sniffed at his cheek and tried to kiss him.

Get away you ass, Suttree said.

Ulysees came over to view him with his quiet cynic's smile. Well, he said. Looking rather affluent there, Bud. He kneaded Suttree's sleeve between his thumb and forefinger. Oy, he said. Iss qvality.

Suttree crossed Gay Street to the Farragut and went downstairs to the barbershop. He passed Tarzan Quinn coming up, freshly powdered, swinging his billyclub by its thong to and fro into and out of his enormous hand.

An aged black took his new coat and he climbed into a chair.

Yessir, said the barber, flinging the apron ticking over him.

Shave, haircut, shine . . . You do manicures?

No, said the barber. We dont have a manicurist.

Okay. Shave, haircut, shine. And dont spare the smellgood.

The barber brought a steaming towel and wrapped his face and tilted him back in the chair. Suttree lay in deep euphoria, his legs crossed at the ankles, his new shoes easy on the nickleplated grating of the footrest. He listened dreamily to the pop of the razor on the strop.

He half dozed in the chair while the barber pulled his face about, the razor slicing off the hot lavendar foam. Peace seeped through to Suttree's bones. The barber raised him up and began to trim his hair with scissors. The black had settled at his feet with his wooden box of polishes and begun to work over the shoes. The second barber read the newspaper. No one spoke. Suttree's dark locks dropped soundlessly to the tiles. Gentle barber. He drifted.

The barber talced the back of his neck and whipped away the apron and stood back. Suttree opened his eyes. He raised the shoes up one and then the other and looked at them. He climbed down from the chair and looked at himself in the mirror.

The old black held his coat while he paid and then helped him on with it and dusted his shoulders with a little broom. Suttree dropped a half dollar into his palm and the old man made a sort of bow and said thank you sir and the barber said come back.

In the streets a colder wind on his shaven nape. Bobbyjohn stood on the corner with Bucket and Hoghead and two boys he did not know. They seized upon him with great joy. Bobbyjohn was offering him two dollars for the coat, waving the money about.

Where's your stick? said Hoghead. You caint go around lookin like that and no stick to beat the women off with.

Old Suttree's caught himself a hell of a fish somewheres.

He and J-Bone ate dinner at Regas. Bobby smiled when she brought them the menu.

What are you goin for, Bud?

I think I'll go for the large fillet steak.

Believe I'll go for the veal cutlet.

Hell, get the steak.

The cutlet's good, Bud.

Get the biggest fucking steak they own.

The steaks arrived on iron platters sizzling in their own juice and there were steaming baked potatoes with pithy cores to melt the butter over and there was sour cream with chives and hot rolls and coffee. Suttree popped a chunk of steak into his mouth and sat back in the chair and closed his eyes, chewing.

Good aint it Bud?

J-Bone dipped a roll into his platter and raised it dripping with dark gravy and loaded it into his jaw. Lordy, he said.

Where we going tonight?

Anywhere suits me. What about the Carnival Club?

Is this Thursday?

Sure is, said J-Bone. The place will be crawling with lovely young cuntlets.

I'm for that, said Suttree.

He woke in Woodlawn among the menhirs of the dead. He raised himself onto one elbow and looked out across the ordered landscape of polished stones, the pale winter's grass and black trees. He brushed the chaff from his sleeve. An oxblood stain was seeping up his white socks from the new shoes. He staggered to his feet, brushing at himself. His trousers were caked with great patches of mud at the knees and he was damp and cold. Suddenly he crammed both fists in his pocket. His eyes wandered in his head as he grappled with the murky history of the prior night. Dim memories. A maudlin madman stumbling among the stones in search of a friend long dead who lies here. He pulled from his watchpocket a small wet folded paper. It was one of the hundred dollar bills somehow put by. Suttree crossed the spiderfrosted grass of the cemetery toward the fence and the road.

The sun was not so high he could not take his bearings by it and he set off in what he figured to be the direction of the town. A bus passed in a blue stink of diesel smoke, the windows filled with faces.

He brushed his hair back and grimaced at the riders. He shaped a curse in the air after them with a leanboned hand.

A half mile down stood a roadside store. Suttree at the drinkbox lifted out an orange bottle and opened it and drank. The woman who kept the store watched him from under her wrinkled eyelids.

I'm not loose from the circus, he said.

What?

I said do you have any aspirins.

She turned and reached a small tin box of them from a shelf behind the counter. Suttree opened the box and emptied the contents into his hand and dropped them into his mouth like peanuts and washed them down with a swig of the drink.

What do I owe you?

Fifteen cents, she said. Old nervous eyes.

Gravegrass clung to his trousers. He pulled the hundred dollar bill from his pocket and spread it out on the counter. She looked at it and she looked at him. She said: I caint change that.

That's all I have.

Well I dont have change for nothin like that.

Well I'll have to owe you then.

He took the bill up and put it back in his pocket.

You'll have to pay, she said. I dont know ye.

I'll write you a check.

She just stood there.

Do you have a counter check?

I dont have no checks.

Do you have a paper bag?

Have what?

A poke.

How big of a one did you want? She was rummaging under the counter.

Any size, said Suttree.

She raised up with a bag. Thisn here's the biggest I got.

That's fine. Do you have a pen?

She had a pen.

Suttree wrote out an enormous I O U across the face of the bag and signed his name and turned the bag around so she could read it. She took small rimless eyeglasses from her apron and bent over the bag. Suttree laid the pen down and left.

He kept off the high roads, going by dogpaths through the hobo

303

jungles down along the railroad tracks. A yardman watched him from the baywindow of a caboose, a bitten sandwich upheld in one hand, his jaws moving slowly. He came out by the L&N depot and went up a brickpaved street past the House Hasson warehouse and over a little concrete bridge with plumbingpipe handrails cold and gritty in his palms. Small waters coiling far below about the feet of the viaduct's diamondshaped stanchions. Along a wall of concrete grown with bright green fur. Suttree climbing toward a watered sun.

He crossed under the Western Avenue viaduct and went up Grand Avenue. A dog went before him at its cambered winking trot. He took off his coat and shook it and put it on again. Ionic order much in evidence in these old streets. Weathercracked columns, plaster capitals clogged shapeless with paint. A dead lot strewn with brickbats and blackened timbers. Walkways of weathered marble, of herringbone brick. The walkway at 1504 where each brick read Knoxville Brick Company, long defunct. Suttree passed under the gray magnolia tree and up the steps to the porch of the tall gray house and in.

At night he leaned in the octagonal windowbay and looked out over the switching yards and the warehouses like a child in a pulpit in the dark of an empty church. He could hear singing from the Grand Avenue Mission down the street where revelers caroled perhaps perverse and secret deities behind their plywood windowpanes.

Next evening he took the bus out Magnolia Avenue and stood before the old brick house where he'd gone to school, the untrue glass with black stars stoned through the panes and the wind cutting along in a razory whistle intermittent with the gnashing of weeds in the dark of the lot. He went in by the back door where the cafeteria once had been. The floorboards creaked underfoot, small life scrabbled away. He placed his hand on the newel post and went up the stairs.

Through old classrooms, the dusty clutter of desks. On the blackboards scrawled obscenities. A derelict school for lechers. Suttree had been sitting at his old desk for some time before he noticed the figure standing in the door.

This old bedroom in this old house where he'd been taught a sort of christian witchcraft had two doors and Suttree rose and went out the other one. He descended the front steps and went to the fireplace where he lifted back the iron mask and on one knee reached up the chimney throat and took down a small billikin carved from some soft wood and detailed with a child's crayon.

When he came past the stairway the priest was mounted on the first landing like a piece of statuary. A catatonic shaman who spoke no word at all. Suttree went out the way that he'd come in, crossing the grass toward the lights of the street. When he looked back he could see the shape of the priest in the baywindow watching like a paper priest in a pulpit or a prophet sealed in glass.

In the spring of his third year on the river there were heavy rains. It rained all through the latter part of March and into April and he had set but one line in the rising river and followed it each day with a cold loathing while the rain fell small and gray for miles upon him. It was cold and damp in the shanty and he kept a fire in the little stove through the bleak afternoons and sat at the table by the window with the lamp lit, gazing out at the swollen river coming down from the gutted upcountry and sliding past with a slaverous mutter and seethe.

Bearing along garbage and rafted trash, bottles of suncured glass wherein corollas of mauve and gold lie exploded, orangepeels ambered with age. A dead sow pink and bloated and jars and crates and shapes of wood washed into rigid homologues of viscera and empty oilcans locked in eyes of dishing slime where the spectra wink guiltily.

One day a dead baby. Bloated, pulpy rotted eyes in a bulbous skull and little rags of flesh trailing in the water like tissuepaper.

Oaring his way lightly through the rain among these curiosa he felt little more than yet another artifact leached out of the earth and washed along, draining down out of the city, that cold and grainy shape beyond the rain that no rain could make clean again. Suttree among the leavings like a mote in the floor of a beaker, come summer a bit of matter stunned and drying in the curing mud, the terra damnata of the city's dead alchemy. The fish he raised up from the flood in this season themselves looked stunned.

He stood hard into the oars to come back against the current. Past the bridge risers where small ugly rips broke on the concrete and the boatshaped upstream face rode in a bone of curling froth. Along this clay shoulder where the river gnawed and pulled with her leathery brown waters.

In the fluted gullies where the river backed or eddied spoondrift lay in a coffeecolored foam, a curd that draped the varied flotsam locked and turning there, the driftwood and bottles and floats and the white bellies of dead fish, all wheeling slowly in the river's suck and the river spooling past unpawled with a muted seething freighting seaward her silt and her chattel and her dead.

One morning while he stood on the gallery in the dim early light watching the river he saw an empty skiff go by. Next came looming out of the yellow mist a patchwork shack composed of old slats and tarpaper and tin snuff signs all mounted in wild haphazard upon a derelict barge and turning with the keelless rotations of a drunken bear, going downriver to founder cumbrously against a pier, list and halt, sidle and grope past with the next wall of the shack coming about and along it like plaster caryatids hung there in a stunned frieze above the licking river the figures of four women and two men, pale, rigid, deathless, wheeling slowly away below the bridge and gone in the mist.

Suttree watched the transit of this foggy apparition with no surprise. Two days later when he went downriver he saw the shantyboat pulled up under some willows on the south bank below the sand and gravel company. There was a line of wash hung out and a small skiff swung at tether below the mooring. Some coon hides were tacked flat to the wall, bleached a pale cream color. You'd have thought them to be wares but the hides were dry and all but hairless and seemed forgotten.

Suttree oared past while a group of wide faces watched from a window. When he came back in the afternoon there was a chair on the roof of the shanty and in it a man sleeping. The wash had been taken down and smoke was rising from a stovepipe elbowed through one wall. The skiff was gone.

As Suttree passed beneath the bridge he saw the skiff coming down. A thin young boy was rowing it. Suttree let one oar trail and lifted a hand in greeting. The boy nodded at him, one eye blueblack and swollen closed, and went on.

In the morning he went down early and as he passed the houseboat he saw a young girl come out along the little veranda and turn and squat, her skirts gathered in the crooks of her elbows. Through the fog Suttree was presented with a bony pointed rump. She pissed loudly into the river and rose and went in again.

He was back before noon with his catch. He came up close by the bank and swung around the houseboat. A woman was peering down at him, a stonejawed and apparently gravid slattern resting her belly on the rim of the washtub and regarding him through clotted rags of hair.

Howdy, he said.

She nodded.

I saw you all come down the other mornin. I live cross the river. He rested an oar under his elbow and pointed.

She said uh-hunh.

Suttree smiled. He said: I figured since we were kind of neighbors

I ought to stop and say hidy anyway.

She reached down into the tub and brought something up from the bottom of it. He's asleep, she said.

The mister is?

Yep.

He dipped the oars to stay against the current. You've got a good-sized family, dont you?

She watched down into the tub. How her face must look back from the dead well of blue washwater, rocking and licking in what shapes. We got four, she said. Three girls. She paused and pushed her nose against her arm and snuffled. And a boy, she said.

I believe I saw him the other day.

You aint the one hit him in the eye are ye?

No mam.

Somebody hit him in the eye, she said. With a beadle of soap-softened wood she subdued the grayish rags that stewed in the pot. She lifted something out and wrung it and laid it on a bench.

Where are you all from?

We was from up around Mascot.

I see, he said.

She glanced down at him and went back to her washing. After a minute she said: Looks like you got you some fish there.

Yes mam. You all like catfish?

We eat it some.

I've got plenty here, if you'd like one for your supper.

She looked down into the bottom of the skiff. What would you have to have for one? she said.

He began to sort among the fish. I'll just give you one, he told her.

Well. I'd rather just to pay ye.

Here. He stood in the skiff and handed up a sleek fourpounder.

She took it expertly behind the gills and looked it over. What do I owe ye? she said.

Not anything.

Well, let me pay ye.

I dont want nothin for it.

Well, she said.

I run a trotline on down a ways.

Well.

I got plenty.

Well, I better put him in here.

He sat down and leaned into the oars, watching her go in with the catfish. Before he had pulled more than a few yards upstream she was out again. He thought she had come back to her washing but she called to him across the water. Hey, she said.

Yes mam.

He's awake now if you wanted to see him.

Well, I dont want to bother him.

He said to thank ye for the catfish.

You welcome. Tell him I'll come by in a day or two.

Well, she said. Come back when you can.

The next day there was no one about but the day following the man was in his chair again reading a newspaper. Suttree hailed him as he came alongside and the man folded the paper and squinted down at him.

Hey, he said.

How you getting along?

Right tolerable. You the feller sent that catfish by the other day?

I just had more than I needed.

Well I wanted to thank ye. My old lady fried it up and we et it for supper and sure enjoyed it.

Good, said Suttree.

He turned his head and spoke down a ventilator pipe rising from the roof. Hey old woman, he said.

A muffled snarl came back.

You got any coffee fixed?

He started to turn back to Suttree and his face flickered a small annoyance. He leaned to speak into the pipe again. Fix some, he said. Then he looked down to where Suttree sat in his skiff. Come up, he said, and take some coffee with us.

I dont want to put you out.

Aint no bother. She's got some ready. Just tie up there. Watch them lines. I got me some thowlines out. Just pull in down there on the lower end. Here, thow the rope.

He had climbed down off the roof and was going along the walkway talking and waving the folded paper about. Suttree pulled the skiff in and tossed his rope.

Come on in, said the man as Suttree climbed aboard. He pushed aside a curtain of knotted twine and ushered him in with a grand expansiveness.

As Suttree entered three girls flew to the far wall of the room whinnying like goats and subsided in a simpering heap together on a bed there. Suttree nodded to the woman and she said him a quiet howdy and pointed out a chair. He looked around. There were beds all along the wall and a table in the center of the room with a faded piece of oilcloth and miscellaneous white crockery draped with breakfast remnants.

Set down, the man said. Get ye a chair. Boy wait till you hear what all happened to us.

Suttree could imagine. He glanced again toward the bed and glimpsed a flash of young thighs and dingy drawers. The three of them together were looking at a magazine and stealing crazed looks at him past the edges of it. He sat in one of the low cane chairs and tilted it backward against the bunk behind him and smiled at the man.

Do you know Doren Lockhart?

No.

Well, he's the one I beat out of forty dollars in this here tong game Sunday afternoon. He's supposed to be a big gambler up there. I knowed he was mad. I busted him plumb out. He tried to get up some money to get back in the game but time he done that me and Gene Edmonds had all the money and was gone. Old Gene was with us. Where's that coffee at, woman?

I caint perk it no faster than what it's perkin.

Anyway we'd drunk some whiskey and everthing and I went to bed. What time was it I went to bed?

He waited a minute and then went on.

About ten oclock. Course I always was a sound sleeper.

A flurry of girls' laughter rose and died.

And time I woke up it was getting on towards daylight and we was comin past Island Home. I looked out the winder and seen trees goin by and I said: Lord God, we're plumb adrift. Neighbor, we was. I come up from there and went on out and about that time they was a airplane took off over on the island and I looked downriver and seen Knoxville comin up and knowed where we was at. That son of a bitch had crep up in the night and sawed us loose.

He leaned forward with his hands on his knees and looked at Suttree with a hard eyed squint as if to see which way lay his sympathies. What about that? he said.

Well, said Suttree.

The woman set a cup of coffee in front of him. You use milk and sugar?

No mam, that's fine like it is.

Bring him some of them cakes.

Have you got any way to get back up there? Suttree asked.

Why hell no. It costes to get a tow if you can get somebody to do it even. What do you think about a son of a bitch would do that?

Suttree regarded him over the rim of the cup. He lowered the cup and cradled it in both hands. Well, he said. I guess I'd call him a poor loser at the least.

You daggone right he is, said the man, leaning back.

What do you aim to do?

Lord I dont know. I thought about huntin me a job down here. You dont know where there is one do ye?

I dont know. You might find something. If you go out Blount Avenue here there's a woolen mill and a fertilizer plant. Then there's the sand and gravel company right here. You could ask around.

Well much obliged. I just need to get set up back upriver so as to start in musselin come summer.

The woman set a plate of cookies on the table.

Start what? Suttree said.

The man looked at him. He looked behind him at the woman and toward the girls on the bed. Then he leaned toward Suttree again. Musselin, he said.

Musselin?

Yeah.

Suttree looked at him. What's that? he said.

The man leaned back and crossed his feet in a chair. Mussel brailin, he said. When the river gets down low towards middle and late summer we go up on the shoals of the French Broad and set us up a mussel camp. I've got everthing. I got a boat for it and everthing.

What do you do with them?

Sell they shells. The womenfolk clean em and me and the boy drags for em.

What do they do with them?

The shells?

Yes.

Different things. Make buttons out of em, the biggest part. Some I reckon they grind for chicken grit.

What are they worth?

They fetch round in about forty dollar a ton.

Forty dollars a ton?

That's right.

That doesnt seem like a whole lot.

The man smiled. Them little fellers is heavier than what you might think. Asides they's more money in it than just that.

The woman poured his cup full. The man didnt seem to notice, sitting there waiting for her elbow to move on out of the way. When she had done he leaned forward. They's more to it than just the shells, good buddy. He looked about craftily. More to it than that.

He stayed to dinner. By then the old man had told him about the pearls and even showed him some. Taking from some secret place on his person a small purse tailored from the scrotum of a treefox and setting out the pearls on the oilcloth. Suttree turned one in his hand and held it to the light.

If we had another hand we could run two boats, the old man said.

Can you make any money at it?

The old man turned away in mirthful derision. Money? Shit, boy. Whyyy . . .

Suttree stared at the pearls. The little cabin had filled with a rich steam of cookery. Plates were clattering and the woman and the oldest girl whispered together at the stove.

How would you go shares if you was interested? the old man said.

Suttree looked up. He looked around the cabin. Shares, he said?

They's six of us. Everbody works.

Let her set the table, Reese, the woman said.

Reese raised his elbows. He hadn't taken his eyes off Suttree. Would you go fifths? Not takin out nothin for ye board.

Suttree scooped the pearls into his palm and funneled them back into the purse. His voice sounded far away. I might go fourths, he said.

A soft young breast crossed his nape. The girl leaned and dealt from a tray of old and mismatched silver.

The man took the purse and hefted it in his hand and eyed Suttree. It's hard work, he said.

Suttree nodded.

The old man grinned. Make ye sleep good of a night.

Suttree had started with a question but the old man suddenly flung his hand across the table. Partner, he said. You're on.

When they sat for dinner it was a tight fit and Suttree looking around the table couldnt help smiling. The boy came in with his swollen eye as they were taking seats and he studied Suttree without much interest. The two younger girls didnt know where to look at all.

This had emboldened the oldest one who set her shoulders and flung her hair back and passed Suttree a platter of biscuits. She was extraordinarily well put together with great dark eyes and hair. The head of the house stood to better grapple with the joint of pork before him. The boy was ladling a great load of beans aboard his plate. Suttree buttered one of the buoyant looking soda biscuits and watched the pale slices of pork fall under the knife, the man turning the roast and finally seizing it in his hands, the white knob of bone coming from its socket with a sucking sound and breaking like a great pearl up through the steaming meat.

He forked the greasy slabs of meat onto what plates he could reach and told the woman at the end of the table to pass hers. Suttree ladled thick gravy onto his pork and biscuits and reached for the pepper. Beans were coming downtable and fat sweet potatoes and coffee was being poured around. He gripped his fork in his fist in the best country manner and fell to.

Dont be shy, called the old man. Eat a plenty.

Suttree nodded and waved his fork.

Harrogate saw them going along Blount Avenue Sunday morning. They wore outfits all cut from the same bolt of cloth and in the church pew standing six across they looked like a strip of gaudy wallpaper cut into those linked dolls madfolk pass their time in fashioning. People could not stop looking. The preacher forwent his station at the door when services were over and there was no one to shake the hands of these new and startling parishioners. Small boys had gathered outside to jeer but the emergence of this little group found them unprepared, inert. They filed out in descending order by altitudes, the father first, out through the sunlit doors in a sextet of calico isotropes and into the street, the elder smiling, along through the crowds and down the road toward the river still single file and with deadpan decorum leaving behind a congregation mute and astounded.

He rowed out to visit. Coming about the end of the shantyboat in his welded skiff and singing out at the woman where she sat on the porch shelling beans.

Howdy! he called.

She sprang like a wounded moose and came up against the rail at the far corner of the catwalk with her eyes walled and her fallen bosom heaving beneath the rag of a shirt she wore. He didnt seem to notice, sitting there with his impassive smile in the center of his suicidal boat with the FORD in chrome letter across the bow and the homemade paddle laid dripping across his knees. Right purty day, aint it? he said.

Lord God, she said, I knowed the law had me. Dont you never come up on me thataway, you hear?

Yes mam, he said, his face a flower in the warm sunshine.

She looked down at him. He just sat there smiling. She took her seat on the box she'd vacated and fell to shelling beans again.

I live crost the river yonder, he said. I seen ye'ns at church Sunday.

She nodded.

Thought I'd come on down and say hidy.

She looked at him with her caved eyes.

So, he said, toying with the paddle. So hidy.

Hidy, she said.

Where's the rest of the family at today?

Gone on over in town.

Left ye by your lonesome huh?

She didnt answer.

He looked about and he eyed the sun's progress. Looks like it's goin to be another warm'n, I'd say.

Perhaps she didnt hear.

Wouldnt you? he said.

She looked down at him. Flushed, her lank hair matted about her sweating face. I reckon, she said.

That's the biggest thing about this here boat. It gets hot as a two-peckered . . . it gets hot as anything. And it settin in the water where you'd allow it'd cool.

Yes, she said.

I like to of drownded in it once.

Uh huh.

It wont float atall.

He took a dip with his paddle to recover the current.

What time you reckon they'll get back?

I dont know.

Does that boy go to school?

He does sometime. He aint now.

I just despise a school. What kind of hides is them?

Coon hides. Or they was.

Harrogate leaned and spat into the river and raised up again. How old's that boy of yourn anyway?

She looked at him. She looked at the contraption in which he sat. She said: He aint old enough to ride in that.

What, this here? Shoot. Why you couldnt sink it with dynamite.

She tilted a paper of shucked beanpods overboard. Harrogate watched them drift away.

Old Suttree's a friend of mine. You know him dont ye?

No.

He et with ye'ns here the other evenin. Runs trotlines. He said he knowed ye.

She nodded her head and tilted the beans in the pan and rose and dumped the debris from the folds of her skirt.

He's a friend of mine, Harrogate said.

She bent and picked up the pan of shelled beans and tossed her hair back from her face.

He's rid in it, said Harrogate. In this here boat. Suttree has.

They were walking along the tracks with the city rat at Suttree's off elbow taking legstretcher steps over every other tie, his hands crammed in his hippockets gripping each a skinny buttock. He watched the ground and shook his head.

What do you say to em?

Say to them?

Yeah. Say.

Hell, say anything. It doesnt matter, they dont listen.

Well you gotta say somethin. What do you say?

Try the direct approach.

What's that?

Well, like this friend of mine. Went up to this girl and said I sure would like to have a little pussy.

No shit? What'd she say?

She said I would too. Mine's as big as your hat.

Aw shit, Sut. Come on, what do you say to em? Boy she's got a big old set of ninnies on her.

Yes she has. You dont think she's too old for you?

She's same age I am.

Well.

How do you get em to take off their clothes. That's what I'd by god like to know.

You take them off.

Yeah? Well what does she do while you're doin that? I mean hell, does she just look out the winder or somethin? I dont understand it at all Sut. The whole thing seems uneasy to me.

They swung off the right of way and went along a dogpath, Suttree grinning. Tell her she sure has got a big old set of ninnies on her, he said.

Shit, said Harrogate. She's liable to smack the fire out of me.

It was midsummer before they went back up the river. They left the crazylooking shanty in Knoxville and went by bus with their bedding and housegoods baled up. Suttree saw them off with promises he'd long regretted.

A week later he got a tow to the forks of the river and began rowing up the French Broad. After nine hours at the oars he pulled into the bank and crawled out with his blanket and slept like a dead man. He had reason to think of the old Bildad up on the Clinch who used to flood his skiff and sleep under water in it to keep the insects off.

When he woke in the smoky dawn he felt alien and tainted, camped there in a wilderness with his little stained boat and his weariness. As if the city had marked him. So that no eldritch daemon would speak him secrets in this wood. He ate two of the sandwiches he'd packed and drank a grape drink, sitting there on the bank and watching a wood duck that floated on the river like a painted decoy block mitered to its double on the pewter calm.

He rowed on upriver until he came to the landing at Boyd's Creek. His hands were puffy and clawed and he wished the skiff at the bottom of the river. He went into the store and drank two cold drinks and got a third one to sip on. Coming back out into the glaring sunlight he saw a thermometer hung in a tin coughsyrup sign on the storefront. The red line in the glass ran from bottom to top and out of sight. He eyed it with baleful bloodfilled eyes and turned and spat a grape-stained clot of mucus at the cooking world. Not even a fly moved.

It was early afternoon when he came upon them. He passed a huge and stinking windrow of shells on the south bank and struggled upstream through faster water, towing the boat up shoals with a rope over his shoulder, clutching and fending among the shore bracken, the water very cold and clear. They were camped like gypsies under a slate bluff and smoke rose among the trees. The skiff at the bank bore a strange rigging of uprights and crosspoles and a travis bar with lines and hooks hanging from it. The boy squatted on a stump watching him. The womenfolk were boiling wash in a big galvanized tub and the old man was asleep under a tree. When she saw Suttree tying up, the woman called Reese, Reese. Two dry flat birdnotes he'd heard all his life. He didnt move.

Suttree came on up the bank. Howdy, he said.

They all nodded. They were shrouded in steam and they looked limp and half fainting. The old woman's long white goat's udders hung half out above the tub and the flesh of her upper arms swung as she wound the water from a pair of jeans. The girl gave him a sort of defeated smile.

Daddy, she called.

Reese opened one eye tentatively from beneath his tree. Yonder's my partner, he sang out.

Hey, said Suttree.

Come set down. Boy we really into em up here. Looky yonder.

Suttree looked. A black slagheap of riven shellfish lay along the riverbank exuding a greenish vapor and quaking gently with flies.

And looky here.

The musselfisher lifted out the little foxcod purse and tilted into his palm a single pearl.

Suttree picked it up and looked at it. It looked a bit lumpy.

What's it worth? he said.

Caint tell. They's lots they go by. He took it and rolled it in his palm and dropped it back into the purse. They aint no tellin what it might be worth, he said.

How many have you found?

Well. That's the only really good'n. I got some others.

Suttree stared bleakly at the levee of shells.

We'll really get into em now though, what with two boats and all.

Suttree turned and looked down at the old man. He was squatting on his heels, having risen that far by way of greeting. Smiling. Optimistic. A pale and bloated tick hung in his scalp like a pendulous wen.

We got to get your boat rigged. I done hunted up some poles and stuff.

Have you got a hammer and nails?

I got some nails comin out of them boards yonder quick as I burn em. We'll get some more. They's plenty of old boards got nails in em.

Suttree was kneading his bloated palms. How do you aim to drive the nails, he said.

Just knock em in with a rock.

Suttree looked at the river. If you just get in your boat you can stretch out and sleep and barring snags wake up sometime back in Knoxville like you'd never been away.

I guess we'll manage, he said.

Why hell yes, said the old man.

Suttree wandered off to the skiff to get his blankets and gear. He took the two cans of beer he had stowed under the rear seat and tied them to a string and lowered them over the side.

The family had put up a rude lean-to against the wall of the bluff. Old roofing tin and random boards and a plywood highway sign that said Slow Construction Ahead. It all looked like it had washed up there in high water. Under the overhang of the bluff were thin home-sewn ticks and quilts and army blankets. Suttree didnt think it would rain anytime soon so he went on down past the camp with his gear to a little knoll that overlooked the river and where there were some small pines and a wind to stand the insects off. He fixed a smooth place on the ground and fluffed up the pineneedles and spread a blanket and sat down. He lay back and stretched out. The river chattered back a querulous babbling from the limestone shoals below the camp. The trees fell and fell down the lightly clouded summer sky.

Reese woke him kicking his foot. Hey, he said.

Suttree rolled over and shaded his eyes.

What you doin?

I was sleeping.

The old man squatted and eyed the river through the trees. We might's well get your boat rigged this afternoon, he said.

Suttree rose heavily. He was hot and sweaty and worn out.

You aim to bed down out here?

If it doesnt rain.

You can sleep up in the camp with us.

I snore, Suttree said.

The old man stood up. Snore? he said. Hell fire, son, you aint never heard a snore. I'll put my old lady up against any three humans or one moose.

Suttree went on up the bank.

He studied the brail rig in the old man's skiff and went into the woods to cast about for suitable saplings to make the uprights. He'd set the boy to straightening nails, beating them out with a rock. The old man had wandered off somewhere.

He sat in the stern of his skiff and trimmed the poles he'd cut, dressing the forks, shaving the lower ends flat to be nailed to the sides of the skiff. The white waxy woodpeelings coiled up cleanly under his knife and he watched them spin and drift on the river. With the point of the knife he bored holes partway through the flats on the butt end so that the wood would not split when it was nailed. The old man had come down the bank and was sitting on his heels nodding at Suttree's work and making encouraging talk. He always expected everyone to be out of heart.

By evening they had the skiff rigged with a ramshackle and barbarous facsimile of a brailboat's gear. Suttree carried the brails aboard and stowed them in the trees of the uprights and Reese eyed the sun.

You want to make a run this evening?

I dont think so.

You and the boy might make just a short run and see how she does.

Suttree stood up in the skiff and stepped ashore. And we might not, he said.

Well. We can get an early start of the mornin.

Suttree didnt answer. He went on toward the camp where smoke was rising from the supper fire.

Hidy, said the girl with studied boldness.

Hey, said Suttree. She was white with flour to her elbows, bent above a breadboard kneading biscuit dough. The two smaller girls were standing behind her and the old woman was at the fire. One of the girls poked her head around and said something and the older girl slapped at her and they fled shrieking with giggles.

Oh you all . . . Mama, make her quit.

You all quit, said the woman. She was stoking the fire and fixing the sheet of tin laid over the rocks. Flames licked from under the edges. There was a kettle and an iron pot on the tin and it sagged badly under the weight.

Is there any coffee? Suttree said.

Is there any coffee Mama?

You know there aint no coffee.

I dont guess there is none, said the girl.

What time do we eat?

In about a hour. It wont be long.

Suttree scratched his jaw and looked about. There was an old mattress in the lean-to and a packingcrate with an oil lamp on it and a miscellany of junk stored along the dark stone wall at the rear. He went down to the river again and stretched out on a cool rock in the shade and looked down into the water. On the rippled silt floor of the eddy a small turtle shifted with uncertain bowlegs. Small bits of wood, twigs, lay furred with silt and a muddog lay inert with its obscene gills branching like bright fungus. Suttree's face shifted and dished. A waterspider crossed on jointed horsehair legs and the river gave off a cool metallic smell. He spat at his trembling visage and sat up and took off his shoes and socks and lowered his feet into the water.

They ate on what looked like an outhouse door. A weathered wooden trestle propped on poles. Suttree was afraid to lean on it. They sat on planks and cinderblocks, the smallest girl's chin just clearing the boards. Suttree was lightheaded with hunger.

The iron pot came aboard and the kettle and pan of biscuits. In the kettle were some rough and hairy greens he'd never met before. In the pot whitebeans. He stirred them but no trace of fat meat turned up. He eyed the boy across the board and began to eat faster.

After supper they sat around the fire while the girls washed the dishes. The old man brought a soft and greasy leather bible from the lean-to and opened it on his knees. When the dishes were done the girls gathered around and the old man commenced to read aloud from the text. Suttree had gone to the river and fetched the two cans of beer. He opened them at the table and carried them to the fire and handed one to the old man. His eyes brightened in the firelight when he saw it. Lord have mercy looky here, he said.

Suttree gestured with his can and drank. The beer was cold and slightly bitter and very good. The old man tilted his beer to drink.

Dont you read scripture and drink that, the woman said.

What?

You heard me. Dont you read scripture and drink that.

Why hell fire, said Reese.

Nor cuss neither. You put that up or finish that beer one.

He looked around to see if anyone might be on his side. Suttree went off down to his little knoll above the river.

They went to sleep like dogs, curling up in their bedding on the ground until they were a scattering of dark shapeless mounds beneath the bluff. The fire had died. Suttree shucked off shoes and trousers and lay in his blanket. The river talked all night in the shoals. Some dogs in the anonymous distance beyond set up a clamor but they were far away and their barking muted by the river fell lost and dreamlike on his ears.

In the morning they were about and breakfasting almost with the first light. Thin cakes of fried cornmeal with sugar syrup. There was still no coffee.

The old man took the girl and went upriver and left Suttree and the boy to themselves. Suttree bailed the boat and stowed the can back under the seat and looked out downstream. A thousand smokes stood on the gray face of the river. After a while the boy emerged from the woods buttoning his trousers and came down the bank and climbed into the skiff.

You ready? he said.

Suttree looked at him. He was sitting in the bow of the skiff with his hands on his knees.

How about casting off for us.

Do what?

How about untying us.

He climbed out and got the rope loose from the stump and threw it into the skiff and knelt in the bow and shoved them off. Suttree let the oars into the river.

The skiff nosed downstream through pales of vapor. A small heron rose clacking from the reeds. The boy swung on it with an imaginary gun. Blam, he said.

I saw ducks on the river coming up, Suttree said.

Boy I bet if I had me a gun I'd kill everthing up here.

He was watching downriver, picking absently at one of the yellow pustules with which his chin was afflicted. After a while he said: What was you in the workhouse for?

Suttree leaned on the oars and looked behind him. They were in faster water and there were little weedy islands in the middle of the river. I was with some guys got caught breaking into a drugstore.

What did you break in for?

They were trying to get some drugs. Pills. They got some cigarettes and stuff. I was outside in the car.

I guess you was keepin the motor runnin and lookout and all.

I was drunk.

The boy looked at him but Suttree had turned to study the water. Across the river a tractor was plowing in the black and fallow bottoms and over the plowed land rim to rim lay a serpentine of mist the course and shape of the river itself like a ghost river there. The sun was a long time coming. In the graygreen light the midsummer corn moved with the first wind and the countryside had a sad and desolate look to it.

Did you go to college? the boy said.

Why?

I just wondered. Gene says you're real smart.

Who, Harrogate?

Yeah.

Well. Some people are smarter than others.

You mean Gene aint real smart?

No. He's plenty smart. You have to be smart to know who's smart and who's not.

I never figured you to be just extra smart.

There you are, said Suttree.

He looked puzzled. Old Gene used to come sniffin around after Wanda, he said. Mama run him off. You got a girl?

No. I used to have one but I forgot where I laid her.

The boy looked at him dully for a minute and then slapped his knee and guffawed. Boy, he said, that's a good'n.

How far down do we go?

We'll run the Gallops first and then go on down to the Wild Bull Shoals.

The Gallops?

That's the next shoals down. Taint far. You say you aint never musseled afore?

No.

Taint nothin to it. Yonder goes a mushrat.

Suttree turned. A dark little shape forded the dawn, a black nose in a wedge of riverwater.

Quick as furs primes I'm goin to be back up here with me some traps.

Suttree nodded, pulling along easily, the oarlocks creaking and the lines of the brail swinging behind the boy's head like a bead curtain. The sun came up. It bored up out of the trees in a greengold light and Suttree's silhouette lay long and narrow down the river among the brail line shadows like a rowing marionette.

He swung the skiff more shoreward. The boy was bent peering down into the water. In the clear shallows suckers trailed by their whiterimmed mouths from the rocks like soft pennants fluttering.

The boy took an empty rubber flashlight from his hippocket and dipping the lens in the river looked down through the gutted barrel at the piscean world below.

Do you see any mussels? Suttree said.

We aint into em yet, the boy said. They godamighty what a catfish.

How deep is it?

Yonder goes a old mudturkle.

Suttree leaned on the oars. How about letting me look, he said.

The boy lifted his head.

I said how about letting me look.

Well. Sure.

Suttree shipped the oars and took the tube from the boy and bent over the side with it. A high sheer rock veered past wrapped in bubbles. Moted panels spun down deeps of dusky jade where dim shoals of fish willowed and flared and drifted back over the cold slate floor of the river. A braided cable among the rocks trailed rags of soft green slime in the current.

I dont see any mussels, he said.

The boy looked out downriver. Keep a lookin, he said. They'll be some directly.

He bent again. A whole tree lay on the bottom of the river, deep in a pool, a murky bole with filaments of moss swaying and a heavy black bass that waited on below. A sandy floor sloped away. Fat suckers sculled. A cloud of bubbles rolled up in the glass and cleared and a green cold slick faired over paler rocks, round river stones and ledges of slate gently sculpted. A seam of black shellfish lay beneath.

Here come some.

He heard the splash of the brail going overboard. The boat rocked and recovered with the boy's standing and Suttree's face dipped in the water. He raised his head and shook the water from the glass and bent to look again. Long greenbrown weeds swung in the current and dimly through the moving water he could see the mussel beds, a slender colony of them dark and quaking among the rocks with their pale clefts breathing, closing, folding slowly fanwise, valved clots of flesh in their keeps of cotyloid nacre. The shadow of the skiff like a nightshade passing swept them shut.

Is they lots?

A few.

The bottom fell away into an opaque green murk. The boat spun slowly.

Suttree raised up and took the oars and straightened the skiff out.

It deeps off here, the boy said.

Yeah.

We'll just go on down.

Okay.

How about lettin me have my looker?

Okay.

They ran downstream a quarter mile, the boy watching the bottom, Suttree at the oars. They swung into a long ropy glide and went rocking down a chute into fast water. The boy raised his head, his forelock dripping. We'll get em now, he called.

Suttree steadied the boat with the oars.

When they drifted out into the slow water at the foot of their run amid flotsam and tranquil spume the boy stood at the transom and hauled the brail aboard and hung it dripping in the uprights with a couple dozen black mussels clamped to the lines. They swung and turned and clacked and the boy took out an enormous brass cookspoon and began to pry them loose. Within minutes they lay like stones in the floor of the skiff and the boy had cast the brail overboard again. He turned to Suttree who was backoaring to stand in the current. His face was flushed and his breath short. That's how we do it, he wheezed.

Is that a pretty good batch for a run?

It aint no more'n average. I've seen em to come up solid with em. Me and Daddy has dredged messes we couldnt lift.

What's the other brail for?

You swap off. You hang up the full brail and thow out the othern.

Well why didnt you throw out the other one?

The boy was watching the river bottom again. He waved one hand in the air to dismiss the subject. I just wanted to show you how to strip the lines, he said.

Suttree edged the boat away from a dimpled suck in the river and they went rocking down the shoals, the sun well up now, the day warming. His hands were like claws on the oars.

They washed out in a slackwater where a gravel bar ran almost to midriver and the boy raised up the brail again and hung it dripping and clicking with mussels in the trees. He and Suttree looked at each other.

These is some jimdandy'ns, the boy said.

Suttree nodded. There were some big as your hand.

Let's swing up and run that bed one more time.

Suttree looked upriver dubiously.

You wont find em much better'n these here.

He swung the skiff and braced his feet and dug into the river. They went up along the inside shore. When they had gained the head of the glide he stood the boat in the current and swung back obliquely across the run while the boy cast over the empty brail.

I thowed one one time a hook got me behind the ear and like to took me with it.

How far down do we go? said Suttree.

You mean this evenin?

Yes.

We'll go on down to the Wild Bull. What Daddy said.

Who the hell is going to row back?

The boy squinted at him there in the sunshine, the spoon poised over the mussel in his hand, the mussels in the skiff floor drying in the sun to a gray slate color. You aint give out are ye? he said.

I've been rowing this damned thing for two days. What do you think?

Well shit, I'll swap off with ye comin back. It aint all that far.

They reached the shoals in the early afternoon. The boy boated the last rackful of mussels and shucked them from the hooks wet and clattering onto the pile in the boat and Suttree stood on one oar to turn them toward the bank. The boat would hardly move it lay so deep in the river with its cargo.

There was but one shovel and it had an old handmade tang about a foot long but no handle other at all. Suttree set the boy to shoveling the mussels out of the boat onto the bank and he himself went up through the woods until he found a good shade tree and he lay flat on his back beneath it and was soon asleep.

He was awakened by cries down toward the river. It occurred to Suttree that he and the boy didnt even know each other's names. He got up and went down through the woods.

Hey, called the boy.

All right, all right.

Hell fire, where'd you get to? I aint shovelin all these here by myself.

Suttree took the shovel from him and stepped into the boat.

I thought you'd run plumb off, the boy said.

My name's Suttree.

Yeah, I know it.

What's yours?

Willard.

Willard. Okay Willard.

Okay what?

Suttree heaved a shovelful of mussels up and looked at the boy. It was hot in the sun. The boy standing there in his rancid overalls looked pale and pitiful and slightly malevolent. Just okay, Willard, he said.

They rowed into camp at dusk sitting side by side on the seat of the skiff each with a sweep in two hands. Suttree staggered up the bank with the rope and tied up and went to the fire and sat and stared into it. Reese emerged from the lean-to in his underwear. Is that you all? he said.

Yeah.

Where you been?

Suttree didnt answer. The boy had come up and was looking around. Where you all been? the man asked him.

Where's everbody at? the boy said.

They've done gone to a social. Where you all been?

Is there anything to eat? Suttree said.

They's some whitebeans and cornbread in the pan.

Is they any onions? the boy said.

No they aint, said Reese. He came over to where Suttree was sitting on a board with his feet stretched out before him. Did you all do any good? he said.

Ask him, said Suttree.

How did you all do?

We done all right. Aint they no milk?

No they aint.

Shit, said the boy.

What?

I said shoot.

You better of.

Did ye'ns get a pretty good mess?

We got about all the boat would hold. How did you all do?

We done all right.

Suttree had taken up a plate and was spooning beans from the pot. Is there any coffee? he said.

No they aint.

He stared sullenly into the fire. No they aint, he said.

He was lying in his blankets out on the knoll when they came back. They came down through the woods by the river swinging a lantern and singing hymns. He lay there listening to this advancing minstrelsy and watching the moon ride up out of the trees. He was hungry and his shoulders ached. His eyelids felt like they were on springs, he couldnt get them to stay shut. After a while he got up.

One of the girls was going toward the river and he called to her. Hey, he said. Is there anything to eat up there?

It was quiet for a minute. The fire had been built back and the flames looked hopeful up there under the rocks. No they aint, she said.

In the morning they were up at some misty hour and were at donning the crazy calico churchclothes. They did not wake him. He raised the edge of his blanket and peered out. Among the slats of the lamplit shed he could see thin flashes of white flesh, birdlike flurryings. The girls emerged in their carboncopy dresses and the boy came out of the woods stiffly and looking churlish and sullen and strange, like a child pervert. They set off upriver through the woods and Suttree sat up in his blanket to better view the spectacle.

They were gone all day. He stirred out and searched through the kitchen things and through the jumble of stuff in the lean-to but he could find nothing to eat other than the cornmeal and a handful of whitebeans that had been left to soak. He made a fire and put the beans on and went off down to the river to look at the skiffs. He squatted on his heels and threw small stones at waterspiders skating on the dimpled river.

In the afternoon he sat in the cool under the bluff. Summer thunderheads were advancing from the south. He leaned back against the rock escarpment. Jagged blades of slate and ratchel stood like stone tools in the loam. Tracks of mice or ground squirrels, a few dry and meatless nuthulls. A dark stone disc. He reached and picked it up. In his hand a carven gorget. He spooned the clay from the face of it with his thumb and read two rampant gods addorsed with painted eyes and helmets plumed, their spangled anklets raised in dance. They bore birdheaded scepters each aloft.

Suttree spat upon the disc and wiped it on the hip of his jeans and studied it again. Uncanny token of a vanished race. For a cold moment the spirit of an older order moved in the rainy air. With a small twig he cleaned each line and groove and with spittle and the tail of his shirt he polished the stone, holding it, a cool lens, in the cup of his tongue, drying it with care. A gray and alien stone of a kind he'd never seen.

He took off his belt and with his pocketknife cut a long thin strip of leather and threaded it through the hole in the gorget and tied the thong and put it around his neck. It lay cool and smooth against his chest, this artifact of dawn where twilight drew across the iron landscape.

He was sitting on a log carving a whistle from willow wood when the family returned from service. He watched them come down through the woods, the six of them indianfile. When they had passed and gone on to the camp he rose and folded away his knife and went after.

Yonder he comes, sang out Reese.

Yeah, said Suttree.

We seen ye was asleep when we left out of here this mornin. Didnt want to bother ye.

The women were gone to the shed to change out of their clothes and Reese had taken a seat under his tree in his suit. Suttree squatted on one knee in front of him and pinned him with a hungry stare.

Look, he said, I dont want to be a bother to anybody but when the hell do we eat around here?

I'm glad you ast me that, said Reese. Somebody has got to go to the store and I was wonderin if you could maybe take the boy and run on over there.

You all just came from over there.

Yes we did. But I'll be danged if I didnt get over there and come to find out I didnt have no money on me. I thought of it quick as we got up to the church there. I'd meant to . . .

All right, said Suttree. He was holding out his hand. Let me have some money.

Reese eased himself up a little bit and leaned forward from the tree. He spoke in a low voice. I wanted to talk to you about that, he said.

Suttree stared at him a minute and then rose and stood looking off toward some brighter landscape beyond them all. Listen, Reese was saying. He tugged at Suttree's trouserleg. Suttree took a step away.

Listen. What it is, we've had so much expense settin up camp and gettin everthing ready, you know. We been up here two weeks now and aint had nothin but outgoes, bound to be a little short, and you a partner, regular partner you know, I thought we could share expense a little until we sold us a load and I could settle with ye. You know.

What the hell would you of done if I hadnt come up here when I did?

Why, somethin would of turned up. Always does. Listen . . .

Suttree had turned out his pockets and was putting together what money he had. A couple of dollars and some change. He dropped it on the ground in front of Reese. How long do you reckon we can eat on that? he said.

We can get something. He looked at the crumpled money lying there. He poked at it, as if it were something dead. It aint a whole lot, is it? he said.

No, said Suttree. It sure as hell aint.

That all you got? Reese squinting up at Suttree.

That's it.

He scratched his head. Well, he said. Listen . . .

I'm listening.

Why dont you and the boy go on over there and get us some bread and some lunchmeat. They's cornmeal and some beans here. Ast the old lady what all she needs real bad. Get a quart of milk if you can. You know.

Suttree stalked off to find the boy.

I just come from there, the boy said.

Well get your ass up cause you're going again.

They aint no need to cuss about it, the boy said. It Sunday and all.

They went off up the path through the woods. She'd written him a list, a pinched scrawl on a piece of paper sack. He balled it in his fist and pitched it into the weeds.

They went through the woods for a half mile and came out onto an old macadam road half grown back in patches of grass, small saplings. They followed it with its tilted slabs of paving through a countryside warped and bleared in the steamy heat. They passed the ruins of an old motel, a broken paintworn sign, a clutch of tiny cabins quietly corroding in an arbor of pines. When they came out onto the highway Suttree could see the little crossroads community at the top of the rise. A handful of houses and a stuccoed roadside grocery store with a gaspump.

He crossed the graveled forebay and entered the store. Old familiar smells. He got a pint of chocolate milk from the cooler and drank it.

You goin to set us up to a dope? the boy said.

Get one.

Let's get us a couple of cakes too and we wont say nothin about it.

Suttree looked at him. He was rummaging among the bottles in the drink case. These here R C's cold? he called out. Suttree went on to the meatcounter.

What for ye? said the storekeeper, appearing behind the case and taking down an apron from a nail.

Slice me a couple of pounds of that baloney, said Suttree.

He hung the apron back.

Slice it thin, said Suttree.

He got some cheese and some bread and a drum of oatmeal and two quarts of milk and some onions. When the merchant had totted up these purchases there was forty cents left. Suttree looked at the rows of coffee in their bags above the merchant's head. The merchant turned to look with him.

What's the cheapest coffee you've got?

Well, let's see. The cheapest I got is the Slim Jim.

Slim Jim?

Slim Jim.

How much is it?

Thirty-nine cents.

Let me have it.

The merchant lifted down a bag of it from the shelf and set it on the counter. It was dusty and he blew on it and gave it a little swat before he lifted it into the grocery bag.

Right, said Suttree. He scooped the bag off the counter and handed it to the boy and they left.

It was evening when they got back. Suttree went down and sat in the dark by the river until supper was ready, the light of the cookfire composing behind him on the high bluff a shadowshow of primitive life. He pitched small round pebbles at the river as if he were feeding it.

They ate sandwiches of fried baloney and bowls of whitebeans. Suttree came to the fire with his cup and held it out. The old woman lifted the potlid and sniffed. Suttree watched her. The plaited hawsers of hair that bound her thin gray skull. She took up her apron in one hand to grip the pot and tilt the hot black coffee out. Suttree went back to the box where he'd been sitting and stirred the coffee and put the spoon in his cuff for safekeeping and lifted the cup and sipped.

He sat very still, then he turned and spat the coffee on the ground. Good God, he said.

What is it? said Reese.

What's happened to this coffee?

I aint drunk none of it.

Suttree swung his nose across the rim of the cup and then pitched the coffee out on the ground and went on eating.

Reese wiped his mouth on his knee and rose. He came back with a cup of the coffee and stood over Suttree blowing at it and then he took a sip.

What is this shit? he said.

Damned if I know. Slim Jim, that's the name of it.

Reese took another sip and then tipped it out on the ground. I dont know what it is, he said. But it aint coffee.

The girl was sitting on the far side of the fire. She flung her black hair. What'd you do to the coffee, Mama? she called.

Reese had gone back to the fire. They had the package up trying to read it. Reese poured the coffee out on the ground. A squabble ensued.

Suttree what is this shit?

I dont know. I bought it for coffee.

It dont even smell like coffee.

They done emptied the coffee out and filled the sack back with old leaves or somethin, said the woman, nodding her head and looking about.

Bring me a cup of it, Willard, the girl called.

Reese cut his eyes about. It might be poison, he said.

Put eggshells in it, Mama, the girl called. That'll rectify it.

Where's she goin to get eggshells at, dumb-ass? They aint no eggs.

The woman reached and swatted the boy in the top of the head with her hand.

Ow, he said.

You mind how you talk to your sister.

Something woke him in the small hours of the morning. Things moving in the dark. He took his flashlight and trained it out along the trees until it ghosted away in the dark fields downriver. He swept it toward the woods and back again. A dozen hot eyes watched, paired and random in the night. He held the light above his head to try and see the shapes beyond but nothing showed save eyes. Blinking on and off, or eclipsing and reappearing as heads were turned. They were none the same height and he tried his memory for anything that came in such random sizes. Then a pair of eyes ascended vertically some five feet and another pair sank slowly to the ground. Weird dwarfs with amaurotic eyeballs out there in the dark on a seesaw sidesaddle. Others began to raise and lower.

Cows. He agreed with himself: It is cows. He switched off the flashlight and lay back. He could smell them now on the cool upriver wind, sweet odor of grass and milk. The damp air was weighted with all manner of fragrance. You can see it in a dog's eyes that he is sorting such things as he tests the wind and Suttree could smell the water in the river and the dew in the grass and the wet shale of the bluff. It was overcast and there were no stars to plague him with their mysteries of space and time. He closed his eyes.

In the morning they took the womenfolk downriver to shuck the mussels there, the girls giggling, the old woman clutching the sides of the boat nervously and staring with her hooded eyes toward the passing shore. That evening after supper he went down to the river with a bar of soap and sat naked in the water off the gravel bar. He washed his clothes and he washed himself and he hung his clothes from a tree and got his towel and dried himself and sat among his blankets. After a while Reese came down through the woods on tiptoe, calling out softly.

Over here, said Suttree.

He crouched in front of Suttree. He looked back over his shoulder toward the camp.

What is it? said Suttree.

We got to go to town.

Okay.

I figure we ought to just go on in the mornin and get done with it.

Suttree nodded.

I started to let Mama and Wanda go, but you caint depend on no women to do business. What do you think?

It suits the hell out of me.

Reese looked toward the fire and looked back. It suits the hell out of me too, he hissed. If I dont get shitfaced drunk they aint a cow in Texas. You ever been to Newport?

Not lately.

Lord they got the wildest little old things runnin around up there. It's a sight in the world.

They have?

You daggone right. The old man checked the camp again and leaned to Suttree's ear. We go up there, Sut, we'll run a pair or two down and put the dick to em. He winked hugely and set one finger to his lips.

They left in the early morning two days later. It had rained all night and the cars came down the long black road like motorboats and passed and diminished in shrouds of vapor. After a while an old man stopped in a model A and they rode on into Dandridge. The old man did not speak. The three of them hunched up like puppets on the front seat watched the summer morning break over the rolling countryside.

They got a ride from Dandridge to Newport on a truck. There was a tractor on the truckbed and it kept shifting in its chains so that the travelers stood back against the stakesides with their hair blowing in the wind lest the thing break loose. They reached Newport around noon and descended blinking and disheveled into the hot street.

The jeweler was sitting in a wire cage at the front of the store and he had what looked like a snuff jar screwed into his eye. The two of them stood there at the window and waited. Yes, the jeweler said. He didnt look up.

Reese laid a pearl on the counter.

The jeweler raised his head and sniffed and took the glass from his eye and donned a pair of spectacles. He reached and picked up the pearl. He rolled it between his thumb and forefinger and looked at it and put it back. He took off his spectacles and put the glass back in his eyes and bent to his work again. I cant use it, he said.

Reese gave Suttree an uneasy wink. He delved up another jewel from his little changepurse and laid it by the first. Larger and more round. Hey, he said.

The jeweler set aside a small pick with which he was sorting something in a boxlid. He looked at the two pearls before him and he looked at Reese. I cant use it.

Reese had fished out meantime his best pearl and this he brought forth and held out in one grimy hand. I guess you cant use this one either, he said in triumph.

The jeweler removed the glass and fitted the spectacles again. He didnt reach for the pearl. He seemed to simply want a better look at these two.

Go ahead, said Reese, grinning and gesturing with the pearl.

Fellers, said the jeweler, those things are not worth anything.

They're pearls, Suttree said.

Tennessee pearls.

Hell, they've got to be worth something.

Well, I hate to say it, but they're not worth a nickel. Oh, you might find somebody that wanted them. Keepsake or something. I've known people to pay three or four dollars for a really nice one that they wanted made into a pin or something, but you might have a shoebox full and I wouldnt give a dime for them.

Reese was still holding out the pearl. He turned to Suttree. He thinks we aint never traded afore, I reckon.

The jeweler had taken off his spectacles and was preparing to look through his glass again.

We may look country, but we aint ignorant, Reese told him.

Let's go, Reese.

You aint never seen no nicer a one than that there.

The jeweler bent with his monocle to his work again.

Suttree took the old man's arm and steered him out the door. Reese was looking over the prize pearl for some undetected flaw. In the street Suttree turned him around and got him by the shoulder. What the hell is going on? I thought you said that big pearl was worth ten dollars?

Shit Sut, dont pay no attention to him, he dont know the first thing about it.

Suttree pointed toward the windowglass. He's a goddamned jeweler. Cant you see the sign? What the hell do you mean he doesnt know?

He's just outslicked hisself is what he's done. He wants us to give him the goddamned pearls. I've traded with these cute sons of bitches afore, Sut. I know.

Let me see those things.

Reese handed him the pearls. Suttree looked them over in the hard light of midday. They looked like pearls. Somewhat gray, somewhat misshapen. Hell, they must be worth something, he said.

Reese took the pearls from him. Course they are, he said. Goddamn, you think I dont know nothin?

How many have you ever sold?

That's all right how many I sold. I sold some.

How many?

Well. I sold one last year for four dollars.

Who to?

Just to somebody.

Suttree was standing looking at the ground and shaking his head. After a while he looked up. Well let's try somewhere else, he said.

They canvassed the three jewelers and two pawnshops and were again on the street. Shadows were tilting on the walk, the day'd grown cooler.

What now? said Suttree.

Let me think a minute, said Reese.

That's all we need.

We aint tried the poolhall.

The poolhall?

Yeah.

Suttree turned and walked away down the street. Reese caught him up and was at his elbow with plans and explanations.

Suttree turned. How much money do you have on you?

He stopped.

Come on. How much?

Why Sut, you know I aint got no money.

Not a dime?

Why no.

Well I've got fifteen cents and I'm going over here and have coffee and doughnuts. You can sit and watch if you like. Then we'd better get on the goddamned road before it gets dark and try and get a ride out of here.

Hell Sut, we caint go back emptyhanded.

But Suttree had already stepped into the street. Reese watched him cross and enter the cafe on the other side.

Suttree borrowed a paper from a stack by the till as he went in and he sat at the counter. A fat man asked him what he would have.

Coffee.

He wrote on the ticket.

Do you have any doughnuts?

Plain or chocolate.

Chocolate.

He wrote that. Suttree craned his neck to see the price.

The fat man went down the counter and Suttree opened his paper.

He drank three cups of coffee and read the paper from front to back. Finally he folded the paper and went to the front and paid his bill and put the paper back and went out. He stood in the street picking his teeth and looking up and down. He waited around for the better part of an hour. The stores were closing. He eyed the failing sun. That son of a bitch, he said.

He was passing a small cafe when something about a figure within stopped him. He stepped back and peered through the glass. At a booth in the little lunchroom was Reese. He was buttering up large chunks of cornbread. Before him sat a platter of steak and gravy with mashed potatoes and beans. A waitress shuffled down the corridor toward him with a tall mug of coffee. Reese looked up to say some pleasantry. His eyes wandered from her to the scowling face at the window and he gave a sort of little jump in his seat and then grinned and waved.

Suttree threw back the door and went down the aisle.

Hey Sut. Where the hell did you get to? I hunted everwhere for you.

Sure you did. Where did you get the money? I thought you were broke.

Set down, set down. Honey? He raised a hand. He pointed at Suttree's head. Bring him what he wants. Boy, I'm glad I found you. Here, tell her what you want.

I dont want a goddamned thing. Listen.

They aint no need to cuss about it, the waitress said.

Suttree ignored her. He leaned to Reese who was loading his jaw with a forkful of steak. You're driving me crazy, he said.

Honey, bring him a cup of coffee.

I dont want a cupping fuck of coffee. Look Reese . . .

Reese lowered his head and gave Suttree a queer clown's wink and nod. Sold em, he whispered. Looky here.

Look at what?

Down here. Looky here.

Suttree had to lean back and look under the table where this grinning fool was holding pinched in his hand so just the corner showed a twenty dollar bill.

What the hell are you hiding it for? Is it counterfeit?

Shhh. Hell no son, it's good as gold.

Who'd you hit in the head?

Old buddy, we goin to take this to the tong games and come off with some real money.

We better get our ass down to the bus station is what we better do.

Honey, bring him a cup of coffee.

He said he didnt want none.

Suttree slumped back in the booth.

Bring him some, said Reese, waving a piece of cornbread. He'll drink it.

They stood in the street under the small lamps. A deathly quiet prevailed over the town.

I wisht it wasnt summer and we could go to the cockfights, Reese said. He sucked his teeth and looked up and down the street. Got to find us a goddamned taxi. He patted his little paunch and belched and squinted about.

Let me have a nickel and I'll go in and call one.

Reese doled the coin easily. Suttree wore a look of dry patience. He went in and called the taxi.

When it arrived Reese opened the front door and hopped in and was whispering loudly to the driver. Suttree climbed in the back and shut the door.

Let me just take you fellers on up to the Green Room, the driver was saying. You can get anything you want up there.

What do you say, Sut?

Suttree looked at the back of Reese's head and then he just looked out the window.

Course you can go anywhere you want, said the driver.

Daggone right you can, said Reese. When ye got the money to do it with. He turned and favored Suttree with a sleazy grin.

What kind of whiskey you boys want? You want bonded or some real good moonshine?

Is it real good sure enough?

Bonded, said Suttree from the back.

They were going by narrow back streets in the small town suppertime dark, by curtained windowlights where families sat gathered. Suttree rolled down the window and breathed the air all full of blossoms.

The driver took them up a gravel drive to the back of an old house. A yellow bulb hung burning from the naked night above them. The driver got out and a man came from the door and the two of them went across the yard and behind a garage. When they came back the driver was holding a pint of whiskey down by the side of his leg.

He got in and palmed the whiskey to Reese. Reese held it to the light and studied the label professionally as he unscrewed the cap.

They went back down the driveway with Reese's head thrown back and the bottom of the bottle standing straight up.

Get ye a drink, he wheezed, poking the bottle over the seat at Suttree.

Suttree drank and handed it back.

Reese held the bottle up and eyed it and held it under the driver's chin. Get ye a drink old buddy, he said.

The driver said he didnt drink on duty.

They drove out through the small streets and struck the highway, Reese and Suttree passing the bottle back and forth and Reese giving the driver a history of himself no part of which was even vaguely true.

Say you all never been to the Green Room? said the driver.

We aint been up here in a long time, said Reese.

They got some little old gals up here will do anything. They'd as soon suck a peter as look at ye.

Reese was elbowing the dark of the cab behind him vigorously. You hear that, Sut? he said.

They went out the highway several miles and turned onto a side-road that had one time been the highway. At the top of the hill stood a squat cinderblock building with neon piping along the roof. The windows were painted black and one of them was broken and fixed back with blocks of wood stovebolted through the holes. There was an iron pole in the drive with a beersign hung from the crosstrees and perhaps half a hundred cars parked in the gravel. The cabdriver switched on the domelight and looked at Reese.

What we owe ye, old buddy?

Let me have five. That'll get the whiskey and everthing.

Reese paid and they stepped out into the gravel. The taxi slewed about in a cloud of dust and flying stones and went back out to the highway. Reese tucked in his shirt and hitched up his trousers and seized the doorhandle to make his entrance but the door was locked.

Ring the buzzer, said Suttree.

He pushed the button and almost immediately the door opened and a man looked at them and stepped back and they entered.

A concrete floor, a horseshoeshaped bar upholstered in quilted black plastic, a gaudy jukebox that played country music. A few sloe-eyed young whores in stage makeup and incredible costumes, ballroom gowns, bathing suits, satin pajamas. They lounged at the bar, they sat in the booths by the wall, they danced with clowns dressed up like farmers wooden clown dances in the shifting jukebox lights. Through a door to the rear Suttree could see thicker smoke yet and the green baize of gaming tables.

Godamighty damn, said Reese reverently. Looky here.

Suttree was looking. He'd been in places like this but not quite. A whole new style seemed to be seeking expression here. They crossed to the bar and were immediately set upon by whores. A blackhaired girl in a chiffon dress with a train that followed her about the floor sweeping up the cigarette butts had Suttree by the elbow. Hidy cutie, she said. Why dont you buy me a drink? Suttree looked down into a pair of enormous painted eyes dripping a black goo. A pair of perfectly round white tits pushed up in the front of her gown. You'll have to see this man here, he said. He's the last of the big spenders.

She immediately turned loose of Suttree and got hold of Reese's arm even though there were two other girls hanging onto him. Hidy cutie, she said. Why dont you buy me a drink?

I'll buy ye'ns all a drink quick as I get done at the tong table, cried Reese.

The bartender was standing at the ready and Suttree held up one hand and caught his eye. He raised his chin to know what Sut would have.

Bourbon and gingerale, said Suttree.

Where you all from, honey? said a blonde who appeared out of the smoke.

Suttree looked at her. Web City, he said.

You're a smart son of a bitch, aint ye?

He watched Reese at the cardtable until he became bored and went back out to the bar. But the whores had thickened and he got another drink and went back into the gambling room again. Reese seemed to have won some money and Suttree tapped him on the shoulder to get some quarters and dimes for the slotmachines. The dealer raised up and eyed him narrowly and told him to back off from the table if he wasnt playing. Reese handed him two dollars over his shoulder and Suttree took the money and went into another room and got change from a lady at a cardtable by the door. There were eight or ten slotmachines along the walls and several young men in dark gabardine shirts and their heads almost shaven were feeding money to the whores and the whores were operating the machines. Suttree won about seven dollars and went back out to the bar and got another drink. He was beginning to feel a little drunk. He bought the black-haired girl a drink and she took him by the arm and they sat in a booth at the far wall and she immediately ordered two more drinks from a waitress dressed in a swimsuit and black net stockings. The black-haired girl put her hand on Suttree's leg and got him by the neck and ran her tongue down his throat. Then she stuck her tongue in his ear and asked him if he wanted to go out in the back.

Reese came reeling through the smoke and the din with a painted childwhore on his arm. She had an eyetooth out and smiled with her cigarette in her mouth to hide the gap.

Looky here, Sut.

Hidy.

Aint that a purty little old thing?

Suttree smiled.

Reese had her by the hand. He leaned toward Suttree. Listen, he said, you wouldnt tell on a feller would ye?

Maybe not. Where's the whiskey?

Here. Hell fire, get ye a drink. He brought the bottle forth from his overalls and handed it over.

You raise tobacco too? the girl said.

Sure, said Suttree.

Reese was making peculiar faces and jerking his shoulder at Suttree. Suttree spun the cap back on the bottle and slid from the booth. I've got to talk to my partner here a minute, he told the girl.

They conferred a few feet from the table. Let's hear the bad news, said Suttree.

Bad news's ass. Looky here.

He was cupping his hand at the mouth of his pocket, a roll of bills crouched there like a pet mouse. Old buddy, I strictly slipped it to em in yonder, he said.

The whore on his arm leaned across to whisper in Suttree's ear. You ought to get with Doreen yonder, she said, nodding toward a puffy blonde at the bar. She's real sweet.

We got to get us another bottle of whiskey, said Reese. Both she and Reese had taken to hoarse stage whispers and Suttree had to bend his head forward to hear them at all what with the howl of electric guitars from the jukebox. As he did so the old man seized him by the head and pulled him close and rasped in his ear: Go on and get her Sut. We'll strictly put the dick to em.

When he woke a light had come on in the cabin and a man and a girl were standing in the door. That goddamned Doreen leaves her goddamned dates in the cabins all the time, the girl said. Suttree groaned and tried to put his head beneath the pillow.

Hey, said the girl. You caint stay here.

His head was at the edge of the thin mattress. He looked down at the floor. The floor was pink linoleum with green and yellow flowers. There was a glass there and a halfpint bottle with a drink in the bottom. He reached down and got the bottle and held it against his naked chest.

Hey, said the girl.

Okay, said Suttree. Let me get my clothes.

He wandered off through the weeds in the dark. Out on the highway the sound of trucktires whined and died in the distance. He fell into a gully and climbed out and went on again.

When he woke it was daylight and he was lying in a field. He rose up and looked out across the sedge. Two little girls and a dog were going along a dirt lane. Beyond them the sunhammered landscape veered away in a quaking shapeless hell. A low gray barn, a fence. A fieldwagon standing in milkweed. Yonder the town. He rose to his feet and stood swaying, a great pain in his eyeballs and upon his skull like the pressure of marine deeps. He tottered off across the fields toward the roadhouse.

He found Reese asleep in a wrecked car behind the cabins. Suttree shook him gently awake into a world he wanted no part of. The old man fought it. He pushed away and buried his head in one arm there on the dusty ruptured seat. Suttree could not help but grin for all that his head hurt so.

Come on, he said. Let's go.

The old man moaned.

What? Suttree said.

You go on and I'll come later, tell em.

Okay. You comfortable?

I'm all right.

You want a sip of this cold lemonade fore I go?

An eye opened. The musty gutted hulk of the car stank of mold and sweat and cheap whiskey. Wasps kept coming in the naked rear window and vanishing through a crack in the domelight overhead.

What? said Reese.

I said would you like a sip of this cold lemonade?

The old man tried to see without moving his head but he gave it up. Shit, he said. You aint got no lemonade.

Suttree pulled him around by one arm. Come on, he said. Get your ass up from there and let's go.

A bloated face turned up. Ah God. Just leave me here to die.

Let's go, Reese.

Where are we at?

Let's go.

He struggled up, looking around.

How you feeling, old partner? said Suttree.

Reese looked up into Suttree's grinning face. He put his hands over his eyes. Where you been? he said.

Come on.

Reese shook his head. Boy, we a couple of good'ns aint we?

You dont have a little drink hid away do you?

Shit.

Here.

He lowered his hands. Suttree was holding the almost empty bottle at him. Why goddamn, Sut, he said. He reached for the bottle with both hands and twisted off the cap and drank.

Leave me corners, said Suttree.

Reese closed his eyes, screwed up his face and shivered and swallowed. He blew and held the bottle up. Goddamn, he said. I dont remember it bein that bad last night.

Suttree took the bottle from him and let the little it held fill up one corner and then he tilted it and drank and pitched the empty bottle out through the open window into the weeds. Well, he said. Think you can make it now?

We'll give it a try.

He pulled himself painfully from the doorless car and stood squinting in the heat little pleased with what he saw. Where do you reckon they sell beer on Sunday up here?

Right here probably, Suttree said, nodding toward the roadhouse.

They passed among the cabins and staggered across the dusty waste of gravel and trash with their tongues out like dogs. Suttree tapped at a door at the rear of the premises. They waited.

Knock again, Sut.

He did.

A slide shot back in the side of the building and a man peered out. What'll you have, boys? he said.

You got any cold beer?

It's all cold. What kind?

What kind? said Suttree.

Any goddamned kind, said Reese.

You got Miller's?

What you want, a sixpack?

Suttree looked at Reese. Reese was looking at him blandly. Suttree said: Have you got any money?

No. Aint you?

He felt himself all over. Not a fucking dime, he said.

The bootlegger looked from one to the other of them.

Where's that pearl? said Suttree.

The old man raised his foot and put it down again. He leaned against the side of the building and raised his foot and reached down in his sock. He held up his purse.

How come you to still have that, said Suttree. Did you not get any poontang last night?

You daggone right I got me some. But I never took off my shoes. He undid the mouth of the thing and rolled out the pearl and held it up. Looky here, he said.

What's that supposed to be? said the bootlegger.

A pearl. Go on. Take a look at it.

You sons of bitches get on away from here, said the bootlegger, and slammed the little window shut.

They looked at each other for a minute and then Suttree squatted in the dust among the flattened cans.

Shit, said Reese.

Suttree palmed his knees and shook his head. We're hellatious traders, he said.

Boy I hate a dumb son of a bitch like that that dont know the value of nothin.

Let's get the hell out of here. It's a long way home.

Coming over the Pigeon River Bridge into Newport a county police cruiser passed them. The old man saw them coming. Wave like they know ye, he said.

Fuck that, said Suttree.

The cruiser went by and Reese waved real big. The cruiser turned at the edge of the bridge and came back and pulled up alongside. A fat deputy looked them over. Who you think you wavin at buddy?

Suttree groaned.

Reese smiled. I thought you was somebody I knowed, he said.

Is that right? Maybe you'd like to come uptown and get a little better aquainted.

He didnt mean anything by it, officer.

The deputy eyed Suttree up and down, little joy in the beholding. I'll be the judge of that, he said. Where you two goin?

Both reckoned one more wrong answer would be all that the law allowed. They looked at each other. Suttree could hear the river beneath them. He saw himself in a swandive, heedless, lost. Under gray swirling waters. He could hear the cruiser's motor idling roughly with its high camshaft. Home, he said.

The driver had said something to the deputy. The deputy looked them over again. Well, he said, you'd better be gettin on there.

Yessir, Suttree said.

Much obliged, your officer, said the old man.

They pulled away and turned at the end of the bridge and came back. The driver glanced at them in passing but they were both looking at the ground.

Bastards, Suttree said. I thought for a minute there we were gone.

I knowed how to handle it, Reese said.

I told you not to wave, goddamnit. And what the hell is your officer supposed to mean?

I dont know. Shit, my head hurts.

He was stumbling along holding the top of his head with both hands. Suttree looked at him in disgust. We'd better get the hell out of here, he said.

We better not go through town.

Dont worry, said Suttree. We're not.

They turned down along the river and Suttree took bearings by the sun and plotted a course crosscountry that should bring them out on the highway on the other side of town. They went wandering mournfully down little dirt tracks and across fields. They went through a shantytown strung out along the edge of a branch, all grass and growing things about the creek and the encampment gone, a land of raw clay strewn with trash, with chickens and scabrous dogs. A cadaverous and darkeyed people watched mutely, furtive and dimly defined in their doorways. Such squalid folk as not even a weed grew among. Reese nodded and howdied to them but they just stared.

They crossed a pasture where grackles blue and metallic in the sun were turning up dried cowpats for the worms beneath and they went on past the back side of a junklot with the sun wearing hard upon them and upon the tarpaper roof of the parts shack and upon the endless fenders and lids of wrecked cars that lay curing paintlorn in the hot and weedy reeks.

They ended up lost in a big alfalfa field. On three sides were woods and on the fourth was where they'd come from.

Which way? Reese said.

Suttree squatted and held his head. Will some son of a bitch please tell me what I'm doing here?

I got to get out of this sun fore my old head pops, said Reese. He looked down. Suttree had tilted forward onto his knees. They looked like castaways. Dont lay down, said Reese, or ye never will get up.

Suttree looked up at him. You would absolutely pull the pope under, he said.

He probably dont even drink. Which way, do ye reckon?

Suttree struggled up and looked around and struck out again.

They crossed into heavy woods and began to climb. The ground was covered with random limestone and there were sinkholes to be fallen into.

You take poison ivy, Sut?

No. Do you?

No. Thank the Lord. I believe this here must be under cultivation.

They went on. They rested more and more going up the ridge. Just sitting in the undergrowth like apes eyeing one another with little expectation of anything and breathing hard. When they got to the top they looked out and they could see below them through the trees a piece of black highway about two miles away.

I dont think I can make it without a drink of water, Suttree said.

Dont drink no water, Sut. It'll make ye drunk all over again.

Suttree glared at him.

When they reached the highway they were staggerfooted and crazy-looking. As far as you could see in either direction there was not so much as a billboard. Suttree sat down by the edge of the road with his feet spread and began to pick at gravels and little straws and things.

Here comes a car, Sut.

Thumb it.

Well get up. He wont stop with somebody setting down.

They watched the driver's eyes. He looked like a skittish horse the way he rolled them and the car swerved out as if he'd keep from being leapt upon by these roadside predators who possibly fared on the flesh of motorists in lonely places.

An hour later they were still standing there. Three cars and one truck had passed. They looked at each other and at themselves. The old man fell to combing his hair with his hands.

We better start walking, Suttree said.

How far from home you reckon we are?

I dont know. Twenty miles. Thirty maybe. Suttree's eyes looked burnt and a crusty paste had formed over his lips.

What time do you reckon it is?

Suttree looked at the sky. Gently quaking like a vat of molten cobalt. Past noon. Maybe two oclock. Let's walk on down around this next curve. Maybe there's a store or something.

The old man shaded his eyes and looked down the hot and smoking road to where it dissolved in a distant haze. The landscape subsequent seemed to shift and veer so that he batted his eyes and made little gestures with his hands as if to shape things right again. I reckon we can try for it, he said.

They set off, stumbling along the roadway with their eyes down. If you keep from looking up for a long time you can surprise yourself with how far you've come. Suttree fell to counting the bottlecaps in the dusty roadside gravel. Then he began to divide them into the rightside ups and the upside downs. Before they reached the curve he called for them to stop.

Reese when he looked at him seemed almost in tears. We nearly to the curve, Sut, he said.

I know. I just want to get rested a minute so that when we look down that next stretch of road and there's nothing there I wont faint.

How long you reckon a feller can sweat like this and nothin to drink without dryin up?

Suttree didnt answer. He was looking back up the road, the accrued flat of the surface making mirages of standing water on the heat-bleared black macadam. A truck was coming down. A phantom truck that augmented itself out of the boiling heat by segments and planes, an old black truck that rode down out of a funhouse mirror, coalesced slowly in the middle distance and pulled to a stop alongside them.

Shithouse mouse, cried Reese, staggering toward the truck.

Suttree thought that if he reached for the vehicle it would resolve itself back into the cooking lobes of his skull from whence it came.

346

But the old man was climbing up, jabbering mindlessly to the driver. Suttree followed. He pulled the door shut after them and it bounced open again.

Raise up on it, said the driver.

He raised up on it and it shut and they pulled away. As bad as they looked, bad as they smelled, this saint seemed not to notice.

How far are you going? Suttree asked.

Sevierville. How far you all?

He was a young boy, hair almost white, a light down at his chin and sidejaws. We'll ride on in with you if you dont mind, Suttree said.

You more'n welcome.

Whew, said Reese. We was about give out.

Around the bend of the road was a store. An orange gaspump standing atilt. Suttree almost croaked out for a brief halt and Reese watched the building go past with sadder eyes yet.

Where you all from? the boy said.

Down around Knoxville. You from up here?

Naw, the boy said. I'm from down around Sevierville. He looked them over. I just come up here to mess around some last night, he said.

They watched the road in silence. Reese looked at the boy. He was wearing clean overall pants and he was leaning up over the wheel and he was chewing tobacco. You ever been to that there Green Room? said Reese.

The boy looked at him sidelong slyly. Shit, he said. Aint that the dangdest place?

You wasnt in there last night was you?

We come in there about three oclock this mornin.

Reese looked at him again. He shook his head. Well, he said. Be proud you wasnt there no earlier. That first shift is pure hell. Aint it Sut?

When they stumbled back into the camp on the river the four women and the boy were waiting for them with grim set mouths.

Boy if you aint a couple of good'ns, she said. Where's them groceries you was goin to bring?

I can explain everthing, Reese said.

Where they at? Hey? Boy if you aint a couple of good'ns.

Reese turned to Suttree. I told you she'd say that. What'd I tell ye?

Standing there with her hands on her hips and that stringy hair and her face a mask of bitterness she looked fearful and Suttree turned away. Reese tried to detain him to verify various lies but he went on toward the lean-to and got his bedding and slouched off toward the river with it. He could hear the debate rising behind him. Suttree'll tell ye. Ast him if you wont believe me.

He lay down in his blankets. It was growing dark, long late mid-summer twilight in the woods. He wanted to go down to the river to bathe but he felt too bad. He turned over and looked at the small plot of ground in the crook of his arm. My life is ghastly, he told the grass.

The girl woke him, shaking him by the shoulder. He'd heard his name called and he rose up wondering. The boy was coming up out of the darkness downriver with a load of pale and misshapen drift-wood like scoured bones from a saint's barrow. At the fire the woman bent and stooped and placed the blackened pots about and the old man squatted on his haunches and rolled one of his limp wet cigarettes and lit it deftly with a coal and watched. All this with a quality of dark ceremony. Suttree walked with the girl to the fire. One of the younger girls came up from the river with the coffeepot dripping riverwater and set it on the stones. She gave him a slow look sideways and arranged the pot with a studied domesticity which in this outlandish setting caused Suttree to smile.

They ate almost in silence, a light smacking of chops, eyes furtive in the light of the lantern. The meal consisted of the whitebeans and cornbread and the boiled chicory coffee. There was about them some-thing subdued beyond their normal reticence. As if order had been forced upon them from without. From time to time the woman awarded to the round dark a look of grim apprehension like a fugitive. When Suttree had finished he thanked her and rose from the table and she nodded and he went off toward the river.

He woke once in the night to the sound of voices, a faint lamenta-tion that might have been hounds beyond the wind but which to him as he lay watching the slow procession of lights on a highway far across the river like the candles of acolytes seemed more the thin clamor of some company transgressed from a dream or children who had died going along a road in the dark with lanterns and crying on their way from the world.

It was the boy came down with poison ivy. First between his fingers, then up his arms and on his face. He'd rub himself with mud, with anything. I seen dogs like that, said the old man. Couldnt get no relief.

His eyes is swoll shut, the woman said at breakfast next morning. The boy came to the fire like a sleepwalker. His arms puffed like adders. He tilted his head a bit to one side to favor the eye he could still see from. The skin of his upper arms had cracked in little fissures from which a clear yellow liquid seeped.

The old man shook his head in disgust. I aint never seen a feller swell up thataway with poison ivy. What all do you reckon's the matter with him?

Just keep him away from me, said Suttree.

I thought you didnt take it, Sut.

I think he's found a new kind.

Shoo, said Wanda. You're a mess.

He came toward her, arms flailing stiffly in a fiend's mime, and she ran screaming.

Well, the old man said. You wont get it just bein in the same boat with him.

I aint goin in no boat, the boy said.

You aint, aint ye?

I caint bend my arms.

Reese had a knife and spoon up in his hands, holding them like candles, waiting for the food. The boy was standing rigidly at the end of the table. You what? Said Reese.

Caint bend my arms, said the boy loftily.

The old man laid down his silver quietly. Well hell's bells, he said. He looked at Suttree. I reckon you and Wanda will have to take it today.

I've got a better idea, Suttree said.

What's that?

You and Wanda.

Well, I thought I'd make the downstream run by myself. I thought I'd let you take the upstream with Wanda on account of she knows it.

The woman swung a bucketful of oatmeal onto the table and the old man seized the ladle and loaded his bowl. Suttree looked down-table at the boy. He was still standing with his arms out at his sides. Wanda was sitting at the table across from him. She did not look up. She seemed to be at grace. Suttree took the ladle and dolloped out the oatmeal. Reese was blowing on his, holding the bowl in both hands and watching Suttree across the rim. Pass the milk, said Suttree.

She sat with her knees together in the stern facing him as he rowed, her hands in her lap, the brail drops swinging behind her from the poles. Suttree seeing new country and asking about things along the shore, which side of an island to take. Her pointing, her young breasts swinging in the light cloth of her dress, turning in the boat, caught up in a childlike enthusiasm, a long flash of white thighs appearing and hiding again. Her bare feet on the silty boards of the skiff's floor crossed one over the top of the other.

She said: Holler when you get tired and I'll spell ye.

That's all right.

I row for Daddy all the time. I can row good.

Okay.

You like to work with Willard?

He's all right.

I dont. I worked with him last summer some. He's a smart aleck.

I guess you got to practice up on your rowing with him.

Shoot. That thing wont do nothin. You know he tried to get me to hide out what pearls we found cleanin shells and we'd slip off and sell em and keep the money?

Suttree grinned. Well, he said. I'd guess old Willard probably doesnt have much luck finding pearls. I'd say that everybody else would find about five to his one.

Shoot, I bet he keeps what good ones he does find and hides em somewheres. Looky yonder at that old snake.

A watersnake was weaving his way upriver by the shore reeds, his sleek chin flat on the water.

I just despise them things, she said.

They wont hurt you.

Shoot. What if one was to bite ye?

They wont bite. They're not poison anyway.

She watched the snake, the tip of her thumb between her teeth.

Let's just row over there and get him and I'll show you, said Suttree, taking a hard turn on the larboard oar.

She squealed and jumped, grabbing at the oars. Suttree could see down the front of her dress all the way to her belly, the skin so smooth, the nipples so round and swollen. Buddy! she said, high and breathless and laughing. She was almost in his lap. You stay away from that thing.

The boat rocked. She steadied herself with a hand on his shoulder, she touched the gunwale and sat down, a shy smile. They looked toward the shore for the snake but the snake was gone. The sun was warm on Suttree's back. He let one oar trail and wet his hand in the river and put it against the back of his neck. You scared the snake off, he said.

You scared me.

Maybe we'll see another one.

You stay away from them things. What if one was to climb in the boat?

I guess you'd be climbing out. Suttree suddenly looked down over the side. Why here he is, he said. Right alongside the boat.

She squealed and stood up, holding her wrists together in front of her, her hands at her mouth.

Suttree shook and jostled the oar. He's coming up the oar, he said.

Buddeee! she wailed, climbing onto the seat in the transom. She peered down into the water. Where? she said.

Suttree had let go the oar and was laughing like a simpleton.

You quit that, she said. You hear? Buddy?

Yes? he said.

You promise me. You hear? Dont do that no more.

Okay, he said. You better sit down before you fall in.

She stepped down and sat, holding the gunwales at either side as if to be ready for rough water. He stood his feet against the struts in the skiff's side and pulled into the current.

They ate their lunch on a grassy knoll above the river. A cool wind that bore an odor of damp moss coming off the water. Reese had gotten credit at the store and there were baloney sandwiches on white bread with mayonnaise and little oatmeal cakes. She sat with her bare feet tucked beneath her and brought these things from a paper grocery sack and laid them out. When they'd eaten he lay back in the grass with his hands behind his head. He watched the clouds. He closed his eyes.

She took the oars as they went back down and Suttree handled the brail bars. She would help him haul the filled brails in, smelling of soap and sweat, her body soft and naked under the dress touching him, the mussels dripping and swinging from the lines and clacking like castanets.

They coaxed the loaded boat through the shallows, walking alongside it on the gravel floor of the river. Suttree raised the front of it by the ring in the prow and ran the water to the rear and grounded the bow of the skiff on a rock. Them leaning over the boat from either side, their heads almost touching, scooping out the water with bailing cans.

Drifting downriver in the lovely dusk, the river chattering in the rips and bats going to and back over the darkening water. Rocking down black glides and slicks, the gravel bars going past and little islands of rock and tufted grass.

When they reached the camp there was no one about. Suttree took the axe and went for wood while she built the fire back.

He came up dragging some dead stumps and found her sitting in front of the fire on a tarpaulin she had spread there. She looked up quickly and smiled. He set one of the stumps in the flames. Hot sparks rose and drifted downwind in the dark. Where is everybody? he said.

I reckon they're at church.

You think Willard went with them?

Mama makes him go. She puts him to work if he tries to lay out.

Suttree sat down on the tarp alongside her.

They could hear the river running on in the dark. He heard her breathing beside him, her breast rising and falling, eyes watching the fire. Suttree rose onto his knees and reached across the flames and jostled the stump forward into a better place. He looked back at her. She had her knees up and her arms locked about them. Her full thighs shone in the firelight, the little wedge of pink rayon that pursed her cleft. He leaned to her and took her face in his hands and kissed her, child's breath, an odor of raw milk. She opened her mouth. He cupped her breast in his palm and her eyes fluttered and she slumped against him. When he put his hand up her dress her legs fell open bonelessly.

This is nothing but trouble, he said.

I dont care.

Her dress was around her waist. Incredible amounts of flesh naked in the firelight. She was warm and wet and softly furred. She seemed barely conscious. He felt giddy. An obscene delight not untouched by just a little sorrow as he pulled down her drawers. Struggling one-handed with buttons. Her thighs were slathered with mucus. She put her arms around his neck. She bowed her back and sucked her breath in sharply.

Hers was a tale of bridled lust. He made her tell him everything. Never a living man. When he rose from between her thighs the fire had died almost to coals. She sat and smoothed her skirt and swept back her hair. She got up and took up her fallen underclothing and went to the lean-to. Suttree saw her go with a basin toward the river and when she returned she had bathed and changed her dress and he had mended back the fire and she came and sat by him and he took her hand.

She came to him again in the night where he slept above the river, waking him with her hands on him and her warm breath. She wanted to sleep with him but he sent her away. She came back again toward the morning and Suttree faced the day on buckling knees. He saw her coming from the river with a pail of water, smiling. He went up to the fire and found Reese squatting there with his arms folded on top of his knees.

Hot nights filled with summer thunder. Heat lightning far and thin and the midnight sky becrazed and mended back again. Suttree moved down to the gravelbar on the river and spread his blanket there under the gauzy starwash and lay naked with his back pressed to the wheeling earth. The river chattered and sucked past at his elbow. He'd lie awake long after the last dull shapes in the coals of the cookfire died and he'd go naked into the cool and velvet waters and submerge like an otter and come up and blow, the stones smooth as marbles under his cupped toes and the dark water reeling past his eyes. He'd lie on his back in the shallows and on these nights he'd see stars come adrift and rifle hot and dying across the face of the firmament. The enormity of the universe filled him with a strange sweet woe.

She always found him. She'd come pale and naked from the trees into the water like some dream old prisoners harbor or sailors at sea. Or touch his cheek where he lay sleeping and say his name. Holding her arms aloft like a child for him to raise up over them the nightshirt that she wore and her to lie cool and naked against his side.

She sat in the bow of the boat going upriver. She traced her cool fingertips along his nape and he turned and squinted at her. Sunlight swarmed on the water. That's going to get you screwed, he said. She knelt forward and ran her velvet tongue between his lips. She smelled of soap and woodsmoke. Tasted of salt.

He turned the skiff toward shore and he spread her naked in the grass, her grave and slightly smiling face pooled in black hair, her perfect teeth, her skin completely flawless, not so much as a mole. The nipples tulipshaped and full and her navel just a slit in her flat little belly. Her smooth thighs, her childlike shamelessness, her little hands dug into his buttocks. Her whimpering like a puppy's.

They swam in the river and slept in the sun. They woke in the hot forenoon and laughed at the hurry with which they worked. Reese came down in the dark to help them moor the loaded skiff and ran his flashbeam over the piles of shellfish and the three of them went up through the trees to the fire.

She sat across from him and watched him and she brought his coffee and pushed a soft young breast against his ear in taking away his empty plate.

I believe that gal's a better cook than her mother, said Reese. What do you think?

Suttree stopped chewing and looked sideways at Reese and then went on chewing again.

That little old gal is special to me, Reese said. She'll just do a man's work.

Suttree spat an insoluble wad of gristle at the dark. The women were laboring up the slope with a washtub of water between them, the girl laughing, the water licking over the sides.

You want some more coffee, Sut? Holler there and tell her to bring the pot.

And across the fire her hot eyes watched him and she seemed half breathless in the things she did. He walked off down by the river with his flashlight, along the path, flicking the light into the dead water by the shore where suckers lay on the bottom, old bottles furred with silt, pale mooneyed shad in catatonia. He turned off the light and sat in the easy dark and listened to a rip in some rocky shoal, a gentle whispering in the reeds where the river ran. A figure came down from the fire and squatted in the grass and rose and went back. The willows at the far shore cut from the night a prospect of distant mountains dark against a paler sky. Halfmoon incandescent in her black galactic keyway, the heavens locked and wheeling. A sole star to the north pale and constant, the old wanderer's beacon burning like a molten spike that tethered fast the Small Bear to the turning firmament. He closed his eyes and opened them and looked again. He was struck by the fidelity of this earth he inhabited and he bore it sudden love.

In the morning the boy helped them unload the mussels, sullen face filled with suspicion, a potential spy. The woman and the younger girls came up the river path with their shelling tools, the woman with her air of habitual rigidity and the girls in lockstep behind. At supper that night Reese said he thought the boy was well enough to work and the boy glared at Suttree across the table.

Two mornings later he was looking at Willard in the rear of the skiff. Willard wore a dark blue hat he'd come by somewhere made of imitation felt and maybe paper. Suttree rowed with his head averted watching the shore. They hardly spoke all day. By the time they'd unloaded the mussels downstream it was getting on toward evening.

Daddy's got a hole baited down here, the boy said. Said for us to run his thowlines.

Suttree leaned on his shovel. You go run them, he said.

Willard clambered ashore and disappeared whistling down the river path. He was gone the better part of an hour and when he came back he was lugging a goodsized spoonbill catfish, relict of devonian seas, a thing scaleless and leathery with a duck's bill and the small eyes harboring eons of night. Suttree shook his head. Some like spirit joined beast and captor. Looky here, called the boy. Suttree sat in the boat with his head in his hands. Darkness settled on them before they'd rowed halfway back to the camp.

They spent the last hour rowing upstream with the boy in the bow sounding with a pole, going up shoals where the oars grated on the gravel bottom and rocks passed along the planks with a slow dull wrenching, fighting off treelimbs that kept boarding them in the dark.

She came down to him at some hour before dawn and lay by him. She put her head against his chest.

We've got to stop this, he said.

Why.

We'll get caught.

I dont care.

You'll get pregnant.

She didnt answer. After a while she said: We could be careful.

There's nothing careful about us.

What are we going to do?

Suttree lay staring up through the trees at the night sky.

Do you not want me to come anymore?

He didnt answer.

Buddy?

No, he said. His voice sounded strange.

She lay there for a long time. They didnt speak. Then she rose and went back up the hill.

He thought she would come the next night anyway but she did not. He woke once and heard a rustle, night wind, a dog in the dark. One of the girls went down to the river and back. He got up and walked down the path and waded out and crouched there looking across the dark current to the darker shapes of trees on the farther shore and the faint shoals of mist.

In the third week of August it began to rain. He and the boy were on the river when it started and the rain was very cold and they tucked their necks against it and put toward shore. Not drops but whole glycerinous clots of water were falling in the river, raising great bladderlike weals that exchanged with constant hissing pops. The boy's hat came slowly and darkly down about his face like a flower in an inkbottle until he looked out from a soggy cowl, his back hunched and his eyes planing about in deep suspicion. Suttree at the oars grinned. The boy half grinned back. His whole head was turning pale blue with hatdye. I aint never seen it rain no harder, have you? he said

What?

I said have you?

No.

They sidled into the bank and Suttree boated the oars and took the rope in his hand and leaped for the bank. He went headlong and slid feetfirst back into the river, his hands dragging up great clawfuls of mud. When he came up he was in water to his chest. The first thing he saw was the boy hugging himself dementedly. He slogged over to the boat and hung his elbows over it. What the fuck are you laughing at, he said.

Whew, gasped the boy. You looked like a big springlizard slippin off into the river.

You simple shit. How about getting that oar and pushing us in.

The boy staggered up still shaking his head and took up the oar. They had drifted under some willows and Suttree was holding to the boat with one elbow and pulling on them. The rain was falling so hard it hurt. He got the boat tied and crawled through the willows and up the bank. There was a thick stand of cedars some little distance up the river and he made for that. Crawling under the trees, driving small birds forth into the weather. Within the copse the day was darker yet but the thick brown compost under him was almost dry and he took off his shoes and emptied out the water and fetched the wadded socks from the toes of them and wrung them out. He took off his shirt and twisted the water from it and put it on again. He heard his name called off down by the river. He heard his name called in the woods. Water was beading down through the cedars and dropping all about him. He parted the boughs and saw the boy going up the river path with his hat hanging about his ears and his face a mottled blue and his arms flailing like an idiot wandered from a pesthouse.

It rained for three days while they sat along the narrow strip of dry earth under the bluff and played cards and while they mended their clothes and Reese whittled first a flute from river cane and then a snake with seedpearl eyes and last a basswood bear he stained with shoeblack for the youngest girl.

It cleared a little on the fourth day and they tried to run their boats in the snarling yellow flood but were glad to give it up. That evening it began to rain again and it never did stop. They laid up in the camp for two weeks and watched the river bloat and swell until it was screaming through the trees below the bluff and the fields crossriver were flooded far as you could see.

The first of these days Reese had kept a watcher posted in the skiff to set forth should anything of value come down but soon the waters grew too treacherous for this commerce. They accumulated a strange collection of goods which he sorted and divided among them guided by inscrutable rules of equity. He'd squat for hours and watch the river pass, pointing sadly at valuables hurtling past with the speed of a train. He'd come back dripping and sit by the fire and shake his head.

They spent three days shoveling at the mussels upstream where the river was sucking away at the edge of the pile and taking back the shells. When they hiked downriver to see about things there they found part of the bank washed out and a great crescentshaped bite gone from their stacks.

At night she watched him with eyes full of questions. All were brought into such close and constant communion by the rain that the configuration of the family seemed to alter. A fraily structured matriarchy showed itself in these latter days, and Suttree reckoned it had always been so. Crouched there under the ledge in the wind's lee while the flames of the small fire lapped back the dark and all around and ceaseless fell the rain in the forest they could have been some band of stone age folk washed up out of an atavistic dream.

In the office of the old motel on the pike Suttree had found a stack of moldering books and he read through them one by one without regard. Lying with his blanket for a laprobe, propped against the rocks. He read *Tom Swift and His Motorcycle* and he read *The Black Brotherhood* and he read *Mildred at Home.* There were about a dozen titles and when he had finished them all he started over again. She read *Mildred at Home* and a story about nurses. She said that she would like to be a nurse. He looked at her. She smiled thinly.

When all were asleep in their places she rose with her blanket folded about her and came from the lean-to and went down the bluff toward the woods. Suttree watched. When she was gone he raised up and looked around. Then he pushed back his blanket and followed her.

He caught her up just beyond the edge of the trees. She was all over him. It was raining lightly and they were both wet. She was naked under her blanket. It fell in a dark pool about her feet. In which he knelt, rain dripping from her nipples, runneling thinly on her pale belly. With his ear to the womb of this child he could hear the hiss of meteorites through the blind stellar depths. She moaned and stood tiptoe, her hands holding his head to her.

These lovers lay crumpled in the dripping wood and listened to the fall of the rain heart on heart. Her wet hair lay across his face like black seaweed. She said his name. He moved as if to rise but she held him.

You'll catch cold, he said.

I dont care.

In their last week on the river two possumhunters came upon their camp. They'd heard hounds coursing on the ridge behind them and the hunters hallooed from the dark before they came up. Two figures shambling in from the night like bad news, bearing a lighted lantern by its long bail, a shotgun held together with tape. They squatted on their haunches side by side like buzzards and smiled around. Suttree looked at them. He looked at one and then he looked at the other. They were alike to the crooks in their stained brown teeth. The creases about their eyes, the quilting of their dry bird necks. They squatted there and bobbed their heads and smiled and spat at the fire and said howdy howdy.

Set and warm, said Reese. Hey old woman. Need some coffee cups over here.

Howdy howdy, said the possumhunters.

We heard ye'ns dogs a while back. Did they not tree?

Naw. Fernon here is got this young bitch keeps a treein flyin squirrels. He's kicked her till she's flat on one side but she dont want to give it up.

Quick as I can see one to shoot I'm goin to tie it round her neck and let her wear it till it rots off. That'll break em ever time. You all got dogs out?

Naw. We just camped up here gettin mussels. Danged if you fellers dont favor one another about as much as anybody I ever saw.

The possumhunters looked at each other and guffawed. Their chins jerked forward as if tied together to a wire and they spat into the fire. We're twins, one of them said.

I allowed maybe ye was.

Most folks caint tell us apart.

Boy you can pull some capers on folks when you look much alike as me and Vernon does.

Reese took cups from the woman and set them on a flat rock by the fire and took up the old blue enamel coffeepot. He gazed at the possumhunters from one to the other. You all aint got the same name have ye? he said.

The possumhunters guffawed and the one with the shotgun elbowed the other one in the ribs. Naw, he said. I'm Vernon and this here is Fernon.

Reese grinned. Suttree was leaning back against the slate of the bluff watching them. They were thin and longboned and squatting there their knees came almost to their ears and their hands lay palm up on the ground before them in the manner of apes.

Lots of folks thinks we got the same name, said the one with the lantern. Their bein so much alike. Dont that coffee smell good.

Just drink all ye want, said Reese, pouring carefully.

They hung their lean faces in their cups and peered over the rims. Reese was full of admiration and kept looking from one to the other of them and shaking his head and looking about at various members of his family to see what they thought.

We dont rightly know which one of us is which noway, said the one with the shotgun. Mama never could tell us apart. They'd just kindly guess. Up till we was long in about four or five years old and could tell our own names. Fore that they aint no tellin how many times we might of swapped.

We had little old bracelets had our names on em but we kicked them off first thing. I caint stand to wear nothin like that nor Vernon neither. I just despise a wristwatch.

One time we was eight year old I fell out of a tree and broke my arm Vernon was at Grandaddy's. They wouldnt let me go for somethin I done. I fell out of a black walnut tree in the back yard and laid there hollerin till Mama come and got me. Well, she run out in the road and stopped a car and they put me in it and took me in to Dr Harrison and we went up the steps to where his office was at and there set Vernon with his own arm broke.

The one with the shotgun grinned and nodded. We'd both fell out of black walnut trees at the identical same minute eight mile apart. I broke my right arm and Fernon his left'n and he's lefthanded and me right.

Pshaw, said Reese.

You dont need to ast us. It was in the papers. You can go look it up your ownself.

We had that piece from the paper a long time.

We can tell what one another is thinkin, said the one with the shotgun. He nodded toward the brother. Me and him can.

Reese looked at him and then he looked at the one with the lantern.

He can think a word and I can tell ye what it is. Or him me, either one.

Caint do it, Reese said.

The possumhunters looked at each other and grinned.

What'll you bet on it?

Well, I dont want to bet nothin. But I'd like to see it done.

They looked at each other again. They had a curious way of turning their heads toward each other, like mechanical dolls. Go on over there Fernon and I'll turn my back.

The one with the shotgun turned around with a lithe swiveling motion. He saw Suttree leaning against the rocks there and winked at him and put his hands over his ears and bent his head. The other one rose and went toward Reese and squatted by him and bent to his ear. Tell me a word, he said.

What kind of word?

Just a word. Whatever. Hush. Whisper it in my ear.

Reese leaned and cupped his hand to the possumhunter's ear and then sat back again. The possumhunter mouthed the word to himself, his eyes aloft. Downriver came the thin cry of hounds and across the flooded fields a yard dog yapped in the distance.

The man with the shotgun raised his head and took his hands from his ears. The boy had come to the fire and was squatting near Reese and the old lady and the girls were watching the hunter with the gun. You got it, Fernon? he cried out.

Yep, said Fernon.

The hunter opened his eyes. He squatted there motionless. His folded shadow skewered by the shotgun leaned across the slates. He looked at Suttree. *Brother,* he said.

Suttree stood up. The hunter spun about and faced his unarmed image across the fire, his sinister isomer in bone and flesh. They hooted like mandrills and pointed with opposing hands at Reese. Reese drew back, his hand to his throat. Suttree took up his bedding and went down the face of the bluff beyond the firelight and through the woods to the river.

In the morning he walked out through the rain to the highway and looked down the long black straight. There had been a high wind in the night and the wet macadam lay enameled up with leaves. He could have just walked off down the road.

The old woman and the girls came in about four oclock with some eggs and things from the farm upriver where they traded and the old woman cast about with her sullen eyes as she did her work, kneading out biscuits and placing them in the iron dutch oven and piling coals with care onto the lid. It was past dark when Reese and the boy came in. They ate supper in silence. The rain that had fallen so small and fine all morning had ceased and Suttree took his bedding off down to the river and lay there with his hands composed upon his chest. Watching up at the starless dark. The shapes of the trees rearing dimly in the lightning. A distant toll of thunder. The sound of the river. Each drift of wind brought rainwater from the trees and it spattered lightly in the leaves and on his face. He'd had enough of rain. The fire had died, he eased toward sleep. The next moment all this was changed forever.

Suttree leaped to his feet. The wall of slate above the camp had toppled in the darkness, whole jagged ledges crashing down, great plates of stone separating along the seams with dry shrieks and collapsing with a roar upon the ground below, the dull boom of it echoing across the river and back again and then just the sifting down of small rocks, thin slates of shale clattering down in the dark. Suttree pulled himself into his trousers and started up through the trees at a run. He heard the mother calling out. Oh God, she cried. Suttree heard it with sickness at heart, this calling on. She meant for God to answer.

Reese! he called. There was no light. He stumbled on a clutch of figures on the ground. A sobbing in the dark. The rain was falling on them. He had not known that it was raining. In a raw pool of lightning an image of baroque pieta, the woman gibbering and kneeling in the rain clutching at sheared limbs and rags of meat among the slabs of rock. One of the younger girls was pulling at her. The boy had come with a flashlight.

Dont, said Suttree.

God almighty, said the boy.

He snatched at the boy's hand. Get that damned light off of her.

Mama. Mama.

Oh God, said Reese.

Suttree turned to see him hobbling toward them holding one knee. He knelt by the woman. Where's that light, he said. I know I seen a light.

Suttree was kneeling by Reese. The cryptic lightning developed a rainveiled face stark and blue upon the ground. He took hold of a pale arm to feel for pulse. The arm was limp and turned the wrong way in his hand and there was no pulse to it. Reese was clawing at the rocks and the woman was moaning and pounding at them with her hand as if they were something dumb that might be driven off. Suttree took the light from the boy and cast it about. A havoc of old crushed signs and lumber. A pot, a mangled lantern. At the far edge of the slide the youngest girl sat dumb and bloody in the rain watching them. He reached and took hold of the topmost slate and raised it and slid it back.

They worked without speaking and when the stones were all shifted the old man got the girl's broken body up some way in his arms and began to stumble off with her. The flashlight lay cocked on the ground and the beam of it angled up toward ultimate night and the rain fell small and slant. He seemed to be making for the river with her but in the loose sand he lost his footing and they fell and he knelt there in the rain over her and held his two fists at his breast and cried to the darkness over them all. Oh God I caint take no more. Please lift this burden from me for I caint bear it.

He left downriver in the dark, the oars aboard, turning slowly in the current, jostling over the shoals. The cottonwoods went by like rows of bones. Come sunrise he was drifting through peaceful farmland upon a river high and muddy. He went along past grazing cows, their cropping in the grass audible above the clank of their bells. They looked up surprised to see him there. The fields were spatched with beds of silt and the shoreline brush wore shapes of wood and rags of paper all among the branches. He passed beneath a concrete bridge and boys fishing called to him but he did not look up. He sat in the skiff and held his hands in his lap with the dark blood crusted on the upturned palms. His eyes beheld the country he was passing through but did not mark it. He was a man with no plans for going back the way he'd come nor telling any soul at all what he had seen.

He lay for days in his cot, no one came. The drums under one corner were banjaxed and the shanty lay tilted in the water so that he had to shore up the legs of his cot on one side with bricks. He did not put out his lines again. The windows in the shanty were mostly broken but he did not turn out to mend them. The river filled with leaves. Long days of fall. Indian summer. He wandered up the hill one evening to look for Harrogate but he did not find him. The musty keep beneath the arches of the viaduct was barren of the city rat's varied furnishings and there was a dog long dead lay there whose yellow ribs leered like teeth through the moldy rug of hide.

He crossed the iron river bridge and went down the steep bank on the far side and came out on the railroad. Dry weeds among the ties, dead shells of milkweed, sumac and mimosa. The old locomotive was half swallowed up in kudzu and enormous lizards lay sunning on the tarred coach roofs.

He went past the high webbed iron wheels, the seized journals and driving rods and the fat coiled springs and past the tender and rotting daycoach with its sunpeeled paint and paneless carriage sashes to the caboose.

There was no one about. He climbed the steps and pushed open the door. The place was littered with trash and the little iron brakeman's stove had been kicked over and lay with the rusted sections of stovepipe in a tip of ash and cinder. On the table in the curious little baywindow lay a seal of yellow candlewax and two burnt matches. The old man's mattress was half off the bunk and there was little trace of his having ever lived there. Suttree kicked at the trash, the cans and papers and rags, and went back out. He followed the old railway trace downriver until he came to the bridge and here he called out the ragpicker.

Who is it?

Suttree.

Come on in.

Come on out.

The old man peered from his enormous vault. He came forth with reluctance. They sat on the ground and the ragman looked at him with his fading eyes. Unkempt baron, he ekes neither tariff nor toll. Where you been? he said.

I was up on the French Broad for a while. What's become of Daddy Watson?

I dont know. I aint seen him.

Well he's not living up here anymore. Dont you know anything about him?

The ragman shook his head. Here today and gone tomorrow, he said. He pointed vaguely toward the ground as if perhaps it were responsible.

Is he dead?

I dont know. I think they come and got him.

Who come and got him?

I dont know.

Shit, said Suttree.

Shit may be, said the ragman. I never took him to raise.

Was it the police?

It might of been any of em. I reckon I'll be next. You aint safe.

I'll agree with that.

What happened to your boatshanty?

It sprang a leak.

I seen it go down some ever day. I looked for it to go plumb in under.

Did he have any kin?

Did who have any kin.

Daddy.

I dont know. Who'd claim it if they was? I might have some myself but you wont see em runnin up and down hollerin it out.

No.

Nor yourn neither maybe.

Suttree smiled.

Aint that right?

That's right.

The ragman nodded.

You're always right.

I been wrong.

What about Harvey. Is he still alive?

You couldnt kill him with a stick.

Harvey's right too.

Drunk son of a bitch.

You're not the only one that's right.

The ragman looked up warily.

We're all right, said Suttree.

We're all fucked, said the ragman.

On a wild night he went through the dark of the apple orchards downriver while a storm swept in and lightning marked him out with his empty sack. The trees reared like horses all about him in the wind and the fruit fell hard to the ground like the disordered clop of hooves.

Suttree stood among the screaming leaves and called the lightning down. It cracked and boomed about and he pointed out the darkened heart within him and cried for light. If there be any art in the weathers of this earth. Or char these bones to coal. If you can, if you can. A blackened rag in the rain.

He sat with his back to a tree and watched the storm move on over the city. Am I a monster, are there monsters in me?

He took to wandering aimlessly in the city. He ate at Comer's hot plates of roast beef or pork with vegetables and gravy and rounds of fried cornbread, Stud jotting down each day the new account and never asking for a dime.

On the streets one day he accosted a ragged gentleman going by in an air of preoccupation. Streets filled with early winter sunshine. Suttree had smiled to see him and he tipped an imaginary cap. Morning, Dr Neal, he said.

The old tattered barrister halted in his tracks and peered at Suttree from under his arched brows. Who'd been chief counsel for Scopes, a friend of Darrow and Mencken and a lifelong friend of doomed defendants, causes lost, alone and friendless in a hundred courts. He pulled at his shapeless nose and waggled one finger. Suttree, he said.

Cornelius. You know my father.

For many years, quite honorably. And his father before him. How is he?

He's well. I see him seldom.

Of course. And what line of work are you yourself in now?

I'm a fisherman.

Into it commercially, is that it?

Yessir.

Now that is interesting. Yes indeed. I'd say a lad with your head on his shoulders should be able to put a wrinkle into it that would make it pay.

It does all right, said Suttree. He was swinging subtly about to recover the wind of the reeking figure he confronted. Studying the patterns of gravy and food on the old lawyer's shirt and tie, his belt of balingtwine. Which had broken one day in the line at the S&W cafeteria leaving him standing there with his tray in his hands, his feet hobbled in his old trousers, his thin old man's shanks the same dirty white as his shirt and as wrinkled.

Always had a warm heart for the outdoor life myself, he said. All sedentaries I suppose. Often wished I'd gone to sea. Have a brother in the navy, lives in the Philippines. He scratched at his unshaven cheek and looked up at Suttree. You stick to your guns, he said. Follow the trade that you favor and you'll have no regrets in your old age.

Suttree wondered what regrets the old lawyer had but he didnt ask.

He took a turn down through the trainyard. He'd a mind to see the station with the fireplaces and the inscriptions from Burns on the mantels, remembering his grandfather stepping down to the platform among the wheeltrucks and the steam and the smiling black porter with the red cap. The old man's cheeks new shaven and the fine red veins like the lines in banknote paper. His hat. His stogie. But when Suttree reached the station it was closed, had long been so. In the fine waiting rooms boxes and cartons piled, great crates in storage. A few abandoned coaches and one pullman stood on a siding and old handbills hung bleached and all but wordless on the notice board. The yard beyond was rafted up with reefers and flatcars, tared hoppers, the romantic stencils broken over the slatted sides of cattlecars, Lackawanna, Lehigh Valley, Baltimore and Ohio, the Route of the Chiefs. He turned on down the tracks toward McAnally.

Where he spoke one day with an old man in a rocking chair. Old man watching out over Grand Avenue from his collapsing porch, taking the sun, a small dog in his lap. Save that he was thin and the dog fat they looked a lot alike. The dog was a drab brown the color of shit and it seemed to have been inflated with a tirepump. Its eyes bulged and it bared its teeth. The old man held the dog and rocked. He claimed that it had saved him from terminal asthma. Suttree regarded the bloated dog doubtfully.

I wouldnt take a war pension for this dog, said the old man.

The dog looked sideways across its shoulder and snarled at Suttree.

When I die he's goin to come to sleep with me. We're to be buried together. It's done arranged.

It is.

I want him just like this. The old man held the dog up in his arms. What if the dog dies first?

What?

I said what if the dog dies first?

The old man regarded him warily.

I mean if the dog dies first are they going to put you to sleep?

Why hell no that's crazy.

I guess maybe you could just have him frozen. Keep him till the time came.

The old man hugged the crazy looking thing to him. Of course I could, he said.

The blind man at Suttree's elbow in the seeping dusk kept close with his mincing blind man's walk and his hands wove images in the air to prove the things he said. They went down by steep little streets and took a trodden path through the winter fields. The blind man to read his way through the thin soles of his old man's kidskin boots, stepping like a heron among the gravelstrewn ties and down the slight embankment.

Inside Jones's shanty he nodded and smiled in the soft archaic lamplight and the smoke. A scene from some old riverfront doggery where cutthroats' eyes swang in the murk as if in appeal from their own depravity. Richard tottering woodenly in these strange surroundings, his hands outheld. Doll closed the door behind them and looked at the blind man and shuffled away. Suttree showed him to a chair and went to the cooler and raised the lid and dredged up two bottles from the water and opened them and went back to the table. The players' eyes flicked, some nodded gravely. Oceanfrog dealt the last card and tightened the deck in his hand and laid it on the table and looked his way and winked. In the yellow pool of light from the lamp overhead the crumpled bills fell like leaves.

When the bottles clicked on the stained stone Richard looked up and smiled and reached and seized his beer with great accuracy. Suttree eased himself into the folding wooden chair, the varnish peened up in little black blisters along the back where it had been salvaged from a riverside revival tent burnt years ago. The sun lay on the water behind them and thin blades of light played through onto the far wall, dicing the smoke, casting the poker table behind frail and luminous bars. Richard felt the shack tilt on the river and said so. He tested the air with his nose like a rabbit. Smokehouse spoke his name passing to the rear with empty bottles clutched in his hands and Richard smiled and raised his bottle and drank.

See if you can cipher the names under the table, Richard.

Richard looked at Suttree or almost at him. Names? he said.

Under the table. He tapped with his knuckle.

Richard ran a yellow hand beneath the marble slab, up among the twobyfours in which it sat. It's a gravestone, he said.

What does it say?

Richard smiled nervously, the paleblue clams in his eyesockets shifting under the useless lids, his ears tuned like a fox's to the world as he hears it. He slid his palm beneath the table and fished a cigarette from his shirtpocket with the other hand. Eighteen and forty-eight, he said. Nineteen ought seven.

Two of the cardplayers raised their hooded eyes to regard the blind man but he minded them not. Williams, he said.

It doesnt say who Williams?

No Sut, it dont.

Is that all it says?

Richard felt along the underside of the table. That's all, he said. He lit his cigarette and plumed two soundless streams of smoke from his nostrils.

Let's move to another table.

They rose and fumbled their way to the next table and sat again, Suttree steering him by the elbow through the chairs.

Who are they? said Richard.

They're just stones. They came off an island down the river before it was flooded.

Richard shook his head. Thisn dont say who.

It must say something.

He read the stone again, he shook his head. It's wore, he said. Near naked. His face wrinkled.

What is it?

Danged old chewin gum.

Let's try another one.

We ought not to be doin this. Drinkin off folks's gravestones.

Why not?

I dont know.

Would you care?

If it was some of my kin I would.

What if it was you?

I aint dead.

If you were dead. And me and Callahan drank off it. Your stone.

I dont know. I'd be dead. I'd drink off Billy Ray's.

I would too, said Suttree.

I'd drink off of it in a minute.

Suttree grinned.

Course maybe if you was dead you'd think different. I mean, if you're dead and all why I expect you got to be pretty religious.

We'd drink you a toast. Have a good time.

Richard smiled wanly. Well, he said. I like a good time well as the next feller.

I'll get us another beer.

But Richard was fumbling in his pockets and he stopped Suttree with his hand. Let me get em Bud, he said. What do they get for a beer down here?

Thirty-five.

Richard frowned. He's high, aint he? I reckon it's on account of the gamblin.

He doesnt have a license.

For gamblin?

For anything. For living.

I never see him uptown he dont say hidy, said Richard. They dont make em no whiter.

He doled the change into Suttree's palm and Suttree went to the box and got two more beers and came back to a new table. He took the blind man by the hand and led him to it. Doll raised her one eye from where she slept in her shapeless chair, her heavy arms folded across her bosom. One of the poker players jacked his chair back and reached for the stove door and opened it and looked in and she rose heavily and made her way across the floor to the coalscuttle. When she came back from tending the stove she wiped the tables that they'd read and eyed them curiously. Richard had his eyes closed and the smoke from his cigarette rose alongside his thin nose. Something had passed out on the river and the shanty lifted and settled in the swells. Richard suddenly placed his hands flat on the table. Then he lifted them off again as if it were hot. He took up his beer in both hands and held it like that. I aint readin no more, he said.

What is it? said Suttree.

The blind man sucked on his cigarette and shook his head. The thin gray webs of flesh in his neck trembled.

What is it? said Suttree.

There was an oil lamp sconced in the wall above the table and the blind man beneath it sat clearly lit. Suttree looked at his dead eyes but there was no way of seeing in. What is it? he said again.

You knowed what it was, didnt ye?

No. I dont know.

You aint done it for meanness?

I swear I dont know what it says. He was running his own hand under the table but he could not read the stone.

Will you keep it to yourself? said Richard.

Yes. What does it say?

Tween you and me?

Yes.

It says William Callahan.

He woke early with the cold and sat in his cot crosslegged swaddled up in his blanket and looking out the small window. The sun kindled the haze into a salmoncolored drop against which the brittle trees stood like burnt lace. Charred looking sparrows japed and chittered on the rail. Suttree parted back the sackcloth curtains to better see downriver and the birds flew. He was still sitting there when someone came aboard and knocked at his door. He leaned and reached his shirt up from the floor. The knocking came again, someone called his name softly as if he ailed.

When he went to the door Reese was standing there. He carried a new cap in his hands and smiled thinly.

Come in, said Suttree.

I aint got but a minute. I come to give ye your shares.

Come in.

He stood in the little room holding his cap, one foot wide to shore himself against the tilted floor. Suttree sought his shoes under the bed and stepped into them sockless and turned and sat on the couch. Sit down, Reese, he said. Sit down.

Reese sat at the little table and took his pocketbook from the bib of his overalls and opened it. He lifted out a sheaf of bills tied with

a dirty string and laid them on the table and folded the pocketbook
and put it away again.

What's that? said Suttree.

That's your shares. We never got sold till last week. We had a awful
lot of trouble.

I dont want it, said Suttree. Put it back in your pocket.

Reese set his lips and shook his head. It's yourn, he said.

Well let me give it to you.

No.

Suttree looked at the money and shook his head. Where are you
living now? he said.

We're back up in Jefferson County. Willard run off.

How are you?

I'm okay. I never did understand that boy. I never would just get
to where I could talk to him but what he'd up and do some hatefulness
and it not a bit of use in the world in it.

Suttree ran his hand through his hair. The old man seemed small
and older yet sitting there.

I never did blame ye for leavin out. Poor luck as we had I reckon
ye'd of done better never to of took up with us to start. Did you ever
know anybody to be so bad about luck?

Suttree said he had. He said that things would get better.

The old man shook his head doubtfully, paying the band of his cap
through his fingers. I'm satisfied they caint get no worse, he said.

But there are no absolutes in human misery and things can always
get worse, only Suttree didnt say so.

In the afternoon he went uptown. He bought a thick army sweater at
Bower's and he paid Stud twenty dollars on his lunch tab and he went
to Regas and ate a steak dinner. When he got home he still had forty
dollars left. As he let himself in at his door he thought he heard his
name called somewhere like those sourceless voices that address our
dreams. He went in and shut the door and lit the lamp and sat on the
cot. As he was taking off his shoes he heard it again. Thin and far,
somewhere in the night. He sat with a shoe in one hand listening.

He put his shoe back on and went out. Blind Richard was hailing
him from the bridge.

What is it? the fisherman called.

The blind man on the bridge raised his thin arm into the lamplight like a supplicant to the chalice of God's bright mercies. A ghost of a voice fell.

Suttree couldnt hear what it said but he cupped his hand to his mouth. No, he called.

His name drifted down from the steel span hung in the night.

Go home Richard. It's late.

The blind man called again but he could not find his way down to the river and Suttree turned his back on him and his cries and went in and shut the door.

$\mathbf{B}$illy Ray Callahan labored for a while as a tilesetter but was fired for drinking. The crewchief stopped him coming from his lunchbreak and confronted him.

You cant drink on the job and put in a day's work. You want to drink you can get your time now.

The crewchief's name was Hicks. Callahan grinned at him. Why Hicks, he said, if I was you I wouldnt be caught without a drink of whiskey on my breath.

Hicks looked suspicious. What do you mean? he said.

Why, so people would think I was drunk instead of just so damned ignorant.

He went to Atlanta looking for work but he didnt find any. He fought two boys from Steubenville Ohio in the alley behind the bus station and left one senseless in the well of a cellar window and went into the men's room and washed his swollen fist with cold water and crossed the station to the gate and boarded the bus back to Knoxville.

Where he worked what jobs he could find, tracking by night his isobar of violence through the streets and taverns. Suttree saw him whip a boy from Vestal named George Holmes, a tall boy who used to like to shoot people. All along the wall by the B&J folks from McAnally and Vestal stood dangerously together and Suttree saw pistols gripped in pockets and out. Callahan hit Holmes twice and Holmes went down. He'd have let it go at that but the crowd called out for more.

Stomp him Red. Stomp his ass.

He gave Holmes a few kicks but Holmes only doubled himself up on the sidewalk. When the police cruiser rounded the corner and came up the hill Callahan took off up Commerce and lay in the parking lot under Junior Long's car. The cruiser went back down the hill with Holmes in the back of it crying and cursing and the crowd had already begun to move away. Holmes had shot a dentist in Vestal not long before this and not long after he shot and killed a man across a cardtable at Ab Franklin's and was sent to the penitentiary. Years later he got out and went back to Franklin's and was shot dead himself over the same table.

The last job Callahan had was running a bootleg joint for a man named Cotton down off Ailor Avenue. Suttree saw him in Comer's and he looked subdued.

I seen ye the other day and you didnt know me, he said.

Bullshit, said Suttree. I never saw you. Where at?

Callahan put his arm around Suttree's shoulder and patted him on the belly. These old summer rabbits, he said. You can set on em and they wont hardly even squeal.

At the woodshed in McAnally they bought whiskey and rolled lightless out the far end of the alley passing the bottle about in the brown paper bag. They drove up Gay Street where Comer's was closing and the hustlers stood about the stairwell, Callahan leaning from the window of the car to hoot at them, and they drove past the little cafes and restaurants where dishwashers were cleaning up in the dim back light and they passed folks coming from the last movie who seemed almost unhinged by what they'd seen or were seeing.

At the West Inn Callahan routed an outland troupe from the premises. And aint they got no beerjoints where you come from? And dont let the door hit ye in the ass goin out. Suttree in the washroom stood slightly drunk and read the legends on the weeping wall. Advised that he was pissing on his shoes. Untrue. Wanted to trade: two blind crabs for one with no teeth. He looked up at the clotted bulb overhead. He buttoned and pushed open the plywood door and went out.

It ended on the Clinton Highway at the Moonlite Diner. Billy Ray smiling and going among the tables while the band played country music. He had his hands in his pockets when the barman confronted him. Small, vicious, quiet. He said: Red, you been stealin money out of them girls' purses.

Callahan rocked back on his heels with his hooligan smile and looked down at his assassin. His pockets were full of the stolen change spoken, he'd drunk their drinks. You're a damned liar, he said goodnaturedly. In the act is wedded the interior man and the man as seen. When he was shot he had his hands in his pockets. The last word came out lie. The roar of the pistol in his face chopped it off and the size of the silence that followed was enormous. Billy Ray was standing there with a small discolored hole alongside his ruined nose. A trickle of thin blood started down his face. The band had finished their set and the people going to the tables paused and looked toward the bar where a small cloud of pale smoke hovered above Billy Ray's shaggy head. They saw him lurch and topple.

Curious the small and lesser fates that join to lead a man to this. The thousand brawls and stoven jaws, the clubbings and the broken bottles and the little knives that come from nowhere. For him perhaps it all was done in silence, or how would it sound, the shot that fired the bullet that lay already in his brain? These small enigmas of time and space and death.

He was lying on his back with one leg doubled under him. He was bleeding from the ears and from the nose and from the hole in his face and he was breathing deeply and regular and he was looking up at the ceiling. The murderer had put the gun back in his pocket and stood looking on like any other spectator. A number of people had already started for the door and when Suttree came up Gary was squatting down looking at Billy Ray as if he did not know what to make of his lying there like that.

Oh my God, said Suttree. Callahan's eyes closed slowly. His whole face was blue and he closed his eyes so that you could not see death come up in them like a face at a window. Suttree pushed through the people and ran for the telephone at the back wall.

They pulled a blanket over him but Suttree drew it back from his face.

Cover him up, said the ambulance attendant.

He's not dead.

They gave Suttree a look much like a shrug and lifted the gurney into the rear of the ambulance and Suttree climbed in and sat on the little banquette at the side and the door closed after him.

Shrieking through the streets of Knoxville, the red domelight sweeping the near walls in narrow places, the windows, faces in cars. Billy Ray turned his head once and arched his neck. The pad beneath him grew black with blood. All through the town tonight are folks lie dying. Sirens in the city like the shriek of jackal birds.

They wheeled him through the emergency room door and into a small white room. There was a steel lamp in the ceiling and a steel table beneath it and there were steel cabinets along one wall. The orderlies lifted Callahan onto the table and wheeled the gurney out again. A nurse looked at him lying there, his chest rising and falling. Someone had put a patch of gauze over the hole in his head and the blood around his ears had blackened and dried. A great rugheaded lout lying there with his heavy hands composed alongside him. She shook her head and closed the door.

Later an orderly came in and looked at him and went out again. He returned with a doctor. The doctor carried a clipboard under his arm and he entered the room and pulled the gauze away from Callahan's face and looked at the hole. He lifted the eyelids and looked in and he lifted the shaggy head and let it back again. The orderly was watching the doctor. The doctor pursed his lips and made a little casual gesture with one hand. He felt Billy Ray's pulse and looked at his watch and raised his eyebrows. He said something to the orderly and then went out again, the orderly behind him, the orderly closing the door.

Suttree and Callahan's older brother Charlie rose from their chairs.

There's nothing we can do for that man, said the doctor.

He's not dead, said Suttree.

No, said the doctor. He's not dead.

The last visitor was an old black orderly, a gentle man who washed the stricken and the dead. He pulled back the gauze and unscrewed the top from a bottle of alcohol and poured it slowly down the hole into Billy Ray's brain.

He lived for another five hours and died sometime before daybreak unattended. They hadnt even taken off his shoes. Charlie had gone home and Suttree and the mother sat in the little waiting room. When the doctor came out and told them he was dead Billy Ray's mother began to cry very quietly. She sat there with her chin quivering and she shook her head slowly from side to side over her dead warrior. Suttree touched her shoulder but she waved him away and she did not look up.

He walked out of the hospital and across the wet grass toward the road. Very slowly the lights of the city were going out, the billboards, the streetlamps. He crossed the river by the high iron bridge, past the orchards in the dark, lights in the water upstream and the sky paling and the night and its disciplines draining away leaving the barren trees as black as iron and a paper city rising in the dawn. A great stillness had fallen. He walked through the dead gray streets. A newspedlar was opening his bale of papers at the corner. The streetsweepers had passed and in the black gutterwater the lights from the polelamps lay like pietins among the darker neon bleedings.

He leaned against the viaduct rail. Spat numbly at the tracks down there. At the dreams implicit in their endless steel reachings. Sectionhands were slouching toward work in the switchingyard. The Watkins man pushed his little trundlecart of nostrums across the bridge, humped between the cart tongues in the wan daybreak. Suttree went down the narrow back path at the end of the bridge. He passed beneath the house of the madman but he was not about at such an hour. Suttree stooped and scrabbled up a half a brickbat and slammed it off the curling clapboards high under the eaves. A crazed putty face slobbered up against the glass, a wild eye cocked there. Suttree turned and went on down the path toward the river.

He spent his days in the poorer quarters of the town seeking out some place with steam heat where he could winter cheaply. The season had grown cold and sunless and a mean wind was in the streets. He found at last a room in the deeps of McAnally. A graylooking woman regarded him sourly through the screendoor.

I came to see about the room, he said.

She sorted a key from among clotted tissues in her apron pocket and unlatched the screendoor and handed it out.

It's around the back, she said.

How much is it?

Five dollars a week.

He thanked her and went around the house by a brick walkway past old gray bushes clogged with leaves and down steps into an unpaved alley. The door was open and he walked in and stood in a dim and musty cellar. A furnace with upflung ductwork like a fat and rusty medusa, a dead iron grin in the doorgrate. He crossed to a painted blue door and peered in. A small cubicle with a concrete floor, an iron cot. He looked back into the furnace room. Some stairs materialized out of the deeper gloom and he crossed to them and mounted upward to a door at the top. Long nailed to. A dead lightbulb hung from a flyspecked cord. He turned in the dark of the landing and came back. The frayed and rotting stair carpet wore blooms of pale blue mold.

In a corner of the cellar was a zinc laundrytub. He tried the taps. A brown liquid spat into the sink and lay there. He went back into the room. There were two small windows let into wells high along one wall, the glass covered with rainspattered sand and hung with spider-webs. Suttree looked out at the brambly undercarriage of a hedge, some whitestalked grass perhaps wild onions. In the wells dry leaves and papers. A weathered wooden firetruck.

He sat on the cot and looked around but there wasnt much to look at and after a while he went back out and around the house to the front door again.

She stood veiled behind the screen holding out her hand for the key.

I'll take it, he said.

Is it just yourself?

Yes mam.

That'll be five dollars.

He had his money out. Crossing the serried palm with wilted green.

Is that everything there is? I mean you dont have an extra rug or something do you?

I'll see if I do. She folded the bill into her apron pocket and faded away down the lightless hall.

He brought his blankets over and things for coffee. He lay in the little room in the dark a long time listening to the noises and he woke all night to the passing of cars in the street. In the gray dawn he felt alien and not unhappy and lay staring up at the pipes in their hangers on the ceiling, wrapped in burlap or canvas and leaking kapok or a white plasterlike substance. What woke him was a clanging of iron from the outer chamber and when he went to the door and looked out there was a small black hunchback with enormous orange teeth gleaming in the firelight at the furnace door.

Hey, said Suttree.

When the black saw him he turned and began to bow and smile and shuffle and make mows until Suttree thought he dealt here with a wandered idiot.

Are you the furnaceman?

Yazzuh yazzuh yazzuh, said the black, removing his coachman's hat with the lacquered black wickerwork vents.

Shit, said Suttree.

Yazzuh.

What time is it? What's your name?

The furnaceman was winching up a watch enormous from the pocket of his trousers. Ten oclock Nelson, he said, holding the face of the watch toward Suttree should there be any question.

Okay Nelson, thanks.

Yazzuh yazzuh, said Nelson.

Suttree pushed the door shut. He held his hand to the ventilator overhead. A faint breath there. He lit his little kerosene stove and took his kettle out to the sink. Nelson was loading scoops of coal through the iron door into the furnace where a sulphurous smoke swirled. He turned and offered up his ape's grimace all teeth and eyes wedged shut and Suttree nodded at him and turned the tap. The water coughed and spattered clots of iron scale into the sink and finally cleared to a silty dun color not unlike the river's and Suttree filled his kettle and clopped in sockless shoes back across the gritty concrete floor to his room again.

The only piece of furniture other than the cot was a small table with threadspool pulls to the one drawer. It was painted blue and in the drawer lay last year's someday news already foxed and yellow. A few silverfish scuttled away. Suttree had set his little burner on the table and he sat on the bed and read the lacy scrap of newsprint while the water boiled. It was dark enough to want a light of some kind but there was no bulb in the ceiling. He heard the fireman clank shut the door and leave and he poured the coffee and stirred in milk from a can and sipped and blew and read of wildness and violence across the cup's rim. As it was then, is now and ever shall. He was dressed and out by eleven oclock feeling very much a resident of the city, which made him smile to himself as might Harrogate. On whom his thoughts ran this brisk November morn.

He carried off scouring powder and soap and brushes from the men's rooms of restaurants. A broom and a mop from a backporch. Get the bucket too. He swept and scrubbed and in the afternoon went into town and bought cheap muslin for curtains and a wall lamp from the dimestore.

That evening he carried up everything from the shanty, toting his boxes aboard the Euclid Avenue bus and kicking them into the empty space behind the driver's seat while he rummaged his pockets for a dime. And went a figure among the figures through the chill and broken lamplight over the old streets, down Ailor Avenue to the Live and Let Live Grocery where he bought eggs and sausage and bread for a latenight breakfast.

Anybody seeing him all that forewinter long going about the sadder verges of the city might have rightly wondered what his trade was, this refugee reprieved from the river and its fishes. Haunting the streets in a castoff peacoat. Among old men in cubbyhole lunchrooms where life's vagaries were discussed, where things would never be as they had been. In Market Street the flowers were gone and the bells chimed cold and lonely and the old vendors nodded and agreed that joy seemed gone from these days none knew where. In their faces signature of the soul's remoteness. Suttree felt their looming doom, the humming in the wires, no news is good.

Old friends in the street that he met, some just from jail, some taken to trades. Earl Solomon studying to be a steamfitter so he said. They look through his books and manuals there in the cold wind and Earl seems uncertain, smiling sadly at it all.

He'd sit on the front bench at Comer's and watch through the window the commerce in the street below, the couples moving toward the boxoffice of the theatre in the rainy evening, the lights of the marquee slurred and burning in the wet street.

There was a letter for him, the stamp canceled by a vicious slash of dried birdlime. He read a few lines backward candled against the light at the window and wadded it and put it in the trash.

One day coming up Market he caught sight of a crowd among which the maddest man of God yet seen had appeared electrically out of the carbonic fog. He was some two thirds of a man tall and heavily set and red all over, this preacher. He had red curly hair on the back of his balding and boiled looking head and his skin was pale red and splotched with huge bloodcolored freckles and he was delivering the word in such fashion as even the oldest codgers on this street long jaded to the crop with crazed gospelarity could scarcely credit. Hucksters left their carts and vans untended. The pencil vendor crouched in his corner came crawling and growling through the crowd. The red reverend had hardly begun. He tore out of his coat and rolled his sleeves.

This aint goin to get it, he said. No. He made a sweeping gesture down Market and toward the markethouse. No. This just aint goin to get it. Friends, this aint where it's at.

The watertruck had passed on Union and a creek came curling down the gutter black and choked with refuse. The preacher scooped a bobbing turnip from the flood and held it aloft. He provideth, he said. He knelt, oblivious to all, offering up the turnip, the water boiling about his thighs and sucking down the storm sewer. He washed the turnip like a raccoon and took a great bite. Here's where it's at, he said, spewing chewed turnip. On your knees in the streets. That's where it's at.

An old man mad as he knelt beside. The preacher passed him the turnip. He give out the loaves and the fishes, he howled. Therefore ast not what shall I put on.

The turnip was going from hand to hand in search of communicants. The old man had crawled into the flooded gutter among the sewage and was demanding baptism. But the preacher had risen with his red hands joined in a demented mudra above his glowing skull and begun a dance of exorcism. In the marketplace, he screamed. But not this buyin and sellin. He had begun to rotate with arms outspread and his small feet mincing like a revolving parody of the crucifixion. His eyes had swiveled back in his head and his lips worked feverishly. He went faster. The old man had arisen dripping and he tried to emulate this new and rufous prophet but he tilted and fell and the preacher had begun to rotate with such speed that the crowd dropped back and some just stayed their hands from clapping.

Suttree went on. A mute and shapeless derelict would stop him with a puffy hand run forth from the cavernous sleeve of an armycoat. Woadscrivened, a paling heart that holds a name half gone in grime. Suttree looked into the ruined eyes where they burned in their tunnels of disaster. The lower face hung in sagging wattles like a great scrotum. Some mumbled word of beggary. To make your heart more desolate.

In the evening he would cross Vine Avenue hill on his way homeward, past the old school he'd attended in his infancy, morguelike with its archives of bitterness, past the church with her pawnshop globes of milkglass lightly decked each with a doily of coalsoot and past old brick apartments where in upper windowcorners a white hand might wipe the glass and glazed in the sash a painted face appear, some wizened whoreclown, will you come up, do you dare? He never. Maybe once. Crossing the Western Avenue viaduct he'd stop and lean upon the concrete balustrade where polished riverstones lay in the cracks and gaze down at the broad sprawl of tracks in the yard and the tarred roofs of railcars, a lonely figure framed against the gray pales of the city's edges where the smokestacks reared against the squalid winter sky like gothic organpipes and black and tuneless flags of soot stood down the wind.

One night he came upon a house aflame and took a seat beyond harm's way to watch. People coming to the front door like ants out of a burning log. Carrying their effects. One struggled with an old man in a nightcap who seemed bent upon incineration, tottering about and mouthing gummed curses backward at the fates so long familiar.

Lights appeared up and down the street. Neighbors in their flannel robes came out to watch. An upper window sagged and buckled and collapsed. Sheets of flame ran up the clapboards and they blistered and curled in the heat. A hot blue light crackled through the orange smoke.

How'd it start?

Suttree looked down. A little man was leaning to him with the question.

I dont know, said Suttree. How all things start.

He rose and went on.

A police cruiser must ask his name, where is he going. Suttree proper and wellspoke, bridling the malice in his heart. Pass on. Down alleyways where cats couple, rows of ashcans and dark low doors. This pane of dusty light.

Suttree stood in a kitchen among fugitives and mistried felons. A stout woman doled beers from a cooler and made change out of an apron pocket in which hung the shape of a small automatic pistol. An emaciated whore eyed him as he entered, a stringy sloe-eyed cunt with false teeth and a razorous pelvis beneath the thin dress she wore. Wallace Humphrey stood in one corner with his eyes half closed and his hands dangling. In his oldfashioned suit he looked like one of those western badmen photographed hanging from barndoors or propped up in shopwindows shot full of holes.

Let me have a Redtop, Suttree said.

She handed him a bottle and held out her wet red hand. Suttree placed a halfdollar in it and got his change and went past the whore toward the living room.

Hey sweetie, she said.

Hey, said Suttree.

Through the smoke he saw friends among the drinkers and he made his way toward them.

Here's old Suttree, called Hoghead.

Welcome to the Buffalo Room, said Bucket.

Where's old J-Bone, Sut?

He's still up in Cleveland.

When's he comin back?

I dont know. I had a letter from him said he was working as an assembler. He said every morning he assembles his ass in a corner and watches the proceedings for eight hours.

Old Richard Harper is back from Chicago, him and Junior. Harper was supposed to get em staked up there and Junior said he like to got em burned at the stake.

Junior said the windy city wasnt ready for Harper. He said they had enough wind as it was.

Get ye a drink here, Sut.

Bucket pulled a pint bottle from behind him and handed it to Suttree and he unscrewed the cap and drank.

Bobbyjohn's old crazy uncle was in here a while ago, Bud, he was goin on about haulin whiskey back in the prohibition. Said they come into Knoxville early one mornin with a load, wasnt daylight yet. Old Tip said he was asleep in the front seat and they was a car backfired and he raised up and shot a woman waitin on the bus. Said he seen her feet stickin out of a hedge.

Suttree grinned and drank from his beer. Figures slouched through the smoke like ghosts and there was about the room that eerie reverence felt in places where great crimes have been done. He stayed till the last cup was drained. Leaning in a doorway in the small hours watching a fat whore humping on a bed that bore the black shoetracks of many a traveler. Drifting with the last customers down the alley toward the street. Giggles and catcalls. The plastic purses of the whores cutting garish curves in the milkblue light of the streetlamps. Plates of white ice broken in the chuckholes. A small coalcolored owl trilled from a lightpole and Suttree looked and saw him fluff against the sky. He called again, called softly. Suttree sat on an old stone curb with his back to the pole, a silent dweller in a singing wood. Newsboys were putting forth with wagons through the murk, old feral fathers wading in the surf of older dawns to launch their tarred boats on some dark and ropy shoal.

An empty beercan rolled in a light tin clank down the street before the dawn wind. Wind cold in his nostrils. He watched the graying in the east, a soiled aurora. The city's fabled salients rising through the mist.

Sunday morning Suttree shuffled down a dim stairwell in the clothes in which he'd slept. Across the street the markethouse stood gaunt and dark in the easy rain. Hunched in front of the hotel in an uncanny silence he sucked his coated teeth. Old awnings covered the barren truckbeds and barrows. You could hear the small heeltaps of an idle whore receding in the streets. Claustral landscape of building faces even to the sky. The heelclicks sing with a stinging sound. Suttree looked upward. The baroque hotel front flaking a peagreen paint. A church clock tolling. Pigeons reel and flap in the bellpeal. In the gutted rooms sad quaking sots are waking to the problem of the Sunday morning drink.

It seemed to rain all that winter. The few snowfalls turned soon to a gray slush, but the brief white quietude among the Christmas buntings and softlit shopwindows seemed a childhood dream of the season and the snow in its soft falling sifting down evoked in the city a surcease nigh to silence. Silent the few strays that entered the Huddle

dusting their shoulders and brushing from their hair this winter
night's benediction. Suttree by the window watched through the
frosted glass. How the snow fell cherry red in the soft neon flush of
the beersign like the slow dropping of blood. The clerks and the
curious are absent tonight. Blind Richard sits with his wife. The
junkman drunk, his mouth working mutely and his neck awry like a
hanged man's. A young homosexual alone in the corner crying. Suttree among others, sad children of the fates whose home is the world,
all gathered here a little while to forestall the going there.

He spent a lot of time in the library reading magazines. An assortment of wildeyed freaks used to frequent the upstairs reading room,
glancing furtively about, their cocks hanging out of their trousers
beneath the tables, eyeing the schoolboys. One evening coming out of
May's cafe and heading toward the B&J he passed two women sailing
along in the other direction. He turned around and followed them
back in. They spoke with yankee accents a jivy kind of talk he thought
he'd listen to and he took the booth behind them and ordered a beer.
Before he'd taken a sip of it one of them turned and fixed him with
an up and down look of brazen appraisal. What's happening in this
town? she said.

Suttree hung his arm over the back of the booth and looked at them.
Not much, he said. Where you all from?

Chicago.

How long you been here?

Off and on for a couple of months.

Off and on is right, sweetie, said the older one. The other one smiled
at Suttree. We're hustlers, she said. But we wont hustle you.

Suttree liked her.

Well, he said. There's usually something going on at the Indian
Rock.

You want to go out there with us?

He rubbed his jaw. The clock hanging from the ceiling turned on
its gilt chain. 11:20.

I'm Joyce and this is Margie, the nice one said.

Hi Joyce. Hi Margie.

What do you think?

Okay, he said. I guess so.

They went in a cab, the three of them in the back and him in the
middle. They were all a little drunk.

She pulled out a handful of money to pay the cab with but he pushed it back and paid himself. The cabdriver hissed at him to bend and hear.

Them old gals is hustlers.

Suttree patted him on the arm.

When he danced with her she pressed her thigh between his legs and breathed against his neck. Hard impress of her pubic bone. She smelled very good. The older one kept cutting in on them and Suttree would have to dance with her. He saw no one he knew except Roop the drummer who kept winking huge hobgoblin winks at him.

You never told me your name, she said.

Bud.

Bud.

Yeah.

Okay Bud.

They'd been drinking whiskey and he found the floor a bit unmanageable but she didnt seem to notice. She nibbled his jugular with crimped lips. I like you, Bud, she said.

How do you know.

I can tell.

Can you feel it in the marrow of your bones?

That's not exactly the spot.

How long are you going to be around?

I dont know. A while. I cant go back to Chicago.

Why not.

A little indictment.

Ah.

I travel around. I'm in and out of Knoxville.

In and out and off and on.

She bit his neck.

Do you want another drink?

I'd love one. Let me get them.

I've got them.

He walked her back to the table and called the waitress.

That girl that was here said to tell you she had to go, the waitress said.

They looked at each other. Suttree ordered ice and drinks and the waitress moved away, writing on her pad, her lips moving.

You didnt say anything to her did you? said Suttree.

No. You know I didnt.

They watched each other over the rims of their half empty glasses. They started giggling.

When they pulled up in the mouth of the alley she put her hand on his leg, apprehensive as a young girl.

It's all right, he said.

What's here?

I live here.

There's no lights.

It's all right.

Why dont we go to my hotel?

Suttree was already out. He had one hand extended to help her out and the other lay on the cold steel top of the taxi. He looked up at the dim and midnight shadowworld of shapes above McAnally, dark nightscape of lightwires and chimneypots. He reached down and took her hand. Look, he said. I'm not Jack the Ripper. I live just down here. It's not much but it's clean and I've got something to drink, a couple of beers I know and a little in the bottom of a bottle of whiskey I think. Come on.

She emerged cautiously from the cab and Suttree held her hand while he paid the driver. He slammed the door shut and the cab pulled away and he took her down the little cinderpath alleyway, taking his key from his pocket, showing her the way.

He opened the door and turned on the light. She stood in a cellar. Fire showed in the slotted mouth of the furnace and a wild melee of piping reeled away over the ceiling, their own shadows dipping in the slight swing of the lightbulb from its cord. A deep musty smell. She turned and looked at him. I must be crazy, she said. Will someone tell me what I'm doing here?

He crossed to the door of his room.

What's that, the coalbin?

He turned the light on in his cubicle and ushered her in. She leaned in the doorway with one hand on his shoulder. Well, she said.

Go ahead.

He closed the door. They sat on the bed and kissed. They fumbled with each other. Mmm, she said. She leaned and licked his ear and whispered in. What you dont do right, she said, you're going to have to do over.

Winter sunlight parried from an upper wall fell over them from the high window. He lay awake in the narrow cot, one hand dangling on the floor. He turned to look at her. Pull back these covers from her chin. Is she gross? Is she horrid? Is she old?

She lay slackmouthed in sleep and not unlovely. He laid his face against her full breasts and slept again.

When he woke she was sitting on the edge of the bed in one of his shirts smiling down at him, her ashblond hair tumbled about her face. She was holding a cup of coffee for him.

Hi, he said.

Hello lover. Are you ready for liquids?

Mggh.

Yes, I know. Just sit up a bit. She fluffed the pillow with one hand and then held the cup to his lips.

What time is it?

Noon.

Do you have to go?

Yes. She brushed back his hair.

He drank the coffee.

I copped one of your shirts, she said.

You wont leave those bumps in it will you?

No, she said, taking the cup. She leaned over him. I wont leave anything messed up or marked on except you. She kissed him. She tasted of mint. She ran her hand down his belly. Oh my, she said.

What do you want? said Suttree grinning.

When he woke again she was dressed and sitting at the table combing her hair. He watched her. She put the comb in her purse and snapped it shut and turned around and came over to the bed.

I've got to go, baby.

Well.

Is that laundry tub what you bathe in?

Yes. Such as it is.

I was stripped off out there washing my pussy when some spade came in. An old guy. He almost fainted.

Marvelous, said Suttree. What did he say?

Well, he had on this crazy hat and he took it off and began to bow and to back out the door saying: Scuse me mam, scuse me mam.

God help him. He'll be more peculiar than ever.

She brushed his hair back. When will I see you?

I dont know.

What are you doing tonight?

Nothing. Are you asking for a date?

Do you mind?

No.

May I see you this evening?

It'll have to be someplace cheap.

I've got some money. Baby dont. I've really got to go. Baby.

She left in midafternoon. He lay in the bed a depleted potentate. He felt very good.

A wan midwinter sun hung low and oblong under the leeward fishshaped clouds. A sun hotjowled and squat in the seeping lavender dusk. Down this narrow street where the chinese sign glows green. She is waiting, cupboarded in one of the high booths. A congenial oriental to bid good evening. Suttree saw her smile from a far corner.

No. With the young lady there.

The waitress smiled.

Hello baby.

Hello.

He slid into the seat opposite but she took his hand. Come sit by me.

He stood up again. Come over here, he said. So we dont bump elbows.

You're a southpaw.

Yes.

She rubbed past him. Nice, she said.

She was wearing a pale yellow knit dress that fit her all over and she looked very good. They sat and looked at each other and she leaned and kissed him.

How long have you been here? he said.

I dont know. Half hour.

I didnt know I was so late.

I dont care. I dont mind waiting for you as long as you come.

Did you get wet?

No. I got a cab. Is it still raining out?

No. What shall we eat?

Do you want me to make a suggestion? She was smiling at him and she had taken his elbow in both hands.

No, he said.

They sat together in the booth looking over the newspapersize menu.

The butterfly shrimp are good.

Why dont you order for us.

Okay. What about the combination platter.

That sounds good. Does it have the sweet and sour pork?

Yes. And let's get some eggrolls.

With hot mustard.

You like hot mustard?

Yes. Do you?

I love it. They have some here that will completely remove your sinuses.

I'm hip.

There was no one else in the restaurant. It grew dark outside the window and she held his arm and they sipped tea and waited for the food to come.

They went to a movie. He smiled at the memories induced. Sitting rigid and frightened alongside some girlchild trying to muster the courage to take her hand.

The two of them whispering sexual slanders concerning the actors into each other's ear, vying to elaborate the most outrageous perversions. They had coffee at the Farragut coffee shop and they walked through the streets in the small rain and muted lights and looked in the shopwindows, wrapped in their coats and huddled close and the smell of her good perfume and her hair. And she who had not stopped smiling like a happy cat the evening long took him by the arm down Gay Street to her hotel and through the steamed glass doors into the lobby, the old white tiles and potted plants and polished brasswork. She sauntered to the desk and got her key and came back and took him by the arm and they went to the elevator with a small tancolored bellhop who had been reading the paper at a table in the lobby.

The old brass lattice door clicked shut and they began to rise. A dim hum of mechanisms, cables that slithered in a steep brick well.

You getting any of this white pussy, James? she said.

James shook his head that he wasnt.

She held Suttree's arm. They got off at the fifth floor and went down a long corridor, a black rubber rug. Past door and door alike with metal numbers nailed on them or missing or askew. She put the key in her door and opened it and held out her hand for him to enter.

Go ahead, he said.

He followed her in and she shut the door and took off her coat and hung it on the back of the door and turned to him and began to unbutton his peacoat. The room was neat and orderly with a great sprawl of cosmetics across the dressing table and bureau top and a portable hairdryer and curlers and some expensive looking clothes hung from the walls. A great stuffed ape with long arms and orange hair sat on the bed.

That's Og, she said.

Who named him that, you?

My girlfriend. She gave him to me.

Margie?

No. Chick in Chicago. Christ, this thing weighs a ton.

Let me get it.

I've got it. You're not wet are you? Your head's wet.

It's all right.

She had a towel and was tousling his hair with it. You look like a little boy, she said. Here. Sit down. Let me see if there's any music on the radio.

Suttree unzipped his shoes and kicked them off and scooted back on the bed and crossed his feet and lifted one of the ape's arms and let it fall again.

You like hillbilly?

Anything.

I used to hate it.

Find something else.

There was a knock on the door and she went to answer it. The elevator man stood with a tin bucket of ice and a pint of whiskey in a paper bag.

Baby, she said, do you want a Coke or something? I didnt think to ask you.

I dont need anything.

She paid the stolid yellow James and shoved the change back at him and shut the door with her elbow. She set the bucket and the package of whiskey on the bedside table and took a pair of glass tumblers from the shelf above the sink and brought them over and filled them with ice. She sat on the edge of the bed and started peeling at the seal on the bottle until Suttree took it from her and twisted the cap loose with his teeth. He poured the drinks and they sat on the bed opposite each other and sipped and looked at each other and smiled.

I wonder if I'm already hungry again or if it's something else, she said.

They say that's the trouble with chinese girls.

What?

An hour later and you're horny again.

She smiled and sipped from her glass. There was altogether too much of her sitting there, the broad expanse of thigh cradled in the insubstantial stocking and the garters with the pale flesh pursed and her full breasts and the sootblack piping of her eyelids, a gaudish rake of metaldust in prussian blue where cerulean moths had fluttered her awake from some outlandish dream. Suttree gradually going awash in the sheer outrageous sentience of her. Their glasses clicked on the tabletop. Her hot spiced tongue fat in his mouth and her hands all over him like the very witch of fuck.

He woke later in the night alone in the bed. She was sitting at the dressing table engaged in alchemic rituals with creams and lotions, she was at brushing her hair. In the dark window and partly obscured by the old lace drapes a red pulse of watered light bloomed and faded and the sound of the rain and the traffic in the wet streets made him sprawl deliciously in the sheets. She was watching him in the glass. She winked. Hi lover, she said.

Hello baby. What time is it?

She bent to see her watch. It's quarter to one, she said. Did you have a good nap?

Mmm.

Would you like a drink?

Yes. I can get it.

No.

She rose and came over to the bed. She was wearing a pale blue negligee that flowed lightly behind her. She came and bent and kissed him and he stroked her breasts and she propped him up with both pillows and fixed the drink and sat on the bed for a moment.

What was all that racket a while ago?

Goddamned Ralph came up here trying to get room rent. You wouldnt believe it. Said you were supposed to be in the date room.

Did you get him straightened out?

She smiled. I told him you were no goddamned date. I think I called him a nigger cocksucker.

How did he go for that?

He didnt say. That fucking James has got a big mouth too.

393

Was that Margie in here?

Yeah. She's jealous.

What, of you or me?

Silly. Her old man put her down I think. She's jealous of me, sure, but that chick is almost fifty years old for Christ sake.

I dont see how she makes it.

She's a hundred dollar a night girl.

Her?

Sure. All she has to do is turn fifty tricks. That's mean isnt it?

What brought you down here?

Money what else. Anyway I cant go back to Chicago for a while.

You said you were under indictment. What for?

Selling my pussy.

Her impish grin. Watching him. He sipped the whiskey. Where's Og? he said.

Oh, he's over here on the floor. I guess his nose is out of joint too. She tucked the covers about Suttree's naked chest and went back to her things at the dresser. He had finished the drink and almost drifted into sleep half sitting there in the sagging bed when she turned off the light and climbed in beside him, her warm soft scented body length to length against his own and her breath in his ear whispering obscene endearments.

The hammering of steampipes woke him in the small hours of the night and he lay in the strange room with the red neon flicker of the hotel sign silent at the window. Silence in the streets. She sprawled like a child, one hand loosely clutched by the side of her sleeping face.

In the morning it was still raining or raining again. Alone in the room, brailed in the soft and springshot bed he listened to the traffic below the window, the muted slicing of tires in the wet. Looking up at the ceiling, the petals of wallpaper hanging, the old and ornate gas fixture with brass cherubs. He eased himself up. Gray rain leaned past the window. There was some sort of horrendous foundrywork going on about the hotwater pipes and a little poppet valve on the radiator was hissing like a kettle. He crossed the cold buckled linoleum with puckered feet and stood naked by the window and watched the Monday morning traffic in the streets below. A different slant on life here. Old whiskey bottles with their bleached labels lying on the wet tar of the rooftops. A glass skylight covered with chickenwire. The cold winter rain falling everywhere over the city.

He put on his clothes and went down the hall to the bathroom. A door with MEN stenciled across it. A tall narrow hall of a room in domino tiles. A yellow tub on clawfeet, a sink and a toilet. Suttree pissed long and loud, peering out through the patterned glass of the window at the winter day.

When he got back to the room it was still empty. He took a towel and a bar of soap and went back down the corridor and had a hot bath. When he returned to the room he tried shaving himself with her electric razor. He looked through her things, careful to leave each as it had been. An eclectic tale of gewgaws, the fine with the shoddy. He borrowed her toothpaste and brushed his teeth with his fingers.

She came in smiling and bearing packages and smelling of perfume and rain. She took off the plastic babushka she wore and shook out her hair and came to him unbuttoning the belted raincoat and looking like a movie whore. She kissed him and said hello.

You havent eaten? I brought you some coffee and the paper.

What time is it?

It's about eleven. Why dont we go over to Regas and have lunch.

Okay.

I'm starving, arent you?

I'm about to faint. What time did you stir out this morning?

I dont know. Nine. Here. Be careful, it's hot.

Thanks.

She took off the coat and shook it and laid it on the bed and went to the dressing table to repair her makeup. She seemed ladylike and efficient in her spikeheeled shoes and her tweed suit. Suttree sat on the bed and sipped the coffee and looked at the paper. She watched him in the mirror. She gave him a big sexy wink.

They went down in the elevator with a young black who kept his eyes averted and she made obscene signals above the back of his small neat head. They crossed the lobby arm in arm like a honeymoon couple and she spoke cheerily to the lolling porter and turned up her collar and they crossed the wet street and ducked into Regas.

The next day they got thrown out of the hotel. Suttree hadnt been back to his room in McAnally and they had bought him new clothes to wear and she had picked out a pigskin shavingbag for him and fitted it with all manner of things that he hardly knew the use of, the powders and colognes and lotions and little chrome tools for the care of the nails. They packed all their things down and into a cab and went to the other end of Gay Street where she talked and gestured by the desk with the black bellcaptain and he sat in the back of the cab half buried in dresses and boxes.

She's wavin you on in, the driver said.

Suttree got out of the cab and entered the little dingy lobby that he'd passed a hundred times or more. The cadaverous keeper of the place knew him from the Huddle across the street. Suttree nodded to him and went over to the bellcaptain.

Bud, this is Jesse, she said.

Hello Jesse.

Jesse's head moved very slightly.

Listen baby, do you want to stay here?

What do you mean?

I mean move out of that cellar and stay here. Look, Jesse is an old friend. He knows me and he knows I'm not interested in turning five dollar tricks with these brokendown whores he runs in here. He's got a room up on the top floor we can have if you want. I think I'm going to Athens tomorrow.

Athens?

Yeah. I talked to the guy down there this morning. He said I could come for two weeks at least. Baby, I could come away from there with a grand if I had someone to take care of it for me.

Suttree, who wasnt all that sure what she was talking about, said that he would.

She was very businesslike. She gave him five dollars and he went out and he and the cabdriver carried in their things and stacked them on chairs and on the desk and draped clothes over the banister rail. The driver fumbled around for change but she waved him off and they went up the stairs with armloads of varied finery.

This place is a real rat trap, she said, wheezing back at him from the third landing. But they dont hassle you.

Suttree muttered into a mound of perfumed garments. They were going past gaping fist holes in the stairwell walls and places in the balustrade ripped bare and mended back with raw twobyfours. Down a narrow ill lit hall to a door where she leaned and held the key for him to take.

It looked like the room they'd left, somewhat smaller, a bit more shabby. They piled everything on the bed and went down to get the rest of it. They strung a piece of wire across a corner of the room to hang the clothes on, fastening one end to the doorhinge and the other to the curtainrod bracket above the window. Suttree looked out on the street below.

She woke him in the cold dark of morning among the pipeclang and the stridence of whores passing in the hallway drunk and she was whimpering with fright. He stroked her naked back while she breathed out a dream in the darkness. We were in a car and they dragged you out, they were taking you away it was awful.

You dont have any little friends I should know about do you?

She stroked his face. It was just a dream, baby.

In the morning he put her on the bus, kissing her there at the steps where the driver stood with his tickets and his puncher and the diesel smoke swirled in the cold, Suttree smiling to himself at this emulation of some domestic trial or lovers parted by fate and will they meet again? She went along the aisle with her overnight bag and sat by the window and made elaborate gestures of enticement at him through the glass like a whore mute or in such outland port as christians reck no word of speech there. Until he blew her a kiss and hunched his shoulders to say that it was cold and went up the steps.

Now at noon each day he wakes to the gray light leaking in past the gray rags of lace at the window and the sound of country music seeping through the waterstained and flowered walls. Walls decked with random flattened roaches in little corollas of oilstain, some framed with the print of a shoesole. In the rooms the few tenants huddle over the radiators, flogging them with mophandles, cooking ladles. They hiss sullenly. The cold licks at the window. In the bathrobe and slippers she has bought for him and carrying his pigskin shavingcase he goes along the corridor like a ghost through ruins, nodding at times to chance farmboys or old recluses with skittish eyes emerging from assignations in the rooms he passes. To the bathroom at the end of the hall that no one used save him, the yellow bowl spidered with cracks, the paintstained tub, the diamond panes in the window looking out on a ledge where pigeons crouched in their feathers lee of the wind. A gravel roof where a rubber ball lay rotting. The city a collage of grim cubes under a sky the color of wet steel in the winter noon.

Down the half wrecked stairs to the lobby where he'd get the morning paper from a rack and nod to the dayclerk and with his coatcollar up step into the brisk street with the wind cool on his shaven cheek and down to the Tennessee Cafe where for thirty cents you could get a stack of hotcakes and coffee cup on cup.

J-Bone was still in Cleveland. Others from McAnally gone north to the factories. Old friends dispersed, perhaps none coming back, or few, them changed. Tennessee wetbacks drifting north in bent and smoking autos in search of wages. The rumors sifted down from Detroit, Chicago. Jobs paying two twenty an hour.

The neon rigging went up early, wan ornaments adorning the bleak afternoon. From the hotel window he watched the traffic and he could see through the shelled brickwork of the Cumberland Hotel half razed across the street the rain falling on the dim jungled shacks of the black settlement along First Creek. The sound of the factory whistles in the long dead afternoon seemed sad beyond all telling. Suttree a sitter at windows, a face untrue behind the cataracted glass, specked with the shadow of motes or sootflecks, eyes vacuous. Watching this obscure and prismatic city eaten by dark to a pale electric superstructure, the ways and viaducts and bridges remarked from gloom by sudden lamps their length and the headlights of traffic going through the plumb uncloven rain and the night.

To come in half drunk at a late hour from the Huddle or what worse place and lie suspended in the bed in this house of derelict pleasures where half the night all through the cardboard chambers doors exchanged and brief ruts spent themselves in the joyless dark and the only sounds ever of desire the sometime cries of buckled tribades in the hours toward dawn when trade was done.

In the middle of the week Dick gave him an envelope postmarked Athens with a loveletter from her and two naked hundred dollar bills inside. He took from behind the cashregister the section of broomhandle the key was tied to and went to the toilet and took out the money and looked at it, such exotic tender with the values printed bold and green. He folded them and put them in his pocket. Tuesday she sent three more. He would lay out the five bills on the bed and he and the stuffed ape would look at them without really understanding them at all.

She arrived in the dark of early Sunday morning in a taxi she had taken from Athens and she was wearing a pair of flannel pajamas and a trenchcoat and she had the plastic overnight bag filled with money. She was slightly drunk. She pushed open the door and stood there framed against the orange and burntlooking hallway in a classic hooker's pose and said: Hey big boy. Suttree rolled over in the bed to see what was happening, and she said: How would you like to get fucked?

Not tonight, honey. I'm expecting her back.

She came across the room shedding her raincoat as she went. You son of a bitch, she said, laughing.

Watch out, you'll bend the tentpole.

You'll think tentpole when I get through with you.

Young lady try to control yourself.

Hello baby.

Hi.

They talked all morning. She told him everything. She was from Kentucky, which surprised him. She liked girls, which didnt. And all the towns and cheap hotels and a couple of lockups and a few sadistic pimps and tricks and the cops and the jails and the nigger bellhops while beyond the window dawn unlocked the city in paling increments of gray.

They went out to breakfast before the day had even well begun, going up to the corner through the fog and the coalsmoke and the smell of roast coffee to hail a cab, Suttree scrubbed and aromatic and pleasantly tired and hungry and her holding his arm.

What am I supposed to do with all this money? he said.

Well. You can buy my breakfast.

Seriously. I feel like every heist artist in town is watching me.

How much do you have?

The five bills you sent.

I didnt mean for you not to spend any of it.

I had some money.

Well, put it in the bank. I've got another three something. I thought maybe, I dont know . . . get an apartment. What do you think?

It's up to you.

No it's not.

Well.

They took a cab to Gatlinburg and stopped at a service station to have chains put on the tires. Suttree got two paper cups of ice and poured the ice from the cups into the glasses she had brought and poured the whiskey over the ice and they settled back with the blanket over their laps and drove into the winter mountains.

The silent cabman carried them through a white silent forest by caves in the roadside cliffs all toothed with ice and the only sound the trudge of the shackled tires in the dry snow of the road. Suttree cozied up with his trollop and his toddy, she looking out with child's eyes at this wonderland. It's fucking beautiful, she said.

They stopped for icicles to cool their drinks. Suttree clambered over a low stone wall and dropped into deep snow. Down the slope the firs stood black and brambly in their white shrouds and a fine mist of snow was blowing with a faint hiss like sand. He pissed a slushy yellow flower in the landscape, standing there with his drink in one hand, looking out on a wild white upland world as old as any thing that was and not unlike it might have looked a million years ago. Just when he would have said that nothing lived in these frozen altitudes two small gray birds flew. They came from a clump of snowbroken heather below and crossed the slope in a loping flight like carnival birds on wires and vanished in the forest.

He walked up the road, his shoes crunching in the packed snow. Under an overhang of icebound rock where sheer palisades of opaque crystal walled up the black forests above and he could hear the wind suck and moan in the trees. He reached to pluck small icicles from the rocks until he'd filled his glass with them.

Back in the cab she covered him with the blanket and rubbed his hands. You're icy cold, she said.

At Newfound Gap there were skiers, a bright group bristling with their poles and skis about the parked cars. They pulled in to watch them, goggled madmen in clouds of powder dropping down through the fir forests at breakneck speed. She clutched his arm, them standing there with their drinks and their breath swirling in the cold.

They went back in the early blue twilight, ghosting down the mountain with frames of snowy woodland veering inverted across the glass. They made love under the blankets in the back seat like schoolchildren and later she sat up and talked into the silent cabman's ear and made him promise not to tell what they had done and he said that he would not.

In the morning she took him shopping. Suttree in gray tweeds being fitted.

I love this, she said.

What, shopping?

For men's things. It's sexy.

They selected shirts and ties and cufflinks. They studied shoes in a glass case. A sleek attendant hovered.

Wednesday noon he appeared at Comer's in a pair of alligator shoes and wearing a camelhair overcoat. A pair of beltless gabardine slacks with little zippers at the sides and a winecolored shirt with a crafty placket requiring no buttons.

Fuckin Suttree's robbed Squiz Green's, said Jake.

Stud grinned and wiped the countertop before him. What'll you have, Sut?

I think I'll go for the steak and gravy.

Ulysses leaned on the counter and studied him. He took Suttree's lapel between his thumb and forefinger and eased the coat open to read the label, nodding sagely, a toothpick in his mouth. Fishing business has picked up a bit, has it? he said.

Fishy business, more likely, said Sexton, posed beneath his picture on the wall in flight gear, tapping his thigh with the wooden triangle and watching down the hall.

Let me have a chocolate milk, said Suttree.

She was gone to Asheville for ten days. He had a radio in the room now and a rug for the floor by the side of the bed for stepping out onto. In the afternoons he'd run down ads in the paper for apartments to let, stalking around in cold and barren corridors with half a heart and listening to the chatter of a graying landlord in houseshoes with his massive ring of keys like some latterday gaoler saying blah blah blah blah blah. When she came back he was still at the hotel.

He showed her the bankbook. It was in her name and there was eleven hundred dollars in the account. She gave it back to him and smiled and pushed his nose.

He watched her while she sat at the mirror and dried and set her hair, himself consumed in womby lassitude there in the sagging bed, watching her scoop great daubs of cream from a pot and slab it onto her arms and her breasts, her eyes turned to his in the mirror where he lay sipping his drink. She had smeared her face with a sizelike caulking that set up in a clown's alabaster mask, crumbling gently in the lines of her smile, a white powder sifting from the cracks. In this theatrical cosmetic she came to the bed and sat lotuslike clad only in her panties and dressed her heels with a stone, her full thigh arched, she bent intently.

He bathed and dressed in his new suit and shoes and the neatly folded silk tie and Suttree and his soiled dove descended the shabby stairwell and stepped into a cab at the curbside to take them to dinner. Later they went out to the American Legion and she won over a hundred dollars at the craptable and put it in the top of her stocking, giving him a big whore's wink while the patrons goggled at that outrageous expanse of flesh. She got a little drunk and they danced and she told him she wanted to make love right there on the floor, whispering in his ear and rubbing her cunt on his thigh until he had to take her home.

In the morning she came up with the papers, still in her nightwear under the raincoat, a jug of cold orange juice and a bottle of aspirin. They sat up in bed together and read the paper and went through the rentals with a pencil. They moved that afternoon.

Lugging stuff out of the taxi and up the cold high stairwell to the apartment on the second floor, Suttree poking around in the kitchen, looking in the empty refrigerator, the cupboards. Sitting in the airy front room above Laurel Avenue and staring into space, detached, a displaced soul musing on the hiatus between himself and the Suttree moving through these strange quarters.

The cabman stood fingering the brass snap on the leather change-pouch at his belt. Suttree looked up.

That's it aint it?

I hope so.

Well.

What do I owe you?

Two forty.

Suttree gave him three dollars and sent him down the stairs. She was hanging stuff in the closet. He stood in the doorway and watched her.

Imagine a closet, she said.

Imagine.

He got ice from the refrigerator and fixed them drinks and came into the bedroom with them.

Is it five oclock yet? she said.

Of course, said Suttree, clicking the glasses.

She went in to the bathroom and he stood at the window looking out, the drink in his hand. He could see an old man washing at a sink, pale arms and a small paunch hung in his undershirt. Suttree toasted him a mute toast, a shrug of the glass, a gesture indifferent and almost cynical that as he made it caused him something close to shame.

Toward the middle of February it grew bitter cold. She went to Chicago and he didnt hear from her for ten days, he thought she'd gone back to her girlfriend. The plumbing froze. He spent long hours in bed, his head hanging over the edge of the covers watching how the purfling of scorpions on the raw and napworn carpet went head and tail. Blue and dusky rose, dirtdulled, a center pattern esoteric and obscure. After a chemical dream, or the dried hand of some eastern adept.

One morning at Ellis and Ernest, sadly miscast among the scrubbed college children, sitting at the long pink marble counter he ordered coffee and flipped open the paper. There was Hoghead's picture. He was dead. Hoghead was dead in the paper.

Suttree laid the paper down and stared out at the traffic on Cumberland Avenue this cold bleak forenoon. After a while he read the piece. His name was James Henry. In the old school photo he appeared childlike and puckish, a composition of spots in black and white and gray. How very like the man. He had been shot through the head with a .32 caliber pistol and he was twenty-one years old forever.

It snowed that night. Flakes softly blown in the cold blue lamplight. Snow lay in pale boas along the black treelimbs down Forest Avenue and the snow in the street bore bands of branch and twig, dark fissures that would not snow full. He trudged home in a light fog of alcohol. A thin and distant bell was sounding and he stopped to listen. Something flew. Nameless bird. Suttree turned his face up to the night. The snowflakes came dodging out of the blackness beyond the lamps to settle on his lashes. Snow falling on Knoxville, sifting down over McAnally, hiding the rents in the roofing, draping the sashwork, frosting the coalpiles in the crabbed dooryards. It has covered up the blood and dirt and claggy sleech in gutterways and laid white lattice on the sewer grates. And snow has made cool bowers in the blackened honeysuckle and it has hid the packingcrates in the hobo jungles and wrought enormous pastry rings of trucktires there. Where the creek addles along gorged with offal. Upon whose surface the flakes impinge softly and are gone. Suttree turning up his collar. In the yards a switchengine is working and the white light of the headlamp bores down the rows of iron gray warehouses in a livid phosphorous tunnel through which the snow falls innocently and unburnt.

The Indian's used shoes creaked in the dry snow like chalk. Over his shoulders he wore a greasy tarpaulin stolen from a donkeyengine at a worksite and his skin was gray with the cold. The snow he stopped to knock from his shoes fell in two broken casts on the hallway floor with the print of the heels and the holes in the shoesoles intact. Leached lines of salt rimed the uppers like creeping frost. He shrugged up the tarp and mounted the dim stairs, a shadow batlike on the flowered wall, a muted creak and cry of tread, a thin clatter of teeth. At the door he breathed on his knuckles and tapped and bent to hear. He tapped again.

Suttree? he said.

But his voice was timid and the sleeper within slept deeply and after a while he descended the stairs and went away in the winter night.

Spring that year came early. There were sunny mornings sitting in the little kitchen drinking coffee and reading the papers. There were flowers in the dooryard, yellow jonquils tottering up through the cinders and loam. She was arrested in New Orleans in early May and he had to wire her five hundred dollars. She came back fat and unchastened. She said that if she ever started to work anywhere bigger than Knoxville would he please kick her ass and little as he liked to promise things he said he would.

He woke in the light of various hours to find her gone, or going, just returned. Sprawled in the heat with her heavy thighs agawp and sweat lightly beaded on her forehead like the dew of fevered dreams. Light tracery of old razor scars on her inner wrists. Her scarred paunch and peltlet of coiled black kid's hair. He tried the weight of her softly coppled rosebud teat in his palm and she shifted languorously, one foot trapped in a tourniquet of bedsheet.

Lying on his back he watched the day's shadows lengthen in the room, the blinds drawn, the muted perplex of traffic in the street below fading slowly. He'd rise from the bed and sit by the window like a fugitive and watch through the dusty slats the deepening eve and the wandlike colored lights come up. He'd shave and dress and go down for the paper, a walk in the streets. To come back and lie on the bed because this room was cooler. Reading the paper mindlessly and listening to the radio with its inane announcements. She seemed always bearing her douchebag about with the hose bobbling obscenely and the bag flapping like a great bladder. Her ablutions were endless. In her bright metal haircurlers she looked like the subject of bizarre experiments upon the human brain. And she was growing fatter. She said: How'd you like to live in a whorehouse? You'd eat too.

He'd go for walks, be gone for hours, come back to eyes huge and tearful or speckled with rage.

Follow now days of drunkenness and small drama, of cheap tears and recrimination and half-so testaments of love renewed.

In the secondbest restaurants of the small metropolis and beertaverns dim and rank with musk as brewery cellars. Where others kept their own counsel and nothing short of mayhem raised an eyebrow ever.

He surveyed the face in the mirror, letting the jaw go slack, eyes vacant. How would he look in death? For there were days this man so wanted for some end to things that he'd have taken up his membership among the dead, all souls that ever were, eyes bound with night.

Climbing again these stairs with their tacked runners of worn carpet, dark varnished wainscot panels finely veined like old paintings, the flowered paper, the light in the ceiling thirty feet above like some dim nebula viewed from the pit. An inexplicable picture in a gilt frame, two birds composed of actual feathers dyed bizarrely like hats and defying forever the orders of taxonomy. Down the hallway to the door with no name where he lived.

He passed the car almost every day going to and from town. It sat in the front row of Ben Clark's lot and it looked vicious and barbaric and feline crouched there among the family sedans. These warm days they had the top down and leaning on the wooden sill you could hang your head over the cockpit and drink in a heady smell of rich leather and admire the cluster of black dial faces in the dashboard like an aircraft and the fine red carpeting to match the hide of the seats and the polished burl walnut and the silver jaguar's head snarling from the center of the steering wheel.

Let me fix you up with that today, said the smiling salesman.

Suttree stood up and stepped back and ran his eye along the sleek cream lacquer flank of the thing. What year is it? he said.

Nineteen fifty. Just got twenty-two thousand on her. Spare's never been on the ground.

Suttree felt himself being slowly anesthetized. The silver wire wheels gleamed in the good spring sun.

Look here, said the salesman, lifting the decklid.

Inside the pristine tire so told. And little tools in a fitted case.

Next he had the long bonnet raised and they walked around it looking in at the polished aluminum camshaft covers and the neat little pots that housed the carburetor dampers.

Crank it up, called the salesman, holding open the little door.

Suttree deep in the leather cockpit turned the key, the fuelpump ticked. He put the gearstick in neutral and pulled the starter. It sounded like a motorboat.

He looked up. What do you want for it?

The little car will go for two bills, said the salesman, leaning confidentially on the door.

Suttree blipped the throttle a couple of times and shut it down. The salesman stood up. Take it for a ride if you like, he said. But Suttree was climbing out. He shut the door and turned and looked down into the car again.

The top's perfect, the salesman was saying, unbuttoning the canvas boot that covered it.

It's all right. Dont bother. I'm going to bring my old lady down to look at it.

It wont be here long my friend.

You may be right, said Suttree.

When she came back from Huntsville she had six hundred dollars. He put her in a cab and they went downtown. I've got something I want to show you, he said.

She walked around it and looked at it and she looked up at Suttree. Well, she said. It's beautiful.

We've got enough money to buy it.

Bullshit.

I'm serious.

She looked at him and at the car and at him again. Well, she said. Let's buy the fucking thing then.

He sought out the salesman while she looked it over. He found him in the little wooden box of an office where a fan stirred the humid air about. He was shuffling through papers and talking on the telephone. He nodded to Suttree and held up a finger. Suttree leaned in the door.

Right, said the salesman, hanging up the telephone. Okay. You ready to take the little car today?

Suttree eased himself into a chair. Look, he said, I've got a little over eighteen hundred dollars. Can we do business?

How much over?

Maybe eighteen and a half.

Eighteen and a half.

Yes.

You want the car?

Yes.

My friend, the little car is yours.

They drove to Asheville North Carolina and spent four days at the Grove Park Inn, a cool room high in the old rough pile of rocks and lunch each noon on the sunny tiled terrace overlooking the golf course and the mountains beyond in range on range of hazy blue. They went about the premises leisurely, these apprentice imposters, or sat by the pool while she told outrageous lies to the other guests. In the cool evenings they cruised through the mountains in the roadster and came back to have drinks in the lounge where a small orchestra played music from another era and older couples twostepped quietly over the dimlit dancefloor.

The summer passed in monotone, days run on days. The apartment was hot and unventilated. Lying in the damp sheets with sweat trickling coldly in the folds of his sated skin he fell victim to a vast inertia. She came naked through the room bearing glasses of iced tea and they sat in the barred and tepid gloom behind drawn blinds and sipped and held the cold glass to their faces. She lay there pale and streaked with sweat, wearing a dreamy cat's look, one leg cocked obscenely, the dark foiled hair below her belly matted, dewbeads nesting there. She placed a cool hand across the nape of his neck. A car started up in the street below and pulled away. In the distance a radio. They lay like fallen statuary. Suttree held a piece of ice against his tongue till it was numb with cold, then leaned and licked her nipple.

You son of a bitch, she said, smiling down at him.

Sunday they drove down to Concord, walked by the lake, scaled slates over the brown water. They came upon a fisherman who showed them his small catch of sauger. The water before him floated with amorphic patches of ambergris where he'd spat. They spoke of fish and weather and the old man looked them over and slyly brought forth a whiskeyjar and offered it. Suttree wiped the rim with his sleevecuff and drank. The fisherman looked at her and gestured slightly with the jar but she smiled no. He nodded gravely, spat and shifted his chaw and drank and hid the jar back beneath his raincoat.

I like a drink, he said, I aint no drunkard.

Suttree nodded.

I's married to one would suck the bottom out of the jar. Looky here.

He showed them a limp photograph of a bureau in a cheap room where five empty fifth bottles stood. I carry it daily, he said. Whenever I get to wishin her back I take it out and look at it. You'd be amazed at what you can learn to yearn for.

He turned to his lines and spoke no more. The floats rode serenely in their half shadows. An osprey was going down the lake. They wished the old man luck.

He showed her cores of flint jutting from the mud and he found an arrowhead knapped from the same black stone and gave it to her. Out there on a mudspit white gulls. Mute little treestumps on twisted legs where the shore had washed from their roots, darkly fluted, waterhewn, bulbed with gross knots. Their grotesque shadows fell long upon the silty water of the bay and down the beach each rock and pebble lay in its own dark lick of shadow so that the strand looked spattered with thrown ink.

I've never seen one before, she said, turning the arrowhead in her hand.

They're everywhere. In the winter when the water is down you can find them.

In the last of the day they walked out on the sandspit, their shoes sinking in the dry loam. He fetched up from among bonewhite driftwood and beachwrack a huge blue musselshell wasted paper thin. She carried it carefully, cradling inside the arrowhead and a strangely veined pebble she'd found that looked back like an eye. The gulls rose by ones, by pairs, all flew, bursting upward and wheeling overhead with the sun white on their cupped underwings and their feathers riffling in the breeze they rode. They went down the lake, balanced on dipping wings, necks craned.

Suttree knelt in the sand and skipped a stone. A curving track of ringshapes. The far shore lay deeply shadowed. The siltbars delicately sutured with the tracks of wharfrats. She had knelt beside him and nibbled at his ear. Her soft breast against his arm. Why then this loneliness?

On Simm's hill they stood looking down at the lights of the city. While the stars scudded and the sedge writhed all about them in the dark. A niggard beacon winked above the black and sleeping hills. In the distance the lights of the fairground and the ferriswheel turning like a tiny clockgear. Suttree wondered if she were ever a child at a fair dazed by the constellations of light and the hurdygurdy music of the merrygoround and the raucous calls of the barkers. Who saw in all that shoddy world a vision that child's grace knows and never the sweat and the bad teeth and the nameless stains in the sawdust, the flies and the stale delirium and the vacant look of solitaries who go among these garish holdings seeking a thing they could not name.

At midnight the fireworks went up. Glass flowers exploding. Slow trail of colors down the sky like stains dispersing in the sea, candescent polyps extinguished in the depths. When it was over he asked her if she was ready to leave. He could feel her breathing under the sweater she wore and he thought she was cold. She turned and put her face against his chest and he held her. She was crying, he didnt know why. Down there the city seemed frozen in a blue void. Senseless patterns like the tracks of animalcules on a slide. After a while she said yes and took his hand and they started down into Knoxville again.

Before cold weather came this all was ended. She had not been out of town for two months, then three. The figures in the savings account book began to unreel backwards. She spoke of getting a job. She drank. They argued.

One drunken Sunday morning at Floyd Fox's, a bootleg shack on a deserted stretch of Redbud Drive, she was taken with what seemed a kind of fit. She screamed at him half coherently and made weird gestures in the air, some threatening, some absurd. He tried to get her into the car. It had rained and they slid about and feinted in the slick red clay while drinkers from McAnally or Vestal sat on crates or rusty metal chairs and watched.

I didnt know they had dancin out here at the Redbud Room, called out a wit from the crowd.

He got her into the car, feet globed with mud. They swerved out of the driveway through deep ribbons of mud and onto the mud-stained blacktop road. She sat silent and sullen, an occasional eerie smile crossing her lips.

They were driving up Island Home Pike toward town when she grabbed the gearstick and tried to force it into reverse. The motor whined, gears ratcheted unmeshed with a thin squawk. Suttree grabbed her wrist and held it and she raised one foot and kicked the knobs off the radio.

You crazy bitch, he said.

But now she slumped in the seat for leverage and kicked out with both feet. The righthand windshield went blind white. She kicked again and it fell out onto the hood and slid off into the street.

He wheeled in to the curb. She was screaming at him something senseless.

You dizzy cunt, he said.

She looked at him almost soberly. It's just a car, she said. It can be fixed.

Across the street old faces at windows watching. Suttree stared at the windshield wiper hanging inside across the dashboard. The twisted stumps of the radio knobs. He looked at her. You're a pain in the ass, he said.

She raised her foot, a huge petulant child, and kicked the rearview mirror askew.

He grabbed her ankle. Quit it, he said.

She was sobbing drunkenly. You son of a bitch, she said. You couldnt say: It's okay honey, or say, or say . . . I guess you're so fucking perfect goddamn you anyway.

A police car pulled up without a sound. Two officers got out, one from either side.

What's the trouble here, said Suttree to himself as they approached, wishing a fissure to open beneath them and swallow all.

The officers looked down at Suttree and his whore.

What's the trouble here?

Suttree gestured helplessly. She got mad and kicked out the windshield, he said.

One of the officers was leaning on the roof, Suttree could see the shape of the elbow in the canvas inches above his head. The other was standing with his arms folded. They didnt say anything. Nor Suttree. All seemed to be waiting for another party to arrive.

Finally the officer leaning on the roof said: You got papers on this car?

Suttree leaned and opened the little wooden glovebox door. He shuffled through papers and handed the title to the policeman. The policeman said: Let me see your license.

He got out his billfold and offered the little card up. The officer inspected these documents and handed them back and straightened up. Is that the windshield back there?

Suttree stuck his head out of the window. Yessir, he said.

Well get it out of the street. Then you'd better get off the street yourself.

Yessir. I will.

They glanced at the car again and shook their heads and got into the cruiser and pulled away. Suttree went up the street and fetched the glass from where it lay limp and shattered in the gutter and brought it back and put it in the trunk and got in and started the motor and pulled away. They were going out Cumberland when she began to tear up the money. He heard a handful of it rip and looked in time to see a green confetti swirl away in the slipstream.

Shit, he said. He cut the wheel and went gliding into a fillingstation. There in the Sunday morning boredom old men were watching out through the plateglass window for something to occur. Here came an exotic automobile coasting in with tattered greenbacks blowing from the window and fluttering in the street, whole handfuls of it, who knows what denominations.

She was sitting there ripping it up and crying and saying that this money would never do anybody any good. The old faces were pressed against the glass, flat bloodless noses. Two small boys were coming across the street at a dead run. Suttree was out and gathering up pieces of tens and twenties from the paving. She had climbed from the car and stood with her hair disarranged, swaying slightly, smiling. The boys were scrabbling in the gutter and watching him like cats. Suttree went around and took the keys out of the car and started to close the door and then he stopped and put the keys back in the car and walked on out across the tarmac to the street. She was shouting at him some half drunken imprecations, all he could make out was his name. He seemed to have heard it all before and he kept on going.

It was still early morning when he made his way down the steep path by the ruins of an old wall. Some ancient city overgrown here. In a sere field worn clothes the wind has tattered hung from a hatted cross. Down there the littoral of siltstained rocks, old plates of paving and chunks of concrete sprouting growths of rusted iron rod. He'd even seen old slabs of masonry screed with musselshells here in the weeds. Coming down the concrete steps with the mangled iron handrail and past old brick cisterns filled with rubble. Past the stone abutment of an earlier bridge on the river and the last ramshackle house and the brown curbstones that had once lined the main street and the old cobblestones and pavingbricks and blackened beams with their axed flats and their mortices, all this detritus slid from the city on the hill.

He had passed the madman's house without regard and the old man must have slacked his vigil for he'd almost reached the street before he heard him cry.

Ah he's back, God spare his blackened soul, another hero home from the whores. Come to cool his heels in the river with the rest of the sewage. Sunday means nothing to him. Infidel. Back for the fishing are ye? God himself dont look too close at what lies on that river bottom. Fit enough for the likes of you. Ay. He knows it's Sunday for he's drunker than normal. It'll take more than helping old blind men cross the street to save you from the hell you'll soon inhabit. Suttree went on toward the street with his fingers in his ears.

Howard Clevinger raised one eyebrow at his appearance in the store. Thought you'd left town, he said.

I'm back.

A thin and fragrant arm descended on Suttree's shoulder in a taffeta whisper, a cufflink coined from a bicycle reflector. An African mask in meretricious harlequinade and ivory teeth beset with gold. Hey baby, where you been so long?

Hello John. Just around.

I been out of town myself.

Where've you been?

I's in Lexington. I seen James Herndon. Sweet Evenin Breeze. She just beautiful, for her age.

Who's the oldest?

Oldest what?

You or her. Him. It.

Hush. That thing is sixty.

How old are you, John?

Trippin Through The Dew ignored the question. He said: You know what they goin to put in the paper when she die? Big headlines.

What's that.

They done got it all ready. Sweet Evenin Breeze Blows No More.

Suttree grinned. The invert was bent double holding himself, his face squinched. He whinnied like a she horse.

What are they going to say about you John?

Sheeit. I aint goin to die.

Maybe not, said Suttree.

The houseboat lay half sunken by one corner and the windows were stoned out and the front door was gone altogether. He entered a scene of old memories and new desolations. Torn playing cards and halfpint whiskey bottles broken in the floor, the stove crammed tight to the maw with trash. He crossed the tilted floor and righted the foodlocker from where it lay on its face among broken glass and rags.

By afternoon he had the place swept out and the mattress on the roof for airing, he sat on the veranda in the sun with a glasscutter and shaped old panes purloined from an empty warehouse and with them glazed the naked sashes of his house. In the days that followed he tarred the seams in the roof and carried on his back a door from a razing beyond First Creek and sawed it down to fit and hung it.

Lastly standing off in the skiff on a warm October morning he fended off from the sheer wall of the dredger's hull and reached down the fireaxe handed him. The drums when he stove them filled and wheezed and sputtered and went slowly from sight in the river. He jostled the new ones into place and called up to the pilothouse. The winch creaked and the houseboat corner settled. Suttree unhooked the cables as soon as there was play enough and they went swinging up toward the deck.

What do I owe you? he called, passing up the axe.

The deckman jerked his thumb toward the pilothouse where the captain watched from his high window.

What do I owe you?

The captain spat. I dont know, he said. What's it worth?

I dont know. I dont want to make you mad.

Would you say five dollars?

I'd say that was fair enough.

He handed up the money to the deckhand. The dredger began to back. Great boils of muddy water churned and broke. Suttree raised a hand and the old pilot rang a small bell. Rafts of straw rose and fell and the ratholes in the bank sucked and popped and the dredger moved out, the deckhand leaning on the rail smoking a cigarette and watching toward the shore.

He bought three five hundred yard spools of nylon trotline and spent two days piecing them with their droppers and leads and hooks. The third day he put out his lines and that night in his shanty with the oil lamp lit and his supper eaten he sat in the chair listening to the river, the newspaper open across his lap, and an uneasy peace came over him, a strange kind of contentment. Small graylooking moths orbited the hot cone of glass before him. He set back the plate with the dimestore silver and folded his hands on the table. A beetle kept crashing into the windowscreen and dropping to the deck below to whirr and rise and crash again.

A clear night over south Knoxville. The lights of the bridge bobbed in the river among the small and darkly cobbled isomers of distant constellations. Tilting back in his chair he framed questions for the quaking ovoid of lamplight on the ceiling to pose to him:

Supposing there be any soul to listen and you died tonight?

They'd listen to my death.

No final word?

Last words are only words.

You can tell me, paradigm of your own sinister genesis construed by a flame in a glass bell.

I'd say I was not unhappy.

You have nothing.

It may be the last shall be first.

Do you believe that?

No.

What do you believe?

I believe that the last and the first suffer equally. Pari passu.

Equally?

It is not alone in the dark of death that all souls are one soul.

Of what would you repent?

Nothing.

Nothing?

One thing. I spoke with bitterness about my life and I said that I would take my own part against the slander of oblivion and against the monstrous facelessness of it and that I would stand a stone in the very void where all would read my name. Of that vanity I recant all.

Suttree's cameo visage in the black glass watched him across his lamplit shoulder. He leaned and blew away the flame, his double, the image overhead. The river spooled past dark and silent. A truck droned on the bridge.

All that season on the river he had warrant to remember in the toils of his trade old days of rain on the window and warmth in the bed with her body and how her eyes rolled back in her head like a turkish beggar's with just the bluish whites shining under the slotted lids and her tongue protruding while she seized her knees and cried out and fell back. Lying there on the drenched sheets like a suicide. Till she could flutter back to life and slur sweet lies into his ear or tell the spinebones in his back with such cool fingers.

In the toils of orgasm—she said, she said—she'd be whelmed in a warm green sea through which, dulled by the murk of it, pass a series of small suns like the footlights of a revolving stage, an electric carousel wheeling in a green ether. Envy's color is the color of her pleasuring, and what is the color of grief? Is it black as they say? And anger always red? The color of that sad shade of ennui called blue is blue but blue unlike the sky or sea, a bitter blue, rue-tinged, discolored at the edges. The color of a blind man's noon is white, and is his nighttime too? And does he feel it with his skin like a fish? Does he have blues, are they bridal and serene, or yellows, sunlike or urinous, does he remember? Neural colors like the fleeting tones of dreams. The color of this life is water.

In the morning he set off down the river to run his lines. A cool morning with mist still rising. Crossriver the cries of hogs in the slaughterhouse chutes like the cries of lepers without the gates. He sat in back of the skiff and sculled it slowly down beneath the bridge. As he passed under he raised his head and howled at the high black nave and pigeons unfolded fanwise from the arches and clattered toward the sun.

A season of death and epidemic violence. Clarence Raby was shot to death by police on the courthouse lawn and Lonas Ray Caughorn lay three days and nights on the roof of the county jail among the gravels and tar and old nests of nighthawks until the search reckoned him escaped from the city. What dreams did he have of the lady Katherine? Suttree saw her one evening in the Huddle with Worm Hazelwood. She had no need to travel about the country robbing people. And news in the papers. A young girl's body buried under trash down by First Creek. Sprout Young, the Rattlesnake Daddy, indicted for the murder.

Suttree found people out of doors that would as soon stayed in. A family of aged black folk sitting in the dark among their furnishings in total silence. Their figures swaddled up in old quilts against the cold and the old man's cigarette rising and falling in slow red arcs. When he passed there in the morning they were all gone to seek help save an old woman who sat in a chair on the sidewalk among the piled and grimy household goods. She watched the passers in the street but none watched back. A starling landed on the old yellow icebox and she struggled up to shoo it away.

The junkman lay among sleeping sots in the jungle nor did he stir when the thief who dropped from the dark of a boxcar door went among them. A hominid composed of smoke sucking out the pockets socklike and boarding loose change and half empty packets of cigarettes. Through dark bowerpaths in the honeysuckle where newsprint crouched like ghosts and smokehounds lay so drunk the flies had shat eggs in their earholes. Pausing here to take some shoes. Emerging from the jungle and disappearing into the dark of the car again and the train shunting into motion again as if it had been waiting him. A dog crossed the tracks and paused to sniff at the old man's feet and moved on.

And in the dawn a female simpleton is waking naked from a gangfuck in the back seat of an abandoned car by the river. She stirs, sweet day has broken. Reeking of stale beer and dried sperm, eyes clogged, used rubbers dangling senselessly from the dashboard knobs. Her clothes lie trampled in the floor. They bear bootprints of mud and dogshit and her cunt looks like a hairclot fished from a draintrap. She sees on rising two black boys crouched on the car fenders like gibbons purloined from the architraves of an old world cathedral. She folds her hands across her breasts and they leap to the ground and scamper hooting through the weeds. In the distance cars are rifling along a highway. She bends moaning to sort among her clothes.

Uptown one evening in the Huddle Suttree found Leonard fresh from the workhouse. Leonard had a job as dishwasher and he had gonorrhea of the colon and was otherwise covered with carbuncles. He hobbled over to Suttree's table and sat uneasily. He told how he had seen the lies run down the lawyer's tongue. Vague but of a substance, they came down like mice and looked about a moment before scuttling off. Leaning over Leonard and wagging a long finger, and is it not true that you sought to conceal the death of your father for the purpose of extorting monies unlawfully from the state? Wild in the eye, thrusting his sweating face into Leonard's smaller one and fixing him with a lidless look of triumph until Leonard half rising from his chair seized the lawyer's cold skull in his two hands and pulled his face down and parted those thin lips with a smoking kiss.

He come up, Sut. Draggin all them chains with him.

Fathers will do that, said Suttree.

I hunted you everwheres.

Suttree didnt ask what for.

The catamite tucked his chair closer and leaned in confidence. I need to ast ye somethin Sut.

Okay.

If you buy somethin and dont pay for it can they take it back?

Sure. Of course they can.

I mean no matter what it is?

Well. I dont know. I guess there are some things it would be hard to repossess. What is it?

Well this guy's been comin to the house . . .

Okay.

Well. You know after they found the old man and we had all that trouble with the law.

Okay.

Well, the old lady went and bought this plot out in Woodlawn so they wouldnt bury him down here in the whatever thing it is here and she bought this whole deal, this guy come out to the house, and he sold her this deal, this plot with anothern alongside of it for her and it had this pet, pet . . .

Perpetual care.

Petual care and got her to sign for it all and she didnt have to pay nothin down nor for the first sixty days I think it was and now she's three months behind on her payments and she owes em sixty-two fifty . . .

Leonard.

Yeah.

Are you trying to tell me they're going to repossess your old man's grave plot?

Can they Sut?

I dont know.

Well I know a guy one time they come and got his teeth he never made the payments.

I'll check on it for you. Did they really say they were going to repossess it?

What they tell me, Sut, if she dont make a payment by the tenth up he comes.

Suttree looked at the earnest pinched face. He shook his head in wonder.

Times been rougher'n a old cob, said Leonard. At our house they have.

What's become of Harrogate? said Suttree.

Leonard grinned. I dont know. I seen him uptown about a month ago he had some old country girl on his arm was about a head taller'n him. I hollered at him was he gettin any of that old long stuff but he didnt know me.

Maybe it was his sister.

May be. She favored him some.

Suttree closed his eyes as if he were trying to picture such a person. He opened them to see Leonard watching him. He looked about him as if he could not place how he came to be there.

And this was Harrogate. Standing in the door of Suttree's shack with a cigar between his teeth. He had painted the black one and it was chalk white and he had grown a wispy mustache. He wore a corduroy hat a helping larger than his headsize and a black gabardine shirt with slacks to match. His shoes were black and sharply pointed, his socks were yellow. Suttree in his shorts leaned against the door and studied his visitor with what the city rat took for wordless admiration.

What say Sut. How in a big rat's ass are ye?

I was okay. Come on in.

Harrogate pinched his hat up by the forecrown and swept it to his chest and entered, ducking slightly as he did so though the lintel of the doorframe was two feet above his head. He laid the hat on the table and hitched his trousers and tucked in his shirt with his thin little hands and puffed on the cigar and grinned and looked about. Good God, said Suttree.

I seen old Rufus said you was back down here.

Suttree shut the door. Sit down, he said.

I hunted you up at Comer's. They said you was into the tall cotton.

Yeah. Well, the market collapsed. Sit down, sit down.

Harrogate pushed his hat to one side to make room for his elbow and sat. You fishin again? he said.

Suttree leaned back on the cot. Fishing again, he said.

I thought you'd give it up.

I did too.

I come by a time or two. Your old boathouse was about in under.

What are you doing, Gene?

Hmm?

I said what are you doing.

Harrogate grinned. I got me a few little routes, he said. He turned the cigar in his teeth and gave Suttree a look of fey cunning. Got me a few little routes.

Suttree waited. The story must be elicited with care. It is that the city rat has a telephone route. With small dimestore sponges through which he's fastened wire loops. He runs his routes with a special hook taped to his forefinger, fetching down the blocks from inside the coinreturns of the telephones, a few nickels clattering into the slot, the sponge poked back.

I dont see how that would pay very much, said Suttree.

Harrogate grinned slyly.

How many phones do you have?

He took the cigar from his teeth. Two hunnerd and eight-six, he said.

What?

I had a twenty-six dollar day Saturday. I just barely could walk for the fuckin nickels in my pockets.

Good God, said Suttree. You've got half the telephones in Knoxville plugged up.

Harrogate grinned. It takes me all day to run em. I put on a few new ones ever day. You get away from uptown they's a lot of hard sidewalk tween telephones. I done wore out two pair of brand new Thom McAn shoes.

Suttree shook his head.

Harrogate tipped the ash from his cigar into his palm and looked up. Listen, he said. You ever lose any money in a telephone why you just let me know. I'll make it back to ye. You hear?

Okay, said Suttree.

Or anybody you know. You just tell me.

All right.

You the only other son of a bitch in the world I'd tell. I mean anybody could get on my route and run it if they knowed about it. They aint no way for me to protect myself.

No.

I got some other deals in mind too. There'll be a deal for you if you want in, Sut. You aint never been nothin but decent to me. I dont mind takin a buddy with me on the way up.

Gene.

Yeah.

You're on your way up to the penitentiary is where you're on your way up to.

Shit, said Harrogate. I have me another day like Saturday I'll buy the goddamned penitentiary.

It's not like the workhouse. They have these coalmines up there for you to work in.

Harrogate smiled and shook his head. Suttree watched him. Smiling a sadder smile.

I saw Leonard the other day and he said he saw you uptown with some girl on your arm.

Shit, said Harrogate easily. Man has a little money about him he can get more pussy than you can shake a stick at.

Suttree tapped at the dosshouse door. The keeper shuffled along the hall and unlatched the door and peered out. He shut one eye, he shook his head. No ragman here. Suttree thanked him and descended into the street again.

It was still raining a cold gray rain when he eased himself down the narrow path at the south end of the bridge and made his way over the rocks to the ragman's home. As he came about the abutment and entered the gloom beneath the bridge three boys darted out the far side and clambered over the rocks and disappeared in the woods by the river. Suttree entered the dim vault beneath the arches. Water ran from a clay drain tile and went down a stone gully. Water gushed from a broken pipe down the near wall and water dripped and spattered everywhere from the dark reaches overhead.

Hello, called Suttree. An echo echoed in the emptiness. He shaded his eyes to see. Hey, he called. He could make out the shape of the old man's bed dimly in the cool dank.

He stood at the foot of the ragpicker's mattress and looked down at him. The old man lay with his eyes shut and his mouth set and his hands lay clenched at either side. He looked as if he had forced himself to death. Suttree looked about at the mounds of moldy rags and the stacked kindling and the racks of bottles and jars and the troves of nameless litter, broken kitchen implements or lamps, a thousand houses divided, the ragged chattel of lives abandoned like his own.

He moved along the side of the bed. The old man had his shoes on, he saw their shape beneath the covers. Suttree pulled a chair up and sat and watched him. He passed his hand across his face and sat forward holding his knuckles. Well, he said. What do you think now? God, you are pathetic. Did you know that? Pathetic?

Suttree looked around.

These boys have been at your things. You forgot about the gasoline I guess. Never got around to it. Did you really remember me? I couldnt remember my bear's name. He had corduroy feet. My mother used to sew him up. She gave you sandwiches and apples. Gypsies used to come to the door. We were afraid of them. My sisters' bears were Mischa and Bruin. I cant remember mine. I tried but I cant.

The old man lay dim and bleared in his brass bed. Suttree leaned back in the chair and pushed at his eyes with the back of his hand. The day had grown dusk, the rain eased. Pigeons flapped up overhead and preened and crooned. The keeper of this brief vigil said that he'd guessed something of the workings in the wings, the ropes and sandbags and the houselight toggles. Heard dimly a shuffling and coughing beyond the painted drop of the world.

Did you ask? About the crapgame? What are you doing in bed with your shoes on?

He passed his hand through his hair and leaned forward and looked at the old man. You have no right to represent people this way, he said. A man is all men. You have no right to your wretchedness.

He wiped his eyes with the heel of his hand.

There's no one to ask is there? There's no . . . He was looking down at the ragman and he raised his hand and let it fall again and he rose and went out past the old man's painted rock into the rain.

She unscrewed the threaded halves of a wooden darningegg and took from inside a single piece of pale brown bone. Her hand closed up about it like a burnt spider and she turned slowly to Suttree where he sat at the table. The specter of things sings in its own ashes. Who has ears to hear it? She let shut her nutshell eyelids. A pair of fat black candles dripped and spat, the wax a gray grease congealing in the saucers where they stood. Her tiny hands with their yellow nails looked like the mummied hands he'd seen crossed on the breast of a dead slave in a wormfluted barrow at the rear of a secondhand furniture store. She had before her an ageblackened box of boardhard leather and now she opened it and began to set out her effects. Much like a priest with his deathbed kit. The candleflames lurched in the shadow of her movements and their own shapes reeled briefly on the wall.

Merceline Essary that they said would not never walk on this earth again by men was doctors come under me and I rewalked her in three days. She originally died in October of last year and she walked to that day.

I can walk, said Suttree.

You can walk, she said. But you caint see where you goin.

Can you?

To know what will come is the same as to make it so.

Suttree smiled. Somewhere in the house clockgears clacked.

She lifted from the hide box a castiron jar and set it on the table in a little stand. She took out a small alcohol burner and filled it from a bottle and lit it and set it beneath the pot. She unrolled and spread a black cloth and put things out upon it and seemed to puzzle over them. A blood agate bored with a small hole, a cracked and yellow tooth that may have been a boar's tusk, a tin box too small to hold anything of christian use. She touched each of these in turn. She looked at Suttree. He sat loosely in his chair with his hands resting on the insides of his thighs. He felt an easy peace settle in his spine. Studying the apposition of these effects for hidden systems, waiting for her to fetch down her purse of bones to see what construction they might have for him, their rorschach text, pattern in a carpet. A figure lifted from a cave floor wherein old fossils lay anachronistically conjoined, taxonic absurdities and enemies of order. But she had taken out an old bottle handblown that held an oily unguent and seemed gone on to philters now, spooning some grim powder from the tin into the pot where the oil began to smoke and sputter with a stench like frying dung.

Suttree seemed unalarmed. She unfolded the hand that held the piece of bone and she put the bone under her tongue and she placed her tiny palm against Suttree's eyes, one, the other. He felt a light tingling in his nape, his eyes lost focus. He leaned back in his lassitude and watched the shapes of the candleflames on the ceiling. She was at her triturations. Spooning to death in a salver a speckled slug, marked like an ocelot, viscous and sticky. A whitish paste. Crooning a low threnody to her pawky trade. She said: Aint no common fire can cruciate a groundpuppy. Fetching the smoking mess from the burner she stirred it with her spoon and she blew out the small blue flame and set the pot within the rack again. Her hands unmindful of the heat. Her movements rapid and sure. She spat through a ringbone into a watchglass and mixed with her finger a paste of something drear and leaned with her thumb to anoint his eyelids. Then she took up the pot again and she spooned out the mess within and swung it toward him.

Open you mouf, she said.

That's hot.

Under his hand the arm he stayed was like a piece of black meerschaum. Aneroid bones, birdhollow. To read the weathers in your heart.

Look here at me, she said.

Cold bloodwebbed globes. Wens clung along the dark and weighted lids.

Open you mouf.

He did. She thrust the spoon against the back of his throat and capsized its cargo down his gullet. A tasteless slime impacted with a harsh grit. He swallowed. She sat back to watch. Nodding her head. Suttree felt himself go queasy. He watched her eyes and her mouth but the words seemed detached. She spoke of a boarcat, black through. Find the bone that will not burn. Suttree had half forgotten the paste on his eyelids and he reached to wonder what had clogged them but she stopped his hand. He shuddered in the grip of grue. Scorpion dust, frogpowder in sowsmilk. Ye'll shit through the eye of a needle at thirty paces. Pieces of a dream unreeled down the back of his brain. He pulled himself up and looked at the old woman. She watched him as if he were a thing in a jar.

What? he said.

She did not say, nor was there any news at all in those faded eyes. What do I do?

You dont do nothin. You will be told.

Will you tell me?

No.

A wave of nausea swept through him. He was going to comment on it but it was gone. And then came another. A shuddering sickness that brought his stomach up tight against his diaphragm.

I dont feel good, he said.

Dont you puke.

I think I might.

She took his wrist in her spider's hand and leveled her eyes at him. Dont you puke, she said.

I need to lie down.

She pushed back her chair without speaking and rose and took his arm. He stood woozily. He wanted mightily to vomit.

She took him across the room to a small cot. He looked like some medieval hero led by a small black gnome. He sat on the cot and lay back with his feet on the floor. She took down a lamp and lit it and put back the glass and turned to watch him. On the mantel a small brass amphora held a dark crepe rose and there was a mounted grackle with dull glass eyes and there were small objects, a box, a pincushion. In the lamplight the glass of the mirror in which these things lay doubled was the color of rhenish wine and it was streaked with mauve and metal blue, with petals of peeling spectra. She stepped from the hearth and crossed the room and went out. In the corner stood a coattree hung with celluloid birds green and yellow, and when the door closed they turned silently in the wind and dark flowers in the old coalscuttle swayed like paper cobras. Suttree stared at the fire within the iron teeth of the grate. She was gone for a long time. When she came back she stooped to look at him. He lay as before. The nausea had passed and he felt more and more removed from all that was. He said: Should I go home?

It dont make no difference where you go.

He went to raise himself up from the cot but when he was half sitting he became unsure as to whether he should walk about. There seemed no purpose to it. He lay back down. After a while he lifted his feet into the cot and stretched out his legs. The shifting of the flames in the coalgrate bloomed on the wall like the pulse of distant lightning. Suddenly the fire seemed to be far away and he seemed to be in another room. He seemed to be somewhere else. He looked at the old black woman. Her eyes were closed but when he looked at her she opened them. She was whispering something silently to herself like one in prayer but it was not prayer.

What is that stuff?

She didnt answer. She turned her face in profile, a black androgynous silhouette.

He felt hollow inside and there seemed to be a cool wind moving through him like wind in a street. A door closed on all that he had been. Look at me, he said.

Hush boy. I dont need to look at you.

Suddenly he realized that this scene was past and he was looking at its fading reality like a watcher from another room. Then he was watching the watcher. He was aware of the light in the room and his hands on the iron of the cot under his thighs but he could not determine where he was. And then he was somewhere else.

He had begun to move. He was wheeling in a vast brown circle and he was moving in a helix outward and each few minutes he would pass again the place where he had been. The shape of the fire in the grate would wheel past and the twin cups of light from the black candles on the table in the corner and the old hag's sere and shrunken face. And pass again.

He felt a laying on of hands, dry claws divesting him. A clammy fear clogged his heart. Unknowing if his eyes saw or saw not. They seemed lidless and opened or closed beheld things all the same. His own hand put out to save him seemed to sink in a nameless mucilage and he lay like a moth in a web. Dust fell from her, her eyes rolled wetly in the red glow from the fireplace. A dried black and hairless figure rose from her fallen rags, the black and shriveled leather teats like empty purses hanging, the thin and razorous palings of the ribs wherein hung a heart yet darker, parchment cloven to the bones, spindleshanked and bulbed of joint. Black faltress, portress of hellgate. None so ready as she. Her long flat nipples swung above him. Black and crepey skin of her neck, the plaguey mouth upon him. A gray and handstitched scar flickered in the light. Where she'd survived some murder. Tin figures, the toadstone, dragged on his chest where they hung from her neck by plaited horsehair strands. In the yard he heard a bird scream. They are not rooks in those obsidian winter trees but stranger fowl, pale lean and salamandrine birds that move by night unburnt through the moon's blue crucible. Suttree craned his neck to breathe. Dead reek of aged female flesh, a stale aridity. Dry wattled nether lips hung from out the side of her torn stained drawers. Her thighs spread with a sound of rending ligaments, dry bones dragging in their sockets. Her shriveled cunt puckered open like a mouth gawping. He flailed bonelessly in the grip of a ghast black succubus, he screamed a dry and soundless scream. In the pale reach of firelight on the ceiling spiders were clambering toward the cracks in the high corners of the room and his spine was sucked from his flesh and fell clattering to the floor like a jointed china snake.

The fire had died in the room, the candles burned to pools of grease in their dishes. Suttree saw with perfect clarity a parade he'd watched through the legs of the crowd like a thing that passed in a forest, the floats of colored crepe and the band with its drum and horns and the polished wine broadcloth and gold braid and the majordomo in a stained shako wielding a baton and prancing and farting like a brewery horse. He saw what had been so how a caravan of pennanted cars wound through the rain on a dark day and how Clayton in corduroy knickers and aviator's cap marched with his sisters in a high ceilinged room where the paneled doors were drawn and a nurse in a white uniform called closeorder drill and tapped out the time with a cane and he could remember the stamped brass grapes of an umbrella stand cool and metallic under his tongue and he knew that in that house some soul lay dying.

He saw a pool of oil on a steel drumhead that lay shirred with the pounding of machinery. He saw the blood in his eyelids where he lay in a field in a summer noon and he saw young boys in a pond, pale nates and small bald cods shriveled with the cold and he saw an idiot in a yard in a leather harness chained to a clothesline and it leaned and swayed drooling and looked out upon the alley with eyes that fed the most rudimentary brain and yet seemed possessed of news in the universe denied right forms, like perhaps the eyes of squid whose simian depths seem to harbor some horrible intelligence. All down past the hedges a gibbering and howling in a hoarse frog's voice, word perhaps of things known raw, unshaped by the constructions of a mind obsessed with form.

He saw white swans flying over a house he'd known as a child, enormous shapes laboring above the chimneypots like farm stock flying in a dream, apparitions of such graceful levity quartering on the winter wind with their long necks craned seaward, shouldering the thin and bitter air. And a mechanical victrola and the bitter taste of the cracked varnish and the small dull tiles in a victorian bathroom and the footed castiron standards of the tub and the smell of tooth-paste and excrement and the languid amber kelp that rose and fell in the swells of a cold gray sea.

And he saw what had been so how the lilies leaned in the hall glass and a door closed and the candleflames trembled and righted again and he could smell the lilies and some other musty smell and he could feel the wirelike plush pricking the undersides of his legs in their short trousers where he sat in a chair with his elbows cocked high as his ears to rest on the dark oak chairarms. He saw a small boy in a schoolyard with a broken arm screaming and how the children watched like animals.

He saw shellfish crusted on the spiles of a wooden bridge and a salt river that ran two ways. Buoybells on a reef where the bones of a schooner broke the shallow surf on the out tide and the sound of the parlous and marbled sea and the seethe of spume and the long clatter of pebbles in the foam. He saw a jar in a garden with mousebones and lint and old sashweights stacked like ingots under a woodshed and the mortised shape of a wagonhub, spokestripped, weatherbleached, oaken, arcane. He saw a dead poodle in a street like a toy dog with its red collar and flannel tongue.

He saw what was so how his sisters came down the steps in their black patentleather shoes and he rode in the car with his mouth on the molding of the rear window and how the cold metal tasted of salt and hummed against his lips and he remembered the attar of rose and candlewax and the facets of a glass doorknob cold and smooth on his tongue.

And he saw old bottles and jars in a row on a board propped up with bricks in a field of sedge and the mixtures of mud and diced weeds within and round white pebbles wherein lay basilisks incubat-ing and secret paths through the sedge and a little clearing with broken bricks, an old limecrusted mortarbox, dry white dogturds. He saw a mooncalf dead in a wet road you could see through it, you could see its bones where it lay pale and blue and naked with eyes as barren as lightbulbs.

And he saw what had been how that old lady who had sat in the stained and cracked photograph like a fierce bird lay cold in state, white satin tucked or quilted and the parched claws that came out of the black stuff of her burial dress looked like the bony hands of some grimmer being crossed at her throat. Black lacquer bier trestled up in a drafty hall and how the rain swung from the rims of the pallbearers' hats.

The coals in the grate had died to the faintest pulse and he lay staring at the ceiling in almost total darkness. He listened for some sound in the house but there was none. He could hear organ music trammeled up out of an old black record on a gramophone somewhere and the slow shuffle of feet over the polished floors and he could see how the wind from the open door raised the figured runner in the hall and he was lifted in his father's arms to see how quietly the dead lay. Suddenly Suttree sat upright. He saw in a small alcove among flowers the sleeping doll, the white bonnet, the lace, the candlelight. Come upon in their wanderings through the vast funeral hall. And the little girl took the thing from its cradle and held it and rocked it in her arms and Clayton said you better put that thing up. She took it through the halls crooning it a lullaby, the long lace burial dress trailing behind her to the floor and Suttree following and a woman saw them pass in the hall and called softly upon God before she ran from the room and someone cried out: You bring that thing here. And they ran down the hall and the little girl fell with it and it rolled on the floor and a man came out and took it away and the little girl was crying and she said that it was just lying in there by itself and the little boy was much afraid.

Suttree rose from the cot and stumbled from the room. He went down the hall in the dark and unlatched the door at the end of it and stepped outside. The rind of a moon lay cocked in the sky and the world looked cold and blue. He could see the stalks of dockweed dead in the yard and beyond them the barren and pestilential locust wood and the trashpapers and newsprint among the boughs like varied birds illshapen pale and restless in the wind. He wandered through the wood as if he meant to read the old bleached news spiked there, the artless felonies, the murder in the streets. His tongue lay swollen in his mouth and his skull vised his brain. He could see figures moving in the woods greenly phosphorescent. He thought he might hear singing and he stood in the dark a long time listening but there was no sound, not even a dog barked. He made his way through a world unreal, through causeways in a darkened town, a gray light moving in the east, past dark brick walls and windows kept by steel grates, their panes opaque with soot. He wandered in the night murk by the river, in the cold damp of dead weeds, the lights on the far shore marking orders he had never seen before.

He lay in his bed half waking. He knew what would come to be that the fiddler Little Robert would kill Tarzan Quinn. A barge passed on the river. He lay with his feet together and his arms at his sides like a dead king on an altar. He rocked in the swells, floating like the first germ of life adrift on the earth's cooling seas, formless macule of plasm trapped in a vapor drop and all creation yet to come.

In the madhouse the walls reek with the odors of filth and terminal ills they've soaked up these hundred years. Stains from the rusted plumbing, the ordure slung by irate imbeciles. All this seeps back constantly above the smell of germicidal cleaning fluids.

A cold and brittle day. The iron gate open and the trees like bare black fossils rising from the dead leaves on the lawn. Walking the long drive, the dark brick buildings on the hill looming dire against the winter sky.

Old scarred marble floors in a cold white corridor. A room where the mad sat at their work. To Suttree they seemed like figures from a dream, something from the past, old drooling derelicts bent above their basketry, their fingerpaints or knitting. He'd never been among the certified and he was surprised to find them invested with a strange authority, like folk who'd had to do with death some way and had come back, something about them of survivors in a realm that all must reckon with soon or late.

In the center of the room sat a nurse at a desk. She read the morning paper where the news was madder yet.

McKellar, Suttree said.

She took off her glasses and rubbed her eyes and pushed the paper back. She opened a ledger and held a pencil above it. Your name, she said.

Suttree. Cornelius Suttree.

You are . . . What?

I beg your pardon?

The nurse looked up at him. What, she said. A nephew?

Yes. Nephew.

You've been here before then.

Not in some years.

She put her glasses on again and laid down the pencil and turned in her chair. That's her with the other lady sitting by the far wall. The two by themselves.

Thank you.

Eyes watched him cross the floor. A lone pacer in a strange knitted cap paused and raised a cautionary finger. Suttree nodded, agreeing as he did on the need for care. The old women sat like almstresses on the floor in their hodden cloaks. He knelt before them and they regarded him mildly. He thought that he might know her in some way but age and madness had outdone all the work of likeness there had ever been and he could not guess. Aunt Alice? he said.

The older lady moved. She made a little motion of gathering the hem of her gown and she looked at him with no change of expression. Yes, she said.

I'm Buddy.

Oh yes. How have you been?

Do you know me?

Are you Buddy?

Yes.

Grace's son.

Suttree smiled, son of Grace. I didnt think you'd know me.

She reached out and took his wrist. Her hand cool and firm. He covered it with his own. She had her eyes fixed on him and would not look elsewhere. They were a pure cold gray and something feral in them but there was no malice there. He looked down at their hands. Hers was trembling, just gently. The old woman sitting by her reached over and put her hand with theirs and nodded her head solemnly. The three of them squatting there on the floor like conspirators pledging themselves.

How have you been, Aunt Alice?

A hollow croak of a voice in the drafty dayroom. He cleared his throat. He turned to see had he attracted attention. An old man in a wheelchair cringing by the wall watched. Chanting to himself some silent doxology.

I'm fine, the old woman said.

Do they treat you well?

Oh, a body ought not to complain.

Does Mother come?

Why she died in twenty-seven.

Does Grace come to see you? Or Helen?

Oh well. She shook her head and smiled. No. They dont come a whole lot.

Docs Martha?

No. John comes much as anybody. He took me out. He took me out in his motorcar.

The old woman with them nodded her head. He did, she said. Her John did. Come in a car and fetched her.

The aunt leaned toward Suttree in confidence. He'd been a drinkin some. But I'd rather for him to of come drunk as for nobody to come sober.

Suttree smiled. They were speaking in hushed tones like people in church. The room was enormously silent. He could hear labored breathing, the rattle of osiers among the basketmakers. The clink of a bucket bail out in the hall somewhere. He looked around at the old room, the pale midwinter light that carried the windows tall and slant to the opposite wall and the plaster banded with the bones of lathing.

I never thought to end my time in such a place as this is, she said. If Allen had lived he never would of let no such a thing happen. He was always so good to me. I was like his little girl almost. I was just little when Daddy died.

What was his name? Your father. I never knew his name.

It was Jeffrey. My brother Jeffrey was Jeffrey Junior. Daddy was old when I was born. I know he'd been too old for service in the war between the states. He was a . . . He was wild. Pretty wild. They always said about him anyways. He was shot in a fracas of some kind. Long fore he married. Come near dyin. So I always wondered about that, had he died none of us would never have been at all and I never could . . . Well, that's a funny thing to think. Maybe we would have just been somebody else. But they said he was, that he had been in trouble, I dont know. I reckon it was so and I reckon Jeffrey must of took after him. I never knew Jeffrey. I was just a baby when . . . When he died.

He was hanged in Rockcastle County Kentucky on July 18 1884.

She didnt answer. She said: Allen always said that Robert favored him. But of course Robert never come back from the war. Lord he wasnt but eighteen poor baby. Allen never got over it. They say he died of cancer and that may be but he never had hardly a well day after they brought Robert home. I believe it killed him as much as anything did. They was nine of us you know. Me and Elizabeth outlived all the boys and now she's gone and I'm in the crazy house. Sometimes I dont know what people's lives are for. She looked at Suttree. Her eyes moved and she smiled.

Daddy kept store you know, and we had this horse his name was Captain and he used to pull the wagon delivered the groceries and he was my pet. He'd foller me around, just foller me around like a dog would. We lived in Sweetwater then. And they was hard times then and we had to sell the store and Daddy had to sell Captain. And they took me up to Nanny's because the man was comin to take him, you see. I was just a little thing. Years later when I was a young girl I was in Knoxville one Saturday and I seen this horse standin in front of a feedstore hitched to a wagon and it was Captain. I run over to him and thowed my arms around him and kissed him and I reckon everbody thought I was crazy, me about full growed standin there in the street huggin a old horse and just a bawlin to beat the band.

She pushed the palm of her hand hard against one cheek. She looked up at Suttree and smiled and she looked at the woman by her side who now was weeping and she gave her a great nudge with her elbow. Lord amercy, she said. You're the silliest thing in here.

The woman shook her head and snuffled and Suttree's aunt smiled at him. I want you to look at this old crazy thing, she said. She dont even know what all she's bawlin about.

Do too, said the woman.

It wasnt the first word she'd said but it was the first Suttree'd heard. She had her hand across her forehead and was rubbing it as if she'd have the skin off. She wore a faint mustache and her gray hair stood about her head electrically. Aunt Alice looked down at her with soft amusement. She brushed her cheeks again and turned to Suttree. Her eye was bright and her expression full of sauce. You're a good lookin somethin, she said. I believe you favor E C. You dont have a motorcar do you?

Suttree said he didnt. He felt himself being drawn into modes for which he had neither aptitude nor will. They were both watching him. The tears were gone. Their eyes seemed filled with expectation and he'd nothing to give. He'd come to take. He pulled away from them and they leaned toward him with their veined old hands groping at the emptiness. He rose. Casting his eyes over this wreckage. What perverted instinct made folks group the mad together? So many. He was the only person in the room standing and now they were watching him, eyes vacant or keen with suspicion or incipient hatred. Or eyes betrayed of any earnestness at all. An air of possible insurrection in the room, wanting just the cue to set these wretches clawing at their keepers. He looked down at the old ladies at his feet. They had their hands to their mouth in identical attitudes. I have to go, he said. I cant stay. He tore his look from theirs and wheeled off through the room. An old man in a striped railroader's hat was holding a huge watch in his hand and following Suttree with his eyes as if he'd time him. Their eyes met across the dayroom and Suttree's face drained to see the old man there and he almost said his name but he did not and he was soon out the door.

He was going from phone to phone in the booths of the Park National Bank and he was whistling to himself when a heavy hand dropped across his shoulder. He stopped and looked down, placing the nearest black wingtip shoe. He leaped up and came down on the shoe with his heel, his knee locked. Small bones cracked under the leather. The hand went away. Harrogate never even saw the man. He crossed Gay Street in the noon traffic over the actual hoods and decklids of idling cars, faces white behind the glass, sounds of buckling sheetmetal.

Suttree sought him out under the viaduct among the debris. Gene? he called. There was no fire, no sign of having been one. Cars rumbled distantly overhead. Hey Gene.

Harrogate crawled out of the concrete pillbox and squatted in the dirt. He was ragged looking and shaking with the cold and he had shaved his mustache off.

Suttree squatted beside him. Well, he said. What are your plans?

The city rat hunched his shoulders. He looked frail and wasted with defeat.

You cant stay down here, you'll freeze.

He shook his head slowly from side to side, staring at the raw ground. I dont know, he said. I been in there all day. I figured the law would of done had me by now.

Suttree stirred the dust with his forefinger. They will, he said. This is no place to hide out.

I know it. How'd you find me?

I didnt have any place else to look. Rufus told me you'd been up there.

Yeah. You caint depend on a nigger for nothin. I didnt know where else to go. All them sons of bitches. Many a time as I drunk whiskey with em. They didnt hardly know me.

Suttree smiled. A fugitive's life is a hard one, he said. What happened to your mustache?

Harrogate rubbed his lip. Shaved it off, he said. Maybe they wont recognize me without it. I dont know. Shit.

Well what are you going to do?

I dont know. I was ashamed to come to you.

Maybe you ought to get out of town for a while.

Where to?

Anywhere. Out of town.

Harrogate looked up at him vaguely. Out of town? he said.

If you stay around here they'll nail your ass.

Hell, Sut. I aint never been out of town. I wouldnt know where to go. I wouldnt know which way to start.

Just get on a bus and go. What difference does it make? You've scuffled in this town for three years, hell, you could make it somewhere else.

I dont have no friends somewhere else.

You dont have any here.

Harrogate shook his head. Shit, he said. Bus? I aint never even been on a goddamned bus.

All you do is get a ticket and get on.

Yeah yeah, sure sure. I'd get on the wrong damned bus or somethin.

There's not any wrong bus. Not for you.

Well how the hell would I know where to get off at? And where would I be when I did?

They'd tell you.

He looked at the ground. Naw, he said. I'd never make it. I'd get lost and never would get home again ever. He shook his head. I dont know, Sut. Seems like everthing I turn my hand to. Dont make no difference what it is. Just everthing I touch turns to shit.

Have you got any money?

Not a cryin dime.

What did you do with all that money you were making?

Spent it, naturally.

You could go on the train.

Do they not charge?

You can sneak on. Get in an empty car over in the yards. I can let you have a few dollars.

Train, said Harrogate, staring off toward the creek.

You could go south for the winter. Someplace where it's not so fucking cold. Hell, Gene. You've got to do something. You cant just sit here.

The city rat made a little shivering motion and drew up his feet but he didnt answer.

Who was it nailed you?

Fuck if I know.

Was it a detective? Plainclothes?

I dont know, Sut. I never seen nothin but his feet. I reckon it was the telephone heat. They tell me when them sons of bitches get on your trail you're completely fucked. They wont rest till they get ye.

Telephone heat?

Harrogate looked up warily. You fuckin ay, he said. Them bastards take it personal. He looked at the ground. I knew that, he said. I knew it, but I went and done it anyways.

Dark was falling over the creek and a cold wind was moving in the dry weeds. On the hill among the shacks a dog had begun to bark. They sat quietly under the viaduct in the deepening chill. After a while Harrogate said: They wouldnt be a soul there that I knowed. I'd bet on it.

Where?

In the workhouse.

There wasnt anybody there you knew the last time.

Yeah.

You're not there yet, anyway.

Me and old crazy Bodine used to have some good times racin scorpions in the kitchen. That was after you'd done left.

Scorpions?

Lizards I guess you call em.

Lizards?

Yeah. We'd get the yard man to get em for us. We'd race em on the kitchen floor. Get a bet up. Shit. I had me one named Legs Diamond that son of a bitch would stand straight up with them old legs just a churnin and quick as he'd get traction he was gone like a striped assed ape. Never would touch down with his front feet.

The city mouse shook his head, deep in the fondness of these recollections like a strange little old man there in the blue winter twilight under the bridge. Remembering the sunlight on the buffed floor and the broomhandles laid out and the chalk marks. Lying like the children they were on the cool floor with their fragile reptiles, the small hearts hammering in the palms of their hands. Holding them by their tiny pumping waists and releasing them at a signal. The lizards rearing onto their hind legs as their feet slipped on the smooth waxed concrete, strange little saurians. Harrogate has tacked the hinder toes of his with syrup and it scampers through the barry light to soundless victory.

Old crazy Leithal King worked in the kitchen after that. I believe he was the biggest fuck-up in the workhouse. Shit. I got tired takin stuff off of him he was so dumb. I used to race lizards with him I'd let him take his pick, we'd have upwards of half a dozen in a kettle. I'd have me some chili pepper in my hand and when I got my lizard I'd rub a little of that in his ass. He'd go like he was on fire. Old Leithal'd get em and wouldnt know how to hold em or nothin, half the time he'd pull their tails off. He raced one one time that son of a bitch stood straight up and went right on over backards, feet just a churnin.

They sat in blackness. Lights were coming on across the cut, blooming among the barren vines like winter fireflies there.

Come on, said Suttree. You can stay at my place till you get sorted out what you're going to do.

I dont want to put nobody out.

Hell with that. Let's go.

He rose reluctantly.

What happened to your cat? said Suttree.

Shit if I know. Seems like when the shit hits the fan they all clear out. Even the goddamn cat.

Suttree never locked his door and the city mouse would come and go at hours convenient to his obscure purposes. He wandered through the wastes like a jackal in the dark, in the keep of old warehouse walls and the quiet of gutted buildings. He was enamored of the night and those quiet regions on the city's inward edges too dismal for dwelling. Down alleyways of flueblack brick. Through a gate unhinged to a garden of gloom.

In the dawn when cold trucks cough and lumber over the cobbles and black men in frayed and partly eaten greatcoats of their country's service stand about the fires in empty trashdrums and spit and speculate and nod there'd shoulder in among them a paler derelict who held his small hands to the flames without a word.

At night sometimes he'd sit by the right of way where the rails go so surgically in the slack gloss of the quartermoon. Curving away to some better land where strangers sit freely without being asked. Among alien shapes in the honeysuckles watching the train pass chuffing and clacking down the cut between the high banks, leaving in the smoke and leaf swirl such utter loneliness that he, who'd come from hiding to see it go, knelt sobbing on the crossties among the lightly whispered collisions of the leaves with a hot and salty sorrow in his throat, his hands dangling and his stained face wretched, watching the barnred hinder carriage shuttle gently from sight beyond the curve.

He was caught at his first robbery. White lights crossed like warring swords the little grocery store and back, his small figure tortured there cringing and blinking as if he were being burnt. He dove headlong through a plateglass window and fetched up stunned and bleeding at the feet of a policeman who stood with a cocked revolver at his head saying: I hope you run. I wish you would run.

He rode handcuffed through the winter landscape to Nashville. It is true that the world is wide. Out there the open ends of cornfield rows wheel past like a turnstile. Dark earth between the dead stalks. The rails at a junction veering in liquid collision and flaring again silently in long vees. His forehead to the cold glass, watching.

They went on through the long afternoon twilight with the old carriage rocking and clicking and a rain that blew down from the north cutting long tears in the dust on the windows. Barren fields falling away desolate and small flocks of nameless birds flaring over the land and against the darkening sky like seafans stamped from black sheet iron the shapes of winter trees against a winter sky.

They passed a house and a woman came from the door and tossed a dishpan of water into the yard and wiped her hand on her apron. He pressed his face to the window, watching her recede quietly in the dusk. The train hooted for a crossing and they passed a little store squatting in the coke and dust beyond the yard and they passed a row of empty coaches, the dead windows clocking by and dicing the scene beyond and the long wail of the engine hanging over the country like a thing damned of all deliverance. Harrogate eased the steel bracelet on his wrist and rested his head against the harsh nap of the seat and slept.

He woke in the night with the train's slowing. Stale smell of smoke and an antique mustiness from the old woodwork of the carriage. The man he was manacled to slept slackjawed. He looked out the window. A long row of lighted henhouses on a hill went by like a passing train itself, row on row of yellow windows backing down the night and drawing off into the darkness. They went through a small town in the mountains, a midnight cafe, empty stools, a dead clock on the wall. As they moved on into the country again the windows became black mirrors and the city rat could see his pinched face watching him back from the cold glass, out there racing among the wires and the bitter trees, and he closed his eyes.

Somnolent city, cold and dolorous in the rain, the lights bleeding in the streets. Cutting through the alley off Commerce he saw a man huddled among the trash and he knelt to see about him. The face came up and the eyes closed. An oiled mask in black against the bricks.

Suttree took him by one arm. Ab, he said.

Can you get me home? A voice from the void, dead and flat and divested of every vanity. Suttree raised up one of the great arms and got it across his shoulder and braced his feet to rise. Sweat stood on his forehead. Ab, he said. Come on.

He opened his eyes and looked about. Are they huntin me? he said.

I dont know. Come on.

He lurched to his feet and stood there reeling while Suttree steadied him by one arm. Their shadows cast by the lamp at the end of the alley fell long and narrow to darkness. As they tottered out of the mouth of the alley a prowlcar passed. Ab sagged, swung back and slammed against the building.

Goddamnit Ab. Straighten up now. Ab.

The cruiser had stopped and was backing slowly. The spotlight came on and sliced about and pinned them against the wall.

Go on, Youngblood.

No.

I aint goin.

You'll be all right in a minute.

With them I aint goin. Go on.

No damnit. Ab. I'll talk to them.

But the black had begun to come erect with a strength and grace contrived out of absolute nothingness and Suttree said: Ab, and the black said: Go on.

All right, said the officer. What's this?

I'm just getting him home, said Suttree. He's all right.

Is that so? He dont look so all right to me. What are you doin with him? He your daddy?

Fuck you, said Ab.

What?

There were two of them now. Suttree could hear the steady guttering of the cruiser's exhaust in the empty street.

What? said the officer.

The black turned to Suttree. Go on now, he said. Go on while ye can.

Officer this man's sick, said Suttree.

He's goin to be sicker, said the cop. He gestured with his nightstick. Get his ass in there.

Bullshit on that, said the other one. Let me call the wagon. That's that big son of a bitch . . .

Jones lurched free and swung round the corner of the alley at a dead run. The two cops tore past Suttree and disappeared after him. The flat slap of their shoes died down the alley in a series of diminishing reports and then there was only the rough drone of the idling cruiser at the curb. Suttree stepped to the car, eased himself beneath the wheel and shut the door. He sat there for a moment, then he engaged the gearbox and pulled away.

He drove to Gay Street and turned south and onto the bridge. The radio crackled and a voice said: Car Seven. He turned left at the end of the bridge, past the abandoned roller rink, a rotting wooden arena that leaned like an old silo. He went down Island Home Pike toward the river. The radio fizzled and crackled. Calling any car in area B. Area B. Come in.

We've got a report of some kind of disturbance at Commerce and Market.

Suttree drove along the lamplit street. There was no traffic. The lights at Rose's came up along his left and the lights from the packing company. The radio said: Car Nine. Car Nine. Suttree turned off down an old ferry road, going slowly, the car rocking and bumping over the ground, out across a field, the headlights picking up a pair of rabbits that froze like plaster lawn figures. The dead and lightly coiling back of the river moving beyond the grass. The sparsely lit silhouette of the city above. The headlights failed somewhere out over the water in a gauzy smear. He brought the car to a stop and shifted it into neutral and stepped out into the wet grass. He pulled the hoodlatch under the dash and walked to the front of the cruiser and raised the hood. He came back to the car and sat in the seat and removed his shoelace. He looked out at the river and the city. One of the rabbits began to lope slowly through the light ground mist toward the dark of the trees.

The radio popped. Wagner? What's the story down there?

Suttree got out and walked around to the front of the car and bent into the motor compartment and pulled back the throttle linkage. The motor rose to a howl and he tied the linkage back with the shoelace, fastening it to the fuel line where it entered the pump. Live flame was licking from the end of the tailpipe. He climbed in and pushed the clutch to the floor and shifted the lever hard up into second in a squawk of gearteeth. The rabbits were both gone. He eased off the seat and stood with one foot on the ground and the other on the clutch. Then he leaped back and slapped the door shut.

For a moment it didnt move. The tires cried in the grass and smoking clods went rifling off through the dark. Then it settled slightly sideways, dished back again, and in a shower of mud and grass moved out across the field. It went low and fast, the headlights rigid and tilting. It tore across the field and ripped through the willows at the river's edge and went planing out over the water in two great wings of spray that seemed pure white and fanned upward twenty feet into the air. When it came to rest it was far out in the river. The headlights began to wheel about downstream. Then they went out. For a while he could see the dark hump of it in the river and then it slowly subsided and was gone. He squatted in the damp grass and looked out. There was no sound anywhere along the river. After a while he rose and started home.

Jones came to bay with his back to a brick wall, standing widefooted and gasping while the officers approached. A bloody dumbshow and no word spoken. The first policeman swung at him with his club and Jones slapped at it, a dead smack of meat in his palm. He swung again and this time the black's hand folded over the club. The policeman had the leather lanyard looped about his wrist and Jones swung him sideways and slammed him against the bricks. Then he jerked him to his knees and was strangling him when the other officer fell upon him and forced him to give it up. Jones kicked them back and the first officer staggered toward the center of the alley and dropped to his knees groaning. A cry of sirens was nearing in the streets. The able officer stepped back in alarm but Jones seized him like some huge black pervert. He struggled to reach for his revolver. By now a patrol car was coming down the alley in a blinding spray of lights. The seized officer gave up trying to loosen his pistol and was hammering away with his billy at the cropped skull above him and his hand and arm were slick with blood.

Men were running in the alley. Jones turned and started off lumbering and huge in the lights like a movie monster. The revolvers in that narrow space crashed like mortars and the bullets caromed and whined and skittered. But before they could get a true aim his knees went under him and he collapsed flailing among the trashcans at the alley's mouth.

The officer who opened the rear door of the paddywagon just closed his eyes. He had no time to fend or hide. Jones's boot caught him in the throat and he went to the pavement without a cry. The other officers received him with billies and slapsticks, his eyes huge and crazed and his jacket spongy with blood launching himself upon them like some unshackled wild man and taking them to the ground with him.

They dragged him bleeding and senseless down the corridor to the tank, his feet scuffing behind. His bearers were bleeding and torn and they cursed every step they took. They pulled him into the empty iron cage and let him fall face down on the concrete. Tarzan Quinn came from the dayroom with a cup of coffee in one hand. The jailer was locking back the hall door, a great ring of keys fastened to him with a chain.

Duck, said Tarzan.

The jailer turned. Yeah, he said.

You let me know when that son of a bitch wakes up.

Sure will, Tarzan.

Tarzan nodded and sipped his coffee. He worked his right fist open and shut and rubbed his palm on the side of his trousers.

She was a long time coming but when she saw him she opened the door and motioned with her head for him to enter. She had a lamp in her hand and she wore an old chenille robe and she had some sort of a nightcap on her head that looked vaguely orthopedic. She shuffled wearily into a chair and put her face in one hand.

He shut the door and leaned against it, watching her. After a while she raised her head and wiped her eye and her mouth. She was looking at the lampflame.

He aint dead is he? she said.

No. I thought maybe he got away but he must be in jail.

Well.

What do you want to do?

Aint nothin to do. Aint no use in goin over there till in the mornin.

I guess not.

She shook her head. They aint no way, she said. Just aint no way.

Do you have any money?

Some. I dont know. Them bondsmens gets it all. I'll have to look and see.

I've got about thirty dollars if you need it.

That wouldnt get him started.

What will they charge him with?

What wont they. Two year ago they tried to get him for temptin murder. It costed me fourteen hunnerd dollar.

I cant go down there with you.

You dont need to go down there.

They may be looking for me.

Dont let em get on you, she said. They never will get off.

A dull glow of coals showed through the drafthole in the stove door but it was cold in the room. She must have followed his thoughts. Come over here by the stove and warm, she said. You want a beer?

No. I've got to go. I've got to figure out what to do.

She shook her head and looked up. Black shining face, those lunettes of flesh ridging the skin and the one webbed and blinking eye.

He fifty-six year old, she said. You know that?

I knew he was something like that.

He caint carry on like this. They'll kill him. You caint tell him.

Suttree looked at the floor.

Well, she said. I thank ye for stoppin.

Do you want me to try and get hold of Oceanfrog?

No. I'll see him.

Well. I'll come by tomorrow.

She rose from the chair and put both hands on the table. Then she sat down again. Suttree opened the door and went out.

He crossed the cold white tiles of the lobby floor and leaned at the desk. There was no one about. He palmed the little bell. Brass through the nickel plate. After a while Jesse came from the rear and nodded with that expression of constrained contempt with which he beheld all life forms not midnight in color.

He be out in a minute.

The clerk came out and went through the little gate and stood facing Suttree.

You got a room? said Suttree.

He reached and took a card from a slot and slid it across the marble counter and laid a pen across it.

Suttree wrote his name and pushed the card back. The clerk didnt look at it. Is it just you? he said.

Just me.

How long?

I dont know. Couple of weeks.

He laid out a key on its fiberboard fob. Twelve bucks, he said.

For a week?

Right.

I only paid fourteen for a double. Last time I was here.

It's twelve bucks.

Suttree counted out the money and took the key and crossed the lobby to the stairs and climbed upward into the gloom. He found the room and went to put the key in the door but it was already ajar. He pushed it open. The latch was smashed, broken hardware hung from the screws. The whole door was cracked through and wobbled sickly when he pushed it shut. He went back down the stairs and dinged on the bell.

The clerk gave him another room and he went up again. It looked out over the alley in the rear of the hotel. There were enormous holes caved in the walls and patched over with cardboard and masking tape. A small iron bed. An oak veneer dresser on tall castered legs. He lay hammocked in the soft mattress and stared at the ceiling. After a while he got up and turned off the light and kicked off his shoes and stretched out again. Cars passed in the streets below. Already a faint gray light from the day to come lay in the eastward windows. He slept.

It was late afternoon when he woke. He shuffled off down the hall to the bathroom. There seemed to be no one about. He went down and got the paper in the lobby and crossed the street and went up to the drugstore where he sat in a back booth and had coffee and doughnuts. He ransacked the paper for news of the night before but there was no word.

With dark he went down to the end of the street and to the river. There was no light at Doll's and no one answered when he rapped at the door. Ab's cat came down from the roof and rubbed against his leg but he had nothing to give it.

It was dark on the river and the only sound was the dripping of the oars and the light rasp of the locks. He foundered among the shore brush with his flashlight and finally located the stake where his trotline was fastened and he hooked the line through the lock in the transom and took the oars again, the flashlight propped on the seat and the line coming up very white from the black water. He stripped the bait from the hooks as they came up and when he reached the farther bank he cut the line. It rifled off into the river with a thin sucking sound and disappeared from sight. Then he rowed down and ran the other line and cut it. By the time he came back upriver with his catch in the floor of the skiff it was past midnight. He lit his lamp and sat on the deck and cleaned the fish, pausing from time to time to warm his stained hands at the lampchimney. He wrapped the fish in newsprint and put them in a box and he went down and drew the skiff ashore and turned it over. Then he went in and got his clothes and the few personal things he owned and blew out the lamp and went across the fields toward the town with these things piled atop the fishbox in front of him.

He went down every night but there was no one home. By day he kept off the streets. There was nothing in the papers. He asked for her at Howard Clevinger's but no one knew where she was. As he turned to leave he saw Oceanfrog going along the street.

Hey baby, the frog said.

What's happening, said Suttree. Where's Ab.

The man's in the hospital.

Is he bad?

I dont know. I aint been out there.

Where's Doll?

She out there with him. Frazer turned up his collar and looked off down the street. He turned back to Suttree. You goin out there? he said.

I dont know.

446

They got a cop on the door.

Ah, said Suttree.

Oceanfrog squinted at him and smiled. He tugged at his collar again and took a step backward preparatory to going on up the street. Thought you ought to know, he said.

Have they been down to my place?

They been there, baby. Hang loose.

He went up the street in his jaunty stride and Suttree looked toward the river and tested the air with his nose in a gesture of some simpler antecedent but the wind and the landscape alike remained cool and without movement.

He'd walk out at night to the end of the bridge and lean on the ironwork and watch the river and the squalor of the life below. He could hear the music from upstairs in the old frame house that Carroll King ran as a nightclub, Paul Jones at the piano full of gin and old offcolor songs. A black girl named Priscilla who worked by day in a laundry.

A few nights later he saw the faintest fall of light on the river from the rear of Jones's place and he descended the little path in the dark.

For a while he thought she wouldnt come to the door. He was almost ready to leave when it swung open.

Her hair lay about her head in greasy black clots as if she were besieged with leeches and her eye was bright and inflamed and swiveled up silently to see him. She crossed her arms and held her shoulders and her breath smoked in the cold.

How is he? said Suttree. Is he here?

She shook her head.

Is he not out of the hospital?

Yes. He's out. The Lord taken him out. She began to cry, standing there in her housecoat and slippers, holding her shoulders. The tears that ran on her pitted cheek looked like ink. She had her eye closed but the lid that covered the naked socket did not work so well anymore and it sagged in the cavity and struggled up and that raw hole seemed to watch him with some ghastly equanimity, an eye for another kind of seeing like the pineal eye in atavistic reptiles watching through time, through conjugations of space and matter to that still center where the living and the dead are one.

That spring he did not go to the river. The shadows of the buildings still harbored a gray chill and the sun sulked smoked and baleful somewhere above the city and in the sparsely weeded clay barrens wasting on the city's perimeter first flowers erupted drunkenly through glass and cinder and came slowly to bloom. The days grew warm and grackles returned, hordes of blue tin birds that weighed the shrieking trees. Small bodies that the cold has kept went soft with rot, a cat's balding hide that tautened and dried cloven to the meatless ribs, an upturned eyesocket filled with rainwater and for all weathers this lipless grin, these bleaching teeth.

He went out seldomer, his money dribbled away. The days grew long and he lay hourlong on his cot. The clerk came and tapped at the door and went away again. One day came an eviction notice.

Then he fell sick. First his nose began to bleed nor could he stop it. The floor lay strewn with wads of wet toiletpaper stained with watered blood. The clerk came and rapped again. Shadow of his shoes in the threshold light. And went away. Things had begun to go peculiar. Grainy underwater singing sounds in his head. He lay on his cot and watched the barren vinework of cracks in the ceiling. Old rags of lace lifted at the window. Cries of children at noon on the Bell House School grounds. Suttree lay naked in fever. Even his eyes were hot. He slept some of the afternoon, waking out of a dream fraught with the odor of a long forgotten blanket whose satin selvedge bore blue ducks. His father's weight tilting the bed, how do you feel son, I dont feel so pretty good. Under the slant ceiling, close by the eaves.

He opened his eyes. The room had a warped look to it. He watched arcana uncoil from out of the rough plaster. Something unseen possessed the troweler's hand. Shapes grimacing in a calcimine moonscape. Record of an old mason long dead it may be. He closed his eyes again. A huge and pulsing thumbwhorl hovered above his swollen lids. He steadied himself with one hand to the wall like a drunk.

The day expired in rose and ashen light. Blue dusk cooled in the room.

He lay in darkness.

After a long time he staggered to the wall and threw the switch. Under the stark bulblight he groped for a towel to wrap his loins and reeled out and down the corridor to the bathroom. There he knelt on the cold white tiles and vomited blood into the toilet. When he came back to his room he sat on the bed and looked at his toes.

Well, he said. You're sick.

A shoe salesman named Thomas E Warren found him shortly after midnight. He thought him drunk. Kneeling, he stirred him by the shoulder. Hey Bud, he said.

Suttree was lying naked on the bathroom floor where he'd come for the cool. Warren got him to his feet and Suttree stared back without comprehension, not having expected anyone from the world of the quick. Down a far wall of his smoking brain withdrew a ghastly company. He disengaged himself from the grip of the living Thomas and tottered to the toilet and sat.

You okay, man?

Yes, said Suttree.

He was alone in the narrow room. Water sluiced down a black pipe past his ear. His head had sagged forward and he was clutching his stomach. He shat a loose and bloody stool.

At the sink he laved cold water over his head. Ahh, he told the drainhole.

I know you're in there, said the clerk from beyond the door.

Suttree opened his eyes. He was lying on his cot and it was day. The door rapping faded. Footsteps in a corridor. He looked toward the window. Are there parades in the street? What is this roaring? Who is this otherbody? I am no otherbody.

He sat. The room reeled. He fell back and laughed briefly into the musty bedding.

All day he lay in a quaintly fevered world, nothing in the room but the sun and himself, making what construction he could of the sounds that carried to him, the hammering of a roofer, the long farting of airbrakes from a truck in the streets, screendoors banging, children called. A blank wall against which to elaborate his pantomimes. A less virulent cast of the grim had come to occupy his mind and there was a time in the early noon when he had hope of his own recovery. But the sounds he heard began to coalesce and rush and he no longer knew if he dreamt or woke.

In the long afternoon he fell prey to strange cravings of the flesh. Out of a pinwheel of brown taffy his medusa beckoned. A gross dancer with a sallow puckered belly, hands cupping a pudendum grown with mossgreen hair, a virid merkin out of which her wet mauve petals smiled and bared from hiding little rows of rubber teeth like the serried jaws of conchshells.

Suttree groaned in his sleep. He lay in a sexual nightmare, an enormous wattled fundament lowering slowly over his head, in the center a withered brown pig's eye crusted shut and hung with puffy blue and swollen lobes. A white gruel welled. He pressed his face against the cool wall. And who is this Mr Bones rising wreathed in pale and bluegreen gas? He comes about tottering and wooden like a dummy on a track and goes past with a slight smile and a bow. Lights run over his wetlooking bones and the feet of small rodents grip from within the chamfers of his eyesockets and in his pale blue teeth are cores of blackened silver packed. In a rattle and clang of wheels and pulleys Father Bones tilts out through saloon doors and is gone, old varnished funhouse skeleton. Suttree in his sleep smiled at such child's fancies. A gray crust broke at his mouthcorners. His eyes snapped open. He sat and reached for the towel. It fell from him and he went out and down the hall naked.

Clotted gouts of gore stained the water in the toiletbowl. Pink, magenta, burgundy.

He stretched himself on the tiles. A faint tang of urine there. Bird shadows on the whited windowglass. Water dripped in the sink. I saw her in an older dream, an older time, moving in an aura of musk, a breath of stale roses, her languid hands swaying like pale birds and her face chalk and lips pink and her nigh-blue hair upbuckled in combs of tortoise, coming down out of her chamber in my unhealed memory clothed in smoke.

Hey Bud. Hey.

It is my old J-Bone and no other.

What the fuck are you doing?

Sicky sick, James.

What the hell have you done to yourself? Can you get up?

I'm all fucked up, James.

I can see that. What is it?

Dear friend, it's checkout time.

J-Bone patted his shoulder. Hang on a minute. I'll be right back.

Suttree opened his eyes. In a minute I am going to have a drink of water. He licked his lips.

J-Bone arrived with a fat cabbie. They pulled Suttree up by the arms and began to work a shirt onto him.

I'd just let him sleep it off, said the cabdriver.

I cant leave him layin in here.

Suttree's arm dropped, his knuckles banged on the floor.

He aint sick is he?

Hold him here a minute while I button these. He just needs to get dried out.

Desist officer. I'll come peaceably.

He better not be sick. You hear?

I've seen him worse than this. Let him back down now.

Has he got any shoes?

I'll find him some. Help me lift him here.

What's this?

What?

Hell, he's bleedin out of his ass.

Maybe he's got piles.

Piles hell. Look at it.

A crimson stain was spreading about Suttree's pale and naked haunches. He lay buttoned up in a shirt with a pair of trousers bunched about his knees. The cabdriver backed toward the door. J-Bone looked like an assassin kneeling there. The cabbie turned and fled down the hall.

Go on then, you son of a bitch, J-Bone called.

Son of a bitch, said Suttree from the floor.

J-Bone pulled him sideways out of the blood and began to wrestle the trousers up around him. He fetched his shoes and got them on. He got him up under the armpits and dragged him out and down the hall and stood in Suttree's bed and pulled him up onto it.

Water Jim. A little old drink.

J-Bone was back in ten minutes with another cabdriver.

Can he walk?

No. Give me a hand with him.

Damn if he aint about as fucked up as anybody I ever saw.

He gets this way.

Suttree's toes left a faint wake in the scurfy warp of the hall carpet. His shoes fell down the stairs like toys. He watched the hard sunlight ascend the stairwell. His head banged something.

You goin with him aint ye?

Yes. I'll ride back here. Go ahead.

That's the drunkest human ever I witnessed, said the driver.

Whose house is this? said Suttree.

Take it easy Bud.

Why I'm all right.

They struggled with him. I was all right, he said.

Rank odor of caustic and drugs. Standing in a white room. He leaned in confidence toward an ear. I'm all right now, he lied. Someone has stole the pins from his kneehinges. He leaned heavily on a steel table. A wall placard listed regulations. In the center of the room the taut white linen of the emergency table. An orderly opened the door and looked at him.

To wish to lie down here is to entertain the illusion that kings may worship, said Suttree.

The orderly closed the door.

Another door closed, door closed, door closed softly in his skull. Light bloomed rose, lime green. He was going out by a long tunnel attended by fading voices and a grainy humming sound and going faster and past gray images that clicked apart in jagged puzzle pieces. Down a corridor that opened constantly before him and dissolved after in iron dark. While the dead wheeled past in floats of sere and faded flower wreaths with little cards on which the ink of the names had run in the rain. Callahan and Hoghead leering with their crazy teeth and little plugs stoppering the holes in their skulls and Bobby Davis on a slab with his torso peppered like a pox victim and Jimmy Smith with broken neck and Aunt Beatrice composed and sedate in grayblack gingham with candlewhite hands enfolding a rose and passing in a glass casket. She cracked one powdered eye, winked hugely and was gone. Suttree said I am going out of the world, a long silent scream on rails down the dark nether slope of the hemisphere that is death's prelude. Attended by ponderous and mercurial figures composed of colored gas and wrenching themselves slowly apart, pale green cerise and bottleblue butyljawed fools that galloped softly and cried out Powww and Boyyy, exulting into the breach with boneless cartoon mouths puckered and wapsy galligaskins, lumbering eternally toward the edge of all.

A quartermoon the color of a broken file lay far down the void. Likecolored figures crossed it. He no longer cared that he was dying. He was being voided by an enormous livercolored cunt with prehensile lips that pumped softly like some levantine bivalve. Into a cold dimension without time without space and where all was motion.

A nurse took Suttree's temperature.

Thank you nurse. Yes, that's fine.

You men can come around to the other side here. Yes. Clear the door there. Thank you.

Suttree opened his eyes. Solemn young men in scrubsuits stood about his bedside watching. He fell back laughing and was gone again. Down a cycloid in a sidecar, a streamlined dreamride through the eye of a poisoned kaleidoscope, cutting a helical course and yawing up the wall at speeds that drained his face and rifling through a hot drift of ether where his ears sang. Attending members appeared over and over, face and figure, a harridan with brown flame for hair reeling past, coming again, a cyclic procession shot through with fleering gas mosaics, and again, slightly mutant, slowly altered, until phased out to abstractions of color and form that severed in elastic parallax like colorplate ghosts in a printing and parted forever. Whereon new forms arose and wheeled all and along, good carousel of crazies. Suttree observed these phenomena with mild interest from his galactic drainsuck. An enormous white doctor crossed his vision and drew away, shrinking rapidly down the small end of a spyglass. Suttree realized his eyes were open. From his incredible heights he watched these bald bipedal mutants struggling down there on the raw and livid rim of consciousness with a sad amusement. His astronomical bias placed him beyond the red shift and he wondered at the geography of these spaces or how does the world mesh with the world beyond the world? A door closed. He eddied up in a backwash, wheeled, drew breath and was gone again.

A black cyclocephalic levered him up and withdrew a bowl of his bowels' blood and carried it out covered with a linen.

A medical cart wheeled in on rubber tires, a stench of sulphur and alcohol. A needle sank in his buttock. He rolled back. He thought he'd seen treebranches in a yard beyond the window. Filled with small figures waiting for he. Wizened and crouching, barbate and cateyed dwarfs with little codpieces of scarlet puce. Who could make them out? An old man lay in the bed next, a gray man sucking air feebly through a slack gray naked mouth. Like me like me. Have they trestled up my bones on a cold stone slab and are they honing small blades against my dismembrance?

Wheezing rubberoid oafs with pendulous girths kept lumbering down a slope one by one in a drifting vapor. Everyone was going on.

When they began packing Suttree in ice he felt an enormous sadness touched with rue. He heard someone say the time but he could not understand. He drifted in a morphine sleep.

Along a wet street, a freshened wind with spits of rain in it. Raw musky smell of the walks. He was in some kind of trouble. Clockshop. A fourlegged clock in a glass bell, a pending treblehook baited with gold balls revolving slowly. Coming to rest. The clock hands too. He looked at his face in the glass. On the wall beyond other clocks are stopping. Me? The shop is closed. A thought to ask. He will not ask, however. Clocks need winding and people to wind them. Someone should be told.

Will the accused please stand.

You have heard the charges against you.

Yes.

Yessir. I come in about eight like I usually do. Seen this feller lookin in the winder and never thought nothin about it. Well, I got in there and I looked at the clock and I seen it wasnt right and I went up to set it and it wasnt runnin. It was wound but it wouldnt run. Then I begun to look around and they was all kinds of peculiarness afoot.

And could you describe these things for us briefly.

Yessir. Well, I kindly hate to . . .

You may speak freely. The accused is securely fettered. Is the accused fettered? Aye, fettered.

Yessir. Well, I commenced lookin about and I seen straightaway they wasnt nary clock in the place knowed what time of day it was. And then I seen Tweetiepie's dead.

You seen Tweetiepie was dead. Were dead.

Yessir.

Let the record show that Tweetiepie is dead.

At the hand of person or persons unknown.

It was him done it settin over there feathered.

Will you identify these remains.

O lordy no I caint bear it I'm so tore up with grief.

Your bird sir?

The same.

Let the record show that the bird is the same bird.

Of course the bird is the same bird, called Suttree, lying thin, white, soft, in a tray of ice, curious tetrapod cooling.

Mr Suttree in what year did your greatuncle Jeffrey pass away?

It was in 1884.

Did he die by natural causes?

No sir.

And what were the circumstances surrounding his death.

He was taking part in a public function when the platform gave way.

Our information is that he was hanged for a homicide.

Yessir.

Are you aware of the penalty fixed upon conviction of lycanthropy? Suttree moaned in the ice. It was never me, he called.

Who segued lithe as an eel from chancery to forest path, abroad by dark tarns in a deep wood where no sun shone and the reeds grew black and fish blind. Until he was stopped by a turtlepedlar bearing a sack of turtles and a rifle gun. Clad in burlap and unshaven he was and in brogans out at the toes and it cold weather.

Harkee stranger, cried the man. A turtle for your soup.

Stranger let me pass for I am weary.

Fifty cents and your choice of the best, ye'll not buy cheaper.

Outbound I am, beyond all wares.

It's hard else could bring you here.

This is no path of my choosing.

Nor mine.

Leeway and ease, the night is coming.

The turtlemonger held forth his sack. Fine turkles, fat turkles. Turkles for the stew.

The dreamer would pass but he has let fall the long dark lilac iron of his riflebarrel to bar the way. An outlaw tollsman reeking of woodsmoke and swamp rot and seeking some chiminage dearer than a path so dark could warrant. Or any path at all.

These be special turkles. Dont pass on without you've give em your consideration.

To this the traveler did consent. The vendor's face grew crafty. The wet sack collapsing aclatter on the ground. He turns back the mouth.

Those are not turtles. Oh God they're not turtles.

Suttree had half reared up in the bed, his swollen tongue gagging his cries. He fell back. Voices spoke beyond a wall. He saw with icy prescience the deathcart before the door, menials entering with a pallet to haul away his puling body and surely the stink of the unshriven dead is a dire stench rising to affront the nostrils of God. Impenitents snatched from the midst of their leprous revels, hard justice. Suttree saw the General pass atop his coalwagon, a paler horse in the traces. He lifted a hand. No fingers to the glove he wore, his cart made no sound. They receded into the vapors till there was just the orange light from the lantern where it swung by its bail from the tailboard.

Down Front Street streetlamps marked the way with measured rings of chromeblue light. The sleepfast shacks lay rotting, dusky sleepers lay within. The dooryard flowers half awake in the lamplight and the city's neon constellations emerging on the night, a pastel alpenglow in which the dust of demolition rose from the jagged ruins of the Cumberland Hotel, the Lyric Theatre.

At the door of the Huddle folk from the looms of McAnally are convened. First among these is a beardless Celt with spattled skin and rebate teeth. Three eyes in his head he has and he is covered over all with orange hair like unto a Cathay ape. At his elbow a stripling with a small and foxy face let into the lower part of a bulbous skull. His towcolored hair is cropped and stands wispily erect and seen from behind he most resembles an enormous dandelion. Suttree smiles to see such friends. The murdered are first to embrace him. Callahan's heavy arm about his shoulder, grinding the scapulae. He speaks through the flarey airholes of his boneless nose to the silverhaired and senatoriallooking barman.

Hey Hatmaker. Tell Hoghead and Donald and Byrd and Bobby and Hugh and Conrad and all of em that they aint barred.

They're dead.

Whoops of laughter among the watchers at the door.

Well you wouldnt bar a dead man would ye?

The tavernkeeper folded his towel and wiped the long mahogony bar. He said that he would not. Suttree among the rabble entered in. Outside the junkman stood alone.

Coin of the realm, coin of the realm, muttered Mr Hatmaker, unmaddened by mercurial bloodliens.

Coin, called Big Frig. Are you holding, fendervendor?

Harvey shuffles forward tugging at his changepurse. A few pieces of Denver silver. Avowing blind faith in deaf deities. He takes a stool at the bar. A fishbowl. He orders.

Big Frig nudges the junkman and leans with a huge horsewink. And make it light on the fish.

Blind Richard at the bar, his eyes batting in the beerlight and the clabbered matter in his sockets shining with a bluish cast leans forward and and takes hold of his mug in both hands. His ears remark the voices in his shoreless void. Alice is eyeing the room with contempt. When the moon shines down upon my Wabash then you'll recognize your Indiana home. The whores at the oval table raise their steins. Names of a thousand malefactors and melancholics incised in the black formica there. Faye wears in her garter a glass syringe. I'd give a hog a rimjob to get high, she says. And have, says Shirley. On film, says Rosie.

The queers in the corner booth turn one to the other in shocked amusement. Their spectacles wink small semaphores. Above them in the gutted cage of an electric fan and trapped in a bias of smokegorged light the execrator crouches and drools and turns to and back.

I didnt do it they only said I did. Twas a little jewdoctor come in the night with tailor's shears.

Oh do hush, says a languorous faggot glancing upward.

Foul perverts one and sundry. Silkbedizen pizzlelickers. Roaming the world. Slaking their hideous gorges with jissom. Oh I shall not be loath to tell. I'll bewray the tribe of them to the high almighty God who ledgers up our deeds in a leatherbound daybook. With marbled endpapers, I'm told.

Harrogate in morningcoat stands easily upon the decked and buntinged bar. He wears a small flag in his lapel. Friends, he says. I come from humble circumstance and rose up in the world by my own efforts. And if I'm to leave my footprints in the sands of time let it be with a pair of workshoes.

Someone was tugging at Suttree's sleeve. A small nun with a bitten face, a smell of scorched black muslin and her dead breasts brailed up in the knitted vest she wore. She tugged with little soricine claws at the bones in his elbow.

Cornelius you come away from here this minute.

Mr Suttree it is our understanding that at curfew rightly decreed by law and in that hour wherein night draws to its proper close and the new day commences and contrary to conduct befitting a person of your station you betook yourself to various low places within the shire of McAnally and there did squander several ensuing years in the company of thieves, derelicts, miscreants, pariahs, poltroons, spalpeens, curmudgeons, clotpolls, murderers, gamblers, bawds, whores, trulls, brigands, topers, tosspots, sots and archsots, lobcocks, smellsmocks, runagates, rakes, and other assorted and felonious debauchees.

I was drunk, cried Suttree. Seized in a vision of the archetypal patriarch himself unlocking with enormous keys the gates of Hades. A floodtide of screaming fiends and assassins and thieves and hirsute buggers pours forth into the universe, tipping it slightly on its galactic axes. The stars go rolling down the void like redhot marbles. These simmering sinners with their cloaks smoking carry the Logos itself from the tabernacle and bear it through the streets while the absolute prebarbaric mathematick of the western world howls them down and shrouds their ragged biblical forms in oblivion.

An orderly was going along the outer hall with mop and bucket. He paused for feet to pass. Clicking down the corridor. Voices. And beyond these sounds like the natter and babble of the damned a muted bedlam of voices that were no right voices. Suttree's hands clutched the stenciled sheets.

Did you hear him a while ago?

Shoo. I never heard such stuff.

He's out of his head.

Your head, said Suttree from the depths.

Lord is he awake?

No. Help me turn him, we got to take his temperature.

A sepia crone darted out from under the lower corner of his right eye and cackled and ducked back. Suttree smiled. Dont pack me, ladies. I'm not gone yet.

Hairy aint it?

Oh hush, Wanita. I'd be ashamed.

Pussy, said Suttree from a new place. Weet pussy. Sweet giggling ensued. His penis rose enormous from between his legs, a delicious spasm and there unfolded from the end of it a little colored flag on a wooden stem, who knows what country?

Lightly tinctured, a flavor of sunlight lay in the room. Water dripped in a bowl. He could hear the flat detonation of tennis shoes along a pavement beyond a wall in a courtyard in another kind of kingdom.

Late in the afternoon he rose and wobbled about the room on naked bony legs, a coarse cotton shift just covering his shanks, some strings dangling. He found a sink in the corner of the room and hung by the taps with his face in the bowl and cold water running over his smoking skull. Blood hammered through bearing bad news. He raised up dripping and urinated a few drops painfully into the sink. He looked about the room. Two other beds, both empty. A steel cart with enameled bedpans. He had lifted his nightie and was palming water over his shrunken gut when a nurse entered the room. He turned. They made their way toward each other, reeling across the floor with outstretched arms.

I've got you, said Suttree.

What were you doing?

Bellycooling. Do I know you?

Be careful.

Listen, said Suttree. We were never promised that our flesh, that our flesh . . .

Hush now. Come on.

I have a thing to tell you. I know all souls are one and all souls lonely.

Here we go.

He paused with one knee in the iron bed. He looked up into an uncertain face. It crumbled away grayly, a dusty hag's mask. He lay back. Sheets clammy with salt damp. They clove to him like windings. She tightened the bed while he fanned his belly with the skirt of his gown.

Quit that, she said.

I will not, he said.

She covered him and went away. He lay half waking in the heat, floating like a vast medusa in tropic seas while at his ear he heard sometimes the curious invocations attendant to his case, two hundred milligrams, good deal of fluid in the pleura. . . .

His dreams were of houses, their cellars and attics. Ultimately of this city in the sea.

Some eastern sea that lay heavily in the dawn. There stood on its farther rim a spire of smoke attended and crowned by a plutonic light where the waters have broke open. Erupting hot gouts of lava and great upended slabs of earth and a rain of small stones that hissed for miles in the sea. As we watched there reared out of the smoking brine a city of old bone coughed up from the sea's floor, pale attic bone delicate as shell and half melting, a chalken shambles coralgrown that slewed into shape of temple, column, plinth and cornice, and across the whole a frieze of archer and warrior and marblebreasted maid all listing west and moving slowly their stone limbs. As these figures began to cool and take on life Suttree among the watchers said that this time there are witnesses, for life does not come slowly. It rises in one massive mutation and all is changed utterly and forever. We have witnessed this thing today which prefigures for all time the way in which historic orders proceed. And some said that the girl who bathed her swollen belly in the stone pool in the garden last evening was the author of this wonder they attended. And a maid bearing water in a marble jar came down from the living frieze toward the dreamer with eyes restored black of core and iris brightly painted attic blue and she moved toward him with a smile.

Suttree surfaced from these fevered deeps to hear a maudlin voice chant latin by his bedside, what medieval ghost come to usurp his fallen corporeality. An oiled thumball redolent of lime and sage pondered his shuttered lids.

Miserere mei, Deus . . .

His ears anointed, his lips . . . omnis maligna discordia . . . Bechrismed with scented oils he lay boneless in a cold euphoria. Japheth when you left your father's house the birds had flown. You were not prepared for such weathers. You'd spoke too lightly of the winter in your father's heart. We saw you in the streets. Sad.

The priest's lamptanned and angular face leaned over him. The room was candlelit and spiced with smoke. He closed his eyes. A cool thumb crossed his soles with unction. He lay aneled. Like a rapevictim.

I am familiar with the burial rites of the nameless and the unclaimed.

What is it? said the priest.

Well may he wonder, praetor to a pederastic deity.

The priest wiped his fingers with bits of bread and rose. By candlelight he put away his effects in a little fitted case and left bearing the candle and followed by a nun and Suttree alone in the dark with his death and who will come to weep the grave of an alias? Or lay one flower down.

He dreamed of a race at the poles who rode on sleds of walrus hide and rucked up horn and ivory all drawn by dogs and bristling with lances and harpoon spears, the hunters shrouded in fur, slow caravans against the late noon winter sunset, against the rim of the world, whispering over the blue snow with their sledloads of piled meat and skins and viscera. Small bloodstained hunters drifting like spores above the frozen chlorine void, from flower to flower of bright vermilion gore across the vast boreal plain.

Down the nightworld of his starved mind cool scarves of fishes went veering, winnowing the salt shot that rose columnar toward rifts in the ice overhead. Sinking in a cold jade sea where bubbles shuttled toward the polar sun. Shoals of char ribboned off brightly and the ocean swell heaved with the world's turning and he could see the sun go bleared and fade beyond the windswept panes of ice. Under a waste more mute than the moon's face, where alabaster seabears cruise the salt and icegreen deeps.

When he woke there were footsteps in the room. Shapes crossed between the light and his thin eyelids. He was going again in a corridor through rooms that never ceased, by formless walls unordered unadorned and slightly moist and warm and through soft doors with valved and dripping architraves and regions wet and bluish like the inward parts of some enormous living thing. A small soul's going. By floodlight through the universe's renal regions. Pale phagocytes drifting over, shadows and shapes through the tubes like the miscellany in a waterdrop. The eye at the end of the glass would be God's.

Suttree saw the faces of the living bend. He closed his eyes. Gray geometric saurians lay snapping in a pit. Far away stood a gold pagoda with a little flutterblade that spun in the wind. He knew that he was not going there. He was awake for days. No one knew. He touched a hand attending him and smiled at its withdrawing. The freaks and phantoms skulked away beyond the cold white plaster of the ceiling. A tantric cat that loped forever in a funhouse corridor. He'd see them again on the day of his death.

One morning the priest came. The bed tilted. Suttree's body ran on it saclike and invertebrate, his drained members cooling on the sheets.

Would you like to confess? said the priest.

I did it, said Suttree.

A quick smile.

I'd like some wine.

Oh you cant have any wine, said a nursevoice.

The priest bent and opened his little leather case and took out a cruet. You had a close call, he said.

All my life. I did.

He tipped winedrops from the birdtongue spout down Suttree's throat. Suttree closed his eyes to savor it.

Do you have any more?

Just a drop. Not too much, I dont think.

That works, Suttree said.

Are you feeling better?

Yes.

God must have been watching over you. You very nearly died.

You would not believe what watches.

Oh?

He is not a thing. Nothing ever stops moving.

Is that what you learned?

I learned that there is one Suttree and one Suttree only.

I see, said the priest.

Suttree shook his head. No, he said. You dont.

The days were long and lonely, no one came.

He watched birds come and go in the tree beyoad the window, like a memory from some childhood scene, dim its purpose.

He was given no food. A strange sour potion to drink. A nurse who came to catheterize him. He'd lain for hours with his cock hanging down the cool throat of a battered tin pitcher.

Catheterina, he said.

My name is Kathy.

We've got to stop meeting like this.

Hush now. Can you lift up some? Lift up some.

Try to control yourself. Damn.

You dont even have a temperature so I know this is all put on.

I hear water running.

Hush.

I never saw a lovelier ass.

I never knew anybody to get sexy being catheterized.

Will you marry me?

Sure.

One night as he lay there he felt suddenly strong enough to rise. He thought he'd dreamed of doing so. He eased his feet over the edge of the bed and stood. He tottered across the room and rested against the wall and came back. And again. He felt giddy.

The next night he went down the corridor. I feel like an angel, he told an old lady with a bucket whom he passed. There was no one about. A porter nodded at the desk. Suttree went out the door.

Down the street in his nightshirt till he came to a phone booth. No coins blocked away in there. He had a tag with the name Johnson on it pinned to the front of him and he took it off and laid it on the little metal shelf beneath the phone and he straightened out the pin and lifted the receiver from the hook. He worked the pin through the insulation of the cord and grounded the end of it against the metal of the coinslot. After a few tries he got a dial tone and he dialed 21505.

Carlights washed across this figure in nightwear crouched in his glass outhouse. He dropped to the floor of the booth. A reek of stale piss. The number was ringing. Suttree wondered what time it might be. It rang for some time.

Hello.

J-Bone.

Bud? That you?

Can you come and get me?

As they descended into McAnally Suttree let his head fall back on the musty plush of the old car seat.

You want some whiskey, Bud? We can get some.

No thanks.

You okay?

Yeah. I'd just like maybe a drink of water.

Mr Johnson like to left us didnt you Mr Johnson?

So they say. Who put the priest on me?

They said you was dyin. I came up last week and you didnt know nothin. I had a little drink hid away too.

Suttree patted J-Bone's knee, his eyes shut. Old J-Bone, he said.

I think you're a lowlife son of a bitch for not bringin us one of them, said Junior.

He opened one eye. One of what?

Them slick little nighties.

Piss on you.

Old Suttree's thinner than Boneyard, said J-Bone.

Old Suttree's all right, said Suttree.

They seemed a long time going. Down over the pocked and gutted streets under random pools of lamplight, blue jagged bowls moth-blown that reeled along the upper window rim by dim strung light-wires. Pale concrete piers veered off, naked columns of some fourth order capped with a red steel frieze. New roads being laid over Mc-Anally, over the ruins, the shelled facades and walls standing in crazed shapes, the mangled iron firestairs dangling, the houses halved, broke open for the world to see. This naked spandrel clinging some-way to sheer wallpaper and mounting upward to terminate in nothing-ness and night like the works at Babel.

They're tearing everything down, Suttree said.

Yeah. Expressway.

Sad chattel stood on the cinder lawns, in the dim lilac lamplight. Old sofas bloated in the rain exploding quietly, shriveled tables sloughing off their papery veneers. A backdrop of iron earthmovers reared against the cokeblown sky.

New roads through McAnally, said J-Bone.

Suttree nodded, his eyes shut. He knew another McAnally, good to last a thousand years. There'd be no new roads there.

At night in the iron bed high in the old house on Grand he'd lie awake and hear the sirens, lonely sound in the city, in the empty streets. He lay in his chrysalis of gloom and made no sound, share by share sharing his pain with those who lay in their blood by the highwayside or in the floors of glass strewn taverns or manacled in jail. He said that even the damned in hell have the community of their suffering and he thought that he'd guessed out likewise for the living a nominal grief like a grange from which disaster and ruin are proportioned by laws of equity too subtle for divining.

The destruction of McAnally Flats found him interested. A thin, a wasted figure, he eased himself along past scenes of wholesale razing, whole blocks row on row flattened to dust and rubble. Yellow machines groaned over the landscape, the earth buckling, the few old coalchoked trees upturned and heaps of slag and cellarholes with vatshaped furnaces squat beneath their hydra works of rusted ducting and ashy fields shorn up and leveled and the dead turned out of their graves.

He watched the bland workman in the pilothouse of the crane shifting levers. The long tethered wreckingball swung through the side of a wall and small boys applauded. Brickwork of dried bloodcakes in flemish bond crumbling in a cloud of dust and mortar. Walls grim with scurf, a nameless crud. Pale spongoid growths that kept in clusters along the damper reaches came to light and all day grimecaked salvagers with hatchets spalled dead mortar from the piled black brick. Gnostic workmen who would have down this shabby shapeshow that masks the higher world of form. And left at eventide these cutaway elevations, little cubicles giving onto space, an iron bedstead, a freestanding stairwell to nowhere. Old gothic soffits hung with tar and lapsing paintflakes. Ragged cats picked their way over the glass and nigger dogs in the dooryards beyond the railsiding twitched in their sleep. Until nothing stood save rows of doors, some bearing numbers, all nailed to. Beyond lay fields of rubble, twisted steel and pipes and old conduits reared out of the ground in clusters of agonized ganglia among the broken slabs of masonry. Where small black hominoids scurried over the waste and sheets of newsprint rose in the wind and died again.

When he went one morning to the river he found the houseboat door ajar and someone sleeping in his bed. He entered in a fog of putrefaction. A hot and heady reek under the quaking tin. So warm a forenoon. He screened his nostrils with his sleeve.

Suttree nudged the sleeper with his toe but the sleeper slept. Two rats came from the bed like great hairy beetles and went rapidly without pause or effort up the wall and through a missing pane of glass as soundlessly as smoke.

He went back out and sat on the rail. He watched the river and he watched the fishing canes wink in the sunlight at the point. Wands dipping and rising, an old piscean ceremony he'd known himself. Pigeons came and went beneath the arches of the bridge and he could hear the rattling whine of a bandsaw at Rose's across the river. Upstream at Ab Jones's no sign of life, he looked. After a while he sucked in a breath and entered the cabin again. He kicked away the covers. A snarling clot of flies rose. Suttree stepped back. Caved cheek and yellow grin. A foul deathshead bald with rot, flyblown and eyeless.

He stood against the wall as long as he could hold his breath. A mass of yellow maggots lay working in one ear and a few flies rattled in the flesh and stood him off like cats. He turned and went out.

A woman was trudging stoically across the fields toward his houseboat. She dipped into the swale on the far side of the tracks and rose up again, crossed the tracks and came on down the barren path toward the river. She was roundshouldered and slumped and she walked with a kind of mindless dedication like a circus bear. Suttree waited on her, pulling the door to at his back.

When she reached the river she looked up at him and shaded her eyes with one hand. Mr Suttree? she said.

Yes.

She looked at the plank doubtfully, then shifted into motion again and came plodding up to the deck. She was sweating and she blew the hair from her eyes and wiped her eyes against her shoulders, one, the other, as if she were used to having things in her hands and had forgotten somewhat the use of them.

I seen ye from over in the store, she said. They told me you come in over there. I was about give up on ye.

Who are you? said Suttree.

I'm Josie Harrogate. I wanted to see you about Gene.

Suttree looked at her. A big rawboned woman, her hair matted over her face. The armpits of her cotton housedress black with sweat. Are you Gene's sister?

Yessir. He's my halfbrother is what he is.

I see.

My daddy died fore Gene was born.

Suttree ran his hand through his hair. Have you been to see him? he said.

No. I allowed maybe you knowed where he was at.

You dont know where he is?

No sir.

Suttree looked off down the river.

Mama died back in the winter I dont reckon he even knows it.

Well. I hate to have to tell you. He's in the penitentiary.

Yessir. Whereabouts?

Petros.

Her lips formed the word but nothing came out. What was it again? she said.

Petros. It's the state penitentiary. Brushy Mountain, it's called.

Brushy Mountain. Where's it at?

Well. It's west of here. About fifty miles I think. You could probably get a bus out there. They could tell you up at the bus terminal.

What's he in for?

Robbery.

She stared fixedly into his eyes to stay his lying or to know it if he did and she said: They aint fixin to electricate him are they?

No. He's in for three to five years. He could get out in eighteen months.

Well how long has he done been in?

A couple or three months.

Well, she said. I sure thank ye. I knowed you was a friend to Gene.

Gene's a good boy, Suttree said.

She didnt answer. She had turned to go but she stopped at the rail. What was that name again? she said.

Brushy Mountain?

No. That othern you said.

Petros.

Petros, she said. She said it again, staring emptily upward. Then she started down the catwalk. There must have been a loose cleat somewhere because going down it she fell. Her feet shot from under her and she sat down. The plank bowed deeply and rose again, lifting her flailing figure. She managed to get a grip and steady herself and she stood carefully and went on, teetering along till she reached the shore.

Are you all right? called Suttree.

She didnt look back. She raised one hand and waved it and went on, stooped and heavy gaited, across the fields and the tracks toward the town.

Suttree went up the river path through dockbloom and wild onion to the old floating roadhouse and tapped a last sad time at the green door. He rested on the railing and he tapped again but no one came. After a while he descended the plankwalk and crossed the fields and the tracks to the store.

She's moved out, said Howard Clevinger.

Yes, said Suttree.

She had a brother in Mascot, I think she went to live with them. Did that woman find you that was huntin you?

She did.

I seen you over there.

Suttree went back out and crossed to the river and sat on a stone and watched the water pass for a long time.

It was just dusk. Hung in the darker wall of the hillside among kudzu and dusty vines a few pale windowlights. The porch at Jimmy Smith's with its yellow light and half shadowed drinkers above the slat railed balustrade. A broken portico not unlike the shorn wreckage in McAnally save pasted up with these small crazed faces peering out. Over the squalid littoral, the wasteclogged river and the immense emptiness of the world beyond. A garish figure was coming along, a hoyden that sallied and fluttered through the one cone of uncashiered lamplight down all Front Street. Trippin Through The Dew in harlequin evening wear. They half circled, regarding one another.

Well I see you're still around anyway, said Suttree.

Honey I'm always here. They cant do without me. He smiled, primlipt and coyly.

Where's your hat this evening?

Oh honey hats are out. They just are. I always thought they were tacky anyway. Except mine of course. He knit his hands and rolled his shoulders and a whinny of girlish laughter went skittering among the little gray shacks and along the quiet twilit riverfront. He sobered suddenly and cocked his head. Where you been? he said.

I was in the hospital. Typhoid fever.

Lord honey I thought you looked peaky. Let me see you. He turned Suttree toward the streetlamp and peered into his eyes with genuine solicitude.

I'm okay, Suttree said.

Sweetie you have just fell off to skin and bones.

I lost about twenty pounds. I've gotten some of it back.

You want to rest and take care of yourself. You hear?

Suttree held out his hand. Tell me goodbye, he said.

Where you goin?

I dont know. I'm leaving Knoxville.

Shoot. He slapped at Suttree's outstretched hand. You aint goin noplace. When? When you goin?

Right now. I'm gone.

The black reached out sadly, his face pinched. They stood there holding hands in the middle of the little street. When you comin back?

I dont guess I'll be back.

Dont tell me that.

Well. Sometime maybe. Take care.

Honey you write and let me know how you gettin on.

Well.

Just a postcard.

Okay.

You need any money?

No. I've got some.

You sure?

I'm okay.

Trippin Through The Dew squeezed his hand and stepped back and gave a sort of crazy little salute. Best luck in the world baby, he said.

Thanks John. You too.

He lifted a hand and turned and went on. He had divested himself of the little cloaked godlet and his other amulets in a place where they would not be found in his lifetime and he'd taken for talisman the simple human heart within him. Walking down the little street for the last time he felt everything fall away from him. Until there was nothing left of him to shed. It was all gone. No trail, no track. The spoor petered out down there on Front Street where things he'd been lay like paper shadows, a few here, they thin out. After that nothing. A few rumors. Idle word on the wind. Old news years in traveling that you could not put stock in.

He took the shortcut up the path behind the houses, avoiding any chance of other meetings in the street. Old broken Thersites would have called down from his high window but he was not well these latter days. Dried vitriol hung in glazen strings from a bush by the side of the house and Suttree even thought he heard muted sounds of grousing in an upper room. He cocked one eye up the high warped clapboard wall to the chamber kept by this old taperheaded troll but no one watched back. The eunuch was asleep in his chair and he stirred and mumbled fitfully as if the departing steps of the fisherman depleted his dreams but he did not wake.

The city ambulance swung down off Front Street and went bobbling over the ground and across the tracks and up the river path until it came to the houseboat. People were watching along the porches and there were people standing around in front of the store watching with grave faces. Two men went in with a canvas stretcher and a blanket and in a few minutes they came out with the body and slid it quickly into the rear of the ambulance. In backing around they got the ambulance stuck in the mud. One wheel shot reams of gouty mire out into the river. The men climbed down and looked. One pushed. The ambulance sank until it was resting on its differential carrier.

After a while three tall colored boys in track shoes came along and pushed the ambulance out.

Who sick? one said.

There was a man dead in there, the driver said.

They looked at each other. How long he been dead?

A couple of weeks.

Shoo, one said, wrinkling his wide nose. That's what that's been.

You dont know who it was do you?

No suh.

Dont know who lived here?

No suh.

Come on Ramsey, we got to go.

I heah you, man.

The driver closed the door and motioned with his hand and the ambulance pulled away. The boys watched them go. Shit, one said. Old Suttree aint dead.

He had a small cardboard suitcase and he came out of the weeds and set it on the edge of the road and straightened up and began combing his hair. He looked about his appearance, propping one foot on the case and bending to scrape beggarlice from his trousers with his thumbnail. New trousers of tan chino. A new shirt open at the neck. His face and arms were suntanned and his hair crudely barbered and he wore cheap new brown leather shoes the toes of which he dusted, one, the other, against the back of his trouserlegs. He looked like someone just out of the army or jail. A car came down the highway and he gestured at it with his thumb and it went on.

Traffic was slow along the road and he was there a long time. It was very hot. You could see his skin through the new shirt. Across the road a construction gang was at work and he watched them. A backhoe was dragging out a ditch and a caterpillar was going along the bank with mounds of pale clay shaling across its canted blade. Carpenters were hammering up forms and a cement truck waited on with its drum slowly clanking. Suttree watched this industry accomplish itself in the hot afternoon. Downwind light ocher dust had sifted all along the greening roadside foliage and in the quiet midafternoon the call of a long sad trainhorn floated over the lonely countryside.

A boy was going along the works with a pail and he leaned to each, ladling out water in a tin dipper. Suttree saw hands come up from below the rim of the pit in parched supplication. When all these had been attended the boy came down along the edge of the ditch and handed up the dipper to the backhoe operator. Suttree saw him take it and tilt his head and drink and flick the last drops toward the earth and lean down and restore the dipper to the watercarrier. They nodded to each other and the boy turned and looked toward the road. Then he was coming down across the clay and over the ruts and laddered tracks of machinery. His dusty boots left prints across the black macadam and he came up to Suttree where he stood by the roadside and swung the bucket around and brought the dipper up all bright and dripping and offered it. Suttree could see the water beading coldly on the tin and running in tiny rivulets and drops that steamed on the road where they fell. He could see the pale gold hair that lay along the sunburned arms of the waterbearer like new wheat and he beheld himself in wells of smoking cobalt, twinned and dark and deep in child's eyes, blue eyes with no bottoms like the sea. He took the dipper and drank and gave it back. The boy dropped it into the bucket. Suttree wiped his mouth on the back of his hand. Thanks, he said.

The boy smiled and stepped back. A car had stopped for Suttree, he'd not lifted a hand.

Let's go, said the driver.

Hello, said Suttree, climbing in, shutting the door, his suitcase between his knees. Then they were moving. Out across the land the lightwires and roadrails were going and the telephone lines with voices shuttling on like souls. Behind him the city lay smoking, the sad purlieus of the dead immured with the bones of friends and forebears. Off to the right side the white concrete of the expressway gleamed in the sun where the ramp curved out into empty air and hung truncate with iron rods bristling among the vectors of nowhere. When he looked back the waterboy was gone. An enormous lank hound had come out of the meadow by the river like a hound from the depths and was sniffing at the spot where Suttree had stood.

Somewhere in the gray wood by the river is the huntsman and in the brooming corn and in the castellated press of cities. His work lies all wheres and his hounds tire not. I have seen them in a dream, slaverous and wild and their eyes crazed with ravening for souls in this world. Fly them.

BLOOD MERIDIAN

OR

THE EVENING REDNESS IN THE WEST

The author wishes to thank the Lyndhurst Foundation, the John Simon Guggenheim Memorial Foundation, and the John D. and Catherine T. MacArthur Foundation. He also wishes to express his appreciation to Albert Erskine, his editor of twenty years.

Your ideas are terrifying and your hearts are faint. Your acts of pity and cruelty are absurd, committed with no calm, as if they were irresistible. Finally, you fear blood more and more. Blood and time.

PAUL VALÉRY

It is not to be thought that the life of darkness is sunk in misery and lost as if in sorrowing. There is no sorrowing. For sorrow is a thing that is swallowed up in death, and death and dying are the very life of the darkness.

JACOB BOEHME

Clark, who led last year's expedition to the Afar region of northern Ethiopia, and UC Berkeley colleague Tim D. White, also said that a re-examination of a 300,000-year-old fossil skull found in the same region earlier shows evidence of having been scalped.

THE YUMA DAILY SUN
June 13, 1982

I

Childhood in Tennessee – Runs away – New Orleans –
Fights – Is shot – To Galveston – Nacogdoches –
The Reverend Green – Judge Holden – An affray – Toadvine –
Burning of the hotel – Escape.

See the child. He is pale and thin, he wears a thin and ragged linen shirt. He stokes the scullery fire. Outside lie dark turned fields with rags of snow and darker woods beyond that harbor yet a few last wolves. His folk are known for hewers of wood and drawers of water but in truth his father has been a schoolmaster. He lies in drink, he quotes from poets whose names are now lost. The boy crouches by the fire and watches him.

Night of your birth. Thirty-three. The Leonids they were called. God how the stars did fall. I looked for blackness, holes in the heavens. The Dipper stove.

The mother dead these fourteen years did incubate in her own bosom the creature who would carry her off. The father never speaks her name, the child does not know it. He has a sister in this world that he will not see again. He watches, pale and unwashed. He can neither read nor write and in him broods already a taste for mindless violence. All history present in that visage, the child the father of the man.

At fourteen he runs away. He will not see again the freezing

3

kitchenhouse in the predawn dark. The firewood, the washpots. He wanders west as far as Memphis, a solitary migrant upon that flat and pastoral landscape. Blacks in the fields, lank and stooped, their fingers spiderlike among the bolls of cotton. A shadowed agony in the garden. Against the sun's declining figures moving in the slower dusk across a paper skyline. A lone dark husbandman pursuing mule and harrow down the rainblown bottomland toward night.

A year later he is in Saint Louis. He is taken on for New Orleans aboard a flatboat. Forty-two days on the river. At night the steamboats hoot and trudge past through the black waters all alight like cities adrift. They break up the float and sell the lumber and he walks in the streets and hears tongues he has not heard before. He lives in a room above a courtyard behind a tavern and he comes down at night like some fairybook beast to fight with the sailors. He is not big but he has big wrists, big hands. His shoulders are set close. The child's face is curiously untouched behind the scars, the eyes oddly innocent. They fight with fists, with feet, with bottles or knives. All races, all breeds. Men whose speech sounds like the grunting of apes. Men from lands so far and queer that standing over them where they lie bleeding in the mud he feels mankind itself vindicated.

On a certain night a Maltese boatswain shoots him in the back with a small pistol. Swinging to deal with the man he is shot again just below the heart. The man flees and he leans against the bar with the blood running out of his shirt. The others look away. After a while he sits in the floor.

He lies in a cot in the room upstairs for two weeks while the tavernkeeper's wife attends him. She brings his meals, she carries out his slops. A hardlooking woman with a wiry body like a man's. By the time he is mended he has no money to pay her and he leaves in the night and sleeps on the riverbank until he can find a boat that will take him on. The boat is going to Texas.

Only now is the child finally divested of all that he has been. His origins are become remote as is his destiny and not again in all the world's turning will there be terrains so wild and barbar-

4

ous to try whether the stuff of creation may be shaped to man's will or whether his own heart is not another kind of clay. The passengers are a diffident lot. They cage their eyes and no man asks another what it is that brings him here. He sleeps on the deck, a pilgrim among others. He watches the dim shore rise and fall. Gray seabirds gawking. Flights of pelicans coastwise above the gray swells.

They disembark aboard a lighter, settlers with their chattels, all studying the low coastline, the thin bight of sand and scrub pine swimming in the haze.

He walks through the narrow streets of the port. The air smells of salt and newsawn lumber. At night whores call to him from the dark like souls in want. A week and he is on the move again, a few dollars in his purse that he's earned, walking the sand roads of the southern night alone, his hands balled in the cotton pockets of his cheap coat. Earthen causeways across the marshland. Egrets in their rookeries white as candles among the moss. The wind has a raw edge to it and leaves lope by the roadside and skelter on in the night fields. He moves north through small settlements and farms, working for day wages and found. He sees a parricide hanged in a crossroads hamlet and the man's friends run forward and pull his legs and he hangs dead from his rope while urine darkens his trousers.

He works in a sawmill, he works in a diptheria pesthouse. He takes as pay from a farmer an aged mule and aback this animal in the spring of the year eighteen and forty-nine he rides up through the latterday republic of Fredonia into the town of Nacogdoches.

———◆•◆———

The Reverend Green had been playing to a full house daily as long as the rain had been falling and the rain had been falling for two weeks. When the kid ducked into the ratty canvas tent there was standing room along the walls, a place or two, and such a heady reek of the wet and bathless that they themselves would sally forth into the downpour now and again for fresh

5

air before the rain drove them in again. He stood with others of his kind along the back wall. The only thing that might have distinguished him in that crowd was that he was not armed.

Neighbors, said the reverend, he couldnt stay out of these here hell, hell, hellholes right here in Nacogdoches. I said to him, said: You goin to take the son of God in there with ye? And he said: Oh no. No I aint. And I said: Dont you know that he said I will foller ye always even unto the end of the road?

Well, he said, I aint askin nobody to go nowheres. And I said: Neighbor, you dont need to ask. He's a goin to be there with ye ever step of the way whether ye ask it or ye dont. I said: Neighbor, you caint get shed of him. Now. Are you going to drag him, *him*, into that hellhole yonder?

You ever see such a place for rain?

The kid had been watching the reverend. He turned to the man who spoke. He wore long moustaches after the fashion of teamsters and he wore a widebrim hat with a low round crown. He was slightly walleyed and he was watching the kid earnestly as if he'd know his opinion about the rain.

I just got here, said the kid.

Well it beats all I ever seen.

The kid nodded. An enormous man dressed in an oilcloth slicker had entered the tent and removed his hat. He was bald as a stone and he had no trace of beard and he had no brows to his eyes nor lashes to them. He was close on to seven feet in height and he stood smoking a cigar even in this nomadic house of God and he seemed to have removed his hat only to chase the rain from it for now he put it on again.

The reverend had stopped his sermon altogether. There was no sound in the tent. All watched the man. He adjusted the hat and then pushed his way forward as far as the crateboard pulpit where the reverend stood and there he turned to address the reverend's congregation. His face was serene and strangely childlike. His hands were small. He held them out.

Ladies and gentlemen I feel it my duty to inform you that the man holding this revival is an imposter. He holds no papers of divinity from any institution recognized or improvised. He is

6

altogether devoid of the least qualification to the office he has usurped and has only committed to memory a few passages from the good book for the purpose of lending to his fraudulent sermons some faint flavor of the piety he despises. In truth, the gentleman standing here before you posing as a minister of the Lord is not only totally illiterate but is also wanted by the law in the states of Tennessee, Kentucky, Mississippi, and Arkansas.

Oh God, cried the reverend. Lies, lies! He began reading feverishly from his opened bible.

On a variety of charges the most recent of which involved a girl of eleven years—I said eleven—who had come to him in trust and whom he was surprised in the act of violating while actually clothed in the livery of his God.

A moan swept through the crowd. A lady sank to her knees.

This is him, cried the reverend, sobbing. This is him. The devil. Here he stands.

Let's hang the turd, called an ugly thug from the gallery to the rear.

Not three weeks before this he was run out of Fort Smith Arkansas for having congress with a goat. Yes lady, that is what I said. Goat.

Why damn my eyes if I wont shoot the son of a bitch, said a man rising at the far side of the tent, and drawing a pistol from his boot he leveled it and fired.

The young teamster instantly produced a knife from his clothing and unseamed the tent and stepped outside into the rain. The kid followed. They ducked low and ran across the mud toward the hotel. Already gunfire was general within the tent and a dozen exits had been hacked through the canvas walls and people were pouring out, women screaming, folk stumbling, folk trampled underfoot in the mud. The kid and his friend reached the hotel gallery and wiped the water from their eyes and turned to watch. As they did so the tent began to sway and buckle and like a huge and wounded medusa it slowly settled to the ground trailing tattered canvas walls and ratty guyropes over the ground.

The baldheaded man was already at the bar when they entered.

7

On the polished wood before him were two hats and a double handful of coins. He raised his glass but not to them. They stood up to the bar and ordered whiskeys and the kid laid his money down but the barman pushed it back with his thumb and nodded.

These here is on the judge, he said.

They drank. The teamster set his glass down and looked at the kid or he seemed to, you couldnt be sure of his gaze. The kid looked down the bar to where the judge stood. The bar was that tall not every man could even get his elbows up on it but it came just to the judge's waist and he stood with his hands placed flatwise on the wood, leaning slightly, as if about to give another address. By now men were piling through the doorway, bleeding, covered in mud, cursing. They gathered about the judge. A posse was being drawn to pursue the preacher.

Judge, how did you come to have the goods on that no-account?

Goods? said the judge.

When was you in Fort Smith?

Fort Smith?

Where did you know him to know all that stuff on him?

You mean the Reverend Green?

Yessir. I reckon you was in Fort Smith fore ye come out here.

I was never in Fort Smith in my life. Doubt that he was.

They looked from one to the other.

Well where was it you run up on him?

I never laid eyes on the man before today. Never even heard of him.

He raised his glass and drank.

There was a strange silence in the room. The men looked like mud effigies. Finally someone began to laugh. Then another. Soon they were all laughing together. Someone bought the judge a drink.

———◆·◆———

It had been raining for sixteen days when he met Toadvine and it was raining yet. He was still standing in the same saloon and he had drunk up all his money save two dollars. The teamster had gone, the room was all but empty. The door stood open and you could see the rain falling in the empty lot behind the hotel. He drained his glass and went out. There were boards laid across the mud and he followed the paling band of doorlight down toward the batboard jakes at the bottom of the lot. Another man was coming up from the jakes and they met halfway on the narrow planks. The man before him swayed slightly. His wet hatbrim fell to his shoulders save in the front where it was pinned back. He held a bottle loosely in one hand. You better get out of my way, he said.

The kid wasnt going to do that and he saw no use in discussing it. He kicked the man in the jaw. The man went down and got up again. He said: I'm goin to kill you.

He swung with the bottle and the kid ducked and he swung again and the kid stepped back. When the kid hit him the man shattered the bottle against the side of his head. He went off the boards into the mud and the man lunged after him with the jagged bottleneck and tried to stick it in his eye. The kid was fending with his hands and they were slick with blood. He kept trying to reach into his boot for his knife.

Kill your ass, the man said. They slogged about in the dark of the lot, coming out of their boots. The kid had his knife now and they circled crabwise and when the man lurched at him he cut the man's shirt open. The man threw down the bottleneck and unsheathed an immense bowieknife from behind his neck. His hat had come off and his black and ropy locks swung about his head and he had codified his threats to the one word kill like a crazed chant.

That'ns cut, said one of several men standing along the walkway watching.

Kill kill slobbered the man wading forward.

But someone else was coming down the lot, great steady sucking sounds like a cow. He was carrying a huge shellalegh. He reached the kid first and when he swung with the club the kid went face down in the mud. He'd have died if someone hadn't turned him over.

When he woke it was daylight and the rain had stopped and

9

he was looking up into the face of a man with long hair who was completely covered in mud. The man was saying something to him.

What? said the kid.

I said are you quits?

Quits?

Quits. Cause if you want some more of me you sure as hell goin to get it.

He looked at the sky. Very high, very small, a buzzard. He looked at the man. Is my neck broke? he said.

The man looked out over the lot and spat and looked at the boy again. Can you not get up?

I dont know. I aint tried.

I never meant to break your neck.

No.

I meant to kill ye.

They aint nobody done it yet. He clawed at the mud and pushed himself up. The man was sitting on the planks with his boots alongside him. They aint nothin wrong with you, he said.

The kid looked about stiffly at the day. Where's my boots? he said.

The man squinted at him. Flakes of dried mud fell from his face.

I'm goin to have to kill some son of a bitch if they got my boots.

Yonder looks like one of em.

The kid labored off through the mud and fetched up one boot. He slogged about in the yard feeling likely lumps of mud.

This your knife? he said.

The man squinted at him. Looks like it, he said.

The kid pitched it to him and he bent and picked it up and wiped the huge blade on his trouserleg. Thought somebody'd done stole you, he told the knife.

The kid found his other boot and came and sat on the boards. His hands were huge with mud and he wiped one of them briefly at his knee and let it fall again.

They sat there side by side looking out across the barren lot. There was a picket fence at the edge of the lot and beyond the fence a boy was drawing water at a well and there were chickens in the yard there. A man came from the dramshop door down the walk toward the outhouse. He stopped where they sat and looked at them and then stepped off into the mud. After a while he came back and stepped off into the mud again and went around and on up the walk.

The kid looked at the man. His head was strangely narrow and his hair was plastered up with mud in a bizarre and primitive coiffure. On his forehead were burned the letters H T and lower and almost between the eyes the letter F and these markings were splayed and garish as if the iron had been left too long. When he turned to look at the kid the kid could see that he had no ears. He stood up and sheathed the knife and started up the walk with the boots in his hand and the kid rose and followed. Halfway to the hotel the man stopped and looked out at the mud and then sat down on the planks and pulled on the boots mud and all. Then he rose and slogged off through the lot to pick something up.

I want you to look here, he said. At my goddamned hat.

You couldnt tell what it was, something dead. He flapped it about and pulled it over his head and went on and the kid followed.

The dramhouse was a long narrow hall wainscotted with varnished boards. There were tables by the wall and spittoons on the floor. There were no patrons. The barman looked up when they entered and a nigger that had been sweeping the floor stood the broom against the wall and went out.

Where's Sidney? said the man in his suit of mud.

In the bed I reckon.

They went on.

Toadvine, called the barman.

The kid looked back.

The barman had come from behind the bar and was looking after them. They crossed from the door through the lobby of the hotel toward the stairs leaving varied forms of mud behind them on the floor. As they started up the stairs the clerk at the desk leaned and called to them.

Toadvine.

He stopped and looked back.

He'll shoot you.

Old Sidney?

Old Sidney.

They went on up the stairs.

At the top of the landing was a long hall with a windowlight at the end. There were varnished doors down the walls set so close they might have been closets. Toadvine went on until he came to the end of the hall. He listened at the last door and he eyed the kid.

You got a match?

The kid searched his pockets and came up with a crushed and stained wooden box.

The man took it from him. Need a little tinder here, he said. He was crumbling the box and stacking the bits against the door. He struck a match and set the pieces alight. He pushed the little pile of burning wood under the door and added more matches.

Is he in there? said the boy.

That's what we're fixin to see.

A dark curl of smoke rose, a blue flame of burning varnish. They squatted in the hallway and watched. Thin flames began to run up over the panels and dart back again. The watchers looked like forms excavated from a bog.

Tap on the door now, said Toadvine.

The kid rose. Toadvine stood up and waited. They could hear the flames crackling inside the room. The kid tapped.

You better tap louder than that. This man drinks some.

He balled his fist and lambasted the door about five times.

Hell fire, said a voice.

Here he comes.

They waited.

You hot son of a bitch, said the voice. Then the knob turned and the door opened.

He stood in his underwear holding in one hand the towel he'd used to turn the doorknob with. When he saw them he turned and started back into the room but Toadvine seized him about the neck and rode him to the floor and held him by the hair and began to pry out an eyeball with his thumb. The man grabbed his wrist and bit it.

Kick his mouth in, called Toadvine. Kick it.

The kid stepped past them into the room and turned and kicked the man in the face. Toadvine held his head back by the hair.

Kick him, he called. Aw, kick him, honey.

He kicked.

Toadvine pulled the bloody head around and looked at it and let it flop to the floor and he rose and kicked the man himself. Two spectators were standing in the hallway. The door was completely afire and part of the wall and ceiling. They went out and down the hall. The clerk was coming up the steps two at a time.

Toadvine you son of a bitch, he said.

Toadvine was four steps above him and when he kicked him he caught him in the throat. The clerk sat down on the stairs. When the kid came past he hit him in the side of the head and the clerk slumped over and began to slide toward the landing. The kid stepped over him and went down to the lobby and crossed to the front door and out.

Toadvine was running down the street, waving his fists above his head crazily and laughing. He looked like a great clay voodoo doll made animate and the kid looked like another. Behind them flames were licking at the top corner of the hotel and clouds of dark smoke rose into the warm Texas morning.

He'd left the mule with a Mexican family that boarded animals at the edge of town and he arrived there wildlooking and out of breath. The woman opened the door and looked at him.

Need to get my mule, he wheezed.

She looked at him some more, then she called toward the back of the house. He walked around. There were horses tethered in the lot and there was a flatbed wagon against the fence with some turkeys sitting on the edge looking out. The old lady had come to the back door. Nito, she called. Venga. Hay un caballero aquí. Venga.

He went down the shed to the tackroom and got his wretched saddle and his blanketroll and brought them back. He found the mule and unstalled it and bridled it with the rawhide hackamore and led it to the fence. He leaned against the animal with his shoulder and got the saddle over it and got it cinched, the mule starting and shying and running its head along the fence. He led it across the lot. The mule kept shaking its head sideways as if it had something in its ear.

He led it out to the road. As he passed the house the woman came padding out after him. When she saw him put his foot in the stirrup she began to run. He swung up into the broken saddle and chucked the mule forward. She stopped at the gate and watched him go. He didnt look back.

When he passed back through the town the hotel was burning and men were standing around watching it, some holding empty buckets. A few men sat horseback watching the flames and one of these was the judge. As the kid rode past the judge turned and watched him. He turned the horse, as if he'd have the animal watch too. When the kid looked back the judge smiled. The kid touched up the mule and they went sucking out past the old stone fort along the road west.

II

Across the prairie – A hermit – A nigger's heart –
A stormy night – Westward again – Cattle drovers – Their kindness –
On the trail again – The deadcart – San Antonio de Bexar –
A Mexican cantina – Another fight – The abandoned church –
The dead in the sacristy – At the ford –
Bathing in the river.

Now come days of begging, days of theft. Days of riding where there rode no soul save he. He's left behind the pinewood country and the evening sun declines before him beyond an endless swale and dark falls here like a thunderclap and a cold wind sets the weeds to gnashing. The night sky lies so sprent with stars that there is scarcely space of black at all and they fall all night in bitter arcs and it is so that their numbers are no less.

He keeps from off the king's road for fear of citizenry. The little prairie wolves cry all night and dawn finds him in a grassy draw where he'd gone to hide from the wind. The hobbled mule stands over him and watches the east for light.

The sun that rises is the color of steel. His mounted shadow falls for miles before him. He wears on his head a hat he's made from leaves and they have dried and cracked in the sun and he looks like a raggedyman wandered from some garden where he'd used to frighten birds.

Come evening he tracks a spire of smoke rising oblique from

among the low hills and before dark he hails up at the doorway of an old anchorite nested away in the sod like a groundsloth. Solitary, half mad, his eyes redrimmed as if locked in their cages with hot wires. But a ponderable body for that. He watched wordless while the kid eased down stiffly from the mule. A rough wind was blowing and his rags flapped about him.

Seen ye smoke, said the kid. Thought you might spare a man a sup of water.

The old hermit scratched in his filthy hair and looked at the ground. He turned and entered the hut and the kid followed.

Inside darkness and a smell of earth. A small fire burned on the dirt floor and the only furnishings were a pile of hides in one corner. The old man shuffled through the gloom, his head bent to clear the low ceiling of woven limbs and mud. He pointed down to where a bucket stood in the dirt. The kid bent and took up the gourd floating there and dipped and drank. The water was salty, sulphurous. He drank on.

You reckon I could water my old mule out there?

The old man began to beat his palm with one fist and dart his eyes about.

Be proud to fetch in some fresh. Just tell me where it's at.

What ye aim to water him with?

The kid looked at the bucket and he looked around in the dim hut.

I aint drinkin after no mule, said the hermit.

Have you not got no old bucket nor nothin?

No, cried the hermit. No. I aint. He was clapping the heels of his clenched fists together at his chest.

The kid rose and looked toward the door. I'll find somethin, he said. Where's the well at?

Up the hill, foller the path.

It's nigh too dark to see out here.

It's a deep path. Foller ye feet. Foller ye mule. I caint go.

He stepped out into the wind and looked about for the mule but the mule wasnt there. Far to the south lightning flared soundlessly. He went up the path among the thrashing weeds and found the mule standing at the well.

A hole in the sand with rocks piled about it. A piece of dry hide for a cover and a stone to weight it down. There was a rawhide bucket with a rawhide bail and a rope of greasy leather. The bucket had a rock tied to the bail to help it tip and fill and he lowered it until the rope in his hand went slack while the mule watched over his shoulder.

He drew up three bucketfuls and held them so the mule would not spill them and then he put the cover back over the well and led the mule back down the path to the hut.

I thank ye for the water, he called.

The hermit appeared darkly in the door. Just stay with me, he said.

That's all right.

Best stay. It's fixin to storm.

You reckon?

I reckon and I reckon right.

Well.

Bring ye bed. Bring ye possibles.

He uncinched and threw down the saddle and hobbled the mule foreleg to rear and took his bedroll in. There was no light save the fire and the old man was squatting by it tailorwise.

Anywheres, anywheres, he said. Where's ye saddle at?

The kid gestured with his chin.

Dont leave it out yonder somethin'll eat it. This is a hungry country.

He went out and ran into the mule in the dark. It had been standing looking in at the fire.

Get away, fool, he said. He took up the saddle and went back in.

Now pull that door to fore we blow away, said the old man.

The door was a mass of planks on leather hinges. He dragged it across the dirt and fastened it by its leather latch.

I take it ye lost your way, said the hermit.

No, I went right to it.

He waved quickly with his hand, the old man. No, no, he said. I mean ye was lost to of come here. Was they a sandstorm? Did ye drift off the road in the night? Did thieves beset ye?

The kid pondered this. Yes, he said We got off the road someways or another.

Knowed ye did.

How long you been out here?

Out where?

The kid was sitting on his blanketroll across the fire from the old man. Here, he said. In this place.

The old man didnt answer. He turned his head suddenly aside and seized his nose between his thumb and forefinger and blew twin strings of snot onto the floor and wiped his fingers on the seam of his jeans. I come from Mississippi. I was a slaver, dont care to tell it. Made good money. I never did get caught. Just got sick of it. Sick of niggers. Wait till I show ye somethin.

He turned and rummaged among the hides and handed through the flames a small dark thing. The kid turned it in his hand. Some man's heart, dried and blackened. He passed it back and the old man cradled it in his palm as if he'd weigh it.

They is four things that can destroy the earth, he said. Women, whiskey, money, and niggers.

They sat in silence. The wind moaned in the section of stovepipe that was run through the roof above them to quit the place of smoke. After a while the old man put the heart away.

That thing costed me two hundred dollars, he said.

You give two hundred dollars for it?

I did, for that was the price they put on the black son of a bitch it hung inside of.

He stirred about in the corner and came up with an old dark brass kettle, lifted the cover and poked inside with one finger. The remains of one of the lank prairie hares interred in cold grease and furred with a light blue mold. He clamped the lid back on the kettle and set it in the flames. Aint much but we'll go shares, he said.

I thank ye.

Lost ye way in the dark, said the old man. He stirred the fire, standing slender tusks of bone up out of the ashes.

The kid didnt answer.

The old man swung his head back and forth. The way of the transgressor is hard. God made this world, but he didnt make it to suit everbody, did he?

I dont believe he much had me in mind.

Aye, said the old man. But where does a man come by his notions. What world's he seen that he liked better?

I can think of better places and better ways.

Can ye make it be?

No.

No. It's a mystery. A man's at odds to know his mind cause his mind is aught he has to know it with. He can know his heart, but he dont want to. Rightly so. Best not to look in there. It aint the heart of a creature that is bound in the way that God has set for it. You can find meanness in the least of creatures, but when God made man the devil was at his elbow. A creature that can do anything. Make a machine. And a machine to make the machine. And evil that can run itself a thousand years, no need to tend it. You believe that?

I dont know.

Believe that.

When the old man's mess was warmed he doled it out and they ate in silence. Thunder was moving north and before long it was booming overhead and starting bits of rust in a thin trickle down the stovepipe. They hunkered over their plates and wiped the grease up with their fingers and drank from the gourd.

The kid went out and scoured his cup and plate in the sand and came back banging the tins together as if to fend away some drygulch phantom out there in the dark. Distant thunderheads reared quivering against the electric sky and were sucked away in the blackness again. The old man sat with one ear cocked to the howling waste without. The kid shut the door.

Dont have no bacca with ye do ye?

No I aint, said the kid.

Didnt allow ye did.

You reckon it'll rain?

It's got ever opportunity. Likely it wont.

19

The kid watched the fire. Already he was nodding. Finally he raised up and shook his head. The hermit watched him over the dying flames. Just go on and fix ye bed, he said.

He did. Spreading his blankets on the packed mud and pulling off his stinking boots. The fluepipe moaned and he heard the mule stamp and snuffle outside and in his sleep he struggled and muttered like a dreaming dog.

He woke sometime in the night with the hut in almost total darkness and the hermit bent over him and all but in his bed.

What do you want? he said. But the hermit crawled away and in the morning when he woke the hut was empty and he got his things and left.

All that day he watched to the north a thin line of dust. It seemed not to move at all and it was late evening before he could see that it was headed his way. He passed through a forest of live oak and he watered at a stream and moved on in the dusk and made a fireless camp. Birds woke him where he lay in a dry and dusty wood.

By noon he was on the prairie again and the dust to the north was stretched out along the edge of the earth. By evening the first of a drove of cattle came into view. Rangy vicious beasts with enormous hornspreads. That night he sat in the herders' camp and ate beans and pilotbread and heard of life on the trail.

They were coming down from Abilene, forty days out, headed for the markets in Louisiana. Followed by packs of wolves, coyotes, indians. Cattle groaned about them for miles in the dark.

They asked him no questions, a ragged lot themselves. Crossbreeds some, free niggers, an indian or two.

I had my outfit stole, he said.

They nodded in the firelight.

They got everthing I had. I aint even got a knife.

You might could sign on with us. We lost two men. Turned back to go to Californy.

I'm headed yon way.

I guess you might be goin to Californy ye own self.

I might. I aint decided.

Them boys was with us fell in with a bunch from Arkansas. They was headed down for Bexar. Goin to pull for Mexico and the west.

I'll bet them old boys is in Bexar drinkin they brains out.

I'll bet old Lonnie's done topped ever whore in town.

How far is it to Bexar?

It's about two days.

It's furthern that. More like four I'd say.

How would a man go if he'd a mind to?

You cut straight south you ought to hit the road about half a day.

You going to Bexar?

I might do.

You see old Lonnie down there you tell him get a piece for me. Tell him old Oren. He'll buy ye a drink if he aint blowed all his money in.

In the morning they ate flapjacks with molasses and the herders saddled up and moved on. When he found his mule there was a small fibre bag tied to the animal's rope and inside the bag there was a cupful of dried beans and some peppers and an old greenriver knife with a handle made of string. He saddled up the mule, the mule's back galled and balding, the hooves cracked. The ribs like fishbones. They hobbled on across the endless plain.

He came upon Bexar in the evening of the fourth day and he sat the tattered mule on a low rise and looked down at the town, the quiet adobe houses, the line of green oaks and cottonwoods that marked the course of the river, the plaza filled with wagons with their osnaburg covers and the whitewashed public buildings and the Moorish churchdome rising from the trees and the garrison and the tall stone powderhouse in the distance. A light breeze stirred the fronds of his hat, his matted greasy hair. His eyes lay dark and tunneled in a caved and haunted face and a foul stench rose from the wells of his boot tops. The sun was just down and to the west lay reefs of bloodred clouds up out of which rose little desert nighthawks like fugitives from some great fire at the earth's end. He spat a dry white spit and clumped the cracked wooden stirrups against the mule's ribs and they staggered into motion again.

He went down a narrow sandy road and as he went he met a deadcart bound out with a load of corpses, a small bell tolling the way and a lantern swinging from the gate. Three men sat on the box not unlike the dead themselves or spirit folk so white they were with lime and nearly phosphorescent in the dusk. A pair of horses drew the cart and they went on up the road in a faint miasma of carbolic and passed from sight. He turned and watched them go. The naked feet of the dead jostled stiffly from side to side.

It was dark when he entered the town, attended by barking dogs, faces parting the curtains in the lamplit windows. The light clatter of the mule's hooves echoing in the little empty streets. The mule sniffed the air and swung down an alleyway into a square where there stood in the starlight a well, a trough, a hitchingrail. The kid eased himself down and took the bucket from the stone coping and lowered it into the well. A light splash echoed. He drew the bucket, water dripping in the dark. He dipped the gourd and drank and the mule nuzzled his elbow. When he'd done he set the bucket in the street and sat on the coping of the well and watched the mule drink from the bucket.

He went on through the town leading the animal. There was no one about. By and by he entered a plaza and he could hear guitars and a horn. At the far end of the square there were lights from a cafe and laughter and highpitched cries. He led the mule into the square and up the far side past a long portico toward the lights.

There was a team of dancers in the street and they wore gaudy costumes and called out in spanish. He and the mule stood at the edge of the lights and watched. Old men sat along the tavern wall and children played in the dust. They wore strange costumes all, the men in dark flatcrowned hats, white nightshirts, trousers that buttoned up the outside leg and the girls with garish painted faces and tortoiseshell combs in their blueblack hair. The kid

22

crossed the street with the mule and tied it and entered the cafe. A number of men were standing at the bar and they quit talking when he entered. He crossed the polished clay floor past a sleeping dog that opened one eye and looked at him and he stood at the bar and placed both hands on the tiles. The barman nodded to him. Dígame, he said.

I aint got no money but I need a drink. I'll fetch out the slops or mop the floor or whatever.

The barman looked across the room to where two men were playing dominoes at a table. Abuelito, he said.

The older of the two raised his head.

Qué dice el muchacho.

The old man looked at the kid and turned back to his dominoes.

The barman shrugged his shoulders.

The kid turned to the old man. You speak american? he said.

The old man looked up from his play. He regarded the kid without expression.

Tell him I'll work for a drink. I aint got no money.

The old man thrust his chin and made a clucking noise with his tongue.

The kid looked at the barman.

The old man made a fist with the thumb pointing up and the little finger down and tilted his head back and tipped a phantom drink down his throat. Quiere hecharse una copa, he said. Pero no puede pagar.

The men at the bar watched.

The barman looked at the kid.

Quiere trabajo, said the old man. Quién sabe. He turned back to his pieces and made his play without further consultation.

Quieres trabajar, said one of the men at the bar.

They began to laugh.

What are you laughing at? said the boy.

They stopped. Some looked at him, some pursed their mouths or shrugged. The boy turned to the bartender. You got something I could do for a couple of drinks I know damn good and well.

One of the men at the bar said something in spanish. The

boy glared at them. They winked one to the other, they took up their glasses.

He turned to the barman again. His eyes were dark and narrow. Sweep the floor, he said.

The barman blinked.

The kid stepped back and made sweeping motions, a pantomime that bent the drinkers in silent mirth. Sweep, he said, pointing at the floor.

No está sucio, said the barman.

He swept again. Sweep, goddamnit, he said.

The barman shrugged. He went to the end of the bar and got a broom and brought it back. The boy took it and went on to the back of the room.

A great hall of a place. He swept in the corners where potted trees stood silent in the dark. He swept around the spittoons and he swept around the players at the table and he swept around the dog. He swept along the front of the bar and when he reached the place where the drinkers stood he straightened up and leaned on the broom and looked at them. They conferred silently among themselves and at last one took his glass from the bar and stepped away. The others followed. The kid swept past them to the door.

The dancers had gone, the music. Across the street sat a man on a bench dimly lit in the doorlight from the cafe. The mule stood where he'd tied it. He tapped the broom on the steps and came back in and took the broom to the corner where the barman had gotten it. Then he came to the bar and stood.

The barman ignored him.

The kid rapped with his knuckles.

The barman turned and put one hand on his hip and pursed his lips.

How about that drink now, said the kid.

The barman stood.

The kid made the drinking motions that the old man had made and the barman flapped his towel idly at him.

Andale, he said. He made a shooing motion with the back of his hand.

The kid's face clouded. You son of a bitch, he said. He started down the bar. The barman's expression did not change. He brought up from under the bar an oldfashioned military pistol with a flint lock and shoved back the cock with the heel of his hand. A great wooden clicking in the silence. A clicking of glasses all down the bar. Then the scuffling of chairs pushed back by the players at the wall.

The kid froze. Old man, he said.

The old man didnt answer. There was no sound in the cafe. The kid turned to find him with his eyes.

Está borracho, said the old man.

The boy watched the barman's eyes.

The barman waved the pistol toward the door.

The old man spoke to the room in spanish. Then he spoke to the barman. Then he put on his hat and went out.

The barman's face drained. When he came around the end of the bar he had laid down the pistol and he was carrying a bungstarter in one hand.

The kid backed to the center of the room and the barman labored over the floor toward him like a man on his way to some chore. He swung twice at the kid and the kid stepped twice to the right. Then he stepped backward. The barman froze. The kid boosted himself lightly over the bar and picked up the pistol. No one moved. He raked the frizzen open against the bartop and dumped the priming out and laid the pistol down again. Then he selected a pair of full bottles from the shelves behind him and came around the end of the bar with one in each hand.

The barman stood in the center of the room. He was breathing heavily and he turned, following the kid's movements. When the kid approached him he raised the bungstarter. The kid crouched lightly with the bottles and feinted and then broke the right one over the man's head. Blood and liquor sprayed and the man's knees buckled and his eyes rolled. The kid had already let go the bottleneck and he pitched the second bottle into his right hand in a roadagent's pass before it even reached the floor and he backhanded the second bottle across the barman's skull and crammed the jagged remnant into his eye as he went down.

The kid looked around the room. Some of those men wore pistols in their belts but none moved. The kid vaulted the bar and took another bottle and tucked it under his arm and walked out the door. The dog was gone. The man on the bench was gone too. He untied the mule and led it across the square.

———————◆◆◆———————

He woke in the nave of a ruinous church, blinking up at the vaulted ceiling and the tall swagged walls with their faded frescos. The floor of the church was deep in dried guano and the droppings of cattle and sheep. Pigeons flapped through the piers of dusty light and three buzzards hobbled about on the picked bone carcass of some animal dead in the chancel.

His head was in torment and his tongue swollen with thirst. He sat up and looked around him. He'd put the bottle under his saddle and he found it and held it up and shook it and drew the cork and drank. He sat with his eyes closed, the sweat beaded on his forehead. Then he opened his eyes and drank again. The buzzards stepped down one by one and trotted off into the sacristy. After a while he rose and went out to look for the mule.

It was nowhere in sight. The mission occupied eight or ten ares of enclosed land, a barren purlieu that held a few goats and burros. In the mud walls of the enclosure were cribs inhabited by families of squatters and a few cookfires smoked thinly in the sun. He walked around the side of the church and entered the sacristy. Buzzards shuffled off through the chaff and plaster like enormous yardfowl. The domed vaults overhead were clotted with a dark furred mass that shifted and breathed and chittered. In the room was a wooden table with a few clay pots and along the back wall lay the remains of several bodies, one a child. He went on through the sacristy into the church again and got his saddle. He drank the rest of the bottle and he put the saddle on his shoulder and went out.

The facade of the building bore an array of saints in their niches and they had been shot up by American troops trying their rifles, the figures shorn of ears and noses and darkly mottled with leadmarks oxidized upon the stone. The huge carved and

26

paneled doors hung awap on their hinges and a carved stone Virgin held in her arms a headless child. He stood blinking in the noon heat. Then he saw the mule's tracks. They were just the palest disturbance of the dust and they came out of the door of the church and crossed the lot to the gate in the east wall. He hiked the saddle higher onto his shoulder and set out after them.

A dog in the shade of the portal rose and lurched sullenly out into the sun until he had passed and then lurched back. He took the road down the hill toward the river, a ragged figure enough. He entered a deep wood of pecan and oak and the road took a rise and he could see the river below him. Blacks were washing a carriage in the ford and he went down the hill and stood at the edge of the water and after a while he called out to them.

They were sopping water over the black lacquerwork and one of them raised up and turned to look at him. The horses stood to their knees in the current.

What? called the black.

Have you seen a mule.

Mule?

I lost a mule. I think he come this way.

The black wiped his face with the back of his arm. Somethin come down the road about a hour back. I think it went down the river yonder. It might of been a mule. It didnt have no tail nor no hair to speak of but it did have long ears.

The other two blacks grinned. The kid looked off down the river. He spat and set off along the path through the willows and swales of grass.

He found it about a hundred yards downriver. It was wet to its belly and it looked up at him and then lowered its head again into the lush river grass. He threw down the saddle and took up the trailing rope and tied the animal to a limb and kicked it halfheartedly. It shifted slightly to the side and continued to graze. He reached atop his head but he had lost the crazy hat somewhere. He made his way down through the trees and stood looking at the cold swirling waters. Then he waded out into the river like some wholly wretched baptismal candidate.

27

III

Sought out to join an army – Interview with Captain White –
His views – The camp – Trades his mule – A cantina in the Laredito –
A Mennonite – Companion killed.

He was lying naked under the trees with his rags spread across the limbs above him when another rider going down the river reined up and stopped.

He turned his head. Through the willows he could see the legs of the horse. He rolled over on his stomach.

The man got down and stood beside the horse.

He reached and got his twinehandled knife.

Howdy there, said the rider.

He didnt answer. He moved to the side to see better through the branches.

Howdy there. Where ye at?

What do you want?

Wanted to talk to ye.

What about?

Hell fire, come on out. I'm white and christian.

The kid was reaching up through the willows trying to get his breeches. The belt was hanging down and he tugged at it but the breeches were hung on a limb.

Goddamn, said the man. You aint up in the tree are ye?

Why dont you go on and leave me the hell alone.

Just wanted to talk to ye. Didnt intend to get ye all riled up.

You done got me riled.

Was you the feller knocked in that Mexer's head yesterday evenin? I aint the law.

Who wants to know?

Captain White. He wants to sign that feller up to join the army.

The army?

Yessir.

What army?

Company under Captain White. We goin to whip up on the Mexicans.

The war's over.

He says it aint over. Where are you at?

He rose and hauled the breeches down from where he'd hung them and pulled them on. He pulled on his boots and put the knife in the right bootleg and came out from the willows pulling on his shirt.

The man was sitting in the grass with his legs crossed. He was dressed in buckskin and he wore a plug hat of dusty black silk and he had a small Mexican cigar in the corner of his teeth. When he saw what clawed its way out through the willows he shook his head.

Kindly fell on hard times aint ye son? he said.

I just aint fell on no good ones.

You ready to go to Mexico?

I aint lost nothin down there.

It's a chance for ye to raise ye self in the world. You best make a move someway or another fore ye go plumb in under.

What do they give ye?

Ever man gets a horse and his ammunition. I reckon we might find some clothes in your case.

I aint got no rifle.

We'll find ye one.

What about wages?

Hell fire son, you wont need no wages. You get to keep everthing you can raise. We goin to Mexico. Spoils of war. Aint a man in the company wont come out a big landowner. How much land you own now?

I dont know nothin about soldierin.

The man eyed him. He took the unlit cigar from his teeth and turned his head and spat and put it back again. Where ye from? he said.

Tennessee.

Tennessee. Well I dont misdoubt but what you can shoot a rifle.

The kid squatted in the grass. He looked at the man's horse. The horse was fitted out in tooled leather with worked silver trim. It had a white blaze on its face and four white stockings and it was cropping up great teethfuls of the rich grass. Where you from, said the kid.

I been in Texas since thirty-eight. If I'd not run up on Captain White I dont know where I'd be this day. I was a sorrier sight even than what you are and he come along and raised me up like Lazarus. Set my feet in the path of righteousness. I'd done took to drinkin and whorin till hell wouldnt have me. He seen somethin in me worth savin and I see it in you. What do ye say?

I dont know.

Just come with me and meet the captain.

The boy pulled at the halms of grass. He looked at the horse again. Well, he said. Dont reckon it'd hurt nothin.

They rode through the town with the recruiter splendid on the stockingfooted horse and the kid behind him on the mule like something he'd captured. They rode through narrow lanes where the wattled huts steamed in the heat. Grass and prickly pear grew on the roofs and goats walked about on them and somewhere off in that squalid kingdom of mud the sound of the little deathbells tolled thinly. They turned up Commerce Street through the Main Plaza among rafts of wagons and they crossed another plaza where boys were selling grapes and figs from little trundlecarts.

A few bony dogs slank off before them. They rode through the Military Plaza and they passed the little street where the boy and the mule had drunk the night before and there were clusters of women and girls at the well and many shapes of wickercovered clay jars standing about. They passed a little house where women inside were wailing and the little hearsecart stood at the door with the horses patient and motionless in the heat and the flies.

The captain kept quarters in a hotel on a plaza where there were trees and a small green gazebo with benches. An iron gate at the hotel front opened into a passageway with a courtyard at the rear. The walls were whitewashed and set with little ornate colored tiles. The captain's man wore carved boots with tall heels that rang smartly on the tiles and on the stairs ascending from the courtyard to the rooms above. In the courtyard there were green plants growing and they were freshly watered and steaming. The captain's man strode down the long balcony and rapped sharply at the door at the end. A voice said for them to come in.

He sat at a wickerwork desk writing letters, the captain. They stood attending, the captain's man with his black hat in his hands. The captain wrote on nor did he look up. Outside the kid could hear a woman speaking in spanish. Other than that there was just the scratching of the captain's pen.

When he had done he laid down the pen and looked up. He looked at his man and then he looked at the kid and then he bent his head to read what he'd written. He nodded to himself and dusted the letter with sand from a little onyx box and folded it. Taking a match from a box of them on the desk he lit it and held it to a stick of sealing wax until a small red medallion had pooled onto the paper. He shook out the match, blew briefly at the paper and knuckled the seal with his ring. Then he stood the letter between two books on his desk and leaned back in his chair and looked at the kid again. He nodded gravely. Take seats, he said.

They eased themselves into a kind of settle made from some dark wood. The captain's man had a large revolver at his belt and as he sat he hitched the belt around so that the piece lay cradled between his thighs. He put his hat over it and leaned back. The kid folded his busted boots one behind the other and sat upright.

The captain pushed his chair back and rose and came around to the front of the desk. He stood there for a measured minute and then he hitched himself up on the desk and sat with his boots dangling. He had gray in his hair and in the sweeping moustaches that he wore but he was not old. So you're the man, he said.

What man? said the kid.

What man sir, said the captain's man.

How old are you, son?

Nineteen.

The captain nodded his head. He was looking the kid over. What happened to you?

What?

Say sir, said the recruiter.

Sir?

I said what happened to you.

The kid looked at the man sitting next to him. He looked down at himself and he looked at the captain again. I was fell on by robbers, he said.

Robbers, said the captain.

Took everthing I had. Took my watch and everthing.

Have you got a rifle?

Not no more I aint.

Where was it you were robbed.

I dont know. They wasnt no name to it. It was just a wilderness.

Where were you coming from?

I was comin from Naca, Naca . . .

Nacogdoches?

Yeah.

Yessir.

Yessir.

How many were there?

The kid stared at him.

Robbers. How many robbers.

Seven or eight, I reckon. I got busted in the head with a scantlin.

32

The captain squinted one eye at him. Were they Mexicans?

Some. Mexicans and niggers. They was a white or two with em. They had a bunch of cattle they'd stole. Only thing they left me with was a old piece of knife I had in my boot.

The captain nodded. He folded his hands between his knees. What do you think of the treaty? he said.

The kid looked at the man on the settle next to him. He had his eyes shut. He looked down at his thumbs. I dont know nothin about it, he said.

I'm afraid that's the case with a lot of Americans, said the captain. Where are you from, son?

Tennessee.

You werent with the Volunteers at Monterrey were you?

No sir.

Bravest bunch of men under fire I believe I ever saw. I suppose more men from Tennessee bled and died on the field in northern Mexico than from any other state. Did you know that?

No sir.

They were sold out. Fought and died down there in that desert and then they were sold out by their own country.

The kid sat silent.

The captain leaned forward. We fought for it. Lost friends and brothers down there. And then by God if we didnt give it back. Back to a bunch of barbarians that even the most biased in their favor will admit have no least notion in God's earth of honor or justice or the meaning of republican government. A people so cowardly they've paid tribute a hundred years to tribes of naked savages. Given up their crops and livestock. Mines shut down. Whole villages abandoned. While a heathen horde rides over the land looting and killing with total impunity. Not a hand raised against them. What kind of people are these? The Apaches wont even shoot them. Did you know that? They kill them with rocks. The captain shook his head. He seemed made sad by what he had to tell.

Did you know that when Colonel Doniphan took Chihuahua City he inflicted over a thousand casualties on the enemy and lost only one man and him all but a suicide? With an army of unpaid irregulars that called him Bill, were half naked, and had walked to the battlefield from Missouri?

No sir.

The captain leaned back and folded his arms. What we are dealing with, he said, is a race of degenerates. A mongrel race, little better than niggers. And maybe no better. There is no government in Mexico. Hell, there's no God in Mexico. Never will be. We are dealing with a people manifestly incapable of governing themselves. And do you know what happens with people who cannot govern themselves? That's right. Others come in to govern for them.

There are already some fourteen thousand French colonists in the state of Sonora. They're being given free land to settle. They're being given tools and livestock. Enlightened Mexicans encourage this. Paredes is already calling for secession from the Mexican government. They'd rather be ruled by toadeaters than thieves and imbeciles. Colonel Carrasco is asking for American intervention. And he's going to get it.

Right now they are forming in Washington a commission to come out here and draw up the boundary lines between our country and Mexico. I dont think there's any question that ultimately Sonora will become a United States territory. Guaymas a U S port. Americans will be able to get to California without having to pass through our benighted sister republic and our citizens will be protected at last from the notorious packs of cut-throats presently infesting the routes which they are obliged to travel.

The captain was watching the kid. The kid looked uneasy. Son, said the captain. We are to be the instruments of liberation in a dark and troubled land. That's right. We are to spearhead the drive. We have the tacit support of Governor Burnett of California.

He leaned forward and placed his hands on his knees. And we will be the ones who will divide the spoils. There will be a section of land for every man in my company. Fine grassland. Some of the finest in the world. A land rich in minerals, in gold and silver I would say beyond the wildest speculation. You're young.

But I dont misread you. I'm seldom mistaken in a man. I think you mean to make your mark in this world. Am I wrong?

No sir.

No. And I don't think you're the sort of chap to abandon a land that Americans fought and died for to a foreign power. And mark my word. Unless Americans act, people like you and me who take their country seriously while those mollycoddles in Washington sit on their hindsides, unless we act, Mexico—and I mean the whole of the country—will one day fly a European flag. Monroe Doctrine or no.

The captain's voice had become soft and intense. He tilted his head to one side and regarded the kid with a sort of benevolence. The kid rubbed the palms of his hands on the knees of his filthy jeans. He glanced at the man beside him but he seemed to be asleep.

What about a saddle? he said.

Saddle?

Yessir.

You dont have a saddle?

No sir.

I thought you had a horse.

A mule.

I see.

I got a old hull on the mule but they aint much left of it. Aint a whole lot left of the mule. He said I was to get a horse and a rifle.

Sergeant Trammel did?

I never promised him no saddle, said the sergeant.

We'll get you a saddle.

I did tell him we might find him some clothes, Captain.

Right. We may be irregulars but we dont want to look like bobtails, do we?

No sir.

We aint got no more broke horses neither, said the sergeant.

Well break one.

That old boy that was so good about breakin em is out of commission.

I know that. Get somebody else.

Yessir. Maybe this man can break horses. You ever break horses?

No sir.

Aint no need to sir me.

Yessir.

Sergeant, said the captain, easing himself down from the desk.

Yessir.

Sign this man up.

———◆◆◆———

The camp was upriver at the edge of the town. A tent patched up from old wagon canvas, a few wickiups made of brush and beyond them a corral in the form of a figure eight likewise made from brush where a few small painted ponies stood sulking in the sun.

Corporal, called the sergeant.

He aint here.

He dismounted and strode toward the tent and threw back the fly. The kid sat on the mule. Three men were lying in the shade of a tree and they studied him. Howdy, said one.

Howdy.

You a new man?

I reckon.

Captain say when we leavin this pesthole?

He never said.

The sergeant came from the tent. Where's he at? he said.

Gone to town.

Gone to town, said the sergeant. Come here.

The man rose from the ground and ambled over to the tent and stood with his hands resting in the small of his back.

This here man aint got no outfit, said the sergeant.

The man nodded.

The captain give him a shirt and some money to get his boots mended. We need to get him somethin he can ride and we need to get him a saddle.

A saddle.

Ought to be able to sell that mule for enough to get him one of some kind.

The man looked at the mule and turned back and squinted at the sergeant. He leaned and spat. That there mule wont bring ten dollars.

What it brings it brings.

They done killed another beef.

I dont want to hear about it.

I caint do nothin with em.

I aint tellin the captain. He'll roll them eyes around till they come unscrewed and fall out in the ground.

The man spat again. Well, that's the gods truth anyway.

See to this man now. I got to get.

Well.

Aint nobody sick is they?

No.

Thank God for that.

He stood up into the saddle and touched the horse's neck lightly with the reins. He looked back and shook his head.

In the evening the kid and two other recruits went into town. He'd bathed and shaved himself and he wore a pair of blue cord trousers and the cotton shirt the captain had given him and save for the boots he looked a new man altogether. His friends rode small and colorful horses that forty days ago had been wild animals on the plain and they shied and skittered and snapped like turtles.

Wait till you get you one of these, said the second corporal. You aint never had no fun.

These horses is all right, said the other.

There's one or two in there yet that might make ye a horse.

The kid looked down at them from his mule. They rode either side like escorts and the mule trotted with its head up, its eyes shifting nervously. They'll all stick ye head in the ground, said the second corporal.

They rode through a plaza thronged with wagons and stock.

With immigrants and Texans and Mexicans and with slaves and Lipan indians and deputations of Karankawas tall and austere, their faces dyed blue and their hands locked about the shafts of their sixfoot spears, all but naked savages who with their painted skins and their whispered taste for human flesh seemed outrageous presences even in that fabled company. The recruits rode with their animals close reined and they turned up past the courthouse and along the high walls of the cárcel with the broken glass imbedded in the topmost course. In the Main Plaza a band had assembled and were at tuning their instruments. The riders turned down Salinas Street past small gaminghouses and coffeestands and there were in this street a number of Mexican harnessmakers and traders and keepers of gamechickens and cobblers and bootmakers in little stalls or shops of mud. The second corporal was from Texas and spoke a little spanish and he meant to trade the mule. The other boy was from Missouri. They were in good spirits, scrubbed and combed, clean shirts all. Each foreseeing a night of drink, perhaps of love. How many youths have come home cold and dead from just such nights and just such plans.

They traded the mule accoutred as it was for a Texas stock saddle, bare tree with rawhide cover, not new but sound. For a bridle and bit that was new. For a woven wool blanket from Saltillo that was dusty new or not. And lastly for a two and a half dollar gold piece. The Texan looked at this small coin in the kid's palm and demanded more money but the harnessmaker shook his head and held up his hands in utter finality.

What about my boots? said the kid.

Y sus botas, said the Texan.

Botas?

Sí. He made sewing motions.

The harnessmaker looked down at the boots. He cupped his fingers in a little gesture of impatience and the kid took off the boots and stood barefoot in the dust.

When all was done they stood in the street and looked at one another. The kid had his new tack slung up on his shoulder.

The second corporal looked at the boy from Missouri. You got any money, Earl?

Not a copper cent.

Well I aint neither. We might's well get our asses back on out to that hole of misery.

The kid shifted the weight of the gear on his shoulder. We got this quarter eagle to drink up yet, he said.

———◆◆———

Already it is twilight down in the Laredito. Bats fly forth from their roostings in courthouse and tower and circle the quarter. The air is full of the smell of burning charcoal. Children and dogs squat by the mud stoops and gamecocks flap and settle in the branches of the fruit trees. They go afoot, these comrades, down along a bare adobe wall. Band music carries dimly from the square. They pass a watercart in the street and they pass a hole in the wall where by the light of a small forgefire an old man beats out shapes of metal. They pass in a doorway a young girl whose beauty becomes the flowers about.

They arrive at last before a wooden door. It is hinged into a larger door or gate and all must step over the foot-high sill where a thousand boots have scuffed away the wood, where fools in their hundreds have tripped or fallen or tottered drunkenly into the street. They pass along a ramada in a courtyard by an old grape arbor where small fowl nod in the dusk among the gnarled and barren vines and they enter a cantina where the lamps are lit and they cross stooping under a low beam to a bar and belly up one two three.

There is an old disordered Mennonite in this place and he turns to study them. A thin man in a leather weskit, a black and straightbrim hat set square on his head, a thin rim of whiskers. The recruits order glasses of whiskey and drink them down and order more. There are monte games at tables by the wall and there are whores at another table who look the recruits over. The recruits stand sideways along the bar with their thumbs in their belts and watch the room. They talk among themselves

39

of the expedition in loud voices and the old Mennonite shakes a rueful head and sips his drink and mutters.

They'll stop you at the river, he says.

The second corporal looks past his comrades. Are you talking to me?

At the river. Be told. They'll jail you to a man.

Who will?

The United States Army. General Worth.

The hell they will.

Pray that they will.

He looks at his comrades. He leans toward the Mennonite. What does that mean, old man?

Do ye cross that river with yon filibuster armed ye'll not cross it back.

Dont aim to cross it back. We goin to Sonora.

What's it to you, old man?

The Mennonite watches the enshadowed dark before them as it is reflected to him in the mirror over the bar. He turns to them. His eyes are wet, he speaks slowly. The wrath of God lies sleeping. It was hid a million years before men were and only men have power to wake it. Hell aint half full. Hear me. Ye carry war of a madman's making onto a foreign land. Ye'll wake more than the dogs.

But they berated the old man and swore at him until he moved off down the bar muttering, and how else could it be?

How these things end. In confusion and curses and blood. They drank on and the wind blew in the streets and the stars that had been overhead lay low in the west and these young men fell afoul of others and words were said that could not be put right again and in the dawn the kid and the second corporal knelt over the boy from Missouri who had been named Earl and they spoke his name but he never spoke back. He lay on his side in the dust of the courtyard. The men were gone, the whores were gone. An old man swept the clay floor within the cantina. The boy lay with his skull broken in a pool of blood, none knew by whom. A third one came to be with them in the courtyard.

It was the Mennonite. A warm wind was blowing and the east held a gray light. The fowls roosting among the grapevines had begun to stir and call.

There is no such joy in the tavern as upon the road thereto, said the Mennonite. He had been holding his hat in his hands and now he set it upon his head again and turned and went out the gate.

IV

Setting forth with the filibusters – On alien ground –
Shooting antelope – Pursued by cholera – Wolves – Wagon repairs –
A desert waste – Night storms – The ghost manada –
A prayer for rain – A desert homestead – The old man – New country –
An abandoned village – Herdsmen on the plain –
Attacked by Comanches.

Five days later on the dead man's horse he followed the riders and wagons through the plaza and out of the town on the road downcountry. They rode through Castroville where coyotes had dug up the dead and scattered their bones and they crossed the Frio River and they crossed the Nueces and they left the Presidio road and turned north with scouts posted ahead and to the rear. They crossed the del Norte by night and waded up out of the shallow sandy ford into a howling wilderness.

Dawn saw them deployed in a long file over the plain, the dry wood wagons already moaning, horses snuffling. A dull thump of hooves and clank of gear and the constant light chink of harness. Save for scattered clumps of buckbrush and pricklypear and the little patches of twisted grass the ground was bare and there were low mountains to the south and they were bare too. Westward the horizon lay flat and true as a spirit level.

Those first days they saw no game, no birds save buzzards. They saw in the distance herds of sheep or goats moving along the skyline in scarves of dust and they ate the meat of wild asses shot on the plain. The sergeant carried in his saddle scabbard a heavy Wesson rifle that used a false muzzle and paper patch and fired a coneshaped ball. With it he killed the little wild pigs of the desert and later when they began to see herds of antelope he would halt in the dusk with the sun off the land and screwing a bipod into the threaded boss on the underside of the barrel would kill these animals where they stood grazing at distances of half a mile. The rifle carried a vernier sight on the tang and he would eye the distance and gauge the wind and set the sight like a man using a micrometer. The second corporal would lie at his elbow with a glass and call the shots high or low should he miss and the wagon would wait by until he had shot a stand of three or four and then rumble off across the cooling land with the skinners jostling and grinning in the bed. The sergeant never put the rifle up but what he wiped and greased the bore.

They rode well armed, each man with a rifle and many with the smallbore fiveshot Colt's revolvers. The captain carried a pair of dragoon pistols in scabbards that mounted across the pommel of the saddle so that they rode at each knee. These guns were United States issue, Colt's patent, and he had bought them from a deserter in a Soledad livery stable and paid eighty dollars in gold for them and the scabbards and the mold and flask they came with.

The rifle the kid carried had been sawed down and rebored till it weighed very light indeed and the mold for it was so small he had to patch the balls with buckskin. He had fired it a few times and it carried much where it chose. It rode before him on the saddlebow, he having no scabbard. It had been carried so before, God's years of it, and the forestock was much worn beneath.

In the early dark the wagon came back with the meat. The skinners had piled the wagonbed with mesquite brush and stumps they'd drug out of the ground with the horses and they unloaded the firewood and commenced cutting up the gutted antelopes in the floor of the wagon with bowieknives and handaxes, laughing and hacking in a welter of gore, a reeking scene in the light of the handheld lanterns. By full dark the blackened ribracks leaned steaming at the fires and there was a jousting over the coals with shaven sticks whereon were skewered gobs of meat and a clank of canteens and endless raillery. And sleep that night on the cold plains of a foreign land, forty-six men wrapped in their blankets under the selfsame stars, the prairie wolves so like in their yammering, yet all about so changed and strange.

They caught up and set out each day in the dark before the day yet was and they ate cold meat and biscuit and made no fire. The sun rose on a column already ragged these six days out. Among their clothes there was small agreement and among their hats less. The little painted horses stepped shifty and truculent and a vicious snarl of flies fought constantly in the bed of the gamewagon. The dust the party raised was quickly dispersed and lost in the immensity of that landscape and there was no dust other for the pale sutler who pursued them drives unseen and his lean horse and his lean cart leave no track upon such ground or any ground. By a thousand fires in the iron blue dusk he keeps his commissary and he's a wry and grinning tradesman good to follow every campaign or hound men from their holes in just those whited regions where they've gone to hide from God. On this day two men fell sick and one died before dark. In the morning there was another ill to take his place. The two of them were laid among sacks of beans and rice and coffee in the supply-wagon with blankets over them to keep them from the sun and they rode with the slamming and jarring of the wagon half shirring the meat from their bones so that they cried out to be left and then they died. The men turned out in the early morning darkness to dig their graves with the bladebones of antelope and they covered them with stones and rode on again.

They rode on and the sun in the east flushed pale streaks of light and then a deeper run of color like blood seeping up in sudden reaches flaring planewise and where the earth drained up into the sky at the edge of creation the top of the sun rose out of nothing like the head of a great red phallus until it cleared the unseen rim and sat squat and pulsing and malevolent behind them. The shadows of the smallest stones lay like pencil lines across the sand and the shapes of the men and their mounts advanced elongate before them like strands of the night from which they'd ridden, like tentacles to bind them to the darkness yet to come. They rode with their heads down, faceless under their hats, like an army asleep on the march. By midmorning another man had died and they lifted him from the wagon where he'd stained the sacks he'd lain among and buried him also and rode on.

Now wolves had come to follow them, great pale lobos with yellow eyes that trotted neat of foot or squatted in the shimmering heat to watch them where they made their noon halt. Moving on again. Loping, sidling, ambling with their long noses to the ground. In the evening their eyes shifted and winked out there on the edge of the firelight and in the morning when the riders rode out in the cool dark they could hear the snarling and the pop of their mouths behind them as they sacked the camp for meatscraps.

The wagons drew so dry they slouched from side to side like dogs and the sand was grinding them away. The wheels shrank and the spokes reeled in their hubs and clattered like loom-shafts and at night they'd drive false spokes into the mortices and tie them down with strips of green hide and they'd drive wedges between the iron of the tires and the suncracked felloes. They wobbled on, the trace of their untrue labors like sidewinder tracks in the sand. The duledge pegs worked loose and dropped behind. Wheels began to break up.

Ten days out with four men dead they started across a plain of pure pumice where there grew no shrub, no weed, far as the eye could see. The captain called a halt and he called up the Mexican who served as guide. They talked and the Mexican gestured and the captain gestured and after a while they moved on again.

This looks like the high road to hell to me, said a man from the ranks.

What does he reckon for the horses to eat?

I believe they're supposed to just grit up on this sand like chickens and be ready for the shelled corn when it does come.

In two days they began to come upon bones and cast-off apparel. They saw halfburied skeletons of mules with the bones so white and polished they seemed incandescent even in that blazing heat and they saw panniers and packsaddles and the bones of men and they saw a mule entire, the dried and blackened carcass hard as iron. They rode on. The white noon saw them through the waste like a ghost army, so pale they were with dust, like shades of figures erased upon a board. The wolves loped paler yet and grouped and skittered and lifted their lean snouts on the air. At night the horses were fed by hand from sacks of meal and watered from buckets. There was no more sickness. The survivors lay quietly in that cratered void and watched the whitehot stars go rifling down the dark. Or slept with their alien hearts beating in the sand like pilgrims exhausted upon the face of the planet Anareta, clutched to a namelessness wheeling in the night. They moved on and the iron of the wagon-tires grew polished bright as chrome in the pumice. To the south the blue cordilleras stood footed in their paler image on the sand like reflections in a lake and there were no wolves now.

They took to riding by night, silent jornadas save for the trundling of the wagons and the wheeze of the animals. Under the moonlight a strange party of elders with the white dust thick on their moustaches and their eyebrows. They moved on and the stars jostled and arced across the firmament and died beyond the inkblack mountains. They came to know the nightskies well. Western eyes that read more geometric constructions than those names given by the ancients. Tethered to the polestar they rode the Dipper round while Orion rose in the southwest like a great electric kite. The sand lay blue in the moonlight and the iron tires of the wagons rolled among the shapes of the riders in gleaming hoops that veered and wheeled woundedly and vaguely navigational like slender astrolabes and the polished shoes of the horses kept hasping up like a myriad of eyes winking across the desert floor. They watched storms out there so distant they could not be heard, the silent lightning flaring sheetwise and the thin black spine of the mountain chain fluttering and sucked away again in the dark. They saw wild horses racing on the plain, pounding their shadows down the night and leaving in the moonlight a vaporous dust like the palest stain of their passing.

All night the wind blew and the fine dust set their teeth on edge. Sand in everything, grit in all they ate. In the morning a urinecolored sun rose blearily through panes of dust on a dim world and without feature. The animals were failing. They halted and made a dry camp without wood or water and the wretched ponies huddled and whimpered like dogs.

That night they rode through a region electric and wild where strange shapes of soft blue fire ran over the metal of the horses' trappings and the wagonwheels rolled in hoops of fire and little shapes of pale blue light came to perch in the ears of the horses and in the beards of the men. All night sheetlightning quaked sourceless to the west beyond the midnight thunderheads, making a bluish day of the distant desert, the mountains on the sudden skyline stark and black and livid like a land of some other order out there whose true geology was not stone but fear. The thunder moved up from the southwest and lightning lit the desert all about them, blue and barren, great clanging reaches ordered out of the absolute night like some demon kingdom summoned up or changeling land that come the day would leave them neither trace nor smoke nor ruin more than any troubling dream.

They halted in the dark to recruit the animals and some of the men stowed their arms in the wagons for fear of drawing the lightning and a man named Hayward prayed for rain.

He prayed: Almighty God, if it aint too far out of the way of things in your eternal plan do you reckon we could have a little rain down here.

Pray it up, some called, and kneeling he cried out among the thunder and the wind: Lord we are dried to jerky down here. Just a few drops for some old boys out here on the prairie and a long ways from home.

Amen, they said, and catching up their mounts they rode on.

Within the hour the wind cooled and drops of rain the size of grapeshot fell upon them out of that wild darkness. They could smell wet stone and the sweet smell of the wet horses and wet leather. They rode on.

They rode through the heat of the day following with the waterkegs empty and the horses perishing and in the evening these elect, shabby and white with dust like a company of armed and mounted millers wandering in dementia, rode up off the desert through a gap in the low stone hills and down upon a solitary jacal, crude hut of mud and wattles and a rudimentary stable and corrals.

Bone palings ruled the small and dusty purlieus here and death seemed the most prevalent feature of the landscape. Strange fences that the sand and wind had scoured and the sun bleached and cracked like old porcelain with dry brown weather cracks and where no life moved. The corrugated forms of the riders passed jingling across the dry bistre land and across the mud facade of the jacal, the horses trembling, smelling water. The captain raised his hand and the sergeant spoke and two men dismounted and advanced upon the hut with rifles. They pushed open a door made of rawhide and entered. In a few minutes they reappeared.

Somebody's here somewheres. They's hot coals.

The captain surveyed the distance with an air of vigilance. He dismounted with the patience of one used to dealing with incompetence and crossed to the jacal. When he came out he surveyed the terrain again. The horses shifted and clinked and stamped and the men pulled their jaws down and spoke roughly to them.

Sergeant.

Yessir.

These people cant be far. See if you can find them. And see if there's any forage here for the animals.

Forage?

Forage.

The sergeant placed a hand on the cantle and looked about at the place they were in and shook his head and dismounted.

48

They went through the jacal and into the enclosure behind and out to the stable. There were no animals and nothing but a stall half filled with dry sotols in the way of feed. They walked out the back to a sink among the stones where water stood and a thin stream flowed away over the sand. There were hoofprints about the tank and dry manure and some small birds ran mindlessly along the rim of the little creek.

The sergeant had been squatting on his heels and now he rose and spat. Well, he said. Is there any direction you caint see twenty mile in?

The recruits studied the emptiness about.

I dont believe the folks here is gone that long.

They drank and walked back toward the jacal. Horses were being led along the narrow path.

The captain was standing with his thumbs in his belt.

I caint see where they've got to, said the sergeant.

What's in the shed.

Some old dry fodder.

The captain frowned. They ought to have a goat or a hog. Something. Chickens.

In a few minutes two men came dragging an old man from the stable. He was covered with dust and dry chaff and he held one arm across his eyes. He was dragged moaning to the captain's feet where he lay prostrate in what looked like windings of white cotton. He put his hands over his ears and his elbows before his eyes like one called upon to witness some appalling thing. The captain turned away in disgust. The sergeant toed him with his boot. What's wrong with him? he said.

He's pissing himself, Sergeant. He's pissing himself. The captain gestured at the man with his gloves.

Yessir.

Well get him the hell out of here.

You want Candelario to talk to him?

He's a halfwit. Get him away from me.

They dragged the old man away. He had begun to babble but no one listened and in the morning he was gone.

They bivouacked by the tank and the farrier saw to the mules and ponies that had thrown shoes and they worked on the wagons by firelight far into the night. They set forth in a crimson dawn where sky and earth closed in a razorous plane. Out there dark little archipelagos of cloud and the vast world of sand and scrub shearing upward into the shoreless void where those blue islands trembled and the earth grew uncertain, gravely canted and veering out through tinctures of rose and the dark beyond the dawn to the uttermost rebate of space.

They rode through regions of particolored stone upthrust in ragged kerfs and shelves of traprock reared in faults and anticlines curved back upon themselves and broken off like stumps of great stone treeboles and stones the lightning had clove open, seeps exploding in steam in some old storm. They rode past trapdykes of brown rock running down the narrow chines of the ridges and onto the plain like the ruins of old walls, such auguries everywhere of the hand of man before man was or any living thing.

They passed through a village then and now in ruins and they camped in the walls of a tall mud church and burned the fallen timbers of the roof for their fire while owls cried from the arches in the dark.

The following day on the skyline to the south they saw clouds of dust that lay across the earth for miles. They rode on, watching the dust until it began to near and the captain raised his hand for a halt and took from his saddlebag his old brass cavalry telescope and uncoupled it and swept it slowly over the land. The sergeant sat his horse beside him and after a while the captain handed him the glass.

Hell of a herd of something.

I believe it's horses.

How far off do you make them?

Hard to tell.

Call Candelario up here.

The sergeant turned and motioned for the Mexican. When he rode up he handed him the glass and the Mexican raised it to his eye and squinted. Then he lowered the glass and watched with his naked eyes and then he raised it and looked again. Then he sat his horse with the glass at his chest like a crucifix.

Well? said the captain.

He shook his head.

What the hell does that mean? They're not buffalo are they?

No. I think maybe horses.

Let me have the glass.

The Mexican handed him the telescope and he glassed the horizon again and collapsed the tube shut with the heel of his hand and replaced it in his bag and raised his hand and they went on.

They were cattle, mules, horses. There were several thousand head and they were moving quarterwise toward the company. By late afternoon riders were visible to the bare eye, a handful of ragged indians mending the outer flanks of the herd with their nimble ponies. Others in hats, perhaps Mexicans. The sergeant dropped back to where the captain was riding.

What do you make of that, Captain?

I make it a parcel of heathen stockthieves is what I make it. What do you?

Looks like it to me.

The captain watched through the glass. I suppose they've seen us, he said.

They've seen us.

How many riders do you make it?

A dozen maybe.

The captain tapped the instrument in his gloved hand. They dont seem concerned, do they?

No sir. They dont.

The captain smiled grimly. We may see a little sport here before the day is out.

The first of the herd began to swing past them in a pall of yellow dust, rangy slatribbed cattle with horns that grew agoggle and no two alike and small thin mules coalblack that shouldered one another and reared their malletshaped heads above the backs of the others and then more cattle and finally the first of the herders riding up the outer side and keeping the stock between themselves and the mounted company. Behind them came a herd of several hundred ponies. The sergeant looked for Candelario. He kept backing along the ranks but he could not find him. He nudged his horse through the column and moved up the far side. The lattermost of the drovers were now coming through the dust and the captain was gesturing and shouting. The ponies had begun to veer off from the herd and the drovers were beating their way toward this armed company met with on the plain. Already you could see through the dust on the ponies' hides the painted chevrons and the hands and rising suns and birds and fish of every device like the shade of old work through sizing on a canvas and now too you could hear above the pounding of the unshod hooves the piping of the quena, flutes made from human bones, and some among the company had begun to saw back on their mounts and some to mill in confusion when up from the offside of those ponies there rose a fabled horde of mounted lancers and archers bearing shields bedight with bits of broken mirrorglass that cast a thousand unpieced suns against the eyes of their enemies. A legion of horribles, hundreds in number, half naked or clad in costumes attic or biblical or wardrobed out of a fevered dream with the skins of animals and silk finery and pieces of uniform still tracked with the blood of prior owners, coats of slain dragoons, frogged and braided cavalry jackets, one in a stovepipe hat and one with an umbrella and one in white stockings and a bloodstained weddingveil and some in headgear of cranefeathers or rawhide helmets that bore the horns of bull or buffalo and one in a pigeontailed coat worn backwards and otherwise naked and one in the armor of a spanish conquistador, the breastplate and pauldrons deeply dented with old blows of mace or sabre done in another country by men whose very bones were dust and many with their braids spliced up with the hair of other beasts until they trailed upon the ground and their horses' ears and tails worked with bits of brightly colored cloth and one whose horse's whole head was painted crimson red and all the horsemen's faces gaudy and grotesque with daubings like a company of mounted clowns, death hilarious, all howling in a barbarous tongue and riding down upon them like a horde from a hell more horrible yet than the brimstone land of christian reckoning, screeching and yammering and clothed in smoke like those vaporous beings in regions beyond right knowing where the eye wanders and the lip jerks and drools.

Oh my god, said the sergeant.

A rattling drove of arrows passed through the company and men tottered and dropped from their mounts. Horses were rearing and plunging and the mongol hordes swung up along their flanks and turned and rode full upon them with lances.

The company was now come to a halt and the first shots were fired and the gray riflesmoke rolled through the dust as the lancers breached their ranks. The kid's horse sank beneath him with a long pneumatic sigh. He had already fired his rifle and now he sat on the ground and fumbled with his shotpouch. A man near him sat with an arrow hanging out of his neck. He was bent slightly as if in prayer. The kid would have reached for the bloody hoop-iron point but then he saw that the man wore another arrow in his breast to the fletching and he was dead. Everywhere there were horses down and men scrambling and he saw a man who sat charging his rifle while blood ran from his ears and he saw men with their revolvers disassembled trying to fit the spare loaded cylinders they carried and he saw men kneeling who tilted and clasped their shadows on the ground and he saw men lanced and caught up by the hair and scalped standing and he saw the horses of war trample down the fallen and a little whitefaced pony with one clouded eye leaned out of the murk and snapped at him like a dog and was gone. Among the wounded some seemed dumb and without understanding and some were pale through the masks of dust and some had fouled themselves or tottered brokenly onto the spears of the savages. Now driving in a wild frieze of headlong horses with eyes walled and teeth cropped and naked riders with clusters of arrows clenched in their jaws and their shields winking in the dust and up the far side of the ruined ranks in a piping of boneflutes and dropping down off the sides of their mounts with one heel hung in the withers strap and their short bows flexing beneath the outstretched necks of the ponies until they had circled the company and cut their ranks in two and then rising up again like funhouse figures, some with nightmare faces painted on their breasts, riding down the unhorsed Saxons and spearing and clubbing them and leaping from their mounts with knives and running about on the ground with a peculiar bandylegged trot like creatures driven to alien forms of locomotion and stripping the clothes from the dead and seizing them up by the hair and passing their blades about the skulls of the living and the dead alike and snatching aloft the bloody wigs and hacking and chopping at the naked bodies, ripping off limbs, heads, gutting the strange white torsos and holding up great handfuls of viscera, genitals, some of the savages so slathered up with gore they might have rolled in it like dogs and some who fell upon the dying and sodomized them with loud cries to their fellows. And now the horses of the dead came pounding out of the smoke and dust and circled with flapping leather and wild manes and eyes whited with fear like the eyes of the blind and some were feathered with arrows and some lanced through and stumbling and vomiting blood as they wheeled across the killing ground and clattered from sight again. Dust stanched the wet and naked heads of the scalped who with the fringe of hair below their wounds and tonsured to the bone now lay like maimed and naked monks in the bloodslaked dust and everywhere the dying groaned and gibbered and horses lay screaming.

V

Adrift on the Bolson de Mapimi – Sproule –
Tree of dead babies – Scenes from a massacre – Sopilotes –
The murdered in the church – Night among the dead – Wolves –
The washers at the ford – Afoot westward – A mirage – An encounter
with bandits – Attacked by a vampire – Digging a well – A crossroads
in the waste – The carreta – Death of Sproule – Under arrest –
The captain's head – Survivors – On to Chihuahua –
The city – The prison – Toadvine.

With darkness one soul rose wondrously from among the new slain dead and stole away in the moonlight. The ground where he'd lain was soaked with blood and with urine from the voided bladders of the animals and he went forth stained and stinking like some reeking issue of the incarnate dam of war herself. The savages had moved to higher ground and he could see the light from their fires and hear them singing, a strange and plaintive chanting up there where they'd gone to roast mules. He made his way among the pale and dismembered, among the sprawled and legflung horses, and he took a reckoning by the stars and set off south afoot. The night wore a thousand shapes out there in the brush and he kept his eyes to the ground ahead. Starlight and waning moon made a faint shadow of his wanderings on the dark of the desert and all along the ridges the wolves were howling and moving north toward the slaughter. He walked all night and still he could see the fires behind him.

With daylight he made his way toward some outcroppings of rock a mile across the valley floor. He was climbing among the strewn and tumbled boulders when he heard a voice calling somewhere in that vastness. He looked out over the plain but he could see no one. When the voice called again he turned and sat to rest and soon he saw something moving along the slope, a rag of a man clambering toward him over the talus slides. Picking his way with care, looking behind him. The kid could see that nothing followed.

He wore a blanket over his shoulders and his shirtsleeve was ripped and dark with blood and he carried that arm against him with his other hand. His name was Sproule.

Eight of them had escaped. His horse had carried off several arrows and it caved under him in the night and the others had gone on, the captain among them.

They sat side by side among the rocks and watched the day lengthen on the plain below.

Did you not save any of your possibles? Sproule said.

The kid spat and shook his head. He looked at Sproule.

How bad is your arm?

He pulled it to him. I've seen worse, he said.

They sat looking out over those reaches of sand and rock and wind.

What kind of indians was them?

I dont know.

Sproule coughed deeply into his fist. He pulled his bloody arm against him. Damn if they aint about a caution to the christians, he said.

They laid up in the shade of a rock shelf until past noon, scratching out a place in the gray lava dust to sleep, and they set forth in the afternoon down the valley following the war trail and they were very small and they moved very slowly in the immensity of that landscape.

Come evening they hove toward the rimrock again and Sproule pointed out a dark stain on the face of the barren cliff. It looked like the black from old fires. The kid shielded his eyes. The scalloped canyon walls rippled in the heat like drapery folds.

It might could be a seep, said Sproule.

It's a long ways up there.

Well if you see any water closer let's make for that.

The kid looked at him and they set off.

The site lay up a draw and their way was a jumble of fallen rock and scoria and deadlylooking bayonet plants. Small black and olivecolored shrubs blasted under the sun. They stumbled up the cracked clay floor of a dry watercourse. They rested and moved on.

The seep lay high up among the ledges, vadose water dripping down the slick black rock and monkeyflower and deathcamas hanging in a small and perilous garden. The water that reached the canyon floor was no more than a trickle and they leaned by turns with pursed lips to the stone like devouts at a shrine.

They passed the night in a shallow cave above this spot, an old reliquary of flintknappings and ratchel scattered about on the stone floor with beads of shell and polished bone and the charcoal of ancient fires. They shared the blanket in the cold and Sproule coughed quietly in the dark and they rose from time to time to descend and drink at the stone. They were gone before sunrise and the dawn found them on the plain again.

They followed the trampled ground left by the warparty and in the afternoon they came upon a mule that had failed and been lanced and left dead and then they came upon another. The way narrowed through rocks and by and by they came to a bush that was hung with dead babies.

They stopped side by side, reeling in the heat. These small victims, seven, eight of them, had holes punched in their underjaws and were hung so by their throats from the broken stobs of a mesquite to stare eyeless at the naked sky. Bald and pale and bloated, larval to some unreckonable being. The castaways hobbled past, they looked back. Nothing moved. In the afternoon they came upon a village on the plain where smoke still rose from the ruins and all were gone to death. From a distance it looked like a decaying brick kiln. They stood without the walls a long time listening to the silence before they entered.

They went slowly through the little mud streets. There were goats and sheep slain in their pens and pigs dead in the mud. They passed mud hovels where people lay murdered in all attitudes of death in the doorways and the floors, naked and swollen and strange. They found plates of food half eaten and a cat came out and sat in the sun and watched them without interest and flies snarled everywhere in the still hot air.

At the end of the street they came to a plaza with benches and trees where vultures huddled in foul black rookeries. A dead horse lay in the square and some chickens were pecking in a patch of spilled meal in a doorway. Charred poles lay smoldering where the roofs had fallen through and a burro was standing in the open door of the church.

They sat on a bench and Sproule held his wounded arm to his chest and rocked back and forth and blinked in the sun.

What do you want to do? said the kid.

Get a drink of water.

Other than that.

I dont know.

You want to try and head back?

To Texas?

I dont know where else.

We'd never make it.

Well you say.

I aint got no say.

He was coughing again. He held his chest with his good hand and sat as if he'd get his breath.

What have you got, a cold?

I got consumption.

Consumption?

He nodded. I come out here for my health.

The kid looked at him. He shook his head and rose and walked off across the plaza toward the church. There were buzzards squatting among the old carved wooden corbels and he picked up a stone and squailed it at them but they never moved.

The shadows had grown long in the plaza and little coils of

dust were moving in the parched clay streets. The carrion birds sat about the topmost corners of the houses with their wings outstretched in attitudes of exhortation like dark little bishops. The kid returned to the bench and propped up one foot and leaned on his knee. Sproule sat as before, still holding his arm.

Son of a bitch is dealin me misery, he said.

The kid spat and looked off down the street. We better just hold up here for tonight.

You reckon it would be all right?

Who with?

What if them indians was to come back?

What would they come back for?

Well what if they was to?

They wont come back.

He held his arm.

I wish you had a knife on you, the kid said.

I wish you did.

There's meat here if a man had a knife.

I aint hungry.

I think we ought to scout these houses and see what all's here.

You go on.

We need to find us a place to sleep.

Sproule looked at him. I dont need to go nowheres, he said.

Well. You suit yourself.

Sproule coughed and spat. I aim to, he said.

The kid turned and went on down the street.

The doorways were low and he had to stoop to clear the lintel beams, stepping down into the cool and earthy rooms. There was no furniture save pallets for sleeping, perhaps a wooden mealbin. He went from house to house. In one room the bones of a small loom black and smoldering. In another a man, the charred flesh drawn taut, the eyes cooked in their sockets. There was a niche in the mud wall with figures of saints dressed in doll's clothes, the rude wooden faces brightly painted. Illustrations cut from an old journal and pasted to the wall, a small picture of a queen, a gypsy card that was the four of cups. There were strings of dried peppers and a few gourds. A glass bottle that held weeds. Outside a bare dirt yard fenced with ocotillo and a round clay oven caved through where black curd trembled in the light within.

He found a clay jar of beans and some dry tortillas and he took them to a house at the end of the street where the embers of the roof were still smoldering and he warmed the food in the ashes and ate, squatting there like some deserter scavenging the ruins of a city he'd fled.

When he returned to the square Sproule was gone. All about lay in shadow. He crossed the square and mounted the stone steps to the door of the church and entered. Sproule was standing in the vestibule. Long buttresses of light fell from the high windows in the western wall. There were no pews in the church and the stone floor was heaped with the scalped and naked and partly eaten bodies of some forty souls who'd barricaded themselves in this house of God against the heathen. The savages had hacked holes in the roof and shot them down from above and the floor was littered with arrowshafts where they'd snapped them off to get the clothes from the bodies. The altars had been hauled down and the tabernacle looted and the great sleeping God of the Mexicans routed from his golden cup. The primitive painted saints in their frames hung cocked on the walls as if an earthquake had visited and a dead Christ in a glass bier lay broken in the chancel floor.

The murdered lay in a great pool of their communal blood. It had set up into a sort of pudding crossed everywhere with the tracks of wolves or dogs and along the edges it had dried and cracked into a burgundy ceramic. Blood lay in dark tongues on the floor and blood grouted the flagstones and ran in the vestibule where the stones were cupped from the feet of the faithful and their fathers before them and it had threaded its way down the steps and dripped from the stones among the dark red tracks of the scavengers.

Sproule turned and looked at the kid as if he'd know his thoughts but the kid just shook his head. Flies clambered over the peeled and wigless skulls of the dead and flies walked on their shrunken eyeballs.

Come on, said the kid.

They crossed the square in the last of the light and went down the narrow street. In the doorway there lay a dead child with two buzzards sitting on it. Sproule shooed his good hand at the buzzards and they bated and hissed and flapped clumsily but they did not fly.

They set forth in the morning with first light while wolves slank from the doorways and dissolved in the fog of the streets. They went by the southwest road the way the savages had come. A little sandy stream, cottonwoods, three white goats. They waded a ford where women lay dead at their wash.

They struggled all day across a terra damnata of smoking slag, passing from time to time the bloated shapes of dead mules or horses. By evening they had drunk all the water they carried. They slept in the sand and woke in the cool early morning dark and went on and they walked the cinderland till they were near to fainting. In the afternoon they came upon a carreta in the trace, tilted on its tongue, the great wheels cut from rounds of a cottonwood trunk and pinned to the axletrees with tenons. They crawled under it for shade and slept until dark and went on.

The rind of a moon that had been in the sky all day was gone and they followed the trail through the desert by starlight, the Pleiades straight overhead and very small and the Great Bear walking the mountains to the north.

My arm stinks, said Sproule.

What?

I said my arm stinks.

You want me to look at it?

What for? You caint do nothin for it.

Well. You suit yourself.

I aim to, said Sproule.

They went on. Twice in the night they heard the little prairie vipers rattle among the scrub and they were afraid. With the dawn they were climbing among shale and whinstone under the wall of a dark monocline where turrets stood like basalt prophets and they passed by the side of the road little wooden crosses propped in cairns of stone where travelers had met with death. The road winding up among the hills and the castaways laboring upon the switchbacks, blackening under the sun, their eyeballs inflamed and the painted spectra racing out at the corners. Climbing up through ocotillo and pricklypear where the rocks trembled and sleared in the sun, rock and no water and the sandy trace and they kept watch for any green thing that might tell of water but there was no water. The ate piñole from a bag with their fingers and went on. Through the noon heat and into the dusk where lizards lay with their leather chins flat to the cooling rocks and fended off the world with thin smiles and eyes like cracked stone plates.

They crested the mountain at sunset and they could see for miles. An immense lake lay below them with the distant blue mountains standing in the windless span of water and the shape of a soaring hawk and trees that shimmered in the heat and a distant city very white against the blue and shaded hills. They sat and watched. They saw the sun drop under the jagged rim of the earth to the west and they saw it flare behind the mountains and they saw the face of the lake darken and the shape of the city dissolve upon it. They slept among the rocks face up like dead men and in the morning when they rose there was no city and no trees and no lake only a barren dusty plain.

Sproule groaned and collapsed back among the rocks. The kid looked at him. There were blisters along his lower lip and his arm through the ripped shirt was swollen and something foul had seeped through among the darker bloodstains. He turned back and looked out over the valley.

Yonder comes somebody, he said.

Sproule didnt answer. The kid looked at him. I aint lyin, he said.

Indians, said Sproule. Aint it?

I dont know. Too far to tell.

What do you aim to do?

I dont know.

What happened to the lake?

I couldnt tell ye.

We both saw it.

People see what they want to see.

Then how come I aint seein it now? I sure as hell want to.

The kid looked out over the plain below.

What if it's indians? said Sproule.

Likely it will be.

Where can we hide at?

The kid spat dryly and wiped his mouth with the back of his hand. A lizard came out from under a rock and crouched on its small cocked elbows over that piece of froth and drank it dry and returned to the rock again leaving only a faint spot in the sand which vanished almost instantly.

They waited all day. The kid made sorties down into the canyons in search of water but he found none. Nothing moved in that purgatorial waste save carnivorous birds. By early afternoon they could see the horsemen on the switchbacks coming up the face of the mountain below them. They were Mexicans.

Sproule was sitting with his legs outstretched before him. I was worried about my old boots lastin me, he said. He looked up. Go on, he said. Save yourself. He waved his hand.

They were laid up under a ledge of rock in a narrow shade. The kid didnt answer. Within the hour they could hear the dry scrabble of hooves among the rocks and the clank of gear. The first horse to round the point of rock and pass through the gap in the mountain was the captain's big bay and he carried the captain's saddle but he did not carry the captain. The refugees stood by the side of the road. The riders looked burnt and haggard coming up out of the sun and they sat their horses as if they had no weight at all. There were seven of them, eight of them. They wore broadbrimmed hats and leather vests and they carried escopetas across the pommels of their saddles and as they rode past the leader nodded gravely to them from the captain's horse and touched his hatbrim and they rode on.

Sproule and the kid looked after them. The kid called out and Sproule had started to trot clumsily along behind the horses.

The riders began to slump and reel like drunks. Their heads lolled. Their guffaws echoed among the rocks and they turned their mounts and sat them and regarded the wanderers with huge grins.

Qué quiere? cried the leader.

The riders cackled and slapped at one another. They had nudged their horses forward and they began to ride them about without aim. The leader turned to the two afoot.

Buscan a los indios?

With this some of the men dismounted and fell to hugging one another and weeping shamelessly. The leader looked at them and grinned, his teeth white and massive, made for foraging.

Loonies, said Sproule. They're loonies.

The kid looked up at the leader. How about a drink of water? he said.

The leader sobered, he pulled a long face. Water? he said.

We aint got no water, said Sproule.

But my friend, how no? Is very dry here.

He reached behind him without turning and a leather canteen was passed across the riders to his hand. He shook it and offered it down. The kid pulled the stopper and drank and stood panting and drank again. The leader reached down and tapped the canteen. Basta, he said.

He hung on gulping. He could not see the horseman's face darken. The man shucked one boot backward out of the stirrup and kicked the canteen cleanly from between the kid's hands leaving him there for a moment in a frozen gesture of calling with the canteen rising and turning in the air and the lobes of water gleaming about it in the sun before it clattered to the rocks. Sproule scrambled after it and snatched it up where it lay draining and began to drink, watching over the rim. The horseman and the kid watched each other. Sproule sat back gasping and coughing.

The kid stepped across the rocks and took the canteen from him. The leader kneed his horse forward and drew a sword from its place beneath his leg and leaning forward ran the blade under the strap and raised it up. The point of the blade was about three inches from the kid's face and the canteen strap was draped across the flat of it. The kid had stopped and the rider raised the canteen gently from his hands and let it slide down the blade and come to rest at his side. He turned to the men and smiled and they once again began to hoot and to pummel one another like apes.

He swung the stopper up from where it hung by a thong and drove it home with the heel of his hand. He pitched the canteen to the man behind him and looked down at the travelers. Why you no hide? he said.

From you?

From I.

We were thirsty.

Very thirsty. Eh?

They didnt answer. He was tapping the flat of the sword lightly against the horn of his saddle and he seemed to be forming words in his mind. He leaned slightly to them. When the lambs is lost in the mountain, he said. They is cry. Sometime come the mother. Sometime the wolf. He smiled at them and raised the sword and ran it back where it had come from and turned the horse smartly and trotted it through the horses behind him and the men mounted up and followed and soon all were gone.

Sproule sat without moving. The kid looked at him but he would look away. He was wounded in an enemy country far from home and although his eyes took in the alien stones about yet the greater void beyond seemed to swallow up his soul.

They descended the mountain, going down over the rocks with their hands outheld before them and their shadows contorted on the broken terrain like creatures seeking their own forms. They reached the valley floor at dusk and set off across the blue and cooling land, the mountains to the west a line of jagged slate set endwise in the earth and the dry weeds heeling and twisting in a wind sprung from nowhere.

They walked on into the dark and they slept like dogs in the sand and had been sleeping so when something black flapped up out of the night ground and perched on Sproule's chest. Fine fingerbones stayed the leather wings with which it steadied as it walked upon him. A wrinkled pug face, small and vicious, bare lips crimped in a horrible smile and teeth pale blue in the starlight. It leaned to him. It crafted in his neck two narrow grooves and folding its wings over him it began to drink his blood.

Not soft enough. He woke, put up a hand. He shrieked and the bloodbat flailed and sat back upon his chest and righted itself again and hissed and clicked its teeth.

The kid was up and had seized a rock but the bat sprang away and vanished in the dark. Sproule was clawing at his neck and he was gibbering hysterically and when he saw the kid standing there looking down at him he held out to him his bloodied hands as if in accusation and then clapped them to his ears and cried out what it seemed he himself would not hear, a howl of such outrage as to stitch a caesura in the pulsebeat of the world. But the kid only spat into the darkness of the space between them. I know your kind, he said. What's wrong with you is wrong all the way through you.

───────◆◆◆───────

In the morning they crossed a dry wash and the kid hiked up it looking for a tank or a hole but there was none. He picked out a sink in the wash and fell to digging with a bone and after he had dug some two feet into the sand the sand turned damp and then a little more and a slow seep of water began to fill into the furrows he dredged with his fingers. He took off his shirt and pushed it down into the sand and watched it darken and he watched the water rise slowly among the folds of cloth until there was perhaps a cupful and then he lowered his head into the excavation and drank. Then he sat and watched it fill again. He did this for over an hour. Then he put on the shirt and went back down the wash.

Sproule didnt want to take off his shirt. He tried sucking up the water and he got a mouthful of sand.

Why dont you let me use your shirt, he said.

The kid was squatting in the dry gravel of the wash. Suck on ye own shirt, he said.

He took off the shirt. It stuck to the skin and a yellow pus ran. His arm was swollen to the size of his thigh and it was garishly discolored and small worms worked in the open wound. He pushed the shirt down into the hole and leaned and drank.

In the afternoon they came to a crossroads, what else to call it. A faint wagon trace that came from the north and crossed their path and went on to the south. They stood scanning the landscape for some guidance in that emptiness. Sproule sat where the tracks crossed and looked out from the great caves in his skull where his eyes lay. He said that he would not rise.

Yonder's a lake, said the kid.

He would not look.

It lay shimmering in the distance. Its edges rimed with salt. The kid studied it and studied the roads. After a while he nodded toward the south. I believe this here is the most traveled.

It's all right, said Sproule. You go on.

You suit yourself.

Sproule watched him set off. After a while he rose and followed.

They had gone perhaps two miles when they stopped to rest, Sproule sitting with his legs out and his hands in his lap and the kid squatting a little ways from him. Blinking and bearded and filthy in their rags.

Does that sound like thunder to you? said Sproule.

The kid raised his head.

Listen.

The kid looked at the sky, pale blue, unmarked save where the sun burned like a white hole.

I can feel it in the ground, said Sproule.

It aint nothin.

Listen.

The kid rose and looked about. To the north a small movement of dust. He watched it. It did not rise nor did it blow away.

It was a carreta, lumbering clumsily over the plain, a small mule to draw it. The driver may have been asleep. When he saw the fugitives in the trace before him he halted the mule and began to saw it around to go back and he did get it turned but by then the kid had seized the raw leather headstall and hauled the animal to a standstill. Sproule came hobbling up. From the rear of the wagon two children peered out. They were so pale with dust, their hair so white and faces pinched, they looked like little gnomes crouched there. At the sight of the kid before him the driver shrank back and the woman next to him set up a high shrill chittering and began to point from one horizon to the other but he pulled himself up into the bed of the cart and Sproule came dragging after and they lay staring up at the hot canvas tarp while the two waifs drew back into the corner and watched blackeyed as woodmice and the cart turned south again and set off with a rising rumble and clatter.

There was a clay jar of water hung by a thong from the bowstay and the kid took it down and drank from it and gave it to Sproule. Then he took it back and drank the rest. They lay in the floor of the cart among old hides and spills of salt and after a while they slept.

It was dark when they entered the town. The jostle of the cart ceasing was what woke them. The kid raised himself up and looked out. Starlight in a mud street. The wagon empty. The mule wheezed and stamped in the traces. After a while the man came from the shadows and led them along a lane into a yard and he backed the mule until the cart was alongside a wall and then he unhitched the mule and led it away.

He lay back in the tilted cartbed. It was cold in the night and he lay with his knees drawn up under a piece of hide that smelled of mold and urine and he slept and woke all night and all night dogs barked and in the dawn cocks called and he heard horses on the road.

In the first gray light flies began to land on him. They touched his face and woke him and he brushed them away. After a while he sat up.

They were in a barren mudwalled courtyard and there was a

house made of reeds and clay. Chickens stepped about and
clucked and scratched. A small boy came from the house and
pulled down his pants and shat in the yard and rose and went
in again. The kid looked at Sproule. He was lying with his face
to the wagonboards. He was partly covered with his blanket
and flies were crawling on him. The kid reached to shake him.
He was cold and wooden. The flies rose, then they settled back.

The kid was standing by the cart pissing when the soldiers
rode into the yard. They seized him and tied his hands behind
him and they looked in the cart and talked among themselves
and then they led him out into the street.

He was taken to an adobe building and put in an empty
room. He sat in the floor while a wild-eyed boy with an old
musket watched him. After a while they came and took him out
again.

They led him through the narrow mud streets and he could
hear music like a fanfare growing the louder. First children
walked with him and then old folk and finally a throng of brown-
skinned villagers all dressed in white cotton like attendants in an
institution, the women in dark rebozos, some with their breasts
exposed, their faces stained red with almagre, smoking small
cigars. Their numbers swelled and the guards with their
shouldered fusils frowned and shouted at the jostlers and they
went on along the tall adobe wall of a church and into the
plaza.

There was a bazaar in progress. A traveling medicine show,
a primitive circus. They passed stout willow cages clogged with
vipers, with great limegreen serpents from some more southerly
latitude or beaded lizards with their black mouths wet with
venom. A reedy old leper held up handfuls of tapeworms from
a jar for all to see and cried out his medicines against them and
they were pressed about by other rude apothecaries and by
vendors and mendicants until all came at last before a trestle
whereon stood a glass carboy of clear mescal. In this container
with hair afloat and eyes turned upward in a pale face sat a
human head.

They dragged him forward with shouts and gestures. Mire, mire, they cried. He stood before the jar and they urged his consideration of it and they tilted it around so that the head should face him. It was Captain White. Lately at war among the heathen. The kid looked into the drowned and sightless eyes of his old commander. He looked about at the villagers and at the soldiers, their eyes all upon him, and he spat and wiped his mouth. He aint no kin to me, he said.

———————◆•◆———————

They put him in an old stone corral with three other ragged refugees from the expedition. They sat stunned and blinking against the wall or roved the perimeter around in the dry tracks of mules and horses and retched and shat while small boys hooted from the parapet.

He fell in with a thin boy from Georgia. I was sickern a dog, the boy said. I was afraid I was goin to die and then I was afraid I wasnt.

I seen a rider on the captain's horse up in the country from here, the kid told him.

Aye, said the Georgian. They killed him and Clark and another boy I never did know his name. We come on into town and the very next day they had us in the calabozo and this selfsame son of a bitch is down there with the guards laughin and drinkin and playin cards, him and the jefe, to see who gets the captain's horse and who gets his pistols. I guess you seen the captain's head.

I seen it.

That's the worst thing I ever seen in my life.

Somebody ought to of pickled it a long time ago. By rights they ought to pickle mine. For ever takin up with such a fool.

They drifted as the day advanced from wall to wall to keep out of the sun. The boy from Georgia told him of his comrades displayed on slabs cold and dead in the market. The captain headless in a wallow half eaten by hogs. He ran his heel out in the dust and gouged a little place for it to rest. They fixin to send us to Chihuahua City, he said.

How do you know?

That's what they say. I dont know.

That's what who says?

Shipman yonder. He speaks the lingo some.

The kid regarded the man spoken of. He shook his head and spat dryly.

All day small boys perched on the walls and watched them by shifts and pointed and jabbered. They'd walk around the parapet and try to piss down on sleepers in the shade but the prisoners kept alert. Some at first threw stones but the kid picked one from the dust the size of an egg and with it dropped a small child cleanly from the wall with no sound other than the muted thud of its landing on the far side.

Now you gone and done it, said the Georgian.

The kid looked at him.

They'll be in here with whips and I dont know what all.

The kid spat. They aint about to come in here and eat no whips.

Nor did they. A woman brought them bowls of beans and charred tortillas on a plate of unfired clay. She looked harried and she smiled at them and she had smuggled them sweets under her shawl and there were pieces of meat in the bottom of the bowls that had come from her own table.

Three days later mounted on little malandered mules they set out for the capital as foretold.

<hr>

They rode five days through desert and mountain and through dusty pueblos where the populace turned out to see them. Their escorts in varied suits of timeworn finery, the prisoners in rags. They'd been given blankets and squatting by the desert fires at night sunblackened and bony and wrapped in these serapes they looked like God's profoundest peons. The soldiers none spoke english and they directed their charges with grunts or gestures. They were indifferently armed and they were much afraid of the indians. They rolled their tobacco in cornhusks and they sat by the fire in silence and listened to the night. Their talk when they talked was of witches or worse and always they sought to parcel from the darkness some voice or cry from among the cries that was no right beast. La gente dice que el coyote es un brujo. Muchas veces el brujo es un coyote.

Y los indios también. Muchas veces llaman como los coyotes.

Y qué es eso?

Nada.

Un tecolote. Nada mas.

Quizás.

When they rode through the gap in the mountains and looked down on the city the sergeant of the expedition halted the horses and spoke to the man behind him and he in turn dismounted and took rawhide thongs from his saddlebag and approached the prisoners and gestured for them to cross their wrists and hold them out, showing how with his own hands. He tied them each in this manner and then they rode on.

They entered the city in a gantlet of flung offal, driven like cattle through the cobbled streets with shouts going up behind for the soldiery who smiled as became them and nodded among the flowers and proffered cups, herding the tattered fortune-seekers through the plaza where water splashed in a fountain and idlers reclined on carven seats of white porphyry and past the governor's palace and past the cathedral where vultures squatted along the dusty entablatures and among the niches in the carved facade hard by the figures of Christ and the apostles, the birds holding out their own dark vestments in postures of strange benevolence while about them flapped on the wind the dried scalps of slaughtered indians strung on cords, the long dull hair swinging like the filaments of certain seaforms and the dry hides clapping against the stones.

They passed old alms-seekers by the church door with their seamy palms outheld and maimed beggars sad-eyed in rags and children asleep in the shadows with flies walking their dreamless faces. Dark coppers in a clackdish, the shriveled eyes of the blind. Scribes crouched by the steps with their quills and inkpots and bowls of sand and lepers moaning through the streets and naked dogs that seemed composed of bone entirely and vendors of tamales and old women with faces dark and harrowed as the land squatting in the gutters over charcoal fires where blackened strips of anonymous meat sizzled and spat. Small orphans were abroad like irate dwarfs and fools and sots drooling and flailing about in the small markets of the metropolis and the prisoners rode past the carnage in the meatstalls and the waxy smell where racks of guts hung black with flies and flayings of meat in great red sheets now darkened with the advancing day and the flensed and naked skulls of cows and sheep with their dull blue eyes glaring wildly and the stiff bodies of deer and javelina and ducks and quail and parrots, all wild things from the country round hanging head downward from hooks.

They were made to dismount and were driven afoot through the crowds and down old stone steps and over a doorsill worn like soap and through an iron sallygate into a cool stone cellar long a prison to take their place among the ghosts of old martyrs and patriots while the gate clanked shut behind them.

When their eyes lost their blindness they could make out figures crouched along the wall. Stirrings in beds of hay like nesting mice disturbed. A light snoring. Outside the rattle of a cart and the dull clop of hooves in the street and through the stones a dim clank of hammers from a smith's shop in another part of the dungeon. The kid looked about. Blackened bits of candlewick lay here and there in pools of dirty grease on the stone floor and strings of dried spittle hung from the walls. A few names scratched where the light could find them out. He squatted and rubbed his eyes. Someone in underwear crossed before him to a pail in the center of the room and stood and pissed. This man then turned and came his way. He was tall and wore his hair to his shoulders. He shuffled through the straw and stood looking down at him. You dont know me, do ye? he said.

The kid spat and squinted up at him. I know ye, he said. I'd know your hide in a tanyard.

VI

In the streets – Brassteeth – Los heréticos –
A veteran of the late war – Mier – Doniphan – The Lipan burial –
Goldseekers – The scalphunters – The judge – Freed from the prison –
Et de ceo se mettent en le pays.

With daylight men rose from the hay and crouched on their haunches and regarded the new arrivals without curiosity. They were half naked and they sucked their teeth and snuffled and stirred and picked at themselves like apes. A chary light had washed a high small window from the dark and an early streetvendor'd begun to cry his wares.

Their morning feed was bowls of cold piñole and they were fitted with chains and routed out into the streets clanking and stinking. Overseen all day by a goldtoothed pervert who carried a plaited rawhide quirt and harried them down the gutters on their knees gathering up the filth. Under the wheels of vending-carts, the legs of beggars, dragging behind them their sacks of refuse. In the afternoon they sat in the shade of a wall and ate their dinner and watched two dogs hung together in the street sidle and step.

How do you like city life? said Toadvine.

I dont like it worth a damn so far.

I keep waitin for it to take with me but it aint done it.

They watched the overseer covertly as he passed, his hands clasped behind his back, his cap cocked over one eye. The kid spat.

I seen him first, said Toadvine.

Seen who first.

You know who. Old Brassteeth yonder.

The kid looked after the sauntering figure.

My biggest worry is that somethin will happen to him. I pray daily for the Lord to watch over him.

How you think you goin to get out of this jackpot that you're in?

We'll get out. It aint like the cárcel.

What's the cárcel?

State penitentiary. There's old pilgrims in there come down the trail back in the twenties.

The kid watched the dogs.

After a while the guard came back along the wall kicking the feet of any who were sleeping. The younger guard carried his escopeta at the ready as if there might be some fabled uprising among these chained and tattered felons. Vamonos, vamonos, he called. The prisoners rose and shuffled out into the sun. A small bell was ringing and a coach was coming up the street. They stood along the curb and took off their hats. The guidon passed ringing the bell and then the coach. It had an eye painted on the side and four mules to draw it, taking the host to some soul. A fat priest tottered after carrying an image. The guards were going among the prisoners snatching the hats from the heads of the newcomers and pressing them into their infidel hands.

When the coach had passed they donned their hats again and moved on. The dogs stood tail to tail. Two other dogs sat a little apart, squatting loosely in their skins, just frames of dogs in napless hides watching the coupled dogs and then watching the prisoners clanking away up the street. All lightly shimmering in the heat, these lifeforms, like wonders much reduced. Rough likenesses thrown up at hearsay after the things themselves had faded in men's minds.

———————◆•◆———————

He'd taken up a pallet between Toadvine and another Kentuckian, a veteran of the war. This man had returned to claim some darkeyed love he'd left behind two years before when Doniphan's command pulled east for Saltillo and the officers had had to drive back hundreds of young girls dressed as boys that took the road behind the army. Now he would stand in the street solitary in his chains and strangely unassuming, gazing out across the tops of the heads of the townspeople, and at night he'd tell them of his years in the west, an amiable warrior, a reticent man. He'd been at Mier where they fought until the draintiles and the gutters and the spouts from the azoteas ran with blood by the gallon and he told them how the brittle old spanish bells would explode when hit and how he sat against a wall with his shattered leg stretched out on the cobbles before him listening to a lull in the firing that grew into a strange silence and in this silence there grew a low rumbling that he took for thunder until a cannonball came around the corner trundling over the stones like a wayward bowl and went past and down the street and disappeared from sight. He told how they'd taken the city of Chihuahua, an army of irregulars that fought in rags and underwear and how the cannonballs were solid copper and came loping through the grass like runaway suns and even the horses learned to sidestep or straddle them and how the dames of the city rode up into the hills in buggies and picnicked and watched the battle and how at night as they sat by the fires they could hear the moans of the dying out on the plain and see by its lantern the deadcart moving among them like a hearse from limbo.

They had gravel enough, said the veteran, but they didnt know how to fight. They'd stick. You heard stories about how they found em chained to the trailspades of their pieces, limberteams and all, but if they was I never seen it. We picked powder

76

in the locks yonder. Blowed them gates open. People in here looked like skinned rats. Whitest Mexicans you'll ever see. Thowed theirselves down and commenced kissin our feet and such. Old Bill, he just turned em all loose. Hell, he didnt know what they'd done. Just told em not to steal nothin. Of course they stole everthing they could get their hands on. Whipped two of em and they both died of it and the very next day another bunch run off with some mules and Bill just flat out hung them fools. Which they did likewise perish of. But I never reckoned I'd be in here my own self.

They were squatting crosslegged by candlelight eating from clay bowls with their fingers. The kid looked up. He poked at the bowl.

What is this? he said.

That's prime bullmeat, son. From the corrida. You'll get it of a Sunday night.

You best keep chewin. Dont let it feel ye to weaken.

He chewed. He chewed and he told them of the encounter with the Comanche and they chewed and listened and nodded.

I'm proud I missed that dance, said the veteran. Them is some cruel sons of bitches. I know of one old boy up on the Llano near the dutch settlements, they caught him, took his horse and all. Left him to walk it. He come crawlin into Fredericksburg on his hands and knees buck naked about six days later and you know what they'd done? Cut the bottoms of his feet off.

Toadvine shook his head. He gestured toward the veteran. Grannyrat here knows em, he told the kid. Fought em. Aint ye, Granny?

The veteran waved his hand. Shot some stealin horses is all. Down towards Saltillo. Wasnt nothin to it. There was a cave down there had been a Lipan burial. Must of been a thousand indians in there all settin around. Had on their best robes and blankets and all. Had their bows and their knives, whatever. Beads. The Mexicans carried everthing off. Stripped em naked. Took it all. They carried off whole indians to their homes and set em in the corner all dressed up but they begun to come apart when they got out of that cave air and they had to be thowed out. Towards the last of it they was some Americans went in there and scalped what was left of em and tried to sell the scalps in Durango. I dont know if they had any luck about it or not. I expect some of them injins had been dead a hundred year.

Toadvine was toweling up grease from his bowl with a folded tortilla. He squinted at the kid in the candlelight. What do you reckon we could get for old Brassteeth's teeth? he said.

———————◆•◆———————

They saw patched argonauts from the states driving mules through the streets on their way south through the mountains to the coast. Goldseekers. Itinerant degenerates bleeding westward like some heliotropic plague. They nodded or spoke to the prisoners and dropped tobacco and coins in the street beside them.

They saw blackeyed young girls with painted faces smoking little cigars, going arm in arm and eyeing them brazenly. They saw the governor himself erect and formal within his silkmullioned sulky clatter forth from the double doors of the palace courtyard and they saw one day a pack of viciouslooking humans mounted on unshod indian ponies riding half drunk through the streets, bearded, barbarous, clad in the skins of animals stitched up with thews and armed with weapons of every description, revolvers of enormous weight and bowieknives the size of claymores and short twobarreled rifles with bores you could stick your thumbs in and the trappings of their horses fashioned out of human skin and their bridles woven up from human hair and decorated with human teeth and the riders wearing scapulars or necklaces of dried and blackened human ears and the horses rawlooking and wild in the eye and their teeth bared like feral dogs and riding also in the company a number of halfnaked savages reeling in the saddle, dangerous, filthy, brutal, the whole like a visitation from some heathen land where they and others like them fed on human flesh.

Foremost among them, outsized and childlike with his naked face, rode the judge. His cheeks were ruddy and he was smiling and bowing to the ladies and doffing his filthy hat. The enormous dome of his head when he bared it was blinding white and perfectly circumscribed about so that it looked to have been painted. He and the reeking horde of rabble with him passed on through the stunned streets and hove up before the governor's palace where their leader, a small blackhaired man, clapped for entrance by kicking at the oaken doors with his boot. The doors were opened forthwith and they rode in, rode in all, and the doors were closed again.

Gentlemens, said Toadvine, I'll guarangoddamntee ye I know what that there is about.

The following day the judge in the company of others stood in the street smoking a cigar and rocking back on his heels. He wore a pair of good kidskin boots and he was studying the prisoners where they knelt in the gutter clutching up the filth with their bare hands. The kid was watching the judge. When the judge's eyes fell upon him he took the cigar from between his teeth and smiled. Or he seemed to smile. Then he put the cigar between his teeth again.

That night Toadvine called them together and they crouched by the wall and spoke in whispers.

His name is Glanton, said Toadvine. He's got a contract with Trias. They're to pay him a hundred dollars a head for scalps and a thousand for Gómez's head. I told him there was three of us. Gentlemens, we're gettin out of this shithole.

We aint got no outfits.

He knows that. He said he'd find anybody that was a guaranteed hand and take it out of their shares. So dont let on like you aint no seasoned indiankiller cause I claimed we was three of the best.

Three days later they rode out singlefile through the streets with the governor and his party, the governor on a pale gray stallion and the killers on their small warponies, smiling and bowing and the lovely darkskinned girls throwing flowers from the windows and some blowing kisses and small boys running alongside and old men waving their hats and crying out huzzahs and Toadvine and the kid and the veteran bringing up the rear, the veteran's feet tucked into tapaderos slung nearly to the ground, so long were his legs, so short the horse's. Out to the edge of the city by the old stone aqueduct where the governor gave them his blessing and drank their health and their fortune in a simple ceremonial and they took the road upcountry.

VII

Black and white Jacksons – A meeting on the outskirts –
Whitneyville Colts – A trial – The judge among disputants –
Delaware indians – The Vandiemenlander – A hacienda –
The town of Corralitos – Pasajeros de un país antiguo – Scene of
a massacre – Hiccius Doccius – A naming of fortunes –
Wheelless upon a dark river – The felon wind – Tertium quid –
The town of Janos – Glanton takes a scalp –
Jackson takes the stage.

In this company there rode two men named Jackson, one
black, one white, both forenamed John. Bad blood lay between them and as they rode up under the barren mountains
the white man would fall back alongside the other and take his
shadow for the shade that was in it and whisper to him. The
black would check or start his horse to shake him off. As if the
white man were in violation of his person, had stumbled onto
some ritual dormant in his dark blood or his dark soul whereby
the shape he stood the sun from on that rocky ground bore
something of the man himself and in so doing lay imperiled. The
white man laughed and crooned things to him that sounded like
the words of love. All watched to see how this would go with
them but none would caution either back from his course and
when Glanton looked to the rear along the column from time to
time he seemed to simply reckon them among his number and
ride on.

Earlier that morning the company had met in a courtyard behind a house on the outskirts of the city. Two men carried from

a wagon a stenciled ordnance box from the Baton Rouge arsenal and a Prussian jew named Speyer pried open the box with a pritchel and a shoeing hammer and handed up a flat package in brown butcherpaper translucent with grease like a paper of bakery goods. Glanton opened the package and let the paper fall to the dirt. In his hand he held a longbarreled sixshot Colt's patent revolver. It was a huge sidearm meant for dragoons and it carried in its long cylinders a rifle's charge and weighed close to five pounds loaded. These pistols would drive the half-ounce conical ball through six inches of hardwood and there were four dozen of them in the case. Speyer was breaking out the gangmolds and flasks and tools and Judge Holden was unwrapping another of the pistols. The men pressed about. Glanton wiped the bore and chambers of the piece and took the flask from Speyer.

She's a stout looker, said one.

He charged the bores and seated a bullet and drove it home with the hinged lever pinned to the underside of the barrel. When all the chambers were loaded he capped them and looked about. In that courtyard other than merchants and buyers were a number of living things. The first that Glanton drew sight upon was a cat that at that precise moment appeared upon the high wall from the other side as silently as a bird alighting. It turned to pick its way among the cusps of broken glass set upright in the mud masonry. Glanton leveled the huge pistol in one hand and thumbed back the hammer. The explosion in that dead silence was enormous. The cat simply disappeared. There was no blood or cry, it just vanished. Speyer glanced uneasily at the Mexicans. They were watching Glanton. Glanton thumbed back the hammer again and swung the pistol. A group of fowl in the corner of the courtyard that had been pecking in the dry dust stood nervously, their heads at varied angles. The pistol roared and one of the birds exploded in a cloud of feathers. The others began to trot mutely, their long necks craned. He fired again. A second bird spun and lay kicking. The others flared, piping thinly, and Glanton turned with the pistol and shot a

82

small goat that was standing with its throat pressed to the wall in terror and it fell stone dead in the dust and he fired upon a clay garraffa that burst in a shower of potsherds and water and he raised the pistol and swung toward the house and rang the bell in its mud tower above the roof, a solemn tolling that hung on in the emptiness after the echoes of the gunfire had died away.

A haze of gray gunsmoke lay over the courtyard. Glanton set the hammer at halfcock and spun the cylinder and lowered the hammer again. A woman appeared in the doorway of the house and one of the Mexicans spoke to her and she went in again.

Glanton looked at Holden and then he looked at Speyer. The jew smiled nervously.

They aint worth no fifty dollars.

Speyer looked grave. What is your life worth? he said.

In Texas five hundred but you'd have to discount the note with your ass.

Mr Riddle thinks that it's a fair price.

Mr Riddle aint payin it.

He's putting up the money.

Glanton turned the pistol in his hand and examined it.

I thought it was agreed, said Speyer.

Aint nothin agreed.

They were contracted for the war. You'll not see their like again.

Not till some money changes hands it aint agreed.

A detachment of soldiers, ten or a dozen of them, entered from the street with their arms at the ready.

Qué pasa aquí?

Glanton looked at the soldiers without interest.

Nada, said Speyer. Todo va bien.

Bien? The sergeant was looking at the dead birds, the goat.

The woman appeared at the door again.

Está bien, said Holden. Negocios del Gobernador.

The sergeant looked at them and he looked at the woman in the door.

83

Somos amigos del Señor Riddle, said Speyer.

Andale, said Clanton. You and your halfassedlookin niggers.

The sergeant stepped forward and assumed a posture of authority. Glanton spat. The judge had already crossed the space between them and now he took the sergeant aside and fell to conversing with him. The sergeant came to his armpit and the judge spoke warmly and gestured with a great expansiveness of spirit. The soldiers squatted in the dust with their muskets and regarded the judge without expression.

Dont you give that son of a bitch no money, said Glanton.

But the judge was already bringing the man forward for a formal presentation.

Le presento al sargento Aguilar, he called, hugging the ragged militant to him. The sergeant held out his hand quite gravely. It occupied that space and the attention of all who stood there like something presented for validation and then Speyer stepped forward and took it.

Mucho gusto.

Igualmente, said the sergeant.

The judge escorted him from one to the next of the company, the sergeant formal and the Americans muttering obscenities or shaking their heads silently. The soldiers squatted on their heels and watched each movement in this charade with the same dull interest and at length the judge hove up before the black.

That dark vexed face. He studied it and he drew the sergeant forward the better for him to observe and then he began a laborious introduction in spanish. He sketched for the sergeant a problematic career of the man before them, his hands drafting with a marvelous dexterity the shapes of what varied paths conspired here in the ultimate authority of the extant—as he told them—like strings drawn together through the eye of a ring. He adduced for their consideration references to the children of Ham, the lost tribes of Israelites, certain passages from the Greek poets, anthropological speculations as to the propagation of the races in their dispersion and isolation through the agency of geological cataclysm and an assessment of racial traits with respect to climatic and geographical influences. The sergeant listened to this and more with great attention and when the judge was done he stepped forward and held out his hand.

Jackson ignored him. He looked at the judge.

What did you tell him, Holden?

Dont insult him, man.

What did you tell him?

The sergeant's face had clouded. The judge took him about the shoulders and leaned and spoke into his ear and the sergeant nodded and stepped back and saluted the black.

What did you tell him, Holden?

That shaking hands was not the custom in your land.

Before that. What did you say to him before that.

The judge smiled. It is not necessary, he said, that the principals here be in possession of the facts concerning their case, for their acts will ultimately accommodate history with or without their understanding. But it is consistent with notions of right principle that these facts—to the extent that they can be readily made to do so—should find a repository in the witness of some third party. Sergeant Aguilar is just such a party and any slight to his office is but a secondary consideration when compared to divergences in that larger protocol exacted by the formal agenda of an absolute destiny. Words are things. The words he is in possession of he cannot be deprived of. Their authority transcends his ignorance of their meaning.

The black was sweating. A dark vein in his temple pulsed like a fuse. The company had listened to the judge in silence. A few smiled. A halfwitted killer from Missouri guffawed softly like an asthmatic. The judge turned again to the sergeant and they spoke together and the judge and he crossed to where the crate stood in the courtyard and the judge showed him one of the pistols and explained its workings with great patience. The sergeant's men had risen and stood waiting. At the gate the judge doled coins into Aguilar's palm and he shook hands formally with each ragged charge and complimented them upon their military bearing and they exited into the street.

At noon that day the partisans rode out each man armed with a pair of the pistols and took the road upcountry as told.

———————◆◆◆———————

The outriders returned in the evening and the men dismounted for the first time that day and recruited their horses in the sparse swale while Glanton conferred with the scouts. Then they rode on until dark and made camp. Toadvine and the veteran and the kid squatted at a small remove from the fires. They did not know that they were set forth in that company in the place of three men slain in the desert. They watched the Delawares, of whom there were a number in the party, and they too sat somewhat apart, crouched on their heels, one pounding coffeebeans in a buckskin with a rock while the others stared into the fire with eyes as black as gunbores. That night the kid would see one of them sort with his hand among the absolute embers for a right coal with which to light his pipe.

They were about in the morning before daybreak and they caught up and saddled their mounts as soon as it was light enough to see. The jagged mountains were pure blue in the dawn and everywhere birds twittered and the sun when it rose caught the moon in the west so that they lay opposed to each other across the earth, the sun whitehot and the moon a pale replica, as if they were the ends of a common bore beyond whose terminals burned worlds past all reckoning. As the riders came up through the mesquite and pyracantha singlefile in a light clank of arms and chink of bitrings the sun climbed and the moon set and the horses and the dewsoaked mules commenced to steam in flesh and in shadow.

Toadvine had fallen in with a fugitive from Vandiemen's Land named Bathcat who had come west on legbail. He was from Wales by birth and he had but three fingers to his right hand and few teeth. Perhaps he saw in Toadvine a fellow fugitive—an earless and branded felon who had chosen in life much as had he—and he offered to wager as to which Jackson would kill which.

I dont know them boys, said Toadvine.

How do ye think then?

Toadvine spat quietly to one side and looked at the man. I wouldnt want to bet, he said.

Not a gaming man?

Depends on the game.

The blackie will do for him. Take your odds.

Toadvine looked at him. The necklace of human ears he wore looked like a string of dried black figs. He was big and raw-looking and one eyelid sagged where a knife had severed the small muscles there and he was furnished with gear of every class, the fine with the shoddy. He wore good boots and he carried a handsome rifle bound with german silver but the rifle was slung in a cutoff bootleg and his shirt was in tatters and his hat rancid.

Ye've not hunted the aborigines afore, said Bathcat.

Who says it?

I know it.

Toadvine didnt answer.

You'll find em right lively.

So I hear.

The Vandiemenlander smiled. Much is changed, he said. When I first come into this country there was savages up on the San Saba had hardly seen white men. They come into our camp and we shared our mess with em and they couldnt keep their eyes off our knives. Next day they brought whole strings of horses into camp to trade. We didnt know what they wanted. They had knives of their own, such as they was. But what it was, you see, was they'd never seen sawed bones in a stew before.

Toadvine glanced at the man's forehead but the man's hat was pushed down almost to his eyes. The man smiled and forked the hat back slightly with his thumb. The print of the hatband lay on his forehead like a scar but there was no mark other. Only on the inside of his lower arm was there tattooed a number which Toadvine would see in a Chihuahua bathhouse and again when he would cut down the man's torso where it hung skewered by its heels from a treelimb in the wastes of Pimeria Alta in the fall of that year.

They rode up through cholla and nopal, a dwarf forest of spined things, through a stone gap in the mountains and down among blooming artemisia and aloe. They crossed a broad plain of desert grass dotted with palmilla. On the slopes were gray stone walls that followed the ridgelines down to where they lay broached and tumbled upon the plain. They did not noon nor did they siesta and the cotton eye of the moon squatted at broad day in the throat of the mountains to the east and they were still riding when it overtook them at its midnight meridian, sketching on the plain below a blue cameo of such dread pilgrims clanking north.

They spent the night in the corral of a hacienda where all night men kept watchfires burning on the azoteas or roofs. Two weeks before this a party of campesinos had been hacked to death with their own hoes and partly eaten by hogs while the Apaches rounded up what stock would drive and disappeared into the hills. Glanton ordered a goat killed and this was done in the corral while the horses shied and trembled and in the flaring light of the fires the men squatted and roasted the meat and ate it with knives and wiped their fingers in their hair and turned in to sleep upon the beaten clay.

At dusk of the third day they rode into the town of Corralitos, the horses shuffling through the caked ash and the sun glaring redly through the smoke. The smelter chimneys were ranged against an ashen sky and the globy lights of the furnaces glowered under the dark of the hills. It had rained in the day and the windowlights of the low mud houses were reflected in pools along the flooded road out of which great dripping swine rose moaning before the advancing horses like oafish demons routed from a fen. The houses were loopholed and parapeted and the air was filled with the fumes of arsenic. The people had turned out to see the Texans, they called them, standing solemnly along the way and noting the least of their gestures with looks of awe, looks of wonder.

They camped in the plaza, blackening the cottonwoods with their fires and driving forth the sleeping birds, the flames lighting up the wretched town to its darkest pens and bringing forth even the blind tottering with their hands outstretched toward that conjectural day. Glanton and the judge with the Brown brothers rode out to the hacienda of General Zuloaga where they were received and given their dinner and the night passed without incident.

In the morning when they had saddled their mounts and were assembled in the square to ride out they were approached by a family of itinerant magicians seeking safe passage up-country as far as Janos. Glanton looked down at them from his place at the head of the column. Their goods were piled up in tattered panniers lashed to the backs of three burros and they were a man and his wife and a grown boy and a girl. They were dressed in fools costumes with stars and halfmoons embroidered on and the once gaudy colors were faded and pale from the dust of the road and they looked a set of right wanderfolk cast on this evil terrain. The old man came forward and took the bridle of Glanton's horse.

Get your hands off the horse, said Glanton.

He spoke no english but he did as he was told. He commenced to put forth his case. He gestured, he pointed back toward the others. Glanton watched him, who knows if he heard at all. He turned and looked at the boy and at the two women and he looked down at the man again.

What are you? he said.

The man held his ear toward Glanton and looked up with mouth agape.

I said what are you? Are you a show?

He looked back toward the others.

A show, said Glanton. Bufones.

The man's face brightened. Sí, he said. Sí, bufones. Todo. He turned to the boy. Casimero! Los perros!

The boy ran to one of the burros and began to tug among the packings. He came up with a pair of bald and bat-eared animals slightly larger than rats and pale brown in color and he

89

pitched them into the air and caught them on the palms of his hands where they began to pirouette mindlessly.

Mire, mire! called the man. He was fishing about in his pockets and soon he was juggling four small wooden balls in front of Glanton's horse. The horse snorted and lifted its head and Glanton leaned over the saddle and spat and wiped his mouth with the back of his hand.

Aint that the drizzlin shits, he said.

The man was juggling and calling back over his shoulder to the women and the dogs were dancing and the women were turning to in preparation of something when Glanton spoke to the man.

Dont start no more of that crazy shit. You want to ride with us you fall in in the back. I promise you nothin. Vamonos.

He rode on. The company clanked into motion and the juggler ran shooing the women toward the burros and the boy stood wide-eyed with the dogs under his arm until the man spoke to him. They rode out through the rabble past great cones of slag and tailings. The people watched them go. Some of the men stood hand in hand like lovers and a small child led forth a blind man on a string to a place of vantage.

———◆◆◆———

At noon they crossed the stony bottom of the Casas Grandes River and they rode along a benchland above the gaunt rill of water past a place of bones where Mexican soldiers had slaughtered an encampment of Apaches some years gone, women and children, the bones and skulls scattered along the bench for half a mile and the tiny limbs and toothless paper skulls of infants like the ossature of small apes at their place of murder and old remnants of weathered basketry and broken pots among the gravel. They rode on. The river led a limegreen corridor of trees down out of the barren mountains. To the west lay the ragged Carcaj and to the north the Animas peaks dim and blue.

They made camp that night on a windy plateau among piñon and juniper and the fires leaned downwind in the darkness and

hot chains of sparks raced among the scrub. The jugglers unloaded the burros and began to set up a large gray tent. The
canvas was scrawled with arcana and it flapped and lurched,
stood towering, luffed and wrapped them about. The girl lay
on the ground holding to one corner. She began to drag through
the sand. The juggler took small steps. The woman's eyes were
rigid in the light. As the company watched the four of them
all clutched to the snapping cloth were towed mutely from
sight beyond the reach of the firelight and into the howling
desert like supplicants at the skirts of some wild and irate
goddess.

The pickets saw the tent lumber horribly away into the night.
When the family of jugglers returned they were arguing among
themselves and the man went again to the edge of the firelight
and peered out upon the wrathful blackness and spoke to it
and gestured with his fist nor would he return until the woman
sent the boy to fetch him. Now he sat staring at the flames
while the family unpacked. They watched him uneasily. Glanton
watched him also.

Showman, he said.

The juggler looked up. He put one finger to his chest.

You, said Glanton.

He rose and shuffled forward. Glanton was smoking a slender
black cigar. He looked up at the juggler.

You tell fortunes?

The juggler's eyes skittered. Cómo? he said.

Glanton put the cigar in his mouth and mimed a deal of cards
with his hands. La baraja, he said. Para adivinar la suerte.

The juggler tossed one hand aloft. Sí, sí, he said, shaking
his head with vigor. Todo, todo. He held up one finger and then
turned and made his way to the trove of shoddy partly off-
loaded from the burros. When he returned he was smiling affably
and manipulating the cards very nimbly.

Venga, he called. Venga.

The woman followed him. The juggler squatted before Glanton and spoke to him in a low voice. He turned and looked at

the woman and he riffled the cards and rose and took her by the hand and led her over the ground away from the fire and seated her facing out into the night. She swept up her skirt and composed herself and he took from his shirt a kerchief and with it bound her eyes.

Bueno, he called. Puedes ver?

No.

Nada?

Nada, said the woman.

Bueno, said the juggler.

He turned with the deck of cards and advanced toward Glanton. The woman sat like a stone. Glanton waved him away.

Los caballeros, he said.

The juggler turned. The black was squatting by the fire watching and when the juggler fanned the cards he rose and came forward.

The juggler looked up at him. He folded the cards and fanned them again and he made a pass over them with his left hand and held them forth and Jackson took a card and looked at it.

Bueno, said the juggler. Bueno. He admonished caution with a forefinger to his thin lips and took the card and held it aloft and turned with it. The card popped once sharply. He looked at the company seated about the fire. They were smoking, they were watching. He made a slow sweep before him with the card outheld. It bore the picture of a fool in harlequin and a cat. El tonto, he called.

El tonto, said the woman. She raised her chin slightly and she began a singsong chant. The dark querent stood solemnly, like a man arraigned. His eyes shifted over the company. The judge sat upwind from the fire naked to the waist, himself like some great pale deity, and when the black's eyes reached his he smiled. The woman ceased. The fire fled down the wind.

Quién, quién, cried the juggler.

She paused. El negro, she said.

El negro, cried the juggler, turning with the card. His clothes snapped in the wind. The woman raised her voice and spoke again and the black turned to his mates.

What does she say?

The juggler had turned and was making small bows to the company.

What does she say? Tobin?

The expriest shook his head. Idolatry, Blackie, idolatry. Do not mind her.

What does she say Judge?

The judge smiled. With his thumb he had been routing small life from the folds of his hairless skin and now he held up one hand with the thumb and forefinger pressed together in a gesture that appeared to be a benediction until he flung something unseen into the fire before him. What does she say?

What does she say.

I think she means to say that in your fortune lie our fortunes all.

And what is that fortune?

The judge smiled blandly, his pleated brow not unlike a dolphin's. Are you a drinking man, Jackie?

No more than some.

I think she'd have you beware the demon rum. Prudent counsel enough, what do you think?

That aint no fortune.

Exactly so. The priest is right.

The black frowned at the judge but the judge leaned forward to regard him. Wrinkle not thy sable brow at me, my friend. All will be known to you at last. To you as to every man.

Now a number of the company seated there seemed to weigh the judge's words and some turned to look at the black. He stood an uneasy honoree and at length he stepped back from the firelight and the juggler rose and made a motion with the cards, sweeping them in a fan before him and then proceeding along the perimeter past the boots of the men with the cards outheld as if they would find their own subject.

Quién, quién, he whispered among them.

They were right loath all. When he came before the judge the judge, who sat with one hand splayed across the broad expanse of his stomach, raised a finger and pointed.

Young Blasarius yonder, he said.

Cómo?

El joven.

El joven, whispered the juggler. He looked about him slowly with an air of mystery until he found with his eyes the one so spoken. He moved past the adventurers quickening his step. He stood before the kid, he squatted with the cards and fanned them with a slow rhythmic motion akin to the movements of certain birds at court.

Una carta, una carta, he wheezed.

The kid looked at the man and he looked at the company about.

Sí, sí, said the juggler, offering the cards.

He took one. He'd not seen such cards before, yet the one he held seemed familiar to him. He turned it upside down and regarded it and he turned it back.

The juggler took the boy's hand in his own and turned the card so he could see. Then he took the card and held it up.

Cuatro de copas, he called out.

The woman raised her head. She looked like a blindfold mannequin raised awake by a string.

Cuatro de copas, she said. She moved her shoulders. The wind went among her garments and her hair.

Quién, called the juggler.

El hombre . . . she said. El hombre más joven. El muchacho.

El muchacho, called the juggler. He turned the card for all to see. The woman sat like that blind interlocutrix between Boaz and Jachin inscribed upon the one card in the juggler's deck that they would not see come to light, true pillars and true card, false prophetess for all. She began to chant.

The judge was laughing silently. He bent slightly the better to see the kid. The kid looked at Tobin and at David Brown and he looked at Glanton himself but they were none laughing. The juggler kneeling before him watched him with a strange intensity. He followed the kid's gaze to the judge and back. When the kid looked down at him he smiled a crooked smile.

Get the hell away from me, said the kid.

The juggler leaned his ear forward. A common gesture and one that served for any tongue. The ear was dark and misshapen, as if in being put forth in this fashion it had suffered no few clouts, or perhaps the very news men had for him had blighted it. The kid spoke to him again but a man named Tate from Kentucky who had fought with McCulloch's Rangers as had Tobin and others among them leaned and whispered to the ragged soothsayer and he rose and made a slight bow and moved away. The woman had ceased her chanting. The juggler stood flapping in the wind and the fire lashed a long hot tail over the ground. Quién, quién, he called.

El jefe, said the judge.

The juggler's eyes sought out Glanton. He sat unmoved. The juggler looked at the old woman where she sat apart, facing the dark, lightly tottering, racing the night in her rags. He raised his finger to his lips and he spread his arms in a gesture of uncertainty.

El jefe, hissed the judge.

The man turned and went along the group at the fire and brought himself before Glanton and crouched and offered up the cards, spreading them in both hands. If he spoke his words were snatched away unheard. Glanton smiled, his eyes were small against the stinging grit. He put one hand forth and paused, he looked at the juggler. Then he took a card.

The juggler folded shut the deck and tucked it among his clothes. He reached for the card in Glanton's hand. Perhaps he touched it, perhaps not. The card vanished. It was in Glanton's hand and then it was not. The juggler's eyes snapped after it where it had gone down the dark. Perhaps Glanton had seen the card's face. What could it have meant to him? The juggler reached out to that naked bedlam beyond the fire's light but in the doing he overbalanced and fell forward against Glanton and created a moment of strange liaison with his old man's arms about the leader as if he would console him at his scrawny bosom.

Glanton swore and flung him away and at that moment the old woman began to chant.

Glanton rose.

She raised her jaw, gibbering at the night.

Shut her up, said Glanton.

La carroza, la carroza, cried the beldam. Invertido. Carta de guerra, de venganza. La ví sin ruedas sobre un rio obscuro . . .

Glanton called to her and she paused as if she'd heard him but it was not so. She seemed to catch some new drift in her divinings.

Perdida, perdida. La carta está perdida en la noche.

The girl standing this while at the edge of the howling darkness crossed herself silently. The old malabarista was on his knees where he'd been flung. Perdida, perdida, he whispered.

Un maleficio, cried the old woman. Qué viento tan maleante . . .

By god you will shut up, said Glanton, drawing his revolver.

Carroza de muertos, llena de huesos. El joven qué . . .

The judge like a great ponderous djinn stepped through the fire and the flames delivered him up as if he were in some way native to their element. He put his arms around Glanton. Someone snatched the old woman's blindfold from her and she and the juggler were clouted away and when the company turned in to sleep and the low fire was roaring in the blast like a thing alive these four yet crouched at the edge of the firelight among their strange chattels and watched how the ragged flames fled down the wind as if sucked by some maelstrom out there in the void, some vortex in that waste apposite to which man's transit and his reckonings alike lay abrogate. As if beyond will or fate he and his beasts and his trappings moved both in card and in substance under consignment to some third and other destiny.

In the morning when they rode out it was that pale day with the sun not risen and the wind had abated in the night and the things of the night were gone. The juggler on his burro trotted out to the head of the column and fell in with Glanton and they rode on together and they were so riding in the afternoon when the company entered the town of Janos.

———————◆•◆———————

An ancient walled presidio composed wholly of mud, a tall mud church and mud watchtowers and all of it rainwashed and lumpy and sloughing into a soft decay. The advent of the riders bruited by scurvid curs that howled woundedly and slank among the crumbling walls.

They rode past the church where old spanish bells seagreen with age hung from a pole between low mud dolmens. Darkeyed children watched from the hovels. The air was heavy with the smoke from charcoal fires and a few old pelados sat mute in the doorways and many of the houses were caved and ruinous and stood for pens. An old man with soapy eyes lurched out at them and held forth his hand. Una corta caridad, he croaked to the passing horses. Por Dios.

In the square two of the Delawares and the outrider Webster were squatting in the dust with a weathered old woman the color of pipeclay. Dry old crone, half naked, her paps like wrinkled aubergines hanging from under the shawl she wore. She stared at the ground nor did she look up even when the horses stood all about her.

Glanton looked down the square. The town appeared empty. There was a small company of soldiers garrisoned here but they did not turn out. Dust was blowing through the streets. His horse leaned and sniffed at the old woman and jerked its head and trembled and Glanton patted the animal's neck and dismounted.

She was in a meatcamp about eight mile up the river, said Webster. She caint walk.

How many were there?

We reckoned maybe fifteen or twenty. They didnt have no stock to amount to anything. I dont know what she was doin there.

97

Glanton crossed in front of his horse, passing the reins behind his back.

Watch her, Cap. She bites.

She had raised her eyes to the level of his knees. Glanton pushed the horse back and took one of the heavy saddle pistols from its scabbard and cocked it.

Watch yourself there.

Several of the men stepped back.

The woman looked up. Neither courage nor heartsink in those old eyes. He pointed with his left hand and she turned to follow his hand with her gaze and he put the pistol to her head and fired.

The explosion filled all that sad little park. Some of the horses shied and stepped. A fistsized hole erupted out of the far side of the woman's head in a great vomit of gore and she pitched over and lay slain in her blood without remedy. Glanton had already put the pistol at halfcock and he flicked away the spent primer with his thumb and was preparing to recharge the cylinder. McGill, he said.

A Mexican, solitary of his race in that company, came forward.

Get that receipt for us.

He took a skinning knife from his belt and stepped to where the old woman lay and took up her hair and twisted it about his wrist and passed the blade of the knife about her skull and ripped away the scalp.

Glanton looked at the men. They were stood some looking down at the old woman, some already seeing to their mounts or their equipage. Only the recruits were watching Glanton. He seated a pistolball in the mouth of the chamber and then he raised his eyes and looked across the square. The juggler and his family stood aligned like witnesses and beyond them in the long mud facade faces that had been watching from the doors and the naked windows dropped away like puppets in a gallery before the slow sweep of his eyes. He levered the ball home and capped the piece and spun the heavy pistol in his hand

and returned it to the scabbard at the horse's shoulder and took the dripping trophy from McGill and turned it in the sun the way a man might qualify the pelt of an animal and then handed it back and took up the trailing reins and led his horse out through the square toward the water at the ford.

They made camp in a grove of cottonwoods across the creek just beyond the walls of the town and with dark they drifted in small groups through the smoky streets. The circus folk had set up a little pitchtent in the dusty plaza and had stood a few poles about mounted with cressets of burning oil. The juggler was beating a sort of snaredrum made of tin and rawhide and calling out in a high nasal voice his bill of entertainments while the woman shrieked Pase pase pase, sweeping her arms about her in a gesture of the greatest spectacle. Toadvine and the kid watched among the milling citizenry. Bathcat leaned and spoke to them.

Look yonder, chappies.

They turned to look where he pointed. The black stood stripped to the waist behind the tent and as the juggler turned with a sweep of his arm the girl gave him a shove and he leaped from the tent and strode about with strange posturings under the lapsing flare of the torches.

VIII

Another cantina, another advisor – Monte – A knifing –
The darkest corner of the tavern the most conspicuous –
The sereño – Riding north – The meatcamp –
Grannyrat – Under the Animas peaks – A confrontation and
a killing – Another anchorite, another dawn.

They paused without the cantina and pooled their coins and Toadvine pushed aside the dried cowhide that hung for a door and they entered a place where all was darkness and without definition. A lone lamp hung from a crosstree in the ceiling and in the shadows dark figures sat smoking. They made their way across the room to a claytiled bar. The place reeked of woodsmoke and sweat. A thin little man appeared before them and placed his hands ceremonially upon the tiles.

Dígame, he said.

Toadvine took off his hat and put it on the bar and swept a clawed hand through his hair.

What have you got that a man could drink with just a minimum risk of blindness and death.

Cómo?

He cocked his thumb at his throat. What have you got to drink, he said.

The barman turned and looked behind him at his wares. He seemed uncertain whether anything there would answer their requirements.

Mescal?

Suit everbody?

Trot it out, said Bathcat.

The barman poured the measures from a clay jar into three dented tin cups and pushed them forward with care like counters on a board.

Cuánto, said Toadvine.

The barman looked fearful. Seis? he said.

Seis what?

The man held up six fingers.

Centavos, said Bathcat.

Toadvine doled the coppers onto the bar and drained his cup and paid again. He gestured at the cups all three with a wag of his finger. The kid took up his cup and drained it and set it down again. The liquor was rank, sour, tasted faintly of creosote. He was standing like the others with his back to the bar and he looked over the room. At a table in the far corner men were playing cards by the light of a single tallow candle. Along the wall opposite crouched figures seeming alien to the light who watched the Americans with no expression at all.

There's a game for ye, said Toadvine. Play monte in the dark with a pack of niggers. He raised the cup and drained it and set it on the bar and counted the remaining coins. A man was shuffling toward them out of the gloom. He had a bottle under his arm and he set it on the tiles with care together with his cup and spoke to the barman and the barman brought him a clay pitcher of water. He turned the pitcher so that the handle of it stood to his right and he looked at the kid. He was old and he wore a flatcrowned hat of a type no longer much seen in that country and he was dressed in dirty white cotton drawers and shirt. The huaraches he wore looked like dried and blackened fish lashed to the floors of his feet.

You are Texas? he said.

The kid looked at Toadvine.

You are Texas, the old man said. I was Texas three year. He held up his hand. The forefinger was gone at the first joint and perhaps he was showing them what happened in Texas or perhaps he merely meant to count the years. He lowered the hand and turned to the bar and poured wine into the cup and took up the jar of water and poured it sparingly after. He drank and set the cup down and turned to Toadvine. He wore thin white whiskers at the point of his chin and he wiped them with the back of his hand before looking up again.

You are socieded de guerra. Contra los barbaros.

Toadvine didnt know. He looked like some loutish knight beriddled by a troll.

The old man put a phantom rifle to his shoulder and made a noise with his mouth. He looked at the Americans. You kill the Apache, no?

Toadvine looked at Bathcat. What does he want? he said.

The Vandiemenlander passed his own threefingered hand across his mouth but he allowed no affinity. The old man's full he said. Or mad.

Toadvine propped his elbows on the tiles behind him. He looked at the old man and he spat on the floor. Craziern a runaway nigger, aint ye? he said.

There was a groan from the far side of the room. A man rose and went along the wall and bent to speak with others. The groans came again and the old man passed his hand before his face twice and kissed the ends of his fingers and looked up.

How much monies they pay you? he said.

No one spoke.

You kill Gómez they pay you much monies.

The man in the dark of the far wall moaned again. Madre de Dios, he called.

Gómez, Gómez, said the old man. Even Gómez. Who can ride against the Tejanos? They are soldiers. Que soldados tan valientes. La sangre de Gómez, sangre de la gente . . .

He looked up. Blood, he said. This country is give much blood. This Mexico. This is a thirsty country. The blood of a thousand Christs. Nothing.

He made a gesture toward the world beyond where all the land lay under darkness and all a great stained altarstone. He turned and poured his wine and poured again from the waterjar, temperate old man, and drank.

The kid watched him. He watched him drink and he watched him wipe his mouth. When he turned he spoke neither to the kid nor Toadvine but seemed to address the room.

I pray to God for this country. I say that to you. I pray. I dont go in the church. What I need to talk to them dolls there? I talk here.

He pointed to his chest. When he turned to the Americans his voice softened again. You are fine caballeros, he said. You kill the barbaros. They cannot hide from you. But there is another caballero and I think that no man hides from him. I was a soldier. It is like a dream. When even the bones is gone in the desert the dreams is talk to you, you dont wake up forever.

He drained his cup and took up his bottle and went softly away on his sandals into the farther dim of the cantina. The man at the wall moaned again and called upon his god. The Vandiemenlander and the barman spoke together and the barman gestured at the dark in the corner and shook his head and the Americans chambered down their last cups and Toadvine pushed the few tlacos toward the barman and they went out.

That was his son, said Bathcat.

Who was?

The lad in the corner cut with a knife.

He was cut?

One of the chaps at the table cut him. They were playin cards and one of them cut him.

Why dont he leave.

I asked him the same myself.

What did he say?

He had a question for me. Said where would he go to?

They made their way through the narrow walled streets toward the gate and the fires of the camp beyond. A voice was calling. It called: Las diez y media, tiempo sereño. It was the watchman at his rounds and he passed them with his lantern calling softly the hour.

In the predawn dark the sounds about describe the scene to come. The first cries of birds in the trees along the river and the clink of harness and the snuffle of horses and the gentle sound of their cropping. In the darkened village roosters have begun. The air smells of horses and charcoal. The camp has begun to stir. Sitting all about in the accruing light are the children from the town. None of the men rising know how long they have been there in darkness and silence.

When they rode through the square the dead squaw was gone and the dust was newly raked. The juggler's lamps were stark and black atop their poles and the fire was cold before the pitchtent. An old woman who had been chopping wood raised up and stood with the axe in both hands as they passed.

They rode through the sacked indian camp at midmorning, the blackened sheets of meat draped across the bushes or hung from poles like strange dark laundry. Deerhides were pegged out on the ground and white or ruddled bones lay strewn over the rocks in a primitive shambles. The horses cocked their ears and stepped quickly. They rode on. In the afternoon black Jackson caught them up, his mount surbated and all but blown. Glanton turned in the saddle and measured him with his eye. Then he nudged his horse forward and the black fell in with his pale wayfellows and all rode on as before.

They did not miss the veteran until that evening. The judge made his way down through the smoke of the cookfires and squatted before Toadvine and the kid.

What's become of Chambers, he said.

I believe he's quit.

Quit.

I believe he has.

Did he ride out this morning?

Not with us he never.

It was my understanding that you spoke for your group.

Toadvine spat. He appears to of spoke for hisself.

When did you last see him.

Seen him yesterday evenin.

But not this morning.

Not this mornin.

The judge regarded him.

Hell, said Toadvine. I allowed you knowed he was gone. It aint like he was so small you never would miss him.

The judge looked at the kid. He looked at Toadvine again. Then he rose and went back.

In the morning two of the Delawares were gone. They rode on. By noon they had begun to climb toward the gap in the mountains. Riding up through wild lavender or soapweed, under the Animas peaks. The shadow of an eagle that had set forth from those high and craggy fastnesses crossed the line of riders below and they looked up to mark it where it rode in that brittle blue and faultless void. They came up through piñon and scruboak and they crossed the gap through a high pine forest and rode on through the mountains.

In the evening they came out upon a mesa that overlooked all the country to the north. The sun to the west lay in a holocaust where there rose a steady column of small desert bats and to the north along the trembling perimeter of the world dust was blowing down the void like the smoke of distant armies. The crumpled butcherpaper mountains lay in sharp shadowfold under the long blue dusk and in the middle distance the glazed bed of a dry lake lay shimmering like the mare imbrium and herds of deer were moving north in the last of the twilight, harried over the plain by wolves who were themselves the color of the desert floor.

Glanton sat his horse and looked long out upon this scene. Sparse on the mesa the dry weeds lashed in the wind like the earth's long echo of lance and spear in old encounters forever unrecorded. All the sky seemed troubled and night came quickly over the evening land and small gray birds flew crying softly after the fled sun. He chucked up the horse. He passed and so passed all into the problematical destruction of darkness.

They camped that night on the foreplain at the foot of a talus slope and the murder that had been reckoned upon took place. The white man Jackson had been drunk in Janos and he had ridden red-eyed and sullen for two days through the mountains. He now sat disheveled by the fire with his boots off drinking aguardiente from a flask, circumscribed about by his companions and by the cries of wolves and providence of night. He was sitting so when the black approached the fire and threw down his apishamore and sat upon it and fell to stoking his pipe.

There were two fires in this camp and no rules real or tacit as to who should use them. But when the white man looked to the other fire he saw that the Delawares and John McGill and the new men in the company had taken their supper there and with a gesture and a slurred oath he warned the black away.

Here beyond men's judgements all covenants were brittle. The black looked up from his pipebowl. About that fire were men whose eyes gave back the light like coals socketed hot in their skulls and men whose eyes did not, but the black man's eyes stood as corridors for the ferrying through of naked and un-rectified night from what of it lay behind to what was yet to come. Any man in this company can sit where it suits him, he said.

The white man swung his head, one eye half closed, his lip loose. His gunbelt lay coiled on the ground. He reached and drew the revolver and cocked it. Four men rose and moved away.

You aim to shoot me? said the black.

You dont get your black ass away from this fire I'll kill you graveyard dead.

He looked to where Glanton sat. Glanton watched him. He put the pipe in his mouth and rose and took up the apishamore and folded it over his arm.

Is that your final say?

Final as the judgement of God.

The black looked once more across the flames at Glanton and then he moved away in the dark. The white man uncocked the revolver and placed it on the ground before him. Two of the others came back to the fire and stood uneasily. Jackson sat with his legs crossed. One hand lay in his lap and the other was outstretched on his knee holding a slender black cigarillo. The nearest man to him was Tobin and when the black stepped out of the darkness bearing the bowieknife in both hands like some instrument of ceremony Tobin started to rise. The white man looked up drunkenly and the black stepped forward and with a single stroke swapt off his head.

Two thick ropes of dark blood and two slender rose like snakes from the stump of his neck and arched hissing into the fire. The head rolled to the left and came to rest at the expriest's feet where it lay with eyes aghast. Tobin jerked his foot away and rose and stepped back. The fire steamed and blackened and a gray cloud of smoke rose and the columnar arches of blood slowly subsided until just the neck bubbled gently like a stew and then that too was stilled. He was sat as before save headless, drenched in blood, the cigarillo still between his fingers, leaning toward the dark and smoking grotto in the flames where his life had gone.

Glanton rose. The men moved away. No one spoke. When they set out in the dawn the headless man was sitting like a murdered anchorite discalced in ashes and sark. Someone had taken his gun but the boots stood where he'd put them. The company rode on. They had not gone forth one hour upon that plain before they were ridden upon by the Apaches.

IX

An ambuscado – The dead Apache – Hollow ground –
A gypsum lake – Trebillones – Snowblind horses – The Delawares
return – A probate – The ghost coach – The copper mines –
Squatters – A snakebit horse – The judge on geological evidence –
The dead boy – On parallax and false guidance in things past –
The ciboleros.

They were crossing the western edge of the playa when Glanton halted. He turned and placed one hand on the wooden cantle and looked toward the sun where it sat new risen above the bald and flyspecked mountains to the east. The floor of the playa lay smooth and unbroken by any track and the mountains in their blue islands stood footless in the void like floating temples.

Toadvine and the kid sat their horses and gazed upon that desolation with the others. Out on the playa a cold sea broke and water gone these thousand years lay riffled silver in the morning wind.

Sounds like a pack of hounds, said Toadvine.

It sounds like geese to me.

Suddenly Bathcat and one of the Delawares turned their horses and quirted them and called out and the company turned and milled and began to line out down the lake bed toward the thin line of scrub that marked the shore. Men were leaping from their horses and hobbling them instantly with loops of rope ready made. By the time the animals were secured and they had thrown themselves on the ground under the creosote bushes with their weapons readied the riders were beginning to appear far out on the lake bed, a thin frieze of mounted archers that trembled and veered in the rising heat. They crossed before the sun and vanished one by one and reappeared again and they were black in the sun and they rode out of that vanished sea like burnt phantoms with the legs of the animals kicking up the spume that was not real and they were lost in the sun and lost in the lake and they shimmered and slurred together and separated again and they augmented by planes in lurid avatars and began to coalesce and there began to appear above them in the dawn-broached sky a hellish likeness of their ranks riding huge and inverted and the horses' legs incredibly elongate trampling down the high thin cirrus and the howling antiwarriors pendant from their mounts immense and chimeric and the high wild cries carrying that flat and barren pan like the cries of souls broke through some misweave in the weft of things into the world below.

They'll swing to their right, called Glanton, and as he spoke they did so, favoring their bow arms. The arrows came lofting up in the blue with the sun on their fletchings and then suddenly gaining speed and passing with a waney whistle like the flight of wild ducks. The first rifle cracked.

The kid was lying on his belly holding the big Walker revolver in both hands and letting off the shots slowly and with care as if he'd done it all before in a dream. The warriors passed within a hundred feet, forty, fifty of them, and went on up the edge of the lake and began to crumble in the serried planes of heat and to break up silently and to vanish.

The company lay under the creosote recharging their pieces. One of the ponies was lying in the sand breathing steadily and others stood that bore arrows with a curious patience. Tate and Doc Irving pulled back to see about them. The others lay watching the playa.

They walked out, Toadvine and Glanton and the judge. They picked up a short rifled musket bound in rawhide and studded about the stock with brassheaded tacks in varied designs. The judge looked north along the pale shore of the dry lake where the heathen had fled. He handed the rifle to Toadvine and they went on.

The dead man lay in a sandy wash. He was naked save for skin boots and a pair of wide Mexican drawers. The boots had pointed toes like buskins and they had parfleche soles and high tops that were rolled down about the knees and tied. The sand in the wash was dark with blood. They stood there in the windless heat at the edge of the dry lake and Glanton pushed him over with his boot. The painted face came up, sand stuck to the eyeball, sand stuck to the rancid grease with which he'd smeared his torso. You could see the hole where the ball from Toadvine's rifle had gone in above the lower rib. The man's hair was long and black and dull with dust and a few lice scuttled. There were slashes of white paint on the cheeks and there were chevrons of paint above the nose and figures in dark red paint under the eyes and on the chin. He was old and he bore a healed lance wound just above the hipbone and an old sabre wound across the left cheek that ran to the corner of his eye. These wounds were decorated their length with tattooed images, perhaps obscure with age, but without referents in the known desert about.

The judge knelt with his knife and cut the strap of the tigreskin warbag the man carried and emptied it in the sand. It held an eyeshield made from a raven's wing, a rosary of fruitseeds, a few gunflints, a handful of lead balls. It held also a calculus or madstone from the inward parts of some beast and this the judge examined and pocketed. The other effects he spread with the palm of his hand as if there were something to be read there. Then he ripped open the man's drawers with his knife. Tied alongside the dark genitals was a small skin bag and this the judge cut away and also secured in the pocket of his vest. Lastly he seized the dark locks and swept them up from the sand and cut away the scalp. Then they rose, and returned, leaving him to scrutinize with his drying eyes the calamitous advance of the sun.

They rode all day upon a pale gastine sparsely grown with saltbush and panicgrass. In the evening they entrained upon a hollow ground that rang so roundly under the horses' hooves that they stepped and sidled and rolled their eyes like circus animals and that night as they lay in that ground each heard, all heard, the dull boom of rock falling somewhere far below them in the awful darkness inside the world.

On the day that followed they crossed a lake of gypsum so fine the ponies left no track upon it. The riders wore masks of bone-black smeared about their eyes and some had blacked the eyes of their horses. The sun reflected off the pan burned the under-sides of their faces and shadow of horse and rider alike were painted upon the fine white powder in purest indigo. Far out on the desert to the north dustspouts rose wobbling and augered the earth and some said they'd heard of pilgrims borne aloft like dervishes in those mindless coils to be dropped broken and bleeding upon the desert again and there perhaps to watch the thing that had destroyed them lurch onward like some drunken djinn and resolve itself once more into the elements from which it sprang. Out of that whirlwind no voice spoke and the pilgrim lying in his broken bones may cry out and in his anguish he may rage, but rage at what? And if the dried and blackened shell of him is found among the sands by travelers to come yet who can discover the engine of his ruin?

That night they sat at the fire like ghosts in their dusty beards and clothing, rapt, pyrolatrous. The fires died and small coals scampered down the plain and sand crept past in the dark all night like armies of lice on the move. In the night some of the horses began to scream and daybreak found several so crazed with snowblindness they required to be shot. When they rode out the Mexican they called McGill was on his third horse in as many days. He could not have blacked the eyes of the pony he'd ridden coming up from the dry lake short of muzzling it like a dog and the horse he now rode was wilder yet and there were only three animals left in the caballado.

That afternoon the two Delawares that had left them a day out of Janos caught them up where they nooned at a mineral well. They had with them the veteran's horse, still saddled. Glanton walked out to where the animal stood and took up the trailing reins and led it to the fire where he removed the rifle from the scabbard and handed it to David Brown and then began to go through the wallet strapped to the cantle and to pitch the veteran's meagre effects into the fire. He undid the girthstraps and loosed the other accoutrements and piled them onto the flames, blankets, saddle, all, the greasy wool and leather sending up a foul gray smoke.

Then they rode on. They were moving north and for two days the Delawares read the smokes on the distant peaks and then the smokes stopped and there were no more. As they entered the foothills they came upon a dusty old diligence with six horses in the traces grazing the dry grass in a fold among the barren scrag.

A deputation cut for the carriage and the horses jerked their heads and shied and went trotting. The riders harried them about the basin until they were circling like paper horses in a windtrap and the diligence rattling after with one broken wheel. The black walked out waving his hat and called them off and he approached the yoked horses with the hat outheld and talked to them where they stood trembling until he could reach the trailing straps.

Glanton walked past him and opened the carriage door. The inside of the coach was splintered up with new wood and a dead man slumped out and hung head down. There was another man inside and a young boy and they lay enhearsed with their weapons in a stink to drive a buzzard off a gutcart. Glanton took the guns and ammunition and handed them out. Two men climbed to the freightdeck and cut away the ropes and the tattered tarp and they kicked down a steamer trunk and an old rawhide dispatch box and broke them open. Glanton cut the straps on the dispatch box with his knife and tipped the box out in the sand. Letters penned for any destination save here began to skitter and drift away down the canyon. There were a few tagged bags of ore samples in the box and he emptied them on the ground and kicked at the lumps of ore and looked about. He looked inside the coach again and then he spat and turned and looked the horses over. They were big American horses but badly used up. He directed two of them cut out of the traces and then he waved the black away from the lead horse and wafted his hat at the animals. They set off down the floor of the canyon, mismatched and sawing in the harness, the diligence swaying on its leather springs and the dead man dangling out of the clapping door. They diminished upon the plain to the west first the sound and then the shape of them dissolving in the heat rising off the sand until they were no more than a mote struggling in that hallucinatory void and then nothing at all. The riders rode on.

All afternoon they rode singlefile up thorugh the mountains. A small gray lanneret flew about them as if seeking their banner and then it shied away over the plain below on its slender falcon wings. They rode on through sandstone cities in the dusk of that day, past castle and keep and windfashioned watchtower and stone granaries in sun and in shadow. They rode through marl and terracotta and rifts of copper shale and they rode through a wooded swag and out upon a promontory overlooking a bleak and barren caldera where lay the abandoned ruins of Santa Rita del Cobre.

Here they made a dry and fireless camp. They sent down scouts and Glanton walked out on the bluff and sat in the dusk watching the darkness deepen in the gulf below to see if any light should show itself down there. The scouting party returned in the dark and it was still dark in the morning when the company mounted and rode out.

They entered the caldera in a condition of half gray dawn, riding singlefile through the shaley streets between rows of old adobes abandoned these dozen years past when the Apaches cut off the wagontrains from Chihuahua and laid the works under siege. The starving Mexicans had set out afoot on the long journey south but none ever arrived. The Americans rode past the slag and rubble and the dark shapes of shaft mouths and they rode past the smeltinghouse where piles of ore stood about and weathered wagons and orecarts bonewhite in the dawn and the dark iron shapes of abandoned machinery. They crossed a stony arroyo and rode on through that gutted terrain to a slight rise where sat the old presidio, a large triangular building of adobe with round towers at the corners. There was a single door in the east wall and as they approached they could see rising the smoke that they had smelled on the morning air.

Glanton pounded on the door with his rawhidecovered club like a traveler at an inn. A bluish light suffused the hills about and the tallest peaks to the north stood in the only sun while all the caldera lay in darkness yet. The echo of his knocking clapped about the stark and riven walls of rock and returned. The men sat their horses. Glanton gave the door a kick.

Come out if you're white, he called.

Who's there? called a voice.

Glanton spat

Who is it? they called.

Open it, said Glanton.

They waited. Chains were drawn rattling across the wood. The tall door creaked inward and a man stood before them at the ready with a rifle. Glanton touched his horse with his knee and it raised its head along the door and forced it open and they rode through.

In the gray murk within the compound they dismounted and tied. A few old freightwagons stood about, some looted of their wheels by travelers. There was a lamp burning in one of the offices and several men stood in the door. Glanton crossed the triangle. The men stepped aside. We thought you was injins they said.

They were four left out of a party of seven that had set out for the mountains to prospect for precious metals. They had been barricaded in the old presidio for three days, fled here from the desert to the south pursued by the savages. One of the men was shot through the lower chest and he lay propped against the wall in the office. Irving came in and looked at him.

What have you done for him? he said.

Aint done nothin.

What do you want me to do for him?

Aint asked you to do nothin.

That's good, said Irving. Because there aint nothing to be done.

He looked at them. They were foul and ragged and half crazed. They'd been making forays at night up the arroyo for wood and water and they had been feeding off a dead mule that lay gutted and stinking in the far corner of the yard. The first thing they asked for was whiskey and the next was tobacco. They had but two animals and one of these had been snakebit in the desert and this thing now stood in the compound with its head enormously swollen and grotesque like some fabled equine idea-tion out of an Attic tragedy. It had been bitten on the nose and its eyes bulged out of the shapeless head in a horror of agony and it tottered moaning toward the clustered horses of the company with its long misshapen muzzle swinging and drooling and its breath wheezing in the throttled pipes of its throat. The skin had split open along the bridge of its nose and the bone shone through pinkish white and its small ears looked like paper spills twisted into either side of a hairy loaf of dough. The American horses began to mill and separate along the wall at its approach and it swung after them blindly. There was a flurry of thumps and kicks and the horses began to circle the com-pound. A small mottled stallion belonging to one of the Delawares came out of the remuda and struck at the thing twice and then turned and buried its teeth in its neck. Out of the mad horse's throat came a sound that brought the men to the door.

Why dont you shoot that thing? said Irving.

Sooner it dies the sooner it'll rot, they said.

Irving spat. You aim to eat it and it snakebit?

They looked at one another. They didnt know.

Irving shook his head and went out. Glanton and the judge

looked at the squatters and the squatters looked at the floor. Some of the roofbeams were half down into the room and the floor was filled with mud and rubble. Into these ruinous works the morning sun now slanted and Glanton could see crouched in a corner a Mexican or halfbreed boy maybe twelve years old. He was naked save for a pair of old calzones and makeshift sandals of uncured hide. He glared back at Glanton with a sort of terrified insolence.

Who's this child? said the judge.

They shrugged, they looked away.

Glanton spat and shook his head.

They posted guards atop the azotea and unsaddled the horses and drove them out to graze and the judge took one of the packanimals and emptied out the panniers and went off to explore the works. In the afternoon he sat in the compound breaking ore samples with a hammer, the feldspar rich in red oxide of copper and native nuggets in whose organic lobations he purported to read news of the earth's origins, holding an extemporary lecture in geology to a small gathering who nodded and spat. A few would quote him scripture to confound his ordering up of eons out of the ancient chaos and other apostate supposings. The judge smiled.

Books lie, he said.

God dont lie.

No, said the judge. He does not. And these are his words.

He held up a chunk of rock.

He speaks in stones and trees, the bones of things.

The squatters in their rags nodded among themselves and were soon reckoning him correct, this man of learning, in all his speculations, and this the judge encouraged until they were right proselytes of the new order whereupon he laughed at them for fools.

That evening the main part of the company quartered themselves on the dry clay of the compound under the stars. Before morning rain would drive them in, huddled in the dark mud cubicles along the south wall. In the office of the presidio they'd built a fire in the floor and the smoke rose through the ruined roof and Glanton and the judge and their lieutenants sat about the blaze and smoked their pipes while the squatters stood off to one side chewing the tobacco they'd been given and spitting at the wall. The halfbreed boy watched them with his dark eyes. To the west among the low dark hills they could hear the howling of a wolf that the squatters did mistrust and the hunters smiled among themselves. In a night so beclamored with the jackal-yapping of coyotes and the cries of owls the howl of that old dog wolf was the one sound they knew to issue from its right form, a solitary lobo, perhaps gray at the muzzle, hung like a marionette from the moon with his long mouth gibbering.

It grew cold in the night and it blew stormy with wind and rain and soon all the wild menagerie of that country grew mute. A horse put its long wet face in at the door and Glanton looked up and spoke to it and it lifted its head and curled its lip and withdrew into the rain and the night.

The squatters observed this as they observed everything with their shifting eyes and one of them allowed that he would never make a pet of a horse. Glanton spat at the fire and looked at the man where he sat horseless in his rags and he shook his head at the wonderful invention of folly in its guises and forms. The rain had slacked and in the stillness a long crack of thunder rolled overhead and clanged among the rocks and then the rain came harder until it was pouring through the blackened opening in the roof and steaming and hissing in the fire. One of the men rose and dragged up the rotted ends of some old beams and piled them onto the flames. The smoke spread along the sagging vigas above them and little streams of liquid clay started down from the sod roof. Outside the compound lay under sheets of water that slashed about in the gusts and the light of the fire falling from the door laid a pale band upon that shallow sea along which the horses stood like roadside spectators waiting an event. From time to time one of the men would rise and go out and his shadow would fall among the animals and they would raise and lower their dripping heads and dap their hooves and then wait in the rain again.

The men who had been on watch entered the room and stood steaming before the fire. The black stood at the door neither in nor out. Someone had reported the judge naked atop the walls, immense and pale in the revelations of lightning, striding the perimeter up there and declaiming in the old epic mode. Glanton watched the fire silently and the men composed themselves in their blankets in the drier places about the floor and soon they were asleep.

In the morning the rain had ceased. The water stood in pools in the courtyard and the snakebit horse lay dead with its shapeless head stretched in the mud and the other animals had gathered in the northeast corner under the tower and stood facing the wall. The peaks to the north were white with snow in the new risen sun and when Toadvine stepped out into the day the sun was just touching the upper walls of the compound and the judge was standing in the gently steaming quiet picking his teeth with a thorn as if he had just eaten.

Morning, said the judge.

Morning, said Toadvine.

Looks fair to clear.

It done has cleared, said Toadvine.

The judge turned his head and looked toward the pristine cobalt keep of the visible day. An eagle was crossing the gorge with the sun very white on its head and tailfeathers.

So it has, said the judge. So it has.

The squatters emerged and stood about the cantonment blinking like birds. They had elected among themselves to join the company and when Glanton came across the yard leading his horse the spokesman for their group stepped forward to inform him of their decision. Glanton didnt even look at him. He entered the cuartel and got his saddle and gear. In the meantime someone had found the boy.

He was lying face down naked in one of the cubicles. Scattered about on the clay were great numbers of old bones. As if he like others before him had stumbled upon a place where something inimical lived. The squatters crowded in and stood about the corpse in silence. Soon they were conversing senselessly about the merits and virtues of the dead boy.

In the compound the scalphunters mounted up and turned their horses toward the gates that now stood open to the east to welcome in the light and to invite their journey. As they rode out the doomed men hosteled in that place came dragging the boy out and laid him in the mud. His neck had been broken and his head hung straight down and it flopped over strangely when they let him onto the ground. The hills beyond the minepit were reflected grayly in the pools of rainwater in the courtyard and the partly eaten mule lay in the mud with its hindquarters missing like something from a chromo of terrific war. Within the doorless cuartel the man who'd been shot sang church hymns and cursed God alternately. The squatters stood about the dead boy with their wretched firearms at rest like some tatterdemalion guard of honor. Glanton had given them a half pound of riflepowder and some primers and a small pig of lead and as the company rode out some looked back at them, three men standing there without expression. No one raised a hand in farewell. The dying man by the ashes of the fire was singing and as they rode out they could hear the hymns of their childhood and they could hear them as they ascended the arroyo and rode up through the low junipers still wet from the rain. The dying man sang with great clarity and intention and the riders setting forth upcountry may have ridden more slowly the longer to hear him for they were of just these qualities themselves.

◆ ◆ ◆

They rode that day through low hills barren save for the scrub evergreens. Everywhere in this high parkland deer leapt and scattered and the hunters shot several from their saddles and gutted and packed them and by evening they had acquired a retinue of half a dozen wolves of varying size and color that trotted behind them singlefile and watched over their own shoulders to see that each should follow in his place.

At dusk they halted and built a fire and roasted the deer. The night was much enclosed about them and there were no stars. To the north they could see other fires that burned red and sullen along the invisible ridges. They ate and moved on, leaving the fire on the ground behind them, and as they rode up into the mountains this fire seemed to become altered of its location, now here, now there, drawing away, or shifting unaccountably along the flank of their movement. Like some ignis fatuus belated upon the road behind them which all could see and of which none spoke. For this will to deceive that is in things luminous may manifest itself likewise in retrospect and so by sleight of some fixed part of a journey already accomplished may also post men to fraudulent destinies.

As they rode that night upon the mesa they saw come toward them much like their own image a party of riders pieced out of the darkness by the intermittent flare of the dry lightning to the north. Glanton halted and sat his horse and the company halted behind him. The silent riders hove on. When they were a hundred yards out they too halted and all sat in silent speculation at this encounter.

Who are you? called Glanton.

Amigos, somos amigos.

They were counting each the other's number.

De dónde viene? called the strangers.

A dónde va? called the judge.

They were ciboleros down from the north, their packhorses laden with dried meat. They were dressed in skins sewn with the ligaments of beasts and they sat their animals in the way of men seldom off them. They carried lances with which they hunted the wild buffalo on the plains and these weapons were dressed with tassels of feathers and colored cloth and some carried bows and some carried old fusils with tasseled stoppers in their bores. The dried meat was packed in hides and other than the few arms among them they were innocent of civilized device as the rawest savage of that land.

They parleyed without dismounting and the ciboleros lighted their small cigarillos and told that they were bound for the markets at Mesilla. The Americans might have traded for some of the meat but they carried no tantamount goods and the disposition to exchange was foreign to them. And so these parties divided upon that midnight plain, each passing back the way the other had come, pursuing as all travelers must inversions without end upon other men's journeys.

X

Tobin – The skirmish on the Little Colorado – The Katabasis –
How came the learned man – Glanton and the judge – A new course –
The judge and the bats – Guano – The deserters –
Saltpeter and charcoal – The malpais – Hoofprints – The volcano –
Brimstone – The matrix – The slaughter of the aborigines.

In the days to follow all trace of the Gileños faded and they pushed deeper into the mountains. By fires of highland driftwood pale as bone they crouched in silence while the flames yawed in the nightwinds ascending those stony draws. The kid sat with his legs crossed mending a strap with an awl he'd borrowed from the expriest Tobin and the frockless one looked on as he worked.

You've done this afore, said Tobin.

The kid wiped his nose with a swipe of his greasy sleeve and turned the piece in his lap. Not me, he said.

Well you've the knack. More so than me. There's little equity in the Lord's gifts.

The kid looked up at him and then bent to his work again.

That's so, said the expriest. Look around you. Study the judge.

I done studied him.

Mayhaps he aint to your liking, fair enough. But the man's a hand at anything. I've never seen him turn to a task but what he didnt prove clever at it.

The kid drove the greased thread through the leather and hauled it taut.

He speaks dutch, said the expriest.

Dutch?

Aye.

The kid looked at the expriest, he bent to his mending.

He does for I heard him do it. We cut a parcel of crazy pilgrims down off the Llano and the old man in the lead of them he spoke right up in dutch like we were all of us in dutchland and the judge give him right back. Glanton come near fallin off his horse. We none of us knew him to speak it. Asked where he'd learned it you know what he said?

What did he say.

Said off a dutchman.

The expriest spat. I couldnt of learned it off ten dutchmen. What about you?

The kid shook his head.

No, said Tobin. The gifts of the Almighty are weighed and parceled out in a scale peculiar to himself. It's no fair accountin and I dont doubt but what he'd be the first to admit it and you put the query to him boldface.

Who?

The Almighty, the Almighty. The expriest shook his head. He glanced across the fire toward the judge. That great hairless thing. You wouldnt think to look at him that he could outdance the devil himself now would ye? God the man is a dancer, you'll not take that away from him. And fiddle. He's the greatest fiddler I ever heard and that's an end on it. The greatest. He can cut a trail, shoot a rifle, ride a horse, track a deer. He's been all over the world. Him and the governor they sat up till breakfast and it was Paris this and London that in five languages, you'd have give something to of heard them. The governor's a learned man himself he is, but the judge . . .

The expriest shook his head. Oh it may be the Lord's way of showin how little store he sets by the learned. Whatever could it mean to one who knows all? He's an uncommon love for the common man and godly wisdom resides in the least of things so that it may well be that the voice of the Almighty speaks most profoundly in such beings as lives in silence themselves.

He watched the kid.

For let it go how it will, he said, God speaks in the least of creatures.

The kid thought him to mean birds or things that crawl but the expriest, watching, his head slightly cocked, said: No man is give leave of that voice.

The kid spat into the fire and bent to his work.

I aint heard no voice, he said.

When it stops, said Tobin, you'll know you've heard it all your life.

Is that right?

Aye.

The kid turned the leather in his lap. The expriest watched him.

At night, said Tobin, when the horses are grazing and the company is asleep, who hears them grazing?

Dont nobody hear them if they're asleep.

Aye. And if they cease their grazing who is it that wakes?

Every man.

Aye, said the expriest. Every man.

The kid looked up. And the judge? Does the voice speak to him?

The judge, said Tobin. He didn't answer.

I seen him before, said the kid. In Nacogdoches.

Tobin smiled. Every man in the company claims to have encountered that sootysouled rascal in some other place.

Tobin rubbed his beard on the back of his hand. He saved us all, I have to give him that. We come down off the Little Colorado we didnt have a pound of powder in the company. Pound. We'd not a dram hardly. There he set on a rock in the middle of the greatest desert you'd ever want to see. Just perched on this rock like a man waitin for a coach. Brown thought him a mirage. Might have shot him for one if he'd had aught to shoot him with.

How come you to have no powder?

Shot it up all at the savages. Holed up nine days in a cave, lost most of the horses. We were thirty-eight men when we left Chihuahua City and we were fourteen when the judge found us. Mortally whipped, on the run. Every man jack of us knew that in that godforsook land somewhere was a draw or a culdesac or perhaps just a pile of rocks and there we'd be driven to a stand with those empty guns. The judge. Give the devil his due.

The kid held the tack in one hand, the awl in the other. He watched the expriest.

We'd been on the plain all night and well up into the next day. The Delawares kept callin halts and droppin to the ground to give a listen. There was no place to run and no place to hide. I dont know what they wanted to hear. We knew the bloody niggers was out there and speakin for myself that was already an abundance of information, I didnt need more. That sunrise we'd looked to be our last. We were all watchin the backtrack, I dont know how far you could see. Fifteen, twenty miles.

Then about the meridian of that day we come upon the judge on his rock there in that wilderness by his single self. Aye and there was no rock, just the one. Irving said he'd brung it with him. I said that it was a merestone for to mark him out of nothing at all. He had with him that selfsame rifle you see with him now, all mounted in german silver and the name that he'd give it set with silver wire under the checkpiece in latin: *Et In Arcadia Ego.* A reference to the lethal in it. Common enough for a man to name his gun. I've heard Sweetlips and Hark From The Tombs and every sort of lady's name. His is the first and only ever I seen with an inscription from the classics.

And there he set. No horse. Just him and his legs crossed, smilin as we rode up. Like he'd been expectin us. He'd an old canvas kitbag and an old woolen benjamin over the one shoulder. In the bag was a brace of pistols and a good assortment of specie, gold and silver. He didnt even have a canteen. It was like . . . You couldnt tell where he'd come from. Said he'd been with a wagon company and fell out to go it alone.

Davy wanted to leave him there. Didnt set well with his honor and it dont to this day. Glanton just studied him. It was a day's work to even guess what he made of that figure on that ground. I dont know to this day. They've a secret commerce. Some terrible covenant. You mind. You'll see I'm right. He called for the last of two packanimals we had and he cut the straps and left the wallets to lay where they fell and the judge mounted up and he and Glanton rode side by side and soon they was conversin like brothers. The judge sat that animal bareback like an indian and rode with his grip and his rifle perched on the withers and he looked about him with the greatest satisfaction in the world, as if everything had turned out just as he planned and the day could not have been finer.

We'd not rode far before he struck us a new course about nine points to the east. He pointed out a range of mountains maybe thirty mile distant and we pulled for those mountains and none of us asked what for. By then Glanton had give him the particulars of the situation in which he'd installed himself but if bein naked of arms in that wilderness and half of all Apacheria in pursuit worried him at all he kept it to himself entire.

The expriest had paused to rekindle his pipe, reaching into the raw fire for a coal as did the red scouts and then setting it back among the flames as if it had a proper place there.

Now what do you reckon it was in them mountains that we set out for? And how did he come to know of it? How to find it? How to put it to use?

Tobin seemed to frame these questions to himself. He was regarding the fire and pulling on his pipe. How indeed, he said. We reached the foothills in the early evenin and rode up a dry arroyo and pushed on I guess till midnight and made camp with neither wood nor water. Come mornin we could see them on the plain to the north maybe ten mile out. They were ridin four and six abreast and there was no short supply of them and they were in no hurry.

The judge had been up all the night by what the videttes said. Watchin the bats. He would go up the side of the mountain and make notes in a little book and then he would come back down. Could not have been more cheerful. Two men had deserted in the night and that made us down to twelve and the judge thirteen. I gave him my best study, the judge. Then and now. He appeared to be a lunatic and then not. Glanton I always knew was mad.

We left out with the first light up a little wooded draw. We were on the north slope and there was willow and alder and cherry growin out of the rock, just little trees. The judge would stop to botanize and then ride to catch up. My hand to God. Pressing leaves into his book. Sure I never saw the equal to it and all the time the savages in plain view below us. Ridin on that pan. God I'd put a crick in my neck I couldnt keep my eyes off of them and they were a hundred souls if they were one.

We come out on some flinty ground where it was all juniper and we just went on. No attempt to put their trackers at fault. We rode all that day. We saw no more of the savages for they were come under the lee of the mountain and were somewhere on the slopes below us. As soon as it was dusk and the bats was about the judge he altered our course again, ridin along holdin onto his hat, lookin up at the little animals. We got broke up and scattered all in the junipers and we halted to regroup and to recruit the horses. We sat around in the dark, no one spoke a word. When the judge got back he and Glanton whispered among themselves and then we moved on.

We led the horses in the dark. There was no trail, just steep scrabbly rock. When we reached the cave some of the men thought that he meant for us to hide there and that he was for a fact daft altogether. But it was the nitre. The nitre, you see. We left all that we owned at the mouth of that cave and we filled our wallets and panniers and our mochilas with the cave dirt and we left out at daybreak. When we topped the rise above that place and looked back there was a great spout of bats being sucked down into the cave, thousands of the creatures, and they continued so for an hour or more and even then it was just that we could no longer see them.

The judge. We left him at a high pass, a little clearwater creek. Him and one of the Delawares. He told us to circle the mountain and to return to that place in forty-eight hours. We unloaded all the containers onto the ground and took the two horses with us and him and the Delaware commenced luggin the panniers and the wallets up that little creek. I watched him go and I said that I would never set eyes on that man again.

Tobin looked at the kid. Never in this world. I thought Glanton would leave him. We went on. The next day on the far side of the mountain we encountered the two lads that had deserted us. Hangin upside down in a tree. They'd been skinned and I can tell ye it does very little for a man's appearance. But if the savages had not guessed it already now they knew for sure. That we'd none of us any powder.

We would not ride the animals. Just lead them, keep them off the rocks, hold their noses if they snuffled. But in those two days the judge leached out the guano with creekwater and woodash and precipitated it out and he built a clay kiln and burned charcoal in it, doused the fire by day and fired it again come dark. When we found him him and the Delaware was settin in the creek stark naked and they appeared at first to be drunk but on what none could surmise. The entire top of that mountain was covered with Apache indians and there set he. He got up when he seen us and went to the willows and come back with a pair of wallets and in one was about eight pounds of pure crystal saltpetre and in the other about three pounds of fine alder charcoal. He'd ground the charcoal to a powder in the hollow of a rock, you could have made ink of it. He lashed the bags shut and put them across the pommel of Glanton's saddle and him and the indian got their clothes and I was glad of it for I never seen a grown man with not a hair to his body and him weighin twenty-four stone which he did then and does now. And by my own warrant, for I added up the counters on the bar with my own and sober eyes at a stockscale in Chihuahua City in that same month and year.

We went down the mountain with no scouts, nothin. Just

straight out. We were dead for sleep. It was dark when we reached the plain and we grouped and took a headcount and then we rode out. The moon was about three quarters full and waxing and we were like circus riders, not a sound, the horses on eggshells. We'd no way of knowin where the savages was. The last clue we'd had of their vicinity was the poor buggers flayed in the tree. We set out dead west across the desert. Doc Irving was before me and it was that bright I could count the hairs on his head.

We rode all night and toward the morning just as the moon was down we come upon a band of wolves. They scattered and come back, not a sound out of them no more than smoke. They'd drift off and quarter around and circle the horses. Bold as brass. We cut at them with our hobbles and they would slip past, you couldnt hear them on the hardpan just their breath or they would mutter and grouse or pop their teeth. Glanton halted and the things swirled around and slank off and come back. Two of the Delawares backtracked off to the left a bit—braver souls than me—and sure they found the kill. Twas a young buck antelope new killed the evenin before. It was about half consumed and we set upon it with our knives and took the rest of the meat with us and we ate it raw in the saddle and it was the first meat we'd seen in six days. Froze for it we were. Foragin on the mountain for piñon nuts like bears and glad to get them. We left little more than bones for the lobos, but I would never shoot a wolf and I know other men of the same sentiments.

In all this time the judge had spoke hardly a word. So at dawn we were on the edge of a vast malpais and his honor takes up a position on some lava rocks there and he commences to give us a address. It was like a sermon but it was no such sermon as any man of us had ever heard before. Beyond the malpais was a volcanic peak and in the sunrise it was many colors and there was dark little birds crossin down the wind and the wind was flappin the judge's old benjamin about him and he pointed to that stark and solitary mountain and delivered himself of an oration to what end I know not, then or now, and he concluded with the tellin us that our mother the earth as he said was round like an egg and contained all good things within her. Then he turned and led the horse he had been ridin across that terrain of black and glassy slag, treacherous to man and beast alike, and us behind him like the disciples of a new faith.

The expriest broke off and tapped the dead pipe against the heel of his boot. He looked at the judge over the way where he sat with his torso bared to the flames as was his practice. He turned and regarded the kid.

The malpais. It was a maze. Ye'd run out upon a little promontory and ye'd be balked about by the steep crevasses, you wouldnt dare to jump them. Sharp black glass the edges and sharp the flinty rocks below. We led the horses with every care and still they were bleedin about their hooves. Our boots was cut to pieces. Clamberin over those old caved and rimpled plates you could see well enough how things had gone in that place, rocks melted and set up all wrinkled like a pudding, the earth stove through to the molten core of her. Where for aught any man knows lies the locality of hell. For the earth is a globe in the void and truth there's no up nor down to it and there's men in this company besides myself seen little cloven hoofprints in the stone clever as a little doe in her going but what little doe ever trod melted rock? I'd not go behind scripture but it may be that there has been sinners so notorious evil that the fires coughed em up again and I could well see in the long ago how it was little devils with their pitchforks had traversed that fiery vomit for to salvage back those souls that had by misadventure been spewed up from their damnation onto the outer shelves of the world. Aye. It's a notion, no more. But someplace in the scheme of things this world must touch the other. And somethin put them little hooflet markings in the lava flow for I seen them there myself.

The judge, he seemed not to take his eyes from that dead cone where it rose off the desert like a great chancre. We followed solemn as owls so that he turned to look back and he did laugh when he seen our faces. At the foot of the mountain we drew lots and we sent two men to go on with the horses. I watched them go. One of them is at this fire tonight and I saw him lead them horses away over the slaglands like a doomed man.

And we were not doomed ourselves I dont reckon. When I looked up he was already upon the slope hand and foot, the judge was, his bag over his shoulder and his rifle for alpenstock. And so did we all go. Not halfway up we could already see the savages out on the plain. We climbed on. I thought at worst we'd throw ourselves into the caldron rather than be taken by those fiends. We climbed up and I reckon it was midday when we reached the top. We were done in. The savages not ten miles out. I looked at the men about me and sure they didnt look much. The dignity was gone out of them. They were good hearts all, then and now, and I did not like to see them so and I thought the judge had been sent among us for a curse. And yet he proved me wrong. At the time he did. I'm of two minds again now.

He was the first to the rim of the cone for all the size of him and he stood gazin about like he'd come for the view. Then he set down and he begun to scale at the rock with his knife. One by one we straggled up and he set with his back to that gapin hole and he was chippin away and he called upon us to do the same. It was brimstone. A weal of brimstone all about the rim of the caldron, bright yellow and shining here and there with the little flakes of silica but most pure flowers of sulphur. We chipped it loose and chopped it fine with our knives till we had about two pounds of it and then the judge took the wallets and went to a cupped place in the rock and dumped out the charcoal and the nitre and stirred them about with his hand and poured the sulphur in.

I didnt know but what we'd be required to bleed into it like freemasons but it was not so. He worked it up dry with his hands and all the while the savages down there on the plain drawin nigh to us and when I turned back the judge was standin, the great hairless oaf, and he'd took out his pizzle and he was pissin into the mixture, pissin with a great vengeance and one hand aloft and he cried out for us to do likewise.

We were half mad anyways. All lined up. Delawares and all. Every man save Glanton and he was a study. We hauled forth our members and at it we went and the judge on his knees kneadin the mass with his naked arms and the piss was splashin about and he was cryin out to us to piss, man, piss for your very souls for cant you see the redskins yonder, and laughin the while and workin up this great mass in a foul black dough, a devil's batter by the stink of it and him not a bloody dark pastryman himself I dont suppose and he pulls out his knife and he commences to trowel it across the southfacin rocks, spreadin it out thin with the knifeblade and watchin the sun with one eye and him smeared with blacking and reekin of piss and sulphur and grinnin and wieldin the knife with a dexterity that was wondrous like he did it every day of his life. And when he was done he set back and wiped his hands on his chest and then he watched the savages and so did we all.

They were on the malpais by then and they had a tracker who followed us every step on that naked rock, fallin back at each blind head and callin out to the others. I dont know what he followed. Scent perhaps. We could soon hear them talkin down there. Then they seen us.

Well, God in his glory knows what they thought. They were scattered out across the lava and one of them pointed and they all looked up. Thunderstruck no doubt. To see eleven men perched on the topmost rim of that scalded atoll like misflown birds. They parleyed and we watched to see would they dispatch any of their number after the horses but they did not. Their greed overcame all else and they started for the base of the cone, scramblin over the lava for to see who would be first.

We had I would suppose an hour. We watched the savages and we watched the judge's foul matrix dryin on the rocks and we watched a cloud that was making for the sun. One by one we give up watchin the rocks or the savages either one, for the cloud did look to be dead set for the sun and it would have took the better part of an hour to have crossed it and that was the last hour we had. Well, the judge was sittin making entries in his little book and he saw the cloud same as every other man and he put down the book and watched it and we did all. No one spoke. There was none to curse and none to pray, we just watched. And that cloud just cut the corner from the sun and passed on and there was no shadow fell upon us and the judge took up his ledger and went on with his entries as before. I watched him. Then I clambered down and tested a patch of the stuff with my hand. There was heat comin off of it. I walked along the rim and the savages was ascendin by every quarter for there was no route to favor on that bald and gravel slope. I looked for rocks of any size to send down but there was none there larger than your fist, just fine gravel and plates of scrag. I looked at Glanton and he was watchin the judge and he seemed to have had his wits stole.

Well the judge closed up his little book and took his leather shirt and spread it out in the little cupped place and called for us to bring the stuff to him. Every knife was out and we went to scrapin it up and him cautionin us not to strike fire on them flints. And we heaped it up in the shirt and he commenced to chop and grind it with his knife. And Captain Glanton, he calls out.

Captain Glanton. Would ye believe it? Captain Glanton, he says. Come charge that swivelbore of yours and let's see what manner of thing we have here.

Glanton come up with his rifle and he scooped his charger full and he charged both barrels and patched two balls and drove them home and capped the piece and made to step to the rim. But that was never the judge's way.

Down the maw of that thing, he says, and Glanton never questioned it. He went down the pitch of the inner rim to where lay the terminus of that terrible flue and he held his piece out over it and pointed it straight down and cocked the hammer and fired.

You wouldnt hear a sound like it in a long day's ride. It give me the fidgets. He fired both barrels and he looked at us and he looked at the judge. The judge just waved and went on with his grindin and then he called us all about to fill our horns and flasks and we did, one by one, circlin past him like communicants. And when all had shared he filled his own flask and he got out his pistols and saw to the priming. The foremost of the savages was not more than a furlong on the slope. We were ready to lay into them but again the judge would not have it. He fired off his pistols down into the caldron, spacin out the shots, and he fired all ten chambers and cautioned us back from sight while he reloaded the pieces. All this gunfire had give the savages some pause no doubt for they very likely reckoned us to be without powder altogether. And then the judge, he steps up to the rim and he had with him a good white linen shirt from out of his bag and he waved it to the redskins and he called down to them in spanish.

Well it would have brought tears to your eyes. All dead save me, he called. Have mercy on me. Todos muertos. Todos. Wavin the shirt. God it set them yappin on the slope like dogs and he turns to us, the judge, with that smile of his, and he says: Gentlemen. That was all he said. He had the pistols stuck in his belt at the back and he drew them one in each hand and he is as eitherhanded as a spider, he can write with both hands at a time and I've seen him to do it, and he commenced to kill indians. We needed no second invitation. God it was a butchery. At the first fire we killed a round dozen and we did not let up. Before the last poor nigger reached the bottom of the slope there was fifty-eight of them lay slaughtered among the gravels. They just slid down the slope like chaff down a hopper, some turned this way, some that, and they made a chain about the base of the mountain. We rested our rifle barrels on the brimstone and we shot nine more on the lava where they ran. It was a stand, what it was. Wagers was laid. The last of them shot was a reckonable part of a mile from the muzzles of the guns and that on a dead run. It was sharp shootin all around and not a misfire in the batch with that queer powder.

The expriest turned and looked at the kid. And that was the judge the first ever I saw him. Aye. He's a thing to study.

The kid looked at Tobin. What's he a judge of? he said.

What's he a judge of?

What's he a judge of.

Tobin glanced off across the fire. Ah lad, he said. Hush now. The man will hear ye. He's ears like a fox.

XI

Into the mountains – Old Ephraim – A Delaware carried off –
The search – Another probate – In the gorge – The ruins – Keet seel –
The solerette – Representations and things –
The judge tells a story – A mule lost – Mescal pits –
Night scene with moon, blossoms, judge – The village – Glanton
on the management of animals – The trail out.

They rode on into the mountains and their way took them
through high pine forests, wind in the trees, lonely birdcalls. The shoeless mules slaloming through the dry grass and
pine needles. In the blue coulees on the north slopes narrow
tailings of old snow. They rode up switchbacks through a lonely
aspen wood where the fallen leaves lay like golden disclets in the
damp black trail. The leaves shifted in a million spangles down
the pale corridors and Glanton took one and turned it like a
tiny fan by its stem and held it and let it fall and its perfection
was not lost on him. They rode through a narrow draw where
the leaves were shingled up in ice and they crossed a high
saddle at sunset where wild doves were rocketing down the
wind and passing through the gap a few feet off the ground,
veering wildly among the ponies and dropping off down into
the blue gulf below. They rode on into a dark fir forest, the
little Spanish ponies sucking at the thin air, and just at dusk as
Glanton's horse was clambering over a fallen log a lean blond

bear rose up out of the swale on the far side where it had been feeding and looked down at them with dim pig's eyes.

Glanton's horse reared and Glanton flattened himself along the horse's shoulder and drew his pistol. One of the Delawares was next behind him and the horse he rode was falling backward and he was trying to turn it, beating it about the head with his balled fist, and the bear's long muzzle swung toward them in a stunned articulation, amazed beyond reckoning, some foul gobbet dangling from its jaws and its chops dyed red with blood. Glanton fired. The ball struck the bear in the chest and the bear leaned with a strange moan and seized the Delaware and lifted him from the horse. Glanton fired again into the thick ruff of fur forward of the bear's shoulder as it turned and the man dangling from the bear's jaws looked down at them cheek and jowl with the brute and one arm about its neck like some crazed defector in a gesture of defiant camaraderie. All through the woods a bedlam of shouts and the whack of men beating the screaming horses into submission. Glanton cocked the pistol a third time as the bear swung with the indian dangling from its mouth like a doll and passed over him in a sea of honey-colored hair smeared with blood and a reek of carrion and the rooty smell of the creature itself. The shot rose and rose, a small core of metal scurrying toward the distant beltways of matter grinding mutely to the west above them all. Several rifleshots rang out and the beast loped horribly into the forest with his hostage and was lost among the darkening trees.

The Delawares trailed the animal three days while the party moved on. The first day they followed blood and they saw where the thing had rested and where the wounds had stanched and the next day they followed the dragmarks through the duff of a high forest floor and the day after they followed only the faintest trace across a high stone mesa and then nothing. They cut for sign until dark and they slept on the naked flints and the next day they rose and looked out on all that wild and stony country to the north. The bear had carried off their kinsman like some fabled storybook beast and the land had swallowed them up beyond all ransom or reprieve. They caught up their horses and turned back. Nothing moved in that high wilderness save the wind. They did not speak. They were men of another time for all that they bore christian names and they had lived all their lives in a wilderness as had their fathers before them. They'd learnt war by warring, the generations driven from the eastern shore across a continent, from the ashes at Gnadenhutten onto the prairies and across the outlet to the bloodlands of the west. If much in the world were mystery the limits of that world were not, for it was without measure or bound and there were contained within it creatures more horrible yet and men of other colors and beings which no man has looked upon and yet not alien none of it more than were their own hearts alien in them, whatever wilderness contained there and whatever beasts.

They cut the trail of the party early the next day and by nightfall of the day following they had overtaken them. The lost warrior's horse stood saddled in the caballado as they had left it and they took down the bags and divided his estate among them and that man's name was never said again. In the evening the judge came to the fire and sat with them and questioned them and made a map upon the ground and scrutinized it. Then he rose and trod it out with his boots and in the morning all rode on as before.

Their way led now through dwarf oak and ilex and over a stony ground where black trees stood footed in the seams on the slopes. They rode through sunlight and high grass and in the late afternoon they came out upon an escarpment that seemed to rim the known world. Below them in the paling light smoldered the plains of San Agustin stretching away to the northeast, the earth floating off in a long curve silent under looms of smoke from the underground coal deposits burning there a thousand years. The horses picked their way along the rim with care and the riders cast varied glances out upon that ancient and naked land.

In the days to come they would ride up through a country where the rocks would cook the flesh from your hand and where other than rock nothing was. They rode in a narrow enfilade along a trail strewn with the dry round turds of goats and they rode with their faces averted from the rock wall and the bake-oven air which it rebated, the slant black shapes of the mounted men stenciled across the stone with a definition austere and implacable like shapes capable of violating their covenant with the flesh that authored them and continuing autonomous across the naked rock without reference to sun or man or god.

They rode down from this country through a deep gorge, clattering over the stones, rifts of cool blue shade. In the dry sand of the arroyo floor old bones and broken shapes of painted pottery and graven on the rocks above them pictographs of horse and cougar and turtle and the mounted Spaniards helmeted and bucklered and contemptuous of stone and silence and time itself. Lodged in faults and crevices a hundred feet above them were nests of straw and jetsam from old high waters and the riders could hear the mutter of thunder in some nameless distance and they kept watch on the narrow shape of sky overhead for any darkness of impending rain, threading the canyon's close pressed flanks, the dry white rocks of the dead river floor round and smooth as arcane eggs.

That night they camped in the ruins of an older culture deep in the stone mountains, a small valley with a clear run of water and good grass. Dwellings of mud and stone were walled up beneath an overhanging cliff and the valley was traced with the work of old acequias. The loose sand in the valley floor was strewn everywhere with pieces of pottery and blackened bits of wood and it was crossed and recrossed with the tracks of deer and other animals.

The judge walked the ruins at dusk, the old rooms still black with woodsmoke, old flints and broken pottery among the ashes and small dry corncobs. A few rotting wooden ladders yet leaned against the dwelling walls. He roamed through the ruinous kivas picking up small artifacts and he sat upon a high wall and sketched in his book until the light failed.

The moon rose full over the canyon and there was stark

silence in the little valley. It may be it was their own shadows kept the coyotes from abroad for there was no sound of them or wind or bird in that place but only the light rill of water running over the sand in the dark below their fires.

The judge all day had made small forays among the rocks of the gorge through which they'd passed and now at the fire he spread part of a wagonsheet on the ground and was sorting out his finds and arranging them before him. In his lap he held the leather ledgerbook and he took up each piece, flint or potsherd or tool of bone, and deftly sketched it into the book. He sketched with a practiced ease and there was no wrinkling of that bald brow or pursing of those oddly childish lips. His fingers traced the impression of old willow wicker on a piece of pottery clay and he put this into his book with nice shadings, an economy of pencil strokes. He is a draftsman as he is other things, well sufficient to the task. He looks up from time to time at the fire or at his companions in arms or at the night beyond. Lastly he set before him the footpiece from a suit of armor hammered out in a shop in Toledo three centuries before, a small steel tapadero frail and shelled with rot. This the judge sketched in profile and in perspective, citing the dimensions in his neat script, making marginal notes.

Glanton watched him. When he had done he took up the little footguard and turned it in his hand and studied it again and then he crushed it into a ball of foil and pitched it into the fire. He gathered up the other artifacts and cast them also into the fire and he shook out the wagonsheet and folded it away among his possibles together with the notebook. Then he sat with his hands cupped in his lap and he seemed much satisfied with the world, as if his counsel had been sought at its creation.

A Tennessean named Webster had been watching him and he asked the judge what he aimed to do with those notes and sketches and the judge smiled and said that it was his intention to expunge them from the memory of man. Webster smiled and the judge laughed. Webster regarded him with one eye asquint and he said: Well you've been a draftsman somewheres and them pictures is like enough the things themselves. But no man can put all the world in a book. No more than everthing drawed in a book is so.

Well said, Marcus, spoke the judge.

But dont draw me, said Webster. For I dont want in your book.

My book or some other book said the judge. What is to be deviates no jot from the book wherein it's writ. How could it? It would be a false book and a false book is no book at all.

You're a formidable riddler and I'll not match words with ye. Only save my crusted mug from out your ledger there for I'd not have it shown about perhaps to strangers.

The judge smiled. Whether in my book or not, every man is tabernacled in every other and he in exchange and so on in an endless complexity of being and witness to the uttermost edge of the world.

I'll stand for my own witness, said Webster, but by now the others had begun to call to him his conceit, and who would want to see his bloody portrait anyway and would there be fights break out in the great crowds awaiting its unveiling and perhaps they could tar and feather the picture, lacking the article itself. Until the judge raised his hand and called for amnesty and told them that Webster's feelings were of a different kind and not motivated by vanity at all and that he'd once drawn an old Hueco's portrait and unwittingly chained the man to his own likeness. For he could not sleep for fear an enemy might take it and deface it and so like was the portrait that he would not suffer it creased nor anything to touch it and he made a journey across the desert with it to where he'd heard the judge was to be found and he begged his counsel as to how he might preserve the thing and the judge took him deep into the mountains and they buried the portrait in the floor of a cave where it lies yet for aught the judge knew.

When he was done telling this Webster spat and wiped his mouth and eyed the judge again. That man, he said, was no more than a ignorant heathen savage.

That's so, said the judge.

It aint like that with me.

Excellent, said the judge, reaching for his portmanteau. You've no objection to a sketch then?

I'll sit for no portrait, said Webster. But it aint like you said.

The company fell silent. Someone rose to stoke the fire and the moon ascended and grew small over the ruined dwellings and the little stream braided over the sands in the valley floor shone like woven metal and save for the sound it made there was no sound other.

What kind of indians has these here been, Judge?

The judge looked up.

Dead ones I'd say, what about you, Judge?

Not so dead, said the judge.

They was passable masons, I'd say that. These niggers hereabouts now aint no kind.

Not so dead, said the judge. Then he told them another story and it was this story.

In the western country of the Alleghenies some years ago when it was yet a wilderness there was a man who kept a harness shop by the side of the Federal road. He did so because it was his trade and yet he did little of it for there were few travelers in that place. So that he fell into the habit before long of dressing himself as an indian and taking up station a few miles above his shop and waiting there by the roadside to ask whoever should come that way if they would give him money. At this time he had done no person any injury.

One day a certain man came by and the harnessmaker in his beads and feathers stepped from behind his tree and asked this certain man for some coins. He was a young man and he refused and having recognized the harnessmaker for a white man spoke to him in a way that made the harnessmaker ashamed so that he invited the young man to come to his dwelling a few miles distant on the road.

This harnessmaker lived in a bark house he had built and he kept a wife and two children all of whom reckoned the old man mad and were only waiting some chance to escape him and the

142

wild place he'd brought them to. They therefore welcomed the guest and the woman gave him his supper. But while he ate the old man again began to try to wheedle money from him and he said that they were poor as indeed they were and the traveler listened to him and then he took out two coins which like the old man had never seen and the old man took the coins and studied them and showed them to his son and the stranger finished his meal and said to the old man that he might have those coins.

But ingratitude is more common than you might think and the harnessmaker wasnt satisfied and he began to question whether he ought not perhaps to have another such coin for his wife. The traveler pushed back his plate and turned in his chair and gave the old man a lecture and in this lecture the old man heard things he had once known but forgotten and he heard some new things to go with them. The traveler concluded by telling the old man that he was a loss to God and man alike and would remain so until he took his brother into his heart as he would take himself in and he come upon his own person in want in some desert place in the world.

Now as he was concluding this speech there passed in the road a nigger drawing a funeral hearse for one of his own kind and it was painted pink and the nigger was dressed in clothes of every color like a carnival clown and the young man pointed out this nigger passing in the road and he said that even a black nigger . . .

Here the judge paused. He had been looking into the fire and he raised his head and looked around him. His narration was much in the manner of a recital. He had not lost the thread of his tale. He smiled at the listeners about.

Said that even a crazy black nigger was not less than a man among men. And then the old man's son stood up and began an oration himself, pointing out at the road and calling for a place to be made for the nigger. He used those words. That a place be made. Of course by this time the nigger and hearse had passed on from sight.

With this the old man repented all over again and swore that the boy was right and the old woman who was seated by the fire was amazed at all she had heard and when the guest announced that the time had come for his departure she had tears in her eyes and the little girl came out from behind the bed and clung to his clothes.

The old man offered to walk him out the road so as to see him off on his journey and to apprise him of which fork in the road to take and which not for there were scarcely any waysigns in that part of the world.

As they walked out they spoke of life in such a wild place where such people as you saw you saw but one and never again and by and by they came to the fork in the road and here the traveler told the old man that he had come with him far enough and he thanked him and they took their departure each of the other and the stranger went on his way. But the harnessmaker seemed unable to suffer the loss of his company and he called to him and went with him again a little way upon the road. And by and by they came to a place where the road was darkened in a deep wood and in this place the old man killed the traveler. He killed him with a rock and he took his clothes and he took his watch and his money and he buried him in a shallow grave by the side of the road. Then he went home.

On the way he tore his own clothes and bloodied himself with a flint and he told his wife they had been set upon by robbers and the young traveler murdered and him only escaped. She began to cry and after a while she made him take her to the place and she took wild primrose which grew in plenty thereabout and she put it on the stones and she came there many times until she was old.

The harnessmaker lived until his son was grown and never did anyone harm again. As he lay dying he called the son to him and told him what he had done. And the son said that he forgave him if it was his to do so and the old man said that it was his to do so and then he died.

But the boy was not sorry for he was jealous of the dead man and before he went away he visited that place and cast away the rocks and dug up the bones and scattered them in the forest and then he went away. He went away to the west and he himself became a killer of men.

The old woman was still living at the time and she knew none of what had passed and she thought that wild animals had dug the bones and scattered them. Perhaps she did not find all the bones but such as she did she restored to the grave and she covered them up and piled the stones over them and carried flowers to that place as before. When she was an old woman she told people that it was her son buried there and perhaps by that time it was so.

Here the judge looked up and smiled. There was a silence, then all began to shout at once with every kind of disclaimer.

He was no harnessmaker he was a shoemaker and he was cleared of them charges, called one.

And another: He never lived in no wilderness place, he had a shop dead in the center of Cumberland Maryland.

They never knew where them bones come from. The old woman was crazy, known to be so.

That was my brother in that casket and he was a minstrel dancer out of Cincinnati Ohio was shot to death over a woman.

And other protests until the judge raised both hands for silence. Wait now, he said. For there's a rider to the tale. There was a young bride waiting for that traveler with whose bones we are acquainted and she bore a child in her womb that was the traveler's son. Now this son whose father's existence in this world is historical and speculative even before the son has entered it is in a bad way. All his life he carries before him the idol of a perfection to which he can never attain. The father dead has euchered the son out of his patrimony. For it is the death of the father to which the son is entitled and to which he is heir, more so than his goods. He will not hear of the small mean ways that tempered the man in life. He will not see him struggling in follies of his own devising. No. The world which he inherits bears him false witness. He is broken before a frozen god and he will never find his way.

What is true of one man, said the judge, is true of many. The people who once lived here are called the Anasazi. The old ones. They quit these parts, routed by drought or disease or by wandering bands of marauders, quit these parts ages since and of them there is no memory. They are rumors and ghosts in this land and they are much revered. The tools, the art, the building—these things stand in judgement on the latter races. Yet there is nothing for them to grapple with. The old ones are gone like phantoms and the savages wander these canyons to the sound of an ancient laughter. In their crude huts they crouch in darkness and listen to the fear seeping out of the rock. All progressions from a higher to a lower order are marked by ruins and mystery and a residue of nameless rage. So. Here are the dead fathers. Their spirit is entombed in the stone. It lies upon the land with the same weight and the same ubiquity. For whoever makes a shelter of reeds and hides has joined his spirit to the common destiny of creatures and he will subside back into the primal mud with scarcely a cry. But who builds in stone seeks to alter the structure of the universe and so it was with these masons however primitive their works may seem to us.

None spoke. The judge sat half naked and sweating for all the night was cool. At length the expriest Tobin looked up.

It strikes me, he said, that either son is equal in the way of disadvantage. So what is the way of raising a child?

At a young age, said the judge, they should be put in a pit with wild dogs. They should be set to puzzle out from their proper clues the one of three doors that does not harbor wild lions. They should be made to run naked in the desert until . . .

Hold now, said Tobin. The question was put in all earnestness.

And the answer, said the judge. If God meant to interfere in the degeneracy of mankind would he not have done so by now? Wolves cull themselves, man. What other creature could? And is the race of man not more predacious yet? The way of the world is to bloom and to flower and die but in the affairs of men there is no waning and the noon of his expression signals the onset of night. His spirit is exhausted at the peak of its achievement. His meridian is at once his darkening and the evening of his day. He loves games? Let him play for stakes. This you see here, these ruins wondered at by tribes of savages, do you not think that this will be again? Aye. And again. With other people, with other sons.

The judge looked about him. He was sat before the fire naked save for his breeches and his hands rested palm down upon his knees. His eyes were empty slots. None among the company harbored any notion as to what this attitude implied, yet so like an icon was he in his sitting that they grew cautious and spoke with circumspection among themselves as if they would not waken something that had better been left sleeping.

The following evening as they rode up onto the western rim they lost one of the mules. It went skittering off down the canyon wall with the contents of the panniers exploding soundlessly in the hot dry air and it fell through sunlight and through shade, turning in that lonely void until it fell from sight into a sink of cold blue space that absolved it forever of memory in the mind of any living thing that was. Glanton sat his horse and studied the adamantine deep beneath him. A raven had set forth from the cliffs far below to wheel and croak. In the acute light the sheer stone wall wore strange contours and the horsemen on that promontory seemed very small even to themselves. Glanton looked upward, briefly, as if there were anything to ascertain in that perfect china sky, and then he chucked up his horse and they rode on.

Crossing the high mesas in the days to follow they began to come upon burnedout pits in the ground where the indians had cooked mescal and they rode through strange forests of maguey —the aloe or century plant—with immense flowering stalks that rose forty feet into the desert air. Each dawn as they saddled their horses they watched the pale mountains to the north and to the west for any trace of smoke. There was none. The scouts would be already gone, riding out in the dark before the sun rose, and they would not return until night, reckoning out the camp in that incoordinate waste by palest starlight or in blackness absolute where the company sat among the rocks without fire or bread or camaraderie any more than banded apes. They crouched in silence eating raw meat the Delawares had killed on the plain with arrows and they slept among the bones. A lobeshaped moon rose over the black shapes of the mountains dimming out the eastern stars and along the nearby ridge the white blooms of flowering yuccas moved in the wind and in the night bats came from some nether part of the world to stand on leather wings like dark satanic hummingbirds and feed at the mouths of those flowers. Farther along the ridge and slightly elevated on a ledge of sandstone squatted the judge, pale and naked. He raised his hand and the bats flared in confusion and then he lowered it and sat as before and soon they were feeding again.

Glanton would not turn back. His calculations concerning the enemy included every duplicity. He spoke of ambushes. Even he in all his pride could not have believed that a company of nineteen men had evacuated an area of ten thousand square miles of every living human. Two days later when the scouts returned in the middle of the afternoon and reported finding the Apache villages abandoned he would not ride in. They camped on the mesa and made false fires and lay all night with their rifles on that stony heath. In the morning they caught up the horses and descended into a wild valley strewn with grass huts and the remains of old cookfires. They dismounted and moved among the shelters, frail structures of saplings and weeds stuck into the ground and bent to at the top to form a rounded hovel over which a few rags of hide or old blankets remained. The grounds were strewn with bones and knappings of flint or quartzite and they found pieces of jars and old baskets and broken stone mortars and rifts of dried beanpods from the mesquite and a child's straw doll and a primitive onestringed fiddle that had been crushed and a part of a necklace of dried melonseeds.

The hovel doors were waist high and faced the east and few of the shelters were tall enough to be stood in. The last one that Glanton and David Brown entered was defended by a large and vicious dog. Brown drew his belt pistol but Glanton stopped him. He dropped to one knee and spoke to the animal. It crouched against the rear wall of the hogan and bared its teeth and swung its head from side to side, the ears flattened alongside its skull.

He'll bite you, said Brown.

Get me a piece of jerky.

He crouched, talking to the dog. The dog watched him.

You wont man that son of a bitch, said Brown.

I can man anything that eats. Get me a piece of jerky.

When Brown came back with the dried meat the dog was looking about uneasily. When they rode west out of the canyon it was trotting with a slight limp at the heels of Glanton's horse.

They followed an old stone trail up out of the valley and through a high pass, the mules clambering along the ledges like goats. Glanton led his horse and called after the others, and yet darkness overtook them and they were benighted in that place, strung out along a fault in the wall of the gorge. He led them cursing upward through the profoundest dark but the way grew so narrow and the footing so treacherous they were obliged to halt. The Delawares came back afoot, having left their horses at the top of the pass, and Glanton threatened to shoot them all were they attacked in that place.

They passed the night each man at the feet of his horse where it stood in the trail between a sheer rise and a sheer fall. Glanton sat at the head of the column with his guns laid out before him. He watched the dog. In the morning they rose and went on, picking up the other scouts and their horses at the top of the pass and sending them on again. They rode through the mountains all that day and if Glanton slept none saw him do so.

The Delawares had reckoned the village empty ten days and the Gileños had decamped in small bands by every egress. There was no trail to follow. The company rode on through the mountains singlefile. The scouts were gone for two days. On the third day they rode into camp with their horses all but ruined. That morning they'd seen fires atop a thin blue mesa fifty miles to the south.

XII

Crossing the border – Storms – Ice and lightning –
The slain argonauts – The azimuth – Rendezvous – Councils of war –
Slaughter of the Gileños – Death of Juan Miguel – The dead in
the lake – The chief – An Apache child – On the desert – Night fires –
El virote – A surgery – The judge takes a scalp – Un hacendado –
Gallego – Ciudad de Chihuahua.

For the next two weeks they would ride by night, they would make no fire. They had struck the shoes from their horses and filled the nailholes in with clay and those who still had tobacco used their pouches to spit in and they slept in caves and on bare stone. They rode their horses through the tracks of their dismounting and they buried their stool like cats and they barely spoke at all. Crossing those barren gravel reefs in the night they seemed remote and without substance. Like a patrol condemned to ride out some ancient curse. A thing surmised from the blackness by the creak of leather and the chink of metal.

They cut the throats of the packanimals and jerked and divided the meat and they traveled under the cape of the wild mountains upon a broad soda plain with dry thunder to the south and rumors of light. Under a gibbous moon horse and rider spanceled to their shadows on the snowblue ground and in each flare of lightning as the storm advanced those selfsame forms rearing with a terrible redundancy behind them like some third aspect of their presence hammered out black and wild upon the

151

naked grounds. They rode on. They rode like men invested with a purpose whose origins were antecedent to them, like blood legatees of an order both imperative and remote. For although each man among them was discrete unto himself, conjoined they made a thing that had not been before and in that communal soul were wastes hardly reckonable more than those whited regions on old maps where monsters do live and where there is nothing other of the known world save conjectural winds.

They crossed the del Norte and rode south into a land more hostile yet. All day they crouched like owls under the niggard acacia shade and peered out upon that cooking world. Dust-devils stood on the horizon like the smoke of distant fires but of living thing there was none. They eyed the sun in its circus and at dusk they rode out upon the cooling plain where the western sky was the color of blood. At a desert well they dismounted and drank jaw to jaw with their horses and remounted and rode on. The little desert wolves yapped in the dark and Glanton's dog trotted beneath the horse's belly, its footfalls stitched precisely among the hooves.

That night they were visited with a plague of hail out of a faultless sky and the horses shied and moaned and the men dismounted and sat upon the ground with their saddles over their heads while the hail leaped in the sand like small lucent eggs concocted alchemically out of the desert darkness. When they resaddled and rode on they went for miles through cobbled ice while a polar moon rose like a blind cat's eye up over the rim of the world. In the night they passed the lights of a village on the plain but they did not alter from their course.

Toward the morning they saw fires on the horizon. Glanton sent the Delawares. Already the dawnstar burned pale in the east. When they returned they squatted with Glanton and the judge and the Brown brothers and spoke and gestured and then all remounted and all rode on.

Five wagons smoldered on the desert floor and the riders dismounted and moved among the bodies of the dead argonauts in silence, those right pilgrims nameless among the stones with their terrible wounds, the viscera spilled from their sides and the naked torsos bristling with arrowshafts. Some by their beards were men but yet wore strange menstrual wounds between their legs and no man's parts for these had been cut away and hung dark and strange from out their grinning mouths. In their wigs of dried blood they lay gazing up with ape's eyes at brother sun now rising in the east.

The wagons were no more than embers armatured with the blackened shapes of hoop-iron and tires, the redhot axles quaking deep within the coals. The riders squatted at the fires and boiled water and drank coffee and roasted meat and lay down to sleep among the dead.

When the company set forth in the evening they continued south as before. The tracks of the murderers bore on to the west but they were white men who preyed on travelers in that wilderness and disguised their work to be that of the savages. Notions of chance and fate are the preoccupation of men engaged in rash undertakings. The trail of the argonauts terminated in ashes as told and in the convergence of such vectors in such a waste wherein the hearts and enterprise of one small nation have been swallowed up and carried off by another the expriest asked if some might not see the hand of a cynical god conducting with what austerity and what mock surprise so lethal a congruence. The posting of witnesses by a third and other path altogether might also be called in evidence as appearing to beggar chance, yet the judge, who had put his horse forward until he was abreast of the speculants, said that in this was expressed the very nature of the witness and that his proximity was no third thing but rather the prime, for what could be said to occur unobserved?

The Delawares went on ahead in the dusk and the Mexican John McGill led the column, dropping from time to time from his horse to lie flat on his belly and skylight the outriders on the desert before them and then remount again without halting his pony or the company which followed. They moved like migrants under a drifting star and their track across the land reflected in its faint arcature the movements of the earth itself. To the west the cloudbanks stood above the mountains like the dark warp of the very firmament and the starsprent reaches of the galaxies hung in a vast aura above the riders' heads.

Two mornings later the Delawares returned from their dawn reconnaissance and reported the Gileños camped along the shore of a shallow lake less than four hours to the south. They had with them their women and children and they were many. Glanton when he rose from this council walked out on the desert alone and stood for a long time looking out upon the darkness downcountry.

They saw to their arms, drawing the charges from their pieces and reloading them. They spoke in low voices among themselves although the desert round lay like a great barren plate gently quaking in the heat. In the afternoon a detachment led the horses out to water and led them back again and with dark Glanton and his lieutenants followed the Delawares out to scout the enemy's position.

They'd driven a stick into the ground on a rise north of the camp and when the angle of the Dipper had swung about to this inclination Toadvine and the Vandiemanlander set the company in motion and they rode forth south after the others trammeled to chords of rawest destiny.

They reached the north end of the lake in the cool hours before dawn and turned along the shore. The water was very black and along the beach there lay a wrack of foam and they could hear ducks talking far out on the lake. The embers of the encampment's fires lay below them in a gentle curve like the lights of a distant port. Before them on that lonely strand a solitary rider sat his horse. It was one of the Delawares and he turned his horse without speaking and they followed him up through the brush onto the desert.

The party was crouched in a stand of willow a half mile from the fires of the enemy. They had muffled the heads of the horses with blankets and the hooded beasts stood rigid and ceremonial behind them. The new riders dismounted and bound their own horses and they sat upon the ground while Glanton addressed them.

We got a hour, maybe more. When we ride in it's ever man to his own. Dont leave a dog alive if you can help it.

How many is there, John?

Did you learn to whisper in a sawmill?

There's enough to go around, said the judge.

Dont waste powder and ball on anything that caint shoot back. If we dont kill ever nigger here we need to be whipped and sent home.

This was the extent of their council. The hour that followed was a long hour. They led the blindfolded horses down and stood looking out over the encampment but they were watching the horizon to the east. A bird called. Glanton turned to his horse and unhooded it like a falconer at morning. A wind had risen and the horse lifted its head and sniffed the air. The other men followed. The blankets lay where they had fallen. They mounted, pistols in hand, saps of rawhide and riverrock looped about their wrists like the implements of some primitive equestrian game. Glanton looked back at them and then nudged forth his horse.

As they trotted out onto the white salt shore an old man rose from the bushes where he'd been squatting and turned to face them. The dogs that had been waiting on to contest his stool bolted yapping. Ducks began to rise by ones and pairs out on the lake. Someone clubbed the old man down and the riders put rowels to their mounts and lined out for the camp behind the dogs with their clubs whirling and the dogs howling in a tableau of some hellish hunt, the partisans nineteen in number bearing down upon the encampment where there lay sleeping upward of a thousand souls.

Glanton rode his horse completely through the first wickiup trampling the occupants underfoot. Figures were scrambling out of the low doorways. The raiders went through the village at full gallop and turned and came back. A warrior stepped into their path and leveled a lance and Glanton shot him dead. Three others ran and he shot the first two with shots so closely executed that they fell together and the third one seemed to be coming apart as he ran, hit by half a dozen pistolballs.

Within that first minute the slaughter had become general.

Women were screaming and naked children and one old man tottered forth waving a pair of white pantaloons. The horsemen moved among them and slew them with clubs or knives. A hundred tethered dogs were howling and others were racing crazed among the huts ripping at one another and at the tied dogs nor would this bedlam and clamor cease or diminish from the first moment the riders entered the village. Already a number of the huts were afire and a whole enfilade of refugees had begun streaming north along the shore wailing crazily with the riders among them like herdsmen clubbing down the laggards first.

When Glanton and his chiefs swung back through the village people were running out under the horses' hooves and the horses were plunging and some of the men were moving on foot among the huts with torches and dragging the victims out, slathered and dripping with blood, hacking at the dying and decapitating those who knelt for mercy. There were in the camp a number of Mexican slaves and these ran forth calling out in spanish and were brained or shot and one of the Delawares emerged from the smoke with a naked infant dangling in each hand and squatted at a ring of midden stones and swung them by the heels each in turn and bashed their heads against the stones so that the brains burst forth through the fontanel in a bloody spew and humans on fire came shrieking forth like berserkers and the riders hacked them down with their enormous knives and a young woman ran up and embraced the bloodied forefeet of Glanton's warhorse.

By now a small band of warriors had mounted themselves out of the scattered remuda and they advanced upon the village and rattled a drove of arrows among the burning huts. Glanton drew his rifle from its scabbard and shot the two lead horses and resheathed the rifle and drew his pistol and began to fire between the actual ears of his horse. The mounted indians floundered among the down and kicking horses and they milled and circled and were shot down one by one until the dozen survivors among them turned and fled up the lake past the groaning column of refugees and disappeared in a drifting wake of soda ash.

Glanton turned his horse. The dead lay awash in the shallows like the victims of some disaster at sea and they were strewn along the salt foreshore in a havoc of blood and entrails. Riders were towing bodies out of the bloody waters of the lake and the froth that rode lightly on the beach was a pale pink in the rising light. They moved among the dead harvesting the long black locks with their knives and leaving their victims rawskulled and strange in their bloody cauls. The loosed horses from the remuda came pounding down the reeking strand and disappeared in the smoke and after a while they came pounding back. Men were wading about in the red waters hacking aimlessly at the dead and some lay coupled to the bludgeoned bodies of young women dead or dying on the beach. One of the Delawares passed with a collection of heads like some strange vendor bound for market, the hair twisted about his wrist and the heads dangling and turning together. Glanton knew that every moment on this ground must be contested later in the desert and he rode among the men and urged them on.

McGill came out of the crackling fires and stood staring bleakly at the scene about. He had been skewered through with a lance and he held the stock of it before him. It was fashioned from a sotol stalk and the point of an old cavalry sword bound to the haft curved from out the small of his back. The kid waded out of the water and approached him and the Mexican sat down carefully in the sand.

Get away from him, said Glanton.

McGill turned to look at Glanton and as he did so Glanton leveled his pistol and shot him through the head. He reholstered the gun and stood his empty rifle upright against the saddle and held it with his knee while he measured powder down the barrels. Someone shouted to him. The horse trembled and stepped back and Glanton spoke to it softly and patched two balls and drove them home. He was watching a rise to the north where a band of mounted Apaches were grouped against the sky.

They were perhaps a quarter mile distant, five, six of them, their cries thin and lost. Glanton brought the rifle to the crook of his arm and capped one drum and rotated the barrels and capped the other. He did not take his eyes from the Apaches. Webster stepped from his horse and drew his rifle and slid the ramrod from the thimbles and went to one knee, the ramrod upright in the sand, resting the rifle's forestock upon the fist with which he held it. The rifle had set triggers and he cocked the rear one and laid his face against the cheekpiece. He reckoned the drift of the wind and he reckoned against the sun on the side of the silver foresight and he held high and touched off the piece. Glanton sat immobile. The shot was flat and dead in the emptiness and the gray smoke drifted away. The leader of the group on the rise sat his horse. Then he slowly pitched sideways and fell to the ground.

Glanton gave a whoop and surged forward. Four men followed. The warriors on the rise had dismounted and were lifting up the fallen man. Glanton turned in the saddle without taking his eyes from the indians and held out his rifle to the nearest man. This man was Sam Tate and he took the rifle and reined his horse so short he nearly threw it. Glanton and three rode on and Tate drew the ramrod for a rest and crouched and fired. The horse that carried the wounded chief faltered, ran on. He swiveled the barrels and fired the second charge and it plowed to the ground. The Apaches reined with shrill cries. Glanton leaned forward and spoke into his horse's ear. The indians raised up their leader to a new mount and riding double they flailed at their horses and set out again. Glanton had drawn his pistol and he gestured with it to the men behind and one pulled up his horse and leaped to the ground and went flat on his belly and drew and cocked his own pistol and pulled down the loading lever and stuck it in the sand and holding the gun in both hands with his chin buried in the ground he sighted along the barrel. The horses were two hundred yards out and moving fast. With the second shot the pony that bore the leader bucked and a rider alongside reached and took the reins. They were attempting to take the leader off the wounded animal in mid-stride when the animal collapsed.

Glanton was first to reach the dying man and he knelt with that alien and barbarous head cradled between his thighs like some reeking outland nurse and dared off the savages with his revolver. They circled on the plain and shook their bows and lofted a few arrows at him and then turned and rode on. Blood bubbled from the man's chest and he turned his lost eyes upward, already glazed, the capillaries breaking up. In those dark pools there sat each a small and perfect sun.

He rode back to the camp at the fore of his small column with the chief's head hanging by its hair from his belt. The men were stringing up scalps on strips of leather whang and some of the dead lay with broad slices of hide cut from their backs to be used for the making of belts and harness. The dead Mexican McGill had been scalped and the bloody skulls were already blackening in the sun. Most of the wickiups were burned to the ground and because some gold coins had been found a few of the men were kicking through the smoldering ashes. Glanton cursed them on, taking up a lance and mounting the head upon it where it bobbed and leered like a carnival head and riding up and back, calling to them to round up the caballado and move out. When he turned his horse he saw the judge sitting on the ground. The judge had taken off his hat and was drinking water from a leather bottle. He looked up at Glanton.

It's not him.

What's not?

The judge nodded. That.

Glanton turned the shaft. The head with its long dark locks swung about to face him.

Who do you think it is if it aint him?

The judge shook his head. It's not Gómez. He nodded toward the thing. That gentleman is sangre puro. Gómez is Mexican.

He aint all Mexican.

You cant be all Mexican. It's like being all mongrel. But that's not Gómez because I've seen Gómez and it's not him.

Will it pass for him?

No.

Glanton looked toward the north. He looked down at the judge. You aint seen my dog have ye? he said.

The judge shook his head. Do you intend to drive that stock?

Until I'm made to quit.

That might be soon.

That might be.

How long do you think it will take these yahoos to regroup?

Glanton spat. It wasnt a question and he didnt answer it. Where's your horse? he said.

Gone.

Well if you aim to ride with us you better be for gettin you another one. He looked at the head on the pole. You was some kind of goddamned chief, he said. He nudged the horse forward with his heels and rode out along the water's edge. The Delawares were wading about in the lake feeling for sunken bodies with their feet. He sat there a moment and then he turned the horse and rode up through the sacked encampment. He rode warily, his pistol across his thigh. He followed the tracks coming down from the desert where they'd ridden in. When he returned he had with him the scalp of the old man who had first stood up out of the bushes at dawn.

Within the hour they were mounted and riding south leaving behind them on the scourged shore of the lake a shambles of blood and salt and ashes and driving before them a half a thousand horses and mules. The judge rode at the head of the column bearing on the saddle before him a strange dark child covered with ash. Part of its hair was burned away and it rode mute and stoic watching the land advance before it with huge black eyes like some changeling. The men as they rode turned black in the sun from the blood on their clothes and their faces and then paled slowly in the rising dust until they assumed once more the color of the land through which they passed.

They rode all day with Glanton bringing up the rear of the column. Toward noon the dog caught them up. His chest was dark with blood and Glanton carried him on the pommel of the saddle until he could recruit himself. In the long afternoon he trotted in the shadow of the horse and in the twilight he trotted far out on the plain where the tall shapes of the horses skated over the chaparral on spider legs.

By now there was a thin line of dust to the north and they rode on into dark and the Delawares dismounted and lay with their ears to the ground and then they mounted up and all rode on again.

When they halted Glanton ordered fires built and the wounded seen to. One of the mares had foaled in the desert and this frail form soon hung skewered on a paloverde pole over the raked coals while the Delawares passed among themselves a gourd containing the curdled milk taken from its stomach. From a slight rise to the west of the camp the fires of the enemy were visible ten miles to the north. The company squatted in their bloodstiffened hides and counted the scalps and strung them on poles, the blueblack hair dull and clotted with blood. David Brown went among these haggard butchers as they crouched before the flames but he could find him no surgeon. He carried an arrow in his thigh, fletching and all, and none would touch it. Least of all would Doc Irving, for Brown called him a mortician and a barber and they kept their distance one from the other.

Boys, said Brown, I'd doctorfy it myself but I caint get no straight grip.

The judge looked up at him and smiled.

Will you do her, Holden?

No, Davy, I wont. But I tell you what I will do.

What's that.

I'll write a policy on your life against every mishap save the noose.

Damn you then.

The judge chuckled. Brown glared about him. Will none of ye help a man?

None spoke.

Damn all of ye then, he said.

He sat and stretched his leg out on the ground and looked at it, he bloodier than most. He gripped the shaft and bore down on it. The sweat stood on his forehead. He held his leg and swore softly. Some watched, some did not. The kid rose. I'll try her, he said.

Good lad, said Brown.

He fetched his saddle to lean against. He turned his leg to the fire for the light and folded his belt and held it and hissed down at the boy kneeling there. Grip her stout, lad. And drive her straight. Then he gripped the belt in his teeth and lay back.

The kid took hold of the shaft close to the man's thigh and pressed forward with his weight. Brown seized the ground on either side of him and his head flew back and his wet teeth shone in the firelight. The kid took a new grip and bore down again. The veins in the man's neck stood like ropes and he cursed the boy's soul. On the fourth essay the point of the arrow came through the flesh of the man's thigh and blood ran over the ground. The kid sat back on his heels and passed the sleeve of his shirt across his brow.

Brown let the belt fall from his teeth. Is it through? he said.

It is.

The point? Is it the point? Speak up, man.

The kid drew his knife and cut away the bloody point deftly and handed it up. Brown held it to the firelight and smiled. The point was of hammered copper and it was cocked in its blood-soaked bindings on the shaft but it had held.

Stout lad, ye'll make a shadetree sawbones yet. Now draw her.

The kid withdrew the shaft from the man's leg smoothly and the man bowed on the ground in a lurid female motion and wheezed raggedly through his teeth. He lay there a moment and then he sat up and took the shaft from the kid and threw it in the fire and rose and went off to make his bed.

When the kid returned to his own blanket the expriest leaned to him and hissed at his ear.

Fool, he said. God will not love ye forever.

The kid turned to look at him.

Dont you know he'd of took you with him? He'd of took you, boy. Like a bride to the altar.

———————◆·◆———————

They rose up and moved on sometime after midnight. Glanton had ordered the fires built up and they rode out with the flames lighting all the grounds about and the shadowshapes of the desert brush reeling on the sands and the riders treading their thin and flaring shadows until they had crossed altogether into the darkness which so well became them.

The horses and mules were ranged far out over the desert and they picked them up for miles to the south and drove them on. The sourceless summer lightning marked out of the night dark mountain ranges at the rim of the world and the halfwild horses on the plain before them trotted in those bluish strobes like horses called forth quivering out of the abyss.

In the smoking dawn the party riding ragged and bloody with their baled peltries looked less like victors than the harried afterguard of some ruined army retreating across the meridians of chaos and old night, the horses stumbling, the men tottering asleep in the saddles. The broached day discovered the same barren countryside about and the smoke from their fires of the night before stood thin and windless to the north. The pale dust of the enemy who were to hound them to the gates of the city seemed no nearer and they shambled on through the rising heat driving the crazed horses before them.

Midmorning they watered at a stagnant pothole that had already been walked through by three hundred animals, the riders hazing them out of the water and dismounting to drink from their hats and then riding on again down the dry bed of the stream and clattering over the stony ground, dry rocks and boulders and then the desert soil again red and sandy and the constant mountains about them thinly grassed and grown with ocotillo and sotol and the secular aloes blooming like phantasmagoria in a fever land. At dusk they sent riders west to build fires on the prairie and the company lay down in the dark and slept while bats crossed silently overhead among the stars. When they rode on in the morning it was still dark and the horses all but fainting. Day found the heathen much advanced upon them. They fought their first stand the dawn following and they fought them running for eight days and nights on the plain and among the rocks in the mountains and from the walls and azoteas of abandoned haciendas and they lost not a man.

On the third night they crouched in the keep of old walls of slumped mud with the fires of the enemy not a mile distant on the desert. The judge sat with the Apache boy before the fire and it watched everything with dark berry eyes and some of the men played with it and made it laugh and they gave it jerky and it sat chewing and watching gravely the figures that passed above it. They covered it with a blanket and in the morning the judge was dandling it on one knee while the men saddled their horses. Toadvine saw him with the child as he passed with his saddle but when he came back ten minutes later leading his horse the child was dead and the judge had scalped it. Toadvine put the muzzle of his pistol against the great dome of the judge's head.

Goddamn you, Holden.

You either shoot or take that away. Do it now.

Toadvine put the pistol in his belt. The judge smiled and wiped the scalp on the leg of his trousers and rose and turned away. Another ten minutes and they were on the plain again in full flight from the Apaches.

On the afternoon of the fifth day they were crossing a dry pan at a walk, driving the horses before them, the indians behind just out of rifle range calling out to them in spanish. From time to time one of the company would dismount with rifle and wiping stick and the indians would flare like quail, pulling their ponies around and standing behind them. To the east trembling in the heat stood the thin white walls of a hacienda and the trees thin and green and rigid rising from it like a scene viewed in a diorama. An hour later they were driving the horses—perhaps now a hundred head—along these walls and down a worn trail toward a spring. A young man rode out and welcomed them formally in spanish. No one answered. The young rider looked down along the creek where the fields were laid out with acequias and where the workers in their dusty white costumes stood poised with hoes among the new cotton or waist-high corn. He looked back to the northwest. The Apaches, seventy, eighty of them, were just coming past the first of a row of jacales and defiling along the path and into the shade of the trees.

The peons in the fields saw them at about the same time. They flung their implements from them and began to run, some shrieking, some with their hands atop their heads. The young Don looked at the Americans and he looked at the approaching savages again. He called out something in spanish. The Americans drove the horses up out of the spring and on through the grove of cottonwoods. The last they saw of him he had drawn a small pistol from his boot and had turned to face the indians.

That evening they led the Apaches through the town of Gallego, the street a mud gutter patrolled by swine and wretched hairless dogs. It appeared deserted. The young corn in the road-side fields had been washed by recent rains and stood white and luminous, bleached almost transparent by the sun. They rode most of the night and the next day the indians were still there.

They fought them again at Encinillas and they fought them in the dry passes going toward El Sauz and beyond in the low foothills from which they could already see the churchspires of the city to the south. On the twenty-first of July in the year eighteen forty-nine they rode into the city of Chihuahua to a hero's welcome, driving the harlequin horses before them through the dust of the streets in a pandemonium of teeth and whited eyes. Small boys ran among the hooves and the victors in their gory rags smiled through the filth and the dust and the caked blood as they bore on poles the desiccated heads of the enemy through that fantasy of music and flowers.

XIII

At the baths – Merchants – Trophies of war – The banquet –
Trias – The ball – North – Coyame – The border – The Hueco tanks –
Massacre of the Tiguas – Carrizal – A desert spring –
The Medanos – An inquest concerning teeth – Nacori – The cantina –
A desperate encounter – Into the mountains –
A village decimated – Mounted lancers – A skirmish –
Pursuing the survivors – The plains of Chihuahua –
Slaughter of the soldiers – A burial – Chihuahua – Westward.

Their progress was swelled by new riders, by boys on mule-back and old men in plaited hats and a deputation that took charge of the captured horses and mules and hazed them on through the narrow streets toward the bullring where they could be kept. The tattered campaigners surged on, some now holding aloft cups that had been pressed upon them, waving to the ladies clustered on the balconies their putrescent hats and elevating the bobbing heads with those strange halflidded looks of ennui into which the features had dried, all so hemmed about now by the citizenry that they seemed the vanguard of some ragged uprising and heralded before by a pair of drummers one witless and both barefoot and by a trumpeter who marched with one arm raised above his head in a martial gesture and playing the while. In this manner they passed through the standing portals of the governor's palace, over the worn stone sills and into the courtyard where the broomed hooves of the mercenaries' shoeless horses subsided upon the cobbles with a curious turtlelike clatter.

Hundreds of onlookers pressed about as the dried scalps were counted out upon the stones. Soldiers with muskets kept back the crowds and young girls watched the Americans with huge black eyes and boys crept forth to touch the grisly trophies. There were one hundred and twenty-eight scalps and eight heads and the governor's lieutenant and his retinue came down into the courtyard to welcome them and admire their work. They were promised full payment in gold at the dinner to be held in their honor that evening at the Riddle and Stephens Hotel and with this the Americans sent up a cheer and mounted their horses again. Old women in black rebozos ran forth to kiss the hems of their reeking shirts and hold up their dark little hands in blessing and the riders wheeled their gaunted mounts and pushed through the clamoring multitude and into the street.

They moved on to the public baths where they descended one by one into the waters, each more pale than the one before and all tattooed, branded, sutured, the great puckered scars inaugurated God knows where by what barbarous surgeons across chests and abdomens like the tracks of gigantic millipedes, some deformed, fingers missing, eyes, their foreheads and arms stamped with letters and numbers as if they were articles requiring inventory. Citizens of both sexes withdrew along the walls and watched the water turn into a thin gruel of blood and filth and none could take their eyes from the judge who had disrobed last of all and now walked the perimeter of the baths with a cigar in his mouth and a regal air, testing the waters with one toe, surprisingly petite. He shone like the moon so pale he was and not a hair to be seen anywhere upon that vast corpus, not in any crevice nor in the great bores of his nose and not upon his chest nor in his ears nor any tuft at all above his eyes nor to the lids thereof. The immense and gleaming dome of his naked skull looked like a cap for bathing pulled down to the otherwise darkened skin of his face and neck. As that great bulk lowered itself into the bath the waters rose perceptibly and when he had submerged himself to the eyes he looked about with considerable pleasure, the eyes slightly crinkled, as if he were smiling under the water like some pale and bloated manatee surfaced in a bog while behind his small and close-set ear the wedged cigar smoked gently just above the waterline.

By now merchants had spread their wares all along the clay tiles behind them, suits of European cloth and cut and shirts of colored silks and closenapped beaver hats and fine spanish leather boots, silverheaded canes and riding crops and silvermounted saddles and carven pipes and hideout guns and a group of Toledo swords with ivory hilts and nicely chased blades and barbers were setting up chairs to receive them, crying out the names of celebrated patrons upon whom they had attended, and all of these entrepreneurs assuring the company of credit on the most generous terms.

When they crossed the square attired in their new haberdashery, some with coatsleeves barely past their elbows, the scalps were being strung about the iron fretwork of the gazebo like decorations for some barbaric celebration. The severed heads had been raised on poles above the lampstandards where they now contemplated with their caved and pagan eyes the dry hides of their kinsmen and forebears strung across the stone facade of the cathedral and clacking lightly in the wind. Later when the lamps were lit the heads in the soft glare of the uplight assumed the look of tragic masks and within a few days they would become mottled white and altogether leprous with the droppings of the birds that roosted upon them.

———◆•◆———

This Angel Trias who was governor had been sent abroad as a young man for his education and was widely read in the classics and was a student of languages. He was also a man among men and the rough warriors he'd hired for the protection of the state seemed to warm something in him. When the lieutenant invited Glanton and his officers to dine Glanton replied that he and his men did not keep separate mess. The lieutenant yielded the point with a smile and Trias had done the same. They arrived in good order, shaved and shorn and turned out in their new boots and finery, the Delawares strangely austere and menacing in their morningcoats, all to gather about the table set for them. Cigars were presented and glasses of sherry poured and the governor standing at the head of the table made them welcome and issued orders to his chamberlain that every need be seen to. Soldiers attended them, fetching extra glasses, pouring the wine, lighting cigars from a wick in a silver holder designed for just that purpose. The judge arrived last of all, dressed in a well-cut suit of unbleached linen that had been made for him that very afternoon. Whole bolts of cloth exhausted and squads of tailors as well in that fabrication. His feet were encased in nicely polished gray kid boots and in his hand he held a panama hat that had been spliced together from two such lesser hats by such painstaking work that the joinery did scarcely show at all.

Trias had already taken his seat when the judge made his appearance but no sooner had the governor seen him than he rose again and they shook hands cordially and the governor had him seated at his right and they at once fell into conversation in a tongue none other in that room spoke at all saving for random vile epithets drifted down from the north. The expriest was sat opposite the kid and he raised his brows and motioned toward the head of the table with a swing of his eyes. The kid, in the first starched collar he'd ever owned and the first cravat, sat mute as a tailor's dummy at that board.

By now the table was fully commenced and there was a tandem run of dishes, fish and fowl and beef and wild meats of the countryside and a roast shoat on a platter and casseroles of savories and trifles and glaces and bottles of wine and brandy from the vineyards at El Paso. Patriotic toasts were drunk, the governor's aides raising their glasses to Washington and Franklin and the Americans responding with yet more of their own country's heroes, ignorant alike of diplomacy and any name at all from the pantheon of their sister republic. They fell to and they continued to eat until they had exhausted first the banquet and then the larder of the hotel altogether. Couriers were sent abroad through the city to fetch more only to have this also vanish and more sent for until Riddle's cook barricaded the door with his body and the soldiers in attendance took to simply dumping great trays of pastries, fried meatskins, rounds of cheese—whatever they could find—out upon the table.

The governor had tapped his glass and risen to speak in his well-phrased english, but the bloated and belching mercenaries were leering about and were calling for more drink and some had not ceased to scream out toasts, now degenerated into obscene pledges to the whores of various southern cities. The bursar was introduced to cheers, catcalls, hoisted bumpers. Glanton took charge of the long canvas bag stamped with the state cartouche and cutting the governor short he rose and dumped the gold out onto the table among the bones and rinds and pools of spilled drink and in a brisk drumhead disbursement divided out the pile of gold with the blade of his knife so that each man was paid his spoken share and no further ceremony to it. A sort of skiffle band had struck up a lugubrious air in one corner of the hall and first up was the judge who ushered the players and their instruments into the adjoining ballroom where a number of ladies who had been sent for sat already about the walls on benches and fanned themselves without apparent alarm.

The Americans debouched into the dancing hall by ones and twos and by groups, chairs pushed back, chairs pushed over to lie where they fell. Wall lamps in their tin reflectors had been lit all about the room and the celebrants foregathered there cast conflicting shadows. The scalphunters stood grinning at the dames, churlishlooking in their shrunken clothes, sucking their teeth, armed with knives and pistols and mad about the eyes. The judge was in close conference with the band and soon a quadrille was struck up. A great lurching and stomping ensued while the judge, affable, gallant, squired first one and then another of the ladies through the steps with an easy niceness. By midnight the governor had excused himself and members of the band had begun to slip away. A blind street harpist stood terrified upon the banquet table among the bones and platters and a horde of luridlooking whores had infiltrated the dance.

Pistolfire soon became general and Mr Riddle, who was acting American consul in the city, descended to remonstrate with the revelers and was warned away. Fights broke out. Furniture was disassembled, men waving chairlegs, candlestands. Two whores grappled and pitched into a sideboard and went to the floor in a crash of brandyglasses. Jackson, pistols drawn, lurched into the street vowing to Shoot the ass off Jesus Christ, the longlegged white son of a bitch. At dawn the shapes of insensate topers lay snoring about the floor among dark patches of drying blood. Bathcat and the harpist lay asleep upon the banquet table in one another's arms. A family of thieves were tiptoeing through the wreckage turning out the pockets of the sleepers and the remains of a bonfire that had consumed a good part of the hotel's furnishings smoldered in the street before the door.

These scenes and scenes like them were repeated night after night. The citizenry made address to the governor but he was much like the sorcerer's apprentice who could indeed provoke the imp to do his will but could in no way make him cease again. The baths had become bordellos, the attendants driven off. The white stone fountain in the plaza was filled at night with naked and drunken men. Cantinas were evacuated as if by fire with the appearance of any two of the company and the Americans found themselves in ghost taverns with drinks on the tables and cigars still burning in the clay ashtrays. Horses were ridden indoors and out and as the gold began to dwindle away shopkeepers found themselves presented with debits scrawled on butcherpaper in a foreign language for whole shelves of goods. Stores began to close. Charcoal scrawls appeared on the limewashed walls. Mejor los indios. The evening streets stood empty and there were no paseos and the young girls of the city were boarded up and seen no more.

On the fifteenth of August they rode out. A week later a company of drovers reported them investing the town of Coyame eighty miles to the northeast.

The village of Coyame had for some years been laid under annual contribution by Gómez and his band. When Glanton and his men rode in they were fallen upon as saints. Women ran alongside the horses to touch their boots and presents of every kind were pressed upon them until each man rode with an embarrassment of melons and pastries and trussed chickens gathered in the bow of his saddle. When they rode out three days later the streets stood empty, not even a dog followed them to the gates.

They traveled northeast as far as the town of Presidio on the Texas border and they crossed the horses and rode dripping through the streets. A soil where Glanton was subject to arrest. He rode out alone on the desert and sat the horse and he and the horse and the dog looked out across the rolling scrubland and the barren peppercorn hills and the mountains and the flat brush country and running plain beyond where four hundred miles to the east were the wife and child that he would not see again. His shadow grew long before him on the banded wash of sand. He would not follow. He had taken off his hat for the evening wind to cool him and at length he put it on again and turned the horse and rode back.

They wandered the borderland for weeks seeking some sign of the Apache. Deployed upon that plain they moved in a constant elision, ordained agents of the actual dividing out the world which they encountered and leaving what had been and what would never be alike extinguished on the ground behind them. Spectre horsemen, pale with dust, anonymous in the crenellated heat. Above all else they appeared wholly at venture, primal, provisional, devoid of order. Like beings provoked out of the absolute rock and set nameless and at no remove from their own loomings to wander ravenous and doomed and mute as gorgons shambling the brutal wastes of Gondwanaland in a time before nomenclature was and each was all.

They killed wild meat and they took what they required by way of commissary from the pueblos and estancias through which they passed. One evening almost within sight of the town of

El Paso they looked off toward the north where the Gileños wintered and they knew they would not be going there. They camped that night at the Hueco tanks, a group of natural stone cisterns in the desert. The rocks about in every sheltered place were covered with ancient paintings and the judge was soon among them copying out those certain ones into his book to take away with him. They were of men and animals and of the chase and there were curious birds and arcane maps and there were constructions of such singular vision as to justify every fear of man and the things that are in him. Of these etchings—some bright yet with color—there were hundreds, and yet the judge went among them with assurance, tracing out the very ones which he required. When he had done and while there yet was light he returned to a certain stone ledge and sat a while and studied again the work there. Then he rose and with a piece of broken chert he scappled away one of the designs, leaving no trace of it only a raw place on the stone where it had been. Then he put up his book and returned to the camp.

In the morning they rode out to the south. Little was said, nor were they quarrelsome among themselves. In three days they would fall upon a band of peaceful Tiguas camped on the river and slaughter them every soul.

On the eve of that day they crouched about the fire where it hissed in a softly falling rain and they ran balls and cut patches as if the fate of the aborigines had been cast into shape by some other agency altogether. As if such destinies were prefigured in the very rock for those with eyes to read. No man stood to tender them a defense. Toadvine and the kid conferred together and when they rode out at noon the day following they trotted their horses alongside Bathcat. They rode in silence. Them sons of bitches aint botherin nobody, Toadvine said. The Vandieman-lander looked at him. He looked at the livid letters tattooed on his forehead and at the lank greasy hair that hung from his earless skull. He looked at the necklace of gold teeth at his chest. They rode on.

They approached those wretched pavilions in the long light of the day's failing, coming up from downwind along the south bank of the river where they could smell the woodsmoke of the cookfires. When the first dogs barked Glanton roweled his horse forward and they came out of the trees and across the dry scrub with the long necks of the horses leaning out of the dust avid as hounds and the riders quirting them on into the sun where the shapes of the women rising up from their tasks stood flat and rigid in silhouette for a moment before they could quite believe in the reality of that dusty pandemoniac pounding down upon them. They stood dumb, barefoot, clad in the unbleached cotton of the country. They clutched cooking ladles, naked children. At the first fire a dozen of them crumpled and fell.

The others had begun to run, old people flinging up their hands, children tottering and blinking in the pistolfire. A few young men ran out with drawn bows and were shot down and then the riders were all through the village trampling down the grass wickiups and bludgeoning the shrieking householders.

Long past dark that night when the moon was already up a party of women that had been upriver drying fish returned to the village and wandered howling through the ruins. A few fires still smoldered on the ground and dogs slank off from among the corpses. An old woman knelt at the blackened stones before her door and poked brush into the coals and blew back a flame from the ashes and began to right the overturned pots. All about her the dead lay with their peeled skulls like polyps bluely wet or luminescent melons cooling on some mesa of the moon. In the days to come the frail black rebuses of blood in those sands would crack and break and drift away so that in the circuit of few suns all trace of the destruction of these people would be erased. The desert wind would salt their ruins and there would be nothing, nor ghost nor scribe, to tell to any pilgrim in his passing how it was that people had lived in this place and in this place died.

The Americans entered the town of Carrizal late in the afternoon of the second day following, their horses festooned with the reeking scalps of the Tiguas. This town had fallen almost to ruin. Many of the houses stood empty and the presidio was collapsing back into the earth out of which it had been raised and the inhabitants seemed themselves made vacant by old terrors. They watched the passing of that bloodstained argosy through their streets with dark and solemn eyes. Those riders seemed journeyed from a legendary world and they left behind a strange tainture like an afterimage on the eye and the air they disturbed was altered and electric. They passed along the ruinous walls of the cemetery where the dead were trestled up in niches and the grounds strewn with bones and skulls and broken pots like some more ancient ossuary. Other ragged folk appeared in the dusty streets behind them and stood looking after.

That night they camped at a warm spring atop a hill amid old traces of spanish masonry and they stripped and descended like acolytes into the water while huge white leeches willowed away over the sands. When they rode out in the morning it was still dark. Lightning stood in ragged chains far to the south, silent, the staccato mountains bespoken blue and barren out of the void. Day broke upon a smoking reach of desert darkly clouded where the riders could count five separate storms spaced upon the shores of the round earth. They were riding in pure sand and the horses labored so hugely that the men were obliged to dismount and lead them, toiling up steep eskers where the wind blew the white pumice from the crests like the spume from sea swells and the sand was scalloped and fraily shaped and nothing else was there save random polished bones. They were all day among the dunes and in the evening coming down from the last low sandhills to the plain below among catclaw and crucifixion thorn they were a parched and haggard lot man and beast. Harpie eagles flew up screaming from a dead mule and wheeled off westward into the sun as they led the horses out onto the plain.

Two nights later bivouacked in a pass in the mountains they could see the distant lights of the city below them. They crouched along a shale ridge in the leeward wall of the gap while the fire sawed in the wind and they watched the lamps winking in the blue floor of the night thirty miles away. The judge crossed before them in the dark. Sparks from the fire ran down the wind. He took his seat among the scrabbled plates of shale out there and so they sat like beings from an older age watching the distant lamps dim out one by one until the city on the plain had shrunk to a small core of light that might have been a burning tree or some solitary encampment of travelers or perhaps no ponderable fire at all.

———————— ◆•◆ ————————

As they rode out through the tall wooden gates of the governor's palace two soldiers who had been standing there counting them past stepped forward and took Toadvine's horse by the head-stall. Glanton passed him on the right and rode on. Toadvine stood in the saddle.

Glanton!

The riders clattered into the street. Glanton just beyond the gates looked back. The soldiers were speaking to Toadvine in spanish and one held an escopeta on him.

I aint got nobody's teeth, Glanton said.

I'll shoot these two fools where they stand.

Glanton spat. He looked down the street and he looked at Toadvine. Then he dismounted and led his horse back into the courtyard. Vamonos, he said. He looked up at Toadvine. Get off your horse.

They rode out of town under escort two days later. Upward of a hundred soldiers herding them along the road, uneasy in their varied dress and arms, wrenching their horses about and booting them through the ford where the American horses had stopped to drink. In the foothills above the aqueduct they reined to one side and the Americans filed past and wound up through the rocks and nopal and diminished among the shadows and were gone.

They rode west into the mountains. They passed through small villages doffing their hats to folk whom they would murder before the month was out. Mud pueblos that lay like plague towns with the crops rotting in the fields and what stock not driven off by the indians wandering at will and none to herd or tend it and many villages almost wholly depopulated of male inhabitants where the women and children crouched in terror in their hovels listening until the last hoofclop died in the distance.

At the town of Nacori there was a cantina and here the company dismounted and crowded through the doorway and took tables. Tobin volunteered to guard the horses. He stood watching up and down the street. No one paid him any mind. These people had seen Americans in plenty, dusty laggard trains of them months out of their own country and half crazed with the enormity of their own presence in that immense and bloodslaked waste, commandeering meal and meat or indulging a latent taste for rape among the sloe-eyed girls of that country. Now it was something near to an hour past noon and a number of workers and tradesmen were crossing the street toward the cantina. As they passed Glanton's horse Glanton's dog rose up bristling. They veered slightly and went on. At the same moment a deputation of dogs of the village had started across the plaza, five, six of them, their eyes on Glanton's dog. As they did so a juggler leading a funeral rounded the corner into the street and taking a rocket from among several under his arm he held it to the cigarillo in his mouth and tossed it into the plaza where it exploded. The pack of dogs shied and scrambled back save for two who continued into the street. Among the Mexican horses tethered at the bar before the cantina several shot out a hind leg and the rest stepped about nervously. Glanton's dog did not take his eyes from the men moving toward the door. None of the American horses even raised an ear. The pair of dogs that had crossed in front of the funeral procession veered off from the kicking horses and came on toward the cantina. Two more rockets exploded in the street and now the rest of the procession had swung into view, a fiddler and a cornetplayer leading with a quick and lively tune. The dogs were trapped between the funeral and the animals of the mercenaries and they halted and flattened their ears and began to sidle and trot. Finally they bolted across the street behind the pallbearers. These details should have stood the workers entering the cantina in better stead. They had turned and they stood now with their backs to the door holding their hats to their chests. The pallbearers passed carrying on their shoulders a bier and the watchers could see in her burial dress among the flowers the graylooking face of a young woman jostling along woodenly. Behind came her coffin, made from rawhide blacked with lampblack, carried by dark-clad porters and looking much like a rude hide boat. At the rear advanced a company of mourners, some of the men drinking, the old women in their dusty black shawls helped weeping over the potholes and children bearing flowers who looked shyly at the spectators in the street as they passed.

Within the cantina the Americans had no more than seated themselves before a muttered insult from a nearby table brought three or four of them to their feet. The kid addressed the table in his wretched spanish and demanded which among those sullen inebriates had spoken. Before any could own it the first of the funeral rockets exploded in the street as told and the entire company of Americans made for the door. A drunk at the table rose to his feet with a knife and lurched after them. His friends called after him but he waved them away.

John Dorsey and Henderson Smith, two boys from Missouri, were the first into the street. They were followed by Charlie Brown and the judge. The judge could see over their heads and he raised one hand to those behind him. The bier was just passing. The fiddler and the cornetist were making little bows to each other and their steps suggested the martial style of the air they played. It's a funeral, said the judge. As he spoke the drunk with the knife now reeling in the doorway sank the blade deep into the back of a man named Grimley. None saw it but the judge. Grimley put a hand on the rough wood frame of the door. I'm killed, he said. The judge drew his belt pistol and leveled it above the heads of the men and shot the drunk through the middle of the forehead.

The Americans outside the door were all but looking down the barrel of the judge's pistol when he fired and most of them dove to the ground. Dorsey rolled clear and got to his feet and collided with the workers who'd been paying their respects to the passing cortege. They were putting their hats on when the judge fired. The dead man fell backward into the cantina, blood spouting from his head. When Grimley turned they could see the wooden handle of the knife protruding from his bloody shirt.

Other knives were already in play. Dorsey was grappling with the Mexicans and Henderson Smith had drawn his bowie and half severed a man's arm with it and the man was standing with the dark arterial blood spraying between his fingers where he tried to hold the wound shut. The judge got Dorsey to his feet and they backed toward the cantina with the Mexicans feinting and jabbing at them with their knives. From inside came the uninterrupted sound of gunfire and the doorframe was filling up with smoke. The judge turned at the door and stepped over the several corpses sprawled there. Inside the huge pistols roared without intermission and the twenty or so Mexicans who'd been in the room were strewn about in every position, shot to pieces among the overturned chairs and the tables with the fresh splinters blown out of the wood and the mud walls pocked everywhere by the big conical bullets. The survivors were making for the daylight in the doorway and the first of these encountered the judge there and cut at him with his knife. But the judge was like a cat and he sidestepped the man and seized his arm and broke it and picked the man up by his head. He put him against the wall and smiled at him but the man had begun to bleed from the ears and the blood was running down between the judge's fingers and over his hands and when the judge turned him loose there was something wrong with his head and he slid to the floor and did not get up. Those behind him had meanwhile met with a great battery of gunfire and the doorway was jammed with the dead and dying when there was suddenly a great ringing silence in the room. The judge stood with his back to the wall. The smoke drifted through like fog and the shrouded figures stood frozen. In the center of the room Toadvine and the kid were standing back to back with their pistols at port like duellists. The judge stepped to the door and shouted across the stacked bodies to the expriest where he stood among the horses with his pistol drawn.

The laggards, Priest, the laggards.

They'd not have shot men in public in a town so large but there was no help for it. Three men were running down the street and two others were legging it across the square. Of other souls abroad there were none. Tobin stepped from between the horses and leveled the big pistol in both hands and began to fire, the pistol bucking and dropping back and the runners wobbling and pitching headlong. He shot the two in the plaza and swung and shot down the runners in the street. The last one fell in a doorway and Tobin turned and drew the other pistol from his belt and stepped to the other side of the horse and looked up the street and across the square for any sign of movement there or among the buildings. The judge stepped back from the doorway into the cantina where the Americans stood looking at each other and at the bodies in a sort of wonder. They looked at Glanton. His eyes cut across the smoking room. His hat lying on a table. He stepped over and got it and set it on his head and squared it. He looked about. The men were reloading the empty chambers in their pistols. Hair, boys, he said. The string aint run on this trade yet.

When they left the cantina ten minutes later the streets were deserted. They had scalped the entire body of the dead, sliding about in a floor that had been packed clay and was now a wine-colored mud. There were twenty-eight Mexicans inside the tavern and eight more in the street including the five the expriest had shot. They mounted up. Grimley sat slumped sideways against the mud wall of the building. He did not look up. He was holding his pistol in his lap and looking off down the street and they turned and rode out along the north side of the plaza and disappeared.

It was thirty minutes before anyone appeared in the street. They spoke in whispers. As they approached the cantina one of the men from inside appeared in the doorway like a bloody apparition. He had been scalped and the blood was all run down into his eyes and he was holding shut a huge hole in his chest where a pink froth breathed in and out. One of the citizens laid a hand on his shoulder.

A dónde vas? he said.

A casa, said the man.

———◆◆———

The next town they entered was two days deeper into the sierras. They never knew what it was called. A collection of mud huts pitched on the naked plateau. As they rode in the people ran before them like harried game. Their cries to one another or perhaps the visible frailty of them seemed to incite something in Glanton. Brown watched him. He nudged forth his horse and drew his pistol and this somnolent pueblo was forthwith dragooned into a weltering shambles. Many of the people had been running toward the church where they knelt clutching the altar and from this refuge they were dragged howling one by one and one by one they were slain and scalped in the chancel floor. When the riders passed through this same village four days later the dead were still in the streets and buzzards and pigs were feeding on them. The scavengers watched in silence while the company picked their way past like supernumeraries in a dream. When the last of them was gone they commenced to feed again.

They went on through the mountains without resting. They trod a narrow trail through a black pine wood by day and by dark and in silence save for the creaking of tack and the breathing of the horses. A thin shell of a moon lay capsized over the jagged peaks. They rode down into a mountain town just before day where there was no lamp nor watchman nor dog. In the gray dawn they sat along a wall waiting for daylight. A rooster called. A door slammed. An old woman came down the lane past the daubed sty walls through the mist carrying a yoke of jars. They rose up. It was cold and their breath plumed about them. They took down the poles in the corral and led the horses out. They rode up the street. They halted. The animals sidled and stamped in the cold. Glanton had reined up and drawn his pistol.

A company of mounted troops passed out from behind a wall at the north end of the village and turned into the street. They wore tall shakos faced with metal plates and horsehair plumes and they wore green coats trimmed with scarlet and scarlet sashes and they were armed with lances and muskets and their mounts were nicely caparisoned and they entered the street sidling and prancing, horsemen riding upon horses, all of them desirable young men. The company looked to Glanton. He holstered the pistol and drew his rifle. The captain of the lancers had raised his sabre to halt the column. The next instant the narrow street was filled with riflesmoke and a dozen of the soldiers lay dead or dying on the ground. The horses reared and screamed and fell back upon each other and men were unhorsed and rose up struggling to hold their mounts. A second fire tore through their ranks. They fell away in confusion. The Americans drew their pistols and booted their horses forward up the street.

The Mexican captain was bleeding from a gunshot wound in the chest and he stood in the stirrups to receive the charge with his sabre. Glanton shot him through the head and shoved him from his horse with his foot and shot down in succession three men behind him. A soldier on the ground had picked up a lance and ran at him with it and one of the riders leaned down out of that wild melee and cut his throat and passed on. In the morning dampness the sulphurous smoke hung over the street in a gray shroud and the colorful lancers fell under the horses in that perilous mist like soldiers slaughtered in a dream wide-eyed and wooden and mute.

Some among the rear guard had managed to turn their mounts and start back up the street and the Americans were clouting back with pistolbarrels the riderless horses and the horses surged and milled with the stirrups kicking out and they trumpeted with their long mouths and trampled underfoot the dead. They beat them back and urged their horses through and up the street to where it narrowed and turned up the mountain and they fired after the fleeing lancers as they skeltered up the trail in a rattle of small stones.

Glanton sent a detachment of five men to follow and he and the judge and Bathcat turned back. They met the rest of the company riding up and they turned back and they went down and looted the bodies where they lay in the street like dead bandsmen and they smashed their muskets against the walls of the houses and broke their swords and lances. As they rode out they met the five scouts returning. The lancers had quit the trail and scattered through the woods. Two nights later camped on a butte looking out over the broad central plain they could see a point of light out on that desert like the reflection of a single star in a lake of utter blackness.

They took council. On that raw tablestone the flames of their balefire swirled and circled and they studied the arrant blackness under them where it fell away like the sheer cloven face of the world.

How far do you make them, said Glanton.

Holden shook his head. They've made half a day on us. They number no more than twelve, fourteen. They wont send men ahead.

How far are we from Chihuahua City?

Four days. Three. Where's Davy?

Glanton turned. How far to Chihuahua, David?

Brown stood with his back to the fire. He nodded. If that's them they could be there in three days.

You reckon we can overhaul them?

I dont know. Might depend on whether they figure us to be after them.

Glanton turned and spat into the fire. The judge raised one pale and naked arm and pursued something in the pit of it with his fingers. If we can be off of this mountain by daylight, he said, I believe we can overtake them. Otherwise we had better make for Sonora.

They may be from Sonora.

Then we'd better go get them.

We could take these scalps to Ures.

The fire swept along the ground, it rose again. We'd better go get them, said the judge.

They rode onto the plain at dawn as the judge had said and that night they could see the fire of the Mexicans reflected in the sky to the east beyond the curve of the earth. All the day following they rode and all that night, jerking and lurching like a deputation of spastics as they slept in their saddles. On the morning of the third day they could see the riders before them on the plain in silhouette against the sun and in the evening they could count their number struggling upon that desolate mineral waste. When the sun rose the walls of the city stood pale and thin in the rising light twenty miles to the east. They sat their horses. The lancers were strung out along the road several miles to the south of them. There was no reason for them to stop and no hope in it any more than there was in the riding but as they were riding they rode and the Americans put their horses forward once again.

For a while they rode almost parallel toward the gates of the city, the two parties bloody and ragged, the horses stumbling. Glanton called out to them to surrender but they rode on. He drew his rifle. They were shambling along the road like dumb things. He pulled up his horse and it stood with its legs spread and its flanks heaving and he leveled the rifle and fired.

They were for the most part no longer even armed. There were nine of them and they halted and turned and then they charged across that intermittent ground of rock and scrub and were shot down in the space of a minute.

The horses were caught and herded back to the road and the saddles and trappings cut away. The bodies of the dead were stripped and their uniforms and weapons burned along with the saddles and other gear and the Americans dug a pit in the road and buried them in a common grave, the naked bodies with their wounds like the victims of surgical experimentation lying in the pit gaping sightlessly at the desert sky as the dirt was pushed over them. They trampled the spot with their horses until it looked much like the road again and the smoking gunlocks and sabreblades and girthrings were dragged from the ashes of the fire and carried away and buried in a separate place and the riderless horses hazed off into the desert and in the evening the wind carried away the ashes and the wind blew in the night and fanned the last smoldering billets and drove forth the last fragile race of sparks fugitive as flintstrikings in the unanimous dark of the world.

They entered the city haggard and filthy and reeking with the blood of the citizenry for whose protection they had contracted. The scalps of the slain villagers were strung from the windows of the governor's house and the partisans were paid out of the all but exhausted coffers and the Sociedad was disbanded and the bounty rescinded. Within a week of their quitting the city there would be a price of eight thousand pesos posted for Glanton's head. They rode out on the north road as would parties bound for El Paso but before they were even quite out of sight of the city they had turned their tragic mounts to the west and they rode infatuate and half fond toward the red demise of that day, toward the evening lands and the distant pandemonium of the sun.

XIV

Mountain storms – Tierras quemadas, tierras despobladas –
Jesús María – The inn – Shopkeepers – A bodega – The fiddler –
The priest – Las Animas – The procession – Cazando las almas –
Glanton takes a fit – Dogs for sale – The judge prestidigitant –
The flag – A shootout – An exodus – The conducta – Blood and
mercury – At the ford – Jackson restored – The jungle –
An herbalist – The judge collects specimens – The point of view for
his work as a scientist – Ures – The populace – Los pordioseros –
A fandango – Pariah dogs – Glanton and judge.

All to the north the rain had dragged black tendrils down from the thunderclouds like tracings of lampblack fallen in a beaker and in the night they could hear the drum of rain miles away on the prairie. They ascended through a rocky pass and lightning shaped out the distant shivering mountains and lightning rang the stones about and tufts of blue fire clung to the horses like incandescent elementals that would not be driven off. Soft smelterlights advanced upon the metal of the harness, lights ran blue and liquid on the barrels of the guns. Mad jackhares started and checked in the blue glare and high among those clanging crags jokin roehawks crouched in their feathers or cracked a yellow eye at the thunder underfoot.

They rode for days through the rain and they rode through rain and hail and rain again. In that gray storm light they crossed a flooded plain with the footed shapes of the horses reflected in the water among clouds and mountains and the riders slumped forward and rightly skeptic of the shimmering cities on the distant shore of that sea whereon they trod miraculous. They climbed up through rolling grasslands where small birds shied away chittering down the wind and a buzzard labored up from among bones with wings that went whoop whoop whoop like a child's toy swung on a string and in the long red sunset the sheets of water on the plain below them lay like tidepools of primal blood.

They passed through a highland meadow carpeted with wild-flowers, acres of golden groundsel and zinnia and deep purple gentian and wild vines of blue morninglory and a vast plain of varied small blooms reaching onward like a gingham print to the farthest serried rimlands blue with haze and the adamantine ranges rising out of nothing like the backs of seabeasts in a devonian dawn. It was raining again and they rode slouched under slickers hacked from greasy halfcured hides and so cowled in these primitive skins before the gray and driving rain they looked like wardens of some dim sect sent forth to proselytize among the very beasts of the land. The country before them lay clouded and dark. They rode through the long twilight and the sun set and no moon rose and to the west the mountains shuddered again and again in clattering frames and burned to final darkness and the rain hissed in the blind night land. They went up through the foothills among pine trees and barren rock and they went up through juniper and spruce and the rare great aloes and the rising stalks of the yuccas with their pale blooms silent and unearthly among the evergreens.

In the night they followed a mountain torrent in a wild gorge choked with mossy rocks and they rode under dark grottoes where the water dripped and spattered and tasted of iron and they saw the silver filaments of cascades divided upon the faces of distant buttes that appeared as signs and wonders in the heavens themselves so dark was the ground of their origins. They crossed the blackened wood of a burn and they rode through a region of cloven rock where great boulders lay halved with smooth uncentered faces and on the slopes of those ferric grounds old paths of fire and the blackened bones of trees assassinated in the mountain storms. On the day following they began to encounter holly and oak, hardwood forests much like those they had quit in their youth. In pockets on the north slopes hail lay nested like tectites among the leaves and the nights were cool. They traveled through the high country deeper into the mountains where the storms had their lairs, a fiery clangorous region where white flames ran on the peaks and the ground bore the burnt smell of broken flint. At night the wolves in the dark forests of the world below called to them as if they were friends to man and Glanton's dog trotted moaning among the endlessly articulating legs of the horses.

Nine days out of Chihuahua they passed through a gap in the mountains and began to descend by a trail that ran carved along the solid stone face of a bluff a thousand feet above the clouds. A great stone mammoth watched from the gray escarpment above them. They picked their way down singlefile. They passed through a tunnel hewn in the rock and on the other side miles below them in a gorge lay the roofs of a town.

They descended by rocky switchbacks and across the beds of streams where small trout stood on their pale fins and studied the noses of the drinking horses. Sheets of mist that smelled and tasted of metal rose out of the gorge and crossed over them and moved on through the woods. They nudged the horses through the ford and down the trace and at three oclock in the afternoon in a thin and drizzling rain they rode into the old stone town of Jesús María.

They clattered over the rainwashed cobbles stuck with leaves and crossed a stone bridge and rode up the street under the dripping eaves of the galleried buildings and along a mountain torrent that ran through the town. Small oremills had been ground into the polished rocks in the river and the hills above the town were everywhere tunneled and scaffolded and scarred with drifts and tailings. The raggletag advent of the riders was howled about by a few wet dogs crouched in doorways and they turned into a narrow street and halted dripping before the door of an inn.

Glanton pounded on the door and it opened and a young boy

looked out. A woman appeared and looked at them and went back in. Finally a man came and opened the gate. He was slightly drunk and he held the gate while the horsemen rode through one by one into the little flooded courtyard and then he closed the gate behind them.

In the morning the rain had stopped and they appeared in the streets, tattered, stinking, ornamented with human parts like cannibals. They carried the huge pistols stuck in their belts and the vile skins they wore were deeply stained with blood and smoke and gunblack. The sun was out and the old women on their knees with bucket and rag washing the stones before the shopdoors turned and looked after them and shopkeepers setting out their wares nodded them a wary good morning. They were a strange clientele among such commerce. They stood blinking before the doorways where finches hung in small withy cages and green and brassy parrots that stood on one foot and croaked uneasily. There were ristras of dried fruit and peppers and clusters of tinware that hung like chimes and there were hogskins filled with pulque that swung from the beams like bloated swine in a knacker's yard. They sent for cups. A fiddler appeared and crouched on a stone doorsill and began to saw out some Moorish folktune and none who passed on their morning errands could take their eyes from those pale and rancid giants.

By noon they'd found a bodega run by a man named Frank Carroll, a low doggery once a stable whose shed doors stood open to the street to admit the only light. The fiddler had followed in what seemed a great sadness and he took up his station just without the door where he could watch the outlanders drink and clack their gold doubloons on the board. In the doorway there was an old man taking the sun and he leaned with a goathorn eartrumpet to the rising din within and nodded in continual agreement although no word was spoken in any language he had understanding of.

The judge had spied the musician and he called to him and tossed a coin that clinked upon the stones. The fiddler held it briefly to the light as if it might not serve and then slipped it away among his clothes and fitted his instrument beneath his chin and struck up an air that was old among the mountebanks of Spain two hundred years before. The judge stepped into the sunlit doorway and executed upon the stones a series of steps with a strange precision and he and the fiddler seemed alien minstrels met by chance in this medieval town. The judge removed his hat and bowed to a pair of ladies detoured into the street to bypass the doggery and he pirouetted hugely on his mincing feet and poured pulque from his cup into the old man's eartrumpet. The old man quickly stoppered the horn with the ball of his thumb and he held the horn with care before him while he augered his ear with one finger and then he drank.

By dark the streets were filled with besotted bedlamites lurching and cursing and ringing the churchbells with pistolballs in a godless charivari until the priest emerged bearing before him the crucified Christ and exhorting them with fragments of latin in a singsong chant. This man was drubbed in the street and prodded obscenely and they flung gold coins at him as he lay clutching his image. When he rose he disdained to take up the coins until some small boys ran out to gather them and then he ordered them brought to him while the barbarians whooped and drank him a toast.

Spectators drifted away, the narrow street emptied. Some of the Americans had wandered into the cold waters of the stream and were splashing about and they clambered dripping into the street and stood dark and smoking and apocalyptic in the dim lampfall. The night was cold and they shambled steaming through the cobbled town like fairybook beasts and it had begun to rain again.

The day that followed was the feast of Las Animas and there was a parade through the streets and a horsedrawn cart that bore a rude Christ in a stained and ancient catafalque. Lay acolytes followed all in company and the priest went before ringing a small bell. A barefoot brotherhood clad in black marched in the rear bearing sceptres of weeds. The Christ jostled past, a poor figure of straw with carven head and feet. He wore a crown of mountain briars and on his brow were painted drops of blood and on his old dry wooden cheeks blue tears. The villagers knelt and blessed themselves and some stepped forward and touched the garment the figure wore and kissed their fingertips. The parade trundled past mournfully and small children sat in the doorways eating pastry skulls and watching the parade and the rain in the streets.

The judge sat alone in the cantina. He also watched the rain, his eyes small in his great naked face. He'd filled his pockets with little candy deathsheads and he sat by the door and offered these to children passing on the walk under the eaves but they shied away like little horses.

In the evening groups of townfolk descended from the cemetery on the side of the hill and later in the dark by candle or lamp light they emerged again and made their way up to the church to pray. None but passed clutches of Americans crazed with drink and these grimy visitants would doff their hats oafishly and totter and grin and make obscene suggestions to the young girls. Carroll had closed his squalid bistro at dusk but opened it again to save the doors being stove. Sometime in the night a party of horsemen bound for California arrived, every man of them slumped in exhaustion. Yet within the hour they'd ridden out again. By midnight when the souls of the dead were rumored to be about the scalphunters were again howling in the streets and discharging their pistols in spite of rain or death and this continued sporadically until dawn.

By noon the day following Glanton in his drunkenness was taken with a kind of fit and he lurched crazed and disheveled into the little courtyard and began to open fire with his pistols. In the afternoon he lay bound to his bed like a madman while the judge sat with him and cooled his brow with rags of water and spoke to him in a low voice. Outside voices called across the steep hillsides. A little girl was missing and parties of citizens had turned out to search the mineshafts. After a while Glanton slept and the judge rose and went out.

It was gray and raining, leaves were blowing down. A ragged

stripling stepped from a doorway by a wooden rainspout and tugged at the judge's elbow. He had two pups in his shirtfront and these he offered for sale, dragging one forth by the neck.

The judge was looking off up the street. When he looked down at the boy the boy hauled forth the other dog. They hung limply. Perros a vende, he said.

Cuánto quieres? said the judge.

The boy looked at one and then the other of the animals. As if he'd pick one to suit the judge's character, such dogs existing somewhere perhaps. He thrust forth the lefthand animal. Cincuenta centavos, he said.

The pup squirmed and drew back in his fist like an animal backing down a hole, its pale blue eyes impartial, befrighted alike of the cold and the rain and the judge.

Ambos, said the judge. He sought in his pockets for coins.

The dogvendor took this for a bargaining device and studied the dogs anew to better determine their worth, but the judge had dredged from his polluted clothes a small gold coin worth a bushel of suchpriced dogs. He laid the coin in the palm of his hand and held it out and with the other hand took the pups from their keeper, holding them in one fist like a pair of socks. He gestured with the gold.

Andale, he said.

The boy stared at the coin.

The judge made a fist and opened it. The coin was gone. He wove his fingers in the empty air and reached behind the boy's ear and took the coin and handed it to him. The boy held the coin in both hands before him like a small ciborium and he looked up at the judge. But the judge had set forth, dogs dangling. He crossed upon the stone bridge and he looked down into the swollen waters and raised the dogs and pitched them in.

At the farther end the bridge gave onto a small street that ran along the river. Here the Vandiemenlander stood urinating from a stone wall into the water. When he saw the judge commit the dogs from the bridge he drew his pistol and called out.

The dogs disappeared in the foam. They swept one and the

next down a broad green race over sheets of polished rock into the pool below. The Vandiemenlander raised and cocked the pistol. In the clear waters of the pool willow leaves turned like jade dace. The pistol bucked in his hand and one of the dogs leaped in the water and he cocked it again and fired again and a pink stain diffused. He cocked and fired the pistol a third time and the other dog also blossomed and sank.

The judge continued on across the bridge. When the boy ran up and looked down into the water he was still holding the coin. The Vandiemenlander stood in the street opposite with his pizzle in one hand and the revolver in the other. The smoke had drifted off downstream and there was nothing in the pool at all.

Sometime in the late afternoon Glanton woke and managed to struggle free of his bindings. The first news they had of him was in front of the cuartel where he cut down the Mexican flag with his knife and tied it to the tail of a mule. Then he mounted the mule and goaded it through the square dragging the sacred bandera in the mud behind him.

He made a circuit of the streets and emerged in the plaza again, kicking the animal viciously in the flanks. As he turned a shot rang out and the mule fell stone dead under him with a musketball lodged in its brain. Glanton rolled clear and scrambled to his feet firing wildly. An old woman sank soundlessly to the stones. The judge and Tobin and Doc Irving came from Frank Carroll's on a dead run and knelt in the shadow of a wall and began to fire at the upper windows. Another half dozen Americans came around the corner at the far side of the square and in a flurry of gunfire two of them fell. Slags of lead were whining off the stones and gunsmoke hung over the streets in the damp air. Glanton and John Gunn had made their way along the walls to the shed behind the posada where the horses were stabled and they began bringing the animals out. Three more of the company entered the yard at a run and commenced to tote gear out of the building and to saddle horses. Gunfire was now continual in the street and two Americans lay dead and others lay calling out. When the company rode out thirty minutes later they ran a gantlet of ragged fusil fire and rocks and bottles and they left six of their number behind.

An hour later Carroll and another American named Sanford who'd been residing in the town caught them up. The citizens had torched the saloon. The priest had baptized the wounded Americans and then stood back while they were shot through the head.

Before dark they encountered laboring up the western slope of the mountain a conducta of one hundred and twenty-two mules bearing flasks of quicksilver for the mines. They could hear the whipcrack and cry of the arrieros on the switchbacks far below them and they could see the burdened animals plodding like goats along a faultline in the sheer rock wall. Bad luck. Twenty-six days from the sea and less than two hours out from the mines. The mules wheezed and scrabbled in the talus and the drivers in their ragged and colorful costumes harried them on. When the first of them saw the riders above them he stood in the stirrups and looked back. The column of mules wound down the trail for a half mile or more and as they bunched and halted there were sections of the train visible on the separate switchbacks far below, eight and ten mules, facing now this way, now that, the tails of the animals picked clean as bones by those behind and the mercury within the guttapercha flasks pulsing heavily as if they carried secret beasts, things in pairs that stirred and breathed uneasily within those bloated satchels. The muleteer turned and looked up the trail. Already Glanton was upon him. He greeted the American cordially. Glanton rode past without speaking, taking the upper side in that rocky strait and shouldering the drover's mule dangerously among the loose shales. The man's face clouded and he turned and called back down the trail. The other riders were now pushing past him, their eyes narrow and their faces black as stokers with gunsoot. He stood down off his mule and drew his escopeta from under the fender of the saddle. David Brown was opposite him at this point, his pistol already in his hand at the off side of his horse. He swung it over the pommel and shot the man squarely in the chest. The man sat down heavily and Brown shot him again and he pitched off down the rocks into the abyss below.

The others of the company hardly turned to advise themselves of what had occurred. Every man of them was firing point blank at the muleteers. They fell from their mounts and lay in the trail or slid from the escarpment and vanished. The drivers below got their animals turned and were attempting to flee back down the trail and the laden packmules were beginning to clamber white-eyed at the sheer wall of the bluff like enormous rats. The riders pushed between them and the rock and methodically rode them from the escarpment, the animals dropping silently as martyrs, turning sedately in the empty air and exploding on the rocks below in startling bursts of blood and silver as the flasks broke open and the mercury loomed wobbling in the air in great sheets and lobes and small trembling satellites and all its forms grouping below and racing in the stone arroyos like the imbreachment of some ultimate alchemic work decocted from out the secret dark of the earth's heart, the fleeing stag of the ancients fugitive on the mountainside and bright and quick in the dry path of the storm channels and shaping out the sockets in the rock and hurrying from ledge to ledge down the slope shimmering and deft as eels.

The muleteers benched out in a swag on the trail where the precipice was almost negotiable and they rode and fell crashing down through the scrub juniper and pine in a confusion of cries while the horsemen herded the lag mules off after them and rode wildly down the rock trail like men themselves at the mercy of something terrible. Carroll and Sanford had become detached from the company and when they reached the bench where the last of the arrieros had disappeared they reined their horses and looked back up the trail. It was empty save for a few dead men from the conducta. Half a hundred mules had been ridden off the escarpment and in the curve of the bluff they could see the broken shapes of the animals strewn down the rocks and they could see the bright shapes of the quicksilver pooled in the evening light. The horses stamped and arched their necks. The

riders looked off down into that calamitous gulf and they looked
at each other but they required no conference and they pulled
the mouths of the horses about and roweled them on down the
mountain.

They caught up with the company at dusk. They were dismounted at the far side of a river and the kid and one of the
Delawares were hazing the lathered horses back from the edge
of the water. They put their animals to the ford and crossed, the
water up under the horses' bellies and the horses picking their
way over the rocks and glancing wildly upstream where a cataract
thundered out of the darkening forest into the flecked and seething pool below. When they rode up out of the ford the judge
stepped forward and took Carroll's horse by the jaw.

Where's the nigger? he said.

He looked at the judge. They were all but at eyelevel and he
on horseback. I dont know, he said.

The judge looked at Glanton. Glanton spat.

How many men did you see in the square?

I didnt have time to take no headcount. There was three or
four shot that I know of.

But not the nigger?

I never saw him.

Sanford pushed his horse forward. There was no nigger in the
square, he said. I seen them shoot them boys and they were ever
one white as you and me.

The judge turned loose Carroll's horse and went to get his
own animal. Two of the Delawares detached themselves from
the company. When they rode out up the trail it was almost
dark and the company had pulled back into the woods and
posted videttes at the ford and they made no fire.

No riders came down the trail. The early part of the night was
dark but the first relief at the ford saw it begin to clear and
the moon came out over the canyon and they saw a bear come
down and pause at the far side of the river and test the air with
his nose and turn back. About daybreak the judge and the Delawares returned. They had the black with them. He was naked

save for a blanket he'd wrapped himself in. He didnt even have boots. He was riding one of the bonetailed packmules from the conducta and he was shivering with cold. The only thing he'd saved was his pistol. He was holding it against his chest under the blanket for he had no other place to carry it.

------ ◆◆ ------

The way down out of the mountains toward the western sea led them through green gorges thick with vines where paroquets and gaudy macaws leered and croaked. The trail followed a river and the river was up and muddy and there were many fords and they crossed and recrossed the river continually. Pale cascades hung down the sheer mountain wall above them, blowing off of the high slick rock in wild vapors. In eight days they passed no other riders. On the ninth they saw an old man trying to get off the trail below them, caning a pair of burros through the woods. As they came abreast of this spot they halted and Glanton turned into the woods where the wet leaves were shuffled up and he tracked down the old man sitting in the shrubbery solitary as a gnome. The burros looked up and twitched their ears and then lowered their heads to browse again. The old man watched him.

Por qué se esconde? said Glanton.

The old man didnt answer.

De dónde viene?

The old man seemed unwilling to reckon even with the idea of a dialogue. He squatted in the leaves with his arms folded. Glanton leaned and spat. He gestured with his chin at the burros.

Qué tiene allá?

The old man shrugged. Hierbas, he said.

Glanton looked at the animals and he looked at the old man. He turned his horse back toward the trail to rejoin the party.

Por qué me busca? called the old man after him.

They moved on. There were eagles and other birds in the valley and many deer and there were wild orchids and brakes of bamboo. The river here was sizeable and it swept past enormous boulders and waterfalls fell everywhere out of the high tangled jungle. The judge had taken to riding ahead with one of the Delawares and he carried his rifle loaded with the small hard seeds of the nopal fruit and in the evening he would dress expertly the colorful birds he'd shot, rubbing the skins with gunpowder and stuffing them with balls of dried grass and packing them away in his wallets. He pressed the leaves of trees and plants into his book and he stalked tiptoe the mountain butterflies with his shirt outheld in both hands, speaking to them in a low whisper, no curious study himself. Toadvine sat watching him as he made his notations in the ledger, holding the book toward the fire for the light, and he asked him what was his purpose in all this.

The judge's quill ceased its scratching. He looked at Toadvine. Then he continued to write again.

Toadvine spat into the fire.

The judge wrote on and then he folded the ledger shut and laid it to one side and pressed his hands together and passed them down over his nose and mouth and placed them palm down on his knees.

Whatever exists, he said. Whatever in creation exists without my knowledge exists without my consent.

He looked about at the dark forest in which they were bivouacked. He nodded toward the specimens he'd collected. These anonymous creatures, he said, may seem little or nothing in the world. Yet the smallest crumb can devour us. Any smallest thing beneath yon rock out of men's knowing. Only nature can enslave man and only when the existence of each last entity is routed out and made to stand naked before him will he be properly suzerain of the earth.

What's a suzerain?

A keeper. A keeper or overlord.

Why not say keeper then?

Because he is a special kind of keeper. A suzerain rules even where there are other rulers. His authority countermands local judgements.

Toadvine spat.

The judge placed his hands on the ground. He looked at his inquisitor. This is my claim, he said. And yet everywhere upon it are pockets of autonomous life. Autonomous. In order for it to be mine nothing must be permitted to occur upon it save by my dispensation.

Toadvine sat with his boots crossed before the fire. No man can acquaint himself with everthing on this earth, he said.

The judge tilted his great head. The man who believes that the secrets of the world are forever hidden lives in mystery and fear. Superstition will drag him down. The rain will erode the deeds of his life. But that man who sets himself the task of singling out the thread of order from the tapestry will by the decision alone have taken charge of the world and it is only by such taking charge that he will effect a way to dictate the terms of his own fate.

I dont see what that has to do with catchin birds.

The freedom of birds is an insult to me. I'd have them all in zoos.

That would be a hell of a zoo.

The judge smiled. Yes, he said. Even so.

In the night a caravan passed, the heads of the horses and mules muffled in serapes, led along silently in the dark, the riders cautioning one to the other with their fingers to their lips. The judge atop a great boulder overlooking the trail watched them go.

In the morning they rode on. They forded the muddy Yaqui River and they rode through stands of sunflowers tall as a man on horseback, the dead faces dished toward the west. The country began to open up and they began to come upon plantings of corn on the hillsides and a few clearings in the wilderness where there were grass huts and orange and tamarind trees. Of humans they saw none. On the second of December of eighteen forty-nine they rode into the town of Ures, capital of the state of Sonora.

They'd not trotted half the length of the town before they

had drawn about them a following of rabble unmatched for variety and sordidness by any they had yet encountered, beggars and proctors of beggars and whores and pimps and vendors and filthy children and whole deputations of the blind and the maimed and the importunate all crying out por dios and some who rode astride the backs of porters and hied them after and great numbers of folk of every age and condition who were merely curious. Females of domestic reputation lounged upon the balconies they passed with faces gotten up in indigo and almagre gaudy as the rumps of apes and they peered from behind their fans with a kind of lurid coyness like transvestites in a madhouse. The judge and Glanton rode at the head of the little column and conferred between themselves. The horses cantered nervously and if the riders roweled an occasional hand clutching at the trappings of their mounts those hands withdrew in silence.

They put up that night at a hostel at the edge of the town run by a German who turned over the premises to them entirely and was seen no more for either service or payment. Glanton wandered through the tall and dusty rooms with their withy ceilings and at length he found an old criada cowering in what must have passed for a kitchen although it contained nothing culinary save a brazier and a few clay pots. He set her to work heating water for baths and pressed a handful of silver coins on her and charged her with setting them some kind of board. She stared at the coins without moving until he shooed her away and she went off down the hallway holding the coins cupped in her hands like a bird. She disappeared up the stairwell calling out and soon there were a number of women busy about the place.

When Glanton turned to go back down the hall there were four or five horses standing in it. He slapped them away with his hat and went to the door and looked out at the silent mob of spectators.

Mozos de cuadra, he called. Venga. Pronto.

Two boys pushed through and approached the door and a number of others followed. Glanton motioned the tallest of them forward and placed one hand on top of his head and turned him around and looked at the others.

Este hombre es el jefe, he said. The jefe stood solemnly, his eyes cutting about. Glanton turned his head around and looked at him.

Te encargo todo, entiendes? Caballos, sillas, todo.

Sí. Entiendo.

Bueno. Andale. Hay caballos en la casa.

The jefe turned and shouted out the names of his friends and half a dozen came forward and they entered the house. When Glanton went down the hall they were leading those animals— known mankillers some—toward the door, scolding them, the least of the boys hardly taller than the legs of the animal he'd taken in charge. Glanton went out to the back of the building and looked about for the expriest whom it pleased him to send for whores and drink but he could not be found. In trying to arrive at a detail which might reasonably be expected to return at all he settled on Doc Irving and Shelby and gave them a fistful of coins and returned to the kitchen again.

By dark there were a half dozen young goats roasting on spits in the yard behind the hostel, their blackened figures shining in the smoky light. The judge strolled the grounds in his linen suit and directed the chefs with a wave of his cigar and he in turn was followed by a string band of six musicians, all of them old, all serious, who stayed with him at every turn some three paces to the rear and playing the while. A skin of pulque hung from a tripod in the center of the yard and Irving had returned with between twenty and thirty whores of every age and size and there were deployed before the door of the building whole trains of wagons and carts overseen by impromptu sutlers crying out each his bill of particulars and surrounded by a shifting gallery of townspeople and dozens of halfbroken horses for trade that reared and whinnied and desolatelooking cattle and sheep and pigs together with their owners until the town that Glanton and the judge had hoped to lay clear of was almost entirely at their door in a carnival underwritten with that mood of festivity and growing ugliness common to gatherings in that quarter of the world. The bonfire in the courtyard had been stoked to such heights that from the street the entire rear of the premises appeared to be in flames and new merchants with their goods and new spectators were arriving regularly together with sullen groups of Yaqui indians in loincloths who would be hired for their labor.

By midnight there were fires in the street and dancing and drunkenness and the house rang with the shrill cries of the whores and rival packs of dogs had infiltrated the now partly darkened and smoking yard in the back where a vicious dogfight broke out over the charred racks of goatbones and where the first gunfire of the night erupted and wounded dogs howled and dragged themselves about until Glanton himself went out and killed them with his knife, a lurid scene in the flickering light, the wounded dogs silent save for the pop of their teeth, dragging themselves across the lot like seals or other things and crouching under the walls while Glanton walked them down and clove their skulls with the huge copperbacked beltknife. He was no more than back inside the house before new dogs were muttering at the spits.

By the small hours of the morning most of the lamps within the hostel had smoked out and the rooms were filled with drunken snoring. The sutlers and their carts were gone and the blackened rings of the burnedout fires lay in the road like bombcraters, the smoldering billets dragged forth to sustain the one last fire about which sat old men and boys smoking and exchanging tales. As the mountains to the east began to shape themselves out of the dawn these figures too drifted away. In the yard at the rear of the premises the surviving dogs had dragged the bones about everywhere and the dead dogs lay in dark shingles of their own blood dried in the dust and cocks had begun to crow. When the judge and Glanton appeared at the front door in their suits, the judge in white and Glanton in black, the only person about was one of the small hostlers asleep on the steps.

Joven, said the judge.

The boy leaped up.

Eres mozo del caballado?

Sí señor. A su servicio.

Nuestros caballos, he said. He would describe the animals but the boy was already on the run.

It was cold and a wind was blowing. The sun not up. The judge stood at the steps and Glanton walked up and down studying the ground. In ten minutes the boy and another appeared leading the two horses saddled and groomed at a nice trot up the street, the boys at a dead run, barefoot, the breath of the horses pluming and their heads turning smartly from side to side.

XV

A new contract – Sloat – The massacre on the Nacozari –
Encounter with Elias – Pursued north – A lottery – Shelby and the
kid – A horse lamed – A norther – An ambush – Escape – War on
the plains – A descent – The burning tree – On the track –
The trophies – The kid rejoins his command – The judge –
A desert sacrifice – The scouts do not return – The ogdoad –
Santa Cruz – The militia – Snow – A hospice – The stable.

On the fifth of December they rode out north in the cold darkness before daybreak carrying with them a contract signed by the governor of the state of Sonora for the furnishing of Apache scalps. The streets were silent and empty. Carroll and Sanford had defected from the company and with them now rode a boy named Sloat who had been left sick to die in this place by one of the gold trains bound for the coast weeks earlier. When Glanton asked him if he were kin to the commodore of that name the boy spat quietly and said No, nor him to me. He rode near the head of the column and he must have counted himself well out of that place yet if he gave thanks to any god at all it was ill timed for the country was not done with him.

They rode north onto the broad Sonoran desert and in that cauterized waste they wandered aimlessly for weeks pursuing rumor and shadow. A few small scattered bands of Chiricahua raiders supposedly seen by herdsmen on some squalid and desolate ranch. A few peons waylaid and slain. Two weeks out they massacred a pueblo on the Nacozari River and two days later as they rode toward Ures with the scalps they encountered a party of armed Sonoran cavalry on the plains west of Baviácora under General Elias. A running fight ensued in which three of Glanton's party were killed and another seven wounded, four of whom could not ride.

That night they could see the fires of the army less than ten miles to the south. They sat out the night in darkness and the wounded called for water and in the cold stillness before dawn the fires out there were still burning. At sunrise the Delawares rode into the camp and sat on the ground with Glanton and Brown and the judge. In the eastern light the fires on the plain faded like an evil dream and the country lay bare and sparkling in the pure air. Elias was moving upon them out there with over five hundred troops.

They rose and began to saddle the horses. Glanton fetched down a quiver made from ocelot skin and counted out the arrows in it so that there was one for each man and he tore a piece of red flannel into strips and tied these about the footings of four of the shafts and then replaced the counted arrows into the quiver.

He sat on the ground with the quiver upright between his knees while the company filed past. When the kid selected among the shafts to draw one he saw the judge watching him and he paused. He looked at Glanton. He let go the arrow he'd chosen and sorted out another and drew that one. It carried the red tassel. He looked at the judge again and the judge was not watching and he moved on and took his place with Tate and Webster. They were joined finally by a man named Harlan from Texas who had drawn the last arrow and the four of them stood together while the rest saddled their horses and led them out.

Of the wounded men two were Delawares and one a Mexican. The fourth was Dick Shelby and he alone sat watching the preparations for departure. The Delawares remaining in the company conferred among themselves and one of them approached the four Americans and studied them each in turn. He walked past them and turned and came back and took the arrow from

Webster. Webster looked at Glanton where he stood with his horse. Then the Delaware took Harlan's arrow. Glanton turned and with his forehead against the ribs of his horse he tightened the girthstraps and then mounted up. He adjusted his hat. No one spoke. Harlan and Webster went to get their animals. Glanton sat his horse while the company filed past and then he turned and followed them out onto the plain.

The Delaware had gone for his horse and he brought it up still hobbled through the wallowed places in the sand where the men had slept. Of the wounded indians one was silent, breathing heavily with his eyes closed. The other was chanting rhythmically. The Delaware let drop the reins and took down his warclub from his bag and stepped astraddle of the man and swung the club and crushed his skull with a single blow. The man humped up in a little shuddering spasm and then lay still. The other was dispatched in the same way and then the Delaware raised the horse's leg and undid the hobble and slid it clear and rose and put the hobble and the club in the bag and mounted up and turned the horse. He looked at the two men standing there. His face and chest were freckled with blood. He touched up the horse with his heels and rode out.

Tate squatted in the sand, his hands dangling in front of him. He turned and looked at the kid.

Who gets the Mexican? he said.

The kid didnt answer. They looked at Shelby. He was watching them.

Tate had a clutch of small pebbles in his hand and he let them drop one by one into the sand. He looked at the kid.

Go on if you want to, the kid said.

He looked at the Delawares dead in their blankets. You might not do it, he said.

That aint your worry.

Glanton might come back.

He might.

Tate looked over to where the Mexican was lying and he looked at the kid again. I'm still held to it, he said.

The kid didnt answer.

You know what they'll do to them?

The kid spat. I can guess, he said.

No you caint.

I said you could go. You do what you want.

Tate rose and looked to the south but the desert there lay in all its clarity uninhabited by any approaching armies. He shrugged up his shoulders in the cold. Injins, he said. It dont mean nothin to them. He crossed the campground and brought his horse around and led it up and mounted it. He looked at the Mexican, wheezing softly, a pink froth on his lips. He looked at the kid and then he nudged the pony up through the scraggly acacia and was gone.

The kid sat in the sand and stared off to the south. The Mexican was shot through the lungs and would die anyway but Shelby had had his hip shattered by a ball and he was clear in his head. He lay watching the kid. He was from a prominent Kentucky family and had attended Transylvania College and like many another young man of his class he'd gone west because of a woman. He watched the kid and he watched the enormous sun where it sat boiling on the edge of the desert. Any roadagent or gambler would have known that the first to speak would lose but Shelby had already lost it all.

Why dont you just get on with it? he said.

The kid looked at him.

If I had a gun I'd shoot you, Shelby said.

The kid didnt answer.

You know that, dont you?

You aint got a gun, the kid said.

He looked to the south again. Something moving, perhaps the first lines of heat. No dust in the morning so early. When he looked at Shelby again Shelby was crying.

You wont thank me if I let you off, he said.

Do it then you son of a bitch.

The kid sat. A light wind was blowing out of the north and some doves had begun to call in the thicket of greasewood behind them.

If you want me just to leave you I will.

Shelby didnt answer.

He pushed a furrow in the sand with the heel of his boot. You'll have to say.

Will you leave me a gun?

You know I caint leave you no gun.

You're no better than him. Are you?

The kid didnt answer.

What if he comes back.

Glanton.

Yes.

What if he does.

He'll kill me.

You wont be out nothin.

You son of a bitch.

The kid rose.

Will you hide me?

Hide you?

Yes.

The kid spat. You caint hide. Where you goin to hide at?

Will he come back?

I dont know.

This is a terrible place to die in.

Where's a good one?

Shelby wiped his eyes with the back of his wrist. Can you see them? he said.

Not yet.

Will you pull me up under that bush?

The kid turned and looked at him. He looked off down-country again and then he crossed the basin and squatted behind Shelby and took him up under the arms and raised him. Shelby's head rolled back and he looked up and then he snatched at the butt of the pistol stuck in the kid's belt. The kid seized his arm. He let him down and stepped away and turned him loose. When he returned through the basin leading the horse the man was crying again. He took the pistol from his belt and jammed it among his belongings lashed to the cantle and took his canteen down and went to him.

He had his face turned away. The kid filled his flask from his own and reseated the stopper where it hung by its thong and drove it home with the heel of his hand. Then he rose and looked off to the south.

Yonder they come, he said.

Shelby raised up on one elbow.

The kid looked at him and he looked at the faint and formless articulation along the horizon to the south. Shelby lay back. He was staring up at the sky. A dark overcast was moving down from the north and the wind was up. A clutch of leaves scuttled out of the willow bracken at the edge of the sand and then scuttled back again. The kid crossed to where the horse stood waiting and took the pistol and stuck it in his belt and hung the canteen over the saddlehorn and mounted up and looked back at the wounded man. Then he rode out.

He was trotting north on the plain when he saw another horseman on the grounds before him perhaps a mile distant. He could not make him out and he rode more slowly. After a while he saw that the rider was leading the horse and after a while he could see that the horse was not walking right.

It was Tate. He sat by the wayside watching the kid as he rode up. The horse stood on three legs. Tate said nothing. He took off his hat and looked inside it and put it on again. The kid was turned in the saddle and he was looking to the south. Then he looked at Tate.

Can he walk?

Not much.

He got down and drew up the horse's leg. The frog of the hoof was split and bloody and the animal's shoulder quivered. He let the hoof down. The sun was about two hours high and now there was dust on the horizon. He looked at Tate.

What do you want to do?

I dont know. Lead him awhile. See how he does.

He aint goin to do.

I know it.

We could ride and tie.

You might just keep ridin.

I might anyway.

Tate looked at him. Go on if you want, he said.

The kid spat. Come on, he said.

I hate to leave the saddle. Hate to leave the horse far as that goes.

The kid picked up the trailing reins of his own animal. You might change your mind about what you hate to leave, he said.

They set out leading both horses. The damaged animal kept wanting to stop. Tate coaxed it along. Come on fool, he said. You aint goin to like them niggers a bit more than me.

By noon the sun was a pale blur overhead and a cold wind was blowing out of the north. They leaned into it man and animal. The wind bore stinging bits of grit and they set their hats low over their faces and pushed on. Dried desert chaff passed along with the seething migrant sands. Another hour and there was no track visible from the main party of riders before them. The sky lay gray and of a piece in every direction as far as they could see and the wind did not abate. After a while it began to snow.

The kid had taken down his blanket and wrapped himself in it. He turned and stood with his back to the wind and the horse leaned and laid its cheek against his. Its eyelashes were thatched with snow. When Tate came up he stopped and they stood looking out downwind where the snow was blowing. They could see no more than a few feet.

Aint this hell, he said.

Will your horse lead?

Hell no. I caint hardly make him foller.

We get turned around we might just run plumb into the Spaniards.

I never saw it turn so cold so quick.

What do you want to do.

We better go on.

We could pull for the high country. As long as we keep goin uphill we'll know we aint got in a circle.

We'll get cut off. We never will find Glanton.

We're cut off now.

Tate turned and stared bleakly to where the whirling flakes blew down from the north. Let's go, he said. We caint stand here.

They led the horses on. Already the ground was white. They took turns riding the good horse and leading the lame. They climbed for hours up a long rocky wash and the snow did not diminish. They began to come upon piñon and dwarf oak and open parkland and the snow on those high meadows was soon a foot deep and the horses were blowing and smoking like steamengines and it was colder and growing dark.

They were rolled in their blankets asleep in the snow when the scouts from Elias's forward company came upon them. They'd ridden all night the only track there was, pushing on not to lose the march of those shallow pans as they filled with snow. They were five men and they came up through the evergreens in the dark and all but stumbled upon the sleepers, two mounds in the snow one of which broke open and up out of which a figure sat suddenly like some terrible hatching.

The snow had stopped falling. The kid could see them and their animals clearly on that pale ground, the men in midstride and the horses blowing cold. He had his boots in one hand and his pistol in the other and he came up out of the blanket and leveled the pistol and discharged it into the chest of the man nearest him and turned to run. His feet slid and he went to one knee. A musket fired behind him. He rose again, running down a darkened slash of piñon and turning out along the face of the slope. There were other shots behind him and when he turned he could see a man coming down through the trees. The man stopped and raised his elbows and the kid dove headlong. The musketball went racketing off among the branches. He rolled over and cocked the pistol. The barrel must have been full of snow because when he fired a hoop of orange light sprang out about it and the shot made a strange sound. He felt to see if the gun had burst but it had not. He could not see the man any more and he picked himself up and ran on. At the foot of the slope he sat gasping in the cold air and pulled on the boots and watched back among the trees. Nothing moved. He rose and stuck the pistol in his belt and went on.

———————◆·◆———————

The rising sun found him crouched under a rocky promontory watching the country to the south. He sat so for an hour or more. A group of deer moved up the far side of the arroyo feeding and feeding moved on. After a while he rose and went on along the ridge.

He walked all day through those wild uplands, eating handfuls of snow from the evergreen boughs as he went. He followed gametrails through the firs and in the evening he hiked along the rimrock where he could see the tilted desert to the southwest patched with shapes of snow that roughly reproduced the patterns of cloud cover already moved on to the south. Ice had frozen on the rock and the myriad of icicles among the conifers glistened blood red in the reflected light of the sunset spread across the prairie to the west. He sat with his back to a rock and felt the warmth of the sun on his face and watched it pool and flare and drain away dragging with it all that pink and rose and crimson sky. An icy wind sprang up and the junipers darkened suddenly against the snow and then there was just stillness and cold.

He rose and moved on, hurrying along the shaly rocks. He walked all night. The stars swung counterclockwise in their course and the Great Bear turned and the Pleiades winked in the very roof of the vault. He walked until his toes grew numb and fairly rattled in his boots. His path upon the rimrock was leading him deeper into the mountains along the edge of a great gorge and he could see no place to descend out of that country. He sat and wrestled off the boots and held his frozen feet each by turn in his arms. They did not warm and his jaw was in a seizure of cold and when he went to put the boots back on again his feet were like clubs to poke into them. When he got them on and stood up and stamped numbly he knew that he could not stop again until the sun rose.

It grew colder and the night lay long before him. He kept moving, following in the darkness the naked chines of rock blown bare of snow. The stars burned with a lidless fixity and they drew nearer in the night until toward dawn he was stumbling among the whinstones of the uttermost ridge to heaven, a barren range of rock so enfolded in that gaudy house that stars lay awash at his feet and migratory spalls of burning matter crossed constantly about him on their chartless reckonings. In the predawn light he made his way out upon a promontory and there received first of any creature in that country the warmth of the sun's ascending.

He slept curled among the stones, the pistol clutched to his chest. His feet thawed and burned and he woke and lay staring up at a sky of china blue where very high there circled two black hawks about the sun slowly and perfectly opposed like paper birds upon a pole.

He moved north all day and in the long light of the evening he saw from that high rimland the collision of armies remote and silent upon the plain below. The dark little horses circled and the landscape shifted in the paling light and the mountains beyond brooded in darkening silhouette. The distant horsemen rode and parried and a faint drift of smoke passed over them and they moved on up the deepening shade of the valley floor leaving behind them the shapes of mortal men who had lost their lives in that place. He watched all this pass below him mute and ordered and senseless until the warring horsemen were gone in the sudden rush of dark that fell over the desert. All that land lay cold and blue and without definition and the sun shone solely on the high rocks where he stood. He moved on and soon he was in darkness himself and the wind came up off the desert and frayed wires of lightning stood again and again along the western terminals of the world. He made his way along the escarpment until he came to a break in the wall cut through by a canyon running back into the mountains. He stood looking down into this gulf where the tops of the twisted evergreens hissed in the wind and then he started down.

The snow lay in deep pockets on the slope and he floundered

down through them, steadying himself along the naked rocks until his hands were numb with cold. He crossed with care a gravel slide and made his way down the far side among the rubble stone and small gnarled trees. He fell and fell again, scrabbling for a handpurchase in the dark, rising and feeling in his belt for the pistol. He was at this work the night long. When he reached the benchland above the canyon floor he could hear a stream running in the gorge below him and he went stumbling along with his hands in his armpits like a fugitive in a madman's waistcoat. He reached a sandy wash and followed it down and it took him at last out upon the desert again where he stood tottering in the cold and casting about dumbly for some star in the overcast.

Most of the snow had blown or melted from off the plain on which he found himself. Tandem storms were blowing down-country from the north and the thunder trundled away in the distance and the air was cold and smelled of wet stone. He struck out across the barren pan, nothing but sparse tufts of grass and the widely scattered palmilla standing solitary and silent against the lowering sky like other beings posted there. To the east the mountains stood footed blackly into the desert and before him were bluffs or promontories that ran out like headlands massive and sombre upon the desert floor. He clopped on woodenly, half frozen, his feet senseless. He'd been without food for almost two days and he'd had little rest. He cited the terrain before him in the periodic flare of the lightning and trudged on and in this manner he rounded a dark cape of rock off to his right and came to a halt, shivering and blowing into his clawed and palsied hands. In the distance before him a fire burned on the prairie, a solitary flame frayed by the wind that freshened and faded and shed scattered sparks down the storm like hot scurf blown from some unreckonable forge howling in the waste. He sat and watched it. He could not judge how far it was. He lay on his stomach to skylight the terrain to see what men were there but there was no sky and no light. He lay for a long time watching but he saw nothing move.

When he went on again the fire seemed to recede before him. A troop of figures passed between him and the light. Then again. Wolves perhaps. He went on.

It was a lone tree burning on the desert. A heraldic tree that the passing storm had left afire. The solitary pilgrim drawn up before it had traveled far to be here and he knelt in the hot sand and held his numbed hands out while all about in that circle attended companies of lesser auxiliaries routed forth into the inordinate day, small owls that crouched silently and stood from foot to foot and tarantulas and solpugas and vinegarroons and the vicious mygale spiders and beaded lizards with mouths black as a chowdog's, deadly to man, and the little desert basilisks that jet blood from their eyes and the small sandvipers like seemly gods, silent and the same, in Jeda, in Babylon. A constellation of ignited eyes that edged the ring of light all bound in a precarious truce before this torch whose brightness had set back the stars in their sockets.

When the sun rose he was asleep under the smoldering skeleton of a blackened scrog. The storm had long passed off to the south and the new sky was raw and blue and the spire of smoke from the burnt tree stood vertically in the still dawn like a slender stylus marking the hour with its particular and faintly breathing shadow upon the face of a terrain that was without other designation. All the creatures that had been at vigil with him in the night were gone and about him lay only the strange coral shapes of fulgurite in their scorched furrows fused out of the sand where ball lightning had run upon the ground in the night hissing and stinking of sulphur.

Seated tailorwise in the eye of that cratered waste he watched the world tend away at the edges to a shimmering surmise that ringed the desert round. After a while he rose and made his way to the edge of the pan and up the dry course of an arroyo, following the small demonic tracks of javelinas until he came upon them drinking at a standing pool of water. They flushed snorting into the chaparral and he lay in the wet trampled sand and drank and rested and drank again.

In the afternoon he started across the valley floor with the weight of the water swinging in his gut. Three hours later he stood in the long arc of horsetracks coming up from the south where the party had passed. He followed the edge of the tracks and sorted out single riders and he reckoned their number and he reckoned them to be riding at a canter. He followed the trace for several miles and he could tell by the alternation of tracks ridden over that all these riders had passed together and he could tell by the small rocks overturned and holes stepped into that they had passed in the night. He stood looking out from under his hand long downcountry for any dust or rumor of Elias. There was nothing. He went on. A mile further and he came upon a strange blackened mass in the trail like a burnt carcass of some ungodly beast. He circled it. The tracks of wolves and coyotes had walked through the horse and boot prints, little sallies and sorties that fetched up to the edge of that incinerated shape and flared away again.

It was the remains of the scalps taken on the Nacozari and they had been burned unredeemed in a green and stinking bonfire so that nothing remained of the poblanos save this charred coagulate of their preterite lives. The cremation had been sited upon a rise of ground and he studied every quarter of the terrain about but there was nothing to be seen. He went on, following the tracks with their suggestion of pursuit and darkness, trailing them through the deepening twilight. With sunset it grew cold, yet nothing like so cold as in the mountains. His fast had weakened him and he sat in the sand to rest and woke sprawled and twisted on the ground. The moon was up, a half moon that sat like a child's boat in the gap of the black paper mountains to the east. He rose and went on. Coyotes were yapping out there and his feet reeled beneath him. An hour more of such progress and he came upon a horse.

It had been standing in the trace and it moved off in the dark and stood again. He halted with his pistol drawn. The horse went past, a dark shape, rider or none he could not tell. It circled and came back.

He spoke to it. He could hear its deep pulmonary breathing out there and he could hear it move and when it came back he could smell it. He followed it about for the better part of an hour, talking to it, whistling, holding out his hands. When he got near enough to touch it at last he took hold of it by the mane and it went trotting as before and he ran alongside and clung to it and finally wrapped his legs about one foreleg and brought it to the ground in a heap.

He was the first up. The animal was struggling to rise and he thought it was injured in the fall but it was not. He cinched his belt about its muzzle and mounted it and it rose and stood trembling under him with its legs spread. He patted it along the withers and spoke to it and it moved forward uncertainly.

He reckoned it one of the packhorses purchased in Ures. It stopped and he urged it forward but it did not go. He brought his bootheels sharply up under its ribs and it squatted on its hindquarters and went crabbing sideways. He reached and undid the belt from its muzzle and kicked it forward and gave it a whack with the belt and it stepped out right smartly. He twisted a good handful of the mane in his fist and jammed the pistol securely in his waist and rode on, perched upon the raw spine of the animal with the vertebra articulating palpable and discrete under the hide.

In their riding they were joined by another horse that came off the desert and walked alongside them and it was still there when dawn broke. In the night too the tracks of the riders had been joined by a larger party and it was a broad and trampled causeway that now led up the valley floor to the north. With daylight he leaned down with his face against the horse's shoulder and studied the tracks. They were unshod indian ponies and there were perhaps a hundred of them. Nor had they joined the riders but rather been joined by them. He pushed on. The little horse that had come to them in the night had moved off some leagues and now paced them with a watchful eye and the horse he rode was nervous and ill for want of water.

By noon the animal was failing. He tried to coax it out of

the track to catch the other horse but it would not quit the course it was set upon. He sucked on a pebble and surveyed the countryside. Then he saw riders ahead of him. They'd not been there, then they were there. He realized it was their vicinity that was the source of the unrest in the two horses and he rode on watching now the animals and now the skyline to the north. The hack that he straddled trembled and pushed ahead and after a while he could see that the riders wore hats. He urged the horse on and when he rode up the party were halted and seated on the ground all watching his approach.

They looked bad. They were used up and bloody and black about the eyes and they had bound up their wounds with linens that were filthy and bloodstained and their clothes were crusted with dried blood and powderblack. Glanton's eyes in their dark sockets were burning centroids of murder and he and his haggard riders stared balefully at the kid as if he were no part of them for all they were so like in wretchedness of circumstance. The kid slid down from the horse and stood among them gaunt and parched and crazedlooking. Someone threw him a canteen.

They had lost four men. The others were ahead on scout. Elias had forced on through the mountains all night and all the day following and had ridden upon them through the snow in the dark on the plain forty miles to the south. They'd been harried north over the desert like cattle and had deliberately taken the track of the warparty in order to lose their pursuers. They did not know how far the Mexicans were behind them and they did not know how far the Apaches were ahead.

He drank from the canteen and looked them over. Of the missing he'd no way of knowing which were ahead with the scouts and which were dead in the desert. The horse that Toadvine brought him was the one the recruit Sloat had ridden out of Ures. When they moved out a half hour later two of the horses would not rise and were left behind. He sat a hideless and rickety saddle astride the dead man's horse and he rode slumped and tottering and soon his legs and arms were dangling and he jostled along in his sleep like a mounted marionette. He woke to find the expriest alongside him. He slept again. When he woke next it was the judge was there. He too had lost his hat and he rode with a woven wreath of desert scrub about his head like some egregious saltland bard and he looked down upon the refugee with the same smile, as if the world were pleasing even to him alone.

They rode all the rest of that day, up through low rolling hills covered with cholla and whitethorn. From time to time one of the spare horses would stop and stand swaying in the track and grow small behind them. They rode down a long north slope in the cold blue evening and through a barren bajada grown only with sporadic ocotillo and stands of grama and they made camp in the flat and all night the wind blew and they could see other fires burning on the desert to the north. The judge walked out and looked over the horses and selected from that sorry remuda the animal least likely in appearance and caught it up. He led it past the fire and called for someone to come hold it. No one rose. The expriest leaned to the kid.

Pay him no mind lad.

The judge called again from the dark beyond the fire and the expriest placed a cautionary hand upon the kid's arm. But the kid rose and spat into the fire. He turned and eyed the expriest.

You think I'm afraid of him?

The expriest didnt answer and the kid turned and went out into the darkness where the judge waited.

He stood holding the horse. Just his teeth glistened in the firelight. Together they led the animal off a little ways and the kid held the woven reata while the judge took up a round rock weighing perhaps a hundred pounds and crushed the horse's skull with a single blow. Blood shot out of its ears and it slammed to the ground so hard that one of its forelegs broke under it with a dull snap.

They skinned out the hindquarters without gutting the animal and the men cut steaks from it and roasted them over the fire and cut the rest of the meat in strips and hung it to smoke. The scouts did not come in and they posted videttes and turned in to sleep each man with his weapons at his breast.

Midmorning of the day following they crossed an alkali pan whereon were convoked an assembly of men's heads. The company halted and Glanton and the judge rode forward. The heads were eight in number and each wore a hat and they formed a ring all facing outward. Glanton and the judge circled them and the judge halted and stepped down and pushed over one of the heads with his boot. As if to satisfy himself that no man stood buried in the sand beneath it. The other heads glared blindly out of their wrinkled eyes like fellows of some righteous initiate given up to vows of silence and of death.

The riders looked off to the north. They rode on. Beyond a shallow rise in cold ash lay the blackened wreckage of a pair of wagons and the nude torsos of the party. The wind had shifted the ashes and the iron axletrees marked the shapes of the wagons as keelsons do the bones of ships on the sea's floors. The bodies had been partly eaten and rooks flew up as the riders approached and a pair of buzzards began to trot off across the sand with their wings outheld like soiled chorines, their boiled-looking heads jerking obscenely.

They went on. They crossed a dry estuary of the desert flat and in the afternoon they rode up through a series of narrow defiles into a rolling hill country. They could smell the smoke of piñonwood fires and before dark they rode into the town of Santa Cruz.

This town like all the presidios along the border was much reduced from its former estate and many of the buildings were uninhabited and ruinous. The coming of the riders had been cried before them and the way stood lined with inhabitants watching dumbly as they passed, the old women in black rebozos and the men armed with old muskets and miquelets or guns fabricated out of parts rudely let into stocks of cottonwood that had been shaped with axes like clubhouse guns for boys. There were even guns among them with no locks at all that were fired by jamming a cigarillo against the vent in the barrel, sending the gunstones from the riverbed with which they were loaded whissing through the air on flights of their own eccentric selection like the paths of meteorites. The Americans pushed their horses forward. It had begun to snow again and a cold wind blew down the narrow street before them. Even in their wretched state they glared from their saddles at this falstaffian militia with undisguised contempt.

They stood among their horses in the squalid little alameda while the wind ransacked the trees and the birds nesting in the gray twilight cried out and clutched the limbs and the snow swirled and blew across the little square and shrouded the shapes of the mud buildings beyond and made mute the cries of the vendors who'd followed them. Glanton and the Mexican he'd set out with returned and the company mounted up and filed out down the street until they came to an old wooden gate that led into a courtyard. The courtyard was dusted with snow and within were contained barnyard fowl and animals— goats, a burro—that clawed and scrabbled blindly at the walls as the riders entered. In one corner stood a tripod of blackened sticks and there was a large bloodstain that had been partly snowed over and showed a faint pale rose in the last light. A man came out of the house and he and Glanton spoke and the man talked with the Mexican and then he motioned them in out of the weather.

They sat in the floor of a long room with a high ceiling and smokestained vigas while a woman and a girl brought bowls of guisado made from goat and a clay plate heaped with blue tortillas and they were served bowls of beans and of coffee and a cornmeal porridge in which sat little chunks of raw brown peloncillo sugar. Outside it was dark and the snow swirled down. There was no fire in the room and the food steamed ponderously. When they had eaten they sat smoking and the women gathered up the bowls and after a while a boy came with a lantern and led them out.

They crossed the yard among the snuffling horses and the boy opened a rough wooden door in an adobe shed and stood by holding the lamp aloft. They brought their saddles and their blankets. In the yard the horses stamped in the cold.

The shed held a mare with a suckling colt and the boy would have put her out but they called to him to leave her. They carried straw from a stall and pitched it down and he held the lamp for them while they spread their bedding. The barn smelled of clay and straw and manure and in the soiled yellow light of the lamp their breath rolled smoking through the cold. When they had arranged their blankets the boy lowered the lamp and stepped into the yard and pulled the door shut behind, leaving them in profound and absolute darkness.

No one moved. In that cold stable the shutting of the door may have evoked in some hearts other hostels and not of their choosing. The mare sniffed uneasily and the young colt stepped about. Then one by one they began to divest themselves of their outer clothes, the hide slickers and raw wool serapes and vests, and one by one they propagated about themselves a great crackling of sparks and each man was seen to wear a shroud of palest fire. Their arms aloft pulling at their clothes were luminous and each obscure soul was enveloped in audible shapes of light as if it had always been so. The mare at the far end of the stable snorted and shied at this luminosity in beings so endarkened and the little horse turned and hid his face in the web of his dam's flank.

XVI

The Santa Cruz valley – San Bernardino – Wild bulls –
Tumacacori – The mission – A hermit – Tubac – The lost scouts –
San Xavier del Bac – The presidio of Tucson – Scavengers –
The Chiricahuas – A risky encounter – Mangas Colorado – Lieutenant
Couts – Recruiting in the plaza – A wild man – Murder of Owens –
In the cantina – Mr Bell is examined – The judge on evidence –
Dogfreaks – A fandango – Judge and meteorite.

It was colder yet in the morning when they rode out. There was no one in the streets and there were no tracks in the new snow. At the edge of the town they saw where wolves had crossed the road.

They rode out by a small river, skim ice, a frozen marsh where ducks walked up and back muttering. That afternoon they traversed a lush valley where the dead winter grass reached to the horses' bellies. Empty fields where the crops had rotted and orchards of apple and quince and pomegranate where the fruit had dried and fallen to the ground. They found deer yarded up in the meadows and the tracks of cattle and that night as they sat about their fire roasting the ribs and haunches of a young doe they could hear the lowing of bulls in the dark.

The following day they rode past the ruins of the old hacienda at San Bernardino. On that range they saw wild bulls so old that they bore spanish brands on their hips and several of these animals charged the little company and were shot down and left on the ground until one came out of a stand of acacia in a wash and buried its horns to the boss in the ribs of a horse ridden by James Miller. He'd lifted his foot out of the near stirrup when he saw it coming and the impact all but jarred him from the saddle. The horse screamed and kicked but the bull had planted its feet and it lifted the animal rider and all clear of the ground before Miller could get his pistol free and when he put the muzzle to the bull's forehead and fired and the whole grotesque assembly collapsed he stepped clear of the wreckage and walked off in disgust with the smoking gun dangling in his hand. The horse was struggling to rise and he went back and shot it and put the gun in his belt and commenced to unbuckle the girthstraps. The horse was lying square atop the dead bull and it took him some tugging to get the saddle free. The other riders had stopped to watch and someone hazed forward the last spare horse out of the remuda but other than that they offered him no help.

They rode on, following the course of the Santa Cruz, up through stands of immense riverbottom cottonwoods. They did not cut the sign of the Apache again and they found no trace of the missing scouts. The following day they passed the old mission at San José de Tumacacori and the judge rode off to look at the church which stood about a mile off the track. He'd given a short disquisition on the history and architecture of the mission and those who heard it would not believe that he had never been there. Three of the party rode with him and Glanton watched them go with dark misgiving. He and the others rode on a short distance and then he halted and turned back.

The old church was in ruins and the door stood open to the high walled enclosure. When Glanton and his men rode through the crumbling portal four horses stood riderless in the empty compound among the dead fruit trees and grapevines. Glanton rode with his rifle upright before him, the buttplate on his thigh. His dog heeled to the horse and they approached cautiously the sagging walls of the church. They would have ridden their horses through the door but as they reached it there was a rifleshot from inside and pigeons flapped up and they slipped down from their mounts and crouched behind them with their rifles. Glanton looked back at the others and then walked his horse forward to where he could see into the interior. Part of the upper wall was fallen in and most of the roof and there was a man lying in the floor. Glanton led the horse into the sacristy and stood looking down with the others.

The man in the floor was dying and he was dressed altogether in homemade clothes of sheephide even to boots and a strange cap. They turned him over on the cracked clay tiles and his jaw moved and a bloody spittle formed along his lower lip. His eyes were dull and there was fear in them and there was something else. John Prewett stood the butt of his rifle in the floor and swung his horn about to recharge the piece. I seen anothern run, he said. They's two of em.

The man in the floor began to move. He had one arm lying in his groin and he moved it slightly and pointed. At them or at the height from which he had fallen or to his destination in eternity they did not know. Then he died.

Glanton looked about the ruins. Where did this son of a bitch come from? he said.

Prewett nodded toward the crumbling mud parapet. He was up yonder. I didnt know what he was. Still dont. I shot the son of a bitch out of there.

Glanton looked at the judge.

I think he was an imbecile, the judge said.

Glanton led his horse through the church and out by a small door in the nave into the yard. He was sitting there when they brought the other hermit out. Jackson prodded him forward with the barrel of his rifle, a small thin man, not young. The one they'd killed was his brother. They had jumped ship on the coast long ago and made their way to this place. He was terrified and he spoke no english and little spanish. The judge spoke to him in german. They had been here for years. The brother had his wits stole in this place and the man now before them in his hides and his peculiar bootees was not altogether sane. They left him there. As they rode out he was trotting up and back in the yard calling out. He seemed not to be aware that his brother was dead in the church.

The judge caught Glanton up and they rode side by side out to the road.

Glanton spat. Ort to of shot that one too, he said.

The judge smiled.

I dont like to see white men that way, Glanton said. Dutch or whatever. I dont like to see it.

They rode north along the river trace. The woods were bare and the leaves on the ground clutched little scales of ice and the mottled and bony limbs of the cottonwoods were stark and heavy against the quilted desert sky. In the evening they passed through Tubac, abandoned, wheat dead in the winter fields and grass growing in the street. There was a blind man on a stoop watching the plaza and as they passed he raised his head to listen.

They rode out onto the desert to camp. There was no wind and the silence out there was greatly favored by every kind of fugitive as was the open country itself and no mountains close at hand for enemies to black themselves against. They were caught up and saddled in the morning before light, all riding together, their arms at the ready. Each man scanned the terrain and the movements of the least of creatures were logged into their collective cognizance until they were federated with invisible wires of vigilance and advanced upon that landscape with a single resonance. They passed abandoned haciendas and roadside graves and by midmorning they had picked up the track of the Apaches again coming in off the desert to the west and advancing before them through the loose sand of the riverbottom. The riders got down and pinched up samples of the forced sand at the rim of the tracks and tested it between their fingers and calibrated its moisture against the sun and let it fall and looked off up the river through the naked trees. They remounted and rode on.

They found the lost scouts hanging head downward from the limbs of a fireblacked paloverde tree. They were skewered through the cords of their heels with sharpened shuttles of green wood and they hung gray and naked above the dead ashes of the coals where they'd been roasted until their heads had charred and the brains bubbled in the skulls and steam sang from their noseholes. Their tongues were drawn out and held with sharpened sticks thrust through them and they had been docked of their ears and their torsos were sliced open with flints until the entrails hung down on their chests. Some of the men pushed forward with their knives and cut the bodies down and they left them there in the ashes. The two darker forms were the last of the Delawares and the other two were the Vandiemenlander and a man from the east named Gilchrist. Among their barbarous hosts they had met with neither favor nor discrimination but had suffered and died impartially.

They rode that night through the mission of San Xavier del Bac, the church solemn and stark in the starlight. Not a dog barked. The clusters of Papago huts seemed without tenant. The air was cold and clear and the country there and beyond lay in a darkness unclaimed by so much as an owl. A pale green meteor came up the valley floor behind them and passed overhead and vanished silently in the void.

At dawn on the outskirts of the presidio of Tucson they passed the ruins of several haciendas and they passed more roadside markers where people had been murdered. Out on the plain stood a small estancia where the buildings were still smoking and along the segments of a fence constructed from the bones of cactus sat vultures shoulder to shoulder facing east to the promised sun, lifting one foot and then the other and holding out their wings like cloaks. They saw the bones of pigs that had died in a claywalled lot and they saw a wolf in a melonpatch that crouched between its thin elbows and watched them as they passed. The town lay on the plain to the north in a thin line of pale walls and they grouped their horses along a low esker of gravel and surveyed it and the country and the naked ranges of mountains beyond. The stones of the desert lay in dark tethers of shadow and a wind was blowing out of the sun where it sat squat and pulsing at the eastern reaches of the earth. They chucked up their horses and sallied out onto the flat as did the Apache track before them two days old and a hundred riders strong.

They rode with their rifles on their knees, fanned out, riding abreast. The desert sunrise flared over the ground before them and ringdoves rose out of the chaparral by ones and by pairs and whistled away with thin calls. A thousand yards out and they could see the Apaches camped along the south wall. Their animals were grazing among the willows in the periodic river basin to the west of the town and what seemed to be rocks or debris under the wall was the sordid collection of leantos and wickiups thrown up with poles and hides and wagonsheets.

They rode on. A few dogs had begun to bark. Glanton's dog was quartering back and forth nervously and a deputation of riders had set out from the camp.

They were Chiricahuas, twenty, twenty-five of them. Even with the sun up it was not above freezing and yet they sat their horses half naked, naught but boots and breechclouts and the plumed hide helmets they wore, stoneage savages daubed with clay paints in obscure charges, greasy, stinking, the paint on the horses pale under the dust and the horses prancing and blowing cold. They carried lances and bows and a few had muskets and they had long black hair and dead black eyes that cut among the riders studying their arms, the sclera bloodshot and opaque. None spoke even to another and they shouldered their horses through the party in a sort of ritual movement as if certain points of ground must be trod in a certain sequence as in a child's game yet with some terrible forfeit at hand.

The leader of these jackal warriors was a small dark man in cast-off Mexican military attire and he carried a sword and he carried in a torn and gaudy baldric one of the Whitneyville Colts that had belonged to the scouts. He sat his horse before Glanton and assessed the position of the other riders and then asked in good spanish where were they bound. He'd no sooner spoken than Glanton's horse leaned its jaw forward and seized the man's horse by the ear. Blood flew. The horse screamed and reared and the Apache struggled to keep his seat and drew his sword and found himself staring into the black lemniscate that was the paired bores of Glanton's doublerifle. Glanton slapped the muzzle of his horse twice hard and it tossed its head with one eye blinking and blood dripping from its mouth. The Apache wrenched his pony's head around and when Glanton spun to look at his men he found them frozen in deadlock with the savages, they and their arms wired into a construction taut and fragile as those puzzles wherein the placement of each piece is predicated upon every other and they in turn so that none can move for bringing down the structure entire.

The leader was the first to speak. He gestured at the bloodied ear of his mount and spoke. angrily in apache, his dark eyes avoiding Glanton. The judge pushed his horse forward.

Vaya tranquilo, he said. Un accidente, nada más.

Mire, said the Apache. Mire la oreja de mi caballo.

He steadied the animal's head to show it but it jerked loose and slung the broken ear about so that blood sprayed the riders. Horseblood or any blood a tremor ran that perilous architecture and the ponies stood rigid and quivering in the reddened sunrise and the desert under them hummed like a snaredrum. The tensile properties of this unratified truce were abused to the utmost of their enduring when the judge stood slightly in the saddle and raised his arm and spoke out a greeting beyond them.

Another eight or ten mounted warriors had ridden out from the wall. Their leader was a huge man with a huge head and he was dressed in overalls cut off at the knees to accommodate the leggingtops of his moccasins and he wore a checked shirt and a red scarf. He carried no arms but the men at either side of him were armed with shortbarreled rifles and they also carried the saddle pistols and other accoutrements of the murdered scouts. As they approached the other savages deferred and gave way before them. The indian whose horse had been bitten pointed out this injury to them but the leader only nodded affably. He turned his mount quarterwise to the judge and it arched its neck and he sat it well. Buenos días, he said. De dónde viene?

The judge smiled and touched the withered garland at his brow, forgetting possibly that he had no hat. He presented his chief Glanton very formally. Introductions were exchanged. The man's name was Mangas and he was cordial and spoke spanish well. When the rider of the injured horse again put forth his claim for consideration this man dismounted and took hold of the animal's head and examined it. He was bandylegged for all his height and he was strangely proportioned. He looked up at the Americans and he looked at the other riders and waved his hand at them.

Andale, he said. He turned to Glanton. Ellos son amigables. Un poco borracho, nada más.

The Apache riders had begun to extricate themselves from among the Americans like men backing out of a thornthicket. The Americans stood their rifles upright and Mangas led the injured horse forward and turned its head up, containing the animal solely with his hands and the white eye rolling crazily. After some discussion it became plain that whatever the assessment of damage levied there was no specie acceptable by way of payment other than whiskey.

Glanton spat and eyed the man. No hay whiskey, he said.

Silence fell. The Apaches looked from one to the other. They looked at the saddle wallets and canteens and gourds. Cómo? said Mangas.

No hay whiskey, said Glanton.

Mangas let go the rough hide headstall of the horse. His men watched him. He looked toward the walled town and he looked at the judge. No whiskey? he said.

No whiskey.

His among the clouded faces seemed unperturbed. He looked over the Americans, their gear. In truth they did not look like men who might have whiskey they hadnt drunk. The judge and Glanton sat their mounts and offered nothing further in the way of parley.

Hay whiskey en Tucson, said Mangas.

Sin duda, said the judge. Y soldados también. He put forward his horse, his rifle in one hand and the reins in the other. Glanton moved. The horse behind him shifted into motion. Then Glanton stopped.

Tiene oro? he said.

Sí.

Cuánto.

Bastante.

Glanton looked at the judge then at Mangas again. Bueno, he said. Tres días. Aquí. Un barril de whiskey.

Un barril?

Un barril. He nudged the pony and the Apaches gave way and Glanton and the judge and those who followed rode single-file toward the gates of the squalid mud town that sat burning in the winter sunrise on the plain.

———◆·◆———

The lieutenant in charge of the little garrison was named Couts. He had been to the coast with Major Graham's command and returned here four days ago to find the town under an informal investment by the Apaches. They were drunk on tiswin they'd brewed and there had been shooting in the night two nights running and an incessant clamor for whiskey. The garrison had a twelvepound demiculverin loaded with musketballs mounted on the revetment and Couts expected the savages would withdraw when they could get nothing more to drink. He was very formal and he addressed Glanton as Captain. None of the tattered partisans had even dismounted. They looked about at the bleak and ruinous town. A blindfolded burro tethered to a pole was turning a pugmill, circling endlessly, the wooden millshaft creaking in its blocks. Chickens and smaller birds were scratching at the base of the mill. The pole was a good four feet off the ground yet the birds ducked or squatted each time it passed overhead. In the dust of the plaza lay a number of men apparently asleep. White, indian, Mexican. Some covered with blankets and some not. At the far end of the square there was a public whippingpost that was dark about its base where dogs had pissed on it. The lieutenant followed their gaze. Glanton pushed back his hat and looked down from his horse.

Where in this pukehole can a man get a drink? he said.

It was the first word any of them had spoken. Couts looked them over. Haggard and haunted and blacked by the sun. The lines and pores of their skin deeply grimed with gunblack where they'd washed the bores of their weapons. Even the horses looked alien to any he'd ever seen, decked as they were in human hair and teeth and skin. Save for their guns and buckles and a few pieces of metal in the harness of the animals there was nothing about these arrivals to suggest even the discovery of the wheel.

There are several places, said the lieutenant. None open yet though, I'm afraid.

They're fixin to get that way, said Glanton. He nudged the horse forward. He did not speak again and none of the others had spoken at all. As they crossed the plaza a few vagrants raised their heads up out of their blankets and looked after them.

The bar they entered was a square mud room and the proprietor set about serving them in his underwear. They sat on a bench at a wooden table in the gloom drinking sullenly.

Where you all from? said the proprietor.

Glanton and the judge went out to see if they could recruit any men from the rabble reposing in the dust of the square. Some of them were sitting, squinting in the sun. A man with a bowieknife was offering to cut blades with anyone at a wager to see who had the better steel. The judge went among them with his smile.

Captain what all you got in them saddlegrips?

Glanton turned. He and the judge carried their valises across their shoulders. The man who'd spoken was propped against a post with one knee drawn up to support his elbow.

These bags? said Glanton.

Them bags.

These here bags are full of gold and silver, said Glanton, for they were.

The idler grinned and spat.

That's why he's a wantin to go to Californy, said another. Account of he's done got a satchel full of gold now.

The judge smiled benignly at the wastrels. You're liable to take a chill out here, he said. Who's for the gold fields now.

One man rose and took a few steps away and began to piss in the street.

Maybe the wild man'll go with ye, called another. Him and Cloyce'll make ye good hands.

They been tryin to go for long enough.

Glanton and the judge sought them out. A rude tent thrown up out of an old tarp. A sign that said: See The Wild Man Two Bits. They passed behind a wagonsheet where within a crude cage of paloverde poles crouched a naked imbecile. The floor of the cage was littered with filth and trodden food and flies clambered about everywhere. The idiot was small and misshapen and his face was smeared with feces and he sat peering at them with dull hostility silently chewing a turd.

The owner came from the rear shaking his head at them. Aint nobody allowed in here. We aint open.

Glanton looked about the wretched enclosure. The tent smelled of oil and smoke and excrement. The judge squatted to study the imbecile.

Is that thing yours? Glanton said.

Yes. Yes he is.

Glanton spat. Man told us you was wantin to go to Californy.

Well, said the owner. Yes, that's right. That is right.

What do you figure to do with that thing?

Take him with me.

How you aim to haul him?

Got a pony and cart. To haul him in.

You got any money?

The judge raised up. This is Captain Glanton, he said. He's leading an expedition to California. He's willing to take a few passengers under the protection of his company provided they can find themselves adequately.

Well now yes. Got some money. How much money are we talking about?

How much have you got? said Glanton.

Well. Adequate, I would say. I'd say adequate in money.

Glanton studied the man. I'll tell you what I'll do with you, he said. Are you wantin to go to Californy or are you just mouth?

California, said the owner. By all means.

I'll carry ye for a hundred dollars, paid in advance.

The man's eyes shifted from Glanton to the judge and back. I like some of having that much, he said.

We'll be here a couple of days, said Glanton. You find us some more fares and we'll adjust your tariff accordingly.

The captain will treat you right, said the judge. You can be assured of that.

Yessir, said the owner.

As they passed out by the cage Glanton turned to look at the idiot again. You let women see that thing? he said.

I dont know, said the owner. There's none ever asked.

By noon the company had moved on to an eatinghouse. There were three or four men inside when they entered and they got up and left. There was a mud oven in the lot behind the building and the bed of a wrecked wagon with a few pots and a kettle on it. An old woman in a gray shawl was cutting up beefribs with an axe while two dogs sat watching. A tall thin man in a bloodstained apron entered the room from the rear and looked them over. He leaned and placed both hands on the table before them.

Gentlemen, he said, we dont mind servin people of color. Glad to do it. But we ast for em to set over here at this other table here. Right over here.

He stepped back and held out one hand in a strange gesture of hospice. His guests looked at one another.

What in the hell is he talkin about?

Just right over here, said the man.

Toadvine looked down the table to where Jackson sat. Several looked toward Glanton. His hands were at rest on the board in front of him and his head was slightly bent like a man at grace. The judge sat smiling, his arms crossed. They were all slightly drunk.

He thinks we're niggers.

They sat in silence. The old woman in the court had commenced wailing some dolorous air and the man was standing with his hand outheld. Piled just within the door were the satchels and holsters and arms of the company.

Glanton raised his head. He looked at the man.

What's your name? he said.

Name's Owens. I own this place.

Mr Owens, if you was anything at all other than a goddamn fool you could take one look at these here men and know for a stone fact they aint a one of em goin to get up from where they're at to go set somewheres else.

Well I caint serve you.

You suit yourself about that. Ask her what she's got, Tommy.

Harlan was sitting at the end of the table and he leaned out and called to the old woman at her pots and asked her in spanish what she had to eat.

She looked toward the house. Huesos, she said.

Huesos, said Harlan.

Tell her to bring em, Tommy.

She wont bring you nothin without I tell her to. I own this place.

Harlan was calling out the open door.

I know for a fact that man yonder's a nigger, said Owens.

Jackson looked up at him.

Brown turned toward the owner.

Have you got a gun? he said.

A gun?

A gun. Have you got a gun.

Not on me I aint.

Brown pulled a small fiveshot Colt from his belt and pitched it to him. He caught it and stood holding it uncertainly.

You got one now. Now shoot the nigger.

Wait a goddamn minute, said Owens.

Shoot him, said Brown.

Jackson had risen and he pulled one of the big pistols from

his belt. Owens pointed the pistol at him. You put that down, he said.

You better forget about givin orders and shoot the son of a bitch.

Put it down. Goddamn, man. Tell him to put it down.

Shoot him.

He cocked the pistol.

Jackson fired. He simply passed his left hand over the top of the revolver he was holding in a gesture brief as flintspark and tripped the hammer. The big pistol jumped and a double handful of Owens's brains went out the back of his skull and plopped in the floor behind him. He sank without a sound and lay crumpled up with his face in the floor and one eye open and the blood welling up out of the destruction at the back of his head. Jackson sat down. Brown rose and retrieved his pistol and let the hammer back down and put it in his belt. Most terrible nigger I ever seen, he said. Find some plates, Charlie. I doubt the old lady is out there any more.

They were drinking in a cantina not a hundred feet from this scene when the lieutenant and a half dozen armed troopers entered the premises. The cantina was a single room and there was a hole in the ceiling where a trunk of sunlight fell through onto the mud floor and figures crossing the room steered with care past the edge of this column of light as if it might be hot to the touch. They were a hardbit denizenry and they shambled to the bar and back in their rags and skins like cavefolk exchanging at some nameless trade. The lieutenant circled this reeking solarium and stood before Glanton.

Captain, we're going to have to take whoever's responsible for the death of Mr Owens into custody.

Glanton looked up. Who's Mr Owens? he said.

Mr Owens is the gentleman who ran the eatinghouse down here. He's been shot to death.

Sorry to hear it, said Glanton. Set down.

Couts ignored the invitation. Captain, you dont aim to deny that one of your men shot him do you?

I aim exactly that, said Glanton.

Captain, it wont hold water.

The judge emerged from the darkness. Evening, Lieutenant, he said. Are these men the witnesses?

Couts looked at his corporal. No, he said. They aint witnesses. Hell, Captain. You all were seen to enter the premises and seen to leave after the shot was fired. Are you going to deny that you and your men took your dinner there?

Deny ever goddamned word of it, said Glanton.

Well by god I believe I can prove that you ate there.

Kindly address your remarks to me, Lieutenant, said the judge. I represent Captain Glanton in all legal matters. I think you should know first of all that the captain does not propose to be called a liar and I would think twice before I involved myself with him in an affair of honor. Secondly I have been with him all day and I can assure you that neither he nor any of his men have ever set foot in the premises to which you allude.

The lieutenant seemed stunned at the baldness of these disclaimers. He looked from the judge to Glanton and back again. I will be damned, he said. Then he turned and pushed past the men and quit the place.

Glanton tilted his chair and leaned his back to the wall. They'd recruited two men from among the town's indigents, an unpromising pair that sat gawking at the end of the bench with their hats in their hands. Glanton's dark eye passed over them and alighted on the owner of the imbecile who sat alone across the room watching him.

You a drinkin man? said Glanton.

How's that?

Glanton exhaled slowly through his nose.

Yes, said the owner. Yes I am.

There was a common wooden pail on the table before Glanton with a tin dipper in it and it was about a third full of wagonyard whiskey drawn off from a cask at the bar. Glanton nodded toward it.

I aint a carryin it to ye.

The owner rose and picked up his cup and came across to the table. He took up the dipper and poured his cup and set the dipper back in the bucket. He gestured slightly with the cup and raised and drained it.

Much obliged.

Where's your ape at?

The man looked at the judge. He looked at Glanton again.

I dont take him out much.

Where'd you get that thing at?

He was left to me. Mama died. There was nobody to take him to raise. They shipped him to me. Joplin Missouri. Just put him in a box and shipped him. Took five weeks. Didnt bother him a bit. I opened up the box and there he set.

Get ye another drink there.

He took up the dipper and filled his cup again.

Big as life. Never hurt him a bit. I had him a hair suit made but he ate it.

Aint everbody in this town seen the son of a bitch?

Yes. Yes they have. I need to get to California. I may charge four bits out there.

You may get tarred and feathered out there.

I've been that. State of Arkansas. Claimed I'd given him something. Drugged him. They took him off and waited for him to get better but of course he didnt do it. They had a special preacher come and pray over him. Finally I got him back. I could have been somebody in this world wasnt for him.

Do I understand you correctly, said the judge, that the imbecile is your brother?

Yessir, said the man. That's the truth of the matter.

The judge reached and took hold of the man's head in his hands and began to explore its contours. The man's eyes darted about and he held onto the judge's wrists. The judge had his entire head in his grip like an immense and dangerous faith healer. The man was standing tiptoe as if to better accommodate him in his investigations and when the judge let go of him he took a step back and looked at Glanton with eyes that were white in the gloom. The recruits at the end of the bench sat watching with their jaws down and the judge narrowed an eye at the man and studied him and then reached and gripped him again, holding him by the forehead while he prodded along the back of his skull with the ball of his thumb. When the judge put him down the man stepped back and fell over the bench and the recruits commenced to bob up and down and to wheeze and croak. The owner of the idiot looked about the tawdry grogshop, passing up each face as if it did not quite suffice. He picked himself up and moved past the end of the bench. When he was halfway across the room the judge called out to him.

Has he always been like that? said the judge.

Yessir. He was born that way.

He turned to go. Glanton emptied his cup and set it before him and looked up. Were you? he said. But the owner pushed open the door and vanished in the blinding light without.

The lieutenant came again in the evening. He and the judge sat together and the judge went over points of law with him. The lieutenant nodded, his lips pursed. The judge translated for him latin terms of jurisprudence. He cited cases civil and martial. He quoted Coke and Blackstone, Anaximander, Thales.

In the morning there was new trouble. A young Mexican girl had been abducted. Parts of her clothes were found torn and bloodied under the north wall, over which she could only have been thrown. In the desert were drag marks. A shoe. The father of the child knelt clutching a bloodstained rag to his chest and none could persuade him to rise and none to leave. That night fires were lit in the streets and a beef killed and Glanton and his men were host to a motley collection of citizens and soldiers and reduced indians or tontos as their brothers outside the gates would name them. A keg of whiskey was broached and soon men were reeling aimlessly through the smoke. A merchant of that town brought forth a litter of dogs one of whom had six legs and another two and a third with four eyes in its head. He offered these for sale to Glanton and Glanton warned the man away and threatened to shoot them.

The beef was stripped to the bones and the bones themselves carried off and vigas were dragged from the ruined buildings and piled onto the blaze. By now many of Glanton's men were naked and lurching about and the judge soon had them dancing while he fiddled on a crude instrument he'd commandeered and the filthy hides of which they'd divested themselves smoked and stank and blackened in the flames and the red sparks rose like the souls of the small life they'd harbored.

By midnight the citizens had cleared out and there were armed and naked men pounding on doors demanding drink and women. In the early morning hours when the fires had burned to heaps of coals and a few sparks scampered in the wind down the cold clay streets feral dogs trotted around the cookfire snatching out the blackened scraps of meat and men lay huddled naked in the doorways clutching their elbows and snoring in the cold.

By noon they were abroad again, wandering red-eyed in the streets, fitted out for the most part in new shirts and breeches. They collected the remaining horses from the farrier and he stood them to a drink. He was a small sturdy man named Pacheco and he had for anvil an enormous iron meteorite shaped like a great molar and the judge on a wager lifted the thing and on a further wager lifted it over his head. Several men pushed forward to feel the iron and to rock it where it stood, nor did the judge lose this opportunity to ventilate himself upon the ferric nature of heavenly bodies and their powers and claims. Two lines were drawn in the dirt ten feet apart and a third round of wagers was laid, coins from half a dozen countries in both gold and silver and even a few boletas or notes of discounted script from the mines near Tubac. The judge seized that great slag wandered for what millennia from what unreckonable corner of the universe and he raised it overhead and stood tottering and then lunged forward. It cleared the mark by a foot and he shared with no one the specie piled on the saddleblanket at the farrier's feet for not even Glanton had been willing to underwrite this third trial.

XVII

Leaving Tucson – A new cooperage – An exchange – Saguaro forests –
Glanton at the fire – Garcia's command – The paraselene – The
godfire – The expriest on astronomy – The judge on the extraterrestrial,
on order, on teleology in the universe – A coin trick –
Glanton's dog – Dead animals – The sands – A crucifixion – The judge
on war – The priest does not say – Tierras quebradas, tierras
desamparadas – The Tinajas Atlas – Un hueso de piedra – The
Colorado – Argonauts – Yumas – The ferrymen – To the Yuma camp.

They rode out at dusk. The corporal in the gatehouse above
the portal came out and called to them to halt but they did
not. They rode twenty-one men and a dog and a little flatbed
cart aboard which the idiot and his cage had been lashed as if
for a sea journey. Lashed on behind the cage rode the whiskey
keg they'd drained the night before. The keg had been dismantled and rebound by a man Glanton had appointed cooper
pro-tem to the expedition and it now contained within it a flask
made from a common sheep's stomach and holding perhaps three
quarts of whiskey. This flask was fitted to the bung at the inside
and the rest of the keg was filled with water. So provisioned
they passed out through the gates and beyond the walls onto
the prairie where it lay pulsing in the banded twilight. The
little cart jostled and creaked and the idiot clutched at the bars
of his cage and croaked hoarsely after the sun.

Glanton rode at the fore of the column in a new Ringgold
saddle ironbound that he'd traded for and he wore a new hat
which was black and became him. The recruits now five in

number grinned at one another and looked back at the sentry. David Brown rode at the rear and he was leaving his brother here for what would prove forever and his mood was foul enough for him to have shot the sentry with no provocation at all. When the sentry called again he swung about with his rifle and the man had the sense to duck under the parapet and they heard no more from him. In the long dusk the savages rode out to meet them and the whiskey was exchanged for upon a Saltillo blanket spread on the ground. Glanton paid little attention to the proceedings. When the savages had counted out gold and silver to the judge's satisfaction Glanton stepped onto the blanket and kicked the coins together with his bootheel and then stepped away and directed Brown to take up the blanket. Mangas and his lieutenants exchanged dark looks but the Americans mounted up and rode out and none looked back save the recruits. They'd become privy to the details of the business and one of them fell in alongside Brown and asked if the Apaches would not follow them.

They wont ride at night, said Brown.

The recruit looked back at the figures gathered about the keg in that scoured and darkening waste.

Why wont they? he said.

Brown spat. Because it's dark, he said.

They rode west from the town across the base of a small mountain through a dogtown strewn with old broken earthenware from a crockery furnace that once had been there. The keeper of the idiot rode downside of the trestled cage and the idiot clutched the poles and watched the land pass in silence.

They rode that night through forests of saguaro up into the hills to the west. The sky was all overcast and those fluted columns passing in the dark were like the ruins of vast temples ordered and grave and silent save for the soft cries of elf owls among them. The terrain was thick with cholla and clumps of it clung to the horses with spikes that would drive through a bootsole to the bones within and a wind came up through the hills and all night it sang with a wild viper sound through that countless reach of spines. They rode on and the land grew more spare and they reached the first of a series of jornadas where there would be no water at all and there they camped. That night Glanton stared long into the embers of the fire. All about him his men were sleeping but much was changed. So many gone, defected or dead. The Delawares all slain. He watched the fire and if he saw portents there it was much the same to him. He would live to look upon the western sea and he was equal to whatever might follow for he was complete at every hour. Whether his history should run concomitant with men and nations, whether it should cease. He'd long forsworn all weighing of consequence and allowing as he did that men's destinies are given yet he usurped to contain within him all that he would ever be in the world and all that the world would be to him and be his charter written in the urstone itself he claimed agency and said so and he'd drive the remorseless sun on to its final endarkenment as if he'd ordered it all ages since, before there were paths anywhere, before there were men or suns to go upon them.

Across from him sat the vast abhorrence of the judge. Half naked, scribbling in his ledger. In the thornforest through which they'd passed the little desert wolves yapped and on the dry plain before them others answered and the wind fanned the coals that he watched. The bones of cholla that glowed there in their incandescent basketry pulsed like burning holothurians in the phosphorous dark of the sea's deeps. The idiot in his cage had been drawn close to the fire and he watched it tirelessly. When Glanton raised his head he saw the kid across the fire from him, squatting in his blanket, watching the judge.

Two days later they encountered a ragged legion under the command of Colonel Garcia. They were troops from Sonora seeking a band of Apaches under Pablo and they numbered close to a hundred riders. Of these some were without hats and some without pantaloons and some were naked under their coats and they were armed with derelict weapons, old fusils and Tower muskets, some with bows and arrows or nothing more than ropes with which to garrote the enemy.

Glanton and his men reviewed this company with stony

amazement. The Mexicans pressed about with their hands outheld for tobacco and Glanton and the colonel exchanged rudimentary civilities and then Glanton pushed on through that importunate horde. They were of another nation, those riders, and all that land to the south out of which they'd originated and whatever lands to the east toward which they were bound were dead to him and both the ground and any sojourners upon it remote and arguable of substance. This feeling communicated itself through the company before Glanton had moved entirely clear of them and each man turned his horse and each man followed and not even the judge spoke to excuse himself from out of that encounter.

They rode on into the darkness and the moonblanched waste lay before them cold and pale and the moon sat in a ring overhead and in that ring lay a mock moon with its own cold gray and nacre seas. They made camp on a low bench of land where walls of dry aggregate marked an old river course and they struck up a fire about which they sat in silence, the eyes of the dog and of the idiot and certain other men glowing red as coals in their heads where they turned. The flames sawed in the wind and the embers paled and deepened and paled and deepened like the bloodbeat of some living thing eviscerate upon the ground before them and they watched the fire which does contain within it something of men themselves inasmuch as they are less without it and are divided from their origins and are exiles. For each fire is all fires, the first fire and the last ever to be. By and by the judge rose and moved away on some obscure mission and after a while someone asked the expriest if it were true that at one time there had been two moons in the sky and the expriest eyed the false moon above them and said that it may well have been so. But certainly the wise high God in his dismay at the proliferation of lunacy on this earth must have wetted a thumb and leaned down out of the abyss and pinched it hissing into extinction. And could he find some alter means by which the birds could mend their paths in the darkness he might have done with this one too.

The question was then put as to whether there were on Mars or other planets in the void men or creatures like them and at this the judge who had returned to the fire and stood half naked and sweating spoke and said that there were not and that there were no men anywhere in the universe save those upon the earth. All listened as he spoke, those who had turned to watch him and those who would not.

The truth about the world, he said, is that anything is possible. Had you not seen it all from birth and thereby bled it of its strangeness it would appear to you for what it is, a hat trick in a medicine show, a fevered dream, a trance bepopulate with chimeras having neither analogue nor precedent, an itinerant carnival, a migratory tentshow whose ultimate destination after many a pitch in many a mudded field is unspeakable and calamitous beyond reckoning.

The universe is no narrow thing and the order within it is not constrained by any latitude in its conception to repeat what exists in one part in any other part. Even in this world more things exist without our knowledge than with it and the order in creation which you see is that which you have put there, like a string in a maze, so that you shall not lose your way. For existence has its own order and that no man's mind can compass, that mind itself being but a fact among others.

Brown spat into the fire. That's some more of your craziness, he said.

The judge smiled. He placed the palms of his hands upon his chest and breathed the night air and he stepped closer and squatted and held up one hand. He turned that hand and there was a gold coin between his fingers.

Where is the coin, Davy?

I'll notify you where to put the coin.

The judge swung his hand and the coin winked overhead in the firelight. It must have been fastened to some subtle lead, horsehair perhaps, for it circled the fire and returned to the judge and he caught it in his hand and smiled.

The arc of circling bodies is determined by the length of

their tether, said the judge. Moons, coins, men. His hands moved as if he were pulling something from one fist in a series of elongations. Watch the coin, Davy, he said.

He flung it and it cut an arc through the firelight and was gone in the darkness beyond. They watched the night where it had vanished and they watched the judge and in their watching some the one and some the other they were a common witness.

The coin, Davy, the coin, whispered the judge. He sat erect and raised his hand and smiled around.

The coin returned back out of the night and crossed the fire with a faint high droning and the judge's raised hand was empty and then it held the coin. There was a light slap and it held the coin. Even so some claimed that he had thrown the coin away and palmed another like it and made the sound with his tongue for he was himself a cunning old malabarista and he said himself as he put the coin away what all men knew that there are coins and false coins. In the morning some did walk over the ground where the coin had gone but if any man found it he kept it to himself and with sunrise they were mounted and riding again.

The cart with the idiot in his cage trundled along at the rear and now Glanton's dog fell back to trot alongside, perhaps out of some custodial instinct such as children will evoke in animals. But Glanton called the dog to him and when it did not come he dropped back along the little column and leaned down and quirted it viciously with his hobble rope and drove it out before him.

They began to come upon chains and packsaddles, singletrees, dead mules, wagons. Saddletrees eaten bare of their rawhide coverings and weathered white as bone, a light chamfering of miceteeth along the edges of the wood. They rode through a region where iron will not rust nor tin tarnish. The ribbed frames of dead cattle under their patches of dried hide lay like the ruins of primitive boats upturned upon that shoreless void and they passed lurid and austere the black and desiccated shapes of horses and mules that travelers had stood afoot. These parched beasts had died with their necks stretched in agony in the sand and now upright and blind and lurching askew with scraps of blackened leather hanging from the fretwork of their ribs they leaned with their long mouths howling after the endless tandem suns that passed above them. The riders rode on. They crossed a vast dry lake with rows of dead volcanoes ranged beyond it like the works of enormous insects. To the south lay broken shapes of scoria in a lava bed as far as the eye could see. Under the hooves of the horses the alabaster sand shaped itself in whorls strangely symmetric like iron filings in a field and these shapes flared and drew back again, resonating upon that harmonic ground and then turning to swirl away over the playa. As if the very sediment of things contained yet some residue of sentience. As if in the transit of those riders were a thing so profoundly terrible as to register even to the uttermost granulation of reality.

On a rise at the western edge of the playa they passed a crude wooden cross where Maricopas had crucified an Apache. The mummied corpse hung from the crosstree with its mouth gaped in a raw hole, a thing of leather and bone scoured by the pumice winds off the lake and the pale tree of the ribs showing through the scraps of hide that hung from the breast. They rode on. The horses trudged sullenly the alien ground and the round earth rolled beneath them silently milling the greater void wherein they were contained. In the neuter austerity of that terrain all phenomena were bequeathed a strange equality and no one thing nor spider nor stone nor blade of grass could put forth claim to precedence. The very clarity of these articles belied their familiarity, for the eye predicates the whole on some feature or part and here was nothing more luminous than another and nothing more enshadowed and in the optical democracy of such landscapes all preference is made whimsical and a man and a rock become endowed with unguessed kinships.

They grew gaunted and lank under the white suns of those days and their hollow burnedout eyes were like those of noctambulants surprised by day. Crouched under their hats they seemed fugitives on some grander scale, like beings for whom the sun hungered. Even the judge grew silent and speculative. He'd spoke of purging oneself of those things that lay claim to a man but that body receiving his remarks counted themselves well done with any claims at all. They rode on and the wind drove the fine gray dust before them and they rode an army of graybeards, gray men, gray horses. The mountains to the north lay sunwise in corrugated folds and the days were cool and the nights were cold and they sat about the fire each in his round of darkness in that round of dark while the idiot watched from his cage at the edge of the light. The judge cracked with the back of an axe the shinbone on an antelope and the hot marrow dripped smoking on the stones. They watched him. The subject was war.

The good book says that he that lives by the sword shall perish by the sword, said the black.

The judge smiled, his face shining with grease. What right man would have it any other way? he said.

The good book does indeed count war an evil, said Irving. Yet there's many a bloody tale of war inside it.

It makes no difference what men think of war, said the judge. War endures. As well ask men what they think of stone. War was always here. Before man was, war waited for him. The ultimate trade awaiting its ultimate practitioner. That is the way it was and will be. That way and not some other way.

He turned to Brown, from whom he'd heard some whispered slur or demurrer. Ah Davy, he said. It's your own trade we honor here. Why not rather take a small bow. Let each acknowledge each.

My trade?

Certainly.

What is my trade?

War. War is your trade. Is it not?

And it aint yours?

Mine too. Very much so.

What about all them notebooks and bones and stuff?

All other trades are contained in that of war.

Is that why war endures?

No. It endures because young men love it and old men love it in them. Those that fought, those that did not.

That's your notion.

The judge smiled. Men are born for games. Nothing else. Every child knows that play is nobler than work. He knows too that the worth or merit of a game is not inherent in the game itself but rather in the value of that which is put at hazard. Games of chance require a wager to have meaning at all. Games of sport involve the skill and strength of the opponents and the humiliation of defeat and the pride of victory are in themselves sufficient stake because they inhere in the worth of the principals and define them. But trial of chance or trial of worth all games aspire to the condition of war for here that which is wagered swallows up game, player, all.

Suppose two men at cards with nothing to wager save their lives. Who has not heard such a tale? A turn of the card. The whole universe for such a player has labored clanking to this moment which will tell if he is to die at that man's hand or that man at his. What more certain validation of a man's worth could there be? This enhancement of the game to its ultimate state admits no argument concerning the notion of fate. The selection of one man over another is a preference absolute and irrevocable and it is a dull man indeed who could reckon so profound a decision without agency or significance either one. In such games as have for their stake the annihilation of the defeated the decisions are quite clear. This man holding this particular arrangement of cards in his hand is thereby removed from existence. This is the nature of war, whose stake is at once the game and the authority and the justification. Seen so, war is the truest form of divination. It is the testing of one's will and the will of another within that larger will which because it binds them is therefore forced to select. War is the ultimate game because war is at last a forcing of the unity of existence. War is god.

Brown studied the judge. You're crazy Holden. Crazy at last.

The judge smiled.

Might does not make right, said Irving. The man that wins in some combat is not vindicated morally.

Moral law is an invention of mankind for the disenfranchisement of the powerful in favor of the weak. Historical law subverts it at every turn. A moral view can never be proven right or wrong by any ultimate test. A man falling dead in a duel is not thought thereby to be proven in error as to his views. His very involvement in such a trial gives evidence of a new and broader view. The willingness of the principals to forgo further argument as the triviality which it in fact is and to petition directly the chambers of the historical absolute clearly indicates of how little moment are the opinions and of what great moment the divergences thereof. For the argument is indeed trivial, but not so the separate wills thereby made manifest. Man's vanity may well approach the infinite in capacity but his knowledge remains imperfect and howevermuch he comes to value his judgements ultimately he must submit them before a higher court. Here there can be no special pleading. Here are considerations of equity and rectitude and moral right rendered void and without warrant and here are the views of the litigants despised. Decisions of life and death, of what shall be and what shall not, beggar all question of right. In elections of these magnitudes are all lesser ones subsumed, moral, spiritual, natural.

The judge searched out the circle for disputants. But what says the priest? he said.

Tobin looked up. The priest does not say.

The priest does not say, said the judge. Nihil dicit. But the priest has said. For the priest has put by the robes of his craft and taken up the tools of that higher calling which all men honor. The priest also would be no godserver but a god himself.

Tobin shook his head. You've a blasphemous tongue, Holden. And in truth I was never a priest but only a novitiate to the order.

Journeyman priest or apprentice priest, said the judge. Men of god and men of war have strange affinities.

I'll not secondsay you in your notions, said Tobin. Dont ask it.

Ah Priest, said the judge. What could I ask of you that you've not already given?

———————◆◆————————

On the day following they crossed the malpais afoot, leading the horses upon a lakebed of lava all cracked and reddish black like a pan of dried blood, threading those badlands of dark amber glass like the remnants of some dim legion scrabbling up out of a land accursed, shouldering the little cart over the rifts and ledges, the idiot clinging to the bars and calling hoarsely after the sun like some queer unruly god abducted from a race of degenerates. They crossed a cinderland of caked slurry and volcanic ash imponderable as the burnedout floor of hell and they climbed up through a low range of barren granite hills to a stark promontory where the judge, triangulating from known points of landscape, reckoned anew their course. A gravel flat stretched away to the horizon. Far to the south beyond the black volcanic hills lay a lone albino ridge, sand or gypsum, like the back of some pale seabeast surfaced among the dark archipelagos. They went on. In a day's ride they reached the stone tanks and the water they sought and they drank and bailed water down from the higher tanks to the dry ones below for the horses.

At all desert watering places there are bones but the judge that evening carried to the fire one such as none there had ever seen before, a great femur from some beast long extinct that he'd found weathered out of a bluff and that he now sat measuring with the tailor's tape he carried and sketching into his log. All in that company had heard the judge on paleontology save for the new recruits and they sat watching and putting to him such queries as they could conceive of. He answered them with care, amplifying their own questions for them, as if they might be apprentice scholars. They nodded dully and reached to touch that pillar of stained and petrified bone, perhaps to sense with their fingers the temporal immensities of which the judge spoke.

The keeper led the imbecile down from its cage and tethered it by the fire with a braided horsehair rope that it could not chew through and it stood leaning in its collar with its hands outheld as if it yearned for the flames. Glanton's dog rose and sat watching it and the idiot swayed and drooled with its dull eyes falsely brightened by the fire. The judge had been holding the femur upright in order to better illustrate its analogies to the prevalent bones of the country about and he let it fall in the sand and closed his book.

There is no mystery to it, he said.

The recruits blinked dully.

Your heart's desire is to be told some mystery. The mystery is that there is no mystery.

He rose and moved away into the darkness beyond the fire. Aye, said the expriest watching, his pipe cold in his teeth. And no mystery. As if he were no mystery himself, the bloody old hoodwinker.

Three days later they reached the Colorado. They stood at the edge of the river watching the roiled and claycolored waters coming down in a flat and steady seething out of the desert. Two cranes rose from the shore and flapped away and the horses and mules led down the bank ventured uncertainly into the eddying shoals and stood drinking and looking up with their muzzles dripping at the passing current and the shore beyond.

Upriver they encountered in camp the remnants of a wagon train laid waste by cholera. The survivors moved among their noonday cookfires or stared hollowly at the ragged dragoons riding up out of the willows. Their chattels were scattered about over the sand and the wretched estates of the deceased stood separate to be parceled out among them. There were in the camp a number of Yuma indians. The men wore their hair hacked to length with knives or plastered up in wigs of mud and they shambled about with heavy clubs dangling in their hands. Both they and the women were tattooed of face and the women were naked save for skirts of willowbark woven into string and many of them were lovely and many more bore the marks of syphilis.

Glanton moved through this balesome depot with his dog at heel and his rifle in his hand. The Yumas were swimming the few sorry mules left to the party across the river and he stood on the bank and watched them. Downriver they'd drowned one of the animals and towed it ashore to be butchered. An old man in a shacto coat and a long beard sat with his boots at his side and his feet in the river.

Where's your all's horses? said Glanton.

We ate them.

Glanton studied the river.

How do you aim to cross?

On the ferry.

He looked crossriver to where the old man gestured. What does he get to cross ye? he said.

Dollar a head.

Glanton turned and studied the pilgrims on the beach. The dog was drinking from the river and he said something to it and it came up and sat by his knee.

The ferryboat put out from the far bank and crossed to a landing upstream where there was a deadman built of driftlogs. The boat was contrived from a pair of old wagonboxes fitted together and caulked with pitch. A group of people had shouldered up their dunnage and stood waiting. Glanton turned and went up the bank to get his horse.

The ferryman was a doctor from New York state named Lincoln. He was supervising the loading, the travelers stepping aboard and squatting along the rails of the scow with their parcels and looking out uncertainly at the broad water. A half-mastiff dog sat on the bank watching. At Glanton's approach it stood bristling. The doctor turned and shaded his eyes with his hand and Glanton introduced himself. They shook hands. A pleasure, Captain Glanton. I am at your service.

Glanton nodded. The doctor gave instructions to the two men

working for him and he and Glanton walked out along the downriver path, Glanton leading the horse and the doctor's dog following some ten paces behind.

Glanton's party was camped on a bench of sand partially shaded by river willows. As he and the doctor approached the idiot rose in his cage and seized the bars and commenced hooting as if he'd warn the doctor back. The doctor went wide of the thing, glancing at his host, but Glanton's lieutenants had come forward and soon the doctor and the judge were deep in discourse to the exclusion of anyone else.

In the evening Glanton and the judge and a detail of five men rode downriver into the Yuma encampment. They rode through a pale wood of willow and sycamore flaked with clay from the high water and they rode past old acequias and small winter fields where the dry husks of corn rattled lightly in the wind and they crossed the river at the Algodones ford. When the dogs announced them the sun was already down and the western land red and smoking and they rode singlefile in cameo detailed by the winey light with their dark sides to the river. Cookfires from the camp smoldered among the trees and a delegation of mounted savages rode out to meet them.

They halted and sat their horses. The party approaching were clad in such fool's regalia and withal bore themselves with such aplomb that the paler riders were hard put to keep their composure. The leader was a man named Caballo en Pelo and this old mogul wore a belted wool overcoat that would have served a far colder climate and beneath it a woman's blouse of embroidered silk and a pair of pantaloons of gray cassinette. He was small and wiry and he had lost an eye to the Maricopas and he presented the Americans with a strange priapic leer that may have at one time been a smile. At his right rode a lesser chieftain named Pascual in a frogged coat out at the elbows and who wore in his nose a bone hung with small pendants. The third man was Pablo and he was clad in a scarlet coat with tarnished braiding and tarnished epaulettes of silver wire. He was barefooted and bare of leg and he wore on his face a pair of round green goggles. In this attire they arranged themselves before the Americans and nodded austerely.

Brown spat on the ground in disgust and Glanton shook his head.

Aint you a crazylookin bunch of niggers, he said.

Only the judge seemed to weigh them up at all and he was sober in the doing, judging as perhaps he did that things are seldom what they seem.

Buenas tardes, he said.

The mogul tossed his chin, a small gesture darkened with a certain ambiguity. Buenas tardes, he said. De dónde viene?

XVIII

**The return to camp – The idiot delivered – Sarah Borginnis –
A confrontation – Bathed in the river – The tumbril burned – James
Robert in camp – Another baptism – Judge and fool.**

W hen they rode out of the Yuma camp it was in the dark
of early morning. Cancer, Virgo, Leo raced the ecliptic
down the southern night and to the north the constellation of
Cassiopeia burned like a witch's signature on the black face of
the firmament. In the nightlong parley they'd come to terms with
the Yumas in conspiring to seize the ferry. They rode upriver
among the floodstained trees talking quietly among themselves
like men returning late from a social, from a wedding or a death.

By daylight the women at the crossing had discovered the
idiot in his cage. They gathered about him, apparently unap-
palled by the nakedness and filth. They crooned to him and they
consulted among themselves and a woman named Sarah Borginnis led them to seek out the brother. She was a huge woman with
a great red face and she read him riot.

What's your name anyways? she said.

Cloyce Bell mam.

What's his.

His name's James Robert but there dont anybody call him it.

256

If your mother was to see him what do you reckon she'd say.

I dont know. She's dead.

Aint you ashamed?

No mam.

Dont you sass me.

I'm not trying to. You want him just take him. I'll give him to you. I cant do any more than what I've done.

Damn if you aint a sorry specimen. She turned to the other women.

You all help me. We need to bathe him and get some clothes on him. Somebody run get some soap.

Mam, said the keeper.

You all just take him on to the river.

Toadvine and the kid passed them as they were dragging the cart along. They stepped off the path and watched them go by. The idiot was clutching the bars and hooting at the water and some of the women had started up a hymn.

Where are they takin it? said Toadvine.

The kid didnt know. They were backing the cart through the loose sand toward the edge of the river and they let it down and opened the cage. The Borginnis woman stood before the imbecile.

James Robert come out of there.

She reached in and took him by the hand. He peered past her at the water, then he reached for her.

A sigh went up from the women, several of whom had hiked their skirts and tucked them at the waist and now stood in the river to receive him.

She handed him down, him clinging to her neck. When his feet touched the ground he turned to the water. She was smeared with feces but she seemed not to notice. She looked back at those on the riverbank.

Burn that thing, she said.

Someone ran to the fire for a brand and while they led James Robert into the waters the cage was torched and began to burn.

He clutched at their skirts, he reached with a clawed hand, gibbering, drooling.

He sees hisself in it, they said.

Shoo. Imagine having this child penned up like a wild animal.

The flames from the burning cart crackled in the dry air and the noise must have caught the idiot's attention for he turned his dead black eyes upon it. He knows, they said. All agreed. The Borginnis woman waded out with her dress ballooning about her and took him deeper and swirled him about grown man that he was in her great stout arms. She held him up, she crooned to him. Her pale hair floated on the water.

His old companions saw him that night before the migrants' fires in a coarse woven wool suit. His thin neck turned warily in the collar of his outsized shirt. They'd greased his hair and combed it flat upon his skull so that it looked painted on. They brought him sweets and he sat drooling and watched the fire, greatly to their admiration. In the dark the river ran on and a fishcolored moon rose over the desert east and set their shadows by their sides in the barren light. The fires drew down and the smoke stood gray and chambered in the night. The little jackal wolves cried from across the river and the camp dogs stirred and muttered. The Borginnis took the idiot to his pallet under a wagonsheet and stripped him to his new underwear and she tucked him into his blanket and kissed him goodnight and the camp grew quiet. When the idiot crossed that blue and smoky amphitheatre he was naked once again, shambling past the fires like a balden groundsloth. He paused and tested the air and he shuffled on. He went wide of the landing and stumbled through the shore willows, whimpering and pushing with his thin arms at things in the night. Then he was standing alone on the shore. He hooted softly and his voice passed from him like a gift that was also needed so that no sound of it echoed back. He entered the water. Before the river reached much past his waist he'd lost his footing and sunk from sight.

Now the judge on his midnight rounds was passing along at just this place stark naked himself—such encounters being commoner than men suppose or who would survive any crossing by night—and he stepped into the river and seized up the drowning idiot, snatching it aloft by the heels like a great midwife and slapping it on the back to let the water out. A birth scene or a baptism or some ritual not yet inaugurated into any canon. He twisted the water from its hair and he gathered the naked and sobbing fool into his arms and carried it up into the camp and restored it among its fellows.

XIX

The howitzer – The Yumas attack – A skirmish – Glanton
appropriates the ferry – The hanged Judas – The coffers – A deputation
for the coast – San Diego – Arranging for supplies – Brown at
the farrier's – A dispute – Webster and Toadvine freed – The ocean –
An altercation – A man burned alive – Brown in durance vile –
Tales of treasure – An escape – A murder in the mountains – Glanton
leaves Yuma – The alcalde hanged – Hostages – Returns to Yuma –
Doctor and judge, nigger and fool – Dawn on the river – Carts without
wheels – Murder of Jackson – The Yuma massacre.

The doctor had been bound for California when the ferry fell
into his hands for the most by chance. In the ensuing months
he'd amassed a considerable wealth in gold and silver and jewelry.
He and the two men who worked for him had taken up residence on the west bank of the river overlooking the ferrylanding
among the abutments of an unfinished hillside fortification made
from mud and rock. In addition to the pair of freightwagons he'd
inherited from Major Graham's command he had also a mountain howitzer—a bronze twelvepounder with a bore the size of
a saucer—and this piece stood idle and unloaded in its wooden
truck. In the doctor's crude quarters he and Glanton and the
judge together with Brown and Irving sat drinking tea and
Glanton sketched for the doctor a few of their indian adventures
and advised him strongly to secure his position. The doctor
demurred. He claimed to get along well with the Yumas. Glanton
told him to his face that any man who trusted an indian was a
fool. The doctor colored but he held his tongue. The judge inter-
vened. He asked the doctor did he consider the pilgrims huddled

on the far shore to be under his protection. The doctor said that he did so consider them. The judge spoke reasonably and with concern and when Glanton and his detail returned down the hill to cross to their camp they had the doctor's permission to fortify the hill and charge the howitzer and to this end they set about running the last of their lead until they had close on to a hatful of rifleballs.

They loaded the howitzer that evening with something like a pound of powder and the entire cast of shot and they trundled the piece to a place of advantage overlooking the river and the landing below.

Two days later the Yumas attacked the crossing. The scows were on the west bank of the river discharging cargo as arranged and the travelers stood by to claim their goods. The savages came both mounted and afoot out of the willows with no warning and swarmed across the open ground toward the ferry. On the hill above them Brown and Long Webster swung the howitzer and steadied it and Brown crammed his lighted cigar into the touch-hole.

Even over that open terrain the concussion was immense. The howitzer in its truck leaped from the ground and clattered smoking backward across the packed clay. On the floodplain below the fort a terrible destruction had passed and upward of a dozen of the Yumas lay dead or writhing in the sand. A great howl went up among them and Glanton and his riders defiled out of the wooded littoral upriver and rode upon them and they cried out in rage at their betrayal. Their horses began to mill and they pulled them about and loosed arrows at the approaching dragoons and were shot down in volleys of pistolfire and the debarkees at the crossing scrabbled up their arms from among the dunnage and knelt and set up a fire from that quarter while the women and children lay prone among the trunks and freightboxes. The horses of the Yumas reared and screamed and churned about in the loose sand with their hoopshaped nostrils and whited eyes and the survivors made for the willows from which they'd emerged leaving on the field the wounded and the dying and the dead. Glanton and his men did not pursue them. They dismounted and walked methodically among the fallen dispatching them man and horse alike each with a pistolball through the brain while the ferry travelers watched and then they took the scalps.

The doctor stood on the low parapet of the works in silence and watched the bodies dragged down the landing and booted and shoved into the river. He turned and looked at Brown and Webster. They'd hauled the howitzer back to its position and Brown sat easily on the warm barrel smoking his cigar and watching the activity below. The doctor turned and walked back to his quarters.

Nor did he appear the following day. Glanton took charge of the operation of the ferry. People who had been waiting three days to cross at a dollar a head were now told that the fare was four dollars. And even this tariff was in effect for no more than a few days. Soon they were operating a sort of procrustean ferry where the fares were tailored to accommodate the purses of the travelers. Ultimately all pretense was dropped and the immigrants were robbed outright. Travelers were beaten and their arms and goods appropriated and they were sent destitute and beggared into the desert. The doctor came down to remonstrate with them and was paid his share of the revenues and sent back. Horses were taken and women violated and bodies began to drift past the Yuma camp downriver. As these outrages multiplied the doctor barricaded himself in his quarters and was seen no more.

In the following month a company from Kentucky under General Patterson arrived and disdaining to bargain with Glanton constructed a ferry downriver and crossed and moved on. This ferry was taken over by the Yumas and operated for them by a man named Callaghan, but within days it was burned and Callaghan's headless body floated anonymously downriver, a vulture standing between the shoulderblades in clerical black, silent rider to the sea.

Easter in that year fell on the last day of March and at dawn on that day the kid together with Toadvine and a boy named Billy Carr crossed the river to cut willow poles at a place where they grew upstream from the encampment of immigrants. Passing through this place before it was yet good light they encountered a party of Sonorans up and about and they saw hanging from a scaffold a poor Judas fashioned from straw and old rags who wore on his canvas face a painted scowl that reflected in the hand that had executed it no more than a child's conception of the man and his crime. The Sonorans had been up since midnight drinking and they had lit a bonfire on the bench of loam where the gibbet stood and as the Americans passed along the edge of their camp they called out to them in spanish. Someone had brought a long cane from the fire tipped with lighted tow and the Judas was being set afire. Its raggedy clothes were packed with squibs and rockets and as the fire took hold it began to blow apart piece by piece in a shower of burning rags and straw. Until at last a bomb in its breeches went off and blew the thing to pieces in a stink of soot and sulphur and the men cheered and small boys threw a few last stones at the blackened remnants dangling from the noose. The kid was the last to pass through the clearing and the Sonorans called out to him and offered him wine from a goatskin but he shrugged up his rag of a coat about his shoulders and hurried on.

By now Glanton had enslaved a number of Sonorans and he kept crews of them working at the fortification of the hill. There were also detained in their camp a dozen or more indian and Mexican girls, some little more than children. Glanton supervised with some interest the raising of the walls about him but otherwise left his men to pursue the business at the crossing with a terrible latitude. He seemed to take little account of the wealth they were amassing although daily he'd open the brass lock with which the wood and leather trunk in his quarters was secured and raise the lid and empty whole sacks of valuables into it, the trunk already holding thousands of dollars in gold and silver coins as well as jewelry, watches, pistols, raw gold in little leather stives, silver in bars, knives, silverware, plate, teeth.

On the second of April David Brown with Long Webster and Toadvine set out for the town of San Diego on the old Mexican coast for the purpose of obtaining supplies. They took with them a string of packanimals and they left at sunset, riding up out of the trees and looking back at the river and then walking the horses sideways down the dunes into the cool blue dusk.

They crossed the desert in five days without incident and rode up through the coastal range and led the mules through the snow in the gap and descended the western slope and entered the town in a slow drizzle of rain. Their hide clothing was heavy with water and the animals were stained with the silt that had leached out of them and their trappings. Mounted U S cavalry passed them in the mud of the street and in the distance beyond they could hear the sea boom shuddering on the gray and stony coast.

Brown took from the horn of his saddle a fibre morral filled with coins and the three of them dismounted and entered a whiskey grocer's and unannounced they upended the sack on the grocer's board.

There were doubloons minted in Spain and in Guadalajara and half doubloons and gold dollars and tiny gold half dollars and French coins of ten franc value and gold eagles and half eagles and ring dollars and dollars minted in North Carolina and Georgia that were twenty-two carats pure. The grocer weighed them out by stacks in a common scale, sorted by their mintings, and he drew corks and poured measures round in small tin cups whereon the gills were stamped. They drank and set down the cups again and he pushed the bottle across the raw sashmilled boards of the counter.

They had drafted a list of supplies to be contracted for and when they'd agreed on the price of flour and coffee and a few other staples they turned into the street each with a bottle in his fist. They went down the plankboard walkway and crossed through the mud and they went past rows of rawlooking shacks and crossed a small plaza beyond which they could see the low sea rolling and a small encampment of tents and a street where the squatting houses were made of hides ranged like curious dorys along the selvage of sea oats above the beach and quite black and shining in the rain.

It was in one of these that Brown woke the next morning. He had little recollection of the prior night and there was no one in the hut with him. The remainder of their money was in a bag around his neck. He pushed open the framed hide door and stepped out into the darkness and the mist. They'd neither put up nor fed their animals and he made his way back to the grocer's where they were tied and sat on the walkway and watched the dawn come down from the hills behind the town.

Noon he was red-eyed and reeking before the alcalde's door demanding the release of his companions. The alcalde vacated out the back of the premises and shortly there arrived an American corporal and two soldiers who warned him away. An hour later he was at the farriery. Standing warily in the doorway peering into the gloom until he could make out the shape of things within.

The farrier was at his bench and Brown entered and laid before him a polished mahogany case with a brass nameplate bradded to the lid. He unsnapped the catches and opened the case and raised from their recess within a pair of shotgun barrels and he took up the stock with the other hand. He hooked the barrels into the patent breech and stood the shotgun on the bench and pushed the fitted pin home to secure the forearm. He cocked the hammers with his thumbs and let them fall again. The shotgun was English made and had damascus barrels and engraved locks and the stock was burl mahogany. He looked up. The farrier was watching him.

You work on guns? said Brown.

I do some.

I need these barrels cut down.

The man took the gun and held it in his hands. There was a raised center rib between the barrels and inlaid in gold the maker's name, London. There were two platinum bands in the patent breech and the locks and the hammers were chased with scrollwork cut deeply in the steel and there were partridges engraved at either end of the maker's name there. The purple barrels were welded up from triple skelps and the hammered iron and steel bore a watered figure like the markings of some alien and antique serpent, rare and beautiful and lethal, and the wood was figured with a deep red feather grain at the butt and held a small springloaded silver capbox in the toe.

The farrier turned the gun in his hands and looked at Brown. He looked down at the case. It was lined with green baize and there were little fitted compartments that held a wadcutter, a pewter powderflask, cleaning jags, a patent pewter capper.

You need what? he said.

Cut the barrels down. Long about in here. He held a finger across the piece.

I cant do that.

Brown looked at him. You cant do it?

No sir.

He looked around the shop. Well, he said. I'd of thought any damn fool could saw the barrels off a shotgun.

There's something wrong with you. Why would anybody want to cut the barrels off a gun like this?

What did you say? said Brown.

The man tendered the gun nervously. I just meant that I dont see why anybody would want to ruin a good gun like this here. What would you take for it?

It aint for sale. You think there's something wrong with me?

No I dont. I didnt mean it that way.

Are you goin to cut them barrels down or aint ye?

I cant do that.

Cant or wont?

You pick the one that best suits you.

Brown took the shotgun and laid it on the bench.

What would you have to have to do it? he said.

I aint doin it.

If a man wanted it done what would be a fair price?

I dont know. A dollar.

Brown reached into his pocket and came up with a handful

of coins. He laid a two and a half dollar gold piece on the bench. Now, he said. I'm payin you two and a half dollars.

The farrier looked at the coin nervously. I dont need your money, he said. You cant pay me to butcher that there gun.

You done been paid.

No I aint.

Yonder it lays. Now you can either get to sawin or you can default. In the case of which I aim to take it out of your ass.

The farrier didnt take his eyes off Brown. He began to back away from the bench and then he turned and ran.

When the sergeant of the guard arrived Brown had the shotgun chucked up in the benchvise and was working at the barrels with a hacksaw. The sergeant walked around to where he could see his face. What do you want, said Brown.

This man says you threatened his life.

What man?

This man. The sergeant nodded toward the door of the shed.

Brown continued to saw. You call that a man? he said.

I never give him no leave to come in here and use my tools neither, said the farrier.

How about it? said the sergeant.

How about what?

How do you answer to this man's charges?

He's a liar.

You never threatened him?

That's right.

The hell he never.

I dont threaten people. I told him I'd whip his ass and that's as good as notarized.

You dont call that a threat?

Brown looked up. It was not no threat. It was a promise.

He bent to the work again and another few passes with the saw and the barrels dropped to the dirt. He laid down the saw and backed off the jaws of the vise and lifted out the shotgun and unpinned the barrels from the stock and fitted the pieces into the case and shut the lid and latched it.

What was the argument about? said the sergeant.

Wasnt no argument that I know of.

You better ask him where he got that gun he's just ruined. He's stole that somewheres, you can wager on it.

Where'd you get the shotgun? said the sergeant.

Brown bent down and picked up the severed barrels. They were about eighteen inches long and he had them by the small end. He came around the bench and walked past the sergeant. He put the guncase under his arm. At the door he turned. The farrier was nowhere in sight. He looked at the sergeant.

I believe that man has done withdrawed his charges, he said. Like as not he was drunk.

———— ◆•◆ ————

As he was crossing the plaza toward the little mud cabildo he encountered Toadvine and Webster newly released. They were wildlooking and they stank. The three of them went down to the beach and sat looking out at the long gray swells and passing Brown's bottle among them. They'd none of them seen an ocean before. Brown walked down and held his hand to the sheet of spume that ran up the dark sand. He lifted his hand and tasted the salt on his fingers and he looked downcoast and up and then they went back up the beach toward the town.

They spent the afternoon drinking in a lazarous bodega run by a Mexican. Some soldiers came in. An altercation took place. Toadvine was on his feet, swaying. A peacemaker rose from among the soldiers and soon the principals were seated again. But minutes later Brown on his way back from the bar poured a pitcher of aguardiente over a young soldier and set him afire with his cigar. The man ran outside mute save for the whoosh of the flames and the flames were pale blue and then invisible in the sunlight and he fought them in the street like a man beset with bees or madness and then he fell over in the road and burned up. By the time they got to him with a bucket of water he had blackened and shriveled in the mud like an enormous spider.

Brown woke in a dark little cell manacled and crazed with

thirst. The first thing he consulted for was the bag of coins. It was still inside his shirt. He rose up from the straw and put one eye to the judas hole. It was day. He called out for someone to come. He sat and with his chained hands counted out the coins and put them back in the bag.

In the evening he was brought his supper by a soldier. The soldier's name was Petit and Brown showed him his necklace of ears and he showed him the coins. Petit said he wanted no part of his schemes. Brown told him how he had thirty thousand dollars buried in the desert. He told him of the ferry, installing himself in Glanton's place. He showed him the coins again and he spoke familiarly of their places of origin, supplementing the judge's reports with impromptu data. Even shares, he hissed. You and me.

He studied the recruit through the bars. Petit wiped his forehead with his sleeve. Brown scooped the coins back into the poke and handed them out to him.

You think we caint trust one another? he said.

The boy stood holding the sack of coins uncertainly. He tried to push it back through the bars. Brown stepped away and held his hands up.

Dont be a fool, he hissed. What do you think I'd of give to have had such a chance at your age?

When Petit was gone he sat in the straw and looked at the thin metal plate of beans and the tortillas. After a while he ate. Outside it was raining again and he could hear riders passing in the mud of the street and soon it was dark.

They left two nights later. They had each a passable saddle-horse and a rifle and blanket and they had a mule that carried provisions of dried corn and beef and dates. They rode up into the dripping hills and in the first light Brown raised the rifle and shot the boy through the back of the head. The horse lurched forward and the boy toppled backward, the entire foreplate of his skull gone and the brains exposed. Brown halted his mount and got down and retrieved the sack of coins and took the boy's knife and took his rifle and his powderflask and his coat and he cut the ears from the boy's head and strung them onto his scapular and then he mounted up and rode on. The packmule followed and after a while so did the horse the boy had been riding.

———————◆◆◆———————

When Webster and Toadvine rode into the camp at Yuma they had neither provisions nor the mules they'd left with. Glanton took five men and rode out at dusk leaving the judge in charge of the ferry. They reached San Diego in the dead of night and were directed to the alcalde's house. This man came to the door in nightshirt and stockingcap holding a candle before him. Glanton pushed him back into the parlor and sent his men on to the rear of the house from whence they heard directly a woman's screams and a few dull slaps and then silence.

The alcalde was a man in his sixties and he turned to go to his wife's aid and was struck down with a pistolbarrel. He stood up again holding his head. Glanton pushed him on to the rear room. He had in his hand a rope already fashioned into a noose and he turned the alcalde around and put the noose over his head and pulled it taut. The wife was sitting up in bed and at this she commenced to scream again. One of her eyes was swollen and closing rapidly and now one of the recruits hit her flush in the mouth and she fell over in the tousled bedding and put her hands over her head. Glanton held the candle aloft and directed one of the recruits to boost the other on his shoulders and the boy reached along the top of one of the vigas until he found a space and he fitted the end of the rope through and let it down and they hauled on it and raised the mute and struggling alcalde into the air. They'd not tied his hands and he groped wildly overhead for the rope and pulled himself up to save strangling and he kicked his feet and revolved slowly in the candlclight.

Válgame Dios, he gasped. Qué quiere?

I want my money, said Glanton. I want my money and I want my packmules and I want David Brown.

Cómo? wheezed the old man.

Someone had lit a lamp. The old woman raised up and saw first the shadow and then the form of her husband dangling from the rope and she began to crawl across the bed toward him.

Dígame, gasped the alcalde.

Someone reached to seize the wife but Glanton motioned him away and she staggered out of the bed and took hold of her husband about the knees to hold him up. She was sobbing and praying for mercy to Glanton and to God impartially.

Glanton walked around to where he could see the man's face. I want my money, he said. My money and my mules and the man I sent out here. El hombre que tiene usted. Mi compañero.

No no, gasped the hanged man. Búscale. No man is here.

Where is he?

He is no here.

Yes he's here. In the juzgado.

No no. Madre de Jesús. No here. He is gone. Siete, ocho días.

Where is the juzgado?

Cómo?

El juzgado. Dónde está?

The old woman turned loose with one arm long enough to point, her face pressed to the man's leg. Allá, she said. Allá.

Two men went out, one holding the stub of the candle and shielding the flame with his cupped hand before him. When they came back they reported the little dungeon in the building out back empty.

Glanton studied the alcalde. The old woman was visibly tottering. They'd halfhitched the rope about the tailpost of the bed and he loosed the rope and the alcalde and the wife collapsed into the floor.

They left them bound and gagged and rode out to visit the grocer. Three days later the alcalde and the grocer and the alcalde's wife were found tied and lying in their own excrement in an abandoned hut at the edge of the ocean eight miles south of the settlement. They'd been left a pan of water from which they drank like dogs and they had howled at the booming surf in that wayplace until they were mute as stones.

Glanton and his men were two days and nights in the streets

crazed with liquor. The sergeant in charge of the small garrison
of American troops confronted them in a drinking exchange on
the evening of the second day and he and the three men with
him were beaten senseless and stripped of their arms. At dawn
when the soldiers kicked in the hostel door there was no one
in the room.

Glanton returned to Yuma alone, his men gone to the gold
fields. On that bonestrewn waste he encountered wretched parcels of foot-travelers who called out to him and men dead where
they'd fallen and men who would die and groups of folks clustered about a last wagon or cart shouting hoarsely at the mules
or oxen and goading them on as if they bore in those frail caissons
the covenant itself and these animals would die and the people
with them and they called out to that lone horseman to warn
him of the danger at the crossing and the horseman rode on all
contrary to the tide of refugees like some storied hero toward
what beast of war or plague or famine with what set to his re-
lentless jaw.

When he reached Yuma he was drunk. Behind him on a string
were two small jacks laden with whiskey and biscuit. He sat
his horse and looked down at the river who was keeper of the
crossroads of all that world and his dog came to him and nuzzled
his foot in the strirrup.

A young Mexican girl was crouched naked under the shade
of the wall. She watched him ride past, covering her breasts with
her hands. She wore a rawhide collar about her neck and she
was chained to a post and there was a clay bowl of blackened
meatscraps beside her. Glanton tied the jacks to the post and
rode inside on the horse.

There was no one about. He rode down to the landing. While
he was watching the river the doctor came scrambling down the
bank and seized Glanton by the foot and began to plead with
him in a senseless jabber. He'd not seen to his person in weeks
and he was filthy and disheveled and he tugged at Glanton's
trouserleg and pointed toward the fortifications on the hill. That
man, he said. That man.

Glanton slid his boot from the stirrup and pushed the doctor away with his foot and turned the horse and rode back up the hill. The judge was standing on the rise in silhouette against the evening sun like some great balden archimandrite. He was wrapped in a mantle of freeflowing cloth beneath which he was naked. The black man Jackson came out of one of the stone bunkers dressed in a similar garb and stood beside him. Glanton rode back up along the crest of the hill to his quarters.

All night gunfire drifted intermittently across the water and laughter and drunken oaths. When day broke no one appeared. The ferry lay at its moorings and across the river a man came down to the landing and blew a horn and waited and then went back.

The ferry stood idle all that day. By evening the drunkenness and revelry had begun afresh and the shrieks of young girls carried across the water to the pilgrims huddled in their camp. Someone had given the idiot whiskey mixed with sarsaparilla and this thing which could little more than walk had commenced to dance before the fire with loping simian steps, moving with great gravity and smacking its loose wet lips.

At dawn the black walked out to the landing and stood urinating in the river. The scows lay downstream against the bank with a few inches of sandy water standing in the floorboards. He pulled his robes about him and stepped aboard the thwart and balanced there. The water ran over the boards toward him. He stood looking out. The sun was not up and there was a low skein of mist on the water. Downstream some ducks moved out from the willows. They circled in the eddy water and then flapped out across the open river and rose and circled and bent their way upstream. In the floor of the scow was a small coin. Perhaps once lodged under the tongue of some passenger. He bent to fetch it. He stood up and wiped the grit from the piece and held it up and as he did so a long cane arrow passed through his upper abdomen and flew on and fell far out in the river and sank and backed to the surface again and began to turn and to drift downstream.

He faced around, his robes sustained about him. He was holding his wound and with his other hand he ravaged among his clothes for the weapons that were not there and were not there. A second arrow passed him on the left and two more struck and lodged fast in his chest and in his groin. They were a full four feet in length and they lofted slightly with his movements like ceremonial wands and he seized his thigh where the dark arterial blood was spurting along the shaft and took a step toward the shore and fell sideways into the river.

The water was shallow and he was moving weakly to regain his feet when the first of the Yumas leaped aboard the scow. Completely naked, his hair dyed orange, his face painted black with a crimson line dividing it from widow's peak to chin. He stamped his feet twice on the boards and flared his arms like some wild thaumaturge out of an atavistic drama and reached and seized the black by his robes where he lay in the reddening waters and raised him up and stove in his head with his warclub.

They swarmed up the hill toward the fortifications where the Americans lay sleeping and some were mounted and some afoot and all of them armed with bows and clubs and their faces blacked or pale with fard and their hair bound up in clay. The first quarters they entered were Lincoln's. When they emerged a few minutes later one of them carried the doctor's dripping head by the hair and others were dragging behind them the doctor's dog, bound at the muzzle, jerking and bucking across the dry clay of the concourse. They entered a wickiup of willowpoles and canvas and slew Gunn and Wilson and Henderson Smith each in turn as they reared up drunkenly and they moved on among the rude half walls in total silence glistening with paint and grease and blood among the bands of light where the risen sun now touched the higher ground.

When they entered Glanton's chamber he lurched upright and glared wildly about him. The small clay room he occupied was entirely filled with a brass bed he'd appropriated from some migrating family and he sat in it like a debauched feudal baron while his weapons hung in a rich array from the finials. Caballo en Pelo mounted into the actual bed with him and stood there while one of the attending tribunal handed him at his right side a common axe the hickory helve of which was carved with pagan motifs and tasseled with the feathers of predatory birds. Glanton spat.

Hack away you mean red nigger, he said, and the old man raised the axe and split the head of John Joel Glanton to the thrapple.

When they entered the judge's quarters they found the idiot and a girl of perhaps twelve years cowering naked in the floor. Behind them also naked stood the judge. He was holding leveled at them the bronze barrel of the howitzer. The wooden truck stood in the floor, the straps pried up and twisted off the pillow-blocks. The judge had the cannon under one arm and he was holding a lighted cigar over the touch-hole. The Yumas fell over one another backward and the judge put the cigar in his mouth and took up his portmanteau and stepped out the door and backed past them and down the embankment. The idiot, who reached just to his waist, stuck close to his side, and together they entered the wood at the base of the hill and disappeared from sight.

<hr />

The savages built a bonfire on the hill and fueled it with the furnishings from the white men's quarters and they raised up Glanton's body and bore it aloft in the manner of a slain champion and hurled it onto the flames. They'd tied his dog to his corpse and it was snatched after in howling suttee to disappear crackling in the rolling greenwood smoke. The doctor's torso was dragged up by the heels and raised and flung onto the pyre and the doctor's mastiff also was committed to the flames. It slid struggling down the far side and the thongs with which it was tied must have burnt in two for it began to crawl charred and blind and smoking from the fire and was flung back with a shovel. The other bodies eight in number were heaped onto the fire where they sizzled and stank and the thick smoke rolled out over the river. The doctor's head had been mounted upon a paling and carried about but at the last it too was thrown onto the blaze. The guns and clothing were divided upon the clay and divided too were the gold and silver out of the hacked and splintered chest that they'd dragged forth. All else was heaped on the flames and while the sun rose and glistened on their gaudy faces they sat upon the ground each with his new goods before him and they watched the fire and smoked their pipes as might some painted troupe of mimefolk recruiting themselves in such a wayplace far from the towns and the rabble hooting at them across the smoking footlamps, contemplating towns to come and the poor fanfare of trumpet and drum and the rude boards upon which their destinies were inscribed for these people were no less bound and indentured and they watched like the prefiguration of their own ends the carbonized skulls of their enemies incandescing before them bright as blood among the coals.

XX

The escape – Into the desert – Pursued by the Yumas – A stand –
Alamo Mucho – Another refugee – A siege – At long taw – Nightfires –
The judge lives – At barter in the desert – How the expriest comes to
advocate murder – Setting forth – Another encounter – Carrizo Creek –
An attack – Among the bones – Playing for keeps – An exorcism –
Tobin wounded – A counseling – The slaughter of the horses –
The judge on torts – Another escape, another desert.

Toadvine and the kid fought a running engagement upriver
through the shore bracken with arrows clattering through
the cane all about them. They came out of the willow brakes and
climbed the dunes and descended the far side and reappeared
again, two dark figures anguishing upon the sands, now trotting,
now stooping, the report of the pistol flat and dead in the open
country. The Yumas who crested out on the dunes were four in
number and they did not follow but rather fixed them upon the
terrain to which they had committed themselves and then turned
back.

The kid carried an arrow in his leg and it was butted against
the bone. He stopped and sat and broke off the shaft a few
inches from the wound and then he got up again and they went
on. At the crest of the rise they stopped and looked back. The
Yumas had already left the dunes and they could see the smoke
rising darkly along the river bluff. To the west the country was
all rolling sandhills where a man might lie in hiding but there
was no place the sun would not find him and only the wind could
hide his tracks.

Can you walk? said Toadvine.

I aint got no choice.

How much water you got?

Not much.

What do you want to do?

I dont know.

We could ease back to the river and lay up, said Toadvine.

Till what?

He looked toward the fort again and he looked at the broken shaft in the kid's leg and the welling blood. You want to try and pull that?

No.

What do you want to do?

Go on.

They mended their course and picked up the trail the wagon parties followed and they went on through the long forenoon and the day and the evening of the day. By dark their water was gone and they labored on beneath the slow wheel of stars and slept shivering among the dunes and rose in the dawn and went on again. The kid's leg had stiffened and he hobbled after with a section of wagontongue for a crutch and twice he told Toadvine to go on but he would not. Before noon the aborigines appeared.

They watched them assemble upon the trembling drop of the eastern horizon like baleful marionettes. They were without horses and they seemed to be moving at a trot and within the hour they were lofting arrows upon the refugees.

They went on, the kid with his pistol drawn, stepping and ducking the shafts where they fell out of the sun, the lengths of them glistening against the pale sky and foreshortening in a reedy flutter and then suddenly quivering dead in the ground. They snapped off the shafts against their being used again and they labored on sideways over the sand like crabs until the arrows coming so thick and close they made a stand. The kid dropped onto his elbows and cocked and leveled the revolver. The Yumas were over a hundred yards out and they set up a cry and Toadvine dropped to one knee alongside the kid. The pistol bucked and the gray smoke hung motionless in the air and one of the savages went down like a player through a trap. The kid had cocked the pistol again but Toadvine put his hand over the barrel and the kid looked up at him and lowered the hammer and then sat and reloaded the empty chamber and pushed himself up and recovered his crutch and they went on. Behind them on the plain they could hear the thin clamor of the aborigines as they clustered about the one he'd shot.

That painted horde dogged their steps the day long. They were twenty-four hours without water and the barren mural of sand and sky was beginning to shimmer and swim and the periodic arrows sprang aslant from the sands about them like the tufted stalks of mutant desert growths propagating angrily into the dry desert air. They did not stop. When they reached the wells at Alamo Mucho the sun was low before them and there was a figure seated at the rim of the basin. This figure rose and stood warped in the quaking lens of that world and held out one hand, in welcome or warning they had no way to know. They shielded their eyes and limped on and the figure at the well called out to them. It was the expriest Tobin.

He was alone and unarmed. How many are ye? he said.

What you see, said Toadvine.

All the rest gone under? Glanton? The judge?

They didnt answer. They slid down to the floor of the well where there stood a few inches of water and they knelt and drank.

The pit in which the well was sunk was perhaps a dozen feet in diameter and they posted themselves about the inner slope of this salient and watched while the indians fanned out over the plain, moving past in the distance at a slow lope. Assembled in small groups at cardinal points out there they began to launch their arrows upon the defenders and the Americans called out the arrival of the incoming shafts like artillery officers, lying there on the exposed bank and watching out across the pit toward the assailants in that quarter, their hands clawed at either side of them and their legs cocked, rigid as cats. The kid held his fire altogether and soon those savages on the western shore who were more favored by the light began to move in.

About the well were hillocks of sand from old diggings and the Yumas may have meant to try to reach them. The kid left his post and moved to the west rim of the excavation and began to fire on them where they stood or squatted on their haunches like wolves out there on the shimmering pan. The expriest knelt by the kid's side and watched behind them and held his hat between the sun and the foresight of the kid's pistol and the kid steadied the pistol in both hands on the edge of the works and let off the rounds. At the second fire one of the savages fell over and lay without moving. The next shot spun another one around and he sat down and then rose and took a few steps and sat down again. The expriest whispered encouragement at his elbow and the kid thumbed back the hammer and the expriest adjusted the hat to shade gunsight and sight eye with the one shadow and the kid fired again. He'd drawn his sight upon the wounded man sitting on the pan and his shot stretched him out dead. The expriest gave a low whistle.

Aye, you're a cool one, he whispered. But it's cunning work all the same and wouldnt it take the heart out of ye.

The Yumas seemed immobilized by these misfortunes and the kid cocked the pistol and shot down another of their number before they began to collect themselves and to move back, taking their dead with them, lofting a flurry of arrows and howling out bloodoaths in their stoneage tongue or invocations to whatever gods of war or fortune they'd the ear of and retreating upon the pan until they were very small indeed.

The kid shouldered up his flask and shotpouch and slid down the pitch to the floor of the well where he dug a second small basin with the old shovel there and in the water that seeped in he washed the bores of the cylinder and washed the barrel and ran pieces of his shirt through the bore with a stick until they came clean. Then he reassembled the pistol, tapping the barrel pin until the cylinder was snug and laying the piece in the warm sand to dry.

Toadvine had made his way around the excavation until he reached the expriest and they lay watching the retreat of the savages through the heat shimmering off the pan in the late sunlight.

He's a deadeye aint he?

Tobin nodded. He looked down the pit to where the kid sat loading the pistol, turning the powderfilled chambers and measuring them with his eye, seating the balls with the sprues down.

How do you stand by way of ammunition?

Poorly. We got a few rounds, not many.

The expriest nodded. Evening was coming on and in the red land to the west the Yumas were gathering in silhouette before the sun.

All night their watchfires burned on the dark circlet of the world and the kid unpinned the barrel from the pistol and using it for a spyglass he went around the warm sand selvage of the well and studied the separate fires for movement. There is hardly in the world a waste so barren but some creature will not cry out at night, yet here one was and they listened to their breathing in the dark and the cold and they listened to the systole of the rubymeated hearts that hung within them. When day broke the fires had burned out and slender terminals of smoke stood from the plain at three separate points of the compass and the enemy had gone. Crossing the dry pan toward them from the east was a large figure attended by a smaller. Toadvine and the expriest watched.

What do you make it to be?

The expriest shook his head.

Toadvine cupped his hand and whistled sharply down at the kid. He sat up with the pistol. He clambered up the slope with his stiff leg. The three of them lay watching.

It was the judge and the imbecile. They were both of them naked and they neared through the desert dawn like beings of a mode little more than tangential to the world at large, their figures now quick with clarity and now fugitive in the strangeness of that same light. Like things whose very portent renders them ambiguous. Like things so charged with meaning that their forms are dimmed. The three at the well watched mutely this transit out of the breaking day and even though there was no longer any question as to what it was that approached yet none would name it. They lumbered on, the judge a pale pink beneath his talc of dust like something newly born, the imbecile much the darker, lurching together across the pan at the very extremes of exile like some scurrilous king stripped of his vestiture and driven together with his fool into the wilderness to die.

Those who travel in desert places do indeed meet with creatures surpassing all description. The watchers at the well rose the better to witness these arrivals. The imbecile was fairly loping along to keep the pace. The judge on his head wore a wig of dried river mud from which protruded bits of straw and grass and tied upon the imbecile's head was a rag of fur with the blackened blood side out. The judge carried in one hand a small canvas satchel and he was bedraped with meat like some medieval penitent. He hove up at the diggings and nodded them a good morning and he and the idiot slid down the bank and knelt and began to drink.

Even the idiot, who must be fed by hand. He knelt beside the judge and sucked noisily at the mineral water and raised his dark larval eyes to the three men crouched above him at the rim of the pit and then bent and drank again.

The judge threw off his bandoliers of sunblacked meat and his skin beneath was strangely mottled pink and white in the shapes of them. He set by the little mud cap and laved water over his burnt and peeling skull and over his face and he drank again and sat in the sand. He looked up at his old companions. His mouth was cracked and his tongue swollen.

Louis, he said. What will you take for that hat?

Toadvine spat. It aint for sale, he said.

Everything's for sale, said the judge. What will you take?

Toadvine looked uneasily at the expriest. He looked down into the well. Got to have my hat, he said.

How much?

Toadvine gestured with his chin at the strings of meat. I reckon you want to trade some of that tug for it.

Not at all, said the judge. Such as is here is for everybody. How much for the hat?

What'll you give? said Toadvine.

The judge studied him. I'll give one hundred dollars, he said.

No one spoke. The idiot crouched on its haunches seemed also to be awaiting the outcome of this exchange. Toadvine took off the hat and looked at it. His lank black hair clove to the sides of his head. It wont fit ye, he said.

The judge quoted him some term in latin. He smiled. Not your concern, he said.

Toadvine put the hat on and adjusted it. I reckon that's what you got in that there satchel, he said.

You reckon correctly, said the judge.

Toadvine looked off toward the sun.

I'll make it a hundred and a quarter and wont ask you where you got it, said the judge.

Let's see your color.

The judge unclasped the satchel and tipped and emptied it out on the sand. It contained a knife and perhaps a half a bucketful of gold coins of every value. The judge pushed the knife to one side and spread the coins with the palm of his hand and looked up.

Toadvine took off the hat. He made his way down the slope. He and the judge squatted on either side of the judge's trove and the judge put forward the coins agreed upon, advancing them with the back of his hand forward like a croupier. Toadvine handed up the hat and gathered the coins and the judge took the knife and slit the band of the hat at the rear and cut through the brim and opened up the crown and then set the hat on his head and looked up at Tobin and the kid.

Come down, he said. Come down and share this meat.

They didnt move. Toadvine already had a piece of it in both hands and was tugging at it with his teeth. It was cool in the well and the morning sun fell only upon the upper rim. The judge scooped the remaining coins back into the satchel and stood it aside and bent to drink again. The imbecile had been watching its reflection in the pool and it watched the judge drink and it watched the water calm itself once more. The judge wiped his mouth and looked at the figures above him.

How are you fixed for weapons? he said.

The kid had set one foot over the edge of the pit and now he drew it back. Tobin did not move. He was watching the judge.

We've just the one pistol, Holden.

We? said the judge.

The lad here.

The kid had risen to his feet again. The expriest stood by him.

The judge in the floor of the well likewise rose and he adjusted his hat and gripped the valise under his arm like some immense and naked barrister whom the country had crazed.

Weigh your counsel, Priest, he said. We are all here together. Yonder sun is like the eye of God and we will cook impartially upon this great siliceous griddle I do assure you.

I'm no priest and I've no counsel, said Tobin. The lad is a free agent.

The judge smiled. Quite so, he said. He looked at Toadvine and he smiled up at the expriest again. What then? he said. Are we to drink at these holes turn about like rival bands of apes?

The expriest looked at the kid. They stood facing the sun. He squatted, the better to address the judge below.

Do you think that there is a registry where you can file on the wells of the desert?

Ah Priest, you'd know those offices more readily than I. I've no claim here. I've told you before, I'm a simple man. You know you're welcome to come down here and to drink and to fill your flask.

Tobin didnt move.

Let me have the canteen, said the kid. He'd taken the pistol from his belt and he handed it to the expriest and took the leather bottle and descended the bank.

The judge followed him with his eyes. The kid circled the floor of the well, no part of which was altogether beyond the judge's reach, and he knelt opposite the imbecile and pulled the stopper from the flask and submerged the flask in the basin. He and the imbecile watched the water run in at the neck of the flask and they watched it bubble and they watched it cease. The kid stoppered the flask and leaned and drank from the pool and then he sat back and looked at Toadvine.

Are you goin with us?

Toadvine looked at the judge. I dont know, he said. I'm subject to arrest. They'll arrest me in California.

Arrest ye?

Toadvine didnt answer. He was sitting in the sand and he made a tripod of three fingers and stuck them in the sand before him and then he lifted and turned them and poked them in again so that there were six holes in the form of a star or a hexagon and then he rubbed them out again. He looked up.

You wouldnt think that a man would run plumb out of country out here, would ye?

The kid rose and slung the flask by its strap over his shoulder. His trouserleg was black with blood and the bloody stump of the shaft jutted from his thigh like a peg for hanging implements upon. He spat and wiped his mouth with the back of his hand and he looked at Toadvine. It aint country you've run out of, he said. Then he made his way across the sink and up the bank. The judge followed him with his eyes and when the kid reached the sunlight at the top he turned and looked back and the judge was holding open the satchel between his naked thighs.

Five hundred dollars, he said. Powder and ball included.

The expriest was at the kid's side. Do him, he hissed.

The kid took the pistol but the expriest clung to his arm whispering and when the kid pulled away he spoke aloud, such was his fear.

You'll get no second chance lad. Do it. He is naked. He is unarmed. God's blood, do you think you'll best him any other way? Do it, lad. Do it for the love of God. Do it or I swear your life is forfeit.

The judge smiled, he tapped his temple. The priest, he said. The priest has been too long in the sun. Seven-fifty and that's my best offer. It's a seller's market.

The kid put the pistol in his belt. Then with the expriest at his elbow importunate he circled the crater and they set out west across the pan. Toadvine climbed up and watched them. After a while there was nothing to see.

That day their way took them upon a vast mosaic pavement cobbled up from tiny blocks of jasper, carnelian, agate. A thousand acres wide where the wind sang in the groutless interstices. Traversing this ground toward the east riding one horse and leading another came David Brown. The horse he led was saddled and bridled and the kid stood with his thumbs in his belt and watched while he rode up and looked down at his old companions.

We heard you were in the juzgado, said Tobin.

I was, said Brown. I aint now. His eyes catalogued them in every part. He looked at the piece of arrowshaft protruding from the kid's leg and he looked into the expriest's eyes. Where's your outfits? he said.

You're lookin at them.

You fall out with Glanton?

Glanton's dead.

Brown spat a dry white spot in that vast and broken plateland. He had a small stone in his mouth against the thirst and he shifted it with his jaw and looked at them. The Yumas, he said.

Aye, said the expriest.

All rubbed out?

Toadvine and the judge are at the well back yonder.

The judge, said Brown.

The horses stared bleakly at the crazed stone floor whereon they stood.

The rest gone under? Smith? Dorsey? The nigger?

All, said Tobin.

Brown looked east across the desert. How far to the well?

We left about an hour past daybreak.

Is he armed?

He is not.

He studied their faces. The priest dont lie, he said.

No one spoke. He sat fingering the scapular of dried ears. Then he turned the horse and rode on, leading the riderless animal behind. He rode watching back at them. Then he stopped again.

Did you see him dead? he called. Glanton?

I did, called the expriest. For he had so.

He rode on, turned slightly in the saddle, the rifle on his knee. He kept watch behind him on those pilgrims and they on him. When he was well diminished on the pan they turned and went on.

———————•◆•———————

By noon the day following they had begun to come again upon abandoned gear from the caravans, cast shoes and pieces of harness and bones and the dried carcasses of mules with the alparejas still buckled about. They trod the faint arc of an ancient lake shore where broken shells lay like bits of pottery frail and ribbed among the sands and in the early evening they descended among a series of dunes and spoilbanks to Carrizo Creek, a seep that welled out of the stones and ran off down the desert and vanished again. Thousands of sheep had perished here and the travelers made their way among the yellowed bones and carcasses with their rags of tattered wool and they knelt among bones to drink. When the kid raised his dripping head from the water a rifleball dished his reflection from the pool and the echoes of the shot clattered about the bonestrewn slopes and clanged away in the desert and died.

He spun on his belly and clambered sideways, scanning the skyline. He saw the horses first, standing nose to nose in a notch among the dunes to the south. He saw the judge clad in the gusseted clothing of his recent associates. He was holding the mouth of the upright rifle in his fist and pouring powder from a flask down the bore. The imbecile, naked save for a hat, squatted in the sands at his feet.

The kid scuttled to a low place in the ground and lay flat with the pistol in his fist and the creek trickling past his elbow. He turned to look for the expriest but he could not find him. He could see through the lattice of bones the judge and his charge on the hill in the sun and he raised the pistol and rested it in the saddle of a rancid pelvis and fired. He saw the sand jump on the slope behind the judge and the judge leveled the rifle and fired and the rifleball whacked through the bones and the shots rolled away over the dunelands.

The kid lay with his heart hammering in the sand. He thumbed back the hammer again and raised his head. The idiot sat as before and the judge was trudging sedately along the skyline looking over the windrowed bones below him for an advantage. The kid began to move again. He moved into the creek on his belly and lay drinking, holding up the pistol and the powderflask and sucking at the water. Then he moved out the far side and down a trampled corridor through the sands where wolves had gone to and fro. Off to his left he thought he heard the expriest hiss at him and he could hear the creek and he lay listening. He set the hammer at halfcock and rotated the cylinder and recharged the empty chamber and capped the piece and raised up to look. The shallow ridge along which the judge had advanced was empty and the two horses were coming toward him across the sand to the south. He cocked the pistol and lay watching. They approached freely over the barren pitch, nudging the air with their heads, their tails whisking. Then he saw the idiot shambling along behind them like some dim neolithic herdsman. To his right he saw the judge appear from the dunes and reconnoitre and drop from sight again. The horses continued on and there was a scrabbling behind him and when the kid turned the expriest was in the corridor hissing at him.

Shoot him, he called.

The kid spun about to look for the judge but the expriest called again in his hoarse whisper.

The fool. Shoot the fool.

He raised his pistol. The horses stepped one and the next through a break in the yellowed palings and the imbecile shambled after and disappeared. He looked back at Tobin but the expriest was gone. He moved along the corridor until he came to the creek again, already slightly roiled from the drinking horses above him. His leg had begun to bleed and he lay soaking it in the cold water and he drank and palmed water over the back of his neck. The marblings of blood that swung from his thigh were like thin red leeches in the current. He looked at the sun.

Hello called the judge, his voice off to the west. As if there were new riders to the creek and he addressed them.

The kid lay listening. There were no new riders. After a while the judge called out again. Come out, he called. There's plenty of water for everybody.

The kid had swung the powderflask around to his back to keep it out of the creek and he held the pistol up and waited. Upstream the horses had stopped drinking. Then they started drinking again.

When he moved out on the far side of the creek he came upon the hand and foot tracks left by the expriest among the prints of cats and foxes and the little desert pigs. He entered a clearing in that senseless midden and sat listening. His leather clothes were heavy and stiff with water and his leg was throbbing. A horse's head came up streaming water at the muzzle a hundred feet away over the bones and dropped from sight again. When the judge called out his voice was in a new place. He called out for them to be friends. The kid watched a small caravan of ants bearing off among the arches of sheepribs. In the watching his eyes met the eyes of a small viper coiled under a flap of hide. He wiped his mouth and began to move again. In a culdesac the tracks of the expriest terminated and came back. He lay listening. It was hours till dark. After a while he heard the idiot slobbering somewhere among the bones.

He heard the wind coming in off the desert and he heard his own breathing. When he raised his head to look out he saw the expriest stumbling among the bones and holding aloft a cross he'd fashioned out of the shins of a ram and he'd lashed them together with strips of hide and he was holding the thing before him like some mad dowser in the bleak of desert and calling out in a tongue both alien and extinct.

The kid stood up, the revolver in both hands. He wheeled. He saw the judge and the judge was in another quarter altogether and he had the rifle already at his shoulder. When he fired Tobin turned around facing the way he'd come and sat down still holding the cross. The judge put down the rifle and took up another. The kid tried to steady the barrel of the pistol and he let off the shot and then dropped to the sand. The heavy ball of the rifle passed overhead like an asteroid and chattered and chopped among the bones fanned over the rise of ground beyond. He raised to his knees and looked for the judge but the judge was not there. He reloaded the empty chamber and began to move again on his elbows toward the spot where he'd seen the expriest fall, taking his bearings by the sun and pausing from time to time to listen. The ground was trampled with the tracks of predators come in from the plains for the carrion and the wind carrying through the breaks bore with it a sour reek like the stink of a rancid dishclout and there was no sound except the wind anywhere at all.

He found Tobin kneeling in the creek bathing his wound with a piece of linen torn from his shirt. The ball had passed completely through his neck. It had narrowly missed the carotid artery yet he could not make the blood to stop. He looked at the kid crouched among the skulls and upturned ribtines.

You've got to kill the horses, he said. You've no other chance out of here. He'll ride you down.

We could take the horses.

Dont be a fool lad. What other bait has he?

We can get out as soon as it comes dark.

Do you think there'll be no day again?

The kid watched him. Will it not stop? he said.

It will not.

What do you think?

I've got to stop it.

The blood was running between his fingers.

Where is the judge? said the kid.

Where indeed.

If I kill him we can take the horses.

You'll not kill him. Dont be a fool. Shoot the horses.

The kid looked off up the shallow sandy creek.

Go on lad.

He looked at the expriest and at the slow gouts of blood dropping in the water like roseblooms how they swelled and were made pale. He moved away up the creek.

When he came to where the horses had entered the water they were gone. The sand on the side where they'd gone out was still wet. He pushed the revolver along before him, moving on the heels of his hands. For all his caution he found the idiot watching him before ever he saw it.

It was sitting motionless in a bower of bones with the broken sunlight stenciled over its vacant face and it was watching like a wild thing in a wood. The kid looked at it and then he shoved on past in the tracks of the horses. The loose neck swiveled slowly and the dull jaw drooled. When he looked back it was still watching. Its wrists were lying in the sand before it and although there was no expression to its face yet it seemed a creature beset with a great woe.

When he saw the horses they were standing on a rise of ground above the creek and looking toward the west. He lay quietly and studied the terrain. Then he moved out along the edge of the wash and sat with his back to the bone salients and cocked the pistol and took a rest with his elbows on his knees.

The horses had seen him come out of the wash and they were watching him. When they heard the pistol cock they pricked their ears and began to walk toward him across the sand. He shot the forward horse in the chest and it fell over and lay breathing heavily with the blood running out of its nose. The other one stopped and stood uncertainly and he cocked the pistol and shot it as it turned. It began to trot among the dunes and he shot it again and its front legs buckled and it pitched forward and rolled onto its side. It raised its head once and then it lay still.

He sat listening. Nothing moved. The first horse lay as it had fallen, the sand about its head darkening with blood. The smoke drifted away down the draw and thinned and vanished. He moved back down the wash and crouched under the ribs of a dead mule and recharged the pistol and then moved on toward the creek again. He did not go back the way he'd come and he did not see the imbecile again. When he came to the creek he drank and bathed his leg and lay listening as before.

Throw that gun out now, said the judge.

He froze.

The voice was not fifty feet away.

I know what you've done. The priest put you up to it and I'll take that as a mitigation in the act and the intent. Which I would any man in his wrongdoing. But there's the question of property. You bring me the pistol now.

The kid lay without moving. He heard the judge wade the creek upstream. He lay counting slowly under his breath. When the roiled water reached him he stopped counting and let go on the current a dry twist of grass and tolled it away downstream. At that same count it was scarcely out of sight among the bones. He moved out of the water and looked at the sun and began to make his way back to where he'd left Tobin.

He found the expriest's tracks still wet where he'd left the creek and the way of his progress marked with blood. He followed through the sand until he came to that place where the expriest had circled upon himself and lay hissing at him from his place of cover.

Did you do for them lad?

He raised his hand.

Aye. I heard the shots all three. The fool as well, aye lad?

He didnt answer.

Good lad, hissed the expriest. He'd bound up his neck in his shirt and he was naked to the waist and he squatted among those rancid pickets and eyed the sun. The shadows were long on the dunes and in the shadow the bones of the beasts that had died there lay skewed in a curious congress of garbled armatures upon the sands. They'd close to two hours till dark and the expriest said so. They lay under the boardlike hide of a dead ox and listened to the judge calling to them. He called out points of jurisprudence, he cited cases. He expounded upon those laws pertaining to property rights in beasts mansuete and he quoted from cases of attainder insofar as he reckoned them germane to the corruption of blood in the prior and felonious owners of the horses now dead among the bones. Then he spoke of other things. The expriest leaned to the kid. Dont listen, he said.

I aint listenin.

Stop your ears.

Stop yours.

The priest cupped his hands over his ears and looked at the kid. His eyes were bright from the bloodloss and he was possessed of a great earnestness. Do it, he whispered. Do you think he speaks to me?

The kid turned away. He marked the sun squatting at the western rim of the waste and they spoke no more until it was dark and then they rose and made their way out.

They stole up from the basin and set off across the shallow dunes and they looked a last time back at the valley where flickering in the wind at the edge of the revetment stood the judge's nightfire for all to see. They did not speculate as to what it fed upon for fuel and they were well advanced on the desert before the moon rose.

There were wolves and jackals in that region and they cried all the forepart of the night until the moon came up and then they ceased as if surprised by its rising. Then they began again. The pilgrims were weak from their wounds. They lay down to rest but never for long and never without scanning the skyline to the east for any figure intruded upon it and they shivered in the barren desert wind coming out of whatever godless quadrant cold and sterile and bearing news of nothing at all. When day came they made their way to a slight rise on that endless flat and squatted in the loose shale and watched the sun's rising. It was cold and the expriest in his rags and his collar of blood hugged himself. On this small promontory they slept and when they woke it was midmorning and the sun well advanced. They sat up and looked out. Coming toward them over the plain in the middle distance they could see the figure of the judge, the figure of the fool.

XXI

Desert castaways – The backtrack – A hideout – The wind takes
a side – The judge returns – An address – Los Diegueños – San
Felipe – Hospitality of the savages – Into the mountains –
Grizzlies – San Diego – The sea.

The kid looked at Tobin but the expriest sat without expression. He was drawn and wretchedlooking and the approaching travelers seemed to evoke in him no recognition. He raised his head slightly and he spoke without looking at the kid. Go on, he said. Save yourself.

The kid took the water bottle from the shales and unstoppered it and drank and handed it across. The expriest drank and they sat watching and then they rose and turned and set out again.

They were much reduced by their wounds and their hunger and they made a poor show as they staggered onward. By noon their water was gone and they sat studying the barrenness about. A wind blew down from the north. Their mouths were dry. The desert upon which they were entrained was desert absolute and it was devoid of feature altogether and there was nothing to mark their progress upon it. The earth fell away on every side equally in its arcature and by these limits were they circumscribed and of them were they locus. They rose and went on. The sky was luminous. There was no trace to follow other than the bits of cast-off left by travelers even to the bones of men drifted out of their graves in the scalloped sands. In the afternoon the terrain began to rise before them and at the crest of a shallow esker they stood and looked back to see the judge much as before some two miles distant on the plain. They went on.

The approach to any watering place in that desert was marked by the carcasses of perished animals in increasing number and so it was now, as if the wells were ringed about by some hazard lethal to creatures. The travelers looked back. The judge was out of sight beyond the rise. Before them lay the whitened boards of a wagon and further on the shapes of mule and ox with the hide scoured bald as canvas by the constant abrasion of the sand.

The kid stood studying this place and then he backtracked some hundred yards and stood looking down at his shallow footprints in the sand. He looked upon the drifted slope of the esker which they had descended and he knelt and held his hand against the ground and he listened to the faint silica hiss of the wind.

When he lifted his hand there was a thin ridge of sand that had drifted against it and he watched this ridge slowly vanish before him.

The expriest when he returned to him presented a grave appearance. The kid knelt and studied him where he sat.

We got to hide, he said.

Hide?

Yes.

Where do you aim to hide?

Here. We'll hide here.

You cant hide, lad.

We can hide.

You think he cant follow your track?

The wind's taking it. It's gone from the slope yonder.

Gone?

Ever trace.

The expriest shook his head.

Come on. We got to get goin.

You cant hide.

Get up.

The expriest shook his head. Ah lad, he said.

Get up, said the kid.

Go on, go on. He waved his hand.

The kid spoke to him. He aint nothin. You told me so your-self. Men are made of the dust of the earth. You said it was no pair . . . pair . . .

Parable.

No parable. That it was a naked fact and the judge was a man like all men.

Face him down then, said the expriest. Face him down if he is so.

And him with a rifle and me with a pistol. Him with two rifles. Get up from there.

Tobin rose. He stood unsteadily, he leaned against the kid. They set out, veering off from the drifted track and down past the wagon.

They passed the first of the racks of bones and went on to where a pair of mules lay dead in the traces and here the kid knelt with a piece of board and began to scoop them a shelter, watching the skyline to the east as he worked. Then they lay prone in the lee of those sour bones like sated scavengers and awaited the arrival of the judge and the passing of the judge if he would so pass.

They'd not long to wait. He appeared upon the rise and paused momentarily before starting down, he and his drooling manciple. The ground before him was drifted and rolling and although it could be fairly reconnoitred from the rise the judge did not scan the country nor did he seem to miss the fugitives from his purview. He descended the ridge and started across the flats, the idiot before him on a leather lead. He carried the two rifles that had belonged to Brown and he wore a pair of canteens crossed upon his chest and he carried a powderhorn and flask and his portmanteau and a canvas rucksack that must have belonged to Brown also. More strangely he carried a parasol made from rotted scraps of hide stretched over a framework of rib bones bound with strips of tug. The handle had been the foreleg of some creature and the judge approaching was clothed in little more than confetti so rent was his costume to accommodate his figure. Bearing before him that morbid umbrella with the idiot in its rawhide collar pulling at the lead he seemed some degenerate entrepreneur fleeing from a medicine show and the outrage of the citizens who'd sacked it.

They advanced across the flats and the kid on his belly in the sand wallow watched them through the ribs of the dead mules. He could see his own tracks and Tobin's coming across the sand, dim and rounded but tracks for that, and he watched the judge and he watched the tracks and he listened to the sand moving on the desert floor. The judge was perhaps a hundred yards out when he stopped and surveyed the ground. The idiot squatted on all fours and leaned into the lead like some naked species of lemur. It swung its head and sniffed at the air, as if it were being used for tracking. It had lost its hat, or perhaps the judge had replevined it, for he now wore a rough and curious pair of pampooties cut from a piece of hide and strapped to the soles of his feet with wrappings of hemp salvaged from some desert wreck. The imbecile lunged in its collar and croaked, its forearms dangling at its chest. When they passed the wagon and continued on the kid knew they were beyond the point where he and Tobin had turned off from the trace. He looked at the tracks. Faint shapes that backed across the sands and vanished. The expriest at his side seized his arm and hissed and gestured toward the passing judge and the wind rattled the scraps of hide at the carcass and the judge and the idiot passed on across the sands and disappeared from sight.

They lay without speaking. The expriest raised himself slightly and looked out and he looked at the kid. The kid lowered the hammer of the pistol.

Ye'll get no such a chance as that again.

The kid put the pistol in his belt and rose onto his knees and looked out.

And what now?

The kid didnt answer.

He'll be waiting at the next well.

Let him wait.

We could go back to the creek.

And do what.

Wait for a party to come through.

Through from where? There aint no ferry.

There's game comes to the creek.

Tobin was looking out through the bones and hide. When the kid didnt answer he looked up. We could go there, he said.

I got four rounds, the kid said.

He rose and looked out across the scavenged ground and the expriest rose and looked with him. What they saw was the judge returning.

The kid swore and dropped to his belly. The expriest crouched. They pushed down into the wallow and with their chins in the sand like lizards they watched the judge traverse again the grounds before them.

With his leashed fool and his equipage and the parasol dipping in the wind like a great black flower he passed among the wreckage until he was again upon the slope of the sand esker. At the crest he turned and the imbecile squatted at his knees and the judge lowered the parasol before him and addressed the countryside about.

The priest has led you to this, boy. I know you would not hide. I know too that you've not the heart of a common assassin. I've passed before your gunsights twice this hour and will pass a third time. Why not show yourself?

No assassin, called the judge. And no partisan either. There's a flawed place in the fabric of your heart. Do you think I could not know? You alone were mutinous. You alone reserved in your soul some corner of clemency for the heathen.

The imbecile stood and raised its hands to its face and yammered weirdly and sat again.

You think I've killed Brown and Toadvine? They are alive as

you and me. They are alive and in possession of the fruits of their election. Do you understand? Ask the priest. The priest knows. The priest does not lie.

The judge raised the parasol and adjusted his parcels. Perhaps, he called, perhaps you have seen this place in a dream. That you would die here. Then he descended the esker and passed once more across the boneyard led by the tethered fool until the two were shimmering and insubstantial in the waves of heat and then they were gone altogether.

They would have died if the indians had not found them. All the early part of the night they'd kept Sirius at their left on the southwest horizon and Cetus out there fording the void and Orion and Betelgeuse turning overhead and they had slept curled and shivering in the darkness of the plains and woke to find the heavens all changed and the stars by which they'd traveled not to be found, as if their sleep had encompassed whole seasons. In the auburn dawn they saw the halfnaked savages crouched or standing all in a row along a rise to the north. They got up and went on, their shadows so long and so narrow raising with mock stealth each thin articulated leg. The mountains to the west were whited out against the daybreak. The aborigines moved along the sand ridge. After a while the expriest sat down and the kid stood over him with the pistol and the savages came down from the dunes and approached by starts and checks across the plain like painted sprites.

They were Diegueños. They were armed with short bows and they drew about the travelers and knelt and gave them water out of a gourd. They'd seen such pilgrims before and with sufferings more terrible. They eked a desperate living from that land and they knew that nothing excepting some savage pursuit could drive men to such plight and they watched each day for that thing to gather itself out of its terrible incubation in the house of the sun and muster along the edge of the eastern world and whether it be armies or plague or pestilence or something altogether unspeakable they waited with a strange equanimity.

They led the refugees into their camp at San Felipe, a collection of crude huts made from reeds and housing a population of filthy and beggarly creatures dressed largely in the cotton shirts of the argonauts who'd passed there, shirts and nothing more. They fetched them a stew of lizards and pocketmice hot in clay bowls and a sort of piñole made from dried and pounded grasshoppers and they crouched about and watched them with great solemnity as they ate.

One reached and touched the grips of the pistol in the kid's belt and drew back again. Pistola, he said.

The kid ate.

The savages nodded.

Quiero mirar su pistola, the man said.

The kid didnt answer. When the man reached for the pistol he intercepted his hand and put it from him. When he turned loose the man reached again and the kid pushed his hand away again.

The man grinned. He reached a third time. The kid set the bowl between his legs and drew the pistol and cocked it and put the muzzle against the man's forehead.

They sat quite still. The others watched. After a while the kid lowered the pistol and let down the hammer and put it in his belt and picked up the bowl and commenced eating again. The man gestured toward the pistol and spoke to his friends and they nodded and then they sat as before.

Qué pasó con ustedes.

The kid watched the man over the rim of the bowl with his dark and hollow eyes.

The indian looked at the expriest.

Qué pasó con ustedes.

The expriest in his black and crusted cravat turned his whole torso to look at the man who'd spoken. He looked at the kid. He'd been eating with his fingers and he licked them and wiped them on the filthy leg of his trousers.

Las Yumas, he said.

They sucked in air and clucked their tongues.

Son muy malos, said the speaker.

Claro.

No tiene compañeros?

The kid and the expriest eyed each other.

Sí, said the kid. Muchos. He waved his hand to the east. Llegaran. Muchos compañeros.

The indians received this news without expression. A woman brought more of the piñole but they had been without food too long to have appetites and they waved her away.

In the afternoon they bathed in the creek and slept on the ground. When they woke they were being watched by a group of naked children and a few dogs. When they went up through the camp they saw the indians sitting along a ledge of rock watching tirelessly the land to the east for whatever might come out of it. No one spoke to them of the judge and they did not ask. The dogs and children followed them out of the camp and they took the trail up into the low hills to the west where the sun was already going.

They reached Warner's Ranch late the following day and they restored themselves at the hot sulphur springs there. There was no one about. They moved on. The country to the west was rolling and grassy and beyond were mountains running to the coast. They slept that night among dwarf cedars and in the morning the grass was frozen and they could hear the wind in the frozen grass and they could hear the cries of birds that seemed a charm against the sullen shores of the void out of which they had ascended.

All that day they climbed through a highland park forested with joshua trees and rimmed about by bald granite peaks. In the evening flocks of eagles went up through the pass before them and they could see on those grassy benches the great shambling figures of bears like cattle grazing on some upland heath. There were skifts of snow in the lee of the stone ledges and in the night a light snow fell upon them. Reefs of mist were blowing across the slopes when they set out shivering in the dawn and in the new snow they saw the tracks of the bears that had come down to take their wind just before daylight.

That day there was no sun only a paleness in the haze and the country was white with frost and the shrubs were like polar isomers of their own shapes. Wild rams ghosted away up those rocky draws and the wind swirled down cold and gray from the snowy reeks above them, a smoking region of wild vapors blowing down through the gap as if the world up there were all afire. They spoke less and less between them until at last they were silent altogether as is often the way with travelers approaching the end of a journey. They drank from the cold mountain streams and bathed their wounds and they shot a young doe at a spring and ate what they could and smoked thin sheets of the meat to carry with them. Although they saw no more bears they saw sign of their vicinity and they moved off over the slopes a good mile from their meatcamp before they put down for the night. In the morning they crossed a bed of thunderstones clustered on that heath like the ossified eggs of some primal groundbird. They trod the shadowline under the mountains keeping just in the sun for the warmth of it and that afternoon they first saw the sea, far below them, blue and serene under clouds.

The trail went down through the low hills and picked up the wagontrack and they followed where the locked wheels had skidded and the iron tires scarred the rock and the sea down there darkened to black and the sun fell and all the land about went blue and cold. They slept shivering under a wooded boss among owlcries and a scent of juniper while the stars swarmed in the bottomless night.

It was evening of the following day when they entered San Diego. The expriest turned off to find them a doctor but the kid wandered on through the raw mud streets and out past the houses of hide in their rows and across the gravel strand to the beach.

Loose strands of ambercolored kelp lay in a rubbery wrack

at the tideline. A dead seal. Beyond the inner bay part of a reef in a thin line like something foundered there on which the sea was teething. He squatted in the sand and watched the sun on the hammered face of the water. Out there island clouds emplaned upon a salmoncolored othersea. Seafowl in silhouette. Downshore the dull surf boomed. There was a horse standing there staring out upon the darkening waters and a young colt that cavorted and trotted off and came back.

He sat watching while the sun dipped hissing in the swells. The horse stood darkly against the sky. The surf boomed in the dark and the sea's black hide heaved in the cobbled starlight and the long pale combers loped out of the night and broke along the beach.

He rose and turned toward the lights of the town. The tide-pools bright as smelterpots among the dark rocks where the phosphorescent seacrabs clambered back. Passing through the salt grass he looked back. The horse had not moved. A ship's light winked in the swells. The colt stood against the horse with its head down and the horse was watching, out there past men's knowing, where the stars are drowning and whales ferry their vast souls through the black and seamless sea.

XXII

Under arrest – The judge pays a call – An arraignment –
Soldier, priest, magistrate – On his own recognizance – He sees a
surgeon – The arrowshaft removed from his leg – Delirium – He
journeys to Los Angeles – A public hanging – Los ahorcados –
Looking for the expriest – Another fool – The scapular – To
Sacramento – A traveler in the west – He abandons his party –
The penitent brothers – The deathcart – Another massacre –
The eldress in the rocks.

Going back through the streets past the yellow windowlights
and barking dogs he encountered a detachment of soldiers
but they took him for an older man in the dark and passed on.
He entered a tavern and sat in a darkened corner watching the
groups of men at the tables. No one asked him what he wanted
in that place. He seemed to be waiting for someone to come for
him and after a while four soldiers entered and arrested him.
They didnt even ask him his name.

In his cell he began to speak with a strange urgency of things
few men have seen in a lifetime and his jailers said that his
mind had come uncottered by the acts of blood in which he had
participated. One morning he woke to find the judge standing at
his cage, hat in hand, smiling down at him. He was dressed in a
suit of gray linen and he wore new polished boots. His coat was
unbuttoned and in his waistcoat he carried a watchchain and a
stickpin and in his belt a leathercovered clip that held a small
silvermounted derringer stocked in rosewood. He looked down

305

the hallway of the crude mud building and donned the hat and smiled again at the prisoner.

Well, he said. How are you?

The kid didnt answer.

They wanted to know from me if you were always crazy, said the judge. They said it was the country. The country turned them out.

Where's Tobin?

I told them that the cretin had been a respected Doctor of Divinity from Harvard College as recently as March of this year. That his wits had stood him as far west as the Aquarius Mountains. It was the ensuing country that carried them off. Together with his clothes.

And Toadvine and Brown. Where are they?

In the desert where you left them. A cruel thing. Your companions in arms. The judge shook his head.

What do they aim to do with me?

I believe it is their intention to hang you.

What did you tell them?

Told them the truth. That you were the person responsible. Not that we have all the details. But they understand that it was you and none other who shaped events along such a calamitòus course. Eventuating in the massacre at the ford by the savages with whom you conspired. Means and ends are of little moment here. Idle speculations. But even though you carry the draft of your murderous plan with you to the grave it will nonetheless be known in all its infamy to your Maker and as that is so so shall it be made known to the least of men. All in the fullness of time.

You're the one that's crazy, said the kid.

The judge smiled. No, he said. It was never me. But why lurk there in the shadows? Come here where we can talk, you and me.

The kid stood against the far wall. Hardly more than a shadow himself.

Come up, said the judge. Come up, for I've yet more to tell you.

He looked down the hallway. Dont be afraid, he said. I'll speak softly. It's not for the world's ears but for yours only. Let me see you. Dont you know that I'd have loved you like a son?

He reached through the bars. Come here, he said. Let me touch you.

The kid stood with his back to the wall.

Come here if you're not afraid, whispered the judge.

I aint afraid of you.

The judge smiled. He spoke softly into the dim mud cubicle. You came forward, he said, to take part in a work. But you were a witness against yourself. You sat in judgement on your own deeds. You put your own allowances before the judgements of history and you broke with the body of which you were pledged a part and poisoned it in all its enterprise. Hear me, man. I spoke in the desert for you and you only and you turned a deaf ear to me. If war is not holy man is nothing but antic clay. Even the cretin acted in good faith according to his parts. For it was required of no man to give more than he possessed nor was any man's share compared to another's. Only each was called upon to empty out his heart into the common and one did not. Can you tell me who that one was?

It was you, whispered the kid. You were the one.

The judge watched him through the bars, he shook his head. What joins men together, he said, is not the sharing of bread but the sharing of enemies. But if I was your enemy with whom would you have shared me? With whom? The priest? Where is he now? Look at me. Our animosities were formed and waiting before ever we two met. Yet even so you could have changed it all.

You, said the kid. It was you.

It was never me, said the judge. Listen to me. Do you think Glanton was a fool? Dont you know he'd have killed you?

Lies, said the kid. Lies, by god lies.

Think again, said the judge.

He never took part in your craziness.

The judge smiled. He took his watch from his waistcoat and opened it and held it to the failing light.

For even if you should have stood your ground, he said, yet what ground was it?

He looked up. He pressed the case shut and restored the

instrument to his person. Time to be going, he said. I have errands.

The kid closed his eyes. When he opened them the judge was gone. That night he called the corporal to him and they sat on either side of the bars while the kid told the soldier of the horde of gold and silver coins hid in the mountains not far from this place. He talked for a long time. The corporal had set the candle on the floor between them and he watched him as one might watch a glib and lying child. When he was finished the corporal rose and took the candle with him, leaving him in darkness.

He was released two days later. A Spanish priest had come to baptize him and had flung water at him through the bars like a priest casting out spirits. An hour later when they came for him he grew giddy with fear. He was taken before the alcalde and this man spoke to him in a fatherly manner in the spanish language and then he was turned out into the streets.

The doctor that he found was a young man of good family from the east. He cut open his trouserleg with scissors and looked at the blackened shaft of the arrow and moved it about. A soft fistula had formed about it.

Do you have any pain? he said.

The kid didnt answer.

He pressed about the wound with his thumb. He said that he could perform the surgery and that it would cost one hundred dollars.

The kid rose from the table and limped out.

The day following as he sat in the plaza a boy came and led him again to the shack behind the hotel and the doctor told him that they would operate in the morning.

He sold the pistol to an Englishman for forty dollars and woke at dawn in a lot underneath some boards where he'd crawled in the night. It was raining and he went down through the empty mud streets and hammered at the grocer's door until the man let him in. When he appeared at the surgeon's office he was very drunk, holding onto the doorjamb, a quart bottle half full of whiskey clutched in his hand.

The surgeon's assistant was a student from Sinaloa who had apprenticed himself here. An altercation ensued at the door until the surgeon himself came from the rear of the premises.

You'll have to come back tomorrow, he said.

I dont aim to be no soberer then.

The surgeon studied him. All right, he said. Let me have the whiskey.

He entered and the apprentice shut the door behind him.

You wont need the whiskey, said the doctor. Let me have it.

Why wont I need it?

We have spirits of ether. You wont need the whiskey.

Is it stronger?

Much stronger. In any case I cant operate on a man and him dead drunk.

He looked at the assistant and then he looked at the surgeon. He set the bottle on the table.

Good, said the surgeon. I want you to go with Marcelo. He will draw you a bath and give you clean linen and show you to a bed.

He pulled his watch from his vest and held it in his palm and read it.

It is a quarter past eight. We'll operate at one. Get some rest. If you require anything please let us know.

The assistant led him across the courtyard to a whitewashed adobe building in the rear. A bay that held four iron beds all empty. He bathed in a large riveted copper boiler that looked to have been salvaged from a ship and he lay on the rough mattress and listened to children playing somewhere beyond the wall. He did not sleep. When they came for him he was still drunk. He was led out and laid on a trestle in an empty room adjoining the bay and the assistant pressed an icy cloth to his nose and told him to breathe deeply.

In that sleep and in sleeps to follow the judge did visit. Who would come other? A great shambling mutant, silent and serene. Whatever his antecedents he was something wholly other than their sum, nor was there system by which to divide him back into his origins for he would not go. Whoever would seek out his history through what unraveling of loins and ledgerbooks must stand at last darkened and dumb at the shore of a void without terminus or origin and whatever science he might bring to bear upon the dusty primal matter blowing down out of the millennia will discover no trace of any ultimate atavistic egg by which to reckon his commencing. In the white and empty room he stood in his bespoken suit with his hat in his hand and he peered down with his small and lashless pig's eyes wherein this child just sixteen years on earth could read whole bodies of decisions not accountable to the courts of men and he saw his own name which nowhere else could he have ciphered out at all logged into the records as a thing already accomplished, a traveler known in jurisdictions existing only in the claims of certain pensioners or on old dated maps.

In his delirium he ransacked the linens of his pallet for arms but there were none. The judge smiled. The fool was no longer there but another man and this other man he could never see in his entirety but he seemed an artisan and a worker in metal. The judge enshadowed him where he crouched at his trade but he was a coldforger who worked with hammer and die, perhaps under some indictment and an exile from men's fires, hammering out like his own conjectural destiny all through the night of his becoming some coinage for a dawn that would not be. It is this false moneyer with his gravers and burins who seeks favor with the judge and he is at contriving from cold slag brute in the crucible a face that will pass, an image that will render this residual specie current in the markets where men barter. Of this is the judge judge and the night does not end.

———— ◆·◆ ————

The light in the room altered, a door closed. He opened his eyes. His leg was swathed in sheeting and it was propped up with small rolls of reed matting. He was desperate with thirst and his head was booming and his leg was like an evil visitant in the bed with him such was the pain. By and by the assistant came with water for him. He did not sleep again. The water that he drank ran out through his skin and drenched the bedding and he lay without moving as if to outwit the pain and his face was gray and drawn and his long hair damp and matted.

A week more and he was hobbling through the town on crutches provided him by the surgeon. He inquired at every door for news of the expriest but no one knew him.

In June of that year he was in Los Angeles quartered in a hostel that was no more than a common dosshouse, he and forty other men of every nationality. On the morning of the eleventh all rose up still in darkness and turned out to witness a public hanging at the cárcel. When he arrived it was paling light and already such a horde of spectators at the gate that he could not well see the proceedings. He stood at the edge of the crowd while day broke and speeches were said. Then abruptly two bound figures rose vertically from among their fellows to the top of the gatehouse and there they hung and there they died. Bottles were handed about and the witnesses who had stood in silence began to talk again.

In the evening when he returned to that place there was no one there at all. A guard leaned in the gatehouse portal chewing tobacco and the hanged men at their rope-ends looked like effigies for to frighten birds. As he drew near he saw that it was Toadvine and Brown.

He'd little money and then he'd none but he was in every dramhouse and gamingroom, every cockpit and doggery. A quiet youth in a suit too large and the same broken boots he'd come off the desert in. Standing just within the door of a foul saloon with his eyes shifting under the brim of the hat he wore and the light from a wallsconce on the side of his face he was taken for a male whore and set up to drinks and then shown to the rear of the premises. He left his patron senseless in a mudroom there where there was no light. Other men found him on their own sordid missions and other men took his purse and watch. Later still someone took his shoes.

He heard no news of the priest and he'd quit asking. Returning to his lodging one morning at daybreak in a gray rain he saw a face slobbering in an upper window and he climbed the stairwell and rapped at the door. A woman in a silk kimono opened the door and looked out at him. Behind her in the room a candle burned at a table and in the pale light at the window a halfwit sat in a pen with a cat. It turned to look at him, not the judge's fool but just some other fool. When the woman asked him what he wanted he turned without speaking and descended the stairwell into the rain and the mud in the street.

With his last two dollars he bought from a soldier the scapular of heathen ears that Brown had worn to the scaffold. He was wearing them the next morning when he hired out to an independent conductor from the state of Missouri and he was wearing them when they set out for Fremont on the Sacramento River with a train of wagons and packanimals. If the conductor had any curiosity about the necklace he kept it to himself.

He was at this employment for some months and he left it without notice. He traveled about from place to place. He did not avoid the company of other men. He was treated with a certain deference as one who had got onto terms with life beyond what his years could account for. By now he'd come by a horse and a revolver, the rudiments of an outfit. He worked at different trades. He had a bible that he'd found at the mining camps and he carried this book with him no word of which could he read. In his dark and frugal clothes some took him for a sort of preacher but he was no witness to them, neither of things at hand nor things to come, he least of any man. They were remote places for news that he traveled in and in those uncertain times men toasted the ascension of rulers already deposed and hailed the coronation of kings murdered and in their graves. Of such corporal histories even as these he bore no tidings and although it was the custom in that wilderness to stop with any traveler and exchange the news he seemed to travel with no news at all, as if the doings of the world were too slanderous for him to truck with, or perhaps too trivial.

He saw men killed with guns and with knives and with ropes and he saw women fought over to the death whose value they themselves set at two dollars. He saw ships from the land of China chained in the small harbors and bales of tea and silks and spices broken open with swords by small yellow men with speech like cats. On that lonely coast where the steep rocks cradled a dark and muttersome sea he saw vultures at their soaring whose wingspan so dwarfed all lesser birds that the eagles shrieking underneath were more like terns or plovers. He saw piles of gold a hat would scarcely have covered wagered on the turn of a card and lost and he saw bears and lions turned loose in pits to fight wild bulls to the death and he was twice in the city of San Francisco and twice saw it burn and never went back, riding out on horseback along the road to the south where all night the shape of the city burned against the sky and burned again in the black waters of the sea where dolphins rolled through the flames, fire in the lake, through the fall of burning timbers and the cries of the lost. He never saw the expriest again. Of the judge he heard rumor everywhere.

In the spring of his twenty-eighth year he set out with others upon the desert to the east, he one of five at hire to see a party through the wilderness to their homes halfway across the continent. Seven days from the coast at a desert well he left them. They were just a band of pilgrims returning to their homes, men and women, already dusty and travelworn.

He set the horse's face north toward the stone mountains running thinly under the edge of the sky and he rode the stars down and the sun up. It was no country he had ever seen and there was no track to follow into those mountains and there was no track out. Yet in the deepest fastness of those rocks he met with men who seemed unable to abide the silence of the world.

He first saw them laboring over the plain in the dusk among flowering ocotillo that burned in the final light like horned candelabra. They were led by a pitero piping a reed and then in procession a clanging of tambourines and matracas and men naked to the waist in black capes and hoods who flailed themselves with whips of braided yucca and men who bore on their naked backs great loads of cholla and a man tied to a rope who was pulled this way and that by his companions and a hooded man in a white robe who bore a heavy wooden cross on his shoulders. They were all of them barefoot and they left a trail of blood across the rocks and they were followed by a rude carreta in which sat a carved wooden skeleton who rattled along stiffly holding before him a bow and arrow. He shared his cart with a load of stones and they went trundling over the rocks drawn by ropes tied to the heads and ankles of the bearers and accompanied by a deputation of women who carried small desert flowers in their folded hands or torches of sotol or primitive lanterns of pierced tin.

This troubled sect traversed slowly the ground under the bluff where the watcher stood and made their way over the broken scree of a fan washed out of the draw above them and wailing and piping and clanging they passed between the granite walls into the upper valley and disappeared in the coming darkness like heralds of some unspeakable calamity leaving only bloody footprints on the stone.

He bivouacked in a barren swale and he and the horse lay down together and all night the dry wind blew down the desert and the wind was all but silent for there was nothing of resonance among those rocks. In the dawn he and the horse stood watching the east where the light commenced and then he saddled the horse and led it down a scrabbled trail through a canyon where he found a tank deep under a pitch of boulders. The water lay in darkness and the stones were cool and he drank and fetched water for the horse in his hat. Then he led the animal up onto the ridge and they went on, the man watching the tableland to the south and the mountains to the north and the horse clattering along behind.

By and by the horse began to toss its head and soon it would not go. He stood holding the hackamore and studying the country. Then he saw the pilgrims. They were scattered about below him in a stone coulee dead in their blood. He took down his rifle and squatted and listened. He led the horse under the shade of the rock wall and hobbled it and moved along the rock and down the slope.

The company of penitents lay hacked and butchered among the stones in every attitude. Many lay about the fallen cross and some were mutilated and some were without heads. Perhaps they'd gathered under the cross for shelter but the hole into which it had been set and the cairn of rocks about its base showed how it had been pushed over and how the hooded alterchrist had been cut down and disemboweled who now lay with the scraps of rope by which he had been bound still tied about his wrists and ankles.

The kid rose and looked about at this desolate scene and then he saw alone and upright in a small niche in the rocks an old woman kneeling in a faded rebozo with her eyes cast down.

He made his way among the corpses and stood before her. She was very old and her face was gray and leathery and sand had collected in the folds of her clothing. She did not look up. The shawl that covered her head was much faded of its color yet it bore like a patent woven into the fabric the figures of stars and quartermoons and other insignia of a provenance unknown to him. He spoke to her in a low voice. He told her that he was an American and that he was a long way from the country of his birth and that he had no family and that he had traveled much and seen many things and had been at war and endured hardships. He told her that he would convey her to a safe place, some party of her countrypeople who would welcome her and that she should join them for he could not leave her in this place or she would surely die.

He knelt on one knee, resting the rifle before him like a staff. Abuelita, he said. No puedes escúcharme?

He reached into the little cove and touched her arm. She moved slightly, her whole body, light and rigid. She weighed nothing. She was just a dried shell and she had been dead in that place for years.

XXIII

On the north Texas plains – An old buffalo hunter –
The millennial herds – The bonepickers – Night on the prairie –
The callers – Apache ears – Elrod takes a stand – A killing –
Bearing off the dead – Fort Griffin – The Beehive – A stageshow –
The judge – Killing a bear – The judge speaks of old times –
In preparation for the dance – The judge on war, destiny, the
supremacy of man – The dancehall – The whore – The jakes and what
was encountered there – Sie müssen schlafen aber Ich muss tanzen.

In the late winter of eighteen seventy-eight he was on the plains of north Texas. He crossed the Double Mountain Fork of the Brazos River on a morning when skim ice lay along the sandy shore and he rode through a dark dwarf forest of black and twisted mesquite trees. He made his camp that night on a piece of high ground where there was a windbreak formed of a tree felled by lightning. He'd no sooner got his fire to burn than he saw across the prairie in the darkness another fire. Like his it twisted in the wind, like his it warmed one man alone.

It was an old hunter in camp and the hunter shared tobacco with him and told him of the buffalo and the stands he'd made against them, laid up in a sag on some rise with the dead animals scattered over the grounds and the herd beginning to mill and the riflebarrel so hot the wiping patches sizzled in the bore and the animals by the thousands and tens of thousands and the hides pegged out over actual square miles of ground and the teams of skinners spelling one another around the clock and the shooting and shooting weeks and months till the bore shot slick and the stock shot loose at the tang and their shoulders were yellow and blue to the elbow and the tandem wagons groaned away over the prairie twenty and twenty-two ox teams and the flint hides by the ton and hundred ton and the meat rotting on the ground and the air whining with flies and the buzzards and ravens and the night a horror of snarling and feeding with the wolves half crazed and wallowing in the carrion.

I seen Studebaker wagons with six and eight ox teams headed out for the grounds not haulin a thing but lead. Just pure galena. Tons of it. On this ground alone between the Arkansas River and the Concho there was eight million carcasses for that's how many hides reached the railhead. Two year ago we pulled out from Griffin for a last hunt. We ransacked the country. Six weeks. Finally found a herd of eight animals and we killed them and come in. They're gone. Ever one of them that God ever made is gone as if they'd never been at all.

The ragged sparks blew down the wind. The prairie about them lay silent. Beyond the fire it was cold and the night was clear and the stars were falling. The old hunter pulled his blanket about him. I wonder if there's other worlds like this, he said. Or if this is the only one.

———◆•◆———

When he came upon the bonepickers he'd been riding three days in a country he'd never seen. The plains were sere and burntlooking and the small trees black and misshapen and haunted by ravens and everywhere the ragged packs of jackal wolves and the crazed and sunchalked bones of the vanished herds. He dismounted and led the horse. Here and there within the arc of ribs a few flat discs of darkened lead like old medallions of some order of the hunt. In the distance teams of oxen bore along slowly and the heavy wagons creaked dryly. Into these barrows the pickers tossed the bones, kicking down the calcined architecture, breaking apart the great frames with axes. The bones clattered in the wagons, they plowed on in a pale dust. He watched them pass, ragged, filthy, the oxen galled and mad-looking. None spoke to him. In the distance he could see a train of wagons moving off to the northeast with great tottering loads of bones and further to the north other teams of pickers at their work.

He mounted and rode on. The bones had been gathered into windrows ten feet high and hundreds long or into great conical hills topped with the signs or brands of their owners. He overtook one of the lumbering carts, a boy riding the near wheel ox and driving with a jerkline and a jockeystick. Two youths squatting atop a mound of skulls and pelvic bones leered down at him.

Their fires dotted the plain that night and he sat with his back to the wind and drank from an army canteen and ate a handful of parched corn for his supper. All across those reaches the yammer and yap of the starving wolves relayed and to the north the silent lightning rigged a broken lyre upon the world's dark rim. The air smelled of rain but no rain fell and the creaking bonecarts passed in the night like darkened ships and he could smell the oxen and hear their breath. The sour smell of the bones was everywhere. Toward midnight a party hailed him as he squatted at his coals.

Come up, he said.

They came up out of the dark, sullen wretches dressed in skins. They carried old military guns save for one who had a buffalo rifle and they had no coats and one of them wore green hide boots peeled whole from the hocks of some animal and the toes gathered shut with leader.

Evenin stranger, called out the eldest child among them.

He looked at them. They were four and a halfgrown boy and they halted at the edge of the light and arranged themselves there.

Come up, he said.

They shuffled forward. Three of them squatted and two stood.

Where's ye outfit? said one.

He aint out for bones.

You aint got nary chew of tobacca about your clothes have ye?

He shook his head.

Nary drink of whiskey neither I dont reckon.

He aint got no whiskey.

Where ye headed mister?

Are you headed twards Griffin?

He looked them over. I am, he said.

Goin for the whores I'll bet ye.

He aint goin for the whores.

It's full of whores, Griffin is.

Hell, he's probably been there more'n you.

You been to Griffin mister?

Not yet.

Full of whores. Full plumb up.

They say you can get clapped a day's ride out when the wind is right.

They set in a tree in front of this here place and you can look up and see their bloomers. I've counted high as eight in that tree early of a evenin. Set up there like coons and smoke cigarettes and holler down at ye.

It's set up to be the biggest town for sin in all Texas.

It's as lively a place for murders as you'd care to visit.

Scrapes with knives. About any kind of meanness you can name.

He looked at them from one to the other. He reached and took up a stick and roused the fire with it and put the stick in the flames. You all like meanness? he said.

We dont hold with it.

Like to drink whiskey?

He's just talkin. He aint no whiskey drinker.

Hell, you just now seen him drink it not a hour ago.

I seen him puke it back up too. What's them things around your neck there mister?

He pulled the aged scapular from his shirtfront and looked at it. It's ears, he said.

It's what?

Ears.

What kind of ears?

He tugged at the thong and looked down at them. They were perfectly black and hard and dry and of no shape at all.

Humans, he said. Human ears.

Aint done it, said the one with the rifle.

Dont call him a liar Elrod, he's liable to shoot ye. Let's see them things mister if you dont care.

He slipped the scapular over his head and handed it across to the boy who'd spoken. They pressed about and felt the strange dried pendants.

Niggers, aint it? they said.

Docked them niggers' ears so they'd know em when they run off.

How many is there mister?

I dont know. Used to be near a hundred.

They held the thing up and turned it in the firelight.

Nigger ears, by god.

They aint niggers.

They aint?

No.

What are they?

Injins.

The hell they are.

Elrod you done been told.

How come them to be so black as that if they aint niggers.

They turned that way. They got blacker till they couldnt black no more.

Where'd you get em at?

Killed them sons of bitches. Didnt ye mister?

You been a scout on the prairies, aint ye?

I bought them ears in California off a soldier in a saloon didnt have no money to drink on.

He reached and took the scapular from them.

Shoot. I bet he's been a scout on the prairie killed ever one of them sons of bitches.

The one called Elrod followed the trophies with his chin and sniffed the air. I dont see what you want with them things, he said. I wouldnt have em.

The others looked at him uneasily.

You dont know where them ears come from. That old boy you bought em off of might of said they was injins but that dont make it so.

The man didnt answer.

Them ears could of come off of cannibals or any other kind of foreign nigger. They tell me you can buy the whole heads in New Orleans. Sailors brings em in and you can buy em for five dollars all day long them heads.

Hush Elrod.

The man sat holding the necklace in his hands. They wasnt cannibals, he said. They was Apaches. I knowed the man that docked em. Knowed him and rode with him and seen him hung.

Elrod looked at the others and grinned. Apaches, he said. I bet them old Apaches would give a watermelon a pure fit, what about you all?

The man looked up wearily. You aint callin me a liar are ye son?

I aint ye son.

How old are you?

That's some more of your business.

How old are you?

He's fifteen.

You hush your damn mouth.

He turned to the man. He dont speak for me, he said.

He's done spoke. I was fifteen year old when I was first shot.

I ain't never been shot.

You aint sixteen yet neither.

You aim to shoot me?

I aim to try to keep from it.

Come on Elrod.

You aint goin to shoot nobody. Maybe in the back or them asleep.

Elrod we're gone.

I knowed you for what you was when I seen ye.

You better go on.

Set there and talk about shootin somebody. They aint nobody done it yet.

The other four stood at the limits of the firelight. The youngest of them was casting glances out at the dark sanctuary of the prairie night.

Go on, the man said. They're waitin on ye.

He spat into the man's fire and wiped his mouth. Out on the prairie to the north a train of yoked wagons was passing and the oxen were pale and silent in the starlight and the wagons creaked faintly in the distance and a lantern with a red glass followed them out like an alien eye. This country was filled with violent children orphaned by war. His companions had started back to fetch him and perhaps this emboldened him the more and perhaps he said other things to the man for when they got to the fire the man had risen to his feet. You keep him away from me, he said. I see him back here I'll kill him.

When they had gone he built up the fire and caught the horse and took the hobbles off and tied it and saddled it and then he moved off apart and spread his blanket and lay down in the dark.

When he woke there was still no light in the east. The boy was standing by the ashes of the fire with the rifle in his hand. The horse had snuffed and now it snuffed again.

I knowed you'd be hid out, the boy called.

He pushed back the blanket and rolled onto his stomach and cocked the pistol and leveled it at the sky where the clustered stars were burning for eternity. He centered the foresight in the milled groove of the framestrap and holding the piece so he swung it through the dark of the trees with both hands to the darker shape of the visitor.

I'm right here, he said.

The boy swung with the rifle and fired.

You wouldnt of lived anyway, the man said.

It was gray dawn when the others came up. They had no

horses. They led the halfgrown boy to where the dead youth was lying on his back with his hands composed upon his chest.

We dont want no trouble mister. We just want to take him with us.

Take him.

I knowed we'd bury him on this prairie.

They come out here from Kentucky mister. This tyke and his brother. His momma and daddy both dead. His grandaddy was killed by a lunatic and buried in the woods like a dog. He's never knowed good fortune in his life and now he aint got a soul in this world.

Randall you take a good look at the man that has made you a orphan.

The orphan in his large clothes holding the old musket with the mended stock stared at him woodenly. He was maybe twelve years old and he looked not so much dullwitted as insane. Two of the others were going through the dead boy's pockets.

Where's his rifle at mister?

The man stood with his hand on his belt. He nodded to where the rifle stood against a tree.

They brought it over and presented it to the brother. It was a Sharp's fifty calibre and holding it and the musket he stood inanely armed, his eyes skittering.

One of the older boys handed him the dead boy's hat and then he turned to the man. He give forty dollars for that rifle in Little Rock. You can buy em in Griffin for ten. They aint worth nothin. Randall, are you ready to go?

He did not assist as a bearer for he was too small. When they set out across the prairie with his brother's body carried up on their shoulders he followed behind carrying the musket and the dead boy's rifle and the dead boy's hat. The man watched them go. Out there was nothing. They were simply bearing the body off over the bonestrewn waste toward a naked horizon. The orphan turned once to look back at him and then he hurried to catch up.

In the afternoon he rode through the McKenzie crossing of the Clear Fork of the Brazos River and he and the horse walked side by side down the twilight toward the town where in the long red dusk and in the darkness the random aggregate of the lamps formed slowly a false shore of hospice cradled on the low plain before them. They passed enormous ricks of bones, colossal dikes composed of horned skulls and the crescent ribs like old ivory bows heaped in the aftermath of some legendary battle, great levees of them curving away over the plain into the night.

They entered the town in a light rain falling. The horse nickered and snuffed shyly at the hocks of the other animals standing at stall before the lamplit bagnios they passed. Fiddlemusic issued into the solitary mud street and lean dogs crossed before them from shadow to shadow. At the end of the town he led the horse to a rail and tied it among others and stepped up the low wooden stairs into the dim light that fell from the doorway there. He looked back a last time at the street and at the random windowlights let into the darkness and at the last pale light in the west and the low dark hills around. Then he pushed open the door and entered.

A dimly seething rabble had coagulated within. As if the raw board structure erected for their containment occupied some ultimate sink into which they had gravitated from off the surrounding flatlands. An old man in a tyrolean costume was shuffling among the rough tables with his hat outheld while a little girl in a smock cranked a barrel organ and a bear in a crinoline twirled strangely upon a board stage defined by a row of tallow candles that dripped and sputtered in their pools of grease.

He made his way through the crowd to the bar where several men in gaitered shirts were drawing beer or pouring whiskey. Young boys worked behind them fetching crates of bottles and racks of glasses steaming from the scullery to the rear. The bar was covered with zinc and he placed his elbows upon it and spun a silver coin before him and slapped it flat.

Speak or forever, said the barman.

A whiskey.

Whiskey it is. He set up a glass and uncorked a bottle and poured perhaps half a gill and took the coin.

He stood looking at the whiskey. Then he took his hat off and placed it on the bar and took up the glass and drank it very deliberately and set the empty glass down again. He wiped his mouth and turned around and placed his elbows on the bar behind him.

Watching him across the layered smoke in the yellow light was the judge.

He was sitting at one of the tables. He wore a round hat with a narrow brim and he was among every kind of man, herder and bullwhacker and drover and freighter and miner and hunter and soldier and pedlar and gambler and drifter and drunkard and thief and he was among the dregs of the earth in beggary a thousand years and he was among the scapegrace scions of eastern dynasties and in all that motley assemblage he sat by them and yet alone as if he were some other sort of man entire and he seemed little changed or none in all these years.

He turned away from those eyes and stood looking down at the empty tumbler between his fists. When he looked up the barman was watching him. He raised his forefinger and the barman brought the whiskey.

He paid, he lifted the glass and drank. There was a mirror along the backbar but it held only smoke and phantoms. The barrel organ was groaning and creaking and the bear with tongue aloll was revolving heavily on the boards.

When he turned the judge had risen and was speaking with other men. The showman made his way through the throng shaking the coins in his hat. Garishly clad whores were going out through a door at the rear of the premises and he watched them and he watched the bear and when he looked back across the room the judge was not there. The showman seemed to be in altercation with the men standing at the table. Another man rose. The showman gestured with his hat. One of them pointed toward the bar. He shook his head. Their voices were incoherent in the din. On the boards the bear was dancing for all that his heart was worth and the girl cranked the organ handle and the shadow of the act which the candlelight constructed upon the wall might have gone begging for referents in any daylight world. When he looked back the showman had donned the hat and he stood with his hands on his hips. One of the men had drawn a longbarreled cavalry pistol from his belt. He turned and leveled the pistol toward the stage.

Some dove for the floor, some reached for their own arms. The owner of the bear stood like a pitchman at a shooting gallery. The shot was thunderous and in the afterclap all sound in that room ceased. The bear had been shot through the midsection. He let out a low moan and he began to dance faster, dancing in silence save for the slap of his great footpads on the planks. Blood was running down his groin. The little girl strapped into the barrel organ stood frozen, the crank at rest on the upswing. The man with the pistol fired again and the pistol bucked and roared and the black smoke rolled and the bear groaned and began to reel drunkenly. He was holding his chest and a thin foam of blood swung from his jaw and he began to totter and to cry like a child and he took a few last steps, dancing, and crashed to the boards.

Someone had seized the pistol arm of the man who'd done the shooting and the gun was waving aloft. The owner of the bear stood stunned, clutching the brim of his oldworld hat.

Shot the goddamned bear, said the barman.

The little girl had unbuckled herself out of the barrel organ and it clattered wheezing to the floor. She ran forward and knelt and gathered the great shaggy head up in her arms and began to rock back and forth sobbing. Most of the men in the room had risen and they stood in the smoky yellow space with their hands on their sidearms. Whole flocks of whores were scuttling toward the rear and a woman mounted to the boards and stepped past the bear and held out her hands.

It's all over, she said. It's all over.

Do you believe it's all over, son?

He turned. The judge was standing at the bar looking down at him. He smiled, he removed his hat. The great pale dome of his skull shone like an enormous phosphorescent egg in the lamplight.

The last of the true. The last of the true. I'd say they're all gone under now saving me and thee. Would you not?

He tried to see past him. That great corpus enshadowed him from all beyond. He could hear the woman announcing the commencement of dancing in the hall to the rear.

And some are not yet born who shall have cause to curse the Dauphin's soul, said the judge. He turned slightly. Plenty of time for the dance.

I aint studyin no dance.

The judge smiled.

The tyrolean and another man were bent over the bear. The girl was sobbing, the front of her dress dark with blood. The judge leaned across the bar and seized a bottle and snapped the cork out of it with his thumb. The cork whined off into the blackness above the lamps like a bullet. He rifled a great drink down his throat and leaned back against the bar. You're here for the dance, he said.

I got to go.

The judge looked aggrieved. Go? he said.

He nodded. He reached and took hold of his hat where it lay on the bar but he did not take it up and he did not move.

What man would not be a dancer if he could, said the judge. It's a great thing, the dance.

The woman was kneeling and had her arm around the little girl. The candles sputtered and the great hairy mound of the bear dead in its crinoline lay like some monster slain in the commission of unnatural acts. The judge poured the tumbler full where it stood empty alongside the hat and nudged it forward.

Drink up, he said. Drink up. This night thy soul may be required of thee.

He looked at the glass. The judge smiled and gestured with the bottle. He took up the glass and drank.

The judge watched him. Was it always your idea, he said, that if you did not speak you would not be recognized?

You seen me.

The judge ignored this. I recognized you when I first saw you and yet you were a disappointment to me. Then and now. Even so at the last I find you here with me.

I aint with you.

The judge raised his bald brow. Not? he said. He looked about him in a puzzled and artful way and he was a passable thespian.

I never come here huntin you.

What then? said the judge.

What would I want with you? I come here same reason as any man.

And what reason is that?

What reason is what?

That these men are here.

They come here to have a good time.

The judge watched him. He began to point out various men in the room and to ask if these men were here for a good time or if indeed they knew why they were here at all.

Everbody dont have to have a reason to be someplace.

That's so, said the judge. They do not have to have a reason. But order is not set aside because of their indifference.

He regarded the judge warily.

Let me put it this way, said the judge. If it is so that they themselves have no reason and yet are indeed here must they not be here by reason of some other? And if this is so can you guess who that other might be?

No. Can you?

I know him well.

He poured the tumbler full once more and he took a drink himself from the bottle and he wiped his mouth and turned to regard the room. This is an orchestration for an event. For a dance in fact. The participants will be apprised of their roles at the proper time. For now it is enough that they have arrived. As the dance is the thing with which we are concerned and contains complete within itself its own arrangement and history and finale there is no necessity that the dancers contain these things within themselves as well. In any event the history of all is not the history of each nor indeed the sum of those histories and none here can finally comprehend the reason for his presence for he has no way of knowing even in what the event consists. In fact, were he to know he might well absent himself and you can see that that cannot be any part of the plan if plan there be.

He smiled, his great teeth shone. He drank.

An event, a ceremony. The orchestration thereof. The overture carries certain marks of decisiveness. It includes the slaying of a large bear. The evening's progress will not appear strange or unusual even to those who question the rightness of the events so ordered.

A ceremony then. One could well argue that there are not categories of no ceremony but only ceremonies of greater or lesser degree and deferring to this argument we will say that this is a ceremony of a certain magnitude perhaps more commonly called a ritual. A ritual includes the letting of blood. Rituals which fail in this requirement are but mock rituals. Here every man knows the false at once. Never doubt it. That feeling in the breast that evokes a child's memory of loneliness such as when the others have gone and only the game is left with its solitary participant. A solitary game, without opponent. Where only the rules are at hazard. Dont look away. We are not speaking in mysteries. You of all men are no stranger to that feeling, the emptiness and the despair. It is that which we take arms against, is it not? Is not blood the tempering agent in the mortar which bonds? The judge leaned closer. What do you think death is, man? Of whom do we speak when we speak of a man who was and is not? Are these blind riddles or are they not some part of every man's jurisdiction? What is death if not an agency? And whom does he intend toward? Look at me.

I dont like craziness.

Nor I. Nor I. Bear with me. Look at them now. Pick a man, any man. That man there. See him. That man hatless. You know his opinion of the world. You can read it in his face, in his stance. Yet his complaint that a man's life is no bargain masks the actual case with him. Which is that men will not do as he wishes them to. Have never done, never will do. That's the way of things with him and his life is so balked about by difficulty and become so altered of its intended architecture that he is little more than a walking hovel hardly fit to house the human spirit at all. Can he say, such a man, that there is no malign thing set against him? That there is no power and no force and no cause? What manner of heretic could doubt agency and claimant alike? Can he believe that the wreckage of his existence is unentailed? No liens, no creditors? That gods of vengeance and of compassion alike lie sleeping in their crypt and whether our cries are for an accounting or for the destruction of the ledgers altogether they must evoke only the same silence and that it is this silence which will prevail? To whom is he talking, man? Cant you see him?

The man was indeed muttering to himself and peering balefully about the room wherein it seemed there was no friend to him.

A man seeks his own destiny and no other, said the judge. Will or nill. Any man who could discover his own fate and elect therefore some opposite course could only come at last to that selfsame reckoning at the same appointed time, for each man's destiny is as large as the world he inhabits and contains within it all opposites as well. This desert upon which so many have been broken is vast and calls for largeness of heart but it is also ultimately empty. It is hard, it is barren. Its very nature is stone.

He poured the tumbler full. Drink up, he said. The world goes on. We have dancing nightly and this night is no exception. The straight and the winding way are one and now that you are here what do the years count since last we two met together? Men's memories are uncertain and the past that was differs little from the past that was not.

He took up the tumbler the judge had poured and he drank and set it down again. He looked at the judge. I been everwhere, he said. This is just one more place.

The judge arched his brow. Did you post witnesses? he said. To report to you on the continuing existence of those places once you'd quit them?

That's crazy.

Is it? Where is yesterday? Where is Glanton and Brown and where is the priest? He leaned closer. Where is Shelby, whom you left to the mercies of Elias in the desert, and where is Tate whom you abandoned in the mountains? Where are the ladies, ah the fair and tender ladies with whom you danced at the governor's ball when you were a hero anointed with the blood of the enemies of the republic you'd elected to defend? And where is the fiddler and where the dance?

I guess you can tell me.

I tell you this. As war becomes dishonored and its nobility called into question those honorable men who recognize the sanctity of blood will become excluded from the dance, which is the warrior's right, and thereby will the dance become a false dance and the dancers false dancers. And yet there will be one there always who is a true dancer and can you guess who that might be?

You aint nothin.

You speak truer than you know. But I will tell you. Only that man who has offered up himself entire to the blood of war, who has been to the floor of the pit and seen horror in the round and learned at last that it speaks to his inmost heart, only that man can dance.

Even a dumb animal can dance.

The judge set the bottle on the bar. Hear me, man, he said. There is room on the stage for one beast and one alone. All others are destined for a night that is eternal and without name. One by one they will step down into the darkness before the footlamps. Bears that dance, bears that dont.

---◆◆---

He drifted with the crowd toward the door at the rear. In the anteroom sat men at cards, dim in the smoke. He moved on. A woman was taking chits from the men as they passed through to the shed at the rear of the building. She looked up at him. He had no chit. She directed him to a table where a woman was selling the chits and stuffing the money with a piece of shingle through a narrow slit into an iron strongbox. He paid his dollar and took the stamped brass token and rendered it up at the door and passed through.

He found himself in a large hall with a platform for the musicians at one end and a large homemade sheetiron stove at the other. Whole squadrons of whores were working the floor. In their stained peignoirs, in their green stockings and meloncolored drawers they drifted through the smoky oil light like makebelieve wantons, at once childlike and lewd. A dark little dwarf of a whore took his arm and smiled up at him.

I seen you right away, she said. I always pick the one I want.

She led him through a door where an old Mexican woman was handing out towels and candles and they ascended like refugees of some sordid disaster the darkened plankboard stairwell to the upper rooms.

Lying in the little cubicle with his trousers about his knees he watched her. He watched her take up her clothes and don them and he watched her hold the candle to the mirror and study her face there. She turned and looked at him.

Let's go, she said. I got to go.

Go on.

You cant lay there. Come on. I got to go.

He sat up and swung his legs over the edge of the little iron cot and stood and pulled his trousers up and buttoned them and buckled his belt. His hat was on the floor and he picked it up and slapped it against the side of his leg and put it on.

You need to get down there and get you a drink, she said. You'll be all right.

I'm all right now.

He went out. He turned at the end of the hallway and looked

back. Then he went down the stairs. She had come to the door. She stood in the hallway holding the candle and brushing her hair back with one hand and she watched him descend into the dark of the stairwell and then she pulled the door shut behind her.

He stood at the edge of the dancefloor. A ring of people had taken the floor and were holding hands and grinning and calling out to one another. A fiddler sat on a stool on the stage and a man walked up and down calling out the order of the dance and gesturing and stepping in the way he wished them to go. Outside in the darkened lot groups of wretched Tonkawas stood in the mud with their faces composed in strange lost portraits within the sashwork of the windowlights. The fiddler rose and set the fiddle to his jaw. There was a shout and the music began and the ring of dancers began to rotate ponderously with a great shuffling. He went out the back.

The rain had stopped and the air was cold. He stood in the yard. Stars were falling across the sky myriad and random, speeding along brief vectors from their origins in night to their destinies in dust and nothingness. Within the hall the fiddle squealed and the dancers shuffled and stomped. In the street men were calling for the little girl whose bear was dead for she was lost. They went among the darkened lots with lanterns and torches calling out to her.

He went down the walkboard toward the jakes. He stood outside listening to the voices fading away and he looked again at the silent tracks of the stars where they died over the darkened hills. Then he opened the rough board door of the jakes and stepped in.

The judge was seated upon the closet. He was naked and he rose up smiling and gathered him in his arms against his immense and terrible flesh and shot the wooden barlatch home behind him.

In the saloon two men who wanted to buy the hide were looking for the owner of the bear. The bear lay on the stage in an immense pool of blood. All the candles had gone out save one and it guttered uneasily in its grease like a votive lamp. In the dancehall a young man had joined the fiddler and he kept the measure of the music with a pair of spoons which he clapped between his knees. The whores sashayed half naked, some with their breasts exposed. In the mudded dogyard behind the premises two men went down the boards toward the jakes. A third man was standing there urinating into the mud.

Is someone in there? the first man said.

The man who was relieving himself did not look up. I wouldnt go in there if I was you, he said.

Is there somebody in there?

I wouldnt go in.

He hitched himself up and buttoned his trousers and stepped past them and went up the walk toward the lights. The first man watched him go and then opened the door of the jakes.

Good God almighty, he said.

What is it?

He didnt answer. He stepped past the other and went back up the walk. The other man stood looking after him. Then he opened the door and looked in.

In the saloon they had rolled the dead bear onto a wagonsheet and there was a general call for hands. In the anteroom the tobacco smoke circled the lamps like an evil fog and the men bid and dealt in a low mutter.

There was a lull in the dancing and a second fiddler took the stage and the two plucked their strings and turned the little hardwood pegs until they were satisfied. Many among the dancers were staggering drunk through the room and some had rid themselves of shirts and jackets and stood barechested and sweating even though the room was cold enough to cloud their breath. An enormous whore stood clapping her hands at the bandstand and calling drunkenly for the music. She wore nothing but a pair of men's drawers and some of her sisters were likewise clad in what appeared to be trophies—hats or pantaloons or blue twill cavalry jackets. As the music sawed up there was a lively cry from all and a caller stood to the front and called out the dance and the dancers stomped and hooted and lurched against one another.

And they are dancing, the board floor slamming under the jackboots and the fiddlers grinning hideously over their canted pieces. Towering over them all is the judge and he is naked dancing, his small feet lively and quick and now in doubletime and bowing to the ladies, huge and pale and hairless, like an enormous infant. He never sleeps, he says. He says he'll never die. He bows to the fiddlers and sashays backwards and throws back his head and laughs deep in his throat and he is a great favorite, the judge. He wafts his hat and the lunar dome of his skull passes palely under the lamps and he swings about and takes possession of one of the fiddles and he pirouettes and makes a pass, two passes, dancing and fiddling at once. His feet are light and nimble. He never sleeps. He says that he will never die. He dances in light and in shadow and he is a great favorite. He never sleeps, the judge. He is dancing, dancing. He says that he will never die.

THE END

EPILOGUE

In the dawn there is a man progressing over the plain by means
of holes which he is making in the ground. He uses an implement
with two handles and he chucks it into the hole and he enkindles
the stone in the hole with his steel hole by hole striking the fire
out of the rock which God has put there. On the plain behind him
are the wanderers in search of bones and those who do not search
and they move haltingly in the light like mechanisms whose
movements are monitored with escapement and pallet so that
they appear restrained by a prudence or reflectiveness which has
no inner reality and they cross in their progress one by one that
track of holes that runs to the rim of the visible ground and which
seems less the pursuit of some continuance than the verification
of a principle, a validation of sequence and causality as if each
round and perfect hole owed its existence to the one before it
there on that prairie upon which are the bones and the gatherers
of bones and those who do not gather. He strikes fire in the hole
and draws out his steel. Then they all move on again.